# DOINGS IN LONDON;

OR,

## Day and Night Scenes

OF THE

## FRAUDS, FROLICS, MANNERS, AND DEPRAVITIES

OF

## THE METROPOLIS.

*By G. SMEETON.*

WITH

### THIRTY-THREE ENGRAVINGS,

BY BONNER, FROM DESIGNS BY MR. R. CRUIKSHANK.

### FOURTEENTH EDITION.

### LONDON :
## PUBLISHED BY HODSON, FEEET STREET,

AND SOLD BY ALL BOOKSELLERS.

### 1850.

# TO THE READER.

PREFACES, says Ward, are now become common to every work, and, like women's faces, are oftentimes found the most promising part of the whole piece. But when a thing is usual, though ever so ridiculous in the eye of reason, a man, like him that spoils his stomach with a mess of porridge before dinner, may plead custom to excuse his error. I therefore hope it will be no offence to conform with others.

It has been my design to scourge vice and villany, without levelling characters at any person in particular. But if any unhappy sinner, through the guilt of his own conscience, take that burden upon his own shoulders which thousands in the town have as much right to bear as himself he has no reason to be angry with me, but may thank himself for making his tender back so fit for the pack-saddle.

It has been *my* aim to show vice and deception in all their *real* deformity; and not by painting in glowing colours the fascinating allurements, the mischievous frolics, and vicious habits of the profligate, the heedless, and the debauched, to tempt youth to commit those irregularities which often lead to dangerous results, not only to themselves, but also to the public.

Historical notices of the former manners and customs of the inhabitants of London, and also topographical elucidations, have been introduced to illustrate the subject, and to give the stranger a better knowledge of the Metropolis.

G. S.

( G. SMEETON. )

# DOINGS IN LONDON;

OR

## 𝕯𝖆𝖞 𝖆𝖓𝖉 𝕹𝖎𝖌𝖍𝖙 𝕾𝖈𝖊𝖓𝖊𝖘

OF THE

## FRAUDS, FOLLIES, MANNERS, AND DEPRAVITIES
## OF THE METROPOLIS.

### 𝕯𝖔𝖎𝖓𝖌𝖘 𝖔𝖋 𝖙𝖍𝖊 𝕽𝖎𝖓𝖌-𝕯𝖗𝖔𝖕𝖕𝖊𝖗𝖘.*

PEREGRINE WILSON was the son of a retired wealthy merchant, of mean sentiments and narrow comprehension, who desired only to be rich, and to conceal his riches. He originally
intended that his son Peregrine should have a very limited
education; but, discovering great strength of memory and
quickness of apprehension, he sent him to the best school
in the west of England. Here he soon found the delights of
knowledge, and felt the pleasure of intelligence, and the
pride of invention; and began soon to pity his father's grossness
of conception. He felt assured, that knowledge is certainly
one of the means of pleasure, and that ignorance is mere
privation, by which nothing can be produced; it is a vacuity in

* See page 8.

1.                                              B

which the soul sits motionless and torpid for want of attraction;
and, without knowing why, we always rejoice when we learn,
and grieve when we forget; that, if nothing counteracts the
natural consequence of learning, we grow more happy as
our minds take a wider range. After being at this seminary
for some years, death deprived him of his father, and he
thus became possessed of a considerable fortune. He then
determined within himself to satisfy his curiosity of knowing what
is done or suffered in the world; and particularly of visiting London, of which he had heard and read such extraordinary narra-
tions; but, bred up as he had been in pastoral simplicity, and so
completely ignorant of the deceptions and frauds practised in the
metropolis, his friends persuaded him against the journey, lest he
should fall a prey to some designing sharper. Still his curiosity
was unabated, and he resolved to keep his design always in view,
and lay hold of any expedient time should offer. Months rolled
on in this state of uncertainty and expectation, without a prospect
of his entering into the world, and discontent by degrees preyed
upon him, when Mentor, his father's former confidential clerk,
came to his memory: delighted with the hope of gaining his
assistance as a guide, he instantly wrote him his request; and,
in a few days, received for answer, that he would willingly comply
with his desire. Peregrine lost no time in commencing his long-
wished-for journey; and, in a few days, entered London, " stunned
by the noise, and offended by the crowds." After taking some
little refreshment at the inn, he hastened to the house of Mentor,
the future guide of his rambles, who received him affectionately,
on account of the great regard in which he held the memory of his
late father. Peregrine thought himself happy in thus having found a
man who knew the world so well, and could skilfully paint the
scenes of life. He found in him a friend to whom he could impart
his thoughts, and whose experience would assist him in his designs.
He asked a thousand questions about things, to which, though
common to most men, his confinement, from childhood, had kept
him a stranger. Mentor pitied his ignorance, and loved his
curiosity. "The world," said Mentor, "on which you are
about entering, you probably figure to yourself smooth and
quiet, as one of the lakes in your native valleys; but you
will find it a sea foaming with tempests, and boiling with whirl-
pools: you will be sometimes overwhelmed by the waves of
violence, and sometimes dashed against the rocks of treachery.
Amidst wrongs and frauds, competition, and anxieties, you will
wish a thousand times for quiet, and willingly quit hope to be
free from fear." " Do not seek to deter me from my purpose,"
said Peregrine; " I am anxious to see what thou hast seen. Whatever be the consequence of my experiment, I am resolved to judge
with my own eyes, of the various conditions of men, and then to
make deliberately my choice of life."*   " I do not wish,' replied

* Johnson.

Mentor, " to alienate you from your intended project, but I must warn you of the doings in London, of the difficulties you will have to encounter. Be tenacious with whom you associate; form not hasty connections; choose your friends among the wise, and your wife among the virtuous." Mentor thus gave him instruction, and so excited his wishes, that Peregrine regretted the necessity of sleep, and longed till the morning should commence his pleasures. It was agreed that they should breakfast the next morning at the Castle and Falcon, Aldersgate Street, it being the inn where Peregrine intended to reside: to this appointment Peregrine was punctual; they conversed over the news of the day while at breakfast, and, when it was over, Peregrine proposed that they should instantly commence their ramble. " But," said Mentor, " before we begin our walks through London—this vast emporium of happiness and misery, splendour and wretchedness, the mart of all the world, the residence of the voluptuous and the frugal, the idle and the busy, the merchant and the man of learning,—it may be well to give you a short sketch of some of its interesting particulars. Notwithstanding politicians and legislators have at various times expressed considerable alarm at the growth of the metropolis, it has still continued advancing, amidst all impediments and interruptions, to a most gigantic size. Conjecture even dares not fix its limits, for every succeeding year we see some waste ground in the suburbs reclaimed and covered with dwellings; some little village or hamlet in the suburbs united by a continuous street to the metropolis; until what once, and that at no remote period, was London and its environs, is now one great compact city, likely to verify the prediction of James the First, that " England will shortly be London, and London England." By the census of 1821, London, including the borough of Southwark, contained the vast number of 161,905 houses, and 3437 other houses were then building; and, when we consider that every month brings a large addition, it probably could not be too much to estimate the metropolis as at present containing 170,000 houses; nor are its limits likely to stop here, but to be extended considerably in succeeding ages.

" Political economists differed widely in their estimates of the number of inhabitants the metropolis contained, and of the progressive ratio of increase. In 1377, London is said to have contained about 35,000 inhabitants. In 1636-7, they amounted to 700,000, within the city walls, according to a census ordered by the Lord Mayor, Sir Edward Bromfield; but this calculation is thought erroneous. In 1746, an historian calculated the population at 992,000; but, eight years after, Dr. Brackenbridge fixed it at only 751,812 persons; and there is strong reason to believe that this estimate is correct. But, to come to more certain data, we find that, according to the census of 1801, London was inhabited by 864,845 persons. In 1811, it had increased to 1,099,104; and, in 1821, to 1,225,964 persons. Yet, while the population rapidly increases in every other part of the metropolis, it decreases in the city. In 1701, it amounted to 139,300; in 1750, to 87,000; and, at the last census, did not exceed 56,174 persons. This diminution is naturally to be ascribed to the great superiority of the streets at the west-end of the town over those in the east; and to the citizens turning their dwelling-houses into warehouses, and taking their families to some village in the environs, being too refined to bear any longer the inconvenience of "Smoky London!" If the corporation do not set about widening their streets, and generally improving the city, it will shortly be inhabited and frequented by few but what the river Thames calls thither: and the present great proud Ludgate Hill will be as neglected, and as nasty, and as filthy, as its neighbour, Watling Street, now is. So you see, my friend Peregrine," said Mentor, "how cities, like nations and empires, rise and fall, flourish and decay! Having now," continued Mentor, "given you a brief history of the number of its houses and inhabitants, I beg to lead you to the character of these inhabitants, and the means they employ to maintain and amuse themselves.

"The metropolis of England is the centre of wisdom and piety, to which the best and wisest men of every land are continually resorting. Many are brought here by the desire of living after their own manner, without observation, and of lying hid in the obscurity of multitudes. All that is good and noble, generous and humane, is to be found in London; yet it is—

"The needy villain's gen'ral home,"

the receptacle of the vicious and depraved of all parts of the world. But, as a glorious set-off to its annual melancholy catalogue of crime, let us reflect on its numerous godlike charities, with which it abounds, and which stud its immediate vicinity like strings of sparkling diamonds. It is a happy reflection, that there is not a calamity that "flesh is heir to," but what will here find an asylum to assuage its anguish. Such is the metropolis of England! the most dangerous city in the world for a stranger to enter, unless he has a friend to advise him, by reason of the numerous and almost incredible frauds, deceptions, schemes, and villanies, daily practised therein. But," continued Mentor, "to believe them, you must see them: so, take thy hat, and I will show thee sights that will create thy wonder, pity, admiration, and disgust!"

At this instant, a young lad presented himself to their notice, and asked whether they would wish to hear him "*Do* the cat's last dying speech?" Having gained their consent, the boy immediately commenced with his right hand to strike his chin with great rapidity, which, aided by his voice, produced the loud, shrill, and discordant yells of a cat, whose body, one would suppose, was jammed under the leg of a chair; and gave other proofs of his powers of imitating the feline species, truly astonishing. "That boy," said

Mentor, " is named Jackson : he was taken before the magistrates at Union Hall, last year, charged, under the Vagrant Act, with sleeping in the open air. One of the constables of Lambeth stated, that on the preceding night, as he was passing along the Bishop's Walk, he heard a noise proceed from a place where timber was deposited, resembling the cries of a cat in great agony. He hastened to the spot, in order to extricate the animal, conceiving it had got jammed between the logs of wood, from its doleful lamentations. On his way thither, however, the cries of distress were changed into the most loud and boisterous squalling he ever heard in his life, as if at least a dozen cats of both sexes were engaged in their noisy amours. He therefore stopped short, not much relishing the idea of approaching too closely, snatched up a brickbat, and flung it at random (the night being too dark to discover objects) towards the place from whence the 'row' proceeded; but he might as well have spared himself the trouble, for the caterwauling, instead of diminishing, increased to a degree that was quite stunning. He therefore plucked up all his courage, and, having cautiously on tip-toe advanced, with a stone in his hand, weighty enough to knock the 'nine lives' out of any poor mouser, he was astonished, on looking about, to see no cat, or any thing in the shape of a cat, but discovered the boy Jackson, lying very comfortably coiled up between two immense beams of timber. He pretended to be asleep at first, but when the constable said he was convinced he was only shamming, and added, that the uproar the cats had been making would have prevented any human being from closing his eyes, ' the boy then admitted,' said the constable, ' to my wonderment, that it was he who had kicked up the disturbance, and imitated the cats to the very life. And so,' added the constable, ' I took him to the watchouse, and locked him up, for lying out in the open air.' "

" The boy, who stood smiling during the constable's statement of his adventures the night before, on being asked how he got his livelihood, replied, ' By chanting the cat's last dying speech.' The magistrates discharged him, after admonishing him not to be found sleeping again in the open air."

Mentor and his young friend now advanced to the street, with an intention of going to see the New London Bridge, and, as they passed along, their attention was attracted by a woman decently dressed, apparently in the greatest distress, with three children apparently starving; which proved to be the celebrated impostor, Jenny Weston, who, in January, 1827, was taken before Mr. White, the magistrate in Queen Square, by Thompson, the street-keeper; from whose statement it appeared, that this lady and her progeny had for a long time imposed on the credulity of John Bull, and that the drama was uncommonly well got up. The prisoner, who was the principal tragedian in the piece, completely deceived him for some time, as well as the public, by her inimitable representation of a distressed mother with three children, starving in the streets. The scene opens thus :—The prisoner is discovered sitting on the steps of Mr. Cockburn, at White-Hall Place, exclaiming, "**My poor children, what shall I do to get you a mouthful of bread?**" when a tall genteel woman, belonging to the company, comes up and says, "God bless me! my poor creature, what is the matter? Here is all I have got about me at present (turning to some stranger passing): did you ever see such a scene of misery?" Here John Bull's heart naturally melts, and his hand goes into his pocket; when a little short woman, genteelly dressed, belonging to the party, comes up, exclaiming "Oh dear, I am afraid the poor woman is in labour! Do get her to a public-house and give her some refreshment; I fear she will die in the streets (by this time a crowd begins to be collected). Here, my poor soul, take this: it is the last penny I have; but some of these good gentlemen will surely give you a trifle." The distressed mother, during this time, is groaning most lamentably, and commences with "God bless you, kind ladies; my poor children have had nothing to eat for some days—may you never know what want is!" The feelings of the auditory are now wound up to the highest pitch, and the pennies, sixpences, perchance a half-crown, flow into the treasury; the distressed mother is removed to a public-house, and the scene closes. The distressed mother and the two ladies then regale themselves with gin, &c., when they remove to some other spot, the drama is again successfully represented, and the performers reap a rich benefit. Thompson said, so completely was the public gulled by the acting of the prisoner and her two lady confederates, that, about three weeks ago, he took the prisoner into custody, when she resisted, appealing to the by-standers, who rescued her; but, in this instance, some of the audience had seen the tragedy so often repeated, that their tears had ceased to flow, and they assisted him.

The magistrate assured the prisoner she should not perform in public again for three months, and she was committed to the House of Correction for that period.

"This case of imposition," said Mentor, " is not a solitary one; innumerable others might be quoted. I recollect, a few months ago, being at the Mansion House, when four Irishwomen were brought before the Lord Mayor, charged with being common impostors, in shamming fits in the public streets, in order to excite compassion; and the four prisoners are as audacious a set of impostors of that kind, as, perhaps, ever were seen. Their operations were carried on in Moorfields, where they had gained many a shilling; but they were observed and followed by a person who had before seen with what ease they made a comfortable livelihood. One of them, in a very miserable dress, lay down on the broad of her back on the pavement, and frothed at the mouth, and kicked and gnashed her teeth in a horrible manner; while another, with difficulty, held the limbs of the sufferer, and called the attention of humane passengers to her distressed condition, which, she said, arose from want of the necessaries of life. A third, who was dressed like a decent servant-maid, and carried a key in her hand, was seen rummaging her pockets, with tears actually in her eyes ; while the fourth stood looking on, with pity in her countenance, in order to increase the crowd. Each fit was sure to produce money. Soon after the first terminated, the four women paired off, and turned into different public-houses, where they swallowed a couple of glasses of gin each, and then returned to their occupations. After the second fit, they were going to have a little more comfort, but they were disturbed. It required the exertions of six officers to convey them to the Compter. They all looked quite mild when brought before the Lord Mayor, who ordered them to prison and good wholesome labour for a month. After they had retired from the bar, and were locked up in the cage, they desired that his lordship should be informed that they would be d——d if they would not require a coach and six horses to convey them to prison. The gaoler, however, altered their opinions upon the subject, by informing them that, if they would not go quietly, they should be tied hand and foot and placed in a cart.

" In 1731, a female, of tolerable appearance, and between thirty and forty years of age, was the cause of much alarm, by pretending to *hang herself*, in different parts of the town. Her method was this : she found a convenient situation for the experiment, and suspended herself; an accomplice, always at hand for the purpose, immediately released her from the rope, and, after rousing the neighbourhood, absconded. Humanity induced the spectators sometimes to take her into their houses, always to relieve her; who were told, when sufficiently *recovered to articulate*, that she had possessed £1500; but that, marrying an Irish captain, he robbed her of every penny, and fled ; which produced despair, and a determination to commit suicide.

" About this period, another impostor levied great contributions on the credulity of John Bull : it was in the person of a little wretch, who pretended to be subject to epileptic fits, and would fall purposely into some dirty pool, whence he never failed to be conveyed to a dry place, or to receive handsome donations. Sometimes he terrified the spectators with frightful gestures and convulsive motions, as if he would beat his head and limbs to pieces, and, gradually recovering, receive the rewards of his performance ; but the frequency of the exploit at length attracted the notice of the police, in which presence the symptoms continued with the utmost violence: the magistrate, however, undertook, upon this occasion, the office of physician, prescribed the Compter (the tread-mill then was not known), and finally the workhouse, where he had no sooner arrived, than, finding it useless to counterfeit, he began to amend, and beat his hemp with double earnestness.

" Of later days, we witnessed the exploits of *Mister Collins*, the celebrated ' Soap-Eater,' who used to pretend to be in fits, and, by putting a quantity of soap in his mouth, and working it into a lather, let it foam out of the sides of his mouth, making it appear exactly as if he was in dreadful convulsive fits. This fellow used principally to exhibit about Lincoln's-Inn Fields."

Peregrine, lost in amazement at the recital of such tales of imposition, seemed to doubt their existence. " I see," said Mentor, " you had little idea of the doings in London ; but these cases of fraud are as nothing to what I shall bring before you, especially when I take you to St. Giles's, and introduce you to the beggars, or *Cadgers*, as they are called.   But we had better now return to the inn to dinner, and, to beguile our time, I will relate to you the exploits of Mr. John Holloway, known well about town, as the celebrated ' Cabbage-Eater,' who has for many years carried on his profession, as a starving mendicant, with great success, although he has been committed above thirty times to the House of Correction, from the different police-offices. While I was waiting at Queen-Square Office, on the 16th of May last (1827), he was brought before the magistrate, by an inspector of nuisances, charged with imposing on the public by the following stratagem :—It appeared, from the statement of Wright, that the prisoner (whom he had repeatedly cautioned) was in the constant habit of attracting a crowd of passengers around him, by pretending to be starved sitting on the pavement, he would procore a large raw cabbage, which, when any person passed, he would begin to tear to pieces in the most ravenous manner with his teeth, and pretend to eat it. The passengers, conceiving he was in a state of starvation, to be driven to eat raw cabbage, generally gave him something ; by which means he reaped a tolerable good harvest, making oftentimes more in a day than the donors themselves.   Yesterday morning he found the prisoner in Wilton Street, Knightsbridge Road, with about thirty persons around him, whose pity seemed to be excited at seeing him devour a raw cabbage ; he immediately took him into custody.   Wright said, that when he took the prisoner into custody, he had his mouth crammed full of raw cabbage, which he spit out. He did not eat a tenth part of the cabbage he pretended, for he always contrived, by some sleight-of-hand trick, to get the greater part out of his mouth before he swallowed it.   The prisoner was committed accordingly."

Mentor and his friend, having returned to the inn, and while waiting for dinner, Peregrine, seeing two men in earnest conversation with a countryman (who seemingly had just arrived in London), and showing him some rings, seals, and other trinkets, asked, what was their business?   " Those men," replied Mentor, " are two of the most notorious ring-droppers* in London.— They are very common offenders, and belong to a set of cheats that frequently trick simple people, both from the country and Londoners, out of their money ; but generally exercise their villanous acts upon young women. Their usual method is, to drop

* See page 1

a ring, or gilt seal, or some trinket, just before their intended victim comes up, when they generally accost her thus : 'Young woman, I have found a ring, and I really believe it is gold, for here is a stamp upon it.' Immediately upon this, an accomplice joins him, who, being asked the question, replies, 'It is gold.' 'Well,' says the former, 'as the young woman saw me pick it up, she has a right to half of it.' As it often happens, the young person has but a few shillings about her. The sharper says, 'If you have a mind for the ring (or whatever it may be), you shall have it for what you have got in your pocket, and what else you can give me ; which sometimes proves to be a good silk-hand-kerchief, or other apparel. The young woman, being about to take the ring, and give the money and things for it, the accomplice says, 'You had better ask a goldsmith if it is gold ;' but, looking about, they perceive none near, upon which they conclude it is good, and so they part.

"I will now," said Mentor, "give you a history of two other similar frauds, that recently transpired.

"A Miss S—— attended at Union Hall, February, 1828, and gave the following account of a gross imposition that had been practised on her. She stated, that, as she was passing over Blackfriars Bridge, a very tall woman, dressed in a black straw bonnet, light shawl, and dark gown, stooped down and picked up a small parcel, exclaiming, at the same time, 'You are entitled to a share, miss.' On opening the parcel, it was found to contain three very handsome-looking rings, apparently set with real stones, and also a bill of parcels for £10. 5s. 6d. en-closed with the jewellery. The woman then said, 'These things are too fine for me ; you shall have them for half their worth.' Miss S——, believing they were the real sort, pulled out her purse, and gave all the money it contained (12 or 13s.) to the woman, and would have given her three times as much if she had had it about her. To her astonishment, however, the woman was satisfied, and both of them separated, mutually pleased with their good fortune. Miss S—— had the curiosity to enter a jeweller's shop to inquire the real value of the rings, when she discovered they were metal and not worth a groat.

"Now, the next history will develop further cunning tricks played off in London on unsuspecting country people. In May, 1827, a simple-looking young Welshman, apparently about twenty years of age, and most respectably dressed, came to the Thames Police Office in a state of distraction, and charged a fellow well known as a *gammoning cove,* who gave his name William Allen, with robbing him of eighteen sovereigns. On being desired to state all the particulars, he said, he was a native of Llechryd, near Cardigan, in Wales; and, intending to go to America, where he was told he had a rich uncle living, he took his passage to London in the True Blue Coach from Bristol, and, immediately on his arrival in the metropolis, in compliance

2.

with his directions, he repaired to the North and South American Coffee-House, to the master of which he was strongly recommended as a countryman. On his calling there, and explaining the object of his visit, the master, being rather busy, told him to go and walk about and look at the shipping till four o'clock, when, on his return, he should be happy to give him every assistance in his power. Being directed towards the London Docks, he proceeded towards the Tower; and, when he got on Tower Hill, he saw the prisoner walking a little before him. Prisoner, when he saw he was observing him, at once ran forward, and apparently took up a piece of paper off the ground, and put it into his pocket. He immediately after pulled it out, and observing his (Stephens's) curiosity excited, opened it cautiously, and showed him a watch, chain, and seals. He then said, ' If you don't tell any person I found this, I will give you half of it.' Stephens said that he did not want it. Prisoner replied, that ' he must have half of it, as he saw him find it;' and, pointing to a respectable-looking man on before him, said, ' That is a gentleman who is a judge of it, and he will value it, if you give him a shilling.' The prisoner called out to this person, and, on his telling him what he wanted him for, the person at first refused, unless he was paid. Stephens said that he did not want to have any thing to do with the watch, and consequently would not have any thing to do with valuing it. At last, after much entreaty, he agreed to give sixpence, the prisoner paying the other sixpence, which, after conversing some time with him, prisoner agreed to do, and he then accompanied them into a public-house, and as he was going in, he observed the wife of the public-house (as he termed her) look very steadfastly at him, upon which he was determined to be cautious what he was about; and, on their entering the parlour, and sitting down, the watch was produced, and the person whom they met on Tower Hill declared it to be a most valuable watch. At this time the prisoner began to sit very close to him. Hearing a good deal of the dexterity of the London pickpockets, he felt his pocket where he kept his sovereigns. He found he had them; but, lest their ingenuity might have abstracted any of them, he pulled out the paper containing the sovereigns, and began to count them, which no sooner did the prisoner perceive, than he snatched them from him, and handed them to his companion, who instantly threw down the watch, and ran out of the room. He endeavoured to follow him, but the prisoner held him by the collar, and prevented him. The noise of the transaction attracting the attention of one of the officers who happened to be passing at the time, he took the prisoner into custody."

The best plan for the country people and others to pursue, is to avoid entering into conversation with any stranger in the streets of London, by which means they will save themselves from being duped, and oftentimes ruined.

While strolling the streets, the attention of Peregrine was drawn by witnessing a crowd assembled round a baker's shop, in consequence of a poor woman complaining that the loaf she held in her hand was bad bread, which the baker refused to exchange. " This case," said Mentor, " is not uncommon in London ; the adulteration of bread is one of the most wicked impositions practised in London. The wretch who improves his circumstances by this detestable method of increasing his profits, is an assassin full as wicked as the celebrated Italian, Tophana : that human fiend poisoned her victims by degrees, suited to the malice of her employers ; the baker, who throws slow poisons into his trough, does worse, for he undermines the constitutions of his supporters, his customers. He that eats bread without butter or meat, throughout London, at the present moment, and afterwards visits a friend in the country, who makes his own, cannot fail of perceiving the delicious sweetness which the mercy of our Creator hath diffused through the invaluable grain that produces it ; the inducement held out to us, to preserve life by the most innocent means, is thus, in a great measure, lost to the inhabitants of London. I lodged a week at a baker's house, in a country town, and, during a lazy fit, strolled into the bakehouse, where bread was mixing ; in an instant, my landlord's countenance changed, and I was rudely desired to leave the place, as he would allow no one to pry into his business. This conduct, from a man who had before behaved with the utmost civility, convinced me all was not right, and that other materials were within view than simple flour, yeast, and a little innocent salt. Let me not, however, be understood to apply this censure indiscriminately ; it is aimed only at the guilty : the honest baker will adopt my sentiments, which are merely an echo of a little work published in 1757, entitled ' Poison Detected ; or, Frightful Truths, and alarming to the British Metropolis,' &c. The author asserts, that ' good bread ought to be composed of flour well kneaded with the slightest water, seasoned with a little salt, fermented with fine yeast or leaven, and sufficiently baked with a proper fire ; but, to increase its weight, and deceive the buyer by its fraudulent fineness, lime, chalk, alum, &c., are constituent parts of that most common food, in London. Alum is a very powerful astringent and styptic, occasioning heat and costiveness ; the frequent use of it closes up the mouths of the small alimentary ducts, and, by its corrosive concretions, seals up the lacteals, indurates every mass it is mixed with upon the stomach, makes it hard of digestion, and consolidates the fæces in the intestines. Experience convinces me (the author was a physician), that any animal will live longer in health and vigour upon two ounces of good and wholesome bread, than upon one pound of this adulterated compound ; a consideration which may be useful, if attended to in the times of scarcity. But it is not alum alone that suffices the lucrative iniquity of bakers : there is also added a considerable portion of lime and chalk ; so that, if alum be prejudicial* alone, what must be the consequences of eating our bread mingled with alum, chalk, and lime. Obstructions, the causes of most diseases, are naturally formed by bread thus abused. I have seen a quantity of lime and chalk, in the proportion of one to six, extracted from this kind of bread : possibly the baker was not so expert at his craft as to conceal it : the larger granules were visible enough ; perhaps a more minute analysis would have produced a much greater proportion of these pernicious materials.' Since the publication of this work, the guilty baker has made great *improvement* in mixing the deadly stuff which he puts into his bread. In the Times of February, 1828, it says, ' Guildhall— Among the affidavits sworn before Mr. Alderman Ansley yesterday, there was one as to the quantity of goods delivered to, and payments made by, a certain baker. There was a statement of the account annexed, in which occurred two items of deliveries, along with sacks of flour, of *five sacks of bones* each time ; some other stuff was also mentioned by an unintelligible name.'

" I will read you," continued Mentor, " an extract from a paper, in a very interesting periodical, called the *Verulam,* on the subject of the quality of bakers' bread. It says,—' Considering the extent to which the manufacture of bread is required for the supply of the metropolis, and the great temptation afforded to fraudulent tradesmen by the laxity of our municipal regulations, it is not at all surprising that the far greater portion of the bread supplied by the London bakers should be very different from what is presumed to be good wholesome bread, made from wheaten flour only. The consequences resulting from the habitual use of impure or unwholesome bread are, according to our view of the subject, of so serious a nature, as to attach a sort of stigma to our local police, in not taking this branch of civil economy under their immediate superintendence. The local magistracy have the power, which, in some few instances they exercise, of directing unwholesome butchers' meat, or putrid fish, to be publicly seized and destroyed. But, with regard to bread—an article of more universal consumption than either of the above varieties of food—the magistrates seem to think it entirely beneath their notice, unless a specific charge be advanced against an individual baker of having such commodities on his premises as are more publicly and commonly known to be ingredients for the adulteration of bread. Instead of leaving the manufacture of meal, or flour, on which the health of a population of more than a million of persons depends, to the integrity of the miller or mealman, we are of opinion that a similar degree of control ought to be vested in some competent authority, like that of the Excise Board, in superintending the manufacture of malt.

" ' We shall not waste the time of our readers by defining the pro-

* Mr. Clarke, of Apothecaries' Hall, says, alum is not at all injurious, in the quantity in which it is used by the bakers ; they only use it when the yeast is bad, and in small quantities—merely one pound to eight bushels of flour, which can do no harm.

perties of so well-known a commodity as wheaten flour. It wil.
be sufficient to point out the effects on the animal economy, of such
compounds as are too generally, or almost uniformly, sold for fine
flour in the metropolis. It is well known that the quality of grain
varies from ten to thirty per cent. in value, not only from the nature
of the soil in which it has been grown, but also from the way in
which it has been harvested. This is, however, a question simply
between the farmer, or corn-factor, and the miller, and with which
the consumer has nothing to do. The next point, however, very
seriously concerns the consumer—whether the miller or mealman supplies the baker, or the private family, with genuine
wheaten flour, or with a compound meal ground up from several
other kinds of grain and pulse of inferior quality?

" 'That the latter system is carried on in almost every extensive
flour-mill throughout the kingdom, we take the liberty of asserting,
without the fear of contradiction. Not only foreign or ship corn of
damaged quality, but beans, peas, and other inferior grain, are
ground up and mixed with more than three fourths of the flour consumed in the metropolis. It is not necessary to designate at length
the names and qualities of the various samples sold by the London
mealmen under the name of " Fine," " Seconds," " Middlings," &c.,
as the very best of these varieties of flour are only *middlings*, if
considered as an article of daily food ; while some of the inferior
kinds, even when made up of grain alone, are very far from affording wholesome food in the different processes of domestic economy.
The case is, however, infinitely worse when pulverized stone is sold
and used to a great extent as wheaten flour. The calcareous class
of earths, as the sub-carbonates and sulphate of lime, as well as
the tenacious white clays termed potters' clay, or pipe-clay, afford
the most perfect imitations of flour, and serve to deceive even the
most experienced eye, when blended with flour in certain proportions. The article known in the meal trade by the name of
" Devonshire white," forms a very large constituent of the flour
used in London by the inferior bakers, but more especially by the
inferior pastry-cooks.

" 'Now, independent of the gross frauds committed on the public
consumer (for the baker is well aware of the admixture of these
pernicious ingredients in flour, and pays for it at a proportionably
low price), the use of flour for food containing even a tenth part of
insoluble earthy matter, must be attended with the worst consequences to the animal functions.

" 'The unwholesomeness of constantly using bakers' bread, is
commonly ascribed to the portion of alum almost universally employed by bakers in the great towns throughout the kingdom. But
we have no hesitation in stating, that much more evil is to be apprehended from the shameful adulterations of flour by the mealmen.
The principal use of alum in bread-making, is that of hardening
the surface of loaves at the instant they are placed into the oven
while the heat expands the pores of the dough, or sponge. **By**

this means, the bread of the public bakers always preserves its form, so as to please the eye, and also allows of the partition or division of the loaves from each other more effectually than what is called "home-baked bread." The use of alum also contributes in a small degree to improve the colour of bread; but its principal value is that of mechanical agency in improving the shape and appearance of bread. The use of this salt in making bread is, however, extremely injurious to the animal functions, from its drying, or styptic properties, occasioning constipation of the viscera; a small quantity, even a few grains, taken daily, being sufficient to derange the digestive powers in a very perceptive degree. Persons having sedentary occupations ought most particularly to abstain from the use of bread containing the smallest portion of alum; for, the digestive functions of such persons being already impaired by want of exercise, in the great majority of instances, bread containing alum acts literally as a slow poison on the temperament of such individuals. It is not merely constipation of the alimentary passages, to be removed by cathartic medicines only, but a derangement, or paralysis, of all the vital functions, which results from the use of bread having alum in its preparation. It is, moreover, worthy of recollection, that flour of inferior quality stands more in need of alum in the process of bread-making than good flour. One of the distinguishing characters of good wheat flour is that of the gluten it contains, by which property it has a sufficient tenacity to form a tough sponge, which prevents the escape of the air and carbonic acid gas, generated by the fermentation or *working* of the sponge: whereas, inferior flour, as bean-flour, though perhaps equal to wheaten flour in colour, having less gluten, is neither so capable of producing a good fermentation, nor by any means furnishing so nutritive a kind of food when made into bread. We are, however, disposed to think, that, although alum is almost universally employed by bakers with the view of improving the appearance of their bread, as well as for the purpose of disguising the use of inferior flour, yet that this salt is not the worst ingredient in the ordinary bread, or seconds, of the London bakers. We believe, as we before stated, that a vast quantity of pulverized earthy matter is employed by the London bakers and pastry-cooks. It is essential that the sponge, or paste, of bakers, should undergo the process of fermentation; therefore, there must be a sufficient portion of vegetable gluten in the mass to answer that purpose, or no raising or leavening of the mass could take place."

"Maton, in his *Tricks of Bakers Unmasked*, says, 'Alum (which is called the *Doctor*), ground and unground, is sold to the bakers at 4d. per pound. Upon a moderate calculation, there are upwards of 700,000 pounds of alum used annually by the London bakers. It would fill a volume to enumerate all the pernicious practices resorted to by bakers: a case was decided a few years ago, against a baker, for mixing pumice-stone, finely pulverized,

with his flour, and making it into bread : when, by the evidence
of a surgeon, it appeared, that, if a *single particle* of the pulverized
ingredient had rested in the bladder, it would have generated stone.'

Mr. Clarke, of Apothecaries' Hall, stated, before the Lord
Mayor, August, 1825, that he had been sent to Hull, by order of
the Lords of the Treasury, to analyze samples of 1467 sacks of
flour, then at the Custom-House there, to be shipped for Spain and
Portugal; and, on examination, he found *one third of it was plaster
of Paris, one third burnt bones and beans*, and the remainder flour
of the worst description.   On his reporting the result of his examination to the Lords of the Treasury, the flour was condemned, and
ordered to be thrown into the sea, and the owner of it fined to the
amount of £10,000.   The value of the flour was between £3,000
and £4,000.    'I have,' continued Mr. Clarke, 'upon several
other occasions, found, in bakers' flour, an immense quantity of
plaster of Paris, burnt stones, and an earthy substance called
Derbyshire Whites, of the most destructive nature, but prepared for
the sole use of bakers, confectioners, and pastry-cooks.   The
colour of all those dreadful ingredients is beautiful; it resembles
that of the finest flour, and the article is impossible to be detected
in its unmade-up state, without a chymical process.

" It no doubt very often happens that, when a poor baker is in
debt to his mealman, he is prevented from returning flour which he is
assured is unwholesome, and is forced to use it against his inclination :

'His poverty, and not his will, consents.'

Talk of the *assassin !* why his deed is innocence itself, when compared with the hellish *doings* of such a mealman; who, for the sake of
a little money, *slowly* murders thousands of his fellow-creatures !

Unfortunately, the wicked practice of mixing impure ingredients in the bread is not the only knavish ' doing' of the unprincipled London bakers.   I will tell you how they ' *do,*' to
*make a small shoulder of mutton grow into a large one.*   Mr. Crust
first buys the smallest shoulder of mutton which he can find;
perhaps it may weigh about four pounds.   When his Sunday's
dishes come in (which, if he be in any thing of a trade, will be
pretty numerous), he changes this four-pound shoulder for a five-
pounder; then he removes his five-pound shoulder to the place of
a six; then substitutes a seven, and so on to eight, nine, and ten !
Thus he makes a clear gain of six pounds of mutton, and changes
his four pounds of carrion for prime meat.—Maton, in his Confessions, says,—'I had not been long in this service, before I
became fully acquainted with London honesty!   For, on the first
Sunday after I entered this service, I had to attend, with the
other men, in the baking of the dishes of meat, and other things
which were brought to the shop; the custom being, to leave the
dish, and receive a ticket in return for it.   As I was the under-
man, it became my duty to take the dishes out of the shop into
the bakehouse; the second hand, as the cant phrase is, shaves

the meat, that is to say, cuts as much off from each joint as he thinks will not be missed; the foreman drains the water off, and puts the dishes in the oven till they require to be turned; after which, the liquid fat is drained from each dish, and the deficiency is supplied with water; this fat is the master's perquisite. It may be plainly seen, between master and man, that, by these perquisites, the public looses at least two ounces on each pound of meat; and, there being a mutual understanding between master and man, there is little fear of detection. My master not only robbed the customers' dishes of the fat, but he robbed me of my perquisite, in taking the lean also. However, I consoled myself with having a good parish pudding on Christmas Day. I told the servant-maid of my intention, and that she should participate in it. On this day of the year, it is known, all persons provide, according to their means, plum-puddings, mince-pies, and joints of meat; and, at an early hour, they were brought into the shop, ready for the oven. My master being jealous of my presence, sent me out to a public-house, telling me, when he wanted me, he would send for me. I thought it strange he should send me to a public-house, when there was so much extra business to be done, and the more so, when I found that my mistress had sent the servant-maid up stairs: after a considerable time had elapsed, I thought my master had forgot to send to me; I returned home, and remained unobserved in the bakehouse for some time, for my master was too busily employed to notice me, in filling his dishes, basins, and tea-saucers, with puddings and mince-meat, and in ornamenting his dough-boards with mutton chops, veal cutlets, and beef steaks, cut most scientifically from the viands before him. There were upwards of twenty puddings from which he had taken toll.' "

Peregrine asked if there was no punishment for bakers acting so dishonestly? " A little," replied Mentor: " for selling their bread short of weight, it is liable to seizure, and the baker is fined; for instance, some time since, a police-officer found on the premises of a baker fifty quartern loaves and twenty half-quarterns, each loaf being deficient of weight, some wanting from *four* to *seven* ounces! The whole deficiency amounted to *one hundred and sixty-nine ounces*. The penalty only amounted to £21. 2s. 6d. All the bread was forfeited, and by the magistrates distributed among the poor. On the same day, a baker was fined by Sir John Eamer, in the mitigated penalty of £10 with costs, for having a quantity of alum, and other mixtures and ingredients, found in his bakehouse, with intent to use the same in adulterating the flour and bread. This is all the punishment the present law inflicts. But the antient way of punishing bakers for want of weight, was by the tumbrel or cucking-stool. This punishment was inflicted on them in the time of King Henry the Third, by Hugh Bigod, brother to the Earl Marshal. In Turkey, when a baker is found selling bread short of weight, he is hung up instantly before his own door : and Massaniello, the fisherman of Naples, the short time he was in power, passed a law, that all bakers who sold bad bread should be baked in their own ovens.

" Such, my friend," continued Mentor, " are a part of the *doings* of the dishonest bakers of London ; shortly, I shall have an opportunity, not only of giving you a further insight into their knavish tricks, but also of making you acquainted with the mode of knowing bad bread from good.

While they were discoursing on the subject, on their way home, their attention was arrested, by witnessing a vast number of persons crowding into an elegantly fitted-up shop. Peregrine asked what place it was : " Why," replied Mentor, " it is worth thy while to see ; so step in, and (throwing open the door) there," said he, ' behold

THE DOINGS IN A GIN-SHOP !'"

Peregrine seemed lost in amazement, while witnessing the wretched motley group, thus so suddenly presented to his view ; the vulgar laugh—the idiotic grin—the drunken brawl—the hysteric

3.                    C

convulsive throb, which emanated from this mass of misery, poverty, and profligacy, filled his mind with horror, pity, and disgust. After recovering himself, he said, " I thought you told me the poorer sort of people in London were wretchedly in need : why, these surely cannot be any of your poor, for they seem to throw their money away with such heedlessness and extravagance ? It they were poor, I think they could not expend so much in drink as they seem to do." " Indeed, they are the poor," said Mentor; " and the major part of them live upon charity, or receive parochial relief. It is well known that, in many cases, the parish officers refuse to relieve the poor with money, but supply them, instead, with coals, bread, and potatoes ; and no sooner do they get them, than they sell them for what they can get, and expend it in this deadly poison—*gin !* They borrow each other's children, in order that they may appear with them before the parish boards, and have a greater claim to obtain a further allowance ; and, the instant they procure it, then it all goes to the gin-shop. Innumerable such cases I might give you, and, 1 assure you, it is no wonder that the poor-rates should increase, and keep pace with the consumption of gin. In 1827, TWELVE MILLIONS OF GALLONS OF GIN were consumed *more than in the preceding year*, and the poor-rates for the same period amounted to the enormous sum of SEVEN MILLION, SEVEN HUNDRED AND EIGHTY-FOUR THOUSAND, THREE HUNDRED AND FIFTY-ONE POUNDS ! but, of this," said Mentor, " we will speak shortly : let us sit down—we shall be hid among the many, while I tell you the characters and callings of some of these poor lost creatures, now before us.

" That fellow with the crutches, in conversation with the woman, is a most notorious beggar : he is possessed of a great property, in the funds, in houses, and out at interest; but more of his history when I shall show you him in his own element, in the back settlements near Diot Street, St. Giles's. The woman he is talking with, is in a good way of busines in the *cadging-line*, together with her husband, who was taken to the Mansion-House, before the Lord Mayor, in 1827, for being found lying on the ground without shoes, stockings, or shirt, shivering as in the most deplorable condition, from the extreme cold. They were old performers, who were never seen in the city except during hard frosts, when the public sympathies were strongly excited by their nakedness, and appearance of extreme misery. They disappear with the frost, because the exposure then excites less sympathy. Some gentlemen who know the imposture, have often been incited to give money to the fellows, as a compensation for their matchless theatrical performance of wretched characters. No estimate can well be made of the receipts of these fellows, but they are known to be such as to induce them to quit good employment, to beg during the inclement season. The Lord Mayor sent him to Bridewell, there to be kept to hard labour.

That little child, without shoes or stockings, with her father's waistcoat on, having no other clothing, is employed by her parents to run about the streets, in a miserable plight, with naked feet, in the frost. A party of such was taken to the Mansion-House, February, 1827; one of them was apprehended sitting in a court, with a basket, which contained the shoes and stockings of the other children, who were running about, and endeavouring to excite compassion by their nakedness. When they had got sufficient money in this manner, ere the day had closed, they put on their shoes and stockings, and returned home. The Lord Mayor remanded them, and ordered their mother to be sent for, that she might be made responsible for their being at large. Several women, the police are aware, live well by the mendicancy of their children, who are compelled to bring home a certain sum, generally 1s. 6d. per day: all they get beyond this they spend themselves. Thus, a mother who has four or five children, can afford, as the officers state, to "stay at home, and drink gin like a lady." The children are flogged if they do not make up the required sum, and, when occasions serve, they do it by pilfering.

He with the flat basket by his side is a well-known beggar, who frequents St. James's Park, and there, by his piteous tale of misery, imposes on the charity of the frequenters of that celebrated promenade: the woman just entering the door with the pattens in her hand, is also a vile impostor; she always appears remarkably decent, and pretends to be a woman who has seen better days, and used, after the death of her husband, to get her livelihood by needle-work, until she unfortunately caught cold, which deprived her of the sight of one eye, and nearly that of the other. This story is all false: she can see as well as anybody; watch her closely, and you will find her slip her patch off her eye, and appear as merry as the most jovial among the company.

That poor dying creature, in the very last state of a consumption, you there see sitting on a tub, and reclining his head on a gin-cask, was, some time since, a respectable master-tradesman in Holborn; but his love for spirituous liquors soon brought his family to the workhouse, and himself to the state you now see him in: he has been known to drink sixteen glasses of gin in the course of a morning. What a contrast between him and the landlord; between the *gin-drinker* and the *gin-seller:* the one, a horrid spectre of disease, worn to the bone! the other, full of the good things of this world, in the very plenitude of health: for he is like the doctor—he never takes any of his own stuff." "And pray," said Peregrine, "why should he not?" "Because, my friend, he knows of what deadly ingredients it is composed. Gin, or *Geneva*, is principally the manufacture of Holland, from whence it derives its name. The Dutch distillers make the best gin from a spirit drawn from wheat, mixed with a third or fourth part of malted barley, and twice rectified over with juniper berries; but, in general, rye meal is used instead of wheat. But it is the common practice in England, in the making of gin, to add *oil of turpentine*, in the proportion of two ounces to ten gallons of raw spirits; highly injurious as this is, it is not, unfortunately, the only prejudicial ingredient which is put in it. When the gin comes from the distiller, the retailer must know how to *manage* it, for there is a great art in the *making-up* of gin: in the first place, he lowers and reduces it in strength, which he does by putting *white quicklime* in water that has been boiled, and letting it stand until properly settled; he then adds the water to his gin, stirring it well about with what they call a rummaging-staff. Well, when their gin is *lowered*, they then *flavour* it, and *make it up;* and, in doing which, the following are among the ingredients used:—

" Oil of vitriol.                   Sulphuric æther.
  Oil of turpentine.                Extract of orace-root.
  Oil of juniper.                   Extract of angelica-root.
  Oil of cassia.                    Extract of capsicums, or
  Oil of carraways.                 Extract of grains of Paradise.
  Oil of almonds.                   Water, sugar, &c."

The extract of *Capsicums,* or extract of *Grains of Paradise,* is known in the trade by the appellation of " The Devil." They are manufactured by putting a quantity of small East India chellies into a bottle of spirits of wine, and keeping it closely stopped for about a month. They are used to impart an appearance of strength, by the hot pungent flavour which they infuse into the spirit requiring their aid: they give a hot taste in the mouth, which passes for strength with the persons imposed upon. The *oil of vitriol,* from its pungency, keeps up the appearance of strength, when applied to the nose, as the extracts of *capsicums,* or of *grains of paradise,* do, when applied to the taste. *Oil of turpentine* and *sulphuric æther* (the turpentine having been changed from its oily state, by means of *lime-water,* the whites of eggs, or *spirits of wine*) are used for the purpose of concealing the *oil of vitriol,* and to give it a delicate taste. The *extracts of orace* and *angelica roots* are used to give a fulness of body and flavour, and, by their relative bitters, keeping the taste as nearly as possible to that of the gin previously to any reduction.

" That the proportions of the different ingredients I have named," says the author of an invaluable treatise lately published, called *Wine and Spirit Adulterations Unmasked* (a work which, to use a homely saying, is ' worth its weight in gold,' and which every family in England ought to be possessed of), " are varied according to the taste of the wholesale dealer or gin-shop keeper, as well as that sometimes several articles are struck out altogether, or their places supplied by others equally deleterious, there can be little doubt; but that the materials are as numerous, and used in as considerable a quantity, is proved beyond all question, by this simple calculation: it requires *forty-eight gallons of water* to reduce one hundred gallons of gin, purchased at its cheapest rate, to one of the prices at which it is advertised (that at *6s. 6d.* per gallon), and the still further addition of *forty-four gallons more of water* (*making a total of ninety-two gallons*), to allow a profit of **1*s*. 6*d*.** per gallon.

"This alone must be conclusive to every mind, that practices, such as I have pointed out, do exist; and, when it is considered that the evil consequences from them fall most heavily on the poorer classes of society, no one will deny that the system calls loudly for the interference of government. The idle reply that, the weaker such a compound as gin is made, the less injuries it is likely to work, is no answer to such a case; because, although strong spirits may be injurious to the health and morals of the lower classes, the drinking such compositions as I have described must also be pernicious to the constitution and comfort of the people; and tends only to enrich a class of the community, who have neither honour nor usefulness enough to entitle them to the wealth they obtain.

"A part of the profits of many of our modern gin-shop keepers," says the same ingenious author, "arises from a mode they have of cheating their poor dram-drinkers out of their fair allowance of gin, &c. It bespeaks the state of refinement to which their ingenuity has arrived, in this respect, and the fact is, of itself, not a little curious. The means by which a certain additional profit is obtained, is technically called in the trade ' by the turn of the glass,' and may be thus explained:—

"The glasses made use of for the poor people to drink their spirits from, are shaped thus:—

The counter of the bar is covered with lead, perforated with holes, having a communication with a cask. Now, as, for obvious reasons, the glasses, although scarcely holding the measure when filled to the brim, are seldom so filled, at least to within the eighth or sixteenth of an inch, from the chances that, in all probability, as much will be spilled, and run into the cask prepared to receive it, a quantity equal to the portion contained in three quarters of an inch or more, at the bottoms of what are termed their half-quartern glasses, is thus saved to the seller, and an extra profit reckoned at about seven and a half per cent. derived therefrom, amounting to not a very inconsiderable sum of money, even where there is only a tolerable consumption."

"I knew," continued Mentor, a gin-shop keeper, who told

me, he had a shopman who saved him from one hundred and fifty to two hundred pounds per annum, by his mode of filling the glasses."

Unfortunately, ministers have lately taken off a great part of the duty on gin, and thus it is vended at a very cheap rate, and which enables thousands to drink it, who could not otherwise afford it. Ministers, being fully aware that one of the causes of the distresses of the present times is the redundancy of the population, perhaps hit upon this scheme to thin them a little. The late Dr. Millar observes—" The intemperate use of spirituous liquors has been found by experience, for many years past, more destructive to the labouring class of people, in cities and manufacturing towns, than all the injuries accruing from unhealthy seasons, impure air, infection, and close confinement to work within doors, or much fatigue without. It not only produces tedious and peculiar maladies, but is often the means of rendering inveterate, or even fatal, many diseases of the throat and lungs; also, fever, and inflammations of the bowels, liver, kidnies, &c. I am convinced, that considerably more than one-eighth of all the deaths that take place in the metropolis, in persons above twenty years old, happen prematurely, through excess in drinking spirits.

" Most of the criminals refer all their misery to the evil of drinking, especially dram-drinking. It is well known that the direct effect of drams is to inflame and excite the passions; the habitual dram-drinker is rendered insensible to the milder feelings of his nature, and regardless of all consequences, whether as affecting this world or another; his reason is, for the time, departed from him, and he is rendered ripe for the most sanguinary and ferocious acts."

" Nearly all the convicts for murder," says Mr. Poynder, in his evidence before the House of Commons, " with whom I have conversed, have admitted themselves to have been under the influence of spirits at the time of the act; and I am fully persuaded, that in all the trials for murder which take place, with very few (if any) exceptions, it would appear on investigation, that the criminal had, in the first instance, delivered up his mind to the brutalizing effect of spirituous liquors.

" With regard to the extensive mischief of drinking among *females*, there is little doubt that to this source must be ascribed most of the evils of prostitution. To the effects of liquor, multitudes of that sex must refer both their first deviation from virtue, and their subsequent continuance in vice; perhaps it would be impossible for them, without the aid of spirituous liquors, to endure the scenes which they are called to witness."

It is worthy to notice the striking difference between *spirits* and *beer*, in the mode of their operation: beer makes persons first heavy, then stupid, and then senseless; the beer-drinker becomes more drunken than the drinker of spirits, and shows his condition more, but is, in that very proportion, more harmless to society:

his very helplessness and inactivity give a sort of pledge for the security of others. In the case of dram-drinking, however, the effects are not besotting or stupifying; spirits are less narcotic, but more exciting than beer; so far from incapacitating for action, they stimulate to it; they increase and irritate the passions; they heat the brain, by inflaming the quality and quickening the circulation of the blood. There is, perhaps, less of gross drunkenness brought before the public eye than when beer was the national liquor; but there is probably, on that very account, so much more drinking and so much more crime.

"But come," says Mentor, "we seem to excite the attention of the landlord, and we had better leave." So, taking a glass of wine, they retired.

At the corner of an adjoining alley, Mentor, perceiving a notorious *Duffer* in conversation with a young man, asked his friend if he was prepared to witness a little more of the shameful doings in London; to which Peregrine acquiescing, they followed them into a public-house, and saw the swindler unfold his parcel, and show his companion some silk handkerchiefs, stockings, &c. Peregrine, on seeing them, felt desirous of becoming a purchaser. "No," said Mentor, "shun that fellow: he is what they call a *Duffer*, and a most notorious one he is. He belongs to a gang who generally ply at the corner of the streets, courts, and alleys, to vend their contraband goods; which mostly consist of silk handkerchiefs made in Spitalfields, and remnants of silk purchased at the piece-brokers, which they declare are just smuggled from France. The *rig*, as it is called, is not half so much practised now as it used to be, on account of French and other silks, gloves, &c. being now so cheap in London; but yet there are always a number of persons in the metropolis, who will eagerly purchase of this sort of depredators, because they think they can purchase them a little cheaper than at a respectable shopkeeper's; little thinking that the goods are sure to be damaged, or of inferior manufacture. The duffer is a crafty rogue, and lays his schemes with great skill. In order to induce you to buy, he presents you with a *real* India handkerchief to look at, the more artfully to draw your attention, which having done, they whisper that they wish you to step with them aside, up a court, or to some public-house, for fear of the revenue officers, who would immediately seize the goods. Having enticed their prey into some such place, they open the handkerchiefs, &c. for your choice and inspection; and, should you buy, it is fifty to one you get the commodity you bartered for, unless you give a very extravagant price indeed. The method they use to elude your attention, is, they wrap up the article in a piece of paper, and put another of inferior value in its room, which they give you, and you put it into your pocket, not thinking of any cheat, until you get home, and begin to inspect and show your great bargain, when you see how you have been duped, but it is then too late for you to retrieve your loss. This trick they play off very successfully in vending silk stockings; for a person bought of these duffers six pairs of silk stockings, and, when he came to inspect them at home, they all wanted the feet. If it should so happen that you detect them in their frauds, and seem to resent it, or expose them, you are sure to get the worst of it: for there are generally several in the gang, hanging about, while the barter is going on, to come up instantly and make a disturbance, and insult you, while the duffer escapes; or, if he finds himself detected, or you should give him any money to change, he asks you to stop while he just goes into a public-house. You see him enter, but, not returning, you find, on inquiry, he has gone out at a back door; and thus you are cheated out of your money. Persons in London will always find it to their interest to make their purchases at respectable shop, kept by tradesmen of character: there they are sure not to be deceived; although they may pay a little more for the article they want, it will invariably, in the end, prove the cheapest. No sooner had the duffer left the room, having previously persuaded the poor dupe he had with him to purchase some of his goods at a most extravagant rate, than two north-country captains came in, and, having called for glasses of grog, their conversation turned upon their acquaintances, their good luck, and their misfortunes: they did not seem to be at all reserved, but addressed themselves frequently to Peregrine and his friend; and, among other topics, they conversed on the cheats of London; when one of them gave an account, how one of their shipmates was met near Rosemary Lane, by a notorious duffer, Simon Solomon, a celebrated seller of mock jewellery: he said his friend had been completely " done" by this old Solomon; who produced a very fashionable watch, which his shipmate bought, as a " dead cheap bargain," for £4, having, with great difficulty, abated him from £5 to that sum; but, on inquiry, he found that " all was not gold that glitters," and that his new purchase was not worth six shillings. "This," replied the other captain, "is nothing to what a friend of mine, a Mevagissey captain, suffered; who, being in the metropolis, went to see the New London Bridge; where a person, habited like the master of a vessel, accosted him as an old acquaintance. Captain—said, 'I never saw you before.' 'Oh,' replied the other, 'I have seen you in the East Indies.' 'That cannot be,' said the Cornishman, 'for I never was there.' 'Well, then,' rejoined the stranger, 'I am sure I have seen you somewhere, for your face is quite familiar to me; but I feel particularly happy in meeting with you now, because 'tis my first voyage to London. I am, like yourself, master of a vessel called the —, now lying at — (mentioning the name of the place), and I want you to go about with me, to show me a little of the town, for every thing is new to me,' &c. He then prevailed on the captain to accompany him to a public-house and take a glass of grog with him; but, on coming out of the inn-door, the sharper (for such he was, though disguised) snatched the captain's pocket-book, containing his freight, out of his coat, and ran off. Of course he pursued him with all possible speed, but, running fast, he unfortunately threw down a female, and, by the time he had assisted her to rise, the robber was out of sight. Captain —— related the circumstance to a broker, who asked him if he could recognise the thief in case of seeing him again: he replied, ' that he could swear to his person among a thousand.' The broker then advised him to look out, and he might probably see him again, not to be harsh, which would cost him dear, but to speak fair, and then the fellow might probably return the money. A few days after, Captain ——, being in a baker's shop, saw the man pass, ran out, and seized him by the collar, saying ' Do you know me?' ' No,' said the robber; ' I never saw you before.' 'Then,' rejoined the captain, ' I know you, for you stole my pocket-book with £59 in it." ' Hush, hush!' said he, ' 'twas £58 (Captain —— recollected having changed a sovereign). I am very sorry,' rejoined the robber; ' 'twas the first time I was ever guilty of such an offence; I beg you not to mention it, for I should be turned out of employ; my character is dearer to me than the money; I have not got it about me, but if you will go with me to my house, you shall have it all ' Captain ——, still holding him by the collar, went with him through a by-lane, where four ruffians assaulted him. The first knocked off his hat, but he took no notice of it; and, though they beat him on the arm, our hero would not let go his hold, but got into a shop, where he called for assistance; the shop-people, mistaking him for the thief, would not interfere. The captain thought he could have mastered any one or two men, but the gang was too numerous; they beat him sadly, and knocked out four of his front teeth; yet he retained his hold, and perhaps would have done so, though murder had ensued, had not one of the villains, when grown weary of the contest, stepped up and unbuttoned the robber's coat, slipped it off his shoulders, left it in the captain's hand, and run off."

The conversation now turned on the various cheats practised in London, when an old gentleman, who had been for some time perusing the newspaper, hearing the remarks, said he had been reading an interesting trial at the Old Bailey, of a man for fraudulently obtaining £50 in bank notes from a countryman, of the name of Edward Darby; and, as it developed a deep-laid scheme to entrap strangers, he would, by their permission, state the particulars, as given in the paper of this day, February 23, 1828. "The circumstances," continued the old gentleman, "as they appeared in evidence, were these:—The prosecutor, Edward Darby, lives near Tiverton, in Devonshire. In the month of January last, he came to town to dispose of some butter, and sold it to Mr. Edwards, a cheesemonger, in Crawford Street, St. Marylebone, for £50, which was paid to him in four Bank of England notes of £10 each, and two of £5. As he was returning home to the Castle and Falcon Inn, Aldersgate Street, where he stopped, he fell in with a man having he appearance of a farmer, near Holborn Bridge, who entered into conversation with him about the prices of corn, and other subjects connected with the country. After proceeding a short distance with the prosecutor, he left him, but met him again in Newgate Street. He immediately resumed conversation with him, and, having ascertained from him that he was about returning to Devon-shire by one of the Company's coaches, he said that he was also returning to that part of the country, to which he belonged, and would be happy to travel by the same coach. This being agreed upon, the farmer next prevailed upon the prosecutor to go into a public-house, near the New Post Office, where they had some brandy and water. Whilst they were there, the prisoner came in, affecting to be rather tipsy, and asked them if they had seen a lady there, saying that he had been with her over night, and intended making her his wife on the following Monday. The prisoner now sat down and began talking about himself: he had had a cross old uncle, he said, who had frequently declared he would not leave his nephew a shilling; and now he had died, leaving him his entire property, amounting to £350 a-year, besides a great deal of ready cash. ' I have just been to the Bank,' he continued, ' and drawn £450.' He then pulled out a handful of what appeared to be Bank notes, and began flourishing them about. The prosecutor then advised him to put his money in his pocket, and the farmer advised him to do the same, adding that he did not seem to be aware of the value of money. ' Money !' said the prisoner, ' oh, I have plenty of money ; here, I don't mind lending any body £50, if he will only give me a proper stamp for it.' After the party had spent about half an hour at this house, the prosecutor rose for the purpose of going to the Spread Eagle, Gracechurch Street, to start by the Company's coach for Bristol. The farmer did the same ; and the prisoner said he would go with them, offering the prosecutor to pay his coach-fare for him. The prosecutor told him he did not want him to pay his coach-fare, and declined the offer. The far-mer then led him through some back streets, which he said was the shortest way to Gracechurch Street, the prisoner still keeping along with them ; and, as they came to a small public-house, the farmer said he wanted to go in there. They accordingly went in, and a servant-girl fetched some brandy and water. The farmer left the room for a few moments, and, upon his return, drew a piece of chalk from his pocket, with which he chalked some lines and figures on the table. He then drew out some papers like notes, and put them into a hat, and the prisoner did the same. The farmer next began to toss a halfpenny with the prisoner, and after they had done this several times, the prisoner, addressing his two companions, said, ' You are gentlemen—I dare say, men of property; I sup-pose you are 'squires.' ' Yes, I am,' said the farmer, ' and so is this gentleman, too.' This was repeated more than once, when the farmer said to the prosecutor, ' Why don't you show your money, and let him see that you are a man of property, as well as himself?' At last the prosecutor, intending to change a £5 note, put his two fingers into his watch-fob, and pulled out his roll of notes, which he placed on the table; when instantly the farmer took it up and threw it into the hat, saying to the prisoner, 'There, you have won; the money is yours.' The prisoner immediately seized the hat and money, and both he and the farmer made off with all the speed they could, the latter being first out at the door. The prosecutor as quickly pursued, and caught hold of the prisoner's coat, on the stairs, by which he held fast, and was thus dragged down and through a narrow passage into the street. Here two other men came up and inquired what was the matter? The prosecutor replied, 'This rogue has robbed me of £50.' 'Well,' said they, 'come along with us, and we will make him give you back every farthing of your money.' 'Why not do it here?' asked the prosecutor. 'Because,' said they, 'it is fitter to be done in a private house.' They then led the way to another public-house; and, as they went along, the two men who had interfered urged the prosecutor to let go his hold of the prisoner's collar, and not make a spectacle of him in the street; but he refused to release his grasp. Upon entering the house, the prosecutor at first declined going up stairs, but at length went up a few steps, when one of the men opened the door, the inside of which was all hung with wet clothes on lines. Upon seeing that, the prosecutor said, 'I will not go in there; it is a bad house you have brought me to; you are all a set of thieves together.' A woman then made her appearance between the lines, and one of the men pulled the door to, which caused the place where they were standing to be rather dark. 'Well,' said the prisoner, 'I'll give you your money,' and he put a roll of notes into the prosecutor's hand. The prosecutor knew they were not his, and insisted upon his own notes being restored to him; upon which, one of the men chucked the prosecutor's hand from the prisoner's collar, and the latter ran down stairs, and out into the street, shutting the door after him. The other two men caught the prosecutor round the legs and threw him down. He got up, however, as fast as he could, and went in pursuit of the prisoner, whom, upon opening the door, he saw running down the street, at the distance of forty or fifty yards. He called 'Stop thief,' and ran after him as fast as he could, until an officer came up to him, to whom he stated what had occurred, and who immediately went in pursuit of the prisoner. Upon the prisoner being stopped, he drew a parcel from his pocket, and threw it on the ground, which turned out to be the prosecutor's roll of notes; whilst those which the prisoner had put into his hand consisted of seven flash notes of 'the bank of elegance,' purporting to be drawn by a hair-dresser in Goswell Street, who thereby 'promised to cut any lady's or gentleman's hair in the first style of fashion, or forfeit the sum of £50.'

"The witnesses for the prosecution were severally cross-examined on behalf of the prisoner, but nothing was elicited to shake the proof of the above facts. A great number of apparently respectable tradesmen appeared on his behalf, and gave him the best possible character for honesty. The jury, without a moment's hesitation, found the prisoner guilty, and the Recorder immediately sentenced him to be transported for life."

The old gentleman, perceiving the interest Peregrine took while hearing the details of this case, and learning that he was a stranger to London, told him, however improbable such transactions might appear to him now, they would be as nothing to what he would soon become acquainted with.

" I remember," continued he, "hearing a trial at the Old Bailey, of one George Smith: he was indicted for stealing fourteen sovereigns, two £10 notes, two £5 notes, and a promissory note, the property of William Gadsby. This case," says he, " is similar to the one I have just read, being one of the modes of raising money, well known in town by the flash name of ' *Gagging;*' and has been practised of late to a considerable extent on simple countrymen, who are strangers to the ' ways of town.' William Gadsby, the prosecutor, gave his evidence to the following effect: I now live as servant with Lord Frederick Bentinck, and have lived for the last thirty years in the family of the Duke of Portland. On the 26th of May last, I was walking in Holborn, about five or six in the afternoon, when the prisoner came up to me, and tapped me on the shoulder, and said, ' Ah, Mr. Gadsby, is this you? How long are you out of Nottinghamshire?' I said, ' I only *cummed* up on Tuesday last, and I go back again on Sunday, but I know nothing at all about you.' ' Oh,' he said, ' why, don't you know a man who has a farm from the Duke of Portland, and he lives near you in the country?' ' Why,' I says, ' you means Ben Smith, that keeps the public-house;' and he says, ' Yes, he is my cousin.' Ben Smith was a fellow-servant of mine in the Duke of Portland's family. ' Well,' I says, ' you may be Ben's cousin, but I don't know you;' and I was for walking away, but he stops me, and says, ' I am surprised you don't know me, as I was down at my cousin's about six weeks ago.' He then said to me, ' Was you at Lincoln fair?' I said, ' No;' and he says, ' But my cousin was, and he had a quarrel there about a horse.' Now, I knowed that this was true, as I had heard this from Smith himself. Prisoner then talked to me on many subjects, and about the state of the country, and several things; so that I had no doubt he was the man he said, and I did not *suspicion* him for a moment. He was dressed just like a farmer. When we were going on, he said, looking up, ' What place is this?' I said, ' This is Holborn. Why, you knows as little about London as I do.' We then walked on, and he says to me, ' There is a long and serious affair between my brother and me, and I want to write a few lines to him by you: let us step into a public-house while I write them.' . said, ' I never go into public-houses;' but I did go into a house, and there we had a pint of beer. Witness then went on to detail,

in a very simple and artless, but rather prolix manner, the circumstances attending the loss of his money. It was to this effect:—
When we went to the public-house, a man, having the appearance
of being drunk, came in and pulled out a large sum of money, notes,
and sovereigns, and began to throw them on the table, and said
that he had been left a large legacy. After a short time, witness
was induced to go into another public-house, where the prisoner
said he would write. There they saw the same man whom they
saw in the other public-house. They were soon joined by two or
three men, having the appearance of gentlemen. Prisoner began
to ' shake in the hat' with the drunken man for money and glasses
round: the latter always lost. He then won a sovereign from
him, but said in a whisper to prosecutor that he would not keep it.
At length the drunken man offered prosecutor some money, and
said he would go down with him to Nottinghamshire. Prisoner
asked witness for a bit of paper to write his address on; and, when
he pulled out his pocket-book to give him the back of a letter, the
drunken man put his hand on it, and said, ' You have got money
also, but not so much as I have.' Prisoner said, ' Yes; he has
got money, to be sure : do you think nobody has got money but
you?' Prisoner then put his hand on the book, and pulled out
some of the notes. Prosecutor told him to let the notes alone,
and put the book up in his side coat pocket. The drunken man then
again offered witness some money, and prisoner took him by the
breast of the coat, and begged him to take it. Witness soon after
went home, and missed his notes and cash, and, in place of it,
found a piece of brown paper rolled up in it. He had no doubt
that the money was taken at the time the prisoner shook his coat.
No other person came so near him. He took prisoner into custody
in four days after.

" Prisoner made a long harangue in his defence, and appealed
to heaven several times for his innocence. He begged of the court
to let him off to his family in Pontefract, and he would lead a
good life for the time to come.

" Some witnesses were called to give prisoner a character: they
had known him for some years, and had heard nothing against him.
One of them admitted that he (prisoner) had once passed by the
name of William Irish.

" The Deputy Recorder summed up, and the jury, without hesitation, found him guilty. He was sentenced to be transported for
life."

The company now, thanking the old gentleman for his information, separated, and Mentor and his friend determined on returning
home ; but, on their way thither, curiosity led them into a mock-
auction room, where the articles were *seemingly* being disposed of
at extremely cheap prices, which excited the surprise of Peregrine,
and made him anxious to become a purchaser. " Do not," said
his friend, " be allured by the fallacious stories of these fellows.
The whole party are a set of arrant cheats ; the major part of the

people in this shop are paid by the proprietor, to attend the sale,
to puff up the goods, and to bid; they place themselves in different
parts of the room, and are all differently clothed—some genteel,
and some shabby: they are called Puffers, or Riggers; and hence
these sales are denominated Rig-sales. Be careful," continued
Mentor, " you do not even look at the auctioneer, for, if he catches
your eye, he will swear you gave him a bidding; and down goes
the hammer, and you are saddled with a trumpery watch, seals,
razors, knives, and forks, or whatever the lot may be, at about ten
times more than it is worth. If you were to complain, the puffers
would all immediately declare they saw you bid; and you must
be contented either to be cheated or ill-used, or perhaps dragged
to the watch-house on a frivolous charge, and kept there till the
morning, when, no one appearing against you, you are discharged.
But, in order that you may be acquainted with their artful stratagems,
I would advise you to read an excellent work, full of information,
called the *Life of George Godfrey*; in which you will find the following correct picture of the swindling *doings* in a mock-auction room :

'The business proceeded with great spirit, and I was perfectly
astonished at the immense bargains which were sold. It appeared that I was not the only one thus affected : a dandy of the
first water was close to me, who frequently held up his hands, as I
really believed, to indicate his sincere amazement, and not to show
the diamond rings which adorned his fingers.

' An elderly gentleman, who wore powder, and looked, I
thought, like a clergyman, was struck in the same way; and,
more than once, the mutual surprise of these very respectable
persons burst forth in expressions like these—each, however,
carefully subduing his voice, so that Mr. Alderton might not be
apprised of their sentiments, as to the sacrifices he was making.

' " Wonderful !" the dandy began.

' " Dirt cheap !" proceeded the clergyman.

' " It is absolutely giving away !" said the former.

' " It *is*, almost," added the man of the church; " I never saw
any thing like it in my life !"

' " Nor I, never," the beau went on ; and then, his curiosity
being evidently wound up to the highest pitch, he eagerly inquired—

' " How does it happen ? What can be the cause of all this ?"

' " The general scarcity of cash," was the reply; " nobody, at
present, has any money."

' They looked at me while they spoke, as appealing to my
judgment, for the reasonableness of what they said. I gave it at
once in their favour, by repeating some of their phrases. Their
manner told, that they considered me to be a most sagacious young
man, and their kindness to me, stranger as I was, won my warm-
est gratitude; for more than once, before expressing themselves
aloud, that others might profit by their experience, they gave me
a little knock with the elbow, and a look, which distinctly told
me, that then was the time to lay out my money to advantage.

'When the sale was over, a considerable portion of the company surrounded Mr. Alderton and Skim, as I judged, for the purpose of paying for their lots. One lady directed that what she had bought might be sent home early on the following morning. The politeness of Mr. Skim, while addressing her, struck me as admirable; and, with a view to improve my own address, I watched it, in order to copy every movement. He begged to be allowed to see her to her carriage. My lady (for, from his thus accosting her, I found that I was feasting my eyes on a person of rank), dispensed with his services, affably, but, at the same time, with an air of dignity, such as I had never in my life had an opportunity of witnessing before.

'The company now grew thin, and I was about to retire, when Skim whispered in my ear, that there was a dinner set out at Mr. Alderton's house, at which I might as well assist.

'I had no great objection to accept such an invitation.

' " Now, then, since you have put off your *knock-out* for an hour or two," said Skim, loud enough to be heard by the whole company, " to have a jolly good *grease* before you go, I will be with you directly."

' I did not exactly know what this meant, nor to whom it was addressed, but it was answered by several voices at the same time.

' " Very well—very well—be quick."

'They then left the room. Skim put away his books, gave a few directions to the porters, which, by the way, he issued in a very lordly tone, most unlike that which he had used while addressing her ladyship, and then prepared for an adjournment to Mr. Alderton's house.

'It was but a step that we had to go, and Skim had only time to mention, that he should presently introduce me to several persons with whom I should have a good deal to do, before that day twelvemoth, when we entered a spacious apartment, laid out for dinner, in which I found half the company I had seen at the sale, and, among them, the lady he had offered to hand to her carriage, the dandy with rings on his fingers, and the gentleman in black, whom I had supposed to be a clergyman.

' All seemed very merry and uproarious. There were several females present; and the reverend person I have mentioned was by no means reserved and measured in his deportment, as he had appeared in the sale-room, half an hour before.

' I felt disposed to retreat.

' " What do you want to go for ?" inquired my friend, " before you have had your dinner ?"

' " Oh !" said I, " it will never do for me to stop, since you have these gentlemen and ladies here. I thought it was quite a different sort of thing."

' " Well, Mr. Skim, is it almost coming ?" inquired the lady, whose dignity I had admired so much.

' " Don't be in such a hurry, Sal; I suppose you had some breakfast this morning," was Skim's answer.

' I stared at this—he saw my amazement, and guessed the cause of it.

' " Zounds !" said he, " you stare like a duck at thunder ? Why, you don't think these are any body, do you ?"

' " Hush !" said I, " they hear you !"

' " Who the devil cares if they do.  What do you know of them ?"

' " Why, at the sale, I stood close to that gentleman with the diamond rings on his fingers, and near the clergyman, sitting just behind him."

' " The gentleman with the diamond rings ! the clergyman ! what are you talking about ? I did not think you knew so little of the town.  All that *gentleman's* diamond rings you may buy for half-a-crown ; and for the clergyman, as you call him, he is no more a parson than you are a pope.  The fact is, most of these are brokers, or tag-rags, who attend our sales, to encourage purchasers to bid up ; these gentry receive, as pay, what we choose to give them. In a common way, we stand a guinea, to be spent among the whole bunch ; but, to-day, we are more civil than usual, as Alderton, knowing some of them may be useful at Haversham's, determined to ask the Jezebels and pickpockets to a dinner, that I might have an opportunity of hinting how they are to act, when we go into the country."

' He then made me advance to the supposed clergyman, to whom he introduced me, by saying—

' " Barker, here is a young one !   He is one of the concern."

' The reverend parson, as I conceived him to be, replied to this by uttering an oath, indicative of extreme surprise, and added—

' " He in the concern !   Why, then, I and Jack Raffles," and here he pointed to the dandy, " have been making pretty fools of ourselves all day ; we made a dead set at him, and I wondered we could not get him to make a single bidding."

Dinner came in, and we were all very jolly.  The clergyman, the dandy, and the lady, Mrs. Sal Briggs, as Skim familiarly called her, were remarkably good company.  My friend, however, whispered to me that I must not make too free with them, as I should often find it necessary to keep them at a distance ; and he especially cautioned me to be on my guard against lending them money ; for, if they succeeded in borrowing, I might consider the transaction as closed, and not a single farthing of what they might do me out of, would any one among them ever return.'

" This, my friend," said Mentor, " is a real history of the shameful stratagems to which the mock auctioneers resort, in order to rob the unwary."

The most decent of these fellows, who attend mock-auctions in the day-time, are at night employed as decoy-ducks at the low " Hells," at the west-end of the town. " And pray," said Peregrine, " what are ' Hells ?' " " They are," replied Mentor, " gambling-houses, and are, says the author of that popular novel, ' *Life in the West*,' most aptly denominated ' Hells,' from the torments and misery with which all players, more or less, are afflicted by them, and from the heartless ' devils' who keep them. These men can view the progressive ruin of their victims with demoniacal satisfaction and delight. They can see, with a fiend-like smile, the glow of health and happiness, with which the cheeks of the visitors are painted on their first entrance, fade to a look of despair and want, blighted by the horrible system that, while it enriches a few low knaves, plunges many reputable families and persons into a chaos of inextricable wretchedness and ruin, and does an incalculable mischief to society. But," continued Mentor, " to give you some idea of these horrid receptacles of vice, I will ask an unfortunate acquaintance of mine, one of the infatuated frequenters at these gambling-houses, to introduce us; for, unless he does so, it will be impossible for us to gain admittance." Mentor accordingly made an appointment with his friend, and Peregrine was thus presented with a correct view of the devilish

DOINGS IN " A HELL."

Mentor's friend whispered to Peregrine, asking what he thought of the scene before him: " Here," continued he, " is, I hope, a

5. D

esson and a warning to you : behold the torture under which that
poor ruined youth suffers; watch the convulsions of his frame—
his trembling limbs—the racking of his mind seems to drive him to
madness; and then witness the cold villanous behaviour of those
by whom he has been robbed and ruined—callous to every sort of
feeling : those two well-dressed sharpers near the door, fearful
that their unhappy victim should escape from the den with a particle of property about him, are conveying away a pocket-book which
they have just taken from his pocket ; and then, when they think
they have completely *cleaned* him out, these hellites will wish to
be freed from his company, and, if he will not go quietly, they will
*turn* him out without the smallest compunction, for a new-comer
might take the alarm by the sight of such ruined men, and the facts
they could unfold."

" A scandalous scene of violence, which often happens at these
places, but seldom becomes publicly known, on account of the
disgrace attending exposure, occurred lately at a low ' hell' in
King Street, St. James's.   A gentleman who had lost considerable
sums of money at various times, announced his full determination
never to come to a place of the sort again with money.   His visits,
therefore, were no longer wanted, and so orders were given to the
porters not to admit him again.   About two o'clock in the night or
Saturday week, he sought admittance, and was refused.   A warn.
altercation took place in the passage between him and the porters,
which brought down some of the proprietors.   One of them, a powerful man, a bankrupt butcher, struck him a tremendous blow, which
broke the bridge of his nose, covered his face with blood, and knocked
him down.   On getting up, he was knocked down again.   He arose
once more, and instantly received another blow, which would have
laid him upon his back, but one of the porters by this time had got
behind him, and, as he was falling, struck him at the back of his head,
which sent him upon his face. The watch had now arrived, into whose
hands the keeper of the ' hell' and the porter were given.   At the
watchhouse they were ordered to find bail.  The gentleman was then
about quitting, when he was suddenly called back.  A certain little
lawyer, who alternately prosecutes and defends keepers of gaming-
houses, was sent for.   He whispered to the ex-butcher to charge
the gentleman with stealing his handkerchief and hat, which, it was
alleged, had been lost in the affray. Though nothing was found upon
the gentleman, who desired to be searched, this preposterous and
groundlsss charge was taken, and the hellites admitted to bail; but
the gentleman, who had been so cruelly beaten, being charged with
a felony on purpose to cause his detention, and the power held by
magistrates to take bail in doubtful cases not extending to night-
constables, he was locked up below, with two wretched men who had
stolen lead, and five disorderlies, his face a mass of blood and
bruises, and there detained till Monday morning, in a most pitiable
condition.   The magistrate before whom the party appeared on
that day, understanding that the affair took place at a gaming-

house, dismissed both complaints, leaving the parties to their remedy at the sessions.

"In these 'low hells,'" said Mentor's friend, "we can only offer you, as a refreshment, tea, biscuits, and liquors; but, were we at some of the high ones, I could present you with tea, coffee, confectionary, and every sort of wine. We play in this room," continued he, "French hazard, rouge et noir, ecarté, &c., and we vary the games occasionally. Whatever you do, my dear sir," addressing himself to Peregrine, "shun gambling as you would the devil; for, when a man once enters a house of play, as the author of *Life in the West* truly says, ' his mind undergoes a complete revolution. As he continues his visits, his feelings as a gentleman, his delicacy of sentiment, his morals, his honour, all gradually give way with his money. The virtues of his mind are destroyed by the disgusting examples before him, of men who, possessing none themselves, laugh them to scorn in others. If he could but see the horrid deformity of these ' hells,' and most of their visitors, surely he would hesitate before he set a foot into them. But, being there, from the instances of vice and folly ever before him, he by degrees, unperceived by himself, becomes an imitator of the most revolting language, and the worst of principles. A mania seizes and clings to him from the first. In spite of his own constant losses, the losses of all around him, the objects of misery, in consequence of their's, ever presenting themselves to his view, he pursues the same head-long course, with a fascination beyond belief. The springs of social life get dried up within him; he no longer is happy in the bosom of his family; he can no longer enjoy the society of a friend, or of a virtuous woman. His whole soul is so engrossed, enchanted, by these most foul and diabolical establishments, that he is too blind to see that they must sooner or later encompass his ruin, and that, when he falls—and fall he will, a gambler falls unpitied and unrelieved. It is a curious feature in the career of a gambler, that he gets reconciled apparently to his degradation and downfall; though now and then a thought of happier days, and of what he might have been, flashes across his mind, and penetrates his heart with a desolate misery. A player's mind is ever under the influence of tumultuous passions, that destroy all repose,—at one moment in an excess of joy at an instance of good fortune, and the next yielding to the bitterest despair for its indurability.'"

"That youth you see in such anguish of mind has hardly reached the age of two-and-twenty: he has lately come into a fortune of £30,000, by the death of a near relation. He is a member of the great 'hell' in St. James's Street, the 'hell' in Waterloo Place, and the 'hell' in Park Place: he lost, a few days since, some thousands at hazard, where they used the loader, or false dice, which bring up certain numbers: they are used only at hazard, and made either low or high dice; and all those sharpers who use them always have a pair of each in their possession, which they

change with great dexterity. They use also cramped boxes; and
they have a means of cogging, or fastening the dice in the box.

"Here, also, hundreds of families are ruined, and thousands of
pounds lost, by playing at the celebrated game of *Rouge et Noir;*
or, Red and Black. It is a modern game. It is so styled, not
from the cards, but from the table on which it is played, being
covered with red and black cloth, as in the following table:—

TABLE.

| | Rouge. | Noir. | |
|---|---|---|---|
| | Rouge. | Noir. | |
| Dealer. | Rouge. | Noir. | Crouper. |
| | | | |
| | Noir. | Rouge. | |
| | Noir. | Rouge. | |
| | Noir. | Rouge. | |

"Any number of persons may play at this game. They are called
punters, and may risk their money on which colour they please.
The stakes are to be placed within the outside line.

"The dealer and croupier being situated opposite to each other,
as marked in the table, the dealer takes six packs of cards, shuffles them, and distributes them in various parcels to the different
punters round the table, to shuffle and mix. He then finally shuffles them, and removes the end cards into various parts of the
three hundred and twelve cards, until he meets with a pictured
card, which he must place upright at the end. This done, he presents the pack to one of the punters, to cut, who places the pictured card where the dealer separates the pack, and that part of
the pack beyond the pictured card, he places at the end nearest
him, leaving the pictured card at the bottom of the pack.

"The dealer then takes a certain quantity of cards, about as many
in number as a pack, and, looking at the first card, to know its colour, puts it on the table with its face downwards; he then takes
two cards, one red and the other black, and sets them back to
back; these cards are turned, and placed conspicuously as often
as the colour varies, for the information of the company.

"The punters having staked their money on either of the colours,
the dealer says—*Votre jeu est il fait?* Is your game made? or,
*Votre jeu est il prêt?* Is your game ready? or, *Le jeu est prêt,
Messieurs.* The game is ready, gentlemen. He then deals the
first card with its face upwards, saying, Noir, and continues dealing, until the cards turned exceed thirty points in number, which he
must mention, as trente et un, or whatever it may be.

"As the aces reckon but for one, no card after thirty can make
up forty; the dealer, therefore, does not declare the tens after thirty-one, or upwards, but merely the units, as two, three, &c., and

always in the French language, as thus: if the number of points on the card dealt for noir, are thirty-five, he says—*cinq*, or five.

" Another parcel is then dealt for rouge in a similar manner: and if the punters' stakes are on the colour that comes to thirty-one, or nearest to it, they win, which is announced by the dealer, who says, *rouge gagne*, red wins; or *noir gagne*, black wins. These two parcels, one for each colour, make a coup.

" The same number of points being dealt for each colour, the dealer says, *apres*, after. This is a doublet, or *un refait*, by which neither party wins, unless both colours are thirty-one, which the dealer announces, by saying, *un refait trente et un*, and he wins half the stakes punted on both colours. He, however, seldom takes the money, but removes it into the middle line, on which colour the punters please; this is called the first prison, or *la premierè prison;* and, if they win their next event, they draw the whole stake. In case of a second doublet, the money is removed into the third line, which is called the second prison, or *la seconde prison*. When this happens, the dealer wins three quarters of the money punted; and if the punters win the next event, their stakes are removed to the first prison.

" The cards are sometimes cut, for which colour shall be dealt first: but, in general, the first parcel is for black, and the second red. After the first card is turned up, no stakes can be made for that event. The punter is at liberty to pay the proportion of his stake lost, or go to prison.

" The banker at this game cannot refuse any stake; and the punter, having won his first stake, may, as at Pharo, make a paro-let, and pursue his luck up to a *soixante et le va*, if he pleases.

" Bankers generally furnish punters with slips of card-paper, ruled in columns, each marked N. or R. at the top, on which accounts are kept, by pricking with a pin.

" The odds against *le refait* being dealt, are reckoned sixty-three to 1; but bankers acknowledge they expect it twice in three deals; and there are generally from twenty-nine to thirty-two coups in each deal. The odds of winning several following times, are the same as at Pharo.

" Such," continued the friend of Mentor, " are some of the doings practised in these ' hells!' but, if your young friend is not already satisfied, I will, on some future day, introduce him to the great ' hell,' in St. James's Street, and there he will have a wider field for witnessing the cold-blooded *doings* of the gambler.

" It is impossible," continued he, " to subdue the passion for gambling. I remember, some short time ago, at Verdun, among other means resorted to in order to plunder the English, a gaming-table was set up for their sole accommodation; and, as usual, led to scenes of great depravity and horror. For instance—' A young man was enticed into this sink of iniquity, when he was tempted to throw on the table a half-crown; he won, and repeated the ex-periment several evenings successfully, till at length he lost. The manager immediately offered him a ' rouleau' of £50; which, in the heat of play, he thoughtlessly accepted, and lost. He then drew a bill on his agent, which his captain indorsed—this he also lost; he drew two others, which met with the same fate; and the next morning he was found dead in his bed, with his limbs much distorted, and his fingers buried in his sides. On his table was found an empty laudanum-bottle, and scraps of paper whereon he had been practising the signature of Captain B. On inquiry, it was found that he had forged that officer's name to the two last bills. Thus did a once respectable young man meet a most dreadful and disgraceful end, from his being exposed, at too early a period in life, to the temptation of gambling. Another circumstance also occurred, the atrocity of which was somewhat tinged with the ludicrous. A clerk, named Chambers, losing his monthly pay, which was his all, at the gaming-table, begged to borrow of the managers; but they knew his history too well to lend without security, and therefore demanded something in pawn. 'I have nothing to give,' replied the youth, 'but my ears.' 'Well,' said one of the witty demons, 'let us have them.' The youth immediately took out of his pocket a knife, and actually cut off all the fleshy part of one of his ears, and threw it on the table, to the astonishment of the admiring gamesters : he received his two dollars, and gambled on. When this circumstance was reported to the senior officer, the hero was sent to Bilche.

"Another curious case occurred in London, some few years ago. Two fellows were observed by a patrole sitting on a lamp-post, in the New Road; and, on closely watching them, he discovered that one was tying up the other (who offered no resistance) by the neck. The patrole interfered, to prevent such a strange kind of murder, and was assailed by both, and pretty considerably beaten for his good offices; the watchmen, however, poured in, and the parties were secured. On examination the next morning, it appeared that the men had been gambling; that one had lost all his money to the other, and had, at last, proposed to stake his clothes. The winner demurred; observing that he could not strip his adversary naked, in the event of his losing. 'Oh,' replied the other, ' do not give yourself any uneasiness about that : if I lose, I shall be unable to live, and you shall hang me, and take my clothes after I am dead; and I shall then, you know, have no occasion for them.' The proposed arrangement was assented to ; and the fellow, having lost, was quietly submitting to the terms of the treaty, when he was interrupted by the patrole, whose impertinent interference he so angrily resented.

"I could,' continued the friend of Mentor, "give a thousand such instances of the fatal love of play, and of the misery which these gambling-houses entail upon numerous families. I recollect being at Marlborough-Street Office, when an elderly gentleman, accompanied by a youth of eighteen years of age, applied for a warrant against the proprietors of a gambling-house in Bury Street, St. James's. The elderly gentleman stated, that the youth was the son of a banker on the continent, and his brother-in-law. He came to this country about four months since, bringing with him £700, given him by his father for his expenses, and had been allured to the gaming-house of Messrs. ————, where he was induced to drink till he became inebriated, and to play at a game he knew nothing of, till he lost his last shilling; in fact, he was robbed of between £500 and £600. A few days since he called on him (the senior gentleman), and asked him to take a walk. They went out together—the youth appeared extremely dejected—he naturally inquired into the cause, and was horrified at discovering that he had called on him to take leave of him for ever—that he was meditating suicide. This led to further inquiries: the youth confessed the cause of his despair. He, in consequence, went to the house, and saw one of the proprietors, who told him he might go and be hanged; they did not care for him or the magistrates.

"The young man stated, that about nine weeks ago he was introduced to the house, and lost a considerable sum of money. He determined never to go into it again, but was constantly waylaid by the persons he met there, until at length he was induced to return. They had also taken him to another gaming-house in the same street, where he lost £150. When he was totally ruined, and they discovered that he had no more to lose, he was kicked out, on questioning the fairness of the play of which he had been a victim. Both the applicants offered to enter into security to prosecute, if the magistrate would grant the warrant.

"In 1716, the barrow-women of London used, generally, to carry dice with them, and children were induced to throw for fruit and nuts, or, indeed, any person of more advanced age. However, the pernicious consequences of the practice beginning to be felt, the Lord Mayor issued an order to apprehend all such offenders, which speedily put an end to street-gambling."

"That man," says Mentor, addressing himself to Peregrine, "who is looking so coolly and callously on the poor creature just ruined, is a notorious fellow at *Gaffing*, one of the ten thousand modes of swindling now practised in London: it is a game in very great vogue among the *macers*, who congregate nightly at the flash-houses. He laughs a great deal, and whistles Moore's melodies, and extracts music from a deal table with his elbow and wrist. This fellow is one of the greatest *Gaffers* in the country. When he hides a halfpenny, and a flat cries 'head' for £10, a 'tail' is sure to turn up. One of his modes of commanding the turn-up is this . he has a halfpenny with two heads, and a halfpenny with two tails. When he gaffs, he contrives to have both halfpence under his hand, and long practice has enabled him to catch up in the wrinkles or muscles of it the halfpenny which it is his interest to conceal. If 'tail' is called, a 'head' appears, and the 'tail' halfpenny runs down his wrist with astonishing fidelity. This ingenious fellow has often won 200 or 300 sovereigns in the course of a night, by gaffing;

but the landlord and other men, who are privy to the robbery, and
' pitch the baby card' (encourage the loser by sham betting),
always come in for the ' regulars' (their share of the plunder).   The
adept to whom we have here particularly alluded, has contrived to
bilk all the turnpikes in the kingdom.   In going to a fight or to a
race-course, when he reaches a turnpike, he holds a shilling between
his fingers, and says to the gate-keeper, ' Here, catch,' and makes
a movement of the hand towards the man, who endeavours to catch
what he sees.   The shilling, however, by a backward jirk, runs
down the sleeve of the coat, as if it had life in it, and the gate-
keeper turns round to look in the dust, when the tall gaffer drives
on, saying, ' Keep the change.'   A young fellow, who formerly
was a marker at a billiard-table, and who has the appearance of a
soft inexperienced country lad, is another great hand at gaffing.
There is a strong adhesive power in his hand, and such exquisite
sensibility about it, that he can ascertain, by dropping his palm,
even upon a worn-out halfpenny or shilling, what side is turned
up.   Indeed, so perfect a master is he in the science, that Breslaw
could never have done more upon cards than he could do with a
pair of ' grays' (gaffing-coins).   A well-known macer, who is
celebrated for slipping an ' old gentleman' (a long card) into the
pack, and is the inheritor by birth of all propensities of this description, although the inheritance is equally divided between his brother
and himself, got hold, a short time ago, of a young fellow who
had £170 in his pocket, and introduced him to one of the ' cock-
and-hen' houses near Drury-Lane Theatre, well primed with wine.
Gaffing was introduced, and the billiard-marker was pitched upon
to *do* the stranger.   The macer ' pitched the baby card,' and of
course lost, as well as the unfortunate victim.   He had borrowed
£10 of the landlord, who was to come in for the ' regulars;' but,
when all was over, the billiard-marker refused to make any division
of the spoil, or even to return the £10 which had been lost to him
in ' bearing up' the cull.   The landlord pressed his demand upon
the macer, who, in fact, privately was reimbursed by the marker;
but he was coolly told, that he ought not to allow such improper
practices in his house, and that the sum was not recoverable, the
transaction being illegal.   The manner in which the gaffing system
is carried on may be judged of from the fact, that, in one of those
abominable places, 116 sovereigns have been lost, by means of
double-headed and double-tailed halfpence, in a single toss."

Satiated with the horrid scene of villainy which they had witnessed, Mentor took leave of his friend; and, on returning with
Peregrine to their inn, the superiority of the streets near the royal
palaces over those at the east-end of the town, attracted the particular notice of Peregrine, who remarked, he had not before any
idea that London was half so splendid, so various, or so populous.
" Yes, my friend," said Mentor, "' the appearance of the streets
of London, on a fine evening,' as the author of Letters from London
says, ' is a sight capable of affording an hour's amusement to the

admirer of arts, the patriot, or the studious philosopher. How beautiful is the appearance of the various shops, so brilliantly illuminated with the pure soft light of gas, and rich with the productions of every clime! what riches glitter in the goldsmith's window! what delicacies tempt the appetite in the confectioner's! and how elegant the views and portraits displayed by the printseller. To the stranger it is a treat worth a long journey from his village (where three or four tradesmen monopolize all the business of the parish, by each one selling in his little dirty shop a vast variety of articles, and where all business closes at sunset), to roam the whole evening through the Strand, and feast his eyes with the luxuries of art. Then, too, how many happy faces throng the streets—the lover of the drama hastening to the theatre, the *bon-vivant* to the tavern, the mechanic to where—

" The busy housewife plies her evening care,
  And children run to lisp their sire's return,
  Or climb his knee, the envied kiss to share ;"

The spruce apprentice to keep his appointment, and give the well-known whistle and tap at the window, which will call forth his rosy lass, smiling and blushing like a " bonny morn in May." Pleasure reigns in every face; for with many of the busy sons of gain business is over for the day; care and the fear of poverty are left at home, and that evening's recreation, which every man looks for in London, occupies the thoughts of all. The stout broad-shouldered young man, with buck-skin breeches, rough great-coat, and seal-skin hat, who inquires the way to *Common* Garden, is a countryman, anxious to see the play : his mind is full of sharpers and pickpockets ; and, if any one chances to touch him in passing, he turns hastily round, and grasps with eagerness the stout cudgel that he carries. " Six to four, sir, and post the *blunt*," says yonder gentleman in the drab coat, top-boots, and fancy hat :—he is a Corinthian, accompanying his friend to Belcher's, in order to learn the news, or make a bet on the next fight : while the three bucks, passing hastily arm in arm, are probably clerks or apprentices, released from desk or counter, to act the gentleman, and cut a swell for a few hours at night. These smile with pleasure, and perhaps *their* hearts are glad—for empty minds are easily delighted. —But how wretched is the fate of the unfortunate women who crowd the streets at this period ! though their hearts are breaking, their faces must still be arrayed in smiles ; exposed to all the dreadful evils of poverty, cold, disease, and shame, they must hide the bitter feelings of their bosoms in an appearance of cheerfulness.

" ' It is well known that the conversation and manners of many of these deluded creatures are so superior as to give evident indications of good education, and induce a belief that they have seen better days. In such cases they are doubly wretched :—surely, some means might be adopted to alleviate, if not altogether prevent, the evils of prostitution. Many attempts have indeed been made, and of late the punishment of the tread-mill has been resorted to.

A novel expedient, indeed, to arrest and send to Brixton a number of miserable creatures, for adopting the only means in their power of obtaining a livelihood, and at the end of the period of their punishment, turning them loose to pursue the same course again. Such an institution as the Magdalen Hospital, but upon more general and liberal principles, might perhaps be of essential service; at any rate, let not their misfortunes be punished by the degrading and useless toil of the wheel.' "

"The street in which you are," says Mentor, "is called Pall Mall. In a most rare book, entitled 'The French Garden for English Ladies and Gentlemen to walke in' (1621), in a dialogue, the lady says, 'If one had *Paille-mals*, it were good to play in this alley, for it is a reasonable good length, straight, and even.' And a note in the margin informs us, 'A *paille-mal* is a wooden hammer, set to the end of a long staffe, to strike a boule with, at which game noblemen and gentlemen in France do play much.' The custom of playing at this game in St. James's Park (of which Charles II. was very fond, and probably introduced it from France) gave name to the fine street adjoining it, still known by the name of 'Pall Mall.'

Pall Mall is celebrated for being the place where the king's palace, called Carlton Palace, lately stood, and where the lamented Princess Charlotte was born. In this street, the brave Duke Schomberg resided; and here, also, the beauteous and fascinating Nell Gwynn lived and died: a woman, as Granger says, who possessed every virtue but that of chastity.

"How is Pall Mall altered from what it was some years past! In 1752, a few persons were at the expense of procuring a Holland smock, a cap, clocked stockings, and laced shoes, which they offered as prizes to any four women who would run for them at three o'clock in the afternoon, in Pall Mall. The race attracted an amazing number of persons, who filled the streets, the windows, and balconies. The *sport* attendant on this curious mode of *killing time* induced Mr. Rawlings, High Constable of Westminster, resident in Pall Mall, to propose a laced hat, as a prize to be run for by five men, which appears to have produced much mirth to the projector; but the mob, ever upon the watch to gratify their propensity for riot and mischief, committed so many excesses, that the magistrates issued precepts to prevent future races.

"Pall Mall is now the fashionable resort of the great, and the would-be-great,—those creatures, who—

'"Big with a million, and a groat to pay,

strut and flutter, like the silly butterfly, bedecked in all the colours of the rainbow, aping the manners of the titled and the wealthy.

"The liveried servants here assume additional consequence and self-importance, and expend more money in extravagancies than half the tradesmen in London; and it will be no wonder that they do so, when I tell you of the daring conduct of some of these

servants in high life, and the means they use to ' raise the wind.'
A respectable tradesmen, who resides in the Strand, had supplied
a baronet, who is now upon a foreign mission, with clothes, &c.,
for several years.   The baronet had occasion to change one of his
principal servants, whose duty it was to examine the bills, and he
happened to get one into his employment who had been in the
habit of levying contributions, in the shape of per-centage, upon
the shopkeepers with whom his former masters were in the habit
of dealing.   The new servant, who expected his commission-money
at the usual time from the tailor, was astonished at not receiving
it with the receipt for the amount of the bill, and expressed himself
strongly upon the subject to the tradesman; but it was in vain—
no commission-money was forthcoming, and the servant determined
to get rid as soon as possible of so unprofitable a customer upon
his master's purse.   New orders were given, but they were not
long executed before the tradesman received instructions to send
in his bill.   He was surprised at this change in the arrangement
of the baronet, who had been in the habit of discharging his bills
at stated periods ; but he did as he was ordered, observing at the
same time to the servant, who told him the baronet's pleasure,
that he was not at all in want of money.   The amount of the bill
was in a few minutes handed over to the tailor, who little thought
that a long time would elapse before he should be again called
upon to serve the family with articles which he had always supplied
of the most unexceptionable materials.

" After having waited for many months for an order without being
noticed, he suspected that there was some foul play, and resolved to beg an interview with the baronet.   This the servant
alluded to was very reluctant to permit.   He made a variety of
excuses, but the tradesman was not to be denied, and he soon
succeeded.   The matter was then explained.   The servant had,
it appeared, ordered in the bill without any instructions from
his master, and, upon receiving it, he took it up in haste to the
baronet, saying, ' Mr. B. has sent in his account, sir, and desired
me to tell you, that he is waiting below for the amount.'   ' Waiting for the amount !' said the baronet, ' what does he mean ?
Tell him not to trouble me now with his account.'—' Oh, but he
says, sir,' observed the servant, ' that he must have it, and that
he will be d——d if he'll go a yard without it.'   This report of
the conduct of the tailor was told with so much apparent indignation, that the baronet never doubted the truth of it, sent a check
for the amount of the bill to the shopkeeper, and ordered that
another should be immediately substituted.   This was just what
the servant wanted.   He soon found a convenient tradesman, who
' tipped' him ten per cent., and made the master pay the commission, by sending him in a considerable overcharge.   It is unnecessary to add, that this flagrant act of dishonesty was punished
by the discharge of the servant, and that the defrauded tradesman
was immediately employed in the usual way.

" One of the most common tricks to which servants who are dissatisfied with the commission given them by their master's tradesmen resort, in order to get rid of such economists, is, that of ' poisoning' the stitches in clothes, in boots, in saddles, &c. Some time ago, one of the high attendants upon an illustrious person ordered home some pantaloons from his tailor. The tradesman was punctual, but the pantaloons had to pass through the hands of the servant before they reached the master; and, as a commission had been refused, the seams were tipped at once with aquafortis. No sooner did the master put his leg into the pantaloons, than it burst through the sides, to the horror of the hon. gentleman, who was preparing to go to a dinner. The servant, however, exercised no judgment in the use of the poison, for he tipped every pair with so unsparing a hand, that his master would, if he had walked out in such clothing, soon have had the cloth flying about his legs. The pantaloons were sent to the maker, who was ordered to account for the bad quality of the article (the cloth having shared the bad character of the stitching). The vile trick was immediately detected, and the tailor, without hesitation, charged the guilty person, in the presence of his master, with having used the aquafortis. The servant could not deny the accusation, and was of course at once dismissed.

" In nine cases out of ten," continued Mentor, " the masters are more to blame for being thus robbed, than the servants for robbing them; for, were they to take the trouble to pay the bills to the tradesmen themselves, and occasionally look to the various items in the accounts, they would soon become acquainted with the fair charges of honest tradesmen, and save themselves from being cheated of hundreds of pounds in the course of a year; but, above all, were they to pay ready money, they would, indeed, soon find a vast difference in the sum total of the annual expenditure of their household. The *fashionable* tradesmen do not care about serving any family, unless they let their accounts run.

" A gentleman of large fortune and estates near Walthamstow, who has, for some time, kept sixteen servants, determined to examine his tradesmen's bills more scrupulously than usual; and, in the course of the alterations which he found it necessary to adopt, he ascertained that no less than fifteen out of his sixteen domestics were in the habit of robbing him. He went to work rapidly: he opened the boxes of his servants, and found some of his property under the lock and key of every one of the ' below-stairs' gentry, with the exception of the groom: out he packed all guilty persons, men and women, without permitting one to sleep in his house another night. ' We do not know whether he learned that his principal servants were allowed a per-centage upon the bills that were annually paid; but, certain it is, that some of his tradespeople felt great disappointment at the change which took place in the arrangements of the mansion. The following accurate list of arrangements, is extracted from that invaluable journal, *The Times.*

" THE HOUSEKEEPER.—This domestic has under her care, and at her special command, the grocer, the butcher, the baker, the green-grocer, the pastry-cook, the oilman, and the fishmonger. In many families the average amount of the bills of those trades-people exceeds £500 a-year, to speak within a very narrow com-pass ; so that the lady who superintends this list pockets at least ten per cent. upon £3,500 a-year, a calculation which makes her mistress of £350 annually, independent of her wages, which are enormously high indeed, proportioned to the expenditure of the family.

" THE BUTLER.—This personage has under his control the boot-maker, the hatter, the wine-merchant, and the tailor. It is estimated that, in some families, the tailor alone pays £200 a-year to the butler, for the custom. How much cabbage is he not entitled to for the important services he renders to this despot of the kitchen ? The intimacy between him and the tradesmen on his list is kept up by an honest interchange of services. The butler looks at the bottom of their bills, without ever glancing at the items, and regularly deducts his ' regulars.' The interposition of any other tradesman is ridiculous. If the master happens to order clothes upon the recommendation of some dashing friend, at the house of a ' snider,' unknown to the butler, this trusty servant, if he does not ' poison' the stitches, is sure to persuade his master that the ' new cut' is most miserably deficient, and absolutely duns him with complaints, until he throws the clothes to the worthy person who is entitled to the ' cast-offs' (the butler himself), and orders the old tradesman to decorate his person once more.

" THE LADY's-MAID rules over the milliner and the silk-mercer. Her profits are very great indeed. She uniformly takes the cus-tom of the family to some one of the ' worthies' whose practices we have described under an appropriate head, and she has for herself all the cast-off clothes, besides her per-centage for the re-commendation. Her power is the greater, as, when she finds it necessary to exercise it, she has to address herself to the vanity of the weaker sex.

" THE COACHMAN.—This potentate settles with the coachmaker, the corn-chandler, and the harness-maker. He is a great ' poi-soner' of stitches, spoiler of corn, and contaminator of varnish, and his horses are sure to eat five times as much as those of other people. The farrier comes under his authority sometimes, but this tradesman more frequently is indebted to the groom, who sickens and shoes the horses as often as he pleases, and regularly demands a moiety of the amount for the medicine and shoes.

" THE GROOM.—This servant plunders most extensively. His profits are not known to his fellow-servants, for he has to look after the horse-dealer, and will not hesitate to hide a spavin for a £10 note. Hay and oats supply him with still more profits. It has been stated to us, that a noble lord, who is connected with one of the great hunts, lost, for some years, by his groom, at the rate of

at least £1,000 annually.  We can readily believe this, as the
facilities for plunder are inconceivably great.

" The depredations committed upon the wealthy and the eminent
in rank by those reptiles, have been going on for a series of years
without interruption.  A little circumstance, which was mentioned
to us by a friend, will give an idea of their extent.  The servant
of an Irish nobleman, who remained in London no more than three
months, was presented by the milkman with a £5 note for the
recommendation which obtained for that paltry tradesman the
custom of the family.  The insolence of the lazy servants of the
residents in the west-end of the town is intolerable.  A gentleman,
who resides in Wimpole Street, turned away six of his servants
for refusing to substitute cold for hot meat at their breakfasts.

" The Steward has the leases under his care, and he never
fails to recommend short leases, in order to increase his profits."

While Peregrine was feasting his eyes on the newly-erected
buildings contiguous to Pall Mall, his curiosity was attracted to
a number of persons, some with rolls of cloth, bandboxes, tables,
chairs, &c., others dressed like butchers, bakers, grocers, hair-
dressers, &c., waiting about the area of a gentleman's house : on
inquiry of some by-standers, he was told, they believed it was
one of those stupid and mischievous pieces of amusement and
folly called a hoax.  Peregrine asked his friend the meaning of it.
" Why," replied Mentor, " it is called, by some, a piece of fun, and
often practised in London by idle people, whose minds are bent on
mischief.  I will tell you of one that was played off some years
ago in South Audley Street.

" Between the hours of nine and ten, one of the party, in spruce
livery and smart cockade, announced himself at the several houses
of those who were to be *rigged* (as the phrase elegantly expresses
it), in the quality of footman to a widow lady of rank, residing in
South Audley Street, stating, at the same time, that his mistress
was about to give an elegant entertainment to a large number of
fashionables : the attendance of Mr. or Mrs. ——— (whosoever he
addressed) would therefore be required, precisely at twelve o'clock,
to take orders.  The lady into whose service our Mercury had
thus volunteered being well known in the fashionable circles,
nothing seemed more probable.  To be sure, this was not the time
for fashionable parties, but, had the fair mistress of that hospitable
mansion thought proper to deviate from the beaten track of etiquette
and ceremony, and collect around her whatever scraps of quality
remain in London during the summer months, who is there that
might dispute her right?—She had long shone the brightest gem
in fashion's circlet; her house was the seat of genius and of taste
—the resort of the great and the gay ; and her heart was the cradle
of hospitality : who, therefore, could doubt for a moment the
instructions of the smart lackey ?  It is unnecessary to say, the
summons was obeyed with punctuality.  At the appointed hour,
the door was besieged by expectant tradesmen of every descrip-

tion. Bakers, butchers, pastry-cooks, confectioners, grocers, fruiterers, fishmongers, poulterers, together with countless myriads of drapers, tailors, shoemakers, dress-makers, milliners, perfumers, frizeurs, and a full band of instrumental performers; the indefatigable footman omitted none: had he served the office from infancy, he could not be more perfectly *au-fait* to the duties of his station. Never before did Audley Street display a more animated or impatient group: the clock of the adjoining church at length tolled the hour of noon; the knocker was immediately assailed with sundry thumps, and the bell-rope kept in a sad state of agitation. Such were the instructions conveyed by the brass-plate on the door —'Knock and ring;' but, though they fully obeyed the injunction of this silent monitor, they might have knocked and rung, and rung and knocked again—

> "From morn till noon,
> From noon to dewy eve,
> A live-long summer's day"—

without either gaining any admission, or receiving any answer. That mansion, which some time ago was wont to peal with sounds of mirth and melody, was now voiceless and silent—silent as the tomb of the Capulets: and well it might; for she, whose presence shed life and animation through its halls, had long since crossed the Channel, and was then, perhaps, enjoying a promenade in the Tuilleries, or whiling away an hour at the Louvre in Paris, unconscious of every thing going forward in Audley Street. This mortifying piece of intelligence was somehow communicated to the impatient assailants; probably by a passing domestic of some neighbouring family; no matter how, but communicated it was; and never were execrations and curses more profusely lavished on any mischief-loving elf—never were they more vainly bestowed: for the smart footman took care to be out of reach, though very probably quite near enough to enjoy the consummation of his arch project. Such are the effects of idleness and the consequence of *ennui;* and yet, perchance, the head in which this foolish trick was hatched, may one day be enclosed in a mitre, or decorated with a Chancellor's wig. Where will the sense be then—within or without?"

While Peregrine and his friend were noticing the various indications of chagrin among the numerous tradesmen who were so mischievously brought together, they were beset by the importunities of a fresh-coloured round-faced boy, between ten and twelve years of age, who told them a most pitiable tale, when he was recognized as the noted juvenile Bampfylde Moore Carew, from Hull, where he was detected in his imposing falsehoods; and whose exploits are thus related by an eye-witness:—His parents, he said, had resided at Manchester, but were dead, and he was left entirely friendless and destitute. He had begged his way, he stated, from Manchester to Hull, hoping to meet with some employment; he had only arrived here on the preceding day, and had passed the night in the streets, being unable to procure sufficient money to pay for a lodging. He complained that he had had nothing to eat that day, and was almost starved. The lady doubted his word, and entered into conversation with him, when his answers to all the questions she asked were so pertinent, and apparently ingenuous, that she could no longer question the truth of his narrative, and directed him to her house, where she gave him his dinner; and, feeling averse to turn him out in his destitute condition, allowed him to remain till she could make some inquiry respecting him. The boy conducted himself with so much propriety, that she felt perfect confidence in the truth of his tale, and, having provided him with a suit of clothes, kept him for two or three days. At the end of this time, circumstances led to the discovery that he had been in the national-school at this place, and the master having been sent for, he immediately recognized him as a boy who was in the school a short time, and who was then given to much deceit and begging. On his parents being visited, they were found to be decent respectable persons, keeping a small shop; and from them it was learnt that the boy, notwithstanding every endeavour on their part to prevent it, had got such a habit of begging, that they found it impossible to break him from it.

Among the crowd who had now assembled around the young impostor, was an *exquisite* of the first order, whose ridiculous appearance and extravagance of dress seemed to draw the attention of all around him, particularly of Peregrine, who eyed him with astonishment and contempt. "That poor creature who seems to draw your attention," said Mentor, "is of a class of non-descripts called *dandies*, the most effeminate, useless, and contemptible creatures in society: they are indeed the baboons and the buffoons of the times and are an order of great antiquity, for we find them in the earliest of the annals of frivolity. However ridiculous they make themselves now appear, they were certainly out-done by their fraternity in former days. I will show you, this evening, a very rare print of a whole-length portrait of a London dandy in 1646, decked out like Solomon in all his splendour. We find dandies as early as Henry I. Their dress in those days approached to that of women. They wore tunics with deep sleeves and mantles with long trains. The peaks of their shoes (pigaciæ) were stuffed with tow, of enormous length, and twisted to imitate the horn of a ram, or the coils of a serpent—an *improvement* lately introduced by Fulk, Earl of Angou, to conceal the deformity of his feet. Their hair was divided in front, and combed on the shoulders, whence it fell in ringlets down the back, and was often lengthened most preposterously by the addition of false curls. This mode of dressing was opposed by the more rigid among the clergy, particularly the manner of wearing the hair, which was said to have been prohibited by St. Paul: 'If a man nourish his hair it is a shame to him.' 1 Cor. xi. 14.— But, after a long struggle, fashion triumphed over the clergy.

The Doings of a London Dandy of 1646.

" I have, hitherto," continued Mentor, " directed your attention principally to the frauds of the metropolis, I will now give you an

7             E

epitome of the ridiculous follies of the London Dandies (or gallants, fops, beaux, or bucks, as they are also sometimes denominated), from the earliest period; which will convince you that mankind is the same in all ages; that the absurdity of dress and frivolity, which you see now daily in London, was cherished with the same zeal, some hundreds of years past.

"Shortly after the reign of Henry I. the London women increased their rotundity with foxes' tails under their garments, and men with absurd short garments, insomuch as it was enacted in 22 Ed. IV., cap. 1, that no manner of person under the estate of a lord, shall wear, from that time, any gown or mantle, but of proper length, upon pain to forfeit to our Sovereign Lord the King, at every default, twenty shillings.

"Among the many capricious shapes which fashion has assumed in London, few, perhaps, are more remarkable than the piked shoes worn in the fifteenth century. They continued in vogue from the year 1382, for nearly a century; and were at length, carried to so ridiculous and extravagant a pitch, as to provoke the interference of the legislature; for the pikes of the shoes and boots were of such a length, says Baker, in his Chronicles, ' that they were fain to be tied to the knees with chains of silver and gilt, or, at least, with silken laces.' By the statute 3 Ed. IV., cap. 5, (1463) it is declared, that, notwithstanding the statutes then in being, 'the commons of the realm did daily wear excessive and inordinate array and apparel, to the great displeasure of God, and impoverishing of this realm of England, and to the enriching of other strange realms and countries, to the final destruction of the husbandry of the said realms;' and it is, therefore, among other provisions, enacted, ' that no knight, under the state of a lord, esquire, gentleman, or other person, should use or wear any shoes or boots having pikes passing the length of two inches, upon pain of forfeiting to the king, for every default, three shillings and four pence.'

"The rage for piked shoes in London does not, however, seem to have been in the least suppressed by this act; for, in two years after, Edward IV. was obliged to issue a proclamation, forbidding the use of pikes of shoes exceeding the length of two inches, under pain of cursing by the clergy, and forfeiting twenty shillings, to be paid, one noble to the king, another to the cordwainers of London, and a third to the chamber of London.

The Londoners appear to have been intimidated by the severe penalties imposed by this proclamation; for of high piked shoes we hear no more after this period : nay, so much did the fashion in London run into a contrary extreme, that, in the reign of Henry V., as Fuller informs us, 'it was fair to be ordered by proclamation, that none should wear their shoes broader at the toes than six inches.'

"The portrait of the London Dandy of 1646 is the exact dress of the fashionables of that time: the long locks of hair, pendent from the temples, with tasty bows of riband tied at the ends, were called by the ladies *Love-Locks;* and the zeal of Prynne thought this so prominant a folly of the time, that he wrote no less than a quarto volume against the *Unloveliness of Love-Locks.* The fashion expired with Charles I. The stars and half-moons on his face are ornamented patches; which mode of embellishing the face, though more simple, is even in vogue to the present hour. It is no uncommon sight in London, to see some men with a piece of sticking-plaster on their face, as an ornament."

" Among the absurdities of fashion, it would be difficult to find one more ridiculous than that of gentlemen wearing spurs on their boots, as part of their walking-dress. Spurs have been, for upwards of two centuries, a favourite article of finery in the dress of a man of fashion. They were frequently gilt, as appears from ' Wit's Recreations :'

> ' As Battus believed for simple truth,
> That yonder gilt spruce and velvet youth
> Was some great personage.'

" It was very fashionable, in London, to have the spurs so made as to rattle or jingle, when the wearer moved.

" In the puritanical times of Oliver Cromwell, several attempts were made to stop the love of dress in London, and ministers of the Gospel were continually both from the pulpit, and in their writings, exclaiming against it; particularly one Thomas Reeve, B. D. who wrote a work, called ' *God's Plea for Nineveh,*' &c. in which is given a rare vocabulary of *dandyism;* I will read it to you : it says—'The kings of Egypt were wont to give unto their queens the tribute of the city Antilla, to buy them girdles; and how much girdles, gorgets, wimples, cowls, crisping-pins, veils, rails, frontlets, bonnets, bracelets, necklaces, slops, slippers, round tires, sweetballs, rings, ear-rings, mufflers, glasses, hoods, lawns, musks, civets, rose-powders, jessamy-butter, complexion-waters, do cost in our days, many a sighing husband doth know by the year's account. What ado is there to spruce up many a woman, either for streets or market, banquets or temples ? She is not fit to be seen, unless she doth appear half naked ; nor to be marked, unless she hath her distinguishing patches upon her: she goeth not abroad till she be feathered like a popinjay, and doth shine like alabaster. It is a hard thing to draw her out of bed, and a harder thing to draw her from the looking-glass : it is the great work of the family to dress her—much chafing and fuming there is before she can be thoroughly tired; her spongings and perfumings, lacings and lickings, clippings and strippings, dentifricings, and daubings, the setting of every hair methodically, and the placing of every beauty-spot topically, are so tedious, that it is a wonder the mistress can sit, or the waiting-made stand, till all the scenes of this fantastic comedy be acted through. Oh, these birds of Paradise are bought at a dear rate ! The keeping of these lannerets is very chargeable ! The wife oftentimes doth wear more gold upon her back, than the husband hath in his purse; and hath more jewels about her neck, than the annual revenue doth amount to. And this is the she-pride; and doth not the he-pride equal it? Yes, the man now is become as feminine as the woman. Men must have their half-shirts and half-arms, a dozen easements above, and two wide luke-homes below: some walk, as it were, in their waistcoats; and others, a man would think, in their petticoats: they must have narrow waists and narrow bands, large cuffs upon their wrists, and larger upon their shin-bones; their boots must be crimped, and their knees guarded. A man would conceive them to be apes, by their coats; soapmen, by their faces; mealmen, by their shoulders; bears, or dogs, by their frizzled hair. And this is my trim man! And oh, that I could end here! but pride doth go a larger circuit: it is travelled amongst the commons; every yeoman in this age must be attired like a gentleman of the first head; every clerk must be as brave as the justice; every apprentice match his master in gallantry; the waiting-gentlewoman doth vie fashions with her lady! and the kitchen-maid doth look like some 'squire's daughter by her habit; the handicraftsmen are all in their colours, and their wives in rich silks.'

" 'The Portrait of a Gallant.—The gallant is counted a wild creature; no wild colt, wild ostrich, wild cat of the mountain, comparable to him; his mind is wholly set upon cut and slashes, knots and roses, patchings and pinkings, jaggings, taggings, borderings, brimmings, half-shirts, half-arms, yawning breasts, gaping knees, arithmetical middles, geometrical sides, mathematical waists, musical heels, and logical toes.' "

" From this period to the commencement of the eighteenth century, we have little to say of the London Dandies; but in the London Evening Post, for 1738, there is a true picture of them. It says:

" I went the other night to the play, with an aunt of mine, a well-bred woman of the last age, though a little formal. When we sat down in the front boxes, we found ourselves surrounded by a party of the strangest fellows I ever saw in my life: some of them had that loose kind of great-coats on, which I have heard called *wrap-rascals*, with gold-laced hats, slouched in humble imitation of stage-coachmen; others, as being grooms, had *dirty* boots and *spurs*, with black caps on, and long whips in their hands; a third sort wore scanty frocks, little shabby hats put on one side, and clubs in their hands. My aunt whispered me, she never saw such a set of slovenly unmannerly *footmen*, sent to keep places, in all her life; when, to her great surprise, she saw those fellows, at the end of the act, *pay the box-keeper for their places!*"

" A newspaper of 1770 gives the following description of a London Dandy: 'A few days ago, a macaroni made his appearance at an assembly-room, dressed in a mixed silk coat, pink satin waistcoat and breeches, covered with an elegant silver net, white silk stockings, with pink clocks, pink satin shoes and large pearl buckles; a mushroom-coloured stock, covered with fine point-lace, hair dressed remarkably high, and stuck full of pearl pins.'

"An advertisement issued in 1703, gives a whole length portrait of the dress of a young dandy. Such a figure would attract much wonder at present in the streets of London. 'He is of a fair complexion, light-brown lank hair, having on a dark-brown frieze coat, double breasted on each side, with black buttons and button-holes; a light drugget waistcoat, *red shag breeches, striped with black stripes,* and *black* stockings.'

"The dandies of 1720 wore the full-curled flowing wig, which fell in ringlets half way down his arms and back; a neckcloth tied tightly round his neck; a coat reaching to his ancles, laced, straight, formal, with buttons to the very bottom, and several on the pockets and sleeves; his shoes were square at the toes, had diminutive buckles, a monstrous flap on the instep, and high heels.

"If we may credit the Flying Post of June 14, 1722, the Bishop of Durham appeared on horseback at a review, in the king's train, 'in a lay habit of purple, with jack boots, and his hat cocked, and black wig tied behind him, like a military officer.'

"The dandies of 1730 laid aside their swords, and took to carrying large oak sticks, *with great heads and ugly faces carved thereon.'*

"Such, my friend," said Mentor, "is a brief history of the dandies of London: let us retire to rest; the morrow will furnish us with sufficient subjects of curiosity." Peregrine withdrew, but the narrative of wonders and novelties filled his mind with perturbation. He revolved all that he had heard, and prepared innumerable questions for the morning.

While Peregrine was waiting for his friend, Mentor, a wretched squalid-looking creature attracted his notice, passing frequently before the window of the inn; who, seeing she had "caught the eye" of Peregrine, with the utmost humility, and putting on a countenance clouded with sorrow and grief, presented him with a letter, portraying a case of the severest distress; while reading it, his heart melting at the recital of such accumulated distress, Mentor entered the room, to whom Peregrine presented the letter, telling him what an object of charity the bearer was. Mentor read the 'case of distress,' when he recollected he heard the same story at a friend's house, a few days before, and the bearer was discovered to be a most notorious impostor: he therefore ordered the waiter to tell the person who had sent in the letter, to walk in; when behold it was the celebrated Molly Jones, one of the most notorious disciples of the begging-letter tribe, the faithful *pal* of the noted Peter Hill, who was charged, some time before, at the office in Marlborough Street, with committing divers frauds on the public. Peter was immediately dismissed with a severe reproof. "Since the days of Bamfylde Moore Carew," said Mentor, "there has not been such an extraordinary mendicant as Peter Hill. On one occasion he gave evidence, under an assumed name, to prove an *alibi* in favour of his brother, and then pretended to be a gentleman of independent property. He was a witness at the Old Bailey, in favour of the female prisoner who was tried under the name of Larkin, and by his testimony he obtained her acquittal. He was again a witness in her behalf; she was then tried under the name of Hartley, for robbing a youth, whom she dragged into a house of bad repute, and robbed of a broach; Hill's evidence then threw so much doubt on the statement of the prosecutor, that the jury returned a verdict of Not Guilty. The officers of the Mendicity Society, were, for a long time, in pursuit of him; but it appears that he was almost always disguised, when he went to the houses of the nobility and gentry to solicit relief. Sometimes he passed for an unfortunate surgeon, at other times a clergyman, a dissenting minister, an actor, a painter, &c. &c.; but the most extraordinary of his performances, which proves that he would have been an adept in the mimic art, was the following, which was related by an officer of the Mendicity Society:—His disguise is a brown scratch wig, and a pair of huge spectacles, which so alter his appearance, that Peter Hill, without his wig, is quite a different person to Peter Hill in full dress. He went with a petition, early one morning, to the Earl of Harrowby; he was then dressed in his usual attire; he professed to be an unbeneficed clergyman, in great distress; and he detailed the distress of himself and family in such moving terms, that the noble earl gave him £1. On the same night the prisoner went again to Lord Harrowby's, disguised in his large hat, wig, and spectacles, with a different coat; and he represented himself to be a miniature-painter, who was unable to work at his trade, in consequence of his sight being so much impaired; and the noble earl did not discover the impostor, but gave him another pound. The Mendicity Society have not less than three hundred cases against him and his coadjutors; and it has been clearly ascertained that they, at one time, raised contributions upon the public, by means of false pretences, to the extent of £20 a day. The prisoners were both apprehended, some time since, by Cousins, the constable of St. Pancras, as they were quarrelling in Tottenham-Court Road, they having both got beastly drunk with the money which they had obtained through the credulity of humane individuals. Some sheets were found in the female's possession, which, it is believed, she had stolen; and, in the possession of Peter Hill, were found the documents which led to his being charged with the frauds imputed to him. They were brought before the magistrate, and the documents were sent to the Mendicity Society's office, and orders given for the prisoners' re-examination on Monday. Mr. Bodkin, the secretary of the society, and several of the gentlemen connected with the institution, attended. Hill, on his former examination, had had no wig, but, on his appearing at the bar, on Monday, his appearance was so much altered, that he could hardly be recognised as the same

person. Mr. Bodkin said, that he should confine the present examination to two cases, in which the prisoner had obtained money
under false pretences; and these cases would be most satisfactorily
brought home to him. Before the witnesses were examined, he
requested that the magistrate (Mr. Roe) would be so kind as to
order the prisoner to take off his wig, because he obtained the
money in question at a time when he did not wear that ornament
to his pericranium. Mr. Roe commanded Hill to take off his wig.
He hesitated for a moment, and, at length, seized it by a side curl,
and dashed it off. The witnesses (two pretty girls) burst into a fit
of laughter, and exclaimed 'That is he.' Cousins proved having
found, on the person of Hill, a note written by him to Barnes, which
is important, so far as it develops the systematic plans of begging-
letter writers :—

" ' Dear sir—I am hard up. Do favour me with a few directions
on the back of this note, and I will call for them in the morning.
" ' Your's truly, P. HILL.
" ' To Mr. Barnes, Tottenham-Court Road, Sat. Aug. 19.'

" Barnes had written an answer on the back of the above note,
and returned it to Hill. His reply is as follows :—

" ' I have put down a few names of persons at Hampstead, as I
know of no other, and, I am sorry to say, I am like yourself; I
have not a shoe to my feet :—Mrs. Todd, opposite the Load of
Hay; Mrs. Battye, Church Row; Mrs. Mellish, ditto; Mrs.
Walker, ditto; Mrs. Swallow, Well Walk; Mrs. Russell, ditto;
Mrs. Johnson, ditto; Mrs. Freer, on the Heath; Mrs Sheppard,
ditto; Mrs. Spedding, ditto; Mrs. Hoare, ditto; Mrs. Babington,
North End; Lockwood, ditto; School, Mrs. Collins, at the back
of the Shepherd; Mrs. Walker, ditto, next door; Mrs. Whit-
marsh, at the back of Well Walk.'

" The following is a copy of the petition :—' It is with an
aching heart, and a mind bordering on despair, that I presume to
address you with these few lines, at the same time indulging a
hope that my situation will plead in extenuation of the liberty I
take, by intruding on the notice of a lady whose characteristic is
that of doing good. Permit me to state, that I emanate from a
respectable family, and am the son of a much-respected clergyman, many years deceased; and it is melancholy to relate, that
my wife, after lying-in with twins, both of whom are since dead,
was seized with a nervous fever, which flew into her brain; and
she was, poor woman, to the great grief of her disconsolate husband, confined in a private mad-house, and from thence removed
to Saint Luke's. I am professionally a miniature-painter, but,
unhappily, have not been able to pursue my avocation, in consequence of a severe attack of the palsy, and an inflammation in
my eyes, which totally prevent me from painting. Should you
think me worthy of your relief, the smallest mite will be received
with gratitude, and you, through life, will have the inexpressible

pleasure of feeling you have relieved a truly wretched and unfortunate fellow-creature, on whom

　　　　" Fortune smiled deceitful at his birth."

　　　' And your petitioner will for ever pray,

　　　　　　　　　　JAMES LOCKYER.'

　　" Peter was sent to the tread-mill.

　　" These begging-letter impostors," continued Mentor, " are very
numerous in London.   I remember, among a multitude of others,
a fellow of the name of Diggles, who gained a very good livelihood by such means : he was apprehended and brought to one
of the police-offices, in consequence of being detected stealing a
box-coat, value four guineas, out of the country-house of Mr.
Drake, hop-merchant, in the Borough.   It appeared that, on
being searched by the officer, there was found upon him a petition
drawn up, with the signatures of a vast number of highly respectable individuals, who had contributed to the relief of the petitioner,
and also nine shillings in silver, together with a certificate of Mr.
Watson, of the Trinity House, of the prisoner having received a
donation of him that very morning.   The magistrate asked the
prisoner who had authorized him to draw up the petition.   The
prisoner replied, that he was permitted to do so by Messrs. Sikes,
the bankers, who knew him perfectly well, and whose name stood
at the head of the petition, as one of his benefactors.   The prisoner was fully committed for stealing the coat.

　　" Innumerable other cases I might recite," said Mentor; " but
these cases will suffice to put you on your guard, and teach you
never to give to any person presenting you with a statement of
their misfortunes, unless it has the name and residence of some
respectable person affixed to it : for then you can go, and inquire
into the truth of the story."

　　Mentor and his young friend, taking some refreshment, the
conversation turned on the virtues and deleterious qualities of
the Beer of London, in consequence of reading the following
judicious remarks on the dreadful effects of beer-drinking, in that
interesting journal—" *The Watchman.*"

　　" Every body exclaims against the monoply of brewers, but no
one, it would appear, is able to devise a remedy, or collect sufficient power to overturn and destroy the monstrous system.   Its
roots are fixed in a soil so tenacious, its ramifications are so extensive, and its abettors and upholders so numerous, so well dis-
ciplined, and so expert, that few men have the courage to assail
the system in the public journals, and fewer still to attack it in
Parliament.

　　" Yet, for all this, the monopoly of the brewers is the most abominable, the most impolitic, and the most injurious and unjust
monopoly that ever existed in this or any other country.   It would
require a volume to explain how this system has been fostered
and matured, how it is fortified, and how it can with impunity de-

fraud the revenue, crush the honest dealer, and pour down the throats of His Majesty's liege subjects so many thousand barrels of mortal poison weekly. We shall endeavour, however, to revive the case, and bring the facts before the public; and, if we fail in arousing such a storm as will break up this monopoly, it will not be for want of exertion or good intention. The system is too monstrous and iniquitious to be much longer tolerated.

"We protest, nevertheless, that we are not urged to the investigation from any personal dread of being found on our mattress some morning the victim of *coculus indicus* and *nux vomica*. Not one drop of the nauseous potion, called porter, passes our lips. We see its effects on the faces of the emaciated wretches who drink it, too visibly, to run any hazard from it by personally patronizing the decoction. The face of a porter-drinker proves that he drinks poison. The hard-working man eats his beef and greens with a fierce appetite, and he floods his meals with a pint, if not more, of this porter. Examine his eyes two hours afterwards: see how blood-streaked they are—see the saffron colour of his lips—see the strain and tension of his muscles—all the indisputable symptoms of his having taken poison. He drinks no gin, no whiskey, no ardent spirits whatever, or, at least, but rarely—his entire tipple is the brewage of Saint Somebody and company— and yet, if ever poison exhibited itself externally, he shows all the external marks of a patient struggling with the effects of an insidious and slow poison. The tall, strong-boned men, who drive drays—the coal-men and barge-men, and many of the hackney-coachmen, are paler in the face than other men. They are perpetually troubled with heartburn and fever, and attribute their malady to any thing but the right cause. Those who drink the larger portion are uniformly the most sallow and emaciated. All these symptoms, we say, are symptoms of poison, and which is only prevented from speedily proving mortal, by the neutralizing effects of the solids they eat, and the constant and hard labour to which they are subject. They, however, never live long. They never reach an average life; and it is proved beyond all cavil, that these once robust and strong-boned men, who never indulge in spirituous liquors to any excess, who are well clothed and lodged, lived from ten to fifteen years less than men similarly employed, and worse fed, do in all the distant parts of the country.

"That the great brewers mix deleterious drugs with their porter is notorious. They are allowed to make 144 gallons of porter out of the quarter of malt, and the publican is allowed to make as many more as he pleases. That the brewers go to the full extent of their licence is proved by their annual returns of porter made and malt consumed. Now, what does this show? First, that the intoxicating effects of their beer are not produced by malt alone. Second, the proportion of the malt to the porter shows, that, if they used malt and hops alone, their porter would scarcely be so strong and intoxicating as the commonest and most watery small

B.

beer. Its present intoxicating effects must be attributed to some other illegal ingredients. A strong man is soon overpowered by it; inebriety from porter is followed by the most injurious consequences; and a strong man never could become intoxicated from small beer, for his stomach would not contain sufficient, nor his circulation diffuse it sufficiently rapid, to cause intoxication.

" What, therefore, do the brewers, the humane brewers, the philanthropic brewers, the saintly brewers, who can weep by the hour over the condition of the ' poor blacks'—what do these pious and humane rogues mix with their beer to cause such EXHILARATING effects on the constitution of their naturally stout and robust *white* brethren! They use, and notoriously use, what is classically called *porter essence.* And of what is this soothing, wholesome, and exhilarating essence composed? Read, you guzzlers—read this, you stupid drinkers of villanous compounds, while you can procure pure water—read this, and then order your coffins, and prepare for your rout to the only portion of the earth which you will be able to call your own.

" The recipe for this celebrated *porter essence* is as follows:— ' Take twenty-eight pounds of Spanish liquorice, and four pounds of *copperas;* boil them together, in a copper pan, in three gallons of water. Then take fifty-six pounds of molasses or treacle, and fifty-six pounds of raw sugar, and boil them till they thicken a good deal; add the mixture above-mentioned, and boil all together two hours. When cold, add the following ingredients, in powder: four pounds of *gentian-root* (ground,) four pounds of *orange pease*, two pounds of ground *calamus-root*, and stir and mix till it becomes like a soft extract.'

" This ' soft extract' is made by the druggists daily, and for the use of the porter brewers alone; and is put up in one, two, or three pound bladders. This is used in certain proportions, according to circumstances, the age, and the strength of the porter. But many more ingredients than these are used. Quassia is used, as well as what is called the *multum powder,* to save hops, and *coculus indicus* and *nux vomica* to save malt; all of which are deleterious, and destructive to animal life in the highest degree.

" We shall here conclude this notice, by extracting the following remarks from a respectable journal, published a few years ago, which throws some important light on the system:—' More than 30,000lbs. of *nux vomica,* and more than 12,000lbs. of *coculus indicus,* are, upon an average, annually imported into Great Britain. They are both highly poisonous drugs; but in small portions may, like some other poisons, be swallowed without producing any other *immediate* effect than a kind of stupid intoxication. Alarming conjectures and suspicions are entertained, and fearful assertions are made, in regard to the use of these drugs in this country; but, nevertheless, the apprehensions of the public seem to rest more upon inference and implication than upon proof. The argument used is this: that neither in England, nor in any other part of the world, is there any known purpose for which the articles in question are used, with the exception of a small quantity occasionally consumed as poison for vermin; ergo, there is good ground for believing that the grand consumption is, for some end or purpose, secret, mysterious, and illegal. Now, the wholesale dealers in *nux vomica* and *coculus indicus* have an easy mode of removing any odium or suspicion attaching to themselves or their supposed customers, and at the same time of making the public mind easy, by plainly stating to what *honest* use such enormous quantities of these highly deleterious drugs are devoted in this or any other country; and we sincerely hope that some one of the many highly respectable individuals engaged in the drug trade, will, through the medium of the papers, give the required explanation.'"

Dr. Paris, in his work on *Diet*, says, porter ought to be made from high-dried malt, and differs from other malt liquors in the proportion of its ingredients, and from the peculiar manner in which it is manufactured. It is certain, he says, that the adulterations are not carried on in the caldrons of the brewer, but in the *barrels of the publican!* The origin of the beer, to be called *entire*, is thus explained. Before the year 1730, the malt liquors generally used in London, were ale, beer, and twopenny; and it was customary to call for a pint, or tankard, of half-and-half, that is, half of ale and half of porter, half of ale and half of twopenny. In the course of time it also became the practice to call for a pint, or tankard, of three-thirds, meaning one third ale, beer, and two-penny; and thus the publican had the trouble of going to three casks, and turning three cocks, for a pint of liquor. To avoid this inconvenience and waste, a brewer, of the name of Harwood, conceived the idea of making a liquor that should partake of the same united flavour of ale, beer, and twopenny. He did so, and succeeded, calling it entire, or entire butt, meaning that it was drawn entirely from one cask or butt; and, as it was a very hearty and nourishing liquor, it obtained the name of *porter*.

One great source of profit to the dishonest publican, though a disgraceful one, is the mode of filling their pots; and in this species of trickery they are as great adepts as the ill-principled gin-shop keeper is with his glasses. I strongly recommend to all publicans the following advice of an honest Quaker: "A Quaker alighting from the Bristol coach, on entering the inn, called for some beer, and, observing the pint deficient in quantity, thus addressed the landlord—'Pray, friend, how many butts of beer dost thou draw in a month?' 'Ten, sir,' replied Boniface. 'And thou wouldst like to draw eleven,' rejoined Ebenezer. 'Certainly,' exclaimed the smiling landlord. 'Then I will tell thee how, friend,' added the Quaker—'fill thy measures.'"

Public-houses were formerly kept by women, hence called alewives, and then hostesses: they are mentioned repeatedly by Shakspeare and other authors.

Among the most celebrated, may be enumerated, *Mother Redcap*, who kept a public-house at the end of Tottenham-Court Road;

it was frequented principally by soldiers, she having been a soldier's wife,—*Mother Louse*, of Oxford,—the celebrated

**Eleanor Rummin.**

of the time of Henry VIII. Skelton, the poet, wrote a poem,
called "The Tunning of Eleanor Rummin."—*Dame Quickly*, the
ale-wife of the Boar's Head in East Cheap, is immortalized by Shakspeare.—And the last eminent ale-wife we have any notice of, is
*Jane Rouse*, who also kept the Boar's Head: she was tried at
the Old Bailey for witchcraft, and executed!

"Dr. Trotter," said Mentor, "remarks, that 'Malt liquors, and
particularly porter, have their narcotic powers much increased by
noxious compounds, which enter them, and the bitters which are
necessary to their preservation, by long use injure the nerves of the
stomach, and add to the stupefactive quality. Malt-liquor drinkers
are known to be prone to apoplexy and palsy, from that very
cause; and purl drinkers, in a still greater degree, a mixture peculiar to this country. This poisonous morning beverage was, till
lately, confined to the metropolis and its vicinity, but has now,
like other luxuries, found its way into the country.'

"A Mr. Child, some time since, published a small treatise, entitled 'Every Man his own Brewer, explaining the Art and
Mystery of Brewing Porter,' &c. in which you will find that the
following articles are used by the brewers of London: they differ
a little from the recipe, as given in the 'Watchman:'

" ' *Treacle.*

" ' *Liquorice-root.*

" ' *Essentia bina ;*' which is moist sugar boiled in an iron vessel, for no copper one could withstand the heat sufficiently, till it comes to a thick syrupy consistence, perfectly black and extremely bitter.

" ' *Colour ;* composed of moist sugar, boiled till it obtains a middle state, between bitter and sweet, and which gives to porter that fine mellow colour, usually so much admired in good porter.

" ' *Capsicum.*

" ' *Spanish liquorice.*

" ' *Cøculus indicus :* dog-poison.

" ' *Salt of tartar.*

" ' *Heading* is a mixture of half alum and half copperas, ground to a fine powder; and it is so called from giving to porter that beautiful head, or froth, which constitutes one of the peculiar properties of porter, and which landlords are so anxious to raise, to gratify their customers.

" ' *Ginger.*

" ' *Lime slacked.*

" ' *Linseed.*

" ' *Cinnamon.*

" ' *Hops and malt.*

" ' *Opium Hyosecamus, Belladona, and Lauvio Ceracus.* These four last articles, Dr. Trotter says, are used by porter-brewers.'

" Who has the credulity to think that such a composition is fitted for human sustenance ! It is only to be equalled by the combined genius of Macbeth's witches. The ingredients thrown into their divining caldron might perhaps be put in competition with it.

" In distilleries and breweries, where hogs and poultry are fed on the sediments of barrels, their liver and other viscera are observed to be enlarged and hardened, like those of the human body; and, were these animals not killed at a certain period, their flesh would be unfit to eat, and their bodies become emaciated.

" ' Two acres of ground,' says the Mechanics' Magazine, ' in Battersea fields, were lately employed in rearing a crop of bearded darnel (*colium temulentum*). The seeds of it, when ground and mixed with wheaten flour, form a bread that has repeatedly occasioned death; and, when steeped with malt, to give potency to beer (which is said to be no unfrequent case), they cannot be much less injurious. The laws of China make it a capital offence to use them in fermented liquors : it would be well if our's did the same.'

" It is a sad pity," continued Mentor, " that people are so wedded to drinking fermented liquors: water is the only drink that helps to digest the food : water is the only drink that quenches the thirst : water is the only beverage that gives health and strength to man : water is the only simple fluid for diluting, moistening, and cooling—the ends of drink appointed by nature. But then, water can be procured without expense; it may be had in almost

every church-yard in London, for the trouble of fetching it; this
is the grand error of water: if it was the same price as that deadly
poison, *gin*, then it would be swallowed by gallons.  I could almost wish that drinking water was a crime, for then millions would
fly to it as their only beverage :

> " ' O madness! to think use of strongest wines
>     And strongest drink our chief support of health,
>     When God, with these forbidden, made choice to rear
>     His mighty champion, strong above compare,
>     Whose drink was only from the *liquid brook*.'

" But," said Mentor, " more of this subject anon : we must haste
away, lest we should be too late for a view of Covent-Garden
Theatre, as you said you wished to see it before you visited it
during a performance."

Scarcely had they reached the street, when they were importuned
by a cleanly-dressed old woman, who was sweeping the road at
Charing Cross. "That old woman," said Mentor, " is well known
as the *money-lending mendicant*.  She has appeared here for years
with her birch-broom, which is generally a tolerably decent one.
There is not an Admiralty clerk, or an army-agent's assistant, of
twenty or thirty years' standing, but is acquainted with her by
sight or from her importunities; indeed, she appears to have a vested
interest in this crossing, for, if she is not here, nobody is.  She attends ' business' from about ten to four o'clock.  After that, she
returns to her apartments in Duck Lane, Westminster, walking
leisurely home by the Horse Guards, across the park, &c.  The
warfare against reticules was not extended to her broom, with
which she walks as if she had a fire-lock.  She then partakes of
a good dinner.  After dinner, she attends to her financial affairs,
in which she is embarked to considerable extent, chiefly in *bill-dis-
counting*—she is deeply engaged in such affairs.  One recent transaction may illustrate the nature of her concern.  She advanced to
a small tradesman, near Peter Street, £50 on a bill, to receive as
remuneration *twenty* per cent.  Part of the money was afterwards
paid, leaving, of course, a balance; and, when that balance was
proffered, she demanded interest on the whole £50, as if no
part of it had been paid; contending that ' it was her *bond* to have
the interest on the £50, till *that* amount was returned;' and because the tradesman urged that he ought only to pay the rate of
interest stipulated for on the amount remaining unpaid, she for-
sooth lodged the affair in the hands of her *attorney*, not far from
Thornhaugh Street.  An attorney then appeared on the other
side, and, unwilling to break an agreement, tendered the balance,
with the twenty per cent. on that only, which it was deemed right
to accept, the ' money-lending mendicant' fearing some proceedings under the still existing usury laws, which might have subjected her to the penalties of thrice the amount of the principal.
This shows what rigid parsimony, even in a street beggar, may
accomplish."

On passing through Covent-Garden Market, Peregrine was surprised with the delicious display of fruit, the fragrancy of the flowers, and the abundance of vegetable productions that were displayed for sale. "This market," said Mentor, "is the principal one for supplying fruit and vegetables in the greatest perfection, to the inhabitants of London. It was formerly part of the garden belonging to a convent, and therefore ought properly to be called Convent Garden : it was given, at the time of the dissolution of monasteries, to the Earl of Bedford, in whose family it still remains.

The fruit and vegetables consumed in the metropolis are principally produced in the environs; and it is calculated there are upwards of six thousand acres of ground cultivated as gardens, within twelve miles of the metropolis, giving employment to thirty thousand people in winter, and three times that number in summer. Numerous calculations have been made of the annual consumption of food in the metropolis, but this is not easily ascertained; as, although we may know the number of cattle and sheep, yet we have no means of learning the weight. Of the cattle sold in Smithfield market, there are the most accurate returns, from which we find that in 1822 the numbers were 149,885 beasts, 24,609 calves, 1,507,065 sheep, and 20,020 pigs. This does not, however, by any means, form the total consumed in London, as large quantities of meat, in carcases, particularly pork, are daily brought from the counties round the metropolis. The total value of the cattle sold in Smithfield is calculated at £8,500,000. It is supposed that a million a year is expended in fruits and vegetables. The consumption of wheat amounts to a million of quarters annually; of this, four fifths are supposed to be made into bread, being a consumption of sixty-four millions of quartern loaves, every year, in the metropolis alone. Until within the last few years, the price of bread was regulated by assize, and it may afford some idea of the vast amount of money paid for the staff of life, when it is stated, that an advance of one farthing on the quartern loaf formed an aggregate increase, in expense for this article alone, of upwards of £13,000 per week. The annual consumption of butter, in London, amounts to about 11,000, and that of cheese to 13,000 tons. The money paid annually for milk, is supposed to amount to £1,250,000. The quantity of poultry annually consumed in London, is supposed to cost between £70,000 and £80,000. There is nothing, however, more surprising, than the sale of rabbits : one salesman in Leadenhall Market, during a considerable portion of the year, is said to sell 14,000 rabbits weekly. The way in which he disposes of them, is by employing between 150 and 200 men and women, who hawk them through the streets. "Such, my friend," said Mentor, "is a brief calculation of London consumption; and, if you were to be in this market between five and six o'clock in the morning in the pea season, it would increase your surprise in imagining how the immense quantity of vegetables here for sale, could be consumed : the money turned here then, in a market morning, is incredible ; and, to give you some idea of the number of persons who frequent it, the landlady of an inn in James Street, has been known to send out *five hundred breakfasts*, before nine o'clock in the morning.

"We will now walk under the Piazza, as it is erroneously called, and that will lead us to

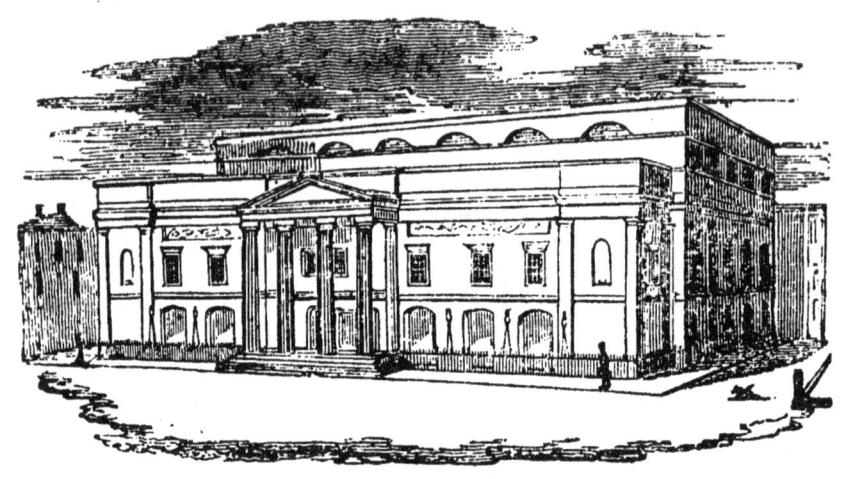

**Covent=Garden Theatre,**

which structure was erected in the year 1809, from designs by Mr. Smirke, jun., architect, on the site of the former theatre, which was destroyed by fire, in September, 1808 ; and the whole of this present edifice was raised within one year. The architect took, for his model, the finest specimen of the Doric from the ruins of Athens—the grand temple of Minerva, situated in the Aeropolis. The interior of the house is splendidly and tastefully ornamented, and is larger than that of Drury; being calculated to hold upwards of 3000 persons, and, when filled, to produce nightly near £700. The original Covent-Garden Theatre was built by subscription, under the direction of Mr. Rich, in 1731, from a de sign by Mr. James Sheppard."

Whilst Peregrine was admiring the architectural beauties of the building, his attention was suddenly called away, by the noise of a number of persons who had assembled in the street, and on inquiring the cause, he was told, the people were waiting to see some culprit come from the police-office there. Peregrine had heard much of the "Doings" in Bow Street, and, expressing a wish to hear some of the examinations, obtained admittance ; when the first case that came before the magistrate, was for obtaining money and other valuables from a servant girl ; who stated, that the old woman at the bar was a celebrated fortune-teller that she had first gained her acquaintance by attending, at her master's house, before the family had risen, and urging her to have her fortune told ; at length, after much persuasion, she consented ; but the fortune-teller told her, before she revealed the secrets of her future destiny, she must deposit in her hands some little token, *to bind the charm*, which the old *lady* said she would invoke the same evening, if I would call at her lodging, and also cast my nativity by her cards, and tell me every particular of the future progress of my life. I accordingly gave her what money I had; but that, she told me, was not enough to buy the ingredients with which she was to compose the charm. I at length gave her four silver tea-spoons, and two table-spoons, which she put carefully in her pocket; and then asked me to let her look at my hand, which I showed her. She told me there were many lines in it, which clearly indicated great wealth and happiness; and, after telling her my name was Martha Carnaby, she took her departure, and I agreed to meet her at her lodgings the same evening; agreeably to her directions, I dressed myself in as fashionable a manner as I could, because I was to see my sweetheart through a mirror, and he was to see me." The poor deluded creature then stated, she attended punctually at the hour appointed, at the old sybil's *sanctum sanctorum*, and seating herself upon an old chair, beheld with astonishment

The Doings of a Fortune-Teller.

" I felt myself," said poor Martha, " on entering the room, all of a *twitter;* the old woman was seated in her chair of state, and, reaching down from the mantle-piece a pack of cards, began, after muttering a few words in a language I could not understand, to lay them very carefully in her lap; she then foretold that I should get married, but not to the person in our house, to whom I expected, but to another young man, whom, if I could afford a trifle, she would show me through her *matrimonial mirror*. To this I consented, and she desired me to shut my eyes and keep my face covered while she made the necessary preparations; and there she kept me, with my face hid in her lap, until I was nearly smothered; when suddenly she told me to turn round, and look through the mirror, which was seen through a hole in a curtain, and I saw a young man pass quickly before me, staring me in the face, at which I was much surprised, she assuring me that would be my husband. It was then agreed she was to call on me the next morning, and return the silver spoons; but your worship," said the poor girl, " she never came; and, as I was afraid my mistress would soon want them, I asked the advice of a woman in our neighbourhood, as to what I had better do, and to whom I related all the circumstances I have told your worship; when the woman asked me how I could have been such a fool as to be duped by that old cheat at the bar; that she was a notorious old woman; that she had in her employ some young man, who was always hid in the room, to overhear the conversation, and to run from out of his hiding-place before the mirror; and that I ought to be thankful I came away as well as I did, as many young girls had been ruined through going to this old creature; that, from her acquaintance with so many servant girls, she always contrived to get from them such intelligence as enabled her to answer those questions as might be put to her, as to the business, name, place of abode, country, and other circumstances of the party applying, the answering of which always convinced the credulous creatures who went to her, of her great skill in the art of astrology; and, when she was right in her guessing, she always took care to have it well published. I knew," continued poor Martha, " if I did not get the spoons, I should lose my place; so at length I summoned courage to tell my mistress and throw myself on her mercy, and she instantly procured a warrant and apprehended this fortune-telling lady; and here she is, your worship," said Martha, hanging down her head, flushed with. shame. The old woman could not deny the charge, only that the spoons were given to her for some *secret* service. This Martha denied; and the fortune-teller was committed for obtaining property under false pretences. The magistrate hoped it would be a lesson to Martha. and to all other foolish girls, never to hearken to those infernal, wicked old wretches, the fortune-tellers—many a girl having lost their character and their virtue by listening to their nonsense. Martha cried, courtesied, and withdrew, to make room for a laughable assault and battery. Mr. Robert Wingrove, a carpet-beater, commonly called Bob Wingrove the *dust-whapper*, charged Mr. Daniel Butcher, " a jolly young waterman," with assaulting him. Bob thus deposed :—

" Your Worship, I beats carpets, and does portering, by which means I was looking out of my window yesterday afternoon, when I saw a *sawant gal* go by, which belongs to a house that I beats for, by which means I runs down stairs to speak to her, and Dan Butcher, this here chap in the scarlet jacket, comes up to me, and, without saying ' *by* your leave,' or ' *with* your leave,' he took me two smacks on the head, right and left."

" Why did he strike you ?" asked the magistrate.

" Ay, that's what I wants to know, your worship !" replies Mr. Bob.

" Then suppose you ask him, now," rejoined his worship ; " ask him, why he gave you the two smacks, as you call them."

Mr. Bob turned and looked Mr. Dan in the face, as though about to put the question to him ; but Mr. Dan smiled him out of countenance, and Mr. Bob, turning back to his worship, said—

" It's no use axing him any thing, your worship, for he's got a spite agen me ever since I was in prison for saying a few words to a *sawant gal,* which brought me here on a peace-warrant, by which means he never sees me, but he peeps through his fingers at me, as much as to say, ' Who peeped through the prison bar?'—He's a great blackguard, though he's a little chap, your worship ; and he never meets my wife, Mrs. Wingrove, but he cries, ' Here's a charming young broom !' when my wife is *not a charming young broom,* as all her neighbours can testify, but as honest a woman as ever broke bread—only that, like *all other women,* your worship, she likes a drop of something comfortable, now and then."

Mr. Bob's landlady corroborated all his evidence, general and particular ; and her evidence closed the case for the prosecution.

Mr. Dan Butcher, in his defence, admitted that he *took* Mr. Bob Wingrove *two smacks in the head,* as that gentleman had deposed ; but he assured his worship, they were in return for *a paunch in the stomach,* which Mr. Bob Wingrove had *lent* him ; and he called two witnesses to prove that Mr. Bob was the aggressor.

Both these witnesses declared, that Dan Butcher was walking quietly under Mr. Bob's window, singing a song, and " giving no offence to nobody," when Mr. Bob ran down stairs, and struck him in the bowels, " without any *privy-cation* whatsoever."

" And pray, what song was he singing?" asked his worship. " I have no doubt it was a song intended to insult him."

" Your worship, I don't know what song it was," replied the first witness ; " it was a funny sort of song enough, and there was a *tithery-um* at the end of it."

The second witness, however, after much pressing, admitted that it was a song, called " *Bob's in the watch-house,*" and made by one of the Hungerford Stairs poets, in commemoration of poor Bob's imprisonment.

Mr. Dan could not deny that he sung this song vexatiously, and he was ordered to find bail—So, then, it was Mr. Bob's turn to sing "*Dan's* in the watch-house."

The next case that was called was John Price, to answer the complaint of John Francis Panchaud, a foreigner, who accused the said landlord with having conspired, with other *gentlemen* unknown, to deprive him of a 10*l.* bank note, at Ascott races, on the preceding Thursday.

In order to a better understanding of this case, and for the benefit of the *greener* lieges of our Sovereign Lord the King, it may be as well to premise that all races, fairs, and other such like conglomerations of those whom Heaven has blessed with more money than wit, are frequented by minor members of "The Fancy," who are technically called *flat-catchers,* and who pick up a very pretty living by a quick hand, a rattling tongue, a deal board, three thimbles, and a pepper-corn. The game they play with these three curious articles, is a sort of Lilliputian game at cups and balls; and the beauty of it lies in dexterously seeming to place the pepper-corn under one particular thimble, getting a *green* one to bet that it is there, and then winning his money by showing that it is not. Every operator at this game is attended by certain of his friends called *eggers* and *bonetters*—the eggers, to *egg* on the green ones to bet, by betting themselves; and the bonnetters, to *bonnet* any green one who may happen to win—that is to say, to knock his hat over his eyes, whilst the operator and the others *bolt* with the stakes. And this pretty little game they call "the *thimble rig*;" and it was by venturing a trifle upon this game that Monsieur Jean François Panchaud lost his 10*l.* note.

On Thursday se'nnight, as aforesaid, M. Panchaud was at Ascott races, and he there saw this landlord defendant, and several other gentlemen, betting away, and apparently winning "lots of sovereigns" at one of these same thimble and pepper-corn boards. "Try your luck, gentlemen!" cried the operator; "I'll bet any gentleman any thing, from half a crown to five sovereigns, that he doesn't name the thimble *as* covers the corn!" M. Panchaud betted half a crown—won it—betted a sovereign—won it:—betted a second sovereign—*lost* it. "Try your luck, gentlemen!" cried the operator again, shifting his thimbles and pepper-corn about the board, here and there and everywhere in a moment; and this done, he offered M. Panchaud a bet of five sovereigns that he could not "name the thimble what covered the corn." "Bet him!—bet him!—why don't you bet him?" said the landlord defendant—*nudging* M. Panchaud on the elbow; and M. Panchaud, convinced in his "own breast" that he knew the right thimble, said, "I shall betta you five sovereign if you will not touch the thimbles again till I name." "Done!" cried the operator; and M. Panchaud was *done*—for, laying down his 10*l.* note, it was caught up by *somebody*, the board was upset, the operator and his friends vanished "like a flash of lightning," and M. Panchaud was left, full of amazement, but with empty pockets, and the landlord defendant standing by his side. " They're a set of rascals ! " said the landlord defendant; but don't fret, my fine fellow ! I'll take you to somebody that shall soon get your money again ; " and, se saying, he boldly led him towards the Royal Stand, where he introduced him to Bishop and J. J. Smith, the police-officers, as a gentleman who had been very ill-used ; at the same time telling them that he had no doubt he could point out the cheats. The affair was immediately mentioned to Sir Richard Birnie ; and, by his direction, Smith accompanied the landlord defendant round the heath in search of the said cheats ; but he did not meet with any that he thought proper to point out. During this perambulation, he admitted to Smith that he had betted at the game at some particular table, in order to induce others to bet, but that he had nothing to do with the one in question. It was afterwards ascertained, however, that he had been seen betting as a decoy at this same table, repeatedly, in the course of the day; and, it being known that the house he keeps in Whitcomb Street is the resort of thieves and cheats of every kind, the present proceeding was instituted against him, as a *particeps criminis* in the robbery of M. Panchaud.

In his defence he denied that he had ever admitted betting at any game of the kind ; and he appealed to M. Panchaud whether he had not manifested the greatest regret at his loss; and whether he did not take him directly to the officers, in the hope of recovering his property.

" Oh ! yes," replied M. Panchaud—" you took me the *wrong way !* The thieves ran one way, and you took me the other, you know, Ahah !—you know what you are about—you took me the *wrong way*—Ahah ! "

The landlord defendant stoutly protested his innocence ; and an old man, a friend of his, gave him an excellent character ; but, maugre all his protestations and the advocacy of his antient friend, the magistrate held that there was sufficient evidence to detain him, and he was detained accordingly.

The business at the office for the morning being over, Mentor and his friend retired to a coffee-house in the neighbourhood, and there the conversation turned upon the examination of the old fortune-teller, and the credulity of the poor girl. " These fortune-tellers or conjurers," said Mentor, " are very famous for the extent of their knowledge, and are as much sought after, by gentle and simple, as the philosophers' stone, and whose predictions are as easily swallowed as the Alcoran by the Mahometans, and are as numerously attended as the court on a levee-day. It is really incredible, in the age of reason as it is called, that so many thousands of people should be so daily gulled and robbed by these really *cunning men !* For poor Martha's case is not a solitary one; very many indeed would be brought to light, only the duped are ashamed for the world to know how they have been cheated.

" Within these few weeks, the two following cases were heard at our public offices :

On Friday, March 21, 1828, a black fellow, named James Carroll, well known as the " Black Magician," was charged at Lambeth-Street Office, with defrauding amorous youths, maids, wives, and widows, of sundry sums of money, under pretence of unravelling to them the mysteries of their approaching fates. The first complainant was a Miss Cecilia Johnson, a pretty little brunette, who said that a few days since, having heard a marvellous account of the " black man's " skill, she went to his house in Leman Row, and applied to him for some information as to " what was to become of her?" He told her a young gentleman was expiring for love of her; he would marry her, and that a large family, and the greatest domestic felicity, would crown their days. Sir Daniel Williams—" Well, Miss, it no doubt was very agreeable; ladies, and young ones especially, wish to hear that young men are dying for them. What did you give him, pray, for this joyous communication?" Cecilia (smiling)—" Only three-pence, your Worship. Ah, Sir! there is no young man dying for me; I wish there was: he is an impostor." This declaration, which was made with much simplicity and guileless sincerity, excited the greatest merriment among those in the office.

The next person whose curiosity outran her judgment, was a staid matronly-looking female, who said that she also consulted the " sable soothsayer," and paid him three-pence for his advice. Sir D. Williams—" Are you a married woman?" " Yes, Sir," replied the matron, " and have a family." " Then, indeed," continued Sir Daniel, " you are a very silly person; there is some excuse for the credulous follies and fancies of young people, but you have none."

At this observation, the matron stood abashed and dumb-foundered. Her place, however, was quickly supplied by a sheepish-looking lad, who was the next to give an account of his experience. Though dull and stupid in appearance, the lad was sharp in practice. He stated, that having some misgivings as to the fortune-teller's predictions, he, in the way of a " lark," went to consult him in his sister's clothes. The primary step of paying the customary fee being gone through, the prisoner commenced his operations by first telling him he was a very pretty girl, and were it not that he was himself unfortunately married, he would select him as a wife; this very flattering declaration he followed up by telling him that he had been very imprudent, and that he was then, without being married, some months gone with child. He thought this was carrying the joke too far, and he at once undisguised himself, and gave the knave into custody.

Sir Daniel—(to the prisoner).—" What have you to say to these charges?" Prisoner—" Vel, your Vorship, you sees as how a number of leddies come to me aboutin deir fortins. I no send

for 'em, and if de vish to hab their fortins told, I can't helps em."
—Sir Daniel—"Ah, but you can: what do you say to taking
the 3d. each?"

The prisoner was mute on this point, as well as on several
others; and under the Vagrant Act he was doomed to a fate
which his divination did not anticipate—14 days' exercise at the
treadmill.

" A few days afterwards, a fortune-teller, of the name of
Stewart, a deaf and dumb man, nearly approximating to his grand
climacteric of sixty years, was brought up to the office in Hatton
Garden, in custody of Waddington and Raven, two of the officers, and charged before Mr. Laing with obtaining money under
false pretences.

" Waddington stated, that having received information of the
prisoner being a fortune-teller, and, in that character, practising
upon the strange credulity of the public, he engaged two females,
whose evidence would be immediately heard, to whom he gave a
certain sum of money, privately marked, with all proper and necessary instructions to detect the impostor, and sent them to his
residence, in Lily Street, Saffron Hill, while he, accompanied by
two other officers, remained in waiting at one of the opposite
houses till the moment approached at which a signal was to be
given to them to enter. The signal was shortly given, and they
accordingly having entered, found the two females sitting at a
table with the prisoner, who was then in the act of divining their
fortunes, and legibly writing them with chalk upon the bottom of a
tea-tray. As soon as they made their appearance in the room, he
instantly recognized them to be officers, and, snatching up a wet
towel that lay beside him, attempted to erase the marks of the
chalk, but, before he could effectually do it, he was secured and
taken into custody.

" The officers stated, that in an ante-room, through which they
passed to the prisoner's *penetrale*, there were several persons, both
male and female, some of whom were very respectably dressed,
and appeared to be considerably above the lower order, in attendance, waiting to have the mysteries of their destinies unfolded
to them, being anxious to know whether that destiny was to be
matrimonial strife or single blessedness through life.

" The two young women, Maria Bullock and Anne Sherwin,
who acted the subordinate part to Waddington, now came forward
and stated, that before the prisoner would consent to tell them
their fortunes, he demanded, by signs, the sum of three shillings
and ninepence halfpenny, which, having been paid him, he wrote
with chalk upon a tea-tray, that the former was to be married in
May, 1829, to a baker of the name of James Thacker; and that
the latter should live till she was fifty years of age, and be then
joined in the bonds of wedlock to a young 'squire of large fortune
When he was asked to disclose the name of the person, and his

address, who had stolen a dozen of silver spoons from Anne
Sherwin's mother, he wrote ' John Baker, a cadger.'

"The prisoner's wife, a very interesting girl, of about eighteen
years of age, who has been married to him only a fortnight, she
being his third wife, and his mother, having given him to understand, by signs, the substance of the above evidence, and the
chief clerk having stated it for him upon paper, he took a pen and
wrote, in very legible characters, ' Pity my case; pity my three
children.' The officers having searched him, and finding the money, which had been previously marked, upon him, Mr. Laing ordered him to be taken to the House of Correction, and confined
to hard labour for the term of three months.

"Fortune-tellers," continued Mentor, "abound in every country; ' they toil not, neither do they spin:' and why should they?
the ingenious rogues can live upon the future hopes of mankind.
Poor human nature, unwilling to submit to that

> "Blindness to the future, wisely given,
> That none might know the secrets hid by Heav'n,"

is perpetually struggling to ' peep through the blanket of the dark,'
and obtain a glimpse of futurity. Innumerable proofs of the utter
impossibility of success, regularly reiterated in every succeeding
age, have given a new direction to its development, without eradi-
cating a delusion that seems to be inherent in our minds. The
practice of paganism long survived its belief, so has that of divination, unless we are to suppose that the young persons of the fair
sex, and the old women of both, are serious proselytes to its efficacy, when they submit the lines of their hand to gipsy judgment,
interpret the cabalistic writing of coffee or tea-grounds in a cup,
or determine their destiny by the casual up-turnings of the cards.
Oh! the profound conception, that we should carry about with us,
in our palm, a manual of futurity, have the whole book of fate engraved upon the narrow space between our fore-fingers and our
thumb, and thus literally and truly make our life and destiny the
work of our own hands! A faith in divination and fatalism can
never want converts, so long as it affords us a convenient scape-
goat for our crimes and follies; and who is there, among us, that
does not lay this flattering unction to his soul, whenever his pride
or self-conceit are wounded. If we succeed in our undertakings,
we very demurely assign the merit to our own talent, prudence,
and forethought; if we fail, our bad luck leaves all the blame of
our bad conduct: we impute our blindness to fortune, and even
make the heavens responsible, if we happen to miss our way upon
earth. There is one sense in which, without the inspiration of
prophecy, or the charge of imposture, we may reasonably and be-
neficially venture to indulge in the mystery of fortune-telling.—
Knowing that, in the established succession of human affairs, certain causes will produce corresponding effects, we may read the
future in the past, and boldly predict, that the spendthrift will come

to want, the debauchee to premature decay, the idler to contempt, the gamester to bitterness of soul, if not to suicide, the profligate to remorse, and the violaters of the laws to punishment; while we may safely augur, that the practice of the opposite virtues will be productive of results diametrically opposite.

" Some years ago, a fellow, called Almanack John, sold, in several parts of London, some ridiculous inventions, which he called *Sigils*, and the possessor of them had only but to fancy they would protect themselves and property. Almanack John was a shoemaker, in the Strand, and obtained great celebrity in this art.

" In the time of Charles II., there was a celebrated fortune-teller, who resided on Clerkenwell Green, well known as Jack Adams, the astrologer. He was chiefly employed in hearsay questions relative to love and marriage, and knew, upon proper occasions, how to soothe the passions, and flatter the expectations of those who consulted him: with him, a woman might have better fortune for five guineas, than for five shillings. When he failed in his predictions, he threw the blame upon wayward and perverse fate! He assumed the character of a learned and *cunning* man; but was no otherwise cunning, than he knew how to overreach those credulous mortals, who were as willing to be cheated, as he was to cheat them. He died very rich.

" Of latter days, we have had Edwards, the Welsh conjurer, who took a poor fool of a Welshman, to a well, made him drink some of the water, repeat the Lord's prayer, and give a piece of paper, and then he was ever to have *good luck!!* for all which *services*, he demanded 16*s.*; but received only 15*s.* 6*d.*, all the dupe had.

" Then there was conjurer Baker, who died in 1819, full of years and iniquities, having, the greater part of his life, practised the gainful tactics of " The Black Art." Such was the fame of this man, when in the West of England (after he had been practising in London), that the educated, as well as the uneducated of all classes, were in the habit of resorting to him from all parts, for the exercise of his cabalistic skill; and, on a Sunday, which was the day for his high orgies, vehicles were found to bring him an eager throng of votaries. Bad crops, lost cattle, lost treasure, and lost hearts, brought their respective sufferers in ceaseless crowds to his door. Charmed powders and mystic lotions were confided in, to the exclusion of rational advice and proper remedies; and the death of the old and young has been the consequent penalty of such deplorable imbecility.

" In a letter from Dublin, January, 1758, we find—' I suppose you have heard of the famous comedian Foote, who is at present in this capital. Being a man of much humour, he took it into his head to hire a private lodging in a remote part of the town, in order to set up the lucrative business of fortune-telling. After he had got his room hung with black, and arranged his dark lantern, with some persons about him who knew the people of fashion in this

10

city, he distribated hand-bills to inform them that there was a
man to be met with at such a place, who wrote down people's
fortune, without asking them any questions. As his room was
quite dark (the light from his lantern excepted), he was in less
danger of being discovered, so that he went on with great success
for many days, and cleared at least, it is said, thirty pounds *per
diem*, at half-a-crown a head.'

" But the greatest fortune-teller, that ever practised in London,
was the celebrated Duncan Campbell, the deaf and dumb fortune-
teller : he published his life, and a very interesting one it is, if you
only believe half what he says."

While Mentor and his friend were ruminating on the multifarious
cheats practised in London, a gentleman of Mentor's acquaintance
entered the room, and joined their company. The conversation
turned on the shameful adulterations of wine, which, when pure,
it was observed, may be said to form one of the blessings of life,
used in moderation, dispensing by its cheering influence an additional zest to several of our social enjoyments; constituting a
luxury, to which more consideration is attached than to almost
any other whatever, and has become, in the existing state of
society, a necessary of life. It has been well observed," said
Mentor, " in an excellent work, ' *The Wine and Spirit Adultera-
tors Unmasked*,' (and to which," addressing himself to Peregrine,
" I drew your attention a few days since, relative to the gin trade),
that so widely diffused, and in such general demand, as wine is,
its abuses, therefore, deserve to be exposed, and a stop put to its
being rendered baneful, without misapplications. No one can
doubt, that an individual thoroughly acquainted with the subject, is fulfilling any more than his duty to the community, when
he holds up to public reprobation, that class of persons, who,
not content with the gains which fair dealing in wine, in its genuine
state, would yield them, seek to reap large and disproportionate
profit, by the most base and fraudulent means, whereby they are
not only undermining the character and livelihood of the honest
tradesman, in respect to his exacting unnecessarily high prices ;
but they are also cheating the pockets of those, who are so easily
gulled, as to put faith in their pretences."

In 1826, a wine-dealer, of the name of Oldfield, had an
information laid against him in the Court of Exchequer, for adulterating certain wines, the mixing of Cape with Sherry, and
selling the mixture as pure Sherry. The mode of doctoring, was
by mixing with the wine a composition made of bitter and sweet
almonds, powdered oyster-shells, and chalk ; the bitter almonds
gave the wine a rough taste, which the sweet almonds in some
degree softened ; the powdered oyster-shells and chalk refined
the mixture. There was a large vat, in which the mixture was
made. The vat was erected for this purpose ; the mixing and
doctoring were both made with the defendant's knowledge and
approbation.

" RED WINE is adulterated, by mixing it with *benecarlo,* a strong coarse Spanish red wine; *fiquera,* a red wine from Portugal; *red cape;* mountain; *sal tartar; gum dragon,* to impart a fulness of flavour, and consistency of body; *berry dye,* a colouring matter extracted from German bilberries; *brandy cowe,* which is obtained from the very staves of the brandy puncheons; as soon as the brandy is racked from the puncheons, four or five gallons of water are immediately put in, and allowed to remain three or four weeks, at the expiration of which time they have imbibed a considerable portion of spirit; and, lastly, *cyder.*

" SHERRY. This most fashionable wine is adulterated with *cape, brandy cowe,* and numerous other ingredients, according to the tastes of the different makers up, and their experience, as to what will best assist in deceiving the public. *Extract of almond cake,* to impart a nutty flavour, is also used; together with, *cherry laurel water ; gum benzoin; lamb's blood,* to -make the brown sherry resemble the desired pale sherry : its properties exceed belief: it is used in the proportion of three pints of blood to every hundred gallons of the compound, if it is to appear as pale sherry; but if it is only meant to pass for amber-coloured sherry, one pint and a half of this delectable ingredient is enough. The whole mixture, however, after laying ten days or so, is bottled off, or racked into quarter casks, &c., and is then considered fit to be advertised, and sold as *genuine.*

" The best manufacture of a fictitious resemblance of *rea.* MADEIRA, is said to consist of a composition of cheap *Vidonia,* with a proportion of about one-twentieth part of *common dry Port,* one-tenth part *Mountain,* and about a fifth-part *Cape ;* when the whole is mixed together, and properly fined, and reduced to the required colour, by means of *lamb's blood,* it is considered excellent ! and puffed off to the public, as *Old London Particular !*

" CLARET is adulterated thus : a small quantity of *Spanish red wine,* and a portion of *rough cyder,* is introduced into a cask, containing inferior claret, a colour being previously added to the cyder, by means of *berry dye,* or *tincture of Brazil wood.*

" *Gooseberry wine* is usually sold at the cheap advertising shops, as a substitute for *sparkling Champagne!*

" *Vidonia wines, Bucellas, Tent, Red Cape,* &c., are all adulterated, before they are vended by the *cheap advertising dealers.*

" Accum, in his ' Culinary Poisons,' (p. 95), says, ' The most dangerous adulteration of wine, is by some preparation of lead, which possesses the property of stopping the progress of ascescence of wine, and also of rendering white wine, when muddy, transparent; I have good reason to state, that lead is certainly employed for this purpose; the effect is very rapid, and there appears to be no other method known of *rapidly recovering ropy wines.* Lead, in whatever state it is taken into the stomach, occasions terrible diseases; and wine, adulterated with the minutest quantity of it, becomes a slow poison !' In Watson's

Chemical Essays (vol. 8, page 369), it is stated, ' That a method of adulterating wine with lead existed at one time so generally in Paris, as to have become quite a common practice.'   In
the Medical Essays, the consequences of the use of this ingredient
are related, in the case of thirty-two persons, having severally
become ill, after drinking white wine that had been adulterated
with lead; and also, that one of them became paralytic, and
another died.

" Peddie, in his *Vintner's Assistant*, says, ' To discover when
lead is dissolved in wine, take of oyster shells and sulphur, equal
parts, mix and beat them together, and, when brought to a white
heat, keep them in that state for about fifteen minutes, and when
cold, pound them together in a mortar, and add an equal quantity
of cream of tartar; put this mixture into a strong bottle with
common water, make it boil for an hour, and, when cold, cork the
bottle, and shake it up; then let it settle; after it is settled, pour
it off in small ounce bottles, and for each ounce of liquor, add
twenty drops of muriatic acid (spirit of salt); this mixture preci-
pitates (or makes fall to the bottom) the least quantity of lead,
copper, &c., from wines and cyder; (but, as iron might accidentally be in the wine, the muriatic acid is added, to prevent it
falling to the bottom, and being mistaken for the precipitate of
lead) if the wine is not adulte.ated, it will remain clear and
bright after the mixture has been added.

" The merchant or dealer who practises this dangerous sophis-
tication, adds the crime of murder to that of fraud, and deliberately scatters the seeds of disease and death among those
consumers who contribute to his emolument.   If to debase the
current coin of the realm, be denounced as a capital offence,
what punishment should be awarded against a practice which
converts into poison a liquor used for sacred purposes?

" The *crusting* of wine-bottles consists of lining the interior
surface of empty wine-bottles, in part with a red crust of super-
tartrate of potash, by suffering a saturated hot solution of this
salt, coloured red with a decoction of Brazil wood, to crystallize
within them; and, after this simulation of maturity is perfected,
they are filled with the compound called port wine.

" Other artisans are regularly employed in straining the lower
extremities of bottle-corks with a fine red colour, to appear, on
being drawn, as if they had been long in contact with the wine.

" The way to detect adulteration of port wine with alum, is
...is :—take some fresh prepared lime-water, mix the suspected
wine with it, in any fair proportion, allow the mixture to stand
about a day; then, if the wine be genuine, a number of crystals
will be found deposited at the bottom of the vessel; if alum be
in the wine, there will be no crystals, but a slimy and muddy
precipitate."

" At no place," said Mentor's acquaintaince, " is more bad
wine drank than in those dreadful sinks of iniquity and debau-

chery, the wine and oyster rooms, politely called saloons. It is monstrous that nuisances of such magnitude should be tolerated in a country calling itself the most moral and decent upon earth; tolerated, too, in the midst of societies of all kinds for the protection of the public morals, and in the face of our bishops, of our great reformists, and the boasted march of social improvement." Is it to be declared of London, what was once said of Rome—the more enlightened, the more depraved? The gambling which is carried on in the private rooms of the wine and oyster houses is just such as that which has so long flourished in the low vicinity of St. James's. Indeed, the constant frequenters of the former have attained the most profound knowledge of the art of robbing at the west-end-of-the-town gaming-houses. The ' legs' visit the saloons every night, in order to pick up new acquaintances amongst the young and inexperienced. They are polite, well-dressed, gentlemanlike persons ; and, if they can trace any thing soft in the countenance of a new visitor, their wits go to work at once to establish an acquaintance with him. Wine is set going, and cards are proposed. The master of the concern soon provides a room, and play advances, accompanied by the certainty of loss to the unfortunate stranger. But if the invitation to play be rejected, they make another plant upon him. The ruffians attack him through a passion of a different kind. They give the word to one of their female *pals*—she throws herself in his way, and prevails upon him to be her companion for the night. She plies him with drink, and, in the morning, the gentlemen, who in vain solicited him to play, call in to pay ' a friendly visit.' Cards are again spoken of and again proposed, with the additional recommendation of the lady, who offers to be the partner of her young friend in the game. The consequence is palpable. Many young noblemen and gentlemen have been plundered, by this scheme, of hundreds, nay, of thousands of pounds. To escape without loss is impossible. They pack and distribute the cards with such amazing dexterity, that they can give a man, as it were, whatever cards they please. A few years ago, some of them were detected in a trick, by which they had won enormous sums. An *ecarté* party, consisting of a nobleman (since deceased), a captain in the army, an Armenian gentleman, and an Irish gentleman, sat down in one of the private chambers attached to one of those large wine and shell-fish rooms. The Armenian and the Irishman were partners, and they were wonderfully successful ; indeed, so extraordinary was their luck in turning up cards, that the captain, who had been on the town for some time, suspected the integrity of his competitors, and, accordingly, handled the cards very minutely. He soon discovered that there was an ' *old gentleman*' (a card somewhat larger and thicker than the rest of the pack, and now in considerable use amongst the ' legs') in the midst of them. The captain and his partner exclaimed, that they were robbed, and the cards were sealed up, and referred to a card-maker for his opinion.

' The old saying,' said the referee, ' that the cards would beat the
card-maker, was never more true than it is in this instance, for this
pack would beat not only me, but the very d—l himself.   There is
not only *an old gentleman*, but *an old lady* (a card broader than
the rest) amongst them.'   The two gentlemen were immediately
accused of the imposition, but they feigned ignorance of the robbery, refused to return a farthing of the *swag*, and charged the
losers with having got up the story in order to recover what they
had fairly lost.   This was a lesson not thrown away upon the nobleman.   He never again appeared in the house where practices
of this description are carried on every night, and where officers
of the police are palmed (bribed) for their forbearance.   At the
game of put, the three is the best card, the two next, and one the
next best.   If a sharper can make certain of having a three every
time his opponent deals, he must have considerably the best of the
game; and this is effected as follows:—the sharper places a three
underneath *an old gentleman*, and it does not signify how much his
opponent shuffles the pack, it is about five to one that he does not
disturb the *old gentleman* or the three.   The sharper then cuts the
cards, which he does by feeling for the *old gentleman;* the three
being then the top card, it is dealt to the sharper by his opponent;
this is one way of securing a three, and this alone is quite sufficient to make a certainty of winning.   The Lord Mayor ordered
the officers to burst open the doors of the Stock Exchange Shades,
if at any time they should suspect that gaming is going forward
there.   Why do not the magistrates of the west end of the town
issue orders to their police to pay an honest and resolute visit to
those infamous abodes, and to rake out the swarms of fellows who
congregate for the purposes of plunder?   The Irishman was intimate with Thurtell the murderer, and is great at the game of
" blind hookey."   In fact, there is no game that is not perfectly
understood by this comely robber.   If the shopkeeper, who can
not account for the decline in his profits, and must call his creditors together if things do not change for the better, would give a
look in occasionally to the houses we have alluded to, he might
recognize amongst the most extravagant of the visitors, a person
whose sole dependence is upon his master, whom he robs to provide himself with the means of living amongst those he and she
devils.   But, without a well-disciplined police, it will be impossible to break down the various base institutions with which London
abounds so much as to make the character of informer honourable.
To the abandonment of that duty is to be ascribed the state of our
prisons, which are always crammed with the victims of flash-cribs,
and brothels, and gambling-dens.   The haberdashers of the metropolis are particularly exposed to plunder at the hands of their
shopmen, who keep up what is called " a pretty game" in the several places which have come under our condemnation.   The facilities are great, and the temptation (the love of a ' *blowing*,')
irresistible to young men under the excitement of liquor, and

acted upon by the intoxicating character of the scene. The system upon which the eminent house of Morrison and Co., of Fore Street, acts, is well worthy of notice. There are upwards of one hundred and fifty men employed every day on the premises. These are divided into companies, each of which has a separate department to attend to, and is under the control of a superintendant, who is responsible for the goods under his care. To steal on the premises, under such an arrangement as exists there, is almost impossible. The security is increased by the example of vigorous industry exhibited by the partners, and the encouragement to study in the hours of relaxation from business. All the persons employed sleep in the premises, where a library is fitted up for their use. Establishments not one tenth of the size, are daily suffering from the dishonesty of servants.

" In the month of November, 1827, a case came on at the Mansion House, which depicted, in a very strong manner, the fatal consequences of visiting these infamous places in the neighbourhood of Covent-Garden.

" A young man, of respectable appearance and connexions, was brought before the Lord Mayor, charged with having embezzled many sums of money, the property of Williams and Co., of Clement's Lane, insurance and ship agents, in whose employment he had acted as confidential clerk for two years. The prisoner seemed to be in the deepest affliction and shame. He held his hands over his face from the beginning to the end of the examination.

" The prisoner was usually employed in collecting the amount of the agency accounts, and it had been lately ascertained that he had been appropriating to his own necessities and debaucheries, various sums of money, which he was in the habit of replacing, with other sums which he collected upon subsequent occasions from other customers to the concern; he of course was obliged, for the purpose of concealing his plans, to make fictitious entries in the books, and he got into his possession, by this practice, some hundreds of pounds, which he spent amongst the most profligate characters.

" While the prisoner was at the bar crying bitterly, and totally inattentive to what was going forward, the prosecutor stated, that he deeply regretted the necessity of proceeding against the unfortunate young man, but he could not help it. He felt it to be a public duty, under all the circumstances, to do so. He lamented the obligation to prosecute the more, as the prisoner had maintained, up to the period of the detection, a most excellent character, and had conducted himself with the greatest propriety in the service of a highly respectable house for upwards of six years. At last, however, the unfortunate young man became connected with some of the well-dressed thieves who infest Mother H.'s, and other flash-houses in the neighbourhood of the theatres, and who led him on in dissipation until they ruined him. At first he began, as appeared from the investigation into the various acts he

committed, by appropriating small sums.  His progress was rapid, and no doubt he would have continued to commit depredations, if not detected, until he had done irreparable mischief."

Peregrine now reminded Mentor, of their appointment to visit

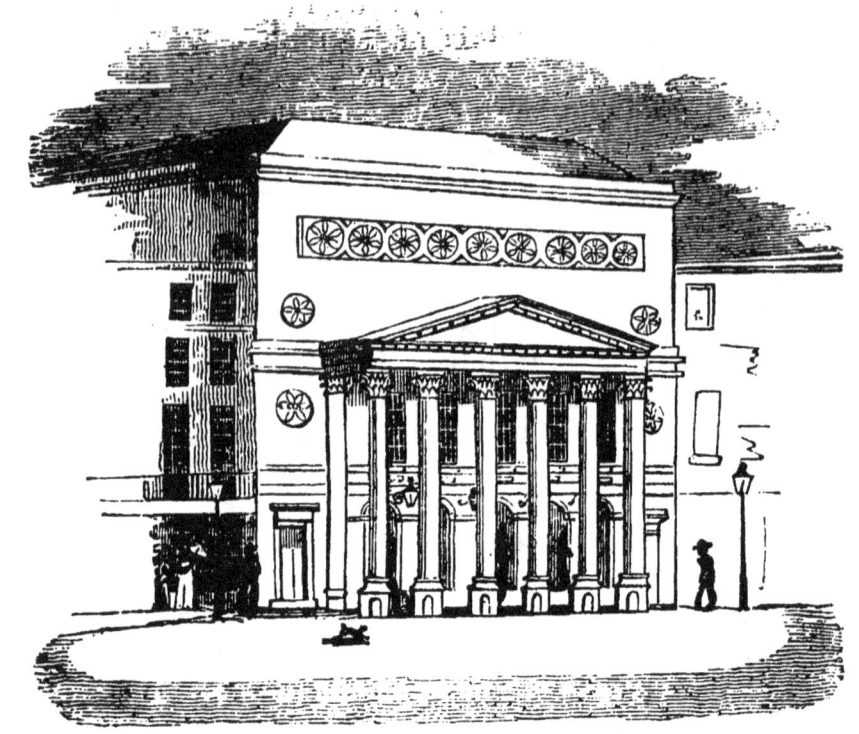

The Theatre-Royal, Haymarket,

To witness the incomparable acting of Liston.  Mentor's acquaintance readily agreed to accompany them, and they proceeded immediately to the theatre: arriving there a short time
before the rising of the curtain, the interval was used by Mentor
giving Peregrine a history of the theatre.  At length the performances commenced, which seemed at first to attract the especial notice of Peregrine, but the gay assemblage of beauty
demanded most of his attention, and, before the conclusion of the
play, entirely engrossed it.  Mentor was aware of the cause of
Peregrine's inattention to the performance: it was a nymph in the
next box, who had caught the eye of the unsuspecting Peregrine;
and she determined not to lose her capture, by any possible means.
She threw around him a halo, the reflection of her incomparable
beauty, which enchanted the object of her desires, and Peregrine's
heart instantly surrendered; for,

> "Who can escape the net which passion throws,
>     Amidst the charms of woman's witchery ?
> Tints like the snow upon the op'ning rose,
>     And looks like gold on Parian masonry."

This was the most pleasing, yet the most painful moment of
Peregrine's life: fondly imagining he already enjoyed

> " A woman's love—that holy flame,
>     Pure as the mighty sun,
> That gladdens as with torch of fame
>     The heart it shines upon."

Upon leaving the theatre, he, unperceived by Mentor, wrote a few lines on the back of the playbill, and put it in the hand of the object of his affection, begging an interview the following morning, in the Green Park. He now hastened to his inn, and, wishing Mentor and his acquaintance a good night, retired to his chamber, anxiously wishing for the return of day: he arose early, and traced his steps to the place of meeting, long before the appointed hour; and, while sitting on one of the benches, anxiously anticipating the pleasure he should experience, in the expected interview, a young man, seemingly from the country, with his dress in great disorder, placed himself by his side, and, without any ceremony, began to tell him of his last night's adventure: that he had only the day before arrived from Suffolk; and on going along Charing Cross, he was accosted by a young woman, who persuaded him to accompany her to an adjoining house, where they were soon joined by another lady; wine was called for, of which he drank till he became almost insensible; they then took his watch from him, and all his money; and "this morning," says he, "I found myself lying on the floor, without a farthing in my pocket. On my making a noise, and complaining of being robbed, a man and woman came up, and demanded five shillings for my night's lodging. I told them how I had been served, at which they laughed at me, and actually took my neckerchief and whip for the five shillings, telling me to think myself well off; and that I was little acquainted with the

Doings in a Brothel

and then pushed me into the street, desiring me to seek for redress

11

G

where I liked. I have," continued the stranger, "strayed here; and Heaven knows what I shall do, for a trifle of money, to enable me to return home." Peregrine felt for his disaster, and counselled with him on the folly of his proceedings; and, putting a sovereign in his hand, wished him a safe return. The stranger thanked him a thousand times, gave him his address, and retired.

And now the hour appointed for the meeting arrived, the lady being punctual to her time: she received Peregrine with a freedom he little anticipated, which created in him much distrust and uneasiness. He fondly imagined her to be,

" **As chaste** as ice, as pure as snow ;"

but he was miserably deceived—she had swerved from the paths of rectitude and virtue: her brightest days were fled, and she was now dragging out a painful existence. They sat for some minutes without either speaking: at length, Peregrine mustered courage enough to ask her name, and to tell her candidly the conquest she had made of him. "I am afraid, sir," said she, "you will feel some degree of disappointment, when you become acquainted with my history; but I will not take advantage of your youth, or your inexperience in life; and, if you will accompany me to my lodgings to breakfast, as we may be overheard here, I will there unfold to you the particulars of my unfortunate career; for there is a pleasure, an inexpressible one, in persons in affliction and sorrow detailing their miseries." Peregrine, after a few moments' consideration, accepted the invitation, and walked with Julia to her home: when breakfast was over, she gave him her history.

" My name, sir, is Julia Desmond; in my youth, I was rich in the choicest gifts of Heaven—health and innocence. My father was a market gardener, and was particularly partial to coursing; and, among the many persons who came to our house on those occasions, was a gentleman, who requested to be allowed to visit me. Our age and expectations in life being nearly equal, were agreeable to the apparent likelihood of our being united. In an unguarded moment, he basely employed the advantages Heaven had bounteously lent him, to my misery and seduction; he coolly turned sensibility and avowed affection against the very heart in which those sensations glowed, excited by himself for a base and unworthy gratification; he planted vice and infamy where virgin purity and spotless innocence had for ever dwelt. To the retributive justice of Heaven in the world to come, I leave the wretch, consoled by the assurance that he will not escape a punishment equal to his crime.

" Finding myself ruined and deserted, I unfolded my wretched state to my mother, who instantly informed my father, from whom I received orders immediately to quit his house. I repaired to the dwelling of a neighbour, and there used every means in my power to gain my father's forgiveness; but no, he was inexorable, and I was obliged to trace my steps to London. I have read," continued Julia, "in the Spectator, that 'of all the hardnesses of heart, there is none so inexcusable as that of parents towards their children. An obstinate, inflexible, unforgiving temper is odious upon all occasions; but here it is unnatural.. The love, tenderness, and compassion, which are apt to arise in us towards those who depend upon us, is that by which the whole world of life is upheld. The Supreme Being, by the transcendant excellency and goodness of his nature, extends his mercy towards all his works; and, because all his creatures have not such a spontaneous benevolence and compassion towards those who are under his care and protection, he has implanted in them an instinct, that supplies the place of this inherent goodness. The man, therefore, who, notwithstanding any passion or resentment, can overcome this powerful instinct, and extinguish natural affection, debases his mind even below brutality, frustrates, as much as in him lies, the great design of Providence, and strikes out of his nature one of the most divine principles that is planted in it. If the father is inexorable to the child who has offended, let the offence be of ever so high a nature, how will he address himself to the Supreme Being, under the tender appellation of father, and desire of him such a forgiveness as he himself refuses to grant?'

"In this distress, I alighted in this wide metropolis—this epitome of the world; and, as I had some knowledge of needle-work, I applied at one of the dress-makers, at the west end of the town, seeing, by the papers, she was in want of hands: here I was engaged at eight shillings a-week, and to work all hours, very often all night, and generally on a Sunday. I was glad, in one respect, I was so fully engaged, as it prevented me from reflecting on my sad fallen state so often as I should otherwise have done. My fellow companions were all kept as close at work as I was, but many of them at less wages, some earning only five shillings per week, out of which they had to find themselves in clothes; for of victuals indeed they had but little,—they existed principally on tea. It is disgraceful the manner in which the poor girls are kept at work at these places: it is no wonder, indeed, so many of them die in declines, and others go on the town; for I know several have taken to that wretched mode of getting a livelihood, through the greatest want. Here is, indeed, the British white slavery; only, with this difference, that their more fortunate sufferers in the West Indies have regular food and appointed hours of work. The world little knows of the disgraceful and inhuman "Doings" at the fashionable dress-makers at the west end of the town.

"But to proceed with my history: after remaining in this situation six months, I fell ill, and, having no money, I gained admittance into an hospital, one of those god-like establishments which abound in London; here I was treated with the utmost care and attention, and I soon recovered my health; upon which, I applied to my old place for employment; but, unfortunately, it was the autumn of the year, and, there being then little doing, they could not engage me. Wherever I thought it possible I could earn a trifle, I made application, but to no purpose: when, one day, walking near the bottom of Piccadilly, near the White-Horse Cellar, an elderly lady, very nicely dressed, accosted me, and entered very familiarly into conversation with me; and, as she seemed a nice motherly woman, I opened my mind freely to her, telling her the whole of my history, in which she seemed to take a very great interest. She advised me, pitied me, and cried for my misfortunes; in fact, she completely gained my confidence. She asked me to take some refreshment, at a pastry-cook's, where she seemed to be well known, entering into conversation with the ladies and gentlemen present. At length, she invited me to her home, telling me, she would find me plenty of employment. Feeling grateful for her kind offer, I accepted it, and I soon arrived at her house, which was very handsomely furnished. On entering, I saw many young ladies, elegantly dressed, who all called her mother, and to whom she seemed very kind. I naturally expected, I was to be engaged to work for these ladies; but when she told me, I should be used as well as her children (as she called them), and be dressed like them, I began to have some doubts that all was right, and to fear that I had got into bad company. My suspicions were soon verified, as in the evening I was to change my clothes, and accompany them to the play; and there they began to show themselves in their true characters. The old lady introduced me to several gentlemen; and, as I was what was termed very handsome, all of them flattered me, and seemed desirous of gaining my favours. I now felt assured that I had been ensnared; and the old lady, seeing me in tears, upbraided me with ingratitude, in acting in the manner I did. I begged of her to let me go, upon which she told me, if I threatened to leave her, she would give me in charge of a police-officer, for stealing the earrings and necklace which I had on. My anguish of mind was now not be described. I was fearful of her putting her threats into execution, although she gave me the rings and necklace. I knew I could get no employment; and then, in a moment of delirium, I threw myself into the vortex of dissipation and ruin.

"I was an involuntary victim. Unkind and cruel as my father had been, I wished to suffer in silence, and not bring additional reproach on him who gave me being.

"In a few days I was placed under the protection of a Lieutenant V——, who behaved to me with great kindness, till he was called to go to India, where he fell at the siege of *Bhurtpoore.*

"The old beldame, under whose roof I took shelter, was, perhaps, the most deceitful, the most wicked, and the most notorious procuress that ever lived. She used regularly to advertise for servants, and have the reference at her green-grocer's: by this scheme she enticed and ruined many young girls; by some of them she gained a vast sum of money, they having taken the fancy of some lecherous old wretch, who always kept 'our mother' in pay for that purpose. She professed to be extremely religious, and it was no uncommon thing to see her go to one of the conventicles in the evening, and then come home and complete the ruin of an unsuspecting innocent girl. An hypocritical villain, the preacher at her chapel, used to visit her frequently; and there they used to sing hymns, and groan, and moan, and cry, and get drunk together: she would boast of the number of years she had lived in the same neighbourhood with respectability; and, as Mother Cole said, during that time, 'no one could say black was the white of her eye.'

"It is a pity," continued Julia, "these old wretches are not now punished in the manner they deserve, I find that formerly they were; particularly Mother Needham, the infamous procuress and brothel-keeper: she was, in every respect, equally notorious with the celebrated Mother Cresswell, who made so conspicuous a figure in the reign of King Charles the Second, and who is said to have died in Bridewell. Mother Needham's exit is more certainly known, which took place in the Gate-House, Westminster, May 5th, 1731. Her personal history is comprised in the following paragraphs from the Grub-Street Journal.

"'March 25, 1731.—The noted Mother Needham was yesterday committed to the Gate House, by Mr. Justice Railton."

"'Ibid.—Yesterday, at the quarter sessions, for the city and liberties of Westminster, the infamous Mother Needham, who has been reported to have been dead for some time, to screen her from several prosecutions, was brought from the Gate-House, and pleaded not guilty to an indictment found against her for keeping a lewd and disorderly house; but, for want of sureties, was remanded back to prison."

"'Ibid.—April 27, 1731. On Saturday ended the quarter sessions for Westminster, &c. The noted Mother Needham, convicted of keeping a lewd and disorderly house in Park Place, St. James's, was fined one shilling, to stand twice in the pillory, and find sureties for her good behaviour for three years."

"'Ibid.—May 6, 1731. Yesterday, the noted Mother Needham stood in the pillory in Park Place, near St. James's Street, and was roughly handled by the populace. She was so very ill that she lay along, notwithstanding which, she was so severely treated, that it is thought she will die in a day or two.' Another account says, 'She lay along on her face in the pillory, and so evaded the law, which requires that her face should be exposed.'

"The memory of this woman is thus perpetuated in the Duncian. l. 323:

'To Needham's quick, the voice triumphant rode,
But pious Needham dropp'd the name of God.

"The note on this passage says she was 'a matron of great fame, and very religious in her way; whose constant prayer it was, that she might get enough by her profession to leave off in time, and make her peace with God. But her fate was not so happy; for, being convicted, and set in the pillory, she was so ill-used by the populace, that it put an end to her days.'

"If the like punishment were to extend to her infamous successors of the present day, the public would not be insulted in seeing their names engraved on brazen plates in some of the most public places in the metropolis.

"Most bawds seem to have some pretence to religion. In Dryden's Wild Gallant, Mother du Lake, being about to drink a dram, is made to exclaim, 'Tis a great way to the bottom; but Heaven is all sufficient to give me strength for it.'

"Pardon me," said Julia, "for this digression,—I will now hasten to the finish of my dismal tale. Since the death of the lieutenant, until the last fortnight, I lived with the old woman; but her ill-usage to me, on account of my not joining willingly in the various debaucheries, became so unbearable, that I left her; and had once more the world before me. I knew not what to do, my character being gone; at length I resolved to take these private lodgings, where I have resided about a month. This," said Julia, is my sad history, and—

> ' Often, when alone,
> I see my heart, as in a mirror shown :
> And spectres oft my fitful fancy cross'd,
> Of broken promises and honour lost ;
> Of good men's pity, and of bad men's sneers,
> My father's anguish, and my mother's tears !'

Poor Julia started from her seat, and, taking up the guitar that was given to her by her father, and which, amidst all her wants, she had preserved with religious care, sung, most plaintively, the following verses of a Scotch ballad :

> ' Wae's me, for my heart is breaking !
> I think on my brithers sma'
> And on my sister grea+
> When I came frae hame awa ;
> And, oh ! how my mither sobbit,
> As she took me from my hand,
> When I left the door o' our ould house,
> To come to this stranger land !

> ' There's nae place like our ain hame ;
> Oh ! I wish that I was there !—
> There's nae hame like our ain hame,
> To be met wi' ony where !—
> And, oh ! that I was back again,
> To our farm and fields so green ;
> And heard the tongues o' my ain folk,
> And *was what I hae' been !'* "

Peregrine felt that he loved Julia, notwithstanding the avowal of her irregularities; and he mingled his tears with hers, while she recited her misfortunes, for he was one of those " who felt for another's woes:" he entered the world with buoyant feelings, fresh and " thick coming fancies," enthusiastic anticipation ; with heart and hand open to the impression and impulses of love, friendship, and generosity; and with a multitude of senses and passions, all promising pleasure in their pursuit and gratification: he found his young pulse bound with delight at the sight of beauty, and experienced a thousand sensations which impelled him to an intimate intercourse of hearts with his fellow-creatures. But he also found it necessary to repress these delightful springings of the heart; to steal his heart against the influence of beauty, and to admit friendship and love only where they are compatible with his interest;—interest, that mainspring of human nature, as it is called, at whose shrine all our best feelings are sacrificed?

Julia had now partially recovered from the paroxysm of grief into which the remembrance of brighter and better days had thrown her, when Peregrine asked her whether he could be of any service in rescuing her from her present wretched mode of living? She thanked him, saying she should be grateful for any situation to snatch her from the one she was now in. At length, the generous-hearted Peregrine agreed to allow her a sufficiency, provided she was determined to leave the paths of vice, until he could do something better for her. Julia's heart was overwhelmed with thanks at this unlooked-for act of benevolence; and she vowed most solemnly nothing on earth should make her continue her present mode of life. Peregrine was happy to see her so repentant, and formed in his mind the pleasure he should feel in rescuing her from ruin.

"I suppose," said Peregrine, "even the short time you have been in London, you have witnessed many sad scenes of depravity." "Yes, I could tell you such tales of scenes that I have witnessed and heard of, 'as would harrow up thy young blood, and make the hair on thy head stand like the quills of the fearful porcupine.' The robberies and ill-usage in these houses exceed belief. In my melancholy hours, I copy out of the daily papers, the various cases brought before the magistrates, of depredations committed in houses of ill fame, and also by the unfortunate prostitutes. From among very many, I will read you the following: the first case shows how the old harpies entice and hide young girls in their wretched houses :—

"'The keeper, according to her own account, of a proper well-regulated house, in Kent Street, in the Borough, for the last three-and-twenty years, appeared at Union Hall, to prefer a complaint against a poor couple, for a riot in the temple in which she presides. It appeared that the daughter of the defendants, a girl not sixteen years of age, had been seduced away from them a few days ago, and that they had learned she had become an inmate of Mother Cole's house. To this abode the parents repaired, to inquire for their child—the poor woman going alone into the house, and the father remaining in the neighbourhood. Mrs. Cole acknoweldged to the afflicted mother that her daughter had been there for a night, and the mother requested to search the house, a liberty which Mother Cole could not allow any person to take, as she had too high a respect for her own character, and for the ladies and gentlemen who frequented her house, to permit any person to enter without the usual fee, or a magistrate's authority, to each of which her doors were always open.   Mother Cole seized the poor woman and thrust her out, and, finding that the appeal to her humanity began to change to a tone of reproach, and, perceiving that she was disposed to resist, dashed the door in her face, and closed it upon one of her legs, with a force that nearly broke it.   The sufferer shrieked out in agony, and the husband ran up, and forced the door so far open as to release his wife from her painful situation.   This was the whole amount of the offence of the unfortunate couple, which was called a riot.

" 'The magistrate inquired whether the daughter of the poor people was in the complainant's house at the time?

" ' Mother Cole declared upon her honour that the young girl was not there, and moreover positively asserted, that she never denied any one's child when it happened to be under her roof; that her house was most respectable, as all who resorted to it would bear testimony.

" ' Here the officers took the liberty of interrupting her, and reminded her that they had on several occasions seached her house, and never failed to find prostitutes in it.

" ' Mother Cole with the greatest effrontery said, she was not accountable for her lodgers, nor for what they might do in their own apartments.   She could answer for it that her own were as pure as any woman's.

" ' The magistrate observed to the depraved brothel-keeper, that he had been acquainted with the infamy of her house for many years, and he should not be surprised if the public indignation were expressed in very substantial terms against it.   He then dismissed the case.'

" The next gives a true picture of a sailor's cruise, and the advantages taken of his thoughtless conduct :—

" In February, 1827, a case that excited much mirth and laughter was heard before the sitting magistrate, R. J. Chambers, Esq.   Three women of the town, named *Montague, Evans*, and *Wright*, were charged with robbing William Dunnick, a sailor, belonging to a ship just arrived from performing a voyage round the world, of £45.

" The complainant, a fine, honest, rough-looking tar, stated the case in his own peculiar manner.   'Your honour,' said he, ' I have just come home, after doubling Cape Horn, and, on the night before, I went up to the other end of the town—I think they call it Bond Street—to see an old messmate of mine.   On coming back, after laying in a pretty good stock of grog, when I got to the Elephant and Castle, or near it, I walked into a pastry-cook's shop to tickle my mouth with ten or a dozen shillings' worth of the good things there.   While I was tucking in, I sees three neat little rigged schooners close alongside, eyeing me from stem to stern. Well, your honour, out I hauls, and soon picked them up, or rather they picked me up. There they are now within them spikes, added he (pointing to the three girls at the bar): they asked me to go home with them, and, as I did not much care about where I went that night, so as I got into a snug harbour, off we tripped in good sailing order, and soon came to an anchor in a d——d bad holding ground. Your honour, I think they call it the Mint. Well, sir, these three pretty damsels set about telling me a long yarn as how they had no grub that day; I puts my hand into my trousers' pocket, and out I hauls a half-sovereign, and desired them to get what belly timber they wanted. One of them then sat on my knee, and pretended to be thankful for what I had given, but in the midst of her caresses, I heard a sovereign fall on the floor, which was picked up by one of them, and when I tried my pockets to see if all was right, I found every sovereign gone.'

" Mr. Chambers—I suppose you were very much intoxicated at the time?

" Sailor—No, your honour; my upper works were all steady enough. I was in very good sailing trim.

" Mr. Chambers—What do you mean by your upper works?

" The sailor (slapping his forehead), I mean your honour, that I had my senses about me—that I had not spliced the main brace so many times that day, as to deprive me of knowledge.

" Mr. Chambers—Can you distinctly swear to the woman that robbed you?

" The sailor, pointing out the prisoner Evans, said he was convinced she was the person who had robbed him, 'but,' added he,

I should not have cared one straw for the loss of the money, had they allowed me to spend it in their company honourably; but to rob me of every farthing I had, and then to leave me to cuddle the bolster alone—this was too bad. I bundled on my jacket, gave a description of the women to a constable, and there they are now before your honour.'

" Mr. Chambers—This is the way with all you sailors—you get drunk, are robbed, and then come here in expectation that I can get back your money. The magistrate then questioned the prisoners; but they protested their innocence, declaring that the sailor was drunk, and lost his money before he accompanied them home.

" Mr. Chambers—Then I shall send the three of you to Brixton, as disorderly prostitutes, for picking up a drunken sailor.

" The complainant expressed his satisfaction at the magistrate's decision, and said that he should like to see them at the wheel, undergoing the punishment which they so richly deserved, for depriving him of the money for which he had toiled both night and day in all climates."

If any thing be wanting to show the callous behaviour of too many of the prostitutes, the following will prove it:—

12

" In December, 1826, a female applied at Union Hall for a war
rant of felony against a man named Gregor M'Gregor, under the
following circumstances :—She stated that, on Christmas eve, the
person whom she accused of having robbed her, called at her
house, accompanied by two females: they retired to a room together, and, having remained in it for some length of time, she heard
his two companions slip down stairs, and, the street-door being
open, they ran out of the house. Soon afterwards, M'Gregor
came blubbering down into the room, wrapped up in a blanket,
and complained that the women with whom he entered, had left
him, taking with them the whole of his clothes, and not leaving
him even his trousers to go home in. She lamented his loss, observing that she could not help his misfortune, and adding that in
future he should be more careful of the company he kept. M'Gregor,
however, instead of receiving her advice with any degree of thankfulness, broke out in his own broad Scotch accent, to abuse her,
and actually accused her of having been concerned with the two
women in depriving him of his garments. She in vain assured him
of the contrary, and requested him to leave her house. ' What,'
said he, ' do you want me to gang home without my breeks ?' ' Certainly,' replied she; ' I have had nothing to do with your breeches,
and I have none to lend you : therefore out of my house you must
and shall pack.' M'Gregor said that he should not quit the house
until he was furnished with covering to enable him to go home;
and, finding at length that there was no prospect of obtaining a
suit, he ran up to the room where he had been divested of all his
clothes by the two women, and, having taken the blankets, sheets,
and counterpane off the bed, he wrapped them tightly round his
body, armed himself with the poker, and rushed down into the
passage, swearing mightily that he would ' smash' the first person
that interrupted him. She (the applicant) was afraid to approach
him, he looked so much like a madman, and he darted out into the
street. She ran after him, and, in the pursuit, he fell into the mud,
from the weight of her bed-clothes. She now thought he could be
easily secured, but she was mistaken, for, on recovering his legs, he
flung off the two blankets (the most cumbersome of the articles in
which he was wrapped up), and afterwards ran with great speed,
so that he completely outstripped all his pursuers, and escaped with
her property. The applicant added, that she had since the occurrence discovered the name and abode of the person by whom she
was robbed, and therefore trusted the magistrate would have no
hesitation in granting her a warrant for his apprehension.

" There was considerable merriment excited in the office during
the applicant's statement against the poor Scotchman, who it appeared was deprived of every article of the dress he had entered
the house in, except his shirt.

" In September, 1827, one of the common prostitutes who infest
the neighbourhood of Whitechapel inveigled a man, named James
Ormston, residing at Berwick-on-Tweed, and prevailed on him to

accompany her to one of her haunts in that sink of iniquity, Wentworth Street. Here he had not been long, when she made several attempts to rifle his pockets of their contents, but finding he was sensible of her manœuvres, and that she could not accomplish her object by stealth, she called out for some assistance, when instantly several of her bullies rushed into the room, and commenced a most furious attack on their victim; he, being a powerful athletic man, kept them at bay for some time. and, perceiving an opportunity, darted out of the aparment to rush down stairs : during his progress to effect this, however, one of his assailants caught him by the neckcloth, and pulled him over the upper bannisters, leaving his person suspended, and, in this situation, he would inevitably have been choked, had not his weight obliged the ruffian to release his hold, and he fell to the ground. After recovering his senses in some degree, he effected an escape into the street: but here again he was beset by his assailants, who were determined not to lose sight of their prey : they a second time surrounded him, and one of them again caught him by the cravat, and endeavoured to strangle him, while the others tore away his waistcoat, in the pocket of which were deposited thirty-one sovereigns, and some silver, with which they got clear off. What is almost incredible in this nefarious transaction, if the truth of the statement was not placed beyond a doubt, is, that though this outrage took place at so early an hour as four o'clock in the evening, and there were hundreds of persons in the street at the time when it occurred, yet none of them offered the least assistance to the sufferer, or resistance to the departure of the thieves, though repeatedly called on most earnestly to do so.

"Some short time since, a young green-horn, fresh from the country, met with a nymph of the pavé in the Haymarket, who kindly offered him a lodging for the night. He at last consented, and, after sundry treats, accompanied her to her lodgings, at No. 2, Union Court, Orchard Street, Westminster, where they reposed for the night. On waking in the morning, the youth was astonished to find that his fair one had decamped, and in her place was a fine baby, fast asleep; he also discovered that she had made free to walk off with his inexpressibles, containing thirteen sovereigns and some silver. In this dilemma, he called the landlady, but no one in the house knew any thing of the transaction. He vowed and swore the child was not his, and he would have nothing to do with it. After a stormy dispute, he ran out of the house, *sans culotte*, to give information to the watchmen, who endeavoured to find the lady, but without success; and he was forced to make the best of his way home in a sad predicament, to ruminate on his folly and repent at leisure.

" A country bumpkin, fresh from his native home, while wandering about gazing at Westminster Abbey, one evening, about dark, was accosted by a nymph of the pavé, who infest the neighbourhood of Tothill Street and its purlieus, and persuaded to accompany her to her lodgings, where he should be made extremely welcome, and accommodated for the night. The countryman, being greatly flattered by the high encomiums passed upon him by the lady, was at length induced to accompany her home to Old Pye Street, Westminster, where he sent for a handsome supper, of which they both partook, and retired for the night. The following morning, great was the countryman's surprise, on examining his pockets, to find himself minus in cash notes about £24, and a watch which he had recently purchased, with three gold seals, for 27 guineas. He accused the nymph with the robbery; this was as stoutly denied, and he was threatened to be thrown out of the window. Not feeling inclined to make his exit in that manner, he quietly went away and got an officer, but on his return the bird was flown, and no discovery could be made; search proved useless, and the countryman returned to his lodgings, having paid dear for his experience."

But, perhaps, the two most desperate amazons that ever walked the streets of London, are, the notorious Lady Barrymore and Kit Bakers, the latter lady having once, in a quarrel with a poor fellow in her lodgings, actually thrown him out of a second-floor window into the street; but, fortunately for her, he was not killed.

It is impossible to portray one half of the fatal effects brought upon mankind by associating with the prostitutes, and which daily experience brings to view, through the depravity of human nature, and the impetuosity of passion in the vicious and abandoned; so that not only the inexperienced countryman, but likewise the citizen who has daily *mementos* before his eyes, falls a victim to the allurements of the insinuating and attractive courtezan, in every state of life.

By the hackneyed one, I mean those nauseating creatures that ply at the corner of streets, alleys, and by-lanes, and at night parade in all places: this class are lost to all shame and decency, and, though pallid with heated lust, are then, *to feed loathsome life*, devoted to every flagitious and wicked purpose for a support; and continually, as it were, forcing men to their disgusting embraces, by every art and trick that wantonness and wickedness can invent: thus compelled by necessity, they prostitute themselves for the smallest consideration, and are affected with diseases incident thereto, from a complication of disorders collected and imbibed by associating with the very scum of the earth, so that they become loathsome and hideous objects to themselves and all around them.

A second class have houses of retreat, where the scenes of wickedness are acted in privacy and security. First being made stupid by the dregs of adulterated wine and stupifying spirits, they are persuaded to spend the evening in those schools of debauchery, to the ruin of their morals, their health, and fortunes. The bawd being the mistress, the prostitute is only a secondary in the place, and, after the man is discharged, the creature supplicates something for her complaisance and condescension. The only difference to be found between these lewd creatures and the former class is their being better habited by the women that have them in pay, and are attended by them and procuresses, to prevent their running away with the clothes they have provided for them, in which they appear gaily to·allure the youths of dissipation, by a display of borrowed plumes to set them off to advantage.

Passion being productive of passion in a greater extreme, they egg him on until he becomes a dupe to their artifices, and work him up to their purpose by their endearments and other fallacious pretences, till, thoroughly absorbed in riot, they take the opportunity to profit by his stay and intoxication, by making the most they can of him, and then send him away as empty in pocket as in knowledge of their schemes and vicious artifices, practised on the unguarded and unthinking part of men that fall into their clutches.

By these means the poor deluded countryman becomes a dupe to the artful courtezan, some of which are scarce in their teens, loses his money, injures his health, and habituates himself to drinking pernicious draughts of poison, contained in their stupifying liquors, which seldom fails of producing the worst and most alarming consequences, exclusive of squandering away fortune, health, and credit, which too often terminates in the loss of life itself.

The bagnio, jelly, and private bagnios, claim attention next, the ladies of which, being one step raised above the street-walkers just mentioned, and yet dependent on procuresses for their attire and appearance in life, being decorated with watches and trinkets, claim a degree of superiority, for which they keep in pay *flash-men*, landlords, and servants, to procure them customers, who make a considerable living out of them, by extracting so much per cent. for their introduction, as the furnishers of clothes do *per* suit *per* day for their dresses. These prostitutes are as much distressed, and in as great misery, as either of the former, and more liable to arrests and inconveniences, and are frequently obliged to submit to the most humiliating means of procuring a wretched subsistence.

"The next class are the prostitutes of fashion, the refuse and cast-off mistresses of men of quality; who, being left with a few clothes and some money, affect grandeur and genteel life, and thereby ensnare the unsuspecting and inconsiderate, who are indifferent about the money squandered upon them, if they can but have the credit of being looked on as persons capable of administering to the foibles and follies of a fine woman, though the refuse of a nobleman. These ladies of pleasure, as they are styled by the *beau monde*, reserve themselves only for such as are able, by ample fortunes, to pay for the favours they bestow; and, being followed by officers, they become toasts, and are thereby sought after by wealthy merchants and tradesmen, to show their taste and breeding, in selecting women of the *Bon Ton* for their leisure moments and hours of indulgence.

"To speak of these ladies as they deserve, I must confess they are the most specious of all prostitutes whatever; for, as amongst thieves, so amongst them, a pretension to honour is to be found, and therefore some dependence is placed on their asseverations, though, in the end, you pay dearly for their condescensions and favours.

Notwithstanding all the artifices, stratagems, and deceptions, practised by these truly unfortunate women, they are objects of peculiar compassion, and, if they are not worthy of our confidence and attention, they are not to be despised or ill used, which is too often done by unfeeling men. It ought to be recollected, they have, poor creatures! enough to bear up against in the bitter recollection of their past and present conduct, the dreadful anxiety of procuring a wretched existence, and the remembrance of better and happier days, and being unprotected and objects of scorn—all these circumstances render them peculiarly worthy of the most compassionate attention of the man of feeling: we ought not to ' break the bruised reed:' and the man who can ill use the unfortunate prostitute, is a million times a greater sinner than the poor, unprotected, forlorn, despised, and neglected object of his savage barbarity. Shun them and their company—their allurements—their fascinations—and their embraces—for ' their touch is death!'—pass them not with curses and taunts, but, like the good Samaritan, pour, if you can, the balm of comfort to their distracted, wretched, and disordered mind.—*The prostitute is the greatest object of pity of any offender in London!*

There is a set of contemptible wretches, who form part of the retinue of the brothel, called bullies, and who depend on the wretched prostitute for support, and whose bread he eats, whose quarrel he fights, and at whose call he is ready to do as commanded. They are creatures of the most vicious and disorderly life, and many of them have lavished their whole substance on the very women who have them in keeping. In general, these kinds of gentry are arrant cowards; for, should they attack a man of spirit, who dares defend himself, they will skulk away on the least resistance, or say they were in jest, and make the most abject submission, or tamely suffer themselves to be kicked down stairs, without the least opposition. On the contrary, if they meet with a man that is intimidated by their blustering, they never fail to abuse and ill-treat him. A countryman was allured by a young wanton, and inveigled to a well-known bagnio in the vicinity of Covent Garden, where they regailed themselves for some time with the best the house afforded, when the lady proposed to adjourn to her own house, to spend the remainder of the evening. Accordingly, the bill was called for and paid, and the couple retired to the lady's lodgings, where they spent the night in joy and festivity. But, lo! when morning came, and the countryman was about to depart, there was a demand of five guineas made by the girl, for lodging, &c. A gratuitous present is also expected for civility, and something for the maid. Being struck with the exorbitance of the demand, he absolutely refused to comply therewith; upon which the bully made his appearance, and, in a peremptory tone, insisted on the lodging being paid for, the lady satisfied, and some acknowledgment to the maid, for the extra trouble she had been at, in attending on him; and swearing if he did not instantly pay the demand, he would run him through the body. The countryman, having a greater regard for his life than he had for his pocket, and more self-love than courage, tamely submitted to the bully's menaces, and, dropping five sovereigns and five shillings on the table, was then turned down stairs.

The following anecdote will show you how these miscreants of bullies are detested by the public:

Some years ago, two loose women had seized upon an inebriated gentleman, and were conveying him to their lodgings at noonday: the populace concluded he would at least be robbed, and determined to rescue him immediately, which they did, and severely ducked the women. Thus far justice proceeded in its due channel; but an unfortunate journeyman cutler happened to exert himself rather too outrageously, and attracted notice: he was observed to hold the woman or women in a manner that might be supposed real efforts of anger, or as efforts intended to mask an intention to release them; the word was instantly given to duck him as *their bully.*—The women were released, and escaped; the cutler was thrown into a horse-pond, in spite of his protestations of innocence; and, when his wife endeavoured to rescue him, she underwent the same discipline.

"Such," continued Julia," is a brief history of the wretched and melancholy doings of the unfortunate prostitute, who too often flies to liquor as a means of deadening, as it were, her sufferings and her poignant feelings. Oh, beware of that seductive vice, sir; hear what Randolph says:

> ' Fly drunkenness, whose vile incontinence
> Takes both away the reason and the sense !
> Consider how it soon destroys the grace
> Of human shape, spoiling the beauteous face,
> Puffing the cheeks, blearing the curious eye,
> Studding the face with vicious heraldry.
> It weaks the brain, it spoils the memory;
> Hast'ning on age and wilful poverty,
> It drowns our better parts, making our name
> To foes a laughter, to our friends a shame.
> 'Tis virtue's poison, and the bane of trust,
> The match of wrath, the fuel unto lust.'

" But even liquor is not so dreadful ' a fuel unto lust,' as that public offence in London, so alarming in its nature, and so mischievous in its effects, and which stands in need of all good men to stop its corroding progress. I mean the exposing to sale, and selling of indecent and obscene prints and books, to the perusal of which, many girls, as well as boys, may lay their ruin. If, at that period of life when children and apprentices stand in need of a parent to advise, a master to restrain, or a friend to admonish and check the first impulse of passion, stimulants like these are held forth to meet their early feelings, what but destruction must be the event? Indeed, by care, parents and masters may prevent youth in some degree from frequenting bad company; they may accustom them to good habits, afford them examples worthy imitation; and, by shutting their doors early, may oblige them to keep good hours: but, alas! what doors, what bolts, what bars can be any security to their innocence, whilst vice, in this deluding form, counteracts all caution, and bids defiance to the force of precept, prudence, and example, by affording such foul, but palatable hints, as are destructive to modesty, sobriety, and obedience."

Peregrine was delighted with the virtuous principles of the unfortunate Julia, and felt unwilling to leave her company; yet prudence dictated they should part. The freedom of behaviour he witnessed in Julia, in the morning, turned now to the most reserved demeanour: she seemed to feel the real value of her new friend, and was determined not to abuse his generous conduct, by holding out any alurements. They parted for the evening, Peregrine providing her with cash sufficient to discharge her arrears of rent, and maintain herself until he should again visit her. He shortly arrived at his inn, and repaired to rest; but his mind was entirely on Julia: to marry her was out of the question; and he thought upon a thousand plans for her relief; and while at breakfast, Mentor entered his room, to whom Peregrine told the whole of his adventure, asking his advice: "That, my young friend," replied he, "I will give you some future day, when I nave further considered the subject, and you have become more collected; but" continued he, "I came to invite you to join a party this evening to visit

The Theatre-Royal, Drury Lane,

as you expressed a strong desire, some few days since, to go there, when one of Shakespeare's plays was performed."

Unfortunately, on account of waiting for some of the party, they found it was too late that evening for the theatre, and agreed, the next day being Sunday, to visit the west end of the town, and witness—

The Doings in Hyde Park.

Which was seen by Peregrine with delight, mingled with pity: he was delighted at the splendid equipages, and the beauty of the ladies; but he looked with pity on the innumerable number of what are termed fashionables, who were there promenading, the monstrocity of their appearance creating in his mind the most sovereign contempt and disgust. Here Peregrine and his friends walked, till they were covered with dust; and, evening drawing in, they repaired to a coffee-house, where it was agreed they should visit Drury Lane the next evening.

"I would advise you," said Mentor to Peregrine, "as it is now the fashion to *butcher* some of Shakspeare's plays, by introducing *modern* music and songs, and other rubbish, to purchase a copy of the play as it used to be performed; and no edition is more worthy your attention, as being critically correct, very neatly printed, and highly embellished, than 'Cumberland's British Theatre;' it also contains judicious remarks on each play, from the pen of a gentleman, who is generally esteemed the first commentator on the stage of the present day; and it is gratifying to reflect, that the patronage of the public keeps pace with the exertions of its spirited publisher and proprietor. The edition has only one fault, and that is, it is too cheap.

13 H

" You will find," continued Mentor, " Drury-Lane Theatre, one of the most splendid in Europe. The whole of the interior of the house presents an appearance of unrivalled splendour, and is replete with every convenience. The grand entrance is in Bridges Street, through a spacious hall, leading to the boxes. This hall is supported by fine Doric columns, and illuminated by two large brass lamps; three large doors lead from this hall into the house, and into a rotunda of great beauty and elegance. On each side of the rotunda, are passages to the great stairs, which are peculiarly grand and spacious; over them is an ornamental ceiling, with a dome light.

" The first Drury-Lane Theatre was built in 1662; destroyed by fire, 1672; rebuilt, 1674; pulled down, 1791; rebuilt, 1794; destroyed by fire, February 24, 1809; and opened on the 10th October, 1812, with the performance of Hamlet, and the farce of the Devil to Pay.

" The footmen, and other livery servants, used formerly to be allowed to sit in the shilling gallery, gratis; but they expressed so unequivocally their displeasure on several occasions, that they were expelled; upon which they threatened to reduce the playhouse to the ground, unless they were reinstated in their rights. Two footmen were committed to Newgate for rioting, and fifty men were stationed in the gallery, when peace was restored.

In 1762, Drury-Lane Theatre was much improved, by lengthening the stage, enlarging the boxes and pit, and rebuilding the galleries: to defray the expenses of these alterations, the managers intimated that nothing under full price would in future be taken during the performance. The audience strongly opposed this innovation, and were determined to enforce their resolution of seeing plays, as usual, at half-price; and, on the commencement of the tragedy of Elvira, they ordered the orchestra to play the music of " Roast Beef," and " Britons Strike Home!" which was complied with. Several fruitless attempts were made to go on with the performance. Mr. Garrick came on the stage, and attempted to speak, but in vain; when the following questions, at length, issued from the pit: " Will you, or will you not, give admittance for half-price after the third act?" The manager again attempted to explain, without effect; *yes*, or *no*, were the only words granted him. *Yes*, accompanied by an expression of indignation, escaped the lips of Roscius, and the theatre shook with sounds of triumph.

" The ridiculous custom of placing two sentinels on the stage, during the performance of plays, was discontinued in 1764; as a soldier, employed for that purpose, highly entertained the audience, by laughing at the character of Sir Andrew Aguecheek, in Twelfth Night, till he actually fell convulsed upon the floor.

" Pantomime was first performed, in the year 1702, at Drury Lane, in an entertainment called *Tavern Bilkers:* it died the fifth night. It was invented by Weaver, a dancing-master of Shrewsbury; who, from the encouragement of the nobility, invented a second, called *Loves of Mars and Venus*, performed at the same theatre, in the year 1716.

"Very considerable improvements were made in Drury-Lane Theatre, previous to the opening for the season of 1775. The frequenters of it, before the above period, describe the interior as very little superior to an old barn.

"Mr. Garrick, whose unrivalled powers as an actor have been the theme of applause and admiration, retired from the stage, at this theatre, in June, 1776, when in full possession of his extraordinary faculties."

Peregrine remarked he had heard much talk of the "Doings" in Drury-Lane Saloon, and expressed a wise to witness the scene: Mentor accordingly accompanied him thither. "That old wretch," said Mentor, "you see in conversation with the little girl, is a constant visitor here: many of such young creatures are procured to satisfy his dreadful passions,—

'It's true—'tis pity;
And pity 'tis, 'tis true!"

That gentleman in the slouched hat, with immoderate whiskers, is a celebrated nobleman; and he, with his back towards you, is one of the first ' Legs' in the kingdom; that lady, sitting down, was once the celebrated mistress of a late unfortunate banker: and that pretty girl, standing near her, is the daughter of a country clergyman. Our friend, Cruikshank, I see, is taking a sketch of the scene; and, when it is finished, I will show it you.

"There is no man breathing," continued Mentor, "but must deplore such scenes of immorality as are nightly exhibited in the saloons of our national theatres. A correspondent, in that valuable journal, the Times newspaper, thus expresses himself on this subject:—'It has often been a matter of wonder to me, that in this age of religion and morality, when every means are tried to make men more religious, more moral, or at all events more decent, so much apathy should exist with respect to the present disgraceful state of the theatres. It is notorious that no respectable female can attend any performance, without being subject to contacts of the most forbidding and offensive description. Not only has each theatre its saloon for the especial convenience of the common prostitutes of the town, but, by the present arrangements, no part of the house is free from their intrusion. The dress-circle I allow, is kept as select as it well can be; but no person can enter the second, except at the risk of being seated by a well-dressed, and, frequently, shameless prostitute, or annoyed by indecent attentions and conversation, particularly at half-price. The third circle is so completely their own, that no woman of respectability would ever knowingly enter it. The lobbies are as bad—the constant parade of women half-dressed, and men half-drunk; through which, and the vestibule, it may be added, issue, at the close of the performance, the whole assemblage of the theatre.

" ' Now, sir, is it not monstrous that a nuisance of this magnitude should be tolerated, in a country calling itself the most moral and decent upon earth; tolerated, too, in the midst of societies of all kinds for the protection of the public morals, and in the face of our bishops, of our great reformists, and the boasted march of social improvement?

" ' It is not the squeamishness of your over-righteous or over-moral people which is outraged; for they have long since been driven from the theatre, partly from this very cause; but it is your respectable play-going people; who, without being "saints," have decency, and delicacy, and religion, and morality enough to be shocked at authorized profligacy, and disgusted with its grossness.

" ' Besides, sir, evil example does wonders : if it shocks one person, it seduces another—

" Vice is a monster of such hideous mien,
As to be hated, needs but to be seen;
But, seen too oft, familiar to her face,
We first endure, then pity, then embrace."

" ' Nor am I to be told that the modest and the virtuous may confine themselves to the first circle : places frequently cannot be got, and, moreover, it may not suit to go " dressed." Besides, this is no answer to my observation on the jumbling together, at the close of the performance, of sisters, wives, mothers, and daughters, with women, whose obscene joke, loud laugh, shameless manners, and disgusting appearance, and frequently besotted paramours, betray, but too well, their misfortunes and their infamy. Nor am I answered by the assertion that these evils are a century old, or that they are not generally felt, because they are not loudly exclaimed against. Age, sir, is no hallower of evil; and, I should have thought, the longer a crying and impudent one of this nature has been permitted to exist, the more imperious is the necessity for its removal. As to the feelings of the public, they too often sleep under the weight of established authorities and customs; and, in this instance, perhaps, people are deterred, because they think it hopeless to attack so formidable a power as a Lord Chamberlain, a host of managers and proprietors, and the manners of a free age to boot. But, I will venture to say, none but libertines will refuse to acknowledge the evil, however the possibility of removing it may be doubted.

" ' We talk, indeed, of the inferior morality of the French; but can we compare with them, in externals, our streets or our theatres? Vice, with them, pays homage to virtue, by being decent. With us, its only antidote is its extreme grossness; which, unfortunately, is no protection, as the tempters and tempted are generally, in point of delicacy, too much on a level.

" ' Vice, I shall be told, always must exist—expel it from the theatre, and you only change its abode; and, if that were true, which I deny, is there nothing gained in forcing it from its licensed and strongest hold, and hunting it into places less public, and therefore less dangerous? Where do half the disorderlies come from, but the theatres? and how are your "Mother H.'s" supported but by them? Rochefoucault wisely says,—" Our qualities, both good and bad, are at the mercy of opportunity." If vice, therefore, must exist, let it riot on in obscurity; but let not a place of public amusement be made the rallying-point and very centre of its attractions.

" ' Convinced, therefore, that the best interests of a nation depend on its moral character, and equally sure of the demoralizing effect of saloons, from the sanction and opportunities they afford to every species of debauchery and vice, and powerfully impressed with the influence which the metropolis extends over the whole country, I would abolish these legalized appendages to the brothel, and, by lessening the facilities, diminish the amount of vice. The inconvenience of the virtuous and vicious being now and then thrown together, would not, I am aware, be provided against by this alteration; but vice in that case might at all events be made to appear decent, and, by proper restraints, the mass would ultimately be driven from the theatre.

" ' The coffers of the manager, I am persuaded, would suffer little; for many people, to my knowledge, abstain from playgoing, because the saloon, avowedly for the purposes of prostitution, is part and parcel of the theatre, and by going to the one they countenance and support the other. But, if the profits were to be affected, is the progress of public virtue and improvement to wait on the prosperity of a playhouse? and are the managers and proprietors to be allowed to thrive by pandering to the bad passions of our nature?

" ' If, however, too many difficulties and objections exist to doing away with saloons altogether, in the name of decency, separate them from the body of the house; or, at all events, stop that free communication, which is fraught with so much indecency and inconvenience. Let a particular part of the house be appropriated to the use of the women: shut them out from the second circle, and, if it be possible, provide against the nuisance of females of the best and worst characters being jostled together on leaving the theatre.

" ' In conclusion, let me ask what title has the press to the guardianship of the public morals, if it allows so glaring a blot as this to escape it? Where is the Bishop of London, that he permits this " high place" of sin to stand out insultingly prominent in the very centre of his diocese? And, lastly, to what purpose do our hundred different moral and religious societies, and particularly that for the suppression of vice, exist, if this canker in the heart of the metropolis is to remain uncured and unregarded?'

This correspondent, he may rest assured, is wrong, in saying " the coffers of the managers would suffer little," by prohibiting such characters as now visit the saloons. Some years ago, a man of the name of R——m, was engaged by the manager of one of our metropolitan theatres, at a salary of £3 per week, to find out the finest women of the town, and present them with tickets of free admission to the theatre: and what was the consequence? Why, the house never paid so well as during that season: there were two audiences, one to witness the performance, and another to gaze on the beauty of the unfortunate creatures who were promenading in the saloon. In fact, persons of authority in the theatres were employed to decide upon the merits of the female visitors to the lobbies; and, if a girl was pronounced "likely to draw friends, she became at once enrolled in the list of the establishment, and thus contributed to the prosperity of her respectable patrons. That pimping plan has been a good deal abated. The lobbies and saloons and upper boxes exhibited such scenes of riot and indecency, that society was shamed into a determination not to wink any longer at the violation of its most sacred compact: respectable men would not allow their families to run the hazard of the pollution, and trembled for the immorality, not of the stage, but of the immense concourse of performers before the curtain. It certainly would be desirable, if such practices were prohibited; but that they are the sources of much wealth to the manager, there can be no doubt; and, when we reflect on the very great salaries *now* paid to the performers, and the various enormous expenses of the theatre, it can be a matter of no surprise, that the saloons are tolerated. Many a young clerk is to be seen in the saloons of the theatres, accompanied by some prostitute, dressed out and supported in her wanton extravagance by the daily plunder of some industrious man. Many a boy has been suddenly transferred from the lobbies to the prison, and from thence to the place of most frightful retribution. Of late years, there has been a most dangerous addition to the vanity which courts the heart and imagination of youth. I mean the accommodation given to persons of both sexes, at all hours of the night, in houses in which, although they are not licensed by the magistrates, wine and spirits are sold, and fighting, and robbery, and drunkenness are to be constantly witnessed. The owners of those hateful places of debauchery contrive to get the consent of some worn-out beggarly vintners, and, upon the authority of that qualification, they open their doors to all well-dressed miscreants, both men and women.

Upon leaving the theatre, Peregrine was warned against the importunities of fellows who ply about the theatres at night, called *dragsmen*—a very dangerous sort of gentry. They are very fond of helping gentlemen into coaches, and paying themselves for their trouble, by *prigging* a watch or a pocket-book; but their chief amusement is *hustling*, an art in which they excel, as they have been known to push a gentleman from one to the other, without letting him fall to the ground, until he has been dispossessed of every thing valuable about him. Their efforts are of course generally confined to *lushy coves* (drunken men), as the gentlemen of the whip on that beat have a sort of reputation to support, and will not countenance an attempt to rob a sober man, inasmuch as he has not been "disgracing himself" with too much "lush."

From the saloon, the depraved characters visit the flash-houses, which are open at all hours, for the most flagitious purposes. Robbers, and gentlemen, and watchmen, and bawds, and bullies, and prostitutes, are received upon equal terms; and, in the event of a quarrel, the keeper of the "crib" invariably lends his aid and authority to the person who calculates upon advantage in the confusion of the fight. In fact, the public-house act is considered, in that provision which inflicts a penalty for late hours, one of the most useful measures ever submitted to, and adopted by, Parliament. The shopman or the clerk must, if he is not satisfied with the obligation to go home at a seasonable hour, turn towards Bow Street, where, although he is sure to be served with liquor at any hour, he is sure (to use the phraseology of the cribs) to be *sarved out* too, and runs the chance of being exposed, as well as plundered and half poisoned. There is a sort of security against citizen visits in the very disgrace which may attend the experiment. We would, however, recommend every man of extensive business to have his eye upon public places in which dissipation forms an essential part of the system.

Some of the officers are to be seen in the flash-houses, drinking with brothel-keepers and hell-keepers inside the bar, while the parlour is crowded with *macers* and *buzzmen*, and prostitutes. At three or four in the morning, there is a general turn-out of the spirit-shops into the coffee-shops, which are accessible even at an earlier hour. It is at the coffee-shops that the gaming-house crimps, or *touters*, as they are more frequently called, are to be seen. Those miscreants are the most abstemious of thieves; always sober, always attentive and polite, to any stranger who has a purse or a gold watch; and they seldom fail to entice to their employers tables, a flat or two, in the course of the morning. Poisonous spirits are supplied at the flash-cribs, and poisonous wines are retailed at the coffee-shops.

In the account of the variety of deceptions by which the visitors of flash-houses, oyster-shops, and coffee-shops, contrive to "draw" any young man of fortune, or any clerk or shopman, whom they induce to rob his master, it is difficult to speak with accuracy, without exciting a feeling very different from that which, in such cases, ought to absorb every other. Some of them sham the man of birth, education, and fortune; others, the simple countryman; and others, the buffoon and devil-may-care-sort of fellow. They are all masters in their way, and there is not one of them who would not cut his brother "macer's" throat for a sovereign, if the gallows (not in its disgrace, but its bodily infliction) were not constantly before his eyes. Such is their love of the crooked path, that they would rob a poor wretch of sixpence, although their pockets were crammed with sovereigns and bank-notes. The "gaffer," of whom I lately spoke, is perhaps more like a human being than any of them. He has been known to give some trifle in charity to those whom he has contributed to make beggars, while others have sneered at the entreaty, and desired an unfortunate gull to hang or drown himself, as he must be a burden to himself, and a bore to every one else.

It is well known, that some of the flash-house keepers not unfrequently join in a little buzzing excursion themselves, as that they treat with contempt the act of Parliament for the regulation of public-houses, by admitting persons at all hours to drink and smoke in their houses. It is true, that the licence of one of these thieving dens is sometimes threatened, and sometimes taken away; but the influence of a large brewer never fails to restore it, and the same iniquity flourishes every night, although for decency's sake the name of the proprietor may undergo a change. No inspector is appointed to visit the "cribs." The watchmen are the only superintendents, and they are always at the command of the landlord. The patrol will not interfere, for there is no adequate remuneration upon the side of morals, and there is no order issued by their superiors. It is admitted universally, by those who are best qualified to judge of the cause of the increase of crime, that houses of this description, and the houses of receivers of stolen goods, hold out the greatest encouragement to the perpetration of the most desperate villanies, and it is well known to the police magistrates, that an effectual check can be given to both sorts of abominations. If inspectors, with good pay for the performance of their duty, are appointed to examine and report the public-houses which are known to harbour the abandoned, the "cribs" must be knocked up, and if, on occasions of robbery, a reward was offered for the receiver, instead of the thief, Petticoat Lane, and Houndsditch, and Whitechapel, and the Jew-streets and alleys in the neighbourhood of the Strand, would no longer be places of refuge and barter for the prosperous ruffian. A perpetual watch would be kept upon the numerous houses where the police are aware "swag" is hourly conveyed. Many of the old-clothes shops would be ransacked, and a general rout would take place amongst the Jews, very few of whom, in that line, ever refused to purchase stolen goods, of whatever description. The principal officers of the police are convinced of the efficacy of such a system, and that robberies cannot be checked without a determined effort to spoil the business of receivers.

While at breakfast the following morning, Peregrine complained that he felt something like gravel at the bottom of his cup: "that, my good friend," said Mentor, "is most probably salt, which many of the ill-principled grocers mix with their sugars: I remember a case, in September, 1825, which came before the Lord Mayor, when Mr. Clarke, of Apothecaries' Hall, the gentleman I mentioned to you some days ago, being asked what he had to say relative to adulterated sugar, replied, ' a lady, who resided, he believed, in

Berwick Street, Soho, applied to Dr. Brookes, to analyze some sugar, which she had purchased in the neighbourhood, and the doctor, not having time to do as she requested, referred her to him. She stated that she was in the habit of sweetening pies and puddings with the sugar of which she produced a sample, for her children, and that her children always fell sick immediately after their meals. She had remarked that it was necessary to use a great quantity of this sugar before it had any effect upon that with which it was mixed, and that, when the pies or puddings tasted sweet, they also tasted salt or brackish. The twang which this commodity gave to tea, was also very extraordinary, and she felt a grievous sickness in her stomach after drinking it. The sugar, nevertheless, was extremely bright. Upon analyzing the commodity, he found that it contained about one-half of common salt, which was about a halfpenny a pound. This ingredient, when applied in such enormous quantities, must excite excessive thirst and fever in children, and could not be very serviceable to grown people, putting out of question the immense per-centage gained upon the adulteration.'

"The exposure of the fraud on the public, by grocers mixing salt with sugar, may probably have a beneficial effect; but there is another practice to which attention should be drawn: that is, the practice of many grocers grinding coffee and sugar together, in the proportion of three fourths of the former, and one fourth of the latter, and retailing this mixture at the price of coffee.

"The Lord Mayor said the public were certainly indebted to Mr. Clarke for this piece of intelligence, and would, no doubt, consider the obligation increased by the information as to the means of discovering the adulteration.

"Mr. Clarke said a person had to do no more, to detect the adulteration, than to put a little of the suspected article into a cup, and pour a little spirits of wine upon it. The sugar would immediately melt, and the salt would remain at the bottom.

" His lordship then asked Mr. Clarke if he had ever analyzed any adulterated tea, to which Mr. Clarke replied that he was at present engaged, by order of government, in analyzing several chests of caper Souchong tea, and, although he had as yet only examined a few of them, yet he found that one-fourth of their contents was *lead ore*, or poison of the rankest description, and he knew from experience, that a great quantity of tea was adulterated in a similar manner, and that the result of his observation convinced him that the greater part of the statements contained in a work published some time since by Mr. Accum, the celebrated chymist, respecting the adulteration of food (although they were disbelieved at the time), were strictly correct, and not at all exaggerated. The adulteration of tea had been carried on to a most surprising extent lately, and he would convince his lordship of the fact, by sending him a sample of the Souchong.

" A long conversation then ensued between Mr. Clarke and his lordship, on the subject of the adulteration of various articles of food, at the close of which his lordship thanked Mr. Clarke for tne valuable information he had given him, when the latter bowed and withdrew.

"The best black tea," said Mentor, "though not much used here, is Pekoe, which is highly esteemed in the northern parts of Europe. Souchong is little inferior to Pekoe, but so little of it is imported, that it is difficult to get it genuine; for what is usually sold as Souchong is in reality the better sort of Congo, the leaf of which is much larger, from its being older before it is pulled.

"The best green tea is Gunpowder, but it is very often mixed with Hyson, rolled up in imitation, and tinged of the proper colour, and with some sort of green dye. It is erroneously stated in some books, that it is greened with verdigris. If this poisonous substance were used, the tea, when poured out, would be black as ink, by the chymical action between the copper and the astringent principle (bannin) of the tea. Hyson is also larger in grain and in leaf than Gunpowder, and will more easily fall to dust on being pressed. This. however, is not so much the case with young Hyson.

"The infusion is deeper-coloured than that of the single, which is also known by the flat leaf, while that of Hyson is round.

"As a ready test of black tea being manufactured from *old tea-leaves, dyed with logwood*, &c., moisten some of the tea, and rub it on white paper, which it will blacken when not genuine. If you wish to be more particular, infuse a quantity of the sample in half a pint of cold soft water, for three or four hours. If the water is then of an amber colour, and does not become red when you drop some oil of vitriol or sulphuric acid in it, you may presume the tea to be good. Adulterated black tea, when infused in cold water, gives it a bluish black tinge, and it becomes instantly red, with a few drops of oil of vitriol. After infusion, some of the largest leaves should be spread out, when the real tea-leaf may be known from that of the sloe, by being larger, longer, more pointed, and more deeply and widely serrated, like the teeth of a saw. There is no difference of the shape in the leaves of green and black tea. The leaves of the sloe and of the privet are, in a slight degree, unwholesome, the former for containing a small proportion of prussic acid.

"When tea is suspected to be coloured by carbonate of copper, take two table spoonsful of liquid ammonia, and half its quantity of water, in a stopped phial, and put a tea spoonful of leaves into it: shake the phial, and, if the least portion of copper be present, the fluid will become of a fine blue; or the tea, thus adulterated, will blacken water impregnated with sulphurated hydrogen gas.

"Common Bohea tea, worth about three or four shillings per pound, is sifted, and the largest reserved for painting, as it is called. Dutch pink and Prussian blue are finely powdered and united together, which form a fine green powder; the tea and the colour are put together into a long leathern bag, and gently shook backward and forward by two persons, until the tea becomes charged with sufficient colour to assume the appearance of fine bloom Hyson, and is then sold for eight or ten shillings the pound : occasionally, the leaves of the black-currant tree are rolled, dried, and broken into fine pieces, which imparts a peculiar and agreeable flavour.

" The Dutch have been long in the habit of drying sage-leaves to resemble tea, for which purpose they collect not only their own, but obtain great quantities from the south of France. They pack them in cases, and take them out to China : for every pound of sage they get four pounds of tea, the Chinese preferring it to the best of their own tea

" It has been known, tnat the thin twigs of the birch and blackthorn have been cut very small, and mixed with the tea.

" These are," continued Mentor, " a few of the frauds practised by ill-principled tea-dealers and grocers. As tea is now so universally drunk, it is interesting to inquire when it was first introduced into Europe, and also into its present enormous consumption. The precise time when the Europeans first became acquainted with this plant, is in some measure involved in obscurity. Anderson observes, that the earliest author he met with, by whom tea is mentioned, is Giovanni Botaro, an Italian, who, in his work, ' Of the Cause of the Magnificence and Greatness of Cities,' published 1590, says, ' The Chinese have a herb, out of which they press a delicate juice, which serves them for drink, instead of wine; it also preserves their health, and frees them from all those evils, that the immoderate use of wine doth breed unto us.' This is evidently descriptive of tea, though it is not mentioned by name. Dr. Lettsom, however, says, that it had been the subject of notice before that period. The editors of the Encyclopedia Britannica state, that it was first imported by the Dutch, in 1610. However, the Dutch East India Company were unquestionably the first who engaged in tea, as an article of commerce; and from the beginning until near the close of the seventeenth century, the whole of the European demand was supplied through the medium of their sales. The quantities, however, that were imported during this period, were very trifling, as it was principally used as a medicine, and failed of obtaining any considerable degree of reputation, owing to the discordant opinions that were held by the faculty, with regard to its properties. The use of tea was known in England long before the company adopted it as an article of their established imports; but when, or by whom, it was first introduced, does not appear with any direct certainty. That tea was considered as a scarce and valuable article in 1664, may be gathered from an entry in the company's records, under the date of June the first, in that year, whereby it appears, that on the arrival of some ships, the master attendant was ordered to go aboard, and inquire what *rarities* of birds, beasts, or other curiosities, there were on board, fit to present to his majesty; and, on the third of September following, there is, in the general books, an entry of two pounds two ounces of *thea* for his majesty, for which the company are charged, in their accounts with the secretary, £4. 5s. The first importation of tea, made by the company, appears to have been in 1669, when two cannisters were received from the factors at Bantam, weighing 143lbs. 8oz.

" The earliest *historical* notice we find of tea, in this country, is in Burnet's History, who states that the illustrious Lord Russell partook of some on the morning of his murder.  This was in 1683.

" In four years, from 1697 to 1700, the average importation from Holland, and the East Indies, amounted to 36,935lbs.  Such was the state of the tea trade in England, at the close of the seventeenth century, at which time it was nearly, if not altogether, unknown in the sister kingdoms of Scotland and Ireland.  It is related, upon good authority, that, in 1685, the widow of the unfortunate Duke of Monmouth sent a pound of tea as a present to some of her noble relatives in Scotland; but, having omitted to transmit the needful directions for its use, the tea was boiled, the iquor thrown away, and the leaves served up as a vegetable.

" In the good happy days of Old England, families sat down to breakfast on beefstakes and wholesome beer; for this was the food of Queen Elizabeth, it being no uncommon circumstance for Essex, Sir Christopher Hatton, Lord Burleigh, and her other ministers, to visit her in her bed-room, and breakfast with her, off good roast beef and knock-me-down ale!  Recollect, reader, this was in the *barbarous* ages, before England became so *refined* as it is at present—before there was so much deceit, humbug, lying, chicanery, pride, dishonesty, trick, fraud, hypocrisy, false religion, and villany, as there is at present among us!!

" Cobbett, in his ' Cottage Economy,' tells you of the *expense* and *time* lost in making and drinking tea: these are his words,— ' I shall suppose the tea to be only five shillings the pound, the sugar only sevenpence, and the milk only twopence per quart. The prices are at the very lowest.  I shall suppose a teapot to cost a shilling, six cups and saucers two shillings and sixpence, and six pewter spoons eighteenpence.  How to estimate the firing I hardly know; but certainly there must, in the course of the year, be two hundred fires made that would not be made, were it not for tea-drinking.  Then comes the great article of all—the *time* employed in this tea-making affair.  It is impossible to make a fire, boil water, make the tea, drink it, wash up the things, sweep up the fireplace, and put all to rights again, in a less space of time, upon an average, than *two hours:* however, let us allow *one hour:* and here we have a woman occupied no less than 365 hours in the year, or thirty whole days, at twelve hours in the day; that is to say, one month out of the twelve in the year, besides the waste of the man's time, in hanging about waiting for the tea!

" ' Now, then, let us take the bare cost of the tea.  I suppose a pound of tea to last twenty days, which is not nearly half an ounce every morning and evening. I allow for each mess half a pint of milk; and I allow three pounds of the red dirty sugar to each pound of tea. The account of expenditure would then stand very high; and to these must be added the amount of the tea-tackle, one set of which will, upon an average, be demolished every year.'

" The China trade being the only monopoly now remaining in the hands of the East India Company, its operation upon the price of tea has been the subject of much observation; for, though it cannot be denied by any one, that by means of the monopoly a tax is levied upon the people of England, for the benefit of the India Company, the amount of that tax is disputed. The company exported from Canton, in the years 1820-21, 1,964,927lbs. of Bohea tea, the prime cost of which was £75,330, which makes something between 9d. and 9¼d. per pound.

" The average price at which this quality of tea was sold in England, in the sales of 1822, was 2s. 5d., 8-10; 2s. 6d., 3-10; 2s. 5d., 5-10; and 2s. 4d., 7-10. On Congou, the species of tea of which the greatest quantity is consumed (about 19 millions out of 27), the sale price, at the company's sales in England, is about 2s. 8d., while the prime cost has been about 1s. 4d. The government duty, moreover, is regulated by the price at the company's sales—95 per cent. on that produce; so that the Bohea, which is bought in China at 9d., costs, duty included, about 5s. at the *wholesale* price in England; and, when duly intermingled with *ash* and *blackthorn*, it may fairly go into the tea-pot at 6s. The company must levy about two millions a-year upon the tea-pot!

" Soon after tea became the fashionable beverage, several gardens, in the outskirts of London, were opened as *tea*-gardens; but the proprietors, finding the visitors wanted something else beside tea, accommodated them with ale, bottled beer, &c. In an old magazine, printed about the year 1789, the writer, speaking of persons whose habit it was to resort to the various tea-gardens near London, on a Sunday, calculates them to amount to 200,000. Of these he considers not one would go away without having spent 2s. 6d., and consequently the sum of £25,000 would have been spent in the course of the day by this number of persons. Twenty-five thousand, multiplied by the number of Sundays in a year, gives, as the annual consumption of that day of rest, the immense sum of £1,300,000. The writer also takes upon himself to calculate the returning situation of these persons, as follows :—sober, 50,000; in high glee, 90,000; drunkish, 30,000; staggering tipsy, 10,000; muzzy, 15,000; dead drunk, 5,000.—Total, 200,000."

" I thank you," said Peregrine, " for this history," and, stirring his tea, said, " What have you to say about the milk and the water : they, surely, are free from adulteration."

" Indeed they are not," replied Mentor ; " milk is well known to be sophisticated ; and, as to the Thames water, good Heaven, what filth is imbibed in it ! So you see, what with the grocer, tea-dealer, milkman, and the water companies, the tea-drinker pours down his ' red lane !' as Dr. Kitchiner calls it, a rare mess of stuff, enough to poison a dog ! Now, with regard to milk,

If,' says a celebrated physician (in recommending milk diet to persons of weakly habits) ' you live in the country, it will be necessary to mix water with your milk : if you live in London, this necessity is anticipated.' No man ever made a more true observation. A cow-keeper sold his farm and stock ; his successor found he was charged for one more cow than was really on the premises, and required an explanation. ' Oh !' said the out-going milk-merchant, ' there's the *blue cow*, with the *iron tail*, in the yard,—she gives half as much as all the rest. And, in an advertisement, for the sale of a dairy, near London, it was particularly mentioned, there was a good *pump* in the yard ! Thus, milk is watered wholesale and retail ; but, as double-watering would give it too azure an appearance, vulgarly called sky-blue, in allusion, perhaps, to the galaxy, or milky way, the retailers boil Spanish liquorice in water, and mix it with the milk, which gives it a sweetish taste, and brownish hue, and thus disguise their delinquency : some also add a quantity of *nice grated chalk !*

" Dr. Smollet, in his Humphrey Clinker, gives the following description of the London milk, in his time :—' But the milk itself should not pass unanalyzed, the produce of faded cabbage-leaves and sour draff, lowered with hot water, frothed with bruised snails ; carried through the streets in open pails, exposed to foul rinsings discharged from doors and windows, spittle and tobacco quids, from foot passengers ; overflowings from mud-carts, spatterings from coach-wheels ; dirt and trash chucked into it by orguish boys for the joke's sake ; the spewings of infants, who have slabbered in the tin-measure, which is thrown back in that condition among the milk, for the benefit of the next customer ; and, finally, the vermin that drops from the rags of the nasty drab that vends that precious mixture, under the respectable denomination of milk-maid.'

" Now, with regard to the Thames water (which is mostly drunk with tea, because it draws the flavour and strength of the leaves better than pump-water), whoever swallows it, quaffs what is impregnated with all the filth of London and Westminster, and charged with the contents of the great common-sewers, which disembogue a pretty particular d—d considerable quantity of filth into the Thames ; the drainings from dunghills and laystalls, the refuse of hospitals, slaughter-houses, colour, lead, and soap works, drug-mills, gas-works, the minerals and poisons used in mechanics and manufacture, enriched with the purifying carcasses of dogs, cats, rats, and men ; and mixed with the scourings of all the washtubs and kennels within the bills of mortality. And this is the agreeable potation extolled by the Londoners, as the finest water in the world!

" In 1827, there was a pamphlet published, called the *Dolphin*, a *brochure* which accused the Grand Junction Water Company of nearly poisoning seven thousand families (whom it furnished at so much per annum), in the city and liberties of Westminster. This little work soon caused inquiry to be made into the state of the water; and a public meeting was held at Willis's Great Room, St. James's, in April, 1827, to 'take into consideration the means of procuring a supply of pure and wholesome water to the inhabitants of the western part of the metropolis.' This meeting, among other resolutions, proposed to petition Parliament to appoint a committee to inquire into the supply of water to the metropolis, and which committee is now sitting.

" Yet, strange as it may appear, Mr. Brande, in the *Quarterly Review of Science*, says—'The result of several experiments upon the Grand Junction water leads us to believe that it is not objectionable, when its mechanical impurities have been separated; we have found none of that abundance of animal and vegetable matter which the said chymists had led us to anticipate. Carbonic acid, carbonate of lime, a little sulphate of lime, and some common salt, are the leading ingredients which we have detected, and these in no alarming relative proportions to the whole mass: a pint, which we have, of the water, yielding upon an average a grain and a half of soluble matter, and always less than two grains.'

" Here, then, we have the broad assertion, published under the authority of a celebrated chymist, that the Thames water, taken up, as it is, near a public sewer, contains little or no matter in solution, but merely minute portions of innocuous saline matter.

" It is well known, and can be attested by numbers, that this water, in warm weather, becomes quickly offensive.

" All voyagers agree that the Thames water, when carried into a warm climate, undergoes a species of fermentation, and emits a large quantity of fetid inflammable gas. Neither of these circumstances could happen, except from some animal or vegetable matter held in solution by the water.

" But, to come to more direct proofs of the same fact. A very simple chymical process, by which this organised matter may be detected and separated from water, consists in merely adding to the water a salt of lead, nitrate, or acetate (sugar) of lead, in solution, collecting the precipitate, and fusing it in contact with a fixed alkali—as common carbonate of potash. This may be done in a tobacco-pipe. By this process it will be found that a portion of lead will be formed, reduced to its metallic state. This, the merest tyro in chymistry knows, could not happen, unless an inflammable substance—that is to say, some animal or vegetable matter—had entered into the composition of the precipitate."

Mr. John Martin has invented a plan for bringing to London, a current of pure water, and, at the same time, materially beautifying the metropolis. Mr. Martin, who disclaims every motive but the public good, proposes that a stream be brought from the Coln (the water of which is excellent), to be taken about three quarters of a mile to the north-east of Denham, just above the point where the Paddington Canal crosses it; conveying it through Uxbridge Common and Furtherfield, near the northern side of Downborn Hill, close to the bank of the canal, near the south side of Massenden Hill, and so on, nearly parallel with the canal, to the reservoir at Paddington, the elevation of which would permit the distribution of the water, without the aid of a steam-engine, to all the western end of the metropolis, except the highest parts of Paddington and Marylebone. In order to combine other objects of utility, as well as ornament, with that of affording a supply of wholesome beverage, Mr. Martin proposes that a large bath should be formed, near the great reservoir, capable of containing one thousand persons, with boxes for the bathers; and he has marked out, upon a map, a route, by which he proposes to carry the stream under Grand Junction Street and the Uxbridge road into Kensington Gardens and the Serpentine, diversifying its course with occasional falls, and pieces of ornamental water. From Hyde Park he would carry it under ground to the gardens of Buckingham Palace, where ‘ the stream might be made to burst out as from a natural cavern, and spread itself into an ornamental water.’ Passing under Constitution Hill, into the Green Park, and ‘ giving motion and wholesomeness to the water stagnant there,’ he proposes that the current should be conveyed under the Mall into the ornamental water now formed or forming in St. James's Park, at the two extremities of which he would place fountains. Finally, he suggests that the stream may flow into the Thames at Whitehall Stairs.

With regard to the dolphin (i. e. the fountain-head of the Grand Junction), it is certainly very strangely placed in the river, off Chelsea Hospital, cheek by jowl with the mighty common sewer, and improved by a fine scum from gas-works, which frequently gives the water, in this part, all the rainbow-hues which Mr. Commissary Webb describes (though from other causes) on the Lake of Geneva. It may be, as it was with some natives, lately, who preferred rotten to fresh eggs, that the natives of Westminster may like water from such a source, better than the tasteless pure element; but, if they do not, the sooner they beg the dolphin to swim a little further up the stream, in all probability, the sooner they will mend their beverage. It appears there is nothing impossible with men of science of the present age; and thus, by the aid of mechanics, a large portion of the New River water is pumped out of the bosom of Old Father Thames, somewhere off Cheapside! How delightful it must be, during the summer heats, and before people go to watering-places, to sit in the heart of

London, and drink cheap champagne, cooled in the icy liquid from the dolphin pipe! A decided enemy to London water, however, declared that it was often so thick and full of foreign matter, that, instead of quenching fires when played upon them from the engines, it actually caught fire and burnt itself! He protested that a quart of it, from the Junction pipe, if forced down the throat, would perfectly supersede the necessity of the stomach-pump: nay, he absolutely swore that he, one morning, actually discovered a drowned kitten (very like a whale) in his basin of tea!!

"I thank you," said Peregrine, "for this your history of London water; and now pray let us trace our steps towards St. Giles's, which being agreed to, they set out on their voyage of discovery to that most delectable region, well known as the Holy Land.

"In order," said Mentor, "that we may obtain an admission to the meeting of beggars, or cadgers, as they are called, we must disguise ourselves, and be dressed in rags; and I will speak to the landlord of the Beggar's Opera, in Church Lane, and, 1 have no doubt, he will gain us an interview." Upon application to the worthy host, he furnished Mentor and Peregrine with such clothes as he was sure would completely prevent them from being discovered, and introduced them the same evening: they paid their *footing*, which was a gallon of beer each, and were then desired to take a seat, if they could find one, and join heartily in

The Merry Doings of the Jovial Beggars.

That little fellow on the right," said Mentor, "sitting on his go-cart, is the celebrated *Andrew Whitson*, the King of the Beggars, and one of the most dissipated of his class.    He is only two feet eight inches in height, thirty-three inches round the body, twenty-two inches round the head, and fourteen inches from the chin to the crown.    From the heel to the knee-joint, he measures sixteen inches, ten from the knee-joint to the hip-bone, and six inches and a quarter round the waist: he is double-jointed throughout, and possesses considerable strength, particularly in the hand: he always sleeps on the floor, and has done so, ever since he was eight years old; and, perhaps, in the course of his life, never stood upright.    His legs are curved, and have the appearance of thin planks, having no calves; the shin-bones were greatly protruded, but he usually covered them with a clean apron.    He has made much use of his time during his intercourse with society, and his mind is stored with information, scarcely inferior to others of his age, in similar walks of life.    He is now (1826), with the exception of Hossey, whom you see sitting on the table, with a pipe in his mouth, and a glass in his hand, and who lost his legs by the fall of some timber, in December, 1784, the only sledge-beggar in London.    Go-cart, Billies-in-bowls, or sledge-beggars, are denominations for those cripples whose misfortunes will not permit them to travel in any other way; the following are the most celebrated of this class:—

" *Philip in the Tub:* a fellow who constantly attended weddings in London, and recited the ballad of " Jesse, or the Happy Pair." Hogarth has introduced him in his wedding of the Industrious Apprentice.

" *Billy in the Bowl,* was famous in Dublin: he left Ireland on the union, and was met in London by a noble lord, who observed, ' So, *you* are here too?'   ' Yes, my lord,' replied Billy, ' the union has brought *us all* over.'

" *John Mac Nally:* who, after scuttling about the streets for some time, discovered the power of novelty, and trained two dogs, Boxer and Rover, to draw him in a sledge, with wheels, by which means he increased his income beyond all belief.

" The celebrated *Jew beggar*, of Petticoat Lane, who was to be seen there and in the neighbourhood, in a go-cart.    His venerable appearance gained him a very comfortable living.

" That beggar you see fiddling, is the equally notorious *Billy Waters,* the king of the beggars elect: he is a most facetious fellow, full of fun and whim, and levies great contributions on the credulity of John Bull, from the singularity of his appearance.

" The woman dancing is known as the *barker:* she gets her living by pretending to be in fits, and barking like a dog: she is well known about Holborn.    When she is tired of the *fit*-trade, she regularly goes over London, early in the morning, to strike out the teeth of dead dogs that have been stolen and killed for the sake of their skins.    These teeth she sells to bookbinders, carvers, and gilders, as burnishing-tools.    At other times, she frequents Thames Street, and the adjoining lanes, inhabited by orange-merchants, and picks up, from the kennels, the refuse of lemons, and rotten oranges ; these she sells to the Jew distillers, who extract from them a portion of liquor, and can thus afford the means of selling, at considerably reduced prices, lemon-drops and orange-juice to the lower order of confectioners. She likewise begs vials, pretending to have an order for medicines at the hospital or dispensary, for her dear husband, or only child, but cannot get the physic without a bottle ; and, when she can, she begs some white linen rags to dress the wounds with ; these she soon turns into money, at the old iron shops—the ' dealers in marine stores.' Very frequently she assumes an appearance of pregnancy, in order to obtain child-bed linen, which she has done nine or ten times over. Her partner is Granne Manoo, in a different dress to that in which he appears in public : he is scarcely out of gaol three months in the year. He scratches his legs about the ancles, to make them bleed, and he never goes out with shoes on his feet. He goes literally so naked, that it is almost disgusting to see him ; and thus he collects a greater quantity of habiliments and shoes than any other man ; these shoes he sells to the people who live in cellars in Monmouth Street, Chick Lane, Rosemary Lane, &c. These persons give them new soles, or otherwise repair them, and are called translators. That man at the back part of the room, has been in the medical line ; he is an Irishman ; he writes a beautiful hand, and gets a good livelihood by writing petitions and begging-letters, for which he obtains sixpence or a shilling each, according to their length.

"I was told," continued Mentor, "by the late Major Hanger, that he accompanied our present king, when Prince of Wales to one of these beggars' carnivals, as they were then called ; and, after being there some time, the chairman, Sir Jeffrey Dunstan, addressing the company, and pointing to the prince, said, 'I call upon that ere gentleman *with a shirt on* for a song.' The prince, as well as he could, got excused, upon Major Hanger promising to sing for him, and he chanted the following ballad, called the ' Beggar's Wedding, or the Jovial Crew,' with great applause :

'Then Tom o' Bedlam winds his horn at best,
Their trumpet 'twas to bring away their feast;
Pick't many bones they had, found in the street,
Carrots kick'd out of kennels with their feet ;
Crusts gather'd up for bisket*, twice so dried,
Alms—tubs, and olla podridas beside,
Many such dishes more ; but I would cumber
Any to name them, more than I can number.
Then comes the banquet, which must never fail,
That the town gave, of Whitbread and strong ale.

* It is seldom the beggars eat the food given to them ; and it is a well-known fact, that they sell their broken bread to biscuit-bakers, who grind it for the purpose of making tops and bottoms

> All was so tipsie, that they could not go,
> And yet would dance, and cry'd for music hoe.
> With tongues and gridiron, they were play'd unto,
> And blind men sung, as they are us'd to do.
> Some whistled, and some hollow sticks did sound,
> And so melodiously they play around :
> Lame men, lame women, manfully cry advance,
> And so, all limping, jovially did dance.' "

The landlord now whispered to Mentor, that it was prudent to leave the company, as they were about fixing their different routes for the ensuing day's business; accordingly, Mentor and Peregrine, drinking to the company, and wishing them "luck till they were tired of it," departed, both of them highly delighted with their entertainment; and, going to a private room, shook off their ragged *toggery*, having previously ordered a supper to be ready for them, which was served up, although in such a house, in a manner that would not have disgraced some of the first coffee-houses : it was agreed that " mine host" was to do them the pleasure of his company, and crack a bottle with them, while he detailed the *doings* of the London Beggars; of whose exploits, and extraordinary mode of gaining a livelihood, few people have any idea.

" I have made," said the landlord, " the history of London Beggars my particular study; and, from the situation I hold, I am enabled to glean many facts, which other people would feel it impossible to do; exclusive of my being possessed of, I believe, every work extant, relative to Mendicity. The beggar's calling, if not one of the most respectable, may, doubtless, be regarded as one of the most ancient. In every part of the globe where man is congregated, the inequality of his condition, the too frequent indolence of his habits, or the shifts to which human misery is occasionally reduced, will compel him to depend for his support on the generosity of his fellow-creatures, and even sometimes lead him to this disgraceful mode of existence. I think," continued the landlord, " there are seven thousand beggars upon the town, daily, and that they each beg two shillings a day, take one with the other,—that is, £700 a day. There are between two hundred and three hundred beggars frequent my house in the course of the day. I am particular as to whom I have to sleep here. In some houses, a fellow stands at the door, and takes the money; for threepence they have straw; for fourpence they have clean straw; and for sixpence, a mattress to sleep on. The servants go and examine all the places, to see that all is free from felony; and then they are let out into the streets, just as you would open tho door of a goal; and at night they come in again. They have a general meeting in the course of the year, and each day they are divided into companies, and each company has its particular walk; the whole company taking the most beneficial walks in turn, keeping it half an hour to three or four hours, as agreed on : their earnings vary much, some as much as five shillings a day. We estimate every one expends about two shillings a day and sixpence for a bed. They start off in parties of four and six together. There are many lodging-houses, besides public-houses; and, perhaps, the most notorious lodging-house in St. Giles's, was kept by the celebrated Mother Cummins. She had come over from Ireland about fifty years ago, in the twenty-ninth year of her age ; and, having entered into matrimonial bonds, she took ' a bit of a shed' in the most obscure part of the Irish regions, in the parish of Bloomsbury ; and, by letting a few beds in shares, without any scrupulousness as to the difference of sex of those who occupied them, contrived to put together as much money as enabled her to speculate more extensively in the accommodation line. She, at last, was able to make up forty beds, and the moderate terms on which she allowed a couple to repose, recommended half-pay officers, and others of that class, to her sheets very frequently. She always boasted of the security of property in her mansion, and she took the most effectual means of maintaining that character, by clapping a padlock upon the door of each room, as soon as she received her demand. The accommodations were furnished at an expense of from sixpence to two shillings per night; so that a bricklayer's labourer, and an Oxford student, sometimes heard each other snore. Mr. Cummins used to assist in the management of the concern. He was a check upon her liberality, which was really great to the poor half-starved wretches in the neighbourhood; but he never dared to interfere, in any serious degree, with her arrangements. Thirty years ago, Mother Cummins took a house in Pratt Place, Camden Town, in which she resided for the purpose of superintending the extensive washing of her *consarn;* and she regularly, every week, drove to town for the linen and woollen in which her customers were wont to repose. Her washerwomen were all decent Irishwomen ; and, upon the wash-days, she was the best customer of the Southampton Arms; but she is gone for ever. She died a most excellent Catholic, never having, as she declared on her death-bed, eaten a bit of meat on a Friday since she was born. After having been waked in the usual way, her remains were allowed the benefit of the air of heaven, all the windows in the house having been thrown up, and open they remained until the body was half way to its everlasting home. On the morning of her funeral, the neighbourhood of Pratt Place was in the greatest bustle. The solemnity which would have been observed in the case of another individual, was thrown aside for bustle and merriment, as if to hail the departure of a gentle spirit for more pure and delightful regions. Even her widower, whose health seemed to flag a good deal, and who was carried to his carriage in his night-cap, as if he was on his journey to eternity, through the hands of a certain important functionary of the law, appeared to partake of the general happiness. The procession moved along until it reached St. Giles's Church, where all the rookeries behind Meux's brewhouse seemed to have disgorged their contents. After the last duties were performed, several glasses of gin were handed into the mourning-coaches; and, towards the conclusion of the day, a general row took place, and many an eye was closed up, and nose distorted, before the police could interfere with effect.

"However wretched and depraved the beggars and inhabitants of these lodging-houses may be, they certainly were worse twenty years ago; for then there was no honour among thieves, the sheets belonging to the lodging-houses having the names of the owners painted on them in large characters of red lead, in order to prevent their being bought, if stolen, thus:

MARY JORDAN,

DIOT STREET.

STOP THIEF.

At this time, the pokers, shovels, tongues, gridirons, and purl-pots, of the public-houses, particularly the Maidenhead, in Diot Street (since pulled down), were all chained to the fire-place. The last cook-shop, where the knives and forks were chained to the table, was on the south side of High Street; it was kept about fifty years ago, by a man of the name of Fossell.

"Most certainly the major part of the London beggars are impostors. I know a man whose leg is in a wooden frame, and when a beadle or officer attempts to apprehend him, he runs faster than any one man in a thousand. He had also a habit of very ingeniously hiding his arm under his clothes, by which it seemed as if he had lost it, which he said he had; and this was his chant:

 ' My larboard eye I lost full soon :
 My starboard arm, on the glorious first of June.

He used to wear a black patch over his left eye, so completely, that it was impossible to detect the imposition, unless you tore off the patch, which he took care you should not do, as he was a strong fellow.

" 'There is also another fellow, who attends the markets, of whom there is a curious anecdote : one of the market-gardeners' wives, who was in the habit of giving him a penny every week, one Saturday, by mistake, gave him a halfpenny and a sovereign, instead of a penny : she soon discovered her loss, and immediately made inquiry for the residence of the beggar; and, at length, was directed to a very genteel house in a court : she doubted the correctness of her direction; but she knocked, and asked for the beggar by his name : his daughter answered, if she would walk in the parlour, he would wait upon her. In a few minutes the beggar made his appearance, very genteelly dressed ; she told him of her mistake, and he immediately went to a beaufet, and, taking down a wooden bowl, said ' If you gave it me this morning, it must be here; as this is all I have earned to-day—seemingly about fifteen shillings—and behold, there was the sovereign, which he handed over to the gardener's wife, saying he was sorry he had given her the trouble; but he never afterwards appeared at that market. Very few of the beggars who pretend to be lame, are so; the life of Bampfylde Moore Carew gives the public a pretty correct insight into the doings of the beggars.

" Many beggars get from ten shillings to twenty shillings a-day; and I have a fellow here who spends fifty shillings a week for his board: he is blind, and has been known to get thirty shillings a day. There is a portrait of James Turner, a beggar, who valued his time at one shilling per hour.

" We had an old woman who kept a night-school, for the purpose of teaching the children the art and mystery of scolding and begging; the academy was principally for females.

" Of the wealth of the London beggars, very many instances might be quoted. I remember a black fellow, who retired to the West Indies with a fortune of £1,500; and then there was the lame baggar, who used to sweep near the turnpike-gate on the Kent Road; he bequeathed £1,500 to a gentleman in the Bank, who had been in the habit of giving him a penny every day for many years, and who attended him in his illness. Jack M'Intire was another rich cadger; he left London, and died in a street in Glasgow; he was found in Bridgegate Street. On being searched, a bag was found on his person, containing bank bills and notes to the value of £238 : there were £225 in bills, and £13 in notes. A silver watch was also found beneath his clothes, if clothes he could be said to have, for certainly a more wretched and destitute-looking creature was never beheld. He was nearly naked, and his body bore every appearance of having been accustomed to all kinds of weather. His aspect was strictly that of an idiot.

" A Scotch beggar, whom I remember, named Curry, was apprehended by the police at Durham, in the act of begging. When searched, he was found to have securites for, and memorandums of various sums of money, deposited and lent, amounting to £900 and upwards !

" Perhaps, a Scotch lad, of the name of George M'Pherson, was one of the most adroit beggars, for his age, that ever walked London streets. He was born in Inverness about sixteen years ago, and his father, who was a tailor at Portray, in the Isle of Skye, dying four years since, Geordie was compelled to become a shepherd-boy, on the estate of Mr. M'Donnell, in Skye. Two years afterwards, through the death of his mother and his master, he was thrown friendless upon the world; and his uncle, a tailor, who lived in that notorious nest of profligacy, Essex Street, Whitechapel, wrote him to come to London. Here he had been but a few days when his uncle also died, leaving, however, nothing behind him to assist our hero, but his wearing apparel and twenty shillings.

" With this little capital, he commenced orange-vender; but

he had not followed this occupation long, when a lad, of the name of Dixon, who was about his own age, and who had been his constant companion since his sojourn in London, informed him he could put him in an easy way of getting money without working. This tempting offer Geordie accepted with gratitude, and declared himself entirely under the direction of his friend, who produced a *Court Guide*, and opened his plan of dividing the metropolis into districts, and picking out the addresses of persons within the division they chose to perambulate each day, upon whom they would call: the one in the character of a shipwrecked and distressed sailor-boy, in want of a few shillings to refit him for service; the other, as a friendless, pennyless Highland lad, come to London to seek employ, in danger of perishing for want, and anxious only to get back to Scotland.

"The scheme was tried, and succeeded beyond expectation, for they generally shared from 7s. to 20s. a day, besides gifts of old clothes, &c. Geordie said he had seen from 5 to £10 at a time in the possession of his companion, who usually secreted his money in a belt, worn round his body, next the skin. M'Pherson sometimes himself pretended to desire to go to sea, and the gentlemen who were prepossessed with his very respectful demeanour, and his seeming youth, piety, and innocence, occasionally accompanied their donations with a recommendation to the Marine Society, which recommendation he, of course, burnt at his earliest convenience. One of these he received from the Rev. Mr. Budd, the Chaplain to Bridewell, who had repeatedly before relieved him with money. From a Mr. Campbell, Geordie obtained money seven or eight times, and a friend of Mr. Campbell's presented him with a sovereign. Mr. Blades, of Ludgate Hill, and Mr. Simpson, the tea-dealer, in New Bridge Street, were among the number of individuals upon whom he had successfully practised. The gains of the day were dissipated at night in the flash-houses in Whitechapel, and Dixon, he says, is such an adept in his line, that he has long been enabled to ' keep his blowing.'

" So far goes Geordie's confessions; but no doubt he has observed the poet's advice—

' Aye free, aff han', your story tell,
    When wi' a bosom crony;
But still keep something to yoursel'
    Ye scarcely tell to ony.'

" We had a Lascar, who sold indecent ballads, for which he got imprisoned, and, when he was liberated, he found 'Othello's occupation gone,' and therefore took upon himself the character of a man who had been taken by the Algerines, who had cut out his tongue: this answered admirably for some time, until he was detected, when he left London; and the last I heard of him was in the following account, in the Nottingham Mercury:—

" ' A lady, of rather dingy appearance, applied to the Rev. Dr. Wilkins for a licence to be married. She blushed with all the sweetness of maiden simplicity whilst making the request, but grew extremely angry with the worthy doctor, when he kindly remonstrated with her respecting the expense, and recommended her to wait for the publication of bans. She boldly replied, that " she was come for a licence, and not for advice; and that her money was as good as any body else's." The rev. gentleman, still wishing to spare them from unnecessary extravagance, and hoping that the parties would think better of it, declined giving the licence till the morning, much to the chagrin of the disappointed *beauty;* for, oh! a sooty *Othello,* who had been a captive at Algiers, had won the heart of this blooming *Desdemona.* She loved him for the dangers he had passed; and he loved her for loving him. He, however, had told her no tale of strange 'ventures, happ'd by land and sea, and mountain waves whose heads touch heaven—he had poured no leprous distilment of soft flattery into the lady's ear—at least, so it may be presumed, for he was reported to be *dumb.* In fact, it was a negro, or mulatto, whom our readers have, no doubt, seen standing in different parts of the town with a placard on his breast, stating that he had been a captive in Algiers, where he had been deprived of his *tongue.* He had gathered £10 by begging, and love, having darted from the bright eyes of Miss Priscilla, in her sixteenth year, shot through the placard, and struck him in the heart. On Tuesday morning, these pair of turtles (we were going to call them *rooks*) received their licence, and were united in the silken bands of Hymen. But *Othello,* or John Smith's misery was at hand. The honey-moon was a new moon to him, that set in *darkness*—

'For scarce had the marriage been bless'd by the priest—
The revelry had not begun,

when the friends of the bride induced her, by their representations, to quit her liege lord, and go with them. But, mark the miracle! though he lost his wife, he found his tongue, and poured forth a flood of lamentations. The *inky* drops rolled down his furrowed cheeks, and in vain he sought the bower of his faithless *Desdemona;* he was not even permitted to take one short, one sad adieu. But even this was denied him, and he quitted Nottingham in despair, as some say, but others believe that, having picked up his speech, the magistrates might very naturally inquire where he found it. He is no doubt gone to practise impositions in some other town, and we hope all young damsels will take warning, and resist his seductive blandishments.'

" Certainly, the beggars must rank foremost in the catalogue of London impostors; and I will read you, from *Smith's Vagabondiana,* the history of some of the most notorious, which must convince you of the folly of people giving money to the beggars in the metropolis:—

" ' Among the cadgers, there are a number of fresh-water sailors

who never saw a vessel but from London Bridge; such an impos
tor was Jack Stuart, who used to travel about London, lead by a
dog. He died in 1815; his funeral was attended by his wife, and his
faithful dog, Tippoo, as chief mourners, accompanied by three blind
beggars, in black cloaks, namely, John Fountain, George Dyball, and
John Jewis; two blind fiddlers, William Worthington and Joseph
Symonds, preceded the coffin, playing the 104th psalm. The whim-
sical procession moved on, amidst crowds of spectators, from
Jack's house, in Charlton Gardens, Somers Town, to the church-
yard of St. Pancras, Middlesex. The mourners afterwards returned to the place from whence the funeral had proceeded, where
they remained the whole of the night, dancing, drinking, swearing,
and fighting, and occasionally chanting Tabernacle hymns. The
conduct of this man's associates in vice, was, however, powerfully
contrasted by the extraordinary attachment and fidelity of Jack's
cur, Tippoo, his long and steadfast guide, who, after remaining
three days upon his master's grave, refusing every sort of food,
died with intermitting sighs and howling sorrow.

" ' Stuart had a pupil, George Dyball, a blind beggar, of considerable notoriety: he sometimes dressed as a sailor, in clean
nankeen trousers and waistcoat; but, like his master, was no
sailor. Stuart taught him to mind, by allowing him to kneel at a
respectful distance, and repeat his supplications. Dyball was
remarkable for his leader, Nelson, whose tricks displayed, in an
extraordinary degree, the sagacity and docility of the canine race.
The dog would, at a word from his master, lead him to any part
of the town he wished to traverse, and at so quick a pace, that both
animals have been observed to get on much quicker than any other
street-walkers. His business was to make a response to his
master's " Pray pity the blind!" by an impressive whine, accompanied with uplifted eyes and an importunate turn of the head;
and, when his eyes have not caught those of the spectators, he
has been seen to rub the tin box against their knees, to enforce
their solicitations. When money was thrown into the box, he
immediately put it down, took out the contents with his mouth,
and, joyfully wagging his tail, carried them to his master; after
this, for a moment or two, he would venture to smell about the
spot: but, as soon as his master uttered, " *Come, sir,*" off he
would go, to the extent of his string, with his tail between his
legs, apprehensive of the effects of his master's corrective switch.
This animal was presented to Dyball by Joseph Symmonds, the
blind fiddler, who received him of James Garland, another blind
beggar, who had taught him his tricks. This custom of teaching
dogs to carry tin boxes in their mouths, is not new: it was a common practice centuries past, as is evident by this print, taken from
an original drawing, of—

A Beggar, of the time of Henry VIII.

"We had a Frenchman, a notorious impostor; he certainly was blind, and used to throw up his eye-balls, to convince the public that he was in darkness. He had a little smattering of English, and used to chant any stuff that came first in his head, but so contrived it, that the last words would seem to tell he had been in the battle of Waterloo. 'Poor fellow,' exclaimed a spectator, he has been in the battle of Waterloo;' 'yes, *my belove friends,* returned the mendicant, ' *de money, de money, go very low, too.*' His hair, which was sometimes bushy, was sometimes put up under his hat, or tied in a tail; and, when he altered his voice, he became a different character—the form of a decrepid vendor of matches.

"Charles Wood, the blind man, who used to go with an organ and a dancing dog, was a constant visitor here. This dog, which was certainly a most extraordinary one, he declared to be ' *The real learned French dog, Bob,*' and extolled his tricks by the following never-failing address: ' *Ladies and gentlemen, this is the real learned French dog; please to encourage him; throw any thing down to him, and see how nimbly he'll pick it up and give it to his poor blind master. Look about, Bob; be sharp, see what you're about, Bob.*' Money being thrown, Bob picks it up, and puts it into his master's pocket. ' *Thank ye, my good masters; should any more ladies and gentlemen wish to encourage the poor dog, he's now quite in the humour; he'll pick it up almost before you can throw it down.*' It is needless to tell you, that this man turned ' a pretty penny' by his French friend.

The following is a side view of this interesting little dog, exhibiting the true cut of his tail:

"There was a chap who used to get a vast sum of money daily, by pretending to be a poor mechanic, and he used to have a written bill in his hat, on which was written, ' out of employment;' this answered his purpose while he kept sober, but he used to get so intolerably drunk, even in the middle of the day, that he could hardly stand. Such are the effects of imposture, and the mischief of ill-directed benevolence.

"Joseph Johnston, a black, is another celebrated beggar : he first showed off on Tower Hill, and afterwards he ventured into the regular streets, and became *a regular chanter*. He built a model of the Ship Nelson, to which, when he placed it on his hat, he could, by a toss of his head, give the appearance of sea motion. He received many wounds while in the merchant service.

"Old Charles Mackey, the celebrated black beggar at the Obelisk, foot of Ludgate Hill, is well known here. He lost an eye, and used to tie his hair, which was almost white, in a tail behind, for his hat to rest on. Charley had a deal of money, and so he ought, for he had the best beat in London.

"But the most notorious black beggar was Toby, as great an impostor as any in London. He had no toes, had his head bound with a white handkerchief, and bent himself almost double to walk upon two hand crutches. Toby generally affected to be tired, whenever he approached a house where good gin was to be procured; and, perhaps, no beggar spent more money in the good things of this world than Toby : he would have his goose, or duck, or turkey, which the cadgers call ' an alderman in chains.'

"The most wicked and unfeeling beggars are those who hire and steel children, for the purpose of begging with, or sending to beg. The oldest they send out to beg, and are sure to beat them when they come home, if they do not bring 2s. 6d. per day; and for the use of them they pay 6d. and 9d. a day each. I know a woman who has sat in the street for these ten years with twin children in her lap, and it answers her purpose famously. A friend of mine," continued the landlord, " brought a child to the out-skirts of London, to put out to nurse, it being in arms, and her health being bad : a respectable woman, in appearance, took charge of it, and all went on well. After a period, my friend, being suddenly summoned to town, went to see a friend before she called on her child. While conversing at the street-door, an old woman with a child in her arms, implored their charity ; the moment my friend saw the child, its remarkable resemblance to her own struck her very forcibly : she gave a trifle, and the beggar departed : the child was no sooner out of sight, than a suspicion passed across her mind, that it must be her own offspring she had put out to nurse : taking a coach, she repaired to the nurse's house with her friend. She found the nurse at home, but not so her child ; in answer to her inquiries after it, the nurse, in much confusion, said, a neighbour had taken it out to give it a little fresh air. Placing herself at the door, and taking care madam nurse did not vanish, my friend's suspicions were confirmed by the return of the identical beggar she had relieved, with the child, clothed in rags. On an explana-tion taking place, it appeared the nurse was in the habit of lending out children entrusted to her care, to beggars, for the purpose of imposture, at so much a day, and that this sort of traffic was a common practice between beggars and nurses.

" Not long since, *William King*, an able-bodied young fellow, was brought before Sir Peter Laurie, charged with begging.

" A gentleman of the Jewish persuasion, stated that, in passing through St. Paul's Church-yard, on Sunday evening, he noticed the prisoner begging, with a child, about eighteen months old, in his arms. As witness approached, the prisoner gave the child a pinch behind, which caused it to cry out piteously. The child cried for its mother, and, as witness passed, he heard the man use a disgusting term to the infant. He watched him for twenty minutes, and, whenever a decent person was approaching, the fellow either pinched or shook the child to make it cry. A gen-tleman was feeling in his coat-pocket to give the prisoner some alms, but witness stepped up to him, and related what he had ob-served, and the prisoner was taken into custody. Three shillings and fourpence in loose copper were found on his person, although he had spent enough of that day's gains to make himself com-pletely drunk.

" ' This is better than working,' observed Sir Peter to the pri-soner, who endeavoured to avoid the subject, by vehemently deny-ing that he had pinched the child.

" The alderman committed him to Bridewell for a month.

" We have likewise," continued the landlord, " many gentry who frequent our houses, that are not beggars ; there are a great number who gain a living by picking up bones about the streets, which they sell to the burners at Haggerstone, Shoreditch, and Battle Bridge, at two shillings a bushel, in which half a bushel is given over, that being bone measure; and they make it answer their purpose very well. There are also the grubbers, or nail-gropers; of these there are few indeed, Mr. M'Adam having nearly annihilated their trade: they procure a livelihood by whatever they find in grubbing out the dirt from between the stones with a crooked bit of iron, in search of the nails that fall from horse-shoes, which are allowed to be the best iron that can be made use of for gun-barrels; and, though the streets are constantly looked over at the dawn of day, by a set of men in search of sticks, handkerchiefs, shawls, &c. that may have been dropped during the night, yet these grubbers now and then find rings that have been drawn with the gloves, or small money that has been dropped in the streets. These heroes are frequently employed to clear gully-holes and common sewers, the stench of which is so great, that their breath becomes pestilential; and its noxious quality on one occasion had so powerful an effect on a man of the name of Dixie, as to deprive him of two of his senses—smelling and tasting; and yet Ned Flowers followed this calling for forty years. But there is still a more wretched class of beings than the Grubbers, who never know the comfort of dry clothes—they are called Mud-Larks: the occupation of these draggle-tailed wretches commences on the banks of the Thames at low water. They go up to their knees in mud to pick up the coals that fall from the barges when at the wharfs. Their flesh and dripping rags are like the coals they carry in small bags across their shoulders, and which they dispose of at a reduced price, to the meanest order of chandler-shop retailers.

"Such, gentlemen," said *mine host*, "is a brief history of the London beggars of the present day; but it is singular that beggars have made no advancement in their trade—the 'march of improvement' has had nothing to do with them; for we find the same schemes of beggary in practice, a little before the reformation, as at the present hour; not a single new one seems to have been invented: the *soap-eater*, the *shamming of fits*, the *creating of wounds*, the *laming of arms, legs*, &c., were then resorted to, as now; so you see there is nothing new under the sun."

" ' Notwithstondynge they go beggynge from dore to dore, because they wyll not werke, and patcheth an olde mantell, or an olde gowne with an hondred colours, and byndeth foule clouts about theyr legges, as who say they be sore; and oftentymes they be more rycher than they that giveth them almesse. They bricke thyre chyldren's members in theyr youthe, because that men sholde have the more pitye of them. They go wepynge and wryngynge of theyr handes, and counterfettynge the sorrowful, praynge for Godde's sake to give them an almesse, and maketh so well the hypocrytes, that there is no man the whiche seeth them, but that he is abused, and must gyve them an almesse. There is some stronge and puysaunt rybaudes, the whiche wyll not laboure, but lyve, as these beggers, without doynge ony thynge, the whiche be dronke oftentymes. They be well at ease to have grete legges and bellyes eten to the bonis; for they wyll not put noo medycynes therto for to hele them, but sooner envemymeth them, and dyvers other begylynges, of whiche I holde my pease. O poore frantyke fooles, the whiche robbeth them that hathe no brede for to ete, and by adventure dare not aske none for shame, the auncyent men, poore wedowes, lazars, and blynde men. Alas! thynke theron, for truely ye shall gyve accomptes before Hym that created us.'

"In the year 1566, Thomas Hannan, Esq., published a very singular and amusing work, entitled, 'A Caveat, or Warning for Common Curseters (runners), vulgarely called Vagabones;' in which he has described the several sorts of thieving, London beggars, and other rogues, with considerable humour, and has collected together a great number of words belonging to what he humourously calls the 'leud, lousey language of these butering luskes and lasy lorrels, wherewith they bye and sell the common people, as they pass through the countrey.' He says, they term this language, *Pedlar's French, or canting*, which had not then been invented above thirty years. It will be proper, on this occasion, to mention only such of Hannan's vagabonds as fall under the begging class. These are, 1. *The Rufflers*, particularly mentioned in the stat. xxvii. Hen. viii. against vagabonds, as fellows pretending to be wounded soldiers. These, says Hannan, 'after a year or two's practice, unless they be prevented by twined hemp, become, 2. *Upright Men*, still pretending to have served in the wars, and offering, though never intending, to work for their living. They decline receiving meat or drink, and take nothing but money by way of charity, but contrive to steal pigs and poultry by night, chiefly plundering the farmers. Of late,' says the author, 'they have been much whipped at fairs. They attack and rob other beggars that do not belong to their own fraternity, occasionally admitting or installing them into it, by pouring a quantity of liquor on their pates, with these words—" I do stall thee, W. T., to the rogue, and that from henceforth it shall be lawful for thee to cant for thy living in all places." All sorts of beggars are obedient to them, and they surpass all the rest in pilfering and stealing. 3. *Hookers*, or *Anglers*. These knaves beg by day, and pilfer at night, by means of a pole, with a hook at the end, with which they lay hold of linen, or any thing hanging from windows, or elsewhere.' The author relates a curious feat of dexterity practised by one of them, at a farm-house, where, in the dead of the night, he contrived to hook off the bed-clothes from three men who were asleep, leaving them in their shirts, and when they awoke from cold, supposing, to use the author's words, "That Robin Goodfellow had been with them that night." 4. *Rogues*, going about with a white handkerchief tied round their head, and pretending to be lame. These people committed various other frauds and impostures, in order to obtain charity. 5. *Pallyards*, with patched garments, collecting, by way of alms, provisions, or whatever they could get, which they sold for ready money ; they are chiefly Welsh, and make artificial sores, by applying spearwort, to raise blisters on their bodies, or else arsenic or ratsbane, to create incurable wounds.  6. *Abraham Men*, pretending to be lunatics, who have been a long time confined in Bedlam, or some other prison, where they have been unmercifully used with blows, &c.  They beg money or provisions at farmers' houses, or bully them by fierce looks and menaces.  7. *Traters*, or fellows travelling about the country with black boxes at the girdle, containing forged briefs, or licences to beg for hospitals.  Some have cloths bound round their legs, and walk as if lame, with staves in their hands, as did this famous

Soap=Eater of the time of Queen Elizabeth,

who pretended also to have fits.  8. *Freshwater Mariners*, or *Whip-jacks*.  9. *The Counterfeit Crank*.  10. *Dommerars*, chiefly Welshmen, pretending to be dumb, and forcibly keeping down their tongues doubled, groaning for charity, and keeping up their hands most piteously, by which means they procure considerable gains.  11. *Demanders for Glymmar*, who are chiefly women that go about with false licences to beg, as sufferers from fire ; glymmar, in pedlar's language, signifying that element.  Many other

**classes** are enumerated in this curious volume, as *Priggers of Prauncers, Swadders, Jackmen, Patricoes, Autem Morts, Walking Morts, Doxies, Dells, Kynchin Morts*, and *Kynchin Coes*."

As every trade had its patron saint, the beggars made choice of St. Martin, who, we are told, having been supplicated by a beggar at a time when he was without money (no uncommon thing for a saint), drew his sword, and divided with him his garment. The cripples likewise have their patron, St. Giles, who, after he had retired to a cave in a solitary desert, was accidentally wounded, while at prayers, by a bowman of the king's party; whereupon, being found unmoved from his position, the king fell at his feet, craved his pardon, and gave orders for the cure of his wound; but the saint preferred remaining a cripple, and received reverence from the king, whom he counselled to build a monastery; the king did so, and Giles became abbot thereof. Our church of St. Giles, Cripplegate, is dedicated to him.

Mentor and his young friend now took their leave of the landlord, and agreed to pay him another visit; when he promised to lay before them further particulars of the metropolitan beggars, with the modes of punishment resorted to, from the earliest period.

The next morning, Peregrine had arranged to pay a visit to Julia Desmond, intending, previously, to consult his friend, Mentor; and, while waiting for him in his parlour, he amused himself by examining his portfolio of prints, among which was a view of

The Doings in Drury Lane Saloon.

and felt delighted with the accuracy with which it was delineated :*

* See page 99.

when Mentor entered the room, and the conversation turned on
the best policy to be pursued by Peregrine, with regard to Julia,
from whom he had received a letter, informing him that she had
had intelligence of the death of her father : "Then," said Mentor,
"now is the time for you to render the poor girl an incalculable
service, by interceding with her mother, to pardon her, and take
her once more under her paternal roof." "To tell you truth," said
Peregrine, "I have already done so; and I expect an answer has
by this time arrived for me, at Julia's lodgings." "You could have
done nothing better," replied Mentor, "and I hope your intercession will be attended with success. I envy you the happiness
and pleasure you must feel, if you can accomplish your intentions.
Go," said Mentor, shaking him by the hand, "go, and perform
one of the acts most acceptable in the eyes of God and man—that
of rescuing from ruin an unfortunate girl : let but such actions as
these be the constant tenor of your life, and then, depend on it,
you will feel that it is possible for a man to be perfectly happy in
this world ; notwithstanding all the ungrateful railings of dissatisfied creatures, who are for ever talking of the miseries of life ;—
yes, our life must be miserable, unless our actions are founded on
virtue. He who gives to the poor, with the hope that it will
alleviate their wants, must feel pleasure in so doing ; because it is
a virtuous action : but he who gives to the poor, that his name
shall appear in print, and he be blazoned forth as a charitable
man, does not receive happiness by so doing, because the action
was not founded on virtue : it was done solely to gain the admiration of the world, and not with the hopes of alleviating the
wants of the applicant. So, if I give alms *secretly*, to spare the
feelings of the petitioner, it is good,—it is a virtuous action, and
renders me happy; but, if I relieve any person in a public
manner, on purpose that all my neighbours may see and know it,
such an action will not produce any happiness, for its intent
was not virtuous. The sympathetic heart of the true Christian is
ever open to the tale of the distressed. "Charity is an emanation
from the choicest attribute of the Deity; it is, as it were, a portion
of divinity, engrafted upon the human stock; it cancels a multitude of transgressions in the possessor, and gives him a foretaste
of celestial joys. It whetted the pious Martin's sword, when he
divided his garment with the beggar, and swelled the royal Alfred's
bosom, while a pilgrim was the partner of his meal; it influenced
the sorrowing widow to cast her mite into the treasury, and held
a Saviour on the cross, when he could have summoned heaven to
his rescue. Its practice was dictated by the law, its neglect has
been censured by the prophets ; and, when the Lord of the vine-
yard sent his only Son, he came not to destroy the law, but to fulfil it. Other virtues may have a limit here, but charity extends
beyond the grave. Faith may be lost in endless certainty, and
hope may perish in the fruition of its object; but charity shall live
for countless ages, for ever blessing and for ever blessed !"

"These words," continued Mentor, "were written by Mr. Hamilton, a Roman Catholic gentleman; and yet there are many people who think it wrong even to associate with persons of his persuasion. But, thank heaven, the sun of intellect is fast dispelling the cloud of bigotry and animosity; and, I hope, the time is not far distant when persons of every religion will look upon each other as brothers, and children of one father. But go, my friend, on your god-like mission, and may it prosper! Meet me again in the morning, and we will fulfil our promise of dining with the worthy landlord in St. Giles's."

Peregrine soon arrived at the lodgings of Julia, whom he found absorbed in tears; and, as he anticipated, a letter from Julia's mother was waiting for him. He found it full of gratitude for his intercession, and good services rendered her unfortunate daughter, to whom she promised a full forgiveness and future protection. The news was received by Julia with profound silence; it seemed to deprive her of utterance; when, throwing herself on the sofa, a flood of tears soon gave her relief. Peregrine stood motionless, gazing on the bewildered Julia, with love, pity, and admiration: at length she broke the silence, by giving utterance to the grateful dictates of her heart, by invoking the Almighty to shower down blessings upon her deliverer.

After a short interval, it was arranged that Julia should return home by the next morning's early coach; and, every thing being arranged, by Peregrine furnishing her with the means of defraying the expenses of her journey (her parents having, some time before, removed above one hundred miles from London), they now sat down to dinner; after which, Julia gave Peregrine the particulars of the expenditure of the money which he had, on his last visit, given her. Among the items, was a trifle for an unfortunate creature, who had been in the London Female Penitentiary, "in which most excellent institution," said Julia, "she had been sheltered and protected, and taught fancy work, at which she excelled. In that asylum for the truly unfortunate, there are one hundred inmates: some are employed in spinning thread and worsted, making child-bed linen, and all kinds of needle-work; others in washing and attending the kitchen, to qualify them for service, when they leave the institution; which is not half so well patronized and supported as it deserves to be. It is, indeed, gratifying to reflect on the many girls they have reclaimed, and made valuable members of society: but it is a pity they have not funds enough to receive any thing like the numerous applicants."

Julia now arose from the table, and retired to make the necessary arrangements for her long-wished-for, yet dreaded interview with her mother. During her absence, Peregrine's mind was wholly absorbed on her; he felt, in spite of all his philosophy, that he loved her, that she had a dominion over him, he before was little aware of, and which he could not control.—He began

K 2

to imagine that, when she was gone, the world would be a blank
to him: he now felt there was no enjoyment in life, without
woman,

"The last and best of all God's works."

How dreary and lone
  The world would appear,
If women were none!

  Without their smile,
Life would be tasteless, vain, and vile;
  A chaos of perplexity,—
A body without a soul 'twould be.

  What are we? what our race?
  How good for nothing and base,
  Without fair woman to aid us!
What could we do? where should we go?
How should we wander in night and woe,
  But for woman to lead us?
How could we love, if women were not?
Love—the brightest part of our lot;
Love—the only charm of living;
Love—the only gift worth giving!
Who would take charge of your house?—Say, who;
Kitchen, and dairy, and money-chest?
Who but the women; who guard them best—
Guard and adorn them, too?
All that is good is theirs, is theirs—
  All we give, and all we get,—
  And if a beam of glory yet
  O'er the gloomy earth appears,
Oh, 'tis theirs! Oh, 'tis theirs!

They are the guard—the soul—the seal
Of human hope and human weal;
They—they—none but they!
Women—sweet women—let none say nay!

Julia had now entered the room; and Peregrine rose to bid her
adieu; and, taking her by the hand, exclaimed, "Farewell, my
poor Julia, may heaven protect thee! Happy indeed should I
have been, could thou but be the partner of my life—' to eat of
my bread, and drink of my cup;' but it must not be!" Julia felt
her fallen state, and, in bitter anguish of mind, took her farewell
of her protector, with a coolness that surprised him:

But such is woman! mystery at best!
Seeming most cold, when most her heart is burning
Hiding the melting passions of her breast
Beneath a snowy cloud, and scarce returning
One glance on him for whom her soul is yearning.
Adoring, yet repelling—proud, but weak—
Conquered—commanding still; enslav'd, yet spurning:
Checking the words her heart would bid her speak;
Love raging in her breast, but vanished from her cheek!

Peregrine proceeded home, and retired to rest; but sleep was
denied him; he arose, and wandered through the streets; at length

he found himself in the Borough; and, to employ his time, strolled into the Town Hall, when a countryman, from the neighbourhood of Folkestone, in Kent, entered the office, in considerable fright, booted and spurred, to request the assistance of an officer in apprehending three men, who had defrauded him of a crown-piece, a silver watch, and his great-coat, in the following manner:—The uninitiated clown in the wiles of the metropolis was travelling from his home, on horseback, towards a cornchandler's in Tooley Street, on business, when he was accosted in the High Street, Borough, by a man habited like himself, and also on horseback; who asked him if he was not travelling towards Tooley Street, from home, naming both places (a knowledge, doubtless, gained by some of his confederates on the road, known among such marauders by the flash term of "Magsmen"), and, answering in the affirmative, his new acquaintance joined his company, and, on their way down Tooley Street, invited him to take some refreshment at the Admiral Hood, in Tooley Street. They had scarcely, however, sat down, before two others, in travelling dresses, came in, and occupied an adjoining box. Some time passed in drinking; a conversation, premeditated, arose, which led to a boast on the part of the new-comers of being able to produce more money than the countryman; who, blind to their intention, deposited a crown-piece and his silver watch in the hat of one of them, as pledges for his return in a few minutes with more money than any of them, and left the house, with the intention of applying to the corn-chandler for the £30 he was indebted to him, with which to return, his first-found acquaintance kindly offering to go with him; but no sooner had they passed out of the front door than the other two left the house by another. Arrived near St. John's burying-ground, the unsuspecting man was suddenly asked by his companion, if he knew the man with whom he had left his watch and money, and, answering that he did not, was advised to hasten back, or he would lose his property, but to lighten himself of his great coat, which he threw off his shoulders, into the hands of his supposed friend, setting out full speed on his return to the public-house, where he arrived in breathless haste to learn the result of his folly, his great-coat sharing the fate of his watch and money.

The simpleton's tale ended, an officer was deputed to assist him in his search after the rogues.

So soon as this case was disposed of, information was given of such a barefaced robbery as, perhaps, never was surpassed. The preceding week, an honest farmer, from the eastern part of the county of Essex, attended, with some stock to dispose of, at Romford market. In the course of the day he met with a person who claimed his acquaintance, and mentioned circumstances that convinced the farmer they must have often met before. The farmer sold his beasts, and retired with his old acquaintance to a public-house, where they drank freely; and they both proceeded on horseback towards Chelmsford. On the road, however, they stopped to bait their horses, and had more drink, until the farmer was too much inebriated to proceed farther that night. They slept in a double-bedded room; and, early in the morning, the farmer being still asleep, his friend dressed himself in his clothes, in the pockets of which his money was deposited, paid the expenses of the night, proceeded to the stable, and was ready to mount the farmer's horse, worth forty guineas, leaving his own old horse and clothes with the farmer in lieu. Just as he was leaving the house, the farmer awoke: and, finding his *quondam* friend and his own clothes and money gone, he got hastily up, put on the clothes left for him, and came down stairs, in time to prevent as he thought, the escape of his old acquaintance. The knave faced him boldly before the landlord and servants, dressed and mounted as we have described, and succeeded in convincing them that the farmer was an impostor; this was easier done, as the parties were strangers in the house. The villain even proposed that they should ride together to Chelmsford, where his identity could be proved by many respectable persons. As matters stood, the farmer agreed to this arrangement, and mounted the rogue's old horse. They had not proceeded far, when the farmer's palfrey became so lame, that he could scarcely walk ; the thief having, while in the stable, driven a nail in the animal's foot. It was then that the cheat applied the spur to the horse he rode, and soon left the farmer to get home as well as he could, minus a suit of clothes, his horse, and about £140 in cash.

Peregrine was now about to retire, when his attention was called to the recital of a novel deception, which had just been practised upon a widow-woman, keeping a hatter's shop in the Walworth Road. A man, with the appearance of a working mechanic, entered the shop, and, desiring to be fitted with a hat, his wish was complied with, and the price agreed upon ; payment was made partly in silver, and the remainder with two supposed 5s. papers of half-pence, one of which was the following day paid to a tax-collector, and from him passed to a liquor-merchant, High Street, Borough, who, on opening it for change, discovered that two pieces of lead pipe, of the requisite length, with a half-penny at each end, formed the whole of the value, and, when taken back to the widow's, proved, to her cost, to be the counter-part of the other paper still in her possession.

Notice was also given to the officers, of a fellow being in town, who was in the practice of visiting, in the evening, various public-houses, imposing on the frequenters of them a tale of the deepest woe ; and, in order to excite their sympathy, offering them his shirt for sale, unbuttoning his waistcoat at the same time to show he had none on ; then, pretending that he was reduced to the most abject misery, he has generally been relieved. A few evenings ago, however, a man, who suspected he was an impostor, made him nearly tipsy, and the fellow then acknowledged, that he had obtained for himself and wife a very comfortable livelihood, and resided in genteel apartments, from whence he sallied every evening, resorting to the above artifice. In the daytime he amused himself *by selling religious tracts.*

An elderly gentleman now made his appearance, and stated, "That, on the preceding Saturday, a person residing at Oakingnam, Berks. was walking along Holborn, when he was accosted by two genteel-dressed men, who, by their insinuating manner, soon got into conversation with him, and at last they adjourned to the Three Tuns Tavern, in Chancery Lane, to procure some refreshment. Some wager was at length proposed, and, as usual, the *pigeon* produced his cash, which amounted to eleven sovereigns, which was deposited in the hands of one of his new acquaintances. All the difficulty was now surmounted, and the *gentlemen* soon found an excuse for leaving their friend for a moment, which they did, together with eleven halfpence, in a piece of brown paper. It is needless to say, that they did not again make their appearance."

The time was now fast approaching for Peregrine to meet his friend, and he hastened to the inn, where Mentor had been waiting for him. After the usual salutations, Mentor inquired as to the success of his affair with Julia. Peregrine informed him of every particular, and of his unfortunate regard for her. Mentor, with the feelings of a father, depictured to him the folly of keeping her in remembrance, as it was impossible for him to introduce her to his family, and strongly urged him to try to forget her; which the better to effect, he laid before him schemes of fresh adventures, which, he was in hopes, from the multifarious characters and variety of scenes that would be presented to his view, might tend to wean his mind from the present object of his affections. Peregrine listened with attention, and assured him he would follow his counsel.

They now agreed to visit St. Giles's once more, to dine with the worthy host of the "Beggars' Opera," and hear the finish of his interesting history. While proceeding along Holborn, they observed a decent woman sitting at a private door, crying most piteously, with two young children at her breast. Peregrine, putting his hand in his pocket, was about to relieve her, which a gentleman prevented, by telling him, that she was a notorious impostor; that her name was M'Gregor, and that, not long since, she was taken, together with another woman, with three children, before the Lord Mayor, when an officer stated, "That it was the practice of the prisoner, Isabella M'Gregor, to post herself near the Bank, or Royal Exchange, in the way of merchants, with her two children at her breast, and to assume the appearance of being in the extremity of illness or distress. The little girl at the bar, who was about twelve or thirteen years of age, was with her, as one of her children, and partook of the mother's extreme misery. At other times, M'Gregor would appear in fits, with her helpless little ones crying or screaming around her. The other prisoner,

Wilson, who was decently dressed, attended, to add to the interest of the scene, by assuming the character of a compassionate passenger, rendering all the assistance in her power, setting an example to the charitable, by administering pecuniary relief, and upbraiding the passers-by for their want of feeling. From the superior style of the performance, it was highly successful, and the officer had seen it repeated at different times and places in the city, the same children crying, and the same humane female passenger administering relief, or actively exciting others to relieve. At last, M'Gregor, the principal character, stopped to have a fit, by the side of the walls of the Bank, when he took the whole into custody, and he found, that the little girl of twelve or thirteen years of age, who pretended to be one of the children of M'Gregor, was the daughter of the feeling passenger, Mrs. Wilson.

"The Lord Mayor said, this species of fraud was increasing daily, and, as it was calculated to steel the heart against objects of real charity, he should commit them all."

Peregrine and his friend having arrived at their place of destination, dinner was served up, and, upon its being over, the landlord proceeded thus to dilate on the modes formerly adopted to prevent mendicity.

"By statute 12 Richard II., c. 6., every beggar who is able to work, shall be put in the stocks; and such as are unable to work, shall repair to their native places, there to remain during their lives.

"The statute 19 Henry VII. enacts, that all beggars be set in the stocks for a day and a night, without other food than bread and water, and then sent to the place of their nativity.

"By the statute 22 Henry VIII., persons unable to work were furnished with licences to beg, within certain districts; and, if they were found begging without such licence, they were to be set in the stocks for three days and three nights, and fed only on bread and water, or else whipped. Persons being 'whole and mighty in body, and able to labour,' and found begging, were to be whipped at the cart's-tail, till blood came, and then dismissed to their own districts. Scholars at the universities, begging without licences, to be punished as above. The licence was in these words:—' Memorandum.—That A. B. of London, for reasonable considerations, is licensed to beg within the county of M.'

"By the 27 Henry VIII., beggars offending, after the first punishment, were to be marked, by cutting off the upper gristle of the right ear; and, if found still loitering in idleness, to be indicted as felons, and, on conviction, to suffer death.

"At the commencement of the reign of Edward VI., it was enacted that any beggar, not being lame or impotent, after loitering or idly wandering for the space of three days, who shall not offer himself to labour, shall, on conviction, be marked with a hot iron with the letter V. on the breast, and shall be a slave for two years, and be fed on bread and water, or refuse of meat, and to be caused to work by beating, chaining, or otherwise ; and, if he shall escape while he is a slave, he is to be sentenced to be marked on the forehead, or ball of the cheek, with a hot iron, with the letter S., and adjudged to be a slave for life.—All masters of such slaves may put a ring of iron about their necks, arms, or legs, for safe custody.

" By the statute of 29 Eliz. c. 4. for the punishment of rogues and sturdy beggars, by which houses of correction were for the first time established, it is enacted, that all persons calling themselves scholars, and going about begging, fellows pretending losses by sea, fortune-tellers, procurers, fencers, bearwards, minstrels, jugglers, &c., able in body, and refusing labour, all persons whatever that beg in any manner, shall be punished by whipping till the blood comes and passed to their parishes, or committed to the house of correction. If any do appear dangerous to the inferior sort of people, or will not be reformed, they shall, if necessary, be banished from the kingdom, or otherwise be sent to the galleys of the kingdom for life, with pain of death, on returning from banishment. No beggars to be imported from Ireland or Scotland. No beggar to be suffered to repair to Bath or Buxton, for cure, unless he forbear to beg.

" Such were the means devised, in former times, to prevent public begging ; and, whatever may have been the other inventions of the idle to obtain bread, that of begging, in all its ramifications, was the most ancient : the fraternity of mendicants have resisted every attempt to dissolve their body, nor will they vanish, till the last day shall remove every living creature from the face of the earth. After the establishment of Christianity, flocks of Christians determined to devote themselves to the service of the Lord *in their way*, and work no more ; such were the pilgrims and friars mendicant. The monasteries afterwards, acting upon a mistaken idea of charity, gave alms, and fed the poor and idle indiscriminately at their gates : thus, a wretch might invigorate his body with the viands of the abbots and monks in the day, and pass the nights in attacks upon the defenceless traveller, perhaps often relieved in presence of the depredator by the blind religious. In vain have the monarch, the law, and the judge, from the days of the aborigines down to the present moment, exerted their authority and terrors to prevent mendicity.

"' I am sorry, gentlemen," said the landlord, " that I cannot now enter upon the history of the ballad-singers, or street minstrels of London—a class of persons possessing curious interest ; but, at a future day, I shall feel a pleasure in giving you all the information in my power on that subject." He now thanked them for their patronage ; and, conducting them safely to the street, bade them farewell. It was now night ; and, as Peregrine was returning to his inn, the description of London at midnight, by Mr. Montgomery, author of that exquisite poem, " The Omnipresence of the Deity," came forcibly to his remembrance :—

13

" How noiseless are the streets ! a few hours gone,
And all was fierce commotion ; car and hoof,
And bick'ring wheel, and crackling stone, and throats
That rang with revelry and woe—were here
Immingled in the stir of life, but now
A deadness mantles round the midnight scene ;
Time, with his awful feet, has paced the world,
And frowned her myriads into sleep ! 'Tis hushed !
Save when a distant drowsy watch-call breaks
Intrusive on the calm ; or rapid cars
That roll them into silence.   Beauteous look !
The train of houses yellow'd by the moon,
Whose tile-roofs slaunting down amid the light,
Gleam like an azure track of waveless sea !

The past !  Oh ! who on London stones can tread,
Nor shadow forth the spirits that have been.
An atmosphere of genius genders here.—
Remembrance of the past ! the storied nurse,
The ancient mother of the mighty, Thou
Unrivalled London ! sages, poets, kings,
And all the giant race of glorious fame,
Whose world-illuming minds, like quenchless stars,
Burn through the wreck of ages,—triumphed here,
Or ravished hence a beam of fame !   And now,
Imagination cites these mighty dead
In dismal majesty from out the tomb !

And who shall paint the midnight scenes of life
In this vast city ?—mart of human kind !
Some weary of woe are lapp'd in sleep,
And blessed in dreams, whose day-life was a curse.
Some, heart-rack'd, roll upon a sleepless couch,
And, from the heated brain, create a hell
Of agonizing thoughts and ghostly fears ;
While Pleasure's moths, around the golden glare
Of princely halls, dance off the dull wing'd hours ;—
And, Oh ! perchance, in some infectious cell,
Far from his home, unaided and alone,
The famished wanderer dies :—no voice to sound
Sweet comfort to his heart,—no hand to smooth
His bed of death,—no beaming eye to bless
The spirit hovering o'er another world !

And shall this city queen,—this peerless mass
Of pillar'd domes, and gray worn towers sublime,
Be blotted from the world, and forests wave
Where once the second Rome was seen ?   Oh ! say,
Will rank grass grow on England's royal streets,
And wild beasts howl where Commerce stalk'd supreme.
Alas ! let mem'ry dart her eagle glance
Down vanish'd time, till summon'd eyes rise
With ruined empires on their wings !  Thought weeps
With patriot truth, to own a funeral day,
Heart of the universe ! shall visit thee,
When round thy wreck some lonely man shall roam,
And, sighing, say,—' 'Twas here vast London stood.' "

Mentor visited his friend Peregrine early the next morning, when
they steered their course to Billingsgate, and arrived when the

market was a scene of bustle and business. They took their breakfast at a coffee-house on the spot, in order to have a better view of the busy scene before them. "There is not," said Mentor, " in any city of Europe, a fish-market that is so badly situated as this Billingsgate. The approaches, you must have perceived, are narrow and few, crowded with waggons and carts, and covered with dirt. It is not half so large as it ought to be, considering it is the only fish-market that has to supply the whole of the metropolis, now consisting of 1,400,000 persons; and it is placed at such a distance from the centre of the population, that one-fifth cannot conveniently go there to purchase their fish; and, that it should frequently be as scarce and as extravagantly high-priced as if we lived 100 or 150 miles in the interior, will excite no astonishment, after the statement of such a fact. Various remedies, for what fish-dealers themselves own to be a serious evil, have been projected. New markets, along the banks of the Thames, to supply the different parts of the metropolis, as well as the suburbs, for miles round, which receive fish from London, have been devised; but all the schemes are abandoned.

" The first record we have of the customs to be paid at Billingsgate, or Belin's-gate (so named after King Belin), is in the reign of Edward III.

" In earlier days, the monarchs took care that their subjects should not suffer from the avarice or combination of dealers, and therefore fixed the price at which commodities should be sold: the following are the terms on which some of the principal fish was obliged to be vended at Billingsgate, in 1296, the time of Edward I.: the prices of the present day are also given:

| | 1296. | | | 1828. | | |
|---|---|---|---|---|---|---|
| | s. | d. | | £. | s. | d. |
| " The best plaice . . . . | 0 | 1½ | —— | 0 | 0 | 6 |
| A dozen of soles . . . | 0 | 3 | —— | 0 | 18 | 0 |
| Best turbot . . . . . | 0 | 6 | —— | 1 | 5 | 0 |
| Best mackarel . . . . | 0 | 0½ | —— | 0 | 1 | 0 |
| Best haddock . . . . | 0 | 2 | —— | 0 | 1 | 0 |
| Best whitings, 4 for . . | 0 | 1 | —— | 0 | 1 | 6 |
| Best fresh salmon, 4 for . | 5 | 0 | —— | 0 | 3 | 0 per lb. |

" In May, 1699, Billingsgate was constituted a free and open market for fish, six days in the week, and on Sundays for mackarel, to be served before and after divine service.

" ' It has been repeatedly remarked,' says that late excellently-good man and magistrate, P. Colquhoun, Esq., in his Treatise on the Police of the Metropolis, ' that there is not, perhaps, a country in the world better situated to be plentifully and constantly supplied with fish than Britain, yet it is well known that in London fish is seldom seen but at the tables of the rich, and, excepting sprats and herrings, which are caught only during a short season, none are tasted by the poor, though fresh fish, of some kind or other, might be sold all the year much cheaper than butchers' meat, if no sinister arts were used to prevent it.

" ' As to fish brought to market by the fishermen, the fishmongers, in conjunction, employ persons, as the buyers at the market, to take up all the best fish, and then divide it among themselves, by such lots or parcels as they thought proper; so that, when it came to their shops, they enhanced the price at pleasure, and were sure not to be undersold.

" ' When a new fish-market was, in the year 1794, attempted to be established in Westminster, the trustees and inhabitants raised a large sum of money by subscription, and purchased fishing-vessels, to be employed solely in supplying this new market. Yet such was the influence of the fishmongers and the fishermen, by their interest, that, though they were bound down under covenant, with large penalties, they broke through them all, so that the market was deserted for want of a supply, and the subscribers ultimately lost their money.'

" Many have been the attempts to put a stop to these frauds and monopolies; but to little purpose.

" Unfortunately," continued Mentor, " these are not the only frauds practised in Billingsgate; for I find that, in May, 1827, a fish-dealer, who is much in the habit of selling stinking fish, was summoned before the Lord Mayor, at the Mansion House, to account to his lordship for having sold, or hawked about for sale, a quantity of that commodity. Mr. Goldham, the active superintendant of the Billingsgate Market, detected the defendant in disposing of some of what the latter called ' his live sole;' but which must have been dead for a considerable length of time.

" The superintendant assured the Lord Mayor, that he found great difficulty in checking the impositions practised by such fellows. The fish was exhibited. It appeared fast approaching to decomposition.

" The Lord Mayor said, that he could at once decide, from the application of no more than one sense, that the ' live sole' was unfit for the use of man.

" The defendant.—The Lord bless you, my lord! the fish is as fresh as any that ever swam. I just had some *on* it for my dinner to-day, and I never tasted better. If you'd only just taste it, you'll find it very good.

" The Lord Mayor said, that the appearance of the fish was quite enough.

" The fish had by this time been long enough in the room to reach the nostrils of all, whereupon the Lord Mayor made a remark upon the effluvia, condemned the fish to the flames, and ordered the defendant to find bail to answer at the sessions any complaint which Mr. Goldham might think proper to bring against him.

" Mr. Goldham observed, that the tricks played by the venders of bad fish were most ingenious, and many an economical lady, who attended the market early in the morning, for the purpose of purchasing a cheap and fresh commodity, returned home with a basket of as stale an article as ever beggar rejected. The cunning fellows, who were on the look-out for ladies of that description, generally painted the gills of the fish they had for sale, and stuffed them with new bowels—the unerring criterion of a recent and wholesome death. As soon, however, as the fish was dished, it was found, in every instance of deception, that there was a more extraordinary contrast between the body of the fish and the bowels than philosophy could account for. It was the practice, also, of the gentlemen of the market, to make their fish fat by stuffing them. In fact, they could alter the appearance of the inhabitants of the waters in such a manner as to make them look as if they were just taken from the hook, or out of the net. This very defendant had played a singular trick off upon a lady, at whose house a party were to dine. He exhibited a large Dutch plaice before her eyes. It was painted and polished outside, and stuffed well with the viscera of a cod fish and turbot. ‘ Bless my soul,’ said the lady, who was attended by a servant in livery, ‘ what sort of a fish is that? I never saw the like before.’ She then turned up the gills, which had just been rubbed over with an oyster-shell of bullock’s blood, and, finding that all was right, she asked the vender the name of the fish. ‘ Oh, ma’am,’ said he, ‘ that’s one of the most delicious fish in the world ; it is a thousand times better than a turbot.’ ‘ Why,’ said the lady, ‘ it is wide, like a turbot.’ ‘ It is a new fish, ma’am,’ said he, ‘ just sprung, and we calls it a *turbanet;* most people would buy this sort, but they can’t afford to do so.’ The lady, determined to astonish her company, purchased the *turbanet;* but how great was her astonishment upon perceiving, when the covers were removed, that she was sitting before a stale Dutch plaice, the smell of which was quite enough to deprive her of every one of her guests.

“ When salmon, turbot, soles, &c., have been long exposed to the air, their gills and eyes lose the rosy brightness which they had when first brought to market. In such cases, ill-principled dealers resort to artifice, squeezing, from a small piece of sponge or rag, concealed in their hand, bullocks’ blood into the gills, and about the mouth and eyes of the fish ; and this they call *painting.*

“ Cod, haddock, and whiting, are *blown,* to make them appear large and plump ; a quill, or the stem of a tobacco-pipe, being inserted into the orifice at the belly of the fish, and a hole being made under the fin, which is next the gill, the breath is blown in, to extend the bulk of the fish. This imposition is detected by placing the thumb on each side of the orifice, and pressing it hard, when the air will be perceived to escape.

“ When lobsters have been kept too long alive, they are called spent lobsters, that is, their flesh becomes flabby and watery, and indeed great part of it turns to water ; to make the most of it, however, and preserve the weight of the fish, the shell-fishmen plug up the holes where the water is likely to escape, with small pieces of wood; so, therefore, as soon as you open the lobster, the water escapes, and a fish weighing a pound in the hand will not produce more than eight ounces of flesh, and that not good. This they call *plugging*.

"The City inspectors of weights and measures, in surveying the Billingsgate Market, in August, 1827, discovered that a novel mode of swindling the public had been carried on there to a great extent, by the second-hand fish-salesmen, in the following manner: At the end of the scale beam a large hook was hung, for the purpose (as a casual observer would suppose), of hanging salmon to weigh, but, in fact, as it turns out, to give the scale a draught of about six ounces, which the hooks generally weigh, and the purchasers are cheated of that quantity in a pound. This system has been carried on with impunity there for a length of time, and numerous have the complaints been to the superintendant of the market, who never before had an opportunity of catching them in the fact: he took, in consequence, several standings from the guilty parties.

"It is not known whether there was a *clerk of the fishmarket* at Genoa, in 1664; but Sir Philip Skippon tells us, in his journal, that whenever a fisherman or fishmonger was guilty of taking or selling unwholesome fish, he expiated the crime, by standing for some time exposed in an iron cage, with his thumbs tied together behind him.

"Mr. Goldham, in his evidence before the House of Commons, May, 1828, relative to the supply of the metropolis with water, thus shows the cause of the falling-off of salmon, smelts, &c., which heretofore were brought in such large quantities to Billingsgate.

"He says, 'My engagement as clerk of the market is to ascertain the quality of the fish, to seize and condemn that which is bad, and to receive the dues, and regulate the market. I was yeoman of the market twenty-five years ago, and at that time there were four hundred fishermen, each having a boat and a boy fishing from about Deptford to Richmond, and the fish they caught were roach, plaice, smelts, flounders, salmon, shads, eels, gudgeon, dace, dabs, &c. These men were apprenticed to the business. They gained their livelihood entirely by fishing in the river. At that time I have known them to take ten salmon, and as many as 3,000 smelts, at one haul, up towards Wandsworth, and as many as 50,000 smelts have been brought daily to Billingsgate; some of these boats would earn as much as £6. per week, and as many as 3,000 salmon have been brought to Billingsgate Market in the season, caught in the river Thames. The Thames salmon were the best salmon, and would frequently fetch 3s. or 4s. per pound. There was no change in the quantity for the first ten or eleven years that I was yeoman. The quantities did not begin to fall off till about fourteen or fifteen years ago; every year since that period, there has been a diminution in the quantity; and now there are not two hundred men engaged in this fishery, and many of them are selling off their nets and boats; last week one man caught only twenty-six smelts, which he sold for 4s. 6d. I reckon that this fishery is gone. There are no salmon now. I consider it impossible there should be any. I have not seen salmon for these ten years, except a straggling fish now and then, caught high up or low down the river. I attribute the cause of the loss of this fishery,—first, to the docks. Near the West-India Docks, there was an inlet of ten or twelve feet water, where the smelts used to resort, but the gates of the dock were occasionally opened, and the water was let out, which was very impure, from the bilge-water and the effect of the copper-bottomed vessels; and this I consider as the cause why all the smelts have left this spot. This water is so impure, that, if a man falls into it, it generally proves fatal. Another reason is, that all the common sewers run into the Thames. There are now a much greater number of drains which run into the common sewers, as well as privies and water-closets: formerly, the scavengers used to carry away the soil at night, but that practice has of late years been much diminished. The filth that they used to carry away is passed by the drains into the sewers. In the river at Billingsgate, we have many Dutch boats with eels; I have been on board, and have seen 4,000 alive in the wells and coffs, and the next morning three-fourths have been dead, and the same proportion of loss has been sustained by all the Dutch vessels. When there is but little water in the river, they do not die so much, as the water is less disturbed; but on heavy rains, after a dry season, the filth which has been accumulating in the drains and sewers is washed into the river, and disturbs the general sediment; the water is thus rendered very impure, and contributes towards producing the above effect. Other causes of the increased impurity of the river, or its being worse than it formerly was, arise from the accumulation of filth brought down by rains after dry weather, the great fall at London Bridge, and the steam-boats stirring up the filth of the Thames, and keeping it in a state of almost continual agitation. Another nuisance is the gas: I have noticed it at twelve o'clock at night; the gas liquor is let out in the middle of the night; the river is often covered with it, having the appearance of an oily substance, in patches of three or four feet square. The tide ebbs seven hours, and goes about three miles per hour, and this will carry it on this side of Gravesend, and, as the tide flows five hours, this substance returns with the tide. As a proof of the impurity of the water in the Thames, the flounders which are brought up from sea-reach, Medway, &c., when they get to Woolwich, fly about in the wells of the boats, through which the water flows, and they turn up and die. Flounders are brought, some from above and some below bridge. I think they will not live in Thames water. They are taken out of the wells about Woolwich, and put on the decks, then into baskets, and brought up dry to market. White bait are obtained in greater abundance than formerly by poachers (viz., fishermen who have been thrown out of their former employ) using unlawful nets; it should, however, be observed, that white bait are taken at particular times of the tide, as they are a salt-water fish, and come and retire with the water, which is partially salt; on this account they are never known above Blackwall. It can be proved that many fishermen have been ruined by the change in the water.'

"I need tell you little more of Billingsgate," said Mentor, "only that it is famous for ladies, who, from time immemorial, have possessed great volubility of tongue, employing vast freedom and elegance of speech, blended with forcible and vituperative similitudes, which far-famed class of the softer sex are hence designated ' Billingsgates,' or more coarsely, perhaps, ' fishfags.' The French call their vulgar fish-women *poissardes*, who were foremost in action at the commencement of their revolution.

"In 1585, there was an ale-house in Billingsgate, where the *arts of cutting purses and picking pockets were taught scientifically.* It was kept by one Wotton, a gentleman born, and once a merchant of good credit, but fallen by time into decay. Here was a regular school for teaching youth the necessary dexterity of hand, which was done by hanging up a pocket and a purse, one containing counters, and the other silver, each of them being ' hung about with hawks' bells,' and having a little bell at top. The pupil was instructed to take out the silver and counters without jingling the bells, which, when he had accomplished, his proficiency was rewarded, by styling him a *nypper* and a *foyster:* the former term signifying a pick-purse or cut-purse, and the latter a pickpocket. This mode of instruction has been notoriously practised in our times, and was brought to a state of great ' scientific' perfection by Barrington. Shakspeare says, ' To have an open ear, a quick eye, and a nimble hand, is necessary for a cut-purse.' Among the most celebrated cut-purses, may be mentioned John Selman, a pupil of Wotton's, who was hung at Charing Cross, the 7th of January, 1612, for robbing a lady of her purse in the king's chapel at Whitehall, upon Christmas Day, in the presence of the king. There is a print of this worthy in a cloak and ruff, with a purse in his hand.

"Ladies, at this period, as at present, did not wear pockets; they carried their money, &c., in a purse, as the ladies now do in their reticules.

"Mary Frith, or, as she was generally called, Moll Cutpurse, was another celebrated professor of the art of cutting purses. She lived near Fleet-Street Conduit, and made it run with wine, on the return of Charles I. from Scotland, in 1638; she took him by the hand, and welcomed him home. In the civil war, the women and maids of every parish went, rank and file, with mattocks, shovels, and baskets, to work at the fortifications round the city of London: Moll was a superintendant over these women. She was a participator in most of the crimes and wild frolics of her times, and kept a regular correspondence with the thieves. Upon a sentence in the Court of Arches, she did penance at Paul's Cross, for wearing indecent apparel. Moll Cutpurse robbed the celebrated General Fairfax on Hounslow Heath: she was the first woman that ever smoked tobacco in England, and was also one of the women barbers of Drury Lane, of whose history I will, some day, give you many interesting particulars. When she found death had ordered her to lay by her pipe and pot, she bequeathed the greater part of her property to her nephew, with an order that he should not lay it out *foolishly*, but get drunk with it while it lasted. She died in 1662, aged 73."

Mentor and Peregrine now took their leave of Billingsgate, intending to return to the Castle and Falcon; but, being overtaken on their way by a violent shower of rain, they sheltered themselves in the parlour of a public-house, and in which room was a window, that gave them a view of the tap-room, where they saw

The Doings of the London Sharpers,

in fleecing a countryman of his money, by playing at cards. "Watch those knaves," said Mentor to Peregrine; "they are of the lowest order of public-house sharpers; frequenters of horse-races, cock-fights, &c.: many of them have run through a fortune in the early part of their lives, by associating with gamblers and sharpers (who, having eased them of their money, in return, complete them for the profession by which they have been ruined), set

19. L

up for themselves, put honour and conscience at defiance, become black-legs, are scouted out of even the gambler's company, and, as a *dernier resorte*, are obliged to take to resorting to low pot-houses, and robbing the poorest and most ignorant of society. That fellow, without a hat, standing behind the countryman, is what they call *working the telegraph :* he is a confederate sharper, and is looking over the novice's hand, and telling his opponent, by his fingers, what cards he holds; while another one is plying the countryman well with liquor. They are playing at Put, at which game there is as much cheating as in any. The game of put is played with an entire pack of cards, generally by two, and sometimes by four persons. At this game the cards rank differently from all others; a tray being the best, then a two, then an ace, then the king, queen, &c.

## Laws of the Game.

### I.

" When the dealer accidentally discovers any of his adversary's cards, the adversary may demand a new deal.

### II.

" When the dealer discovers any of his own cards in dealing, he must abide by the deal.

### III.

" When a faced card is discovered during the deal, the cards must be re-shuffled and dealt again.

### IV.

" If the dealer gives his adversary more cards than are necessary, the adversary may call a fresh deal, or suffer the dealer to draw the extra cards from his hand.

### V.

" If the dealer gives himself more cards than are his due, the adversary may add a point to his game, and call a fresh deal, if he pleases, or draw the extra cards from the dealer's hand.

### VI.

" No by-stander must interfere, under penalty of paying the stakes.

## VII.

" Either party saying ' I put,' that is, I play, cannot retract, but must abide the event of the game, or pay the stakes.

### TWO-HANDED PUT.

" The game consists of five points: they are generally marked with counters, or money, as at whist.

" On the commencement of the game, the parties cut for deal, as at whist. The deal is made by giving three cards, one at a time, to each player. The non-dealer then examines his cards, and, if he thinks them bad, he is at liberty to put them upon the pack, and his adversary scores one point to his game. This, however, should never be done. It is always best to play the first card; and, whether your opponent wins it, passes it, or plays one of equal value to it (which is called a tie), you are at liberty to put, or not, just as you please, and your adversary only wins one point.

" If your opponent should say, ' I put,' you are at liberty either to play or not. If you do not play, your adversary adds a point to his game; and, if you do play, whoever wins three tricks, or two out of three, wins five points, which is the game. It sometimes happens that each party wins a trick, and the third is a tie; in that case neither party scores any thing.

### Four-handed Put

" Is played exactly the same as two-handed, only each person has a partner; and, when three cards are dealt to each, one of the players gives his partner his best card, and throws the other two away; the dealer is at liberty to do the same to his partner, and *vice versa*. The two persons who have received their partners' cards, play the game, previously discarding their worst card, for the one they have received from their partners. The game then proceeds as at two-handed put.

" There are as many kinds of gambling as there are trades," said Mentor, " and they move in as many spheres, from the most noble duke or duchess, to the most abandoned chimney-sweeper; pretenders to honour and honesty, versed in various tricks and arts, by which many, among both nobility and gentry, have squandered away their fortunes in accomplishing themselves for the epithet of a complete gambler, or, in the true sense of the word, an expert gambler.

" If instances were necessary to prove the assertion, I could produce hundreds within my own knowledge, many not above a twelvemonth ago, that have been ruined by the pernicious itch for gaming. Young noblemen and gentlemen, just come to clear estates and affluent fortunes, have, in the hour of dissipation, been waylaid by gamblers, and, through their arts, frauds, and deceptions, have been stripped of the last shilling. Tradesmen and others, though not exactly in the same way, yet in ways similar to the before-mentioned, have been tricked by the gamblers of their all, the consequences whereof have been emigration, bankruptcy, or imprisonment. The lower class of mankind, having had their share of the supposed run of ill luck, or frowns of fortune, as they call it, and not knowing when they are imposed on, have become sufferers in the last degree: many of whom, in order to retrieve their losses, have had recourse to picking of pockets, shop-lifting, and such like offences, till, emboldened by success, and for some time escaping detection, they have then set ont on greater exploits, such as breaking into houses by night, robbing on the highway, &c., till at length they finish their career at Newgate : when they have declared, that the love of gambling was the first step that led them on to the commission of greater crimes, for which they now justly suffer.

" In this great city are several houses not only converted, but others built, for the assembly of gamblers, into which, however, none under a certain degree are admitted unless a friend of a subscriber is introduced as a novice in the art, in order to be initiated in those rules of fraud and cunning they square their actions by : his admittance may be effected at the expense of five or ten thousand pounds, and a qualification is given of his adeptness in the science, which will enable him to exhibit with eclat at Newmarket or York races.

" In short, there are so many gamblers to be met with in every circle about this polite town, that to give an account of them would take up more time than we have at present leisure to apply to it. I wish rather to point out the method of avoiding cheats and their machinations, than to portray the various modes of accomplishing their unlawful practices; and, as I have given some account of the most glaring, I hope you will be thereby warned against the delusive frauds and insinuations of the gambler of every denomination.

" You will perceive," said Mentor, " when these sharpers have cleaned out the countryman, as it is called, that they will then sneak off one by one, from the table, leaving the poor dupe minus all his property." In a short time, they perceived the countryman stake all his money, and in a few minutes his opponent very deliberately took all the stakes, and, putting them into his pocket, and he walked off, leaving his two companions; but they shortly after followed him. Peregrine, seeing the poor fellow in distress, asked him to walk into the parlour, when he told his tale of woe: that he had that day arrived from Lincolnshire, and on alighting from the coach, was accosted by one of the sharpers, who, hearing where he came from, claimed an acquaintance, saying he knew his father, and many other people in the village, upon which, said the countryman, ' I asked him if he could recommend me to a safe house to reside in while I remained in London, and he brought me here, where, after we had drank a pint of ale, in comes the two other men, one shortly after the other. They seemed to be all strangers, but in the course of conversation, one of them challenged either of the others to play a game at put, which the man who brought me to the house declined, telling me at the same time, he was sorry he had no money to spare, else he would play him, but that, if I was any thing of a hand, he would advise me to play him for a trifle ; and which, after some hesitation, I agreed to. I won,' continued he, ' the first dozen games, when it was proposed by the man I was playing with, to play for twenty pounds, which, as I had been so lucky, I agreed to, and then I lost the whole, leaving me only a few shillings : but what surprises me most is,' said the countryman, ' what has become of my friend who brought me here.' ' Friend !' said Mentor, ' why, my good fellow, they were all three arrant knaves and companions, and their operations were planned immediately you entered this house.' The poor countryman seemed lost in surprise, when he was told how he had been duped; he said what made the matter worse was, that he had been entrusted with the money by his father, to pay a salesman in Smithfield for some cattle he had bought. Mentor and Peregrine advised him instantly to return home, and congratulated him that the loss was no greater. The score for liquor, amounting to seven shillings, they had also left the countryman to discharge, which, as he had hardly as much left, Peregrine and Mentor jointly paid for him, for which he seemed very grateful, promising to return home, but lamenting his hard fortune the little time he had been in London ; he then took his leave. Mentor and his friend followed shortly afterwards, and on going along Lombard Street, Peregrine remarked, whilst witnessing the number of banking-houses, that money was the cause of every ill— the very seed of human misery, and that it was a mistaken notion to suppose it commanded happiness—that it brought with it, in general, a thousand curses worse than poverty. I remember reading," continued Peregrine, " a poem on the Pleasures of Poverty, wherein it says,—

Of all the plagues that torture hapless man,
　Those that relate to money are the worst ;
And ever since the coining pest began,
　Of mortal evils it has stood the first :
So hard to get—to keep, so hard to plan,
　The very metal seems to be accurs'd ;
That even those who have the most, but find
It leaves a lasting fever in the mind.

Else, why should thousands squander it so fast:
   Drink—gamble—try a hundred ways to spend it:
If 'twere good, they'd strive to make it last;
   Not mar their health—toil day and night to end it.
Some risk it wholesale on a desperate cast—
   Take shares in theatres, build bridges, lend it—
Others, as if they could not bear their sight on't,
Bury it, where the sun can shed no light on't.

Some, when they've got it, don't know what to do
   To keep it from the prying eyes of men!
Try ev'ry art to shut it out from view,
   Yet seem to wish to find it safe again:
Hide it in garrets, walls, and cellars, too,
   Like some black proof of crime, from mortal ken!
Which proves that its possession but disgraces,
Or else why put it in such secret places?

The wealthy scarcely know if those who speak
   Their friendship, act from interest or love;
They know not how the smile that decks the cheek,
   The touchstone of adversity might prove;
But they who kindly come the poor to seek,
   To sooth—to aid—regard alone must move;
They who have nothing in the world to spare,
May deem sincere the friendship that they share.

He who increaseth wealth, increaseth sorrow—
   And yet man lays up all his treasure here;
His joys, his hopes, still hang upon the morrow
   Nor often are more certain, nor more near.
'Twere better toil like slaves, or beg, or borrow,
   Than waste the day in care—the night in fear;
Dreaming of debtors, composition, losses—
And all the thousand terms of money's crosses.

All things alarm the money'd man—the wind,
   Raging at night, appals his soul with fears;
He dreads, when morning comes, that he shall find
   Barns, or old houses, blown about his ears:
If it be moonlight, then his anxious mind
   Thinks of his tenants—reckons their arrears—
And deems that he shall find them gone next day,
And neither goods nor chattels left to pay."

" Pr'ythee, my friend," said Mentor, " do not rail so against money. You must consider our ancestors had as great a veneration for this sort of *dirt*, as you call it, as the present age can possibly bear towards it, as you may find by the excellent virtues they ascribe to it in their old sayings: therefore, instead of slighting it, endeavour to get it, and never rail against it till you are assured you have enough to serve your turn. To despise riches when they are out of your power, savours more of envy than philosophy; but to seem not to value wealth when you have it in possession, is proof of generosity."

Peregrine and Mentor had now arrived at the inn, and, in the course of conversation after dinner, relative to the transaction they had witnessed that morning of the sharpers and the countryman, the argument turned on the frequency, increase, and cause of crime, in the metropolis. " From what has been said, as well as in consequence of the number of criminals and frequency of crime," said Mentor, " which have been voluminously dwelt upon by various writers, the uninvestigating inhabitant, or the inconsiderate isitor of the metropolis, might be tempted to conclude that within its limits there was no safety for property or life. But, although there certainly are numerous classes of persons, consisting of plunderers in every shape, from the midnight robber and murderer, to the poor perpetrators of petty pillage,—from the cultivated swindler and sharper, to the daring street pickpocket,—and although thousands of men and women, following the occupation of roguery and prostitution, daily rise scarcely knowing how they are to procure existence for the passing hour ; yet we submit that it ought to be matter of especial surprise that so little open and daring inroad is made upon our persons as we pass along the streets, or upon property exposed in carts, warehouses, &c., when the extent of the population, merchandise, and commerce, is considered. There are thousands of persons residing within this metropolis, of which it may be said, from the early and late hours, the night and day work necessarily pursued in so trading a city, that it never sleeps ; who have been for years compelled to pass along the streets without ever being robbed or seriously molested. Robbers lay wait for the timid and the unwary,—the dissolute and the drunken ; they seldom intercept the man that is steadily pursuing his course without intermingling with suspicious company, or passing along by-streets. At night, persons should always prefer the leading public streets. In them, there are few lurking-holes ; and besides, in cases of attack, there are almost sure to be passengers travelling along who will render assistance when they hear calls for help. Much depends on a person's own resolution and discretion. If he resist attacks, he will generally drive off interlopers ; and, if he keep the public roads, and avoid companionship in the dead hours of the night, he may be watched as a likely object of plunder, but he is tolerably sure of escaping robbery.

" Amidst so vast a population, and where there are so many opportunities for villains to practise their depredations, and screen themselves from detection, it is not surprising that so many rogues by profession are collected together, and that, out of a great number, so few are punished. To this great hive of human beings, the most vicious, as well as the most learned, will resort, as the best field of exertion. Mr. Colquhoun has enumerated and described eighteen different classes of cheats and swindlers, who infest the metropolis, and prey upon the honest and unwary ; besides persons who live by gambling, coining, housebreaking, robbery, and plunder on the river. Although there may be, as there undoubtedly is, great truth, that villains of such descriptions intermingle with honest, hard-working, or unsuspecting persons, we must again caution the reader against implicitly relying on round numbers and calculations in the lump, on subjects regarding which no human being has ever yet gained accurate information.

"Robbery and theft, in many instances, have been reduced to a regular system. Houses, intended to be entered during the night, are previously reconnoitred and examined for days preceding. If one or more of the servants are not already associated with the depredators, the most artful means are used to obtain their assistance; and, when every previous arrangement is made, the mere operation of robbing a house becomes a matter of little difficulty. This information should serve as a caution to every person in the choice both of male and female servants, since the latter, as well as the former, are sometimes accomplices in the most atrocious robberies.

"Night coaches promote, in many instances, the perpetration of burglaries and other felonies. Bribed by a high reward, the coachmen enter into the pay of nocturnal depredators, and wait in the neighbourhood until the robbery is completed, and then draw up, at the moment the watchmen are going their rounds, or off their stands, for the purpose of conveying the plunder to the house of the receiver, who is generally waiting the issue of the enterprise.

"The sharpers, swindlers, and rogues of various descriptions have undergone something like a classification by different writers; and, although such an effort must necessarily be imperfect, partially to follow the example in this place may not be without its use. The following is a list of some of the species of cloaked marauders that beset the unwary in this great metropolis; they deceive none but the ignorant and unthinking—those, however, afford too rich a harvest;—

"1. Sharpers who obtain licences to become pawnbrokers. These are uniformly receivers of stolen goods; and, under this cover, do much mischief.

"2. Swindlers who obtain licences to act as hawkers and pedlars. These men establish fraudulent raffles, substitute plated goods for silver, sell and utter base coin, deal in smuggled goods, and receive stolen goods, with a view to disposing of them in the country.

"3. Swindlers who take out licences as auctioneers. These men open shops in different parts of the metropolis, with persons at the door, usually denominated *barkers*.

"4. Swindlers who raise money by pretending to be discounters of bills, and money-brokers. These chiefly prey upon young men of property, who have lost their money by gambling, or spent it in extravagant amusements.

"5. Jews, who are found in every street, lane, and alley, in and near the metropolis; and, under the pretence of purchasing old clothes, and metals of various sorts, prowl about the houses of men of rank and fortune, holding out temptations to their servants to pilfer and steal small articles, which they purchase at a trifling portion of their value. It is calculated that fifteen hundred of these people have their daily rounds.

"6. Swindlers who associate together for the purpose of defrauding tradesmen of their goods. One assumes the character of a merchant, hires a genteel house, with a counting-house, and every appearance of business: one or two of his associates take upon themselves the appearance of clerks, while others occasionally wear a livery; and sometimes a carriage is set up, in which the ladies of the party visit the shops, in the style of persons of fashion, ordering goods to their apartments. Thus circumstanced, goods are obtained on credit, which are immediately pawned or sold, and the produce used as the means of obtaining more, and procuring recommendations, by offering to pay ready money, or discount bills. After circulating notes to a considerable amount, and completing their system of fraud, by possessing as much of the property of others as is possible, without risk of detection, they decamp, assume new characters, and generally elude all pursuit.

"7. Sharpers, who take elegant lodgings, dress fashionably, and assume false names. These men pretend to be related to persons of real credit and fashion, produce letters familiarly written, to prove intimacy, show these letters to tradesmen and others, on whom they mean to practise, and, when they have secured their good graces, purchase wearing apparel and other articles, and then disappear with the booty.

"Besides these descriptions of rogues who 'live by their wits,' there are villains who associate systematically together, for the purpose of discovering and preying upon persons from the country, or any other ignorant person who is supposed to have money, or who has visited London with the view of selling goods; who prowl about the streets where shopmen and boys are carrying parcels, and who attend inns at the time that coaches and waggons are loading and unloading. These have recourse to a variety of stratagems, according to the peculiar circumstances of the case, and, in a multitude of instances, succeed.

There are many female sharpers, who dress elegantly, personate women of fashion, attend masquerades; and instances have been known, in which, by extraordinary effrontery, they have forced themselves into the circle at St. James's. One is said to have appeared, in a style of peculiar elegance, on the king's birth-day, in the year 1795, and to have pilfered, in conjunction with her husband, who was dressed as a clergyman, to the amount of £1,700, without discovery or suspicion. Houses are kept where female cheats dress and undress for public places. Thirty or forty of these often attend masquerades, in different characters, where they generally realize a considerable booty.

"Mr. Randle Jackson, the worthy magistrate of Surry, has recently published a pamphlet, in the form of a report to the magistracy of that county, on the increase and extent of crime, with its causes and probable remedies. The convictions in England and Wales, we

20

are a   red by Sir Eardly Wilmot, were, in 1810, 3,158; and, in 1826, 11,095, almost fourfold in sixteen years: while, during the same period, the population increased not more than about one-third!

"The author ascribes the present apparent degeneracy of the people of England to the following causes—but there is one subject he has forgotten—viz. the diminished rate of wages, throughout the country, in proportion to the prices of human sustenance.

"Those causes will be found to differ much in their degree; and, although several of them will point out their own remedies, your committee will defer the consideration of those remedies until they shall come to their third or remedial proposition.

"Among such causes your committee rank the following—namely,

"The almost unchecked parading of the streets by the notoriously dissolute and abandoned of both sexes.

"The multitude of gin-shops.

"The want of due control over public-houses.

"The existence of unlicensed wine-rooms, flash-houses, and other receptacles for known thieves and loose women.

"Public fairs in London and its immediate neighbourhood.

"The utter fearlessness of punishment on the part of offenders.

"And, above all, the constant and daily addition of expert and hardened criminals, who are in a state of continual return from short transportations, from the hulks, the Penitentiary, and from gaols and houses of correction. On the remedies, the author thus expresses himself:

"'As far as the state of the streets contribute to crime, it can only be counteracted by a vigilant and efficient police, removing from them the openly abandoned of both sexes. To accomplish this, it might, perhaps, require some further legislative interference or exposition of the law respecting vagrants and reputed thieves, strictly to justify their apprehension, as well as a much more efficient night and day patrol than exist at present. But, when apprehended, whither, alas! would you send them? As the law stands at present, after a few short weeks of maintenance at the expense of the county, they return, for ever branded with infamy, cut off from all hope of employment, advanced in the knowledge of every thing that is bad and wicked, and left with scarcely any alternative but plunder or starvation.'

"Upon that source and nurse of crime, the multitude of gin-shops, your committee can say no more than that they concur in the opinion of a former committee, whose reports stand in the Appendix as ratified and confirmed by the sessions; and believe with them, that there is no hope of relief, but by limiting the sale of gin, and other spirituous liquors, to the bona-fide keepers of taverns, inns, coffee-houses, and ale-houses, as directed by the 16th Geo. II., cap 8, and to such of them only as shall have sufficient accommodations and stock of good malt liquor, for those who prefer drinking it; and who, instead of the present gin-closets in alleys and obscure places, will confine the sale of spirits to a tap-room of suitable size, in which the bar should, as formerly, be placed open to observation.

" ' The want of due control over public-houses, as well as the existence of unlicensed wine-rooms, flash-houses, and other receptacles for known thieves and abandoned characters, will fall generally under the consideration of public-houses, which it is proposed to defer; especially as a bill is now pending in Parliament which is said to have for its object a material alteration with respect to the authority of magistrates in granting or withholding of licences, when it will be important to consider the suggestions of different members of your committee on that head.

" ' Your committee have nothing to add upon the subject of fairs. They have no wish to oppose such innocent recreations as relieve the monotony of labour, or give joy to the youthful part of society. It is only when fairs are not effectually superintended by the police, that they become, as has been fatally experienced, the means of disorder, violence, and crime.'

" It would be idle," said Mentor, " to deny, that diminising the number of gin-shops, those nurseries of vice and wickedness, would be one of the efficient remedies; and, not only lessening the number of shops, but also increasing the price of gin, making it at the present rate of brandy; for, I ask any man, OF WHAT USE IS GIN ? Are there any benefits derived from it ? To be sure, it brings in revenue to the state—but ministers ought to remember it debases the mind of the people, and that it is the cause of such dreadful crime : ten murders out of twelve may be ascribed to the horrid habit of the perpetrators being drinkers of ardent spirits. It was truly said, some time ago, in the House of Commons, of the distilleries, that ' they take the bread from the people, and convert it into poisons !' I wish the ministers of this country would but visit the gin-shops of the metropolis, and there view the tremendous collection of misery and mischief.—Intemperance ! Poverty ! Villany ! Murder ! Desolation ! Good God ! what an assemblage is here ? how dreadful, and how real ! Can it be read without concern, or is it possible it should be seen with indifference ?* It was but last week," continued Mentor, " I lent a poor hard-working man, with a large family, a few pounds, to prevent his goods being seized for poor-rates ; and the very next morning, I saw many persons, who were in weekly receipt of money from the overseers of the poor, reeling drunk out of a gin-shop !—A people corrupted by strong drink cannot long remain a free people.

" The amelioration of the present criminal code has engaged the attention of some of the wisest men. Foreigners say the laws of England are written in blood, alluding to the frequency of our executions. That hanging is the worst use you can make of man, is acknowledged by many ; and, indeed, except in cases of murder,

* See page 17 of this work.

our religion does not warrant us in taking the human life.—
Mr. Harmer gives it as his opinion, that hard labour would
more effectually prevent crime, than the dread of an ignominious
death; for laziness is the mother of crime, and, to a lazy fellow,
death is far preferable to hard labour. England prides itself
on being a civilized and refined nation; yet no stranger would
think so, were he to witness the executions at the Old Bailey
(which, unfortunately, take place so repeatedly), and see with
what carelessness and disregard the people witness the dreadful
fulfilment of the law. Women—I almost blush to say it—generally are among the spectators; and they, together with the majority of the men and boys, leave the dreadful scene with as much
apathy as if they had seen the ascent of a balloon, or any thing
else of a trivial nature. Most certainly, a repetition of the sight
tends to deaden the feelings, and render the mind callous, instead
of its being a lesson or warning to prevent people from violating
the laws.— Indeed, it must be the habituating himself to such sights,
that makes the executioner, or Jack Ketch, as he is called, go so
cold-bloodedly through his business : for, if the sheriffs could not
get any body to do that dreadful work for them, they must do it
themselves; and then we should see how differently they would
go about it.

"The executioner is now called Jack Ketch; but this title is
not of very remote origin : for it appears that, in 1534, the name
of the public executioner was *Dun*, and the executioners, long
after that period, went by the same name; for Mr. Butler, 1663,
in his Proposals for Farming Liberty of Conscience, among many
resolutions, gives the following : 'To be delivered from the hand
of Dun, that uncircumcised Philistine.'—Dun's predecessor was
Gregory Brandon; and from him the hangmen were called Gregory, for some time. But this hero did not hold the office any
vast while; for, in 1662, Jack Ketch was advanced to that office,
and who has left his name to his successors ever since.

"The present Jack Ketch is *Ould Tom Cheshire*. 'Tom' is
nearly seventy years of age, and *looks* the character which he plays
in the great drama of the world admirably. He deduces his
descent from a family, of course, 'of the highest respectability,' in
the county of Worcester, and in his younger days served his
country, in the support of those laws which he now *finishes*, in
the navy.

"On the morning of an execution, while the wretched convicts
were ruminating, in the dark and cold solitude of their cells, on
the few minutes left to them of mortality, 'Tom' was amusing the
turnkeys, in a room near to the drop, in the detail of a few of the
incidents which have marked his eventful life, till the keeper entered the room, and a new halter was shown to the orator. He
examined it with a scrutinizing eye, and, untwisting a part of it,
applied it to his nose, for, no doubt, the smell of a well-twisted
rope is as pleasant to 'Tom's' olfactory nerves, as 'the sweet

south, breathing o'er a bed of violets.' Twice and thrice was the rope snuffed at, when, at last, he held it at arm's length from him, and broke out in the following eloquent cord criticism :—' Vy, I say, master, it smells o' junk, and b'en't twisted as a hauter should be ; now, here's one (making an extract from his pocket) summut like ; it cost me eighteen-pence. I've tried all them there ropes with my own weight, at a three-foot or three-foot-two drop, and they'll bear any chuck.' Then turning round, and addressing a respectable builder of the town, he added, ' I'm a droll hand to go loose.' There seemed to be a general coincidence of opinion in this remark.

" ' Tom' was asked how many of his fellow-creatures he had relieved of their worldly cares ?

" ' Vy, I've knocked off somewhere about five hundred and fifty, and never had a haccident, because I always carries a good rope. These three (adverting to the unfortunate sufferers about to be consigned to his merciless hands) makes three more, and then I've another at Oxford, and three more a' Wensday at New-gate,—so it's busy work.' A loud yell, which ' Tom,' no doubt, would call a laugh, marked the wretch's exultation at the thriving state of his trade.

" In the course of the morning, ' Ould Tom' had made an in-spection of the dreadful machine on which he was about to operate. He was asked whether he approved the plan of it ?

" ' I calls it a foolish sort of thing; it's like going up a church steeple to get a top on it.' It was intimated to him, for ' Tom has always an eye to business, that one of the culprits had a good watch in his pocket, which, by the bye, was not the fact, and was named solely to excite his unfeeling rapacity. ' Then it belongs to me, and as soon as he's off, I'll bone it. I don't much mind their clothes, and if their friends wants 'em, they shall have 'em for a fair price.'

" ' Tom' now thrust his legs nearly into the ash-hole of the fire-grate, and rubbing them with his hands (which seemed not to have come in contact with soap for the last year), with an expression of the highest satisfaction at his exploits, he entered into a long narrative of some of the principal executions at which he had at-tended :—' I did the business for Mester Fontilry (Fauntleroy) in style ; every body said I did it well ; and it was a good job, for I got above £3 for his clothes. I tucked up Thistlewood, and all them chaps, and held all their heads (another yell) in this here hand,' spreading out his arm. ' There was a lot on 'em ; they never complain after me !' ' Tom,' of course, judged this to be a palpable hit, and its excellence called forth a reiterated howl exultation.

In this heartless way did ' *Mister* Thomas Cheshire,' so he designates himself, proceed, till it was announced that the prisoners had finished their last devotions in the chapel, and then he hurried out to pinion them, with an alacrity which showed that his horrible mode of life was to him a real pleasure!

"I think," continued Mentor, "this delectable biographical sketch, must convince the most fastidious, that no human being could talk so unfeelingly, unless his senses and feelings had become so deadened by the continual practice of such a wretched calling; and therefore the more frequently a person witnesses executions, the sooner their feelings become blunt and callous."

"Enough of this subject," said Peregrine; "let us haste to the Borough, and keep good our appointment with your cousin." To this proposal, Mentor acquiesced, and on their road thither, their curiosity led them into Union-Street Office, where several decent-looking women were attending before the magistrate, for the purpose of making the following complaint, and obtaining redress :—After much whispering among them, one of the women, who was impelled forward by her companions towards the magistrate's table, dropped a low courtesy, requesting, on the behalf of herself and fellow-sufferers, to state a shameful imposition which had been practised upon them all by a barber. This person called at her house a few days ago, and, having requested an interview, which he said was of serious moment, was shown into the parlour. He commenced by entreating her pardon for the liberty he was about to take in asking her to take off her cap. She did as he wished, and, having a good head of hair, he praised its beautiful colour and softness, adding, that if he could prevail upon her kindness to permit him to cut it off, she should have a guinea and two false fronts to conceal that which she would lose in case she accepted of the bargain. Being in want of money at the time, the poor woman consented, and he immediately drew forth from his pocket a pair of scissors, and cut all her hair off close round. "See, your worship," said she, "see what he has done," and, taking her bonnet and cap off, exhibited her bare head, with the little left upon it by the barber, sticking up like pig's bristles. There was a general roar of laughter in the office, as the lady turned her body round, to enable the magistrate to see the manner in which the fellow had cropped her." She continued—"As soon as the barber had clipped her so closely as not even to leave as much over her temples as would bear a curl-paper, he thrust the whole of her hair into the crown of his hat, and ran out of the house, without giving her a half-penny for that of which he had deprived her.—She had not seen him since until that morning, when she was informed he had served many other females in the same manner."

Several of her fellow-sufferers here stood forward, and displayed their heads, shorn of hair, to the magistrate, all of whom were docked as closely of their hair as the former lady.—They all declared that, since their husbands had found out the scandalous way they had been tricked out of their locks, they had been quite miserable. The officer said that within the last few days many complaints had been made to him by respectable females, who had had their hair cut short off by a fellow answering the description of the one alluded to by the present complainants. If the magistrates approved of it, he (the officer) would apprehend the man, and he would also bring forward a score of women besides those present, to prefer charges against him. The magistrate expressed his surprise how women of the least particle of common understanding could allow their hair to be cut off under such circumstances. It was, he observed, a description of offence that had never before been brought under his notice; however, as the ladies had been so cruelly treated as to be deprived of so great an ornament, he (the magistrate) would, in the event of the offender being taken into custody, punish him in such a manner as would effectually check such practices. The women then retired, thanking the magistrate for his condescension in listening to their complaints.

Scarcely had these foolish women retired, when a poor fellow, a native of the Island of Sumatra, in the East Indies, appeared before the sitting magistrate, to solicit his advice as to the means of recovering a sum of money from the proprietor of a travelling caravan, for exhibiting him as a ' *Wild Indian.*' When he was engaged, the showman stipulated that he should allow his nose and ears to be pierced, for the purpose of introducing large brass rings into them; his mustachios and beard were also suffered to grow to an amazing length, in order the better to pass off for an Indian warrior, just arrived from the back settlements of America. He was to have twenty shillings a week, and support himself in victuals. For the first four months, he was paid pretty regularly, but afterwards he received his wages by *dribs* and *drabs,* until at length they were stopped altogether; and, at the conclusion of the last Bartholomew Fair, he was sent adrift starving, without being paid his arrears, amounting to between two and three pounds. He said he had been basely treated by Mr. Moon; for that person had made plenty of money by showing him up; and, at the last Bartholomew fair, between 12 and 1500 people paid their sixpences each to see him.

The magistrate asked him whether he appeared at the fair in the dress he now wore?

" No, sir," said he, in a very different tone, " I was then strapped up in a buffalo-skin, and marched up and down in the caravan with a large club in my hands, with which Mr. Moon told his customers I had vanquished and killed more than a hundred of my enemies. A tomahawk was also put into my hands, and with this instrument the showman declared to all that I had scalped hundreds of my own countrymen, with whom, he said, I had been at war a few months previous to the time I was then imposing upon the public.

The magistrate then directed him to the Court of Requests, where he could take out a summons against the person who was in his debt.

" This imposition of the poor Indians reminds me," said Mentor, " of the following anecdote, recorded in a York paper, January, 1827 :—A woman in the York poorhouse has given to the master there a strange account of herself, and of another female impostor, who formerly travelled with Cooke's equestrian troop. They appeared as men of colour, and in all the feats of the most dexterous horsemanship were not to be surpassed by any others of the company.   In addition to this, being dressed in male attire, and having their persons stained black, suspicion of their real sex was readily subdued, by an allowance for the difference of personal appearance which opposite climates generally occasion.   The real name of the woman now in the poorhouse is Ellen Lowther, but when with Cooke's company she called herself John Clifford—she is of eastern origin, though born in England; her grandfather, she says, was called Signor Rammapattan; he was brought to England from Bengal, by the late Lord Lowther, and, when they arrived in London, his lordship changed his name to Lowther; he afterwards resided in the north of England, and was killed by a pitman at Sutherland, when he was one hundred and six years and nine months old.   Her father, she says, lives at Tadcaster.   She represents herself as being but twenty years of age, and, having commenced her equestrian performances at five years old, she has been with the two Cookes fifteen years.   As might have been expected, this vagabond way of life led to vice and immorality, and the woman (alias John Clifford) was removed to the parish of St. Martin, Coney Street, in a state of pregnancy, and thence to the workhouse, where, on the 2d inst. " John" was delivered of a still-born male child.   The other woman, who passed for a black man, in the same company, went by the name of Pablo Paddington, and effected the deception so dexterously, as to have even deceived those about her; and, by assiduous attentions, gained the affections of a Miss King, who also travelled with Mr. Cooke.   The courtship thus commenced was carried on for some time, till scandal whispered in the ears of the unsuspecting fair one, that her favourite *Pablo* was too much a man of the world, possessing more of female acquaintance than was consistent with his solemn promises and plighted vows.   A lover's quarrel was the consequence;  and slighted attachment led to some estrangement of the lady's affections.   Misfortunes, however, often overtake the faithless, and the fair are sometimes, in those cases, too ready to forgive.   This was the case with the parties in question.   *Pablo* had his arm broken soon after, and pity again called forth the tender affections of Miss King, who, during her lover's illness, attended him with peculiar care.

Mentor remarked, that the public would indeed be surprised, did they know of half the impositions practised in the various shows at fairs and other places.   A man some short time since had an exhibition of a non-descript animal, found near Worthing, in Sussex, that had upwards of a thousand eyes, which, in fact, was a lump of stone, with thousands of exceedingly small fish

of the limpet species, adhering to it : this show pleased the cockneys for some time ; but, on Sir Joseph Bankes visiting the exhibition, he immediately discovered the cheat, when the extraordinary non-descript instantly disappeared.

On Mentor and his friend returning home, their attention was
drawn to a vast assemblage of persons in a church-yard ; and,
upon inquiry, they found it was a parishioner haranguing those
around him on

### The Doings of Select Vestrymen.

"The feastings of these (mostly self-constituted) bodies,"
said Mentor, "are certainly very scandalous. It is, indeed,
astonishing, how respectable men can so far disgrace themselves, in
guttling and guzzling at the parish expense. They must have their
Easter dinner ! their venison feast ! dinners on auditing accounts .
visitation dinners ! St. Thomas's-Day dinners ! &c. &c. &c. ! ! !
while they rigidly refuse the deserving poor in their workhouses,
any little extra luxury ! Such proceedings must for ever rank
among the most shameful ' Doings in London !'

" It will no longer excite wonder in the minds of people, why
some districts should be so heavily taxed with parish rates more
than others, when they peruse the following modest items of ex-·
penditure of a select vestry dinner, and which was incurred *in a
five-mile visit to a few pauper children!*

21, M

|                                        | £. | s. | d. |
|----------------------------------------|----|----|----|
| Dinner and desert for 18 *gentlemen*   | 9  | 9  | 0  |
| Lemon                                  | 0  | 1  | 0  |
| Ten bottles of Bucellas                | 3  | 0  | 0  |
| Two ditto of Sherry                    | 0  | 12 | 0  |
| Punch                                  | 0  | 12 | 0  |
| Four bottles of Champagne              | 2  | 8  | 0  |
| Soda                                   | 0  | 16 | 0  |
| *Rose Water*                           | 0  | 2  | 0  |
| Ice for wine                           | 0  | 2  | 0  |
| Twelve bottles of Port                 | 3  | 12 | 0  |
| Five bottles of Sauterne               | 2  | 0  | 0  |
| Noyeau                                 | 0  | 18 | 0  |
| Glass                                  | 0  | 5  | 6  |
| Tea and coffee                         | 1  | 7  | 0  |
| Three servants' dinners                | 0  | 7  | 6  |
| Waiters                                | 0  | 9  | 0  |
|                                        | 26 | 1  | 0  |

To which are to be added, for coach-hire and turnpikes   8  11  6

Grand total   £34  12  6

Such-like extravagances are, most assuredly, one of the causes of the vast increase of poor-rates, which have now grown to so an alarming a height. In 1688, the poor's-rate amounted to three quarters of a million of money; while, in 1827, the sum of six million, one hundred and seventy-nine thousand, eight hundred and seventy-seven pounds, eleven shillings, was levied in England and Wales for the relief of the poor.

"Select vestries are differently constituted: some are established by local acts of Parliament, with very extensive powers; others are self-constituted, while others are formed according to the pro-visions of Mr. Sturges Bourne's General Act: these last-mentioned being certainly most in the spirit of the British Constitution, because the select are annually chosen by householders, of a certain rate; and the reports of their proceedings are published: but the best of all are open vestries, like the respectable parish of St. Olave, Southwark, where the annual income and expenditure is printed, and a copy sent to every housekeeper.—This is as it should be; and the consequence is, the poor-rates are paid cheerfully, because it is certain they are not wasted on dinners for the officers, but the ut-most economy is used in every department. It would be well if some of the *great* parishes, at the west end of the town, were to follow the above example; but it would puzzle one that I could mention, to do so; and, if the inhabitants had but gained the cause they so nobly contended for, a precious mass of extrava-gance and negligence would have been brought to light.

"If any proof was wanting of the evils resulting from select ves-tries, it would be found in the fact that, in the county of Lancaster, where there are 213 select vestries, and £347,911. 18s being expended for the relief of the poor, in the year ending March 25, 1827, the poor-rates *increased* forty seven per cent. ; while, in Middlesex, where there are 17 select vestries, and £711,871. 16s. expended for the poor, the rates increased only ten per cent. Again, in the West Riding of Yorkshire, with 146 select vestries, and an expenditure of £388,730. 9s., the rates increased 31 per cent. ; while, in Kent, with 58 select vestries, and £392,253. 16s. expended for the poor, the rates increased only three per cent. And this is the case with nearly all the other counties, saving Berks, Southampton, and Suffolk, wherein the poor-rates have diminished in a small degreee.

" As the condition of the poor and the indigent not only constitutes an important feature in the state of society, but also in the character of the government under which we live, it would be interesting to give you some statements regarding the actual extent and progress of pauperism and mendicity.

" Poverty has been well defined to be that condition in society in which the individual has no surplus labour in store ; and, consequently, no property but what is derived from the constant exercise of industry in the various occupations of life : that is, the state of every one who must labour for subsistence. Indigence, on the other hand, is that condition which implies want, misery, and distress. Indigence, therefore, and not poverty, is the evil against which good government must guard. Where indigence exists, the burden of what are called paupers must follow ; or, which possibly is much worse, mendicity will ensue. Pauperism and mendicity have, of late years, become such evils as to call for Parliamentary investigation, in the hopes of checking the calamities by improved legislation.

" On the subject of pauperism, facts have been developed that excite attention and demand further inquiry. The number of persons relieved permanently, on an average of the years 1815, 1816, 1817, was 36,034; occasionally, being parishioners, 81,282; total relieved, 117,316 :—so that the number of persons relieved from the poor-rates appears to have been 11⅔ nearly in each 100 of the resident population—while the number relieved in 1803, was nearly 7⅓ in each 100 ; and that, while the population has increased about one-sixth, the number of parishioners relieved has advanced from 7⅓ to 11⅔ in each 100. The total of the money raised by the poor-rates was £679,284, being at the rate of 13s. 5½d. per head on the population, or 2s. 5d. in the pound of the total amount of the sum of £5,603,057, as assessed to the property-tax in 1815. The amount raised by the same rates, in 1813, was £471,938 ; being at the rate of 10s. 11¼d. per head. This, therefore, exhibits an increase of nearly *one-half* in the amount of money raised to relieve paupers, and 2s. 6½d. on the rate, per head, on the population. In such manner," continued Mentor, "have the poor-rates increased to their present enormous amount."

"While Mentor and Peregrine were thus conversing, the latter was agreeably surprised by a visit from a young friend, who had come to London to finish his education as a surgeon, and attend the lectures on anatomy. After the usual salutations, the conversation turned on the present application to Parliament, relative to the faculty being supplied with subjects for dissection. "I think,' said Peregrine's friend, "it is a disgrace to England, that there is no *public* theatre for lecturing on anatomy in London. Nearly all that is done is done secretly. It has been well said, in the London Medical Journal, that 'it is a remarkable fact, that, while the medical profession ranks higher in England than in any other country in Europe—giving to the honourable and learned practitioner in the healing art a more eligible station in society than he could enjoy in any part of the continent—yet, that the means of attaining that knowledge on which his science, his usefulness, and, consequently, his moral weight in the community, depend, are, in no other country, so dangerous in the pursuit, or so difficult in the attainment. Much of this certainly depends upon the system of exhumation to which we are driven, as a matter of necessity; and which, revolting as it is to the feelings, and contrary to the laws of the land, will always be viewed by the public with abhorrence. This practice, from its very nature, requires that the lowest and most abandoned should be employed in it, because none else will undertake a business so unpopular, and connected with such hazard. Accordingly, the common executioner is not an object of greater antipathy than the resurrection-men; who are, indeed, regarded by the vulgar as so entirely beyond the pale of the law, that they may be shot with impunity, if surprised in the fulfilment of their unhallowed calling.

"'Less than a century ago, the same horror of dissection which continues among us, likewise prevailed in some of those countries where public feeling has since undergone a complete revolution. In Italy, for instance, this was the case till the time of Benedict the Fourteenth. He, only a private gentleman by birth, by his superior talents and assiduity, raised himself successively, through different gradations, until at length he mounted the papal throne, where his zeal in the reformation of abuses acquired him the designation of the Protestant Pope. While pursuing his studies at Bologna, his native city, he had often witnessed the extreme difficulty and risk young men were exposed to in procuring bodies for dissection; and the subject occupied his attention after he had attained the tiara. The plan which he adopted was that of endeavouring to undermine the prejudice, by removing some of the circumstances which supported it; and with this view he issued a decree, by which it was prohibited, in express terms, to deliver over for dissection the body of any felon, how heinous soever his crime. All were amazed at this edict, but most of all the doctors, who beheld in it nothing short of an absolute prohibition of anatomy, and the consequent ruin of their art. In a short time after, there followed another papal decree, but extending only to Bologna, that no patients should be admitted into any of the hospitals without giving their own previous consent, and obtaining the concurrence of their friends, that, in the event of death, their bodies should be dissected; at the same time enjoining the utmost decorum to be observed in conducting the process. The effect of this decree, as might have been expected, was, in the first instance, to render the hospitals nearly deserted. No abatement from the letter of the edict was permitted, and, after a time, the necessities of the living became more imperious than their prejudices with regard to their treatment when dead, and the public charities became filled as before. In order to allay the apprehension of any unnecessary indignity to the body, the relations of the deceased were permitted to be present; while, at stated times, these dissections were conducted in public, and all persons engaged in scientific pursuits invited to attend. These judicious measures had the effect, not only of reconciling the Bolognese to the innovation, but of attracting students from every part of Italy; so that the neighbouring states were soon compelled to adopt the same method, or to behold their anatomical schools deserted. Might not some advantage be derived from the views of this enlightened pontiff? Is it not impolitic to constitute dissection an aggravation of punishment for the most heinous crimes? At all events, the law at present is imperfect, because the provision it affords is quite inadequate to the demand it creates. The legislature requires (through the medium of certain established authorities) that any one who practises the healing art shall have professed dissection for a given period, while it affords no means— that is, no sufficient means—of complying with this enactment; and, consequently, bodies are procured elsewhere—that is, by methods not only not countenanced by authority, but which are positively illegal. In other words, the enactments of the legislature can only be carried into effect by violating the law.

" ' The necessity of some reformation in this respect is too generally acknowledged to require that we should insist upon it: the great object is, to determine the means by which it may be best accomplished. It has been proposed, we understand, to give for dissection the bodies of those who die in the hulks, or similar situations, and of persons dying in workhouses, when they are not claimed; of all persons who commit suicide; to allow individuals to dispose of their own bodies before death, and to empower their executors, under certain circumstances, to do so afterwards. It is not easy, perhaps, to say what effect the latter of these methods might have. In London, no doubt, there are many who would dispose of the bodies of their relatives, if authorized by law to do so; but the first is calculated to foster, rather than abate, those feelings which, after all, appear to us to constitute the great obstacle to be overcome. It is scarcely credible that, if the idea of indignity attached to dissection were removed, those who, while living, submit their persons to an examination necessary to the restoration of health—who consent to undergo the most formidable operations—and who often present themselves, without shrinking, to the knife of the surgeon—should show such an abhorrence of the same treatment after death, when they can no longer feel it. Perhaps one of the considerations which influence the mind, under such circumstances, is the implied absence of the burial service and funeral rites; but were bodies supplied under the sanction of the law, there would be no necessity for these being omitted: indeed, the price paid for the privilege of dissection might enable the friends themselves to have these ceremonies performed, instead of their being done by the parish, against which there is generally a great dislike.

"'There having been a motion for the appointment of a committee, to inquire into this subject, and as the matter has met with the consideration it deserves, from some of the leading men on both sides of the house, we are inclined to hope that some effectual means may be devised for remedying the evil. The question, however, is by no means so simple as it might at first appear. The practice of dissection seems repugnant to the strongest prejudices of the people in this country,—a repugnance which is by no means limited to the lower classes of the community, but which at present pervades nearly all, and which has unfortunately been increased, if not originally produced, by dissection having been made to constitute part of the punishment of the most aggravated felonies, and thus associated in the public mind with crime and degradation.

"'It is matter open to discussion, and ought, in our opinion, to be made the subject of deliberate investigation, whether this part of the law ought not either to be abrogated, or rendered more efficient, by extending the penalty of dissection to all who have forfeited their lives. The latter would unquestionably produce the more immediate relief; but it is questionable whether the former would not ultimately prove the more beneficial, by removing a principal source of that abhorrence which at present exists against the examination of bodies after death.

"'Some who have spoken in Parliament seem to have rather odd notions on the subject. Thus, Sir J. Yorke is reported to have said, that one of the best means was, to allow the poor to sell their own bodies; and that a pauper would not resist the temptation o. £10, while alive, on condition of leaving his body, after death, to the surgeon. Does he really suppose that any surgeon would be such a noodle as to pay £10 on these conditions, and to purchase of the living man the reversion of his body? Does Sir J. Yorke intend that we should buy a poor man alive, and kill him when we want him? We can only make the bargain with a healthy man (the objection to which is, that they may die at a distant period) or with a sick man who might recover, or with one dying of a fatal disease, the effect of which on the patient's mind would probably be of the most unfavourable nature.

"'It appears to us, that the only rational method would be, to appoint a committee to call evidence, and investigate the matter coolly, aided by the opinions of those best able to assist them.'

" Certain it is, the surgeons will, in ' spite of old Harry,' have subjects for dissection." " And it is very proper they should," rejoined Mentor; " all the precautions with patent coffins will never prevent it. I remember the riots which took place in London, in 1795, upon this very subject. Twenty of the parishes of the metropolis and its neighbourhood coalesced to prevent the robbery of churchyards. They set forth the dreadful scene that had just taken place in Lambeth burial-ground. One night three men were discovered conveying away five human bodies in three sacks. In consequence of this, people of all descriptions, whose friends had been recently buried there, assembled on the ground the next morning, and demanded to be allowed to examine the graves. This being refused, a furious contest took' place between the populace and the peace-officers, who were soon overpowered. The assailants now rushed into the burial-ground, and began to tear open the graves, when an immense number of the coffins were found to be empty. Many of the people, in a kind of phrenzy, snatched up the empty coffins of their deceased relations, and ran with them through the neighbouring streets. The committee proceeded to state, that they had ascertained that the grave-digger was the chief robber; and that eight eminent surgeons were in the habit of buying these bodies : that they retained in their pay fifteen body-stealers, and five shillings were given to the grave-diggers for each corpse they permitted to be taken. Thirty burying-grounds had been robbed. The surgeons paid for each adult corpse, if not green or putrid, two guineas and a crown; and for persons under age, six shillings for the first foot, and ninepence per inch for all above it. One eminent quack, who styled himself an Articulator, was proved to have made a wanton use of these bodies, by using the skulls for nail-boxes, soap-trays, &c., and his child had an infant's skeleton to play with as a doll. The committee also stated, that much of the human flesh had been converted into an adipose substance resembling spermaceti, and burnt as candles, whilst some had been converted into soap.

" It is not long since," continued Mentor, " that an extraordinary attempt was thus made to steal a dead body for the surgeons. In April, 1827, a gentleman of very respectable appearance was proceeding through Russell Square, when he was seized with a fit of apoplexy, which caused him to fall down in a state of insensibility. A crowd of persons immediately surrounded him, and rendered every assistance, and ultimately conveyed him to the house of a medical gentleman in the neighbourhood, where, on examination, he was found to be quite dead. The body was conveyed to St. Giles's workhouse, where, on being searched, a pair of silver spectacles, and nine shillings in silver, were found in the pockets, but nothing whatever to lead to a discovery of who or what he was. The parish-officers instantly forwarded information of the circumstance to the coroner, to hold an inquest, and caused bills to be printed and circulated, giving an accurate description of the deceased's dress and person, in order that it might be claimed by his friends. The coroner attended, and the jury, after investigating the matter, returned a verdict of 'Died by the visitation of God.'

" Immediately after the inquest, a female of respectable demeanour called at the workhouse, in a state of the most anxious agitation, and requested to have a sight of the deceased's body, stating that she felt assured that it was her uncle, who had been missing from his home since Wednesday morning last. Her request was of course immediately granted, and, on entering the dead-house, where the body lay, on beholding the countenance, she gave a shriek, and exclaimed, ' My uncle, my dear uncle !' and, embracing the body, she caressed it repeatedly, and appeared to be almost heart-broken with grief. Indeed, the officers had considerable difficulty in causing her to quit the place, prior to doing which, she steadfastly gazed on the remains of her ' dear uncle,' and at length was obliged to be supported from the place. When in the governor's room, she, with the most urgent entreaties, requested that the body might be sent home immediately, as his family were in the utmost distress on account of the melancholy circumstance. This, however, was prudently avoided, until proper inquiries were made; and, on being asked for the address of the deceased, she said, ' Mr. Williams, Blackfriars Road.' Previous to her leaving the place, a young man, who had to transact some business at the workhouse, entered, and, hearing that the lady had made application for a dead body in the workhouse, his mind was instantly struck with suspicion, as he identified her as the person whom he had seen a short time before conversing at the corner of Belton Street, Long Acre, with as notorious a resurrection-man as any in London; and he intimated his suspicions to the parish-officers, who determined on being on the alert. The beadle, and the young man who made the discovery, repaired to Blackfriars Road, when, on making inquiry, they found that it was kept by an honest blacksmith, who knew nothing at all of Mr. Williams, or the death of any of his relations. They, however, traced the applicant to a brothel in Dawson Street, Kent Road, and ascertained that she was a complete adept in such practices, and was connected with a gang of resurrection-men, and that her husband had been transported. This information they imagined to be sufficiently strong to warrant the detention of the woman, until the matter was thoroughly investigated, as it was anticipated that she could be traced, so as to link her with an organized gang of ' body-snatchers,' who have indulged in similar practices with impunity, through the medium of her assistance. In the course of the investigation, several well-known resurrection-men were observed lurking about the neighbourhood, no doubt waiting to ascertain the result of their fair colleague's application; and, on being spoken to upon the subject, by one of the beadles, they attacked him with the most violent abuse. It is presumed that, had she gained her point with the parish-officers, by having their consent to take the body away, she would have called in her companions, who were in readiness, and the body would have been consigned *instanter* to one of the dissecting-rooms of a celebrated anatomist, not far distant from St. Giles's, at the west-end of the town."

"As you are talking of body-stealing," said Peregrine, "I will read you that clever *jeu d'esprit*, written by Mr. Hood, on the subject. It is an admirable burlesque parody on Mallet's poem of William and Mary:—

' 'Twas in the middle of the night,
  To sleep young William tried;
When Mary's ghost came stealing in,
  And stood at his bedside.

"Oh! William dear! Oh! William, dear,
  My rest eternal ceases;
Alas! my everlasting peace
  Is broken into pieces.

I thought the last of all my cares
  Would end with my last minute;
But, though I went to my long home,
  I did'nt stay long in it.

The body-snatchers they have come
  And made a snatch at me:
It's very hard these kind of men
  Won't let a body be.

You thought that I was buried deep,
  Quite decent-like, and chary;
But from her grave in Mary-Bonne,
  They've come and boned your Mary.

The arm that used to take your arm,
  Is took to Dr. *Vyse*;
And both my legs are gone to walk
  The hospital at *Guy's*.

I vow'd that you should have my hand,
  But fate gives us denial;
You'll find it there at Dr. *Bell's*,
  In spirits and a vial.

As for my feet—the little feet,
  You used to call so pretty,
There's one I know, in Bedford Row,
  The other's in the city.

I can't tell where my head is gone,
  But Doctor *Carpue* can;
As for my trunk, it's all pack'd up
  To go by Pickford's van.

I wish you'd go to Mr. P.
  And save me such a ride—
I don't half like the outside place
  They've took for my inside.

> The cock it crows—I must be gone ;
>   My William we must part ;
> But I'll be your's in death, although
>   *Sir Astley* has my heart.
>
> Don't go to weep upon my grave,
>   And think that there I be :
> They hav'nt left an atom there
>   Of my anatomie.' "

" Instances have been known," said Peregrine's friend, " o persons having voluntarily sold their bodies to be anatomized, after their death ; particularly one James Brooke, who, in 1736, sent the following letter to Mr. Goldwyr, surgeon, of Salisbury, which was found among that gentleman's papers :—

' *To Mr. Edward Goldwyr, at his house in the close of Salisbury.*

' Sir,—Being informed you are the only surgeon in this city (or county) that anatomises men, and I being under the unhappy circumstance, and in a very mean condition, would gladly live as long as I can, but by all appearance I am to be executed next March, having no friends on earth that will speak a word to save my life, nor send me a morsel of bread to keep life and soul together, until the fatal day : so, if you will vouchsafe to come hither, I will gladly sell my body (being whole and sound), to be ordered at your discretion ; knowing that it will rise at the general resurrection, as well from your house, as from the grave. Your answer will highly oblige your's, &c.

'                                           ' James Brooke.'

' *Fisherton-Anger Goal,*
    *October 3, 1736.*'

" But, perhaps one of the most extraordinary circumstances transpired in London, a few months since : it was this—' A poor fellow of the name of John, who used to attend horses, died in distress ; and his faithful and affectionate *rib*, not having the means of burying him, hit upon a notable expedient to save herself the trouble and expense of a funeral, and all " that solemn mockery of woe," by offering his body to the surgeons for dissection : the bargain was soon struck, and poor John was taken away. The neighbours were surprised they saw no preparation for John's funeral, especially as they had subscribed towards defraying the expenses of burying him ; and much more so, when they ascertained he was missing : at length, she acknowledged that she had sold him, saying, she had no idea the " *nottamizers*" would have given so much for John's body ; and that she was sure, her poor husband, if he knew it, would feel happy he had been made the means of adding to her comforts ; " for," said she, wiping her eyes, " he, *poor soul, was a kind and an indulgent husband !*" The neighbours thought this a very strange mode of showing her affection to her husband, and deprecated most loudly her unfeeling behaviour: indeed, she was forced immediately to leave the neighbourhood, or else, in a short time, most likely, she would have been herself a subject for the "*nottamizers.*"'

There is no doubt, many people are privy to the stealing of their friends' bodies; and it is not long since a corpse was left in a room, with the window a little way open, when, in the morning, on looking into the coffin, the body was gone. It must have been taken down stairs. "This circumstance," said Mentor, "reminds me of an anecdote, of a person, who, on passing a church-yard, and seeing a funeral, asked who's it was? 'It is our parish lawyer,' replied a by-stander. 'What!' said the other, 'do *you* bury *your* lawyers?' 'Yes, certainly,' said he, 'pray, what do *you* do with them?' 'Why,' he replied, 'when they die, we put them in a room over night, and throw open the window, and in the morning we are sure to find the lawyer gone; the only disagreeable thing is, the room smells rather of *brimstone!*'"

"In London," said Mentor's friend, "even the poor surgeons are cheated: you probably remember the transaction of Mr. B., the celebrated anatomist, and the body-stealers: it is thus related, and may be relied on as a fact:—

> A man at a tavern made so free,
>   With Perkins' best entire,
> He fell from his seat, and asleep laid he,
>   Before the parlour fire.
>
> The landlord, who wish'd to shut up shop,
>   Cried, "Hang this drunken clown!
> Whoe'er will turn him out *neck and crop*,
>   I'll give him half-a-crown."
>
> A wag, who was taking his parting cup,
>   Cried, "Done—just give me a sack,
> I'll put him in gently, tie him up,
>   And take him away on my back."
>
> So said, so done—at a surgeon's door,
>   He gives a gentle kick;
> "I've brought you a subject—five pounds—no more,
>   Here—give me the cash—be quick!"
>
> The bargain is struck—the money is paid,
>   The fellow cries out, "All's right!"
> The drunken man on the floor is laid,
>   And the surgeon says, "Good night."
>
> But either the jostling had conquer'd the beer,
>   Or by time its strength had fled;
> For noises came to the surgeon's ear,
>   That a body can't make that's dead.
>
> Enraged at the trick, he follow'd the man,
>   And cried, "How dare you connive
> At an action so base?—but I'll foil your plan;
>   Why, knave! the fellow's alive!"

    " Alive ! you don't say so," he dryly said,
       (It seemed not the least to daunt him) :
    " He'll keep the better—don't be afraid,
       You can kill him whenever you want him." '

"This is the way," said Peregrine's friend, laughing, "the surgeons are served in London ; and dearly, indeed, they pay for subjects, at the mention of which so many people shudder. Some say, if the doctors are in want of subjects, let them begin by giving the bodies of their deceased relations, and leaving their own persons for dissection ; but, were they to do so, it would contribute little towards remedying the evil ; for the idea is founded upon the erroneous supposition that they have not, generally speaking, the same feelings as the rest of mankind. There are few medical men so much above or below the common weakness of our nature, as not to admit the force of the general sentiment ; and where, in a few instances, they have left their bodies for dissection, it has been looked upon rather as a mark of eccentricity than of superior mind. Besides, this and all similar views of the subject have the great fault of regarding the dead and not the living. It is the feelings of the survivors which alone we have to consider, and which would be as much outraged by the dissection of a ' doctor' as of any other individual. Trace to its source the general sentiment of repugnance to dissection—remove this, if possible, and nothing further is required. But, if this cannot be done, then, the necessity of anatomical pursuits being granted, let the supply of the necessary means come from those who have no friends to claim an interest in them. As society is constituted, the number so situated, we fear, is far greater than would be required.

"What a dreadful state we should be in," said Mentor, " were it not for the skill of the regular-bred practitioners ; we should be then under the care of that murdering class of impostors, the quack doctors ; for the man who, without experience or education, undertakes to administer remedies for the diseases of the human body, of which he is ignorant, is a curse and a pest to society, and an enemy to all around him. Quackery is an ancient profession in London. In King Edward the Fourth's reign, several practisers of physic were examined by the college, and found so unfit for the practice of that art, that they were rejected ; some were punished according to public statutes, and others fined. In the fourth year of this king's reign, in the month of September, one Grig, a poulterer of Surrey, taken among the people for a prophet, in curing of divers diseases, by words and prayers, and saying he would take no money, &c., was, by command of the Earl of Warwick and others of the council, set on a scaffold in the town of Croydon, in Surrey, with a paper on his breast, wherein was written his deceitful and hypocritical dealings : and after that, on the eighth of September, set on a pillory in Southwark, being then our Lady Fair there kept, and the Mayor of London, with his brethren, the aldermen, riding through the fair, the said Grig asked them and all the citizens forgiveness. Of the like counterfeit physician, saith Stowe, have I noted in the summary of my Chronicles, anno 1382, to be set on horseback, his face to the horse's tail, the same in his hand as a bridle, a collar of jordans about his neck, a whetstone on his breast, and so led through the city of London, with ringing of basins, and banished.

"Henry VIII. despised them, and endeavoured to suppress their nostrums, by establishing censors in physic.

"Quack doctors used formerly to go about, attended by their servants; and the first itinerant doctor on record is the celebrated Andrew Borde, and from this man is derived the name of Merry Andrew, for he was as facetious as he was erudite: his speeches, from the singularity of their style, were received with universal approbation by the people, and the cures he performed were very many, he being a man of most extraordinary attainments.

"It was truly said by the notorious quack, Dr. Rock (who shines so conspicuously in Hogarth's prints), when asked how he, who was so utterly ignorant of physic and surgery, could have amassed such a fortune by *doctoring*, thus replied (taking the person to the window): there, said he, out of every thousand people that pass, nine hundred are fools, and they are my customers; the other hundred go to the regular M. D's. If people would but apply, in the first instance, to men of acknowledged medical skill, instead of going to cheap quacks, what money it would save them; and hundreds of persons would be saved from a premature grave, or from passing a lingering life of misery and pain.

"Among the many eminent quacks, were *Doctor* Benjamin Thornhill, the *seventh son of the seventh son*, and *Doctor* Bossy, also the *seventh son of the seventh son:* this latter was the last mountebank doctor who exhibited in the British metropolis, and his public services ceased about forty years ago. Every Thursday, his stage was erected opposite the north-west colonnade, Covent Garden. The platform was about six feet from the ground, was covered, open in front, and was ascended by a broad step-ladder. On one side was a table, with medicine-chest and surgical apparatus, displayed on a table with drawers. In the centre of the stage was an arm-chair, in which the patient was seated; and, before the doctor commenced his operations, he advanced, taking off his gold-laced hat, and, bowing right and left, began addressing the populace, which crowded before his booth. The following dialogue, *ad literatim,* will afford the reader a characteristic specimen of the customs in London of the last age. It should be observed, the doctor was a humourist.—An aged woman was helped up the ladder, and seated in the chair,—she had been deaf, nearly blind, and was lame to boot; indeed, she might be said to have been visited with Mrs. Thrale's *three* warnings, and death would have walked in at the door, only that Dr. Bossy blocked up the passage. The doctor asked questions with an audible voice, and the patient responded—he usually repeating the response in his Anglo-German dialect. *Doctor*—dis a poora voman vot is—how old vosh you? *Old woman*—I be almost eighty, sir; seventy-nine last Lady-Day, old style. *Doctor*—Ah, tat is an incurable disease. *Old woman* —Oh, dear! Oh, dear! say not so—incurable! Why, you have restored my sight—I can hear again, and I can walk without my crutches. *Doctor* (smiling)—No, no, good voman, old age is vot is incurable, but, by the plessing of God, I vill cure you of vot is elshe. Dis poora woman vos lame, and deaf, and almost blind. How many hossipals have you been in? *Old Woman*— Three, sir; St. Thomas's, St. Bartholomew's, and St. George's.— *Doctor*—Vot, and you found no relief? vot none—not at alls? *Old Woman*—No, not at all, sir. *Doctor*—And how many medical professioners have attended you? *Old Woman*—Some twenty or thirty, sir. *Doctor*—O mine Gote! Three sick hossipals and dirty (thirty) doctors! I should vonder vot if you have not enough to kill you twenty time. Dis poora voman has become mine patient. Doctor Bossy gain all patients bronounced ingurables; pote, mid de plessing of Brovidence, I shall make short work of it, and set you upon your legs again. Coode beoples, dis poora vomans vas teaf as a toor nail: (holding up his watch to her ear, and striking the repeater), gan you hear dat pell? *Old woman*—Yes, sir. *Doctor*—O den, be thankful to Gote. Can you valk round dis chair? (offering his arm). *Old woman*—Yes, sir. *Doctor*—Sit you town again, good voman. Can you see? *Old woman*— Pretty so-so, doctor. *Doctor*—Vot gan you see, good woman? *Old woman*—I can see the baker there (pointing to a mutton-pie-man, with the pie-board on his head—all eyes were towards him). *Doctor*—And vat else gan you see, good vomans? *Old woman*— The poll-parrot there (pointing to Richardson's hotel). ' Lying old ——,' screamed Richardson's poll-parrot; all the crowd shouted with laughter. Dr. Bossy waited until the laugh had subsided, and looking across the way, significantly shook his head at the parrot, and gravely exclaimed, laying his hand on his bosom, ' 'tis no lie, you silly pird, 'tis all true as de gospel.' Those who knew Covent Garden half a century ago cannot have forgotten the famed Dr. Bossy."

Peregrine and his friend enjoyed Mentor's description of poor Dr. Bossy; and the latter, taking up the tankard, and drinking a good draught of Calvert's entire, asked whether Mentor thought Bossy recommended his patients to drink London porter. " I cannot answer that question," replied Mentor; " perhaps the price was too high for his patients; but, if it was for them, it was not for the generality of the people, it we are to judge from the immense quantity of it brewed. The prices of this important article of consumption were regulated by statute, as early as the reigns of Henry III. and Henry I., which enacted that they should rise or fall with the price of corn. The scale of prices may be seen in Strype's Stowe.

" In 1468 (8 Edward IV.), according to an assize then made,

it was ordained—that, if the brewer bought the quarter of malt for *two shillings*, he was to sell a gallon of the best ale for a *halfpenny*, and was to make forty-eight gallons of a quarter of malt. If the quarter of malt was three shillings, the gallon was to be three farthings; if four shillings the quarter, one penny the gallon; ' and so on of the shilling the farthing.' To prevent frauds, both as to quality and quantity, no brewer was to sell ale till the aletaster had tasted it; and he was to have ' mesurys assized and asselid.' A breach of these ordinances subjected the brewer, for the first and second offences, to fines, and, for the third, to the punishment, ' first of the lockyng-hole, and aftyr to the pillory.'

"The great breweries, or ' bere-houses,' as they are called in the map of London, in *Civitatus Orbem*, &c., stood on the Thames side, below St. Catherine's, though they afterwards extended from thence, westwards, as far as Milford Stairs; and they were, as well as the beer they brewed, under the control of the officers of the crown. Henry VII., in 1492, licensed one John Merchant, a Fleming, to export fifty tons of ale, called beer; and, according to Maitland, in the same reign, Geoffrey Gate, probably one of these officers, ' spoiled the brewhouses at St. Catherine's twice, either for sending too much abroad unlicensed, or for brewing it too weak for their home customers.' The demand for this article from foreign parts increased to a high degree in the reign of Elizabeth, particularly about the year 1580; but the exportation of it was often prohibited by royal proclamation, as a cause, in times of scarcity, of enhancing the price of corn. ' Yet, even upon prohibition,' Stowe tells us, ' special licences were granted by the Lord Treasurer. Thus, he allowed one Lystel, in the month of November, to brew and transport 500 tons of beer, for the queen's use; and, in the same month, another ship was laded with 350 barrels of beer to Embden; and, in the same month again, a ship of Amsterdam laded 300 barrels more; and, in the same month, four ships of Embden were laded with 800 barrels more, which shows in what request our English beer was then abroad.'

"In 1585, the quantity of beer, *strong* and *small*, brewed in London, in one year, by the twenty-six brewers in the city, suburbs, and Westminster (whereof the one half were strangers, the other English), was thus calculated:—Most of them brewed, in general, six times a week, and twenty quarters at a time, which yielded, in small beer, at least 100 barrels, and 60 in strong. One with another, they brewed 420 barrels weekly a-piece, which amounted to 2,496 barrels yearly; so that the whole number of brewers brewed, at that rate, 648,960 barrels. The quantities sent abroad, near the same time, were estimated in a similar manner, viz.: ' That there were twenty great brewhouses, or more, situate on the Thames side, from Milford Stairs, in Fleet Street, to below St. Catherine's, which brewed yearly the quantity of seven or eight brewings of sweet beer, or strong beer, that passed to Hoad, Embden, the Low Countries, Calais, Dieppe, and thereabouts; and account but 600 brewings, it makes 26,000 barrels ; which, at seven to a tun, make 3,771 tuns.'

"The contrast in modern times is amazing. In the year ending June, 1760, 425,959 barrels of beer were brewed. From Midsummer, 1786, to Midsummer, 1787, the number of barrels of strong beer alone, brewed in London, was 1,176,856 : of these, Whitbread's house (which then stood first) brewed 150,280 barrels; Calvert's (Felix), 131,043 barrels ; and Thrale's (now Barclay and Perkins), 105,559 barrels ; and the duty on the malt, for the preceding year, was one million and a half of money. In the year ending July 5, 1827, 1,412,590 barrels of beer were brewed. The sight of a London brewhouse presents a magnificence unspeakable. The vessels evince the extent of the trade.

"Vessels of beer and ale were not gauged by statute before the 23d of Henry VIII. Defects were punishable, upon presentment of juries, by the magistrates. The price of a quarter of wheat was then 6s. 8d. ; the quarter of malt, 4s. or 5s. ; and a quarter of oats cost 2s. 8d. The price of a cwt. of the best hops was 6s. or 6s. 8d. Beer sold for—

The last for { Barrels, at 9s. / Kilderkins, at 5s. } { And the barrel of the best beer, or ale, sold then for 3s. 8d. or 4s. The 1½d. beer for 3s.

In the beginning of the same reign (1512), the remaining stock of malt liquor in the cellar of one of the noblemen of the court is valued as follows :—

"'Of ale, vij gallons, after ijd. the gallon, xiiijd.

"'Of beire, xiiij hogisheds, *dimid'* conteyning D. iiij score, xvj gallons, after *obol' quadr'* the gallon, xliiijs. vjd.'

"N.B.—Malt was then 4s. a quarter, and hops 13s. 4d. the cwt. It was probably a scarce season for the latter article.

"Ale and beer at this time, and long afterwards, were the common beverage for breakfast, and were generally accompanied by dried or salted fish, and meat. A quart of beer is the quantity ordered to be brought to my Lord of Northumberland's table, every morning at breakfast, in the reign of Henry VII., and a pottle to each person of his household. The common people are also spoken of, somewhat later, as consuming great quantities of beer, double and single (*i. e.* strong and small.) 'This they do not,' says a contemporary writer, 'drink out of glasses, but from earthen pots with silver handles and covers, and this even in houses of persons of middling fortune ; for, as to the poor, the covers of their pots are only pewter, and in some places, such as villages, their pots for beer are only made of wood.'

"Our ancestors were not unacquainted with some of the modern methods of adulterating this article. In the reign of Elizabeth, the brewers were complained of for brewing towards, the close of the year, with bad, or what was called weavy malt, being the bottom and sweepings of their granaries, to make room to bring in new corn. It was also reported that they put in darnel rosin, lime, and chalk, and such like; 'to make,' says Stowe, 'the drinkers thirsty, that they might drink the more; and that for cheapness, when hops were dear, they put into their drink, broom, bay-berries, ivy-berries, and such like things.'"

At this instant, a respectable gentleman, a Quaker, entered the coffee-room, in a state of great vexation. "Friends," said he, "I have been sorely used: I have just been made a sufferer, by the

Doings of the London Pickpockets.

This afternoon, on my way from the Bank, coming along some of the by-streets, a fellow, with a cigar in his mouth, came close up to me, and puffed a cloud of noxious smoke in my face; when, on raising both my hands, instinctively, as it were, to preserve my eyes, I felt a tug at my coat-pocket; but, before I could recover myself (for I was astounded at the singularity of the attack, and the pain in my eyes was very acute), the villains were off, and ran, I suppose, down some of the courts. I then found I was robbed of my pocket-book." "I hope, sir," said Mentor, "there was not much property in it." "I thank thee, friend," said the gentleman, "there were but a few notes, and some private memorandums, which I had put very carelessly in my coat-pocket; for, certainly, in London, where a person has money about him, he ought always to place it where he can, as he walks, feel that it is safe: for instance, inside his waistcoat, and button his coat, keeping his arm over where he knows the money

23.                                    N

is, not in a stiff manner, so as it might appear he was guarding his property, but in a free position: if he does so, and never looks into print or other shops, or stops to witness sights, or disturbances, or accidents, but goes straight forward, until he has paid away, or deposited his money safely at home, it is a hundred chances if ever he is robbed. If a stranger wants to see any sights in London, let him look at them when he has no property about him. It is also a very careless custom of country people and strangers, when they receive any money at a banker's, to come out of the office with the money in their hands, and place it in their pockets in the streets: this has been the cause of many persons being robbed; for the thieves are always on the look-out for *flats*, as they call them. It is best, when at the banker's, or any other place where you are receiving money, to deposit it safely while in the office, and to go straight forward home, as I just mentioned. I knew," continued the friend, " a poor man, a master of a Sunderland collier, who had received £40 in Lombard Street, and, when he arrived on board his ship in the river, he, to his grief and astonishment, found he had been robbed of all the money. He immediately went to the police-officers, who asked him whether he recollected stopping any where in the streets; he said, he was satisfied the money was in his breeches' pocket, for, to be certain, he counted it in the street, and buttoned up his breeches' pocket; and that he only stopped a few minutes to see two men fight on Tower Hill. ' Now, captain,' said one of the police-officers, ' you were watched counting your bank-notes, and where you put them; and the pickpockets had not an opportunity, before you arrived on Tower Hill, of robbing you; when some of the party made a show of a fight, to draw your attention, in which, unfortunately, they succeeded; and there they robbed you. But yours is a case of almost every day's occurrence. The cause of countrymen being often robbed, arises chiefly from their over-caution. It was but the other day, a trusty old man was sent to receive £2000, which he did in two notes: the anxiety of having so much property about him, made him almost every minute put his hand in his pocket, to feel that it was safe; but, by the time he got to Burlington Gardens, he ascertained that he had lost the money; for, by so repeatedly placing his hand in his breeches' pocket, and it being a very hot day, and he walking fast, it is supposed, he drew the notes out, his hands being in a state of perspiration. Fortunately for his employer, a poor washerwoman's boy found the two notes, who immediately hastened with them to the place where they were advertised to be taken, and received a reward of £100. It appeared, also, that the lad, although his mother was in a state of poverty, had received a very good education, and was of an undeniable character; he was therefore received at the office of the gentleman whose property the notes were, and where he now is, a man of worth and respectability,—*such are the good effects of honesty!*' This police-officer told my friend," continued the Quaker gentleman, " that the very day previous, a north-country captain, while going along Wapping, it raining at the time, was overtaken by a mob of people witnessing the dancing of some chimney-sweepers: on an instant, he was surrounded by a party of young fellows, who pressed closely on him, and kept both his arms up, in holding his umbrella; when, all on an instant, they liberated him, and, in a few minutes, after casting his eyes down, he found his watch, with the appendages of five large seals and two keys, were all vanished."

" The love for thieving," said Mentor, " is, I think, born with many people. They only value that which they have had the pleasure of thieving; as has been evinced in the cases of many persons of property and of consequence being detected repeatedly in the act of pilfering. Mr. Cunningham, a surgeon in a convict-ship, in his work, entitled *Two Years in New South Wales*, says, ' Thieves generally affect to consider all the rest of mankind equally criminal with themselves, only being either lucky enough not to be found out, or committing actions which (though equally bad in the eye of the Divinity) are not so tangible in that of men. It is their constant endeavour to reduce every one, in fact, to the same level with themselves, while fate, they believe, impels them on to do the deeds for which the world condemns them :—to thieve is their destiny, and against this how can they contend? Indeed, the conscience-comforting doctrine of predestination derives very considerable force from the fact, that no convict-ships have been lost since the first settling of the colony; demonstrating, what a safe conveyance such a ship is, seeing there are too many destined to be hanged aboard, for her company to run any risk of being drowned. The life of a thief is indeed calculated like the success of a new play; and such a one is said to have a good or a bad run, according to the length of time he has been able to evade the penalties of transportation or the gallows. You will often hear old acquaintances, when they meet during fresh debarkments, from England to Botany Bay, on inquiring how Bill or Sam such a one fares, and hearing he is still " a-going at it," exclaim, in surprise, " What a lucky dog! what a good run he has had !" Of all those I ever heard of,' continues Mr. Cunningham, ' who have manifested the " ruling passion strong in death," George Breadman proved one of the staunchest. He was a poor *yokel*, foisted upon me in the *last stage of consumption*, and who remained bed-ridden until our arrival in the colony. He fell away so fast that I never expected to land him alive, and certainly it required the most anxious attention to retain the glimmering spark. I fortunately, however, possessed a very facetious fellow among the batch, to whom this poor dying creature became strongly attached, never being a day happy whereon his friend neglected to visit him, and often begging me to send this man to him for company, which I gladly did, seeing it invariably put him in good spirits. Wondering what could be the cause of this extraordinary liking, I inquired, and found that Breadman had been a great pig-stealer in his day, which, being considered a very *vulgar* calling among the professional classes (particularly among the *townies*), he could get no one to listen to his adventures except this joker, who would laugh with and quiz him on the particular subjects of his achievements; praise the wonderful expertness with which he had *done* the farmers out of their grunters, and propose a partnership concern on reaching the colony, if the pigs there were found to be worth stealing! I really believe the poor creature was kept in existence a full month solely by the exhilirating conversation of his companion. On anchoring at Sydney, no time was lost in conveying Breadman ashore, he being so weak that he could not even sit up without fainting: yet, in this pitiable state, supporting himself round the hospital-man's neck, while the latter was drawing on his trousers for him, the expiring wretch mustered strength enough to stretch out his pale trembling hand toward the other's waistcoat-pocket, and pick it of a pocket-comb and penknife! Next morning *he was a corpse*, thus dying as he had lived. Yet, during his whole illness, this man would regularly request some of the *sober-minded rogues to read the Scriptures* to him, and *pray by his bed-side!* Indeed, ill practices become ultimately so *habitual* with many, as to be no longer deemed such: and hence, no wonder we so often see *religion* and *knavery* intimately blended.'

" To what magnitude thieves would carry their depredations," observed the Quaker, " if it was not for the publicity given to their exploits by the newspapers!" " They would, indeed," rejoined Mentor; " and, *apropos*, I have in my pocket-book a clever burlesque narrative of a professional meeting of thieves, which I copied from a Sunday paper, called Bell's Dispatch. I preserved it on purpose to read it to you (addressing himself to Peregrine). It is necessary to remark, that it was written at the time when the judges prohibited the publishing of police reports previous to the trial of the parties accused. It is as follows:—

" Monday last a meeting was held at the sign of the Nimble-fingers, in Rosemary Lane, by the thieves, pickpockets, duffers, swindlers, housebreakers, footpads, bludgeon-men, and other rogues of the metropolis, for the purpose of passing a vote of thanks to the Judges, for their spirited and praiseworthy attempt to abolish the publication of Police Reports. Bill Soames having been called to the chair by acclamation, opened the business of the day in a neat and appropriate speech.—The chairman proceeded to take a view of thieving, from the earliest period down to the present time, observing, at some length, on the antiquity of the custom, which was coeval with property itself. What were called honest men must live, however, as well as prigs*; it was but fair they should, and laws were accordingly invented for their protection. He did not object to laws; quite the contrary, he approved of laws; no rogue, who knew his own interests, would object to laws—were it not for laws, every man would be on his guard, and would take care of himself, and instant punishment

* Thieves—See Jonathan Wild's definition of this word.

would be inflicted on the detected thief; but under laws, he meant such laws as those of England, when caught in the fact, how many chances of escape presented themselves to the thief. A word, a letter, a slip of the pen in framing the indictment, prove a loop-hole for the prisoner's escape. These, and a thousand others, were the chances in favour of the detected thief. Now and then, punishment overtakes a thief, and it is well that it should do so; were it not for the gallows, all men would be thieves, and then what would become of the profession? Why, it would resemble a fish-pond of pikes; it would be over-run, over-stocked, like the law, the army, the navy, and the church. Occasional punishments, therefore, were like high duties to certain trades; they secured a sort of monopoly to the adventurous, and deterred small souls from embarking in concerns above their resources. He liked, then, to see honest men in the world, and he liked to see such laws as those of England framed for their protection—that was all fair. But he did not like the tell-tale practice they were that day met to condemn—the tell-tale practice, he would call it, of police-reporting. Formerly, a gentleman contrived some stratagem to take in the unwary, which lasted him his life; but now the trick which is invented and successfully practised to-day, is blown all over the town in twenty-four hours, and is no trick for to-morrow; nay, it is at the Land's End and Johnny Groat's House in a week; every mop-squeezer in London is up to the most knowing go, a few hours after it has first been shown up at a police-office exa-mination. Prigs had fine invention—no man was fit for the busi-ness without it; but no invention could stand this daily demand. They cannot be eternally shifting their ground or contriving new tricks for every day in the year. Let them look at the swindlers, the duffers, the brick-bat parcel folks, and others in that line; they hit on a clever scheme to-day and do a little business, but to-mor-row comes a police report, and every one is up to it, and on his guard. What with the gas and the newspapers, with lighting the streets by night and blabbing by day, a thief's business was not now what it was formerly. Leave the law to itself to take its course, as it used to do, and leave the attorneys for the prosecu-tion to hunt up what evidence they can ferret out, and to get their honest earnings by it; this was the good old plan. We are all innocent, gentlemen, in the eye of the law, and is it not a shame that people should suspect us of being thieves against a maxim of the constitution [much applause]! Folks were getting so woundy suspicious now, there was no doing business with them, and all along with those cursed reports in the papers. But what would be the upshot of all this here? Why, there would be no thieves, and then what would become of the lawyers? It did his heart good, however, to see that the Judges had taken the matter up. The Judges, God bless them, would give fair play to the thieves [loud and continued acclamations of applause]; and it was right they should do so, for if there were no thieves there would be no

Judges.   He concluded by proposing a toast (pipes, tobacco, and punch had been introduced)—

" ' The abolition of Police Reports," with nine times nine.

" ' Tune—" Let us take the road."

" ' After the uproar had subsided, Filch, a well-known public character, rose and observed, that he had not, like the honourable chairman, the gift of the gab, but he should just say a few words about this here matter.   A prig was for all the world like a fox, the cunningest chap as is—the fox is caught in a trap; vell, he's taken good care of and clapped in a bag, to be turned out afore the hounds, the 'squire and big-wigs all agog to ride after him; but they gives him good law, and that's a main good start, and off he sets, as thof the devil was ater him.   Now, if so be a clod with a long pole vere to come across of the wermin, and to floor the fox with a lick on the pate, blow him, vat a row the sporting gemmen would make—how the vips and tongues would go to work on him for spoiling the run; they loves to catch the wermin in their own way, and vould sooner see him bolt clean away than catch him contrary to sportsman's law. It's just for all the world the same when the law gets hold of a prig—first, the beak catches him in a trap, and, lord! what a mortal sight of care he takes of him.   " Mind, don't say nothing to hurt yourself, my honest fellow," says he; " take care you don't commit yourself, whatever you do"—'cause, if he did, 'twould spoil the run.   Then comes the trial, like the hunt, and we are slipped out of the bag with plenty of law and its odds, but with that start we gets clean off: but here comes the *press-gang*, like the clod with the pole, and hits us an ugly vipe with its news. " Blow me tight," says the huntsman, and that's the judge, " but that's foul, rat me if it ant."   " Vy, did not you vant to catch him?" says the clod.   " Not that vay, you son of a ——," says the judge; " ferret me, if I don't set my hounds on you, you nation spoil-sport, for a poaching wagabond, as you be, and be hanged to you, to go and catch the wermin in that ere manner; vy, it's not giving him a fair run, I'm blowed if it is ;" and then he takes and wallops the clod.   Fair play's a jewel, and lawyers serve the thieves as 'squires do foxes; they preserves 'em all carefully for their own sport, and loves to give them a sight of chances to get off, for that makes the fun of the run.   And lord, gemmen, vhen ve sees the court a setting at sizes, with its counsels and judges all so big and grand like, ve should take a pride to think it's ve that keeps 'em all; they owes all to us; ve causes it all; and they should be grateful; and now, gemmen, having no more to say at this present, I propose a toast, I am certain sure you will all drink with hearty good will—the law, gemmen.

" ' The law'—Air " The Rogues' March.'"

" ' Mr. Chousen, a swindler, in very extensive business, then rose, and observed, that the exposure of their private affairs in the public prints was fatal to the prosperity of the profession.   The measure meditated by the judges of putting down those obnoxious publications, could alone save them from impending ruin. He begged to offer a toast that could not be other than acceptable to the meeting.

" ' The wooden heads of old England.'—Tune, " Ye Gentlemen of England."

" ' Jack Midnight, a housebreaker of note, said, that among prigs there could be but one opinion concerning the injurious tendency of police reports, which were as barking dogs and gaslights to their operations. If the judges had not humanely considered their hard case, he, for one, should have been compelled to adopt another line of business. He had some thoughts of practising, according to the Court of Chancery law, that is to say, of burglariously entering and robbing houses of ill-fame, and forcibly taking from dwelling-houses in general all species of property of a paw-paw nature, or *contra bonos mores*. Our fine houses were rich in plunder of this description, the forcible abstraction of which would, by the famous decision of the Court of Chancery on literary property, be regarded as no crime, or rather as a decided public benefit. The speaker gave, as a toast, " The beauty of appropriation."

" ' Air—" At the silent midnight hour."

" ' Billy Brainem, a footpad, then rose and observed, what a singular blessing it was, that in this country punishments were regarded with more horror than crimes. The extreme severity of punishments softened the hearts of prosecutors, and was the best safety of the prig. He therefore proposed—" The Criminal Code."

" ' Air—" The groans of the dying."

" ' Mr. Filch again got on his legs, and moved that the thanks of this meeting be given to the judges for their spirited, praiseworthy, and truly constitutional attempt to put down the publication of police reports ; and that a committee, consisting of the following persons, be appointed to convey the same :—Bill Soames, Nimming Ned, Lady Barrymore, Filch, Billy Brainem, and Light-Fingered Jack.

" ' Lady Barrymore seconded the motion, observing, that no lady had suffered more than herself in reputation, from the publication of the police reports.

" ' Billy Brainem moved, as an amendment, that with the first-fruits of their industry, after the suppression of police reports, a piece of plate should be purchased and presented to the judges, in commemoration of the signal service they had rendered to the profession.

" ?Lady Barrymore did not like the idea of shelling out ; she thought the money would be better laid out in *blue ruin*.

" ' Filch—It's no expense ; we can always steal the plate again vhen ve vants it.

" ' The amendment was carried.

" 'On which Lady Barrymore knocked down the chairman, and the meeting was tumultuously adjourned.

" ' A large body of watchmen attended the meeting, but were not permitted to mix in the deliberations, as not being strictly professional; in the course of the proceedings, however, Filch proposed the toast of " The Watchmen."

" ' Air—" Charley is my darling." '

"The landlady of the house where I reside while in town, said Peregrine's friend, " was lately robbed in a singular manner, which shows how careful all persons ought to be who let lodgings: she told me that a young female, apparently about eighteen or twenty years of age, who represented herself as being a servant to an elderly lady of an independent fortune, went and took lodgings for the said lady and herself, and, in order to gain her point, had recourse to the following stratagem :—She went about eleven o'clock in the morning, and, after inquiring the terms, went away with a pretence to inform her mistress, who, she said, was lodging at Brompton Row, near Hyde Park, and where a satisfactory character would be given, if required. After the lapse of about two hours, the said female returned, and said that her mistress would make trial of her choice, and that she was to stop and get a good fire in the sitting-room,—that she would follow with the luggage, and, to satisfy the landlady, would pay a month's lodgings in advance, and that, if she found herself comfortable, she should continue them. After the girl had made the fire, she asked the landlady to lend her a basket and basin to fetch some meat in, from an eating-house in the street, to be ready for her mistress on her arrival, which the latter readily complied with; but, not returning after a sufficient time had elapsed, the landlady began to think that all was not right, and, on examining the premises, found that she had decamped with two silver table-spoons, two tea-spoons, a pair of silver sugar-tongs, and a tortoise-shell tea-caddy.

" The young thief was of middle stature, but rather slender, a fresh-coloured good-looking girl, and rather prepossessing in her manners; had on a black bonnet, a white spotted shawl, a red gown, with black stripes, and a white apron."

Mentor observed, " That cases of robbing ready-furnished lodgings were unfortunately very common; to recite half the instances, would almost fill a volume. Indeed, very few persons are greater sufferers, by the vicious artifices of the swindler. I remember," continued Mentor, " about two months since, a lady, elegantly dressed, took expensive lodgings at the house of a tradesman in the Strand. On the credit of her appearance, she obtained goods from several shopkeepers, without prompt payment. She appeared *en famille*, and no person imagined her *accouchement* far distant. A milliner and dress-maker, near Essex Street, was employed to make her a morning-dress, and other articles, which came to 8*l.* She carried the things home, and the lady's daughter said, her *mamma*, being indisposed, had retired to her chamber; therefore begged she would call again next morning. The young woman went the following day, and saw the lady, who expressed herself quite satisfied with the dress, and gave another order, observing, 'When you have finished this dress, bring your bill, and take the money.' After leaving the house, she reflected, being but lately engaged in business, that she ought not to execute the second order unless the first was paid for; she, consequently, returned, and informed the daughter, that she really had not the means of purchasing materials for the last order, unless the lady would pay her for the dress sent home. The daughter acquiesced in the reasonable representations made by the dress-maker, and appointed her to come at nine o'clock on Thursday morning, when she said the money should be ready. The young woman was punctual; but, instead of paying for her goods, she found the family of the tradesman, who kept the house, in great consternation. At eight o'clock the preceding evening, the lady was delivered of a fine infant, and at dead of night, before any person in the house was stirring, she contrived to remove the child, herself, her daughter, and a trunk, containing every article she had of value, as it is supposed, to a coach, in which she drove off before the family could have the least suspicion of her departure. The servant in the house first discovered the ladies' apartment unoccupied, and the street-door open. Besides eight weeks' arrears of board and lodging, she has left unpaid debts amounting to a considerable sum.

"There is also," continued Mentor, "a species of swindling now in practice, which cannot be made too public, as it has hitherto been very successful. Two persons, forming, it is supposed, part of a gang, go and take lodgings in respectable houses, and advertise for 'several respectable young women, who may be taught a genteel business, at which they can earn from 15*s.* to 25*s.* per week, and have constant employment." The advertisers generally have numerous applicants, from each of whom they obtain 1*l.* as a premium for teaching young women to bind shoes. About a fortnight ago, a man and woman, calling themselves Mr. and Mrs. Bennet, went to a house, and, after viewing a suite of apartments, took them for twelve months certain. In consequence of an advertisement of the description before alluded to, five young women were engaged to work at the above-mentioned house; but, after the swindlers had obtained various articles of jewellery and wearing apparel, to the amount of about 6*l.*, from the landlady, they decamped, leaving the young women the dupes of their artifices, their lodging and every other demand unpaid, and taking with them also several articles of value. During their stay, the female requested to have the initials H. I. J. erased from a dozen silver spoons and other articles, under the specious pretext that they were the property of her first husband. From the circumstance of the parties

24.

having an abundance of plate and linen with them, no suspicions were entertained of their respectability."

The following case is somewhat similar.—" A man and woman, who stated their names to be Mr. and Mrs. Bull, and of decent exterior, lately took lodgings, and introduced themselves as being in the fancy line; that they had just arrived from Bristol, where they had a house, and moreover, that they carried on a flourishing business in the above line in Paris. The female mentioned to the landlady, that their luggage had not arrived from Bristol, and begged of her to lend them the linen requisite for their use, until their boxes reached them, which were daily expected by the waggon. They had with them a large box, which seemed to contain nothing but some working-implements. On the following Monday, a very pompous advertisement appeared, purporting to teach young ladies a very lucrative and advantageous business in a very short time. This seemed to take with the ladies; for upwards of one hundred in the course of the week made application into the nature of the employment, and a considerable number of them engaged to learn the business; different sums of money were exacted from them as the terms of their initiation, according to the nature of their agreements. No less than fifteen were set down to work in the house, for which purpose the parlour and bed-rooms were put in requisition, and turned into workshops, to the great annoyance of the landlady. Those females who were unfortunate enough not to find room on the premises, were obliged, in addition to the sum paid for learning the business, to leave a handsome deposit for the work which they took out. All went on very smoothly for a few weeks, when, on the ladies coming as usual to their regular employment, they had the unwelcome intelligence doled out to them, that their employers had decamped the evening before, no one knew whither."

But, of all depredations, none is more in practice than that of robbing dwelling-houses; and the public, and servants in particular, cannot be too much on their guard against the admission into their masters' houses, of a gang of itinerant venders of different articles,—such as fruit, oranges and lemons, wooden and earthenware, and other such commodities,—who at present infest the metropolis and its environs, and assume these businesses as a mere cloak, to enable them the more easily to obtain access to the premises, and carry on without detection their game of plunder. In many instances, though not themselves the actual perpetrators of the robberies, they are what are called the *putters-up*, by describing to their companions in crime the situation of the houses, and the means through which an easy entrance can be obtained to them. They also find out, from the servants, the time at which the family retires for the night, or whether they are in the country, or get at such information as very much assists their purposes. Complaints are every day made, when too late, of robberies accomplished through their instrumentality.

"It is a pity," said Mentor, "that servants are not made better acquainted with the schemes of plunder practised in London; among them may be mentioned the following :—

"A system of fraud is now practising in the metropolis, by a set of swindlers, at gentlemen's private houses and offices, by which they levy very considerable contributions on the public. Their plan is to watch the absence of the master from home, then ascertain his name, and, after a reasonable lapse of time, apply at the house with a small parcel, and inquire if he has returned home. Being answered in the negative, the fellow instantly replies "Oh, then, I was desired to apply to the servant for payment." In most instances the demand is thoughtlessly complied with. Upon inspection, the parcel is found to contain some trifling article, of little or no value. This trick was successfully played off, at an office in Somerset House, after the close of business, and, during the absence of the gentleman residing there, some shillings were obtained from the servant, for a small bottle of ink; which, he pretended, was ordered from a stationer in Throgmorton Street.

"A few evenings ago, one of those many ingenious devices that are daily practised by the thieves of the metropolis, for the purpose of plundering dwelling-houses, was carried into successful effect at the residence of a lady of fortune, living in Pall Mall. Just as the family had finished dinner (about seven o'clock), a man knocked at the street-door, and handed in a letter, addressed to Mrs. M., which, he said, required an answer, and which the servant, who had been waiting at dinner, carried in to his mistress, leaving the man standing at the street-door. Mrs. M., having read the first few lines of a very long epistle, saw that it was an application from the writer, who said that he had been recommended to Mrs. M.'s family to be hired as a footman, and she desired the servant to say that she was not in want of any footman, at the same time observing that houses were frequently robbed by persons bringing letters on such pretences. The servant having delivered his mistress's answer to the fellow, who still stood at the hall-door, the latter, with the most cool effrontery, requested that, as the contents of his letter could not be complied with, it might be given back to him, which was accordingly done, and he took his departure, without having excited the slightest suspicion as to his having accomplished any robbery. Soon after he was gone, however, the servant had occasion to go into the pantry, where a quantity of plate lay, part of which had been just removed from the dinner-table, when he found that the whole, in value upwards of £100, had been carried off, consisting chiefly of very massive sets of spoons and forks, king's pattern, marked with the initial M. only, together with a silver teapot, cream-jug, &c. It was clear that the fellow who brought the letter did not himself commit the robbery; but, no doubt, while he stood at the street-door, waiting a reply to his letter, he let some person into the house, who knew where the plate generally lay at that hour, and, proceeding directly to the pantry, had time to carry away his spoil, unperceived by the servants.

" About twelve o'clock on a Sunday, while the family were at church, and no person in the house, but one female servant, two men, disguised as fashionably dressed females, inquired for Mrs. G. ; and, on being told by the servant, that she was not at home, they asked permission to wait in the house until she should return, which, however, the girl very properly refused to grant, as they were entire strangers to her. The prisoners then endeavoured to induce her out of the passage ; but, in resisting their attempts, she lifted up the veil which hung over the face of one of them, and discovered, by a black beard, that it was the face of a man. She then called out ' Thieves ! Robbers !' &c. as loud as she could, and, the hall-door being open, the people in the street heard her cries. The thieves on this alarm ran out of the house, and were joined by another, who, it appeared, had been waiting outside, and all three ran away together: they were, however, pursued by several persons, and, after a short chase, taken into custody.

" During the pursuit, one was seen to fling away a large pistol from under his shawl, which was picked up, and the one who was not dressed in female attire was also observed to throw away some housebreaking implements, which were also picked up and produced.

" The prisoners appeared at the bar in their female apparel— namely, bombasin gowns, silk shawls, Leghorn bonnets, lace veils and caps, with a profusion of artificial curls and ringlets hanging down their faces. In their defence, they said, that they went to the house merely to have a lark with the servant, and not with any intent to commit a robbery."

There are no thieves against whom servants ought to be more on their guard, than those fellows who go out on the *morning sneak*, as it is termed : that is, watching gentlemen's servants, when they open the house early in the morning, and perhaps leave the area-gate open, they sneak down, and steal what may be in the kitchen, while the servant is lighting the parlour fire ; or else they steal, if they can, the bolts of the shutters, in order that, at night, they may the more easily enter the premises. Many robberies are thus committed ; and many a good servant suspected, by the depredations of dustmen, or sweeps, who purloin spoons, or any thing they can lay their hands on ; and, because they are missing, the poor servant is supposed to have carelessly lost them, and is discharged. It is incredible the property that is carried away with the dust; and the following case will give you some idea of the profits of *dust-sifting* :—" Some time ago, a decent-looking woman was put to the bar, charged with felony, by Mary Collins, a *dust-sifter*, whose evidence was remarkable for the extraordinary disclosures it incidentally contained of the large profits obtained from the apparently humble vocation of dust-sifting. The detail will be at once interesting and instructive to the public. The complainant stated, that the prisoner had been employed by her to sit up with a sick child, and that, during the time she was thus employed, an old pocket, containing a great variety of valuables, was abstracted from its usual place of deposit. The prisoner having access to the place, suspicion fell upon her. The contents of the pocket were thus described :—One coral necklace, large beads ; one ditto, with pearl clasp ; several handsome brooches ; five gold seals ; some gold rings ; several gold shirt-pins ; a quantity of loose beads ; broken bits of gold and silver, &c. The magistrate expressed his surprise at her having such a motley assortment of valuables by her. *Complainant*—Your worship, we find them amongst the dust. *Magistrate*—Indeed! what, all these articles? *Complainant*—Oh, your worship, that's nothing; we find many more things than them : we find almost every small article that can be mentioned. We are employed by the dust-contractor, who allows us 8*d.* per load for sifting, besides which, we have all the spoons and other articles which we find among the dust. *Magistrate*—That's dustman's law, I suppose ; but pray, how many silver spoons may you find in the course of the year? *Complainant*—It is impossible to say : sometimes more, and sometimes less.

The magistrate declared, that what she had been telling him was quite novel to him. The urbane manner of the worthy magistrate won upon the old lady, and made her quite communicative. She had followed her occupation eight years, and what with the " perquisites" (*id est*, articles found), and the saving from " hard labour," she had realized quite enough to think about house-building, and had then a house erecting, which she expected would cost her at least £300. She had deposited £100 in the hands of Mr. Kelly, in part-payment, and, as a proof that all was not vaunting, she produced her box, in which was counted thirty-nine sovereigns, two five-pound bank-notes, and several guineas and half-sovereigns. She produced, also, a variety of duplicates of different found articles, which she disposed of by pledging to different pawnbrokers. They consisted of finger-rings, silver table and tea spoons, silver forks, gold brooches, &c. In respect to the poor woman accused, no evidence was adduced to corroborate the suspicion, and she was therefore discharged.

" The recital of the many acts of deception we have just heard," said Peregrine, addressing himself to the Quaker gentleman, " makes us deplore that so much ingenuity and industry should have been devoted to the perpetration of such bad practices." " It does truly, friend," replied the gentleman ; " and it is singular, that many men who are too lazy to work at any honest employment, yet will toil day and night, undergo every fatigue, brave every danger, and persevere with a zeal that in any other cause would do them honour—to accomplish the robbery they have in view : it must be the pleasure they inwardly feel in possessing that which they know belongs to another, that makes them show such energy, which in all honest engagements they are so totally devoid of." "It is indeed astonishing," said Peregrine; "but come sir," taking up his glass of wine, "I have the pleasure of drinking to you, wishing you a long continuance of health." "I thank thee, friend, for thy good wishes," replied the gentleman, "I will join thee in a bottle;" but I cannot return the compliment, for *we* never drink healths, although the custom is as ancient as the time of the Greeks and Romans, who used at their meals to make libations, pour out, and even drink wine in honour of the Gods, as well as drinking to the healths of their benefactors and acquaintances. Besides which, the men of gallantry (as we learn from Martial) used to take off as many glasses to their respective mistresses as there were letters in the name of each. The *Tatler* (No. 24) gives a curious account of the origin of the word ' Toast,' as used in the drinking of healths. It states that it had its rise from an accident at Bath, in the reign of Charles II. It happened that, on a public day, a celebrated beauty of those times was in the Cross Bath, and one of the crowd of her admirers took a glass of the water in which the fair one stood, and drank her health to the company. There was in the place a gay fellow, half fuddled, who offered to jump in, and swore, though he liked not the *liquor,* he would have the *toast.* He was opposed in his resolution; yet this whim (says the paper in question) gave foundation to the present honour which is done to the lady we mention in our liquor, who has ever since been called a toast. There are writers, however, who dispute this origin of the term, and assign it (used in this sense) a much more ancient one—an opinion apparently corroborated in the following lines of Hudibras, which was published before the period alluded to:

' Who would not rather suffer whipping,
Than swallow *toasts of bits of ribbin.*'

And indeed the Tatler's anecdote seems likelier to have been a *consequence,* than the *cause,* of this singular use of the word."

One Stephen Perlin, a French ecclesiastic, who was in London in the reign of King Edward VI. speaks, perhaps in just terms, of what was a great fault in the character of the English then, and is so now—the fondness for drink : he says "The English are great drunkards. In drinking or eating, they will say to you a hundred times, ' *I drink to you;*' and you should answer them in their language, ' *I pledge you.*' When they are drunk, they will swear death and blood that you shall drink all that is in your cup."

"The word *pledge,*" continued the Quaker, "is probably derived from the French ' pleige,' a surety or gage. The expression of ' I'll pledge you,' is by most writers deduced from the time of the Danes' ruling in England. It being said to have been common with those ferocious people to stab a native, in the act of drinking, with a knife or dagger; hereupon people would not drink in company, unless some one present would be their pledge, or surety, that they should receive no hurt whilst they were in their draught;

and hence is thought to come the following expression from Shak speare, in his *Timon of Athens :—*

"If I
Were a huge man, I should fear to drink at meals,
Lest they should spy my windpipe's dangerous notes :
Great men should drink *with harness on their throats.*"

"The old manner of pledging each other, according to Strutt (an eminent investigator of antiquities of this kind), was, the person who was going to drink, asked any one of the company who sat near him, whether he would *pledge* him; on which he answered that he would, and held up his knife or sword, to guard him whilst he drank; for, whilst a man is drinking, he is necessarily in an unguarded posture, exposed to the treacherous stroke of some hidden, or secret enemy. The same author, to corroborate what he advances, gives, in the part of his works mentioning this custom, a print, from an illuminated drawing of the time; in the middle of which is a figure, going to drink, addressing himself to his companion, who seems to tell him that he pledges him, holding up his knife in token of his readiness to assist and protect him. Some authors say the custom took rise from the murder of Edward the Martyr, who was barbarously stabbed in the back, on horseback, by an assissin, whilst drinking at Corfe Castle, the residence of Elfrida, the widow of Edgar.

"The term 'hob-nob,' is said to be a north-country expression, and to mean sometimes 'a venture, rashly.' And the question, '*will you hob-nob with me?*' Grose explains, in his Classical Dictionary of the Vulgar Tongue, as being one formerly in fashion at polite tables, signifying a request or challenge to drink a glass of wine with the proposer. He says further, that in the days of Queen Bess, when great chimneys were in fashion, there was at each corner of the hearth, or grate, a small elevated projection, called the *hob,* and behind it a seat. In winter-time, the beer was placed on the hob to warm, and the cold beer, or that not intended to be warmed, was set on a *small table,* reported to have been called a *nob.* So that the question, will you have *hob* or *nob?* seems only to have meant, will you have warm or cold beer: *i. e.* beer from the *hob,* or beer from the *nob.*

"Formerly, in the churches in London, and other parts of England, a whip was hung up to punish all drunkards. The emblem of them was a barrel standing on end, with a bung-hole above, and a spigot beneath. Accordingly, a tub was put over them, with holes made for the head and hands, and so they were obliged to walk through the streets."

"I wish," said Mentor, "the ancients had left us also some effective punishment for impostors, as well as drunkards; for really the metropolis swarms with them. In addition to the very many cases I have already made you acquainted with, Peregrine, I will tell how a friend of mine, Mr. L., was deceived by a fellow of the name of Patrick Murphy, who for the last three years has picked up a good deal of money by a troublesome cough, attended with spitting of blood : he was brought before the magistrate at the instance of my friend, who stated that he had been several times imposed upon by this worthy and his malady. Several months ago, he saw him in St. James's Park, coughing violently, and spitting blood, and surrounded by several respectable people, who were giving him money. Mr. L. also gave him money, and moreover offered his assistance, if he would try to walk to some place where he might be taken care of. To this friendly offer, Pat Murphy replied only by a fit of more coughing, and an intimation that *walking* was quite out of the question in his case ; but upon Mr. L. stating his intention of going for some constables to carry him, he took to his heels, and scampered away up Constitution Hill, as if nothing at all was the matter with him. This conduct determined my friend to punish him, should he ever have an opportunity, and seeing him again next day, displaying his cough, &c. in Russell Court, he caused him to be apprehended. Patrick, in his defence, assured the magistrate, that the gentleman was mistaken in the Park story, and said he certainly had been very ill a long time—the more was his misfortune. The magistrate prescribed him two months' exercise in the Cold-Bath *treading-mill*; and told him he had no doubt it would restore his health.

"The way this impostor contrives to spit blood, is by always having in his mouth a small bladder of bullock's or sheep's blood, and which, whenever he wants any, he squeezes with his teeth, and it gives him as much as needs his present purpose.

"You probably remember, Peregrine, I told you, some days past, of that sad fellow, the *cabbage-eater\**." "I do well remember his history," replied Peregrine ; "but what about him ?" "Why," said Mentor, "he has been taken again before the magistrate, by the officers of that very useful association—the Mendicity Society ; when it was stated, that since his liberation recently from gaol, he had left off raw cabbage-eating, and was to be seen daily about the town now, picking up any description of offal that came in his way, and pretending to devour it voraciously. That morning he was watched, and observed to pick up the head of a mackerel that was lying in the kennel, with which he smeared his mouth so as to impress a belief that he had swallowed it. Many persons, believing this, gave him money ; and, when the officer who apprehended him made his appearance, he endeavoured to escape, and, on examining his pockets, the head of the fish, which he was supposed to have devoured, was found therein.—He was committed for three months to Brixton.

And there is another species of imposition that cannot be made too public : it is this—Boys and grown persons are frequently seen to grope about kennels and hunt on the pavement for money that some lad, who is said to have been sent on an

* See page 8 of this work.

errand by his parents, has lost, and, from the dread of chastisement, they pretend to fear returning home. In many of these cases, humane persons have been induced to reimburse him, and the boy has been enabled fearlessly to proceed to his home. These misfortunes have now become very prevalent, and have been resorted to by sharpers connected with children, who are disposed of in various parts of the metropolis to practise this system of imposition.

"In truth, friend," said the Quaker, "although every means are used to give publicity to such disgraceful doings, in order that the public may be on their guard, it seems there are some people that will never gain wisdom; and those must be left to their fate. But I beg, now, my friends, to wish thee farewell, thanking thee for thy company;" and, after a cordial shake of the hand, he withdrew. Mentor, Peregrine, and his friend Wilmot soon followed, having previously agreed to be present the next day at a sparring exhibition. Accordingly, they met the following morning, and repaired to Windmill Street, Haymarket, to witness

The Doings in the Tennis Court;

There being a grand display of the manly art of boxing, for the benefit of a celebrated pugilist.

They were highly delighted with the setting-to of Spring and Peter Crawley, as well as the wind-up of Jem Ward and Jack Carter. At the conclusion of the sports, Mentor, Peregrine, and his friend Wilmot retired to the ex-champion Cribb's, where they had an opportunity of witnessing the general unassuming behaviour of the pugilists.   Having called for some refreshments, which were served in the first style by the worthy host, the conversation turned upon boxing.

"Figg," observed Mentor, "erected, in 1725, the first amphitheatre for sparring in England, at the top of Wells Street, Oxford Road, then called Marybone Fields, which seems to have been much frequented, if we can judge by the following lines, composed by one of the writers in the Spectator :—

> ' Long was the great Figg, by the prize-fighting swains,
> Sole monarch acknowledged of Marybon plains,
> To the towns far and near did his valour extend,
> And swam down the river from Thame to Gravesend.
> There lived Mr. Sutton, pipe-maker by trade,
> Who, hearing that Figg was thought such a stout blade,
> Resolv'd to put in for a share of his fame,
> And so sent to challenge the champion of Thame.
> With alternate advantage two trials had pass'd,
> When they fought out the rubbers Wednesday last.
> To see such a contest the house was so full,
> There hardly was room left to thrust in your scull.'

"In 1781, Figg opened an exhibition-room for sparring in Catherine Street, Strand, which was a favourite resort for many years, until the Fives' Court, St. Martin's Street, Leicester Square, was found more advantageous.   It was here I witnessed," continued Mentor, "the sparring between Molineux and Cribb. I got into the gallery, commanding a fine view of the stage and all the proceedings of the day.   So crowded was the court,  so closely wedged together were the spectators, that when, on the cry of 'hats off,' all eyes were raised and directed towards the stage, the vast and crowded area below seemed thickly paved with human faces :—

> The Fives' Court rush—the flash—the rally,
> The noise of 'Go it, Jack'—the stop—the blow—
> The shout—the chattering hit—the check—the sally!

"This, then, said I, mentally to myself, is the Fives' Court— the amphitheatre wherein the free gladiators try their skill previous to more serious combats : here, for many years past, the leary professors of that art so necessary to *men*, and so much despised by canting *hypocrites*, have displayed in public the science gained by long and patient practice in private.   Here the slaughtering Jem Belcher peeled, and here his first conqueror, the gallant Pearce, exhibited his finished person ;—on that stage, rendered as it were a classic spot by the efforts of those *giants of the ring*, Cribb, Molineux, Spring, Randal, Turner, &c., and others, having put in many a striking claim to distinction.

"Here were to be seen some of the first noblemen in the land, huddled together with the vilest blackguards—but Fives' Court is no more!  The improvements in the neighbourhood caused its walls to be levelled with the ground ; and the amateurs and professors of boxing have since resorted to this Tennis Court, the first benefit being for the black, Richmond, on February 28, 1820.

" It was Broughton who introduced the use of gloves in sparring. The Roman gladiators used to arm their hands with a tremendous kind of cæstus, composed of several thicknesses of raw hides, strongly fastened together in a circular form, and tied to the hand and part of the fore-arm.

" Sir John Perrot fought the first boxing-match upon record, in Southwark, where he beat two of the king's yeomen of the guards, an action which brought him into public notice at that time. He was the supposed son of Henry VIII. by Mary, wife to Thomas Perrot, Esq., of Haroldstone, in the county of Pembroke. In his stature and high spirit he bore a strong resemblance to that monarch. At the beginning of the reign of Mary, he was sent to prison for harbouring Protestants; but, by the interference of friends, he was discharged. He assisted at the coronation of Queen Elizabeth, who sent him to Ireland as Lord President of Munster, where he grew very unpopular by reason of his haughty conduct; he was recalled, unjustly accused, and condemned of treason. In 1592 he was tried by a special commission, brought in guilty of high treason, and sentenced to die. He was, however, respited by favour of the queen, but died of a broken heart in the Tower.

" Much has been said," continued Mentor, " both for and against the art of boxing; but it must be admitted it is in perfect unison with the feelings of Englishmen. It is from such open and manly contests in England, that the desperate and fatal effects of human passion are in a great measure, if not totally, prevented. The sons of our nobility and gentry now universally acquire the art. The national character for skill in this science is universal in foreign countries. This opinion is highly convenient, and is often sufficient to protect our countrymen from insult. Foreigners, in general, know nothing of it; they handle their arms like the flapping of the wings of a duck, and, they are conscious, but with little effect; and they dare not await the assault of the British batteringram, preparing to be put in motion. When they hear the blessing which an Englishman in his wrath pronounces on their eyes, and see his uplifted arm, it is as if they heard the roar, and were about to encounter the paw, of a lion. Thus, a Briton, trusting in native strength, moves among them like Achilles amongst the Trojans.

" I agree with the opinion of that late revered patriot, Whitbread, in thinking that such combats ought not to be prohibited, but winked at as the most innocent mode of abating the violence of human passions. It might be well, perhaps, if men were to become gentle as lambs (yet even lambs butt and box together), but men are still far from that meekness of temper, and we must allow passion to work itself off.

" I venture to affirm that the common people, in settling their disputes by the fist, act much more wisely, humanely, and philosophically , than the nobility and gentry, who decide their quarrels by more deadly weapons. Lead is very unwholesome to the constitution, and, taken inwardly, every medical man knows, often proves fatal, and there is no way so dangerous of administering this remedy as from the mouth of a pistol. This remedy for abating the violence of human passions is, therefore, worse than the disease. Steel is very little better : the surgical operations which the offended parties perform upon one another are often highly injurious. A sword is a very fearful kind of thing ; it is very handsome in the hands of an officer, and is a very useful instrument of war at such places as Trafalgar and Waterloo; but ought never to be used by one fellow subject against another. It is, after all, but a piece of cold, very cold iron, and, as Hudibras says—

> ' Ah me ! what troubles do environ,
> The man who meddles with cold iron.'

" It is at all times much better for men to appeal to the fist in the centre of the ring, before a jury of their countrymen to see fair play, than to have recourse to such deadly weapons.

" If we look abroad, into foreign countries, we shall see the desperate and fatal effects of human passion, for want of a regular and innocent mode of working itself off. In some countries, men administer the poisonous draught, and dreadful and secret vengeance is thus taken; in others, as in Portugal and Spain, and in Italy, and formerly before the French system of police, the dagger has, from time to time immemorial, administered to offended pride, the vengeance of death. In Holland, the peasants were wont to fight at snick-en-snee: that is, to cut each other with knives. In France, from the military habits of the people, the use of the sword is not unusual, even with the lower orders, and death often ensues, or, what is worse, the parties are maimed for life. In the southern states of North America, the practice of gouging, or forcing out the eyes, is not unusual : all these substitutes are infinitely worse than a moderate hammering in a fair contest with the fist, in which each party may acknowledge himself best, when he feels he has enough; animosity ceases, and in a few days every thing is over.

" There is something fair and honourable in an appeal to pugilistic strength and science. It is done openly, not in secret ; it is in the presence of umpires to see justice done; no foul blow must be struck; a man is not to be struck when he is falling; he is helped up, and time is given him to recover ; and, when he allows himself to be pronounced vanquished, his person is secure against all further violence. Voltaire was much delighted with the sight of a pugilistic contest in London ! and, in his works, describes it as a decided proof of the love of justice and fair play in the British populace.

" A spirit of humanity towards an enemy is hereby engendered : he is not to be struck when on the ground, and every act of generous forbearance meets with the applause which is its due. No sailors or soldiers show so much mercy to a fallen foe, as the British; and it is to their early acquaintance with the ring that they owe this quality.

"There is something nobly generous implanted in the breasts )f the British youth, by the custom of shaking hands with their antagonist, before they begin to decide any dispute with their fists; and the same manly and truly English token of good-will and forgiveness is resorted to, when the battle is ended. What a glorious sight it is to see two youths, after a boxing-match, approach each other, and offer the hand of friendship, as a token and proof that no animosity exists in the breast of either party; and that all their differences are forgotten and forgiven.

"This custom of shaking hands is exclusively British. Mons. Grossby, in his Travels, thus humorously describes it: 'To take a man by the hand,' says he, ' and shake it till his shoulder is almost dislocated, is one of the grand testimonies of friendship which the English give each other, when they happen to meet. This they do very coolly: there is not any great expression of friendship in their countenances, yet the whole soul enters into the hand which gives the shake; and this supplies the place of the embraces and salutes of the French.'

"It is well known, as I before remarked, that the English nation are, by pre-eminence, above all nations, ancient and modern, a *boxing nation;* and London is, in a pre-eminent degree, the metropolis of pugilistic science—the grand centre of the amateurs and performers. Boxing, throughout England generally, and in London in particular, is an elementary part of education; and behold the consequence,—no people on earth are so distinguished for generosity of feeling, for humanity, for charity towards distress, as the English; and, whilst we are proud of every inch of land that may be called England—of our metropolis, we are more than usually proud; for it is the concentration of all that is noble in human nature, and its whole population are actuated by a love of justice, benevolence, charity, and humanity, of which the limits of the habitable world alone form the boundary.

"There are many persons who despise all English sports and pastimes, as not consistent with the present *refined* state of society; and that they tend to blunt the feelings. Our present king knows the value of such recreations to his people. ' Meddle not with the pastimes of the people,' said his majesty to some puritanical would-be emaculates, who were railing against the various modes of amusement.

"Let us take a glance at the effects of the present *refined* state of society, and of those of the *barbarous* ages, when boxing, bear and bull-baiting, &c., were witnessed without fainting. In the first place—at what period did the people live, who founded most of those charitable institutions, such as alms-houses, hospitals, &c., which are in London and its vicinity? Why, in the *barbarous* ages. Old Coram, the founder of the Foundling Hospital, was a frequenter at Figg's; yet his heart was in the right place. Guy, the founder of Guy's Hospital, too, was of the old school; there was none of the present *refinement* about him. Dean Collett founded St. Paul's School; yet he was of the bull and bear-fighting period: and a thousand other instances might be quoted, of the real genuine truly British charitable disposition of persons who lived in the *barbarous* ages, as they are falsely called. Read the histories of those splendid monuments of charity, the alms-houses; and you will find the founders were of olden times.—Where are the proofs of individual charitable munificence of the present *refined* age? It would take some time to find them. It is, indeed, a sad *pity*, that so *much refinement* produces so *little charity*; and that *crime* keeps pace with *refinement*. Oh, no! it is not refinement the present age possesses: it is pride, beggarly pride—puritanical pride—cold-blooded pride—that is now making such rapid strides in society in England, and not refinement. The good old blunt feeling is giving way to a narrow-minded jealousy, and to a total want of confidence.

" What has become of the English cheer, of the gambols, of the feastings, of the hospitality among neighbours and tenants, which marked the period of good Queen Bess? Where are they to be found now? No where.—The people are too *refined* to attend to such affairs now a-days: and, as to asking them to witness a bear-bait, why they would swoon at the very mention of it.

" It is true, that, in the reign of Elizabeth, the practice of bear-baiting, and the fighting of other beasts, was carried to a great extent, as may be inferred from many black-letter advertisements in those times. The following may be taken as proofs of the truth of the remark.

"' At the boarded house in Marybone Fields, on Monday, the 24th of this instant (July), will be a match fought between the wild and savage panther and twelve English dogs, for £300. This match was made between an English gentleman and a foreigner; the latter was praising the boldness and fierceness of the panther, and said he would lay the above-named sum that he would beat any twelve dogs we had in England. The English gentleman laid the wager with him; the other has brought the panther; and, notwithstanding the boldness of the creature, he desires fair play for his money, and but one dog at a time. First gallery, 2s. 6d.; second gallery, 2s. No persons admitted on the stage but those belonging to the dogs. The doors to be open at three o'clock, and the panther will make his appearance on the stage at five precisely.

"' Note. Also a bear to be baited, and a mad green bull to be turned loose in the gaming-place, with fireworks all over him, and a comet at his tail, and bull-dogs after him; a dog to be drawn up with fireworks after him in the middle of the yard; and an ass to be baited upon the same stage.'—*Weekly Journal*, July 22, 1721.

"' At the particular request of several persons of distinction, the celebrated white sea-bear, which has been seen and admired by the curious in most parts of England, will be baited at Mr. Broughton's Amphitheatre, this day, being the 29th instant. This creature is now supposed to be arrived at his utmost strength and perfection, so that he will afford extraordinary entertainment, and *behave* himself in such a manner as to fill those who are lovers of diversion of this kind with delight and astonishment. Any person who brings a dog will be admitted gratis.'—*Daily Advertiser*, January 29, 1747.

" ' We hear there will be a large he-tiger baited on Wednesday next at Mr. Broughton's Amphitheatre, in Oxford Road, being the first that was ever baited in England. He is the largest that was ever seen here, being eight feet in length. He is one of the fiercest and swiftest of savage beasts, and it is thought will afford good sport.'

" We cannot have a better idea of the amusements of the days of good Queen Bess, than from the following passage in one of Rowland White's letters to Sir Robert Sydney:—' Her majesty is very well: this day she appoints a Frenchman to do feats upon a rope in the Conduit Court; to-morrow she hath commanded the bears, the bull, and the ape, to be baited in the tilt-yard; upon Wednesday she will have solemn *dawncing*.'—1600.

" The following is a copy of an advertisement from a bear-garden, kept by Alleyn the performer :—

" ' To-morrow, being Thursdaie, shall be seen at the bear-garden on the Bankside, a greate match plaid by the gamesters of Essex, who hath challenged all comers whatsoever, to plaie five dogges at the single beare, for £5; and also to wearie a bull dead at the stake; and for their better content shall have pleasant sport with the horse and ape, and whipping of the blind bear.'

" Hentzner's Itinerary explains blind-bear whipping in the following manner :—' Whipping a blind bear is performed by five or six men standing circularly with whips, with which they flagellate his loins without any mercy, as he cannot escape from them by reason of his chains.' Such was the rage for the baiting of bears and other animals in those times, that persons were empowered to seize and take away such bears, bulls, and dogs, as were thought meet for the royal service. In the old records, we find an engagement signed by certain persons of the town of Manchester, wherein they promise to send up yearly, ' A masty dogge or bytche, to the bear-garden, between Midsomer and Michaelmasse?' Alleyn, the *great* keeper of the bear-garden, in a petition addressed to James the First, complains of the loss which he had sustained in consequence of that monarch's prohibition of public baitings on Sundays in the afternoon. In this curious petition, the writer mentions the loss of a ' goodly *beare* of George Stone, who was killed before the King of Denmark.' And also of ' little Bess of Bromley, who fought, in one day, twenty double and single courses with the best dogs in the country.' "

Pipes and tobacco were introduced after dinner; and, as Mentor and his friends would not appear singular, they too "blowed a clowd;" but not very cheerfully on the part of Peregrine. "Perhaps, Sir," said a gentleman to him, "you have a dislike to tobacco?" "Not exactly," replied Peregrine; for he was ashamed to acknowledge he had never smoked a pipe. "There is nothing more astonishing in the history of the human mind," said the gentleman, (a person of great literary attainments) than that unaccountable sort of prejudice, which some people evince at the introduction of any thing to which they have not been accustomed, be the thing ever so good or advantageous. This kind of feeling occasioned it to be debated, on first adopting the use of potatoes, whether they were really fit for food, or were not rather a vegetable poison; it occasioned the resistance of small-pox inoculation years ago, and of the vaccine in the present day, as "flying in the face of God," to adopt a phrase of some old ladies, as great fatalists in these matters as the Turks; but it is in no instance more strikingly exhibited than in that of the first bringing of *Tobacco* into this country. Who would have thought that a king of England, two centuries back, and that one of the poorest and neediest of our monarchs, would have written a tract, in the bitterest style of invective, expressly to hinder the use of a commodity, the duties on which now yield to the state more than the amount of his whole revenue. Not but we believe, could his majesty have been sensible of what it might have been made to produce (such was his love or want of money), he would have spoken of it in more moderate terms than he has done in the following extract. The king we allude to is James I., who, in his "Counter-blast to Tobacco," says,—

"'That it is not only a common herbe, which, though under divers names, grows almost every where, but was first found out by the barbarous Indians; and asks his good countrymen to consider what 'honours or policy can move them to imitate the manners of such wild, godlesse, and slavish people?' He proceeds: —'It is not long since the first entry of this abuse amongst us here (as this present age can very well remember, both the first author, and forms of its introduction); and now many in this kingdome have had such continuall use of this unsavourie smoke, that they are not able to forbeare the same, no more than an old drunkard can abide to be long sober. How several are, by this custome, disabled in their goods, let the gentrie of this land bear witnesse; some of whom bestow £300, some £400 a-year, on this precious stinke. And is it not great vanitie and uncleanlinesse that at the table, a place of respect, men should sit tossing of tobacco-pipes, and smoking of tobacco, one to another; making the filthy stinke thereof to exhale across the dishes, and infect the wine. But no other time nor action is exempted from the publicke use of this uncivill tricke; for a man cannot heartily welcome his friende at his home, but straight they must in hand wi'h tobacco; yea, the mistresse cannot in more mannerly kind entertaine her servant, than by giving him, out of her faire hand, a pipe of tobacco.—A weed,' he adds, 'the smoaking whereof is loathsome to the eye, hateful to the nose, harmfull to the braine, dangerous to the lungs, and, in the blacke stinking fumes thereof, nearest resembles the Stigion smoke of the pit that is bottomlesse.' He is still more bitter in his 'Witty Apophthayms,' in which he avers that 'Tobacco is the lively image and pattern of hell; for that it has, by alllusion, in it all the parts and vices of the world, whereby hell may be gained. For, first, it is smoke; so are all the vanities of this world. Secondly, it delighteth them that take it; so do all the pleasures of the world. Thirdly, it maketh men drunken and light in the head; so do all the vanities of this world. Fourthly, he that taketh tobacco saith he cannot leave it; it doth bewitch him—even so the pleasures of the world make men loth to leave them; and, further, besides all this, it is like hell in the very substance of it; for it is a stinking loathsome thing; and so is hell.' And further, his majesty professed, that 'where he to invite the devil to a dinner, he should have three dishes: first, a pig; second, a poll of ling and mustard; and, third, a pipe of tobacco for digesture.'

"The king's aversion was adopted by his courtiers, as a matter of courtesy, who all pretended a great horror of smoking. The people generally, however, paid no attention to this, or all the other methods which were used to discountenance it; and, in some respects, even carried it to a greater excess than at present, particularly by smoking tobacco in the theatres. Malone (Hist. of the English Stage), mentioning the custom, in Shakspeare's time, of spectators being allowed to sit on the stage during performances, says, ' They were attended by pages, who furnished them with pipes and tobacco, which were smoked there, as well as in other parts of the house :—

> " When young Roger goes to see a play,
>     His pleasure is, *you place him on the stage.*
> The better to demonstrate his array,
>     And how he sits, *attended by his page.*
> That only serves to fill those pipes with smoke,
>     For which he pawned hath his riding-cloak."
>                     *Springs to catch Woodcocks*—1613.

" And earlier, in Skialethia, a collection of epigrams and satires, 1598 :—

> " See you him yonder, who sits o'er the stage,
>     With his *tobacco-pipe* now at his mouth?"

"This, however, was a custom much excepted against by some, as appears from a satirical epigram, by Sir John Davis, 1598 :—

> " Who dares affirm that Sylla dares not fight?
> He that *dares take tobacco on the stage*;
> ———— Dares dance in Paul's,' &c.

26.

" But Hentzner's account, at this same period (1598), which Mr. Malone has omitted to quote, as to the custom mentioned, is far more explicit and amusing. Speaking of the London playhouse then, he says, ' Here, and every where else, the English are constantly smoking of tobacco, and in this manner :—they have pipes *on purpose*, made of clay; into the further end of which they put *the* herb, so dry, that it may be rubbed into powder; and, putting fire to it, they draw the smoke into their mouths, which they puff out again through their nostrils, like funnels, along with it plenty of phlegm and defluxion of the head.'—*Paul Hentzner's Journey into England*, 1598.

" Sir Walter Raleigh is well known to have first introduced the use of tobacco into England, and is the person King James hints at, when he speaks of the first author and introduction of it being then well remembered; and is said to have been so partial to it, that he took, says a nearly contemporary writer, ' a pipe of tobacco a little before he went to the scaffold, which some formal persons were scandalized at; but, I thinke,' he adds, ' 'twas well and properly done to settle his spirits.' And the same author adds the following curious anecdotes on this subject: ' In my part of North Wilts (Malmsbury hundred), it were brought into fashion by Sir Walter Long. They had, at first, *silver pipes*; the ordinary sorte made use of a walnut-shell and a straw. I have heard my grandfather, Lyte, say that one pipe was handed from man to man round the table. Sir Walter Raleigh, standing at a stand at Sir Robert Poyntz' Parke, at Acton, took a pipe of tobacco, which made the ladies quit it till he had done. Within these thirty-five years,' he adds (about 1680), ' it was sold then for its weight in silver. I have heard some of our old yeomen neighbours say, that when they went to Malmsbury or Chippenham market, they culled out their biggest shillings to lay in the scales against the tobacco. Now the customs of it are th. greatest his majesty (Charles II.) hath."

" Now, I am one," continued the gentleman, " who thinks that King James, although he has been called a second Solomon, was none of the wisest.

" Barton, in his Anatomie of Melancholy, calls tobacco the divine, rare, super-excellent tobacco; a sovereign remedy for all disorders; a virtuous herb, if opportunely taken, and medicinally used; but as it is commonly used by most men, it is a plague, a mischief, a violent purger of goods, lands, health : hellish, develish, and damned tobacco, the ruin and overthrow of body and soul.

" Raphall Thorias, who wrote a book called Hymnus Tabaci, has this invective against tobacco :—

> Let it be damned to hell! and called from thence,
> Proserpine's wine, the furies' frankincense,
> The Devil's addle eggs; or else to these,
> A sacrifice grim Pluto to appease,
> A deadly weed, which its beginning had,
> From the foam Cerberus, when the cur was mad.'

Howell, in his Letters, 1678, says—'Tobacco is good for many things, if moderately taken : it helps digestion ; it makes one void rheum ; it is a good companion to one that has been long poring over a book, and stupified with study ; it quick'neth him, and dispels those clouds that usually oversets the brain. The smoke of tobacco is one of the wholesomest scents that is, against all contagious airs, for it over-masters all other smells. Tobacco is good to fortify and preserve the eyesight, the smoke being let in round about the balls of the eyes once a week, and frees them of all heum, and

> " Plumb-tree gum, such as is in old men's eyes."

Besides, being taken into the stomach, it will heal and cleanse it. In Barbary, and other parts of Africa, they put the tobacco under the tongue, which affords them perpetual moisture, and takes off the edge of the appetite for some days.'

" My pipe," continued the gentleman, " is one of my greatest luxuries : it is the—

> Charm of the solitude I love,
> My pleasing pipe ; my glowing stove !
> My head of rheum is purged by thee,
> My heart of vain anxiety.
> Tobacco ! fav'rite of my soul !
> When round my head thy vapours roll,
> When lost in air they vanish too,
> An emblem of my life I view.
> I view, and hence, instructed, learn,
> To what myself shall shortly turn—
> Myself,—a kindled coal to-day,
> That wastes in smoke, and fleets away.
> Swiftly as then, confusing thought,
> Alas ! I vanish into naught.

" Some say tobacco takes its name from its being first discovered in 1520, near Tobasco, in the Gulf of Mexico. Others say, it is named from Tobago, one of our West India islands, whence it was first brought to England in 1585, by Sir Francis Drake, the great circumnavigator, and that Sir Walter Raleigh taught the English how to smoke it. .

" That King James was not the only mortal enemy to tobacco, is evident, from the following singular will : Peter Campbell, a Derbyshire gentleman, made his will 20 Oct. 1616, and therein was the following extraordinary clause. 'Now for all such household goods at Darby, where John Hoson hath an inventory, my will is, that my son Roger shall have them all toward house-keepinge, on this condition, that yf, at any tyme hereafter, any of his brothers or sisters, shall fynd him *taking of tobacco*, that then he or she so fynding him, and making just proofe thereof to my executors, shall have the said goods, or the full value thereof, according as they shall be praysed, which said goods shall presently after my death be valued and praysed by my executors for that purpose.' "

"I was reading the other day," said Mentor, "that every professed, inveterate, and incurable snuff-taker, at a moderate computation, takes one pinch in ten minutes. Every pinch, with the agreeable ceremony of blowing and wiping the nose, and other incidental circumstances, consumes a minute and a half.

"One minute and a half, out of every ten, allowing sixteen hours to a snuff-taking day, amounts to two hours and twenty-four minutes out of every natural day, or one day out of every ten.

"One day out of every ten amounts to thirty-six days and a half in every year.

"Hence, if we suppose the practice to be persisted in forty years, two entire years of the snuff-taker's life will be dedicated to tickling his nose, and two more to blowing it.

"The expense of snuff, snuff-boxes, and handkerchiefs, encroaches as much on the income of the snuff-taker, as it does on his time ; and, by the money thus lost to the public, a fund might be constituted for the discharge of the national debt.

"Certainly, so many people would not take snuff, if they knew how much of it was adulterated. The following is the manner *genuine* Macouba is made :—Cheap tobacco-powder, savine, yellow sand, old rotten wood, and almost any vegetable substance, both dry and green, mixed into a body, and coloured with red ochre, amber, or other noxious red or brown colour, moistened with water or molasses. The whole is passed through a hair sieve, to mix it more intimately, then placed in a heap for some time, to sudorify, or sweat, as the snuff-takers have it, which makes it all over equally moist, and imitates the oiliness which the real Havannah possesses. It is then placed in cannisters, or jars, and an ill-printed label in Spanish pasted outside. This is the *genuine* Macouba sold in London ; and much of it is exported in large quantities to the East Indies, too."

Cribb's celebrated dwarf, which he humanely keeps in his service, having entered the room with some liquor, attracted the notice of Peregrine, not only from the smallness of his stature, but from his symmetry, and his neatness of dress. "These dwarfs," said Mentor, "are very curious proofs of the freaks of nature ; and their history is full of interest, which, some day, I will lay fully before you, when we go and visit the various exhibitions in the metropolis ; but certainly one of the greatest curiosities ever witnessed in London, was the celebrated Matthew Buckinga, 'the wonderful little man of Nuremburg,' as he was styled : he was really a singular creature, being born without hands, thighs, or feet; and yet he could play at skittles and nine pins, was a good musician, and a respectable mechanic, in constructing machines to perform on all sorts of music.

"Among the most remarkable of his drawings, is his own portrait, and in the wig he has most ingeniously contrived that its curls should exhibit, in several lines, the 27th, 121st, 128th, 130th, 140th, 149th, and the 150th psalm, concluding with the Lord's

Prayer. He was only twenty-nine inches high.—I bought, this morning, this specimen of his writing."

*This was Written by Matthew Buchinger born Without Hands or Feet 1674 Germany*

" Do but observe," said Peregrine, " how smart the dwarf is about his shoes ; he seems a patron of those illuminators, the blacking gentry." " He does, indeed," replied Mentor ; and it is astonishing how the public allow themselves to be humbugged by purchasing blacking at such an enormous rate. The bottles seem large to the sight, tall and big ; but, if you take the trouble to dissect one, Master Wilmot, you will find great ingenuity displayed : the inside shows a regular row of projected lines, like the worm of a screw, to prevent the bottle holding too much ; the top of the bottle is wide, but it slopes gently, so that the bottom is considerably less than the top : which bottom is completely convex : and, on breaking the bottle, you will find it immensely thick ; so that a pint bottle holds barely half a pint. It is no wonder these gentry can ride in their carriages, when their profits are so immense. In these hard times, and when the lustre of the shoe is such an indispensable part of the dress, it is surprising persons do not make their own blacking ; which, if they were to do, they would find, where much is used, it would save them money. The following is a good receipt to make the *real Japan:*

" Take three ounces of ivory black, two ounces of coarse sugar, one ounce of sulphuric acid, one ounce of muriatic acid, one lemon, one table-spoonful of sweet oil, and one pint of vinegar. First mix the ivory black and sweet oil together, then the lemon and sugar with a little vinegar, to qualify the blacking ; then add the sulphuric and muriatic acids, and mix them well altogether. The sugar, oil, and vinegar, prevent the acids from injuring the leather, and add to the lustre of the blacking.

Mentor proposed, as the company in the room was highly diverting, and much information could be gained by joining in the conversation, that they should stay and take tea there, which was agreed to; and, during their repast, Peregrine's friend remarked how excellent the bread was; and that to get it in such perfection in London was a great luxury. "The history of this important necessary of life," replied Mentor, "is at all times interesting; and I have lately made myself acquainted with several particulars as to the weight, price, and quality, of the different kinds of loaf made anciently. In old times, it appears that wheat was by no means the general bread corn used (and, indeed, is hardly yet in some northern countries), but that rye, barley, or oats, were the common food of the middle or lower ranks of people, who now (in the southern parts of England, at least) disdain any but the finest wheaten bread. Even as late as the reign of Queen Elizabeth, when great advances had been made in luxury and refinement, the lower sort of people fed upon what would at this time scarcely be offered to dogs. This we learn from several contemporary authorities, and particularly from the description of England, prefixed to *Hollingshead's Chronicles* (edition 1582), where we are told that ' the bread through the land is made of such grain as the soile yieldeth. Neverthelesse the gentilitie commonlie provide themselves sufficientlie of wheat for their own table, whilst their household and poore neighbours, in some shires, are forced to content themselves with rie or barleie,—yea, and in time of dearthe, manie with bread made either of beans, peason, or otes, or of altogether, and some acorns among. I will not say that this extremitie is oft so well to be seene in time of plentie, as of dearth, but if I should, I could easily bring my trial.' He afterwards speaks of the artificer and poor labouring man, as seldom able to taste any other than the bad bread above mentioned; and proceeds to describe more particularly the several sorts of bread usually made in England, viz., *manchet, cheat,* or wheaten bread, another inferior sort of wheaten bread, called *ravelled,* and lastly, *brown bread,* ' of which,' says the writer, ' we have two sorts, one baked up as it cometh from the mill, so that neither the bran nor the floor are anie whit diminished; the other hath little or no floure baked therein at all, and it is not only the worst and weakest of all the other sorts, but also appointed in time for servants, slaves, and the inferior kinds of people to feed upon. Hereunto likewise because it is drie and brickle in the working. Some adde a portion of rie meale in our time, whereby the rough drinesse thereof is somewhat qualified, and then it is called *mascelin,*—that is, bread made of mingled corne. Albeit that divers do sow or mingle wheat and rie, and sell the same at the markets, under the aforesaid name.' He adds, ' in champeigne countries, much rie and barleie bread is eaten.' By which addition of ' the rie meale in our time,' it may fairly be concluded that it was then no distant period when the bran corn was baken for servants.

" In the ancient ordinance for the Assize and Weight of Bread, copied in Strype's Stowe, from the ' Old Book of Customs,' at Guildhall, the weight and price of the different sorts of loaf in use are stated, taking the price of wheat from three shillings to twenty shillings per quarter. The species of loaf named is, ' the *ferthing simnel;* the *ferthing whyt loof cocket;* the *penny whyt loof;* and the *penny whet loof of all graynis.*' By this ordinance it was fixed, that ' *the halfpenny loof whyt of Stratford*' was to ' way two ouncis more than the *halfpenny whyt loof of London;* the halfpenny whet loof three ouncis more; the penny whet loof six ouncis more; the three halfpenny whyt loof as much as the London penny whet loof; and the loof all graynis, as much as the penny whet loof, and the halfpenny whyt loof.' The comparison of the *London* bread with that of *Stratford,* here mentioned, arose, it seems, from the bakers' having lived in former times at Stratford-le-Bow, who supplied the city with bread, and which they brought in carts to the London markets.

" These ordinances were confirmed by Queen Elizabeth and her council, towards the latter part of her reign; and, again, in that of her successor, James, in a book called ' The Book of Assize,' by which it was ordered, that no other bread should be baked, and sold publicly, than ' symnel bread and wastel; white wheaten, household, and horse-bread.' And bakers were restrained, upon pain of forfeiture, from making any loaves of a larger size (except at Christmas time), than the farthing white bread, halfpenny white, halpenny wheaten, penny wheaten bread, penny household, and two-penny household loaves.

" In 1468, it is mentioned in a book of the ancient laws and orders as to bread, " that alle maner of bakers dwellyng out of the cities and burgh townes, as bakers dwellyng in villagis, &c. their peny lof be what corn soever it be, be it white brede or browne, should weigh more than the peny lof in the town or city by x's, and the halfpenny lof by v's.' And the reason assigned, is, ' because they bere nat sich chargis as bakers in the citees doon, and townes.' In another old assize, ' *the ferthing wastel*' is mentioned, the *symnel* (siminell) and the halfpenny wheaten, or ' cribel-lofe.'

" To prevent the imposition of a bad or spurious article upon the public, and particularly of the lower sort, it was, by another regulation, ordered, that no bran loaf should be made that ' was worse in breaking than it appeared with outside,' (not deceptively made). And the bakers were forbid by the same, to go into St. Michael's (Cornhill) church-yard, or the markets of West Chepe (Cheapside), Gracechurch, or Belingsgate, nor to Botolph Wharf, nor Queen Hythe, nor aboard of any ship, to buy corn, ' before the first ringing.' This was probably intended to afford a fair competition in the market, and prevent forestalling. ' For there appears of old,' says the commentator on Stowe just quoted, ' to have been bells rung in several church-steeples of the city, as Bow, for one, at certain hours of the day, and that both for devotion and business; and before the first ringing in the morning, none might go out to buy provisions.' By this regulation, also (and it confirms the statement just made as to the very bad quality of some of the bread at this time), bakers were not to make meal of Felger,* of sticks (probably meaning bark), of straw, nor of rushes. And, in regard to short weight, it ordained that the baker, if there lacked an ounce-weight in a loaf, should be fined twenty pence; if an ounce and a half, two shillings; and if he ' should bake over the assize, then he should be judged into the pillory.'

' Manchet loaves, and wastel bread, are mentioned by Shakspeare, as also in a Christmas Carol of the thirteenth or fourteenth centuries, translated from the old Norman French, by Mr. Douce, in his illustrations of that author, in the following lines :—

> ' His liberal board is deftly spread
> With manchet loaves, and wastel bread.'

" A physician, who wrote in 1572, speaks of the Yorkshire bread as the finest he then knew of. ' Bred,' says he, ' of dyvers graines, of dyvers formes, in dyvers places be used; some in form of manchet, used of the quality; some of greate loves, as is usual among yeomenry; some between both, as with the franklings; some in forme of cakes, as at weddings; some roundes of hogs, as at upsittings; some seninels, cracknels, and buns, as in the Lent; some in brode cakes, as the oten cakes in Kendall, on yrons; some on slate-stones, as in Hye Peke; some in frying-pans, as in Derbyshire; some between yrons, as wapons; some in round cakes, as byskets for the ships. But these and all other the mayn bread of Yorkshire excelleth, for that it is of the finest floure of the wheat well-tempered, best baked, a patterne of all others the fineste.' And one Perlin, a French ecclesiastic, and traveller here, in the reign of Edward VI., says (notwithstanding what has been stated), that the bread eaten in London was much whiter than that commonly made in France, although it was as cheap as that sold there. We may presume, however, that he only partook, while in England, of the better sort of bread. He adds, ' They (the Londoners) have a custom of eating with their beer very soft saffron cakes, in which there are likewise raisins, which give a relish to the beer.' "

The hilarity of the company was heightened by the inimitable comic powers of one of the party, in reciting a ludicrous description of " Going to a Mill," written by the celebrated Pierce Egan; and, to give a zest to the treat, the worthy landlord also chaunted : in this manner they passed a very pleasant evening. At length, it was time for the company to separate, which they did, in the utmost good humour, all seemingly highly delighted with the entertainment. Mentor parted with his friends, Peregrine and Wilmot, until the next day, when they agreed to go in search of fresh adventures.

* ' Farinare faciant felgere.'

On their way home, Peregrine and his friend Wilmot, having stopped at the corner of a street, were rudely desired by a watchman *to move on*, at the same time putting his lantern up to their faces, which Wilmot, considering a great insult, instantly demolished it with his walking-stick; upon which round went the watchman's rattle, and a host of charleys came to his assistance, and walked them off to where they might see—

**The Doings in a Watchhouse.**

His honour, the constable of the night, was a miserable half-starved tailor, proud, insolent, and saucy, with a nose as long as a rolling-pin, set with carbuncles and rubies, looking as fresh as the gills of an angry turkey-cock. After taking about twenty puffs at his pipe, he very leisurely, resting his arm on the chair, asked the watchman what the *fellars* had been at. "Breaking my lantern, sir, and also the king's peace," said the watchman. "The king's peace!" replied the tailor; "it is indeed a shame his majesty's sleep should be disturbed at this time of night—shut them up below, traitors and villains." "I beg your pardon," said Peregrine, "we have committed no offence." "No offence!" quoth the constable, "do you call breaking the peace of the king, no offence? Away with you." The watchhouse-keeper was about placing them in the black-hole, but giving him some *sterling* reasons why they should not be so incarcerated, they were handed to a small two-bedded room, for the use of which they were

27                      P

charged the moderate sum of five shillings each. Here they remained till the morning, and, as a memento of their feelings on the unjust behaviour of the constable, Wilmot wrote the following lines with his pencil, which he affixed to the wall of the room, addressed—

### TO THE CONSTABLE OF THE NIGHT.

May rats and mice
Consume his shreds,
His patterns and his measures ;
May nits and lice
Infest his bed,
And care confound his pleasures.

May his long bills
Be never paid ;
And may his helpmate horn him ;
May all his ills
Be public made,
And may his workmen scorn him.

May cucumbers
Be all his food,
And small beer be his liquor ;
Lustful desires
Still fire his blood,
But may his reins grow weaker

When old, may he
Reduced be,
From constable to beadle,
And live until
He cannot feel
His thimble from his needle.

About ten o'clock, a hackney-coach was brought to the watchhouse, into which Peregrine, Wilmot, and the watchhouse-keeper got, and drove off to the police-office. Peregrine having caused a letter to be conveyed to Mentor, relating the adventure, he was found waiting their arrival ; and, it being a regular charge, it was obliged to go before the magistrate, else Mentor would have been happy to have settled it without the *beak's* assistance. An officer in court, learning the nature of their business, told them it would be better to retire to an adjoining public-house, and he would call them in time to meet the charge : they cordially thanked him for his consideration, and left the court, under the care of the watchhouse-keeper, and, while in the parlour of the public-house, they learned the particulars of the multifarious business that was to come on for hearing before the magistrate that morning.—Among them a man was charged by a sailor with the trick of duffing. The complainant, a few days preceding, was crossing Tower Hill, where he was met by the prisoner, who appeared in the garb of a sailor, and, calling him aside, said, " Shipmate, do you want a watch ? I have one that cost me £14, but, being in want of money, you shall have it for £6." At this moment an old clothesman stepped up and said, "I'll give you £7 for it." The duffer answered, "Be-gone, you rascal : I've been once tricked by a Jew, and shall never deal with one again." The associate departed, and the tar, become the dupe of the prisoner, purchased the watch for six sovereigns. The sailor shortly after called at a watchmaker's, where he discovered that the watch was hardly worth twenty shillings. Some time after, he happened to meet the prisoner near the same place, and, on threatening to charge him with the fraud, he said, "If you come with me to my house, and give me up the watch, I'll give you a note of hand for the money." The com-plainant consented. On the note falling due, he demanded pay-ment of it, when he was turned out of doors by the prisoner, who told him to get the money "how he could."

Another case was of a servant girl, who applied for advice, as to what steps she could pursue to apprehend a man who had de-frauded her of £6, the amount of all her savings since she had been in service. The fellow, the complainant said, was one of those people called " Duffers," and the girl, being at her master's street-door, he forced his way in, and insisted on showing her his valuable assortment of shawls and gold watches, which, he said, from particular circumstances, he was enabled to dispose of re-markably cheap. After much persuasion, he prevailed on the foolish woman to purchase what she supposed was a camel's-hair shawl and a gold watch for £6; and, on showing her prize shortly afterwards to a neighbour, it was readily discovered that she had parted with her money for trash, which, at its utmost value, was not worth more than a pound.

The officer now entered the room, telling Mentor and his friends that their case was expected to be called next, and re-quested them to be ready; they immediately accompanied him to the office, where a laughable charge of crim. con. was being heard.

Mr. Daniel Sullivan, greengrocer, fruiterer, coal and po-tatoe-merchant, salt fish and Irish pork-monger, was brought before the magistrate on a peace-warrant, issued at the suit of his wife, Mrs. Mary Sullivan,

Mrs. Sullivan is an Englishwoman, who married Mr. Sullivan for love, and has been " blessed with many children by him." But, notwithstanding, she appeared before the magistrate with her face all scratched and bruised, from the eyes, downward, to the very tip of her chin; all which scratches and bruises, she said, were the handiwork of her husband.

The unfortunate Mary, it appeared, married Mr. Sullivan about seven years ago; at which time he was as polite a young Irishman as ever handled a potatoe on this side channel; he had every thing snug and comfortable about him, and his purse and person, taken together, were quite *ondeniable*. She, herself, was a young woman genteelly brought up—abounding in friends, and acquaintance, and silk gowns, with three good bonnets always in use, and black velvet shoes to correspond—welcome wherever she went, whether to dinner, tea, or supper, and made much of by every body. St. Giles's bells rang merrily at their wedding; a fine fat leg of mutton and capers, plenty of pickled salmon, three ample dishes of salt fish and potatoes, with pies, puddings, and porter of the best, were set forth for the bridal supper; all the most considerablist families in Dyott Street and Church Lane were invited, and every thing promised a world of happiness; and, for five whole years, they were happy. "She loved," as Lord Byron would say, "She loved and was beloved; she ador'd, and she was worshipped;" but Mr. Sullivan was too much like the hero of his lordship's tale—his affections could not "hold the bent;" and the sixth year had scarcely commenced, when poor Mary discovered that she had "outlived his liking." From that time to the present he had treated her continually with the greatest cruelty; and, at last, when by this means he had reduced her from a comely young person to a mere handful of a poor creature, he beat her, and turned her out of doors.

This was Mrs. Sullivan's story; and she told it with such pathos, that all who heard it pitied her—except her husband.

It was now Mr. Sullivan's turn to speak. Whilst his wife was speaking, he stood with his back towards her, his arms folded across his breast, to keep down his choler, biting his lips, and staring at the blank wall; but the moment she ceased, he abruptly turned round, and, curiously enough, asked the magistrate whether *Misthress* Sullivan had done *spaking*?

"She has," replied his worship; "but suppose you ask her whether she has any thing more to say."

"I shall, sir," replied the angry Mr. Sullivan—"Misthress Sullivan, had you any more of it to say?"

Mrs. Sullivan raised her eyes to the ceiling, clasped her hands together, and was silent.

"Very well, then," continued he; "will I get lave to spake, your honour?"

His honour nodded permission, and Mr. Sullivan immediately began a defence, to which it is impossible to do justice; so exuberantly did he suit the action to the word, and the word to the action. "Och! your honour, there is something the matter with me," he began; at the same time putting two of his fingers perpendicularly over his forehead to intimate that Mrs. Sullivan had played him false. He then went into a long story about a *Misther* Burke, who lodged in in his house, and had taken the liberty of assisting him in his conjugal duties, "without any *lave* from *him* at all." "It was one night in *partickler*," he said, "that he went, he himself, went to bed betimes in the little back parlour, quite entirely sick with the headache. *Misther* Burke was out from home, and, when the shop was shut up, Mrs. Sullivan went out too; but he didn't much care for that, *ounly* he thought she might as well have stayed at home, and so he couldn't go to sleep for thinking of it. Well, at one o'clock in the morning," he continued, lowering his voice into a sort of loud whisper, " at one o'clock in the morning, Misther Burke lets himself in with the key that he had, and goes up to bed, and I thought nothing at all; but presently I hears something come tap, tap, tap, at the street-door. The minute after comes down Misther Burke, and opens the door, and sure it was Mary—Misthress Sullivan that is, more's the pity! and d—l-a-bit she came to see after me at all in the little back parlour, but up stairs she goes up after Misther Burke.—' Och!' says I, ' but there's something the matther with me this night!' and I got up with the nightcap o'th' head of me, and went into the shop to see for a knife, but I couldn't get one by no manes. So I creeps up stairs, step by step, step by step (here Mr. Sullivan walked on tip-toe all across the office to show the magistrate how quietly he went up the stairs), and when I gets to the top I sees 'em, by the *gash* (gas) coming through the chink in the windy-curtains—I sees 'em, and ' Och, Misthress Sullivan !' says he; and ' Och, Misther Burke !' says she ; and ' Och, botheration !' says I to myself, ' and what will I do now ?' " He saw enough to convince him that he was dishonoured ; that, by some accident or other, he disturbed the guilty pair ; whereupon Mrs. Sullivan crept under Mr. Burke's bed to hide herself; that Mr. Sullivan rushed into the room and dragged her from under the bed, by her " wicked leg ;" and that he felt about the round table in the corner, where Mr. Burke kept his bread and cheese, in the hope of finding a knife.

" And what would you have done with it if you had found it ?" asked his worship."

" Is it what I would have done with it, your honour asks ?" exclaimed Mr. Sullivan, almost choked with rage. " Is it what I would have done with it?—ounly that I'd have *dagged* it into the heart of 'em at that same time ?" As he said this, he threw himself into an attitude of wild desperation, and made a tremendous lunge, as if in the very act of slaughter.

To make short of a long story, he did not find the knife, Mr. Burke barricadoed himself in his room, and Mr. Sullivan turned his wife out of doors.

The magistrate ordered him to find bail to keep the peace towards his wife and all the king's subjects: and told him, if his wife was indeed what he had represented her to be, he must seek some less violent mode of separation than the *knife*.

No sooner was this case disposed of, than another, developing the extreme folly of young countrymen, and showing how they are fleeced at a certain game, once all the *go*, but now rapidly going out, was next brought under the notice of the magistrate; thus :—

A poor harmless translator of old shoes was placed at the bar by a city officer, upon a charge of having stolen, or otherwise improperly obtained, a check for £300, from one John Freshfield, *Esquire.*

This John Freshfield, Esq. was a diminutive forked-radish sort of a young man; very fashionably attired—or, as he would say, *kiddily togg'd;* and, though it was scarcely noon, rather *queer* in the *attic*—that is to say, not exactly sober.

He stated his case in this manner:—" Here—I wish this fellow to say how he got hold o' my check for three hundred—that's all, you know, let him come that, and I shall be satisfied—*rum go*—had it last night, miss'd it this morning; d—d *rum go.* Here—here it is, see! payable at Hankey's—all right; *grabbed* him myself. Went to Hankey's two hours 'fore Bank opened—waited two hours—sat upon little stool,—wouldn't be done, you know.—In he comes with it—*grabs* him! There he was—looked like a fool. Hollo! says I—how did you come by it? *Mum.* Hadn't a word, you know. Only let him come it now—all about it, and I'm satisfied. Don't like to be done—*a rum go,* but can't stand it. That's all."

The city officer said he had been sent for to Hankey's, to take the prisoner into custody; and, having done so, he carried him before the Lord Mayor: but, as it appeared the offence, if there was any, had been committed in the county, his lordship had referred the matter to Bow Street.

The magistrate asked to see the " check," as the esquire called it. The officer produced it, and it proved to be not a check, but an acknowledgment from Messrs. Hankey and Co., that they had received £300 from John Freshfield, Esq., for which they would account to him on demand.

" Pray, have you an account at Hankey's, Mr. Freshfield?" asked the magistrate.

Mr. Freshfield replied, " Who—I? not a bit of it. I'm from the country, you know. D—n town—had enough of it almost. Diddled in this manner. It's a *sick'ner.* Got it again, though—only want to know how that fellow—the long one there—came by it. Put the *blunt* at Hankey's to be safe—'cause wouldn't be done, and then lost the check! that's a *rum go,* isn't, your worship?"

The magistrate asked the prisoner how he came by it?

He said he lodged at *Mister* Burn's, the *fighting man,* and two gentlemen there, whom he did not know, gave him the " check" to get cashed.

His worship directed an officer to go to Burn's house, and inquire about it.

In about half an hour he returned, with *Mister* Burn in company.

" Burn, do you know any thing of this business?" asked the magistrate. " Who was it gave this paper to the man at the bar?"

" Who gave it him, your worship?" said Mister Burn; " why, I did." " *You* did! and pray how did you come by it?"—" Why, I won it, your worship—won it by *shaking in the hat!*" replied Mister Burn, squeezing the sides of the hat together, and giving it a hearty shake, to show his worship the trick of it.

The real truth was, the *swell* called upon *Ben,* praised his prowess as a boxer, and he, being a *little* man with a *big* heart, was in want of a teacher who could qualify him not to be nice in giving a stone or two away to a countryman. Ben stroked his forehead, and nodded assent with a *congee* or two. The 'squire said he had come to London for a day or two's *lark;* he had been at Spring's new house, and another or two, and would Ben go and take champagne with him? "To be sure," said Ben; "I like a swell's company;" and, after spattering a little broad Durham, off they went. Nothing less than *goblets* would do for the wine, and the 'squire proposed tossing for a sovereign a time. At it they went, and played for several hours, and changed their game to *magging in the shallow,* or, in other words, to shaking in the hat. Ben won £150, after several hours' play, and they had the last shake for the £300 at two and three, which the 'squire lost, and paid Burn the check or receipt, on his undertaking not to make a talk about it. When the effluvia of the champagne became cooler with soda, the 'squire stopped payment of the check at Hankey's. They travelled in a coach together, *seeing life* all night, and the 'squire made two other matches afterwards, for Spring to fight Burn on Monday, and to bring another man to beat him in half an hour.

The magistrate looked at Mr. Freshfield, who looked at Mr. Burn, who looked boldly round at every body, as if nothing was the matter; and at last Mr. Freshfield ejaculated, "Well, that is a *rum go,* however! D—me, never thought of that, you know. Don't believe it, though. Coming it strong, eh! Burn! may be, though—won't be sure."

After soliloquizing some time in this style, he began a long history of his having gone from Burn's to Spring's, and Spring's to Burn's, and betting upon the "match for Monday;" and taking the long odds at one place, and giving them at another, till the magistrate and every body else was quite weary of it. So his worship discharged the prisoner, recommended *Mister* Burn not to addict himself to "shaking in the hat," directed the city officer to return Mr. Freshfield his £300 "check," and advised Mr. Freshfield to put it into his pocket, and return to his home in the country as soon as possible.

Peregrine and Wilmot were now ordered to attend before the magistrate, when the watchman opened the business, by telling his worship, that these *swells* were in a state of *bastely* drunkenness, *extramely* disorderly, infesting my *bate,* by laughing and talking in it: it was King Street, your honour, the same I'm now spaking about. Well, your honour, they, the self-same gentlemen, were, as I said, *braking* the king's peace, *becase* it was in King Street: and *becase* I tould 'em to *hobscond,* and not remain there like *bastes,* they, one of 'em, the biggest of the two, without saying, "by *yer lave,*" took my lantern a mighty *dacent* stroke, which shivered it thus, your worship (holding up the lantern); and then they kicked up a *hubbaboo, clane* contrary to all sorts of *dacency;*

and I and my comrades took 'em both, and lodged 'em in the watchhouse, and that's all the matter, your worship.—The magistrate asked Peregrine and Wilmot what they had to say to the story of the watchman; when the former assured his worship, that there was no truth in the watchman's statement, but the breaking of the lantern, and that would not have been done, had he not rudely put it so close to their faces. "You must pay for the lantern, young gentlemen, and then you are discharged," said the magistrate; which being done, they left the office, asking the officer, who had been so kind as to attend them, to go and take some refreshment with them; which invitation he accepted.

Mentor jocularly complimented Peregrine and his friend, on the happy termination of their exploit. "Not so happy," said Peregrine: "it is scandalous a person should be dragged through the streets, and lodged in a watch-house, merely on the word of a vagabond watchman." 'I should have liked," said Wilmot," to have given my friend, the tailor constable, a good drubbing. I never shall forget the insolence with which he ordered us, last night, to be taken away—I"—"Hold your tongue," said Mentor, "here comes the officer: he is a civil communicative fellow; and I have no doubt will give us some information relative to the thieves and disorderlies:" while they were having a luncheon, the officer, addressing himself to Mentor, said, "I suppose these two gentlemen are from the

affirmative, telling him he should feel obliged by his giving them a description of the thieves and swindlers they saw at the office this morning. "Most of them are going to prison; but if you wish it, I will accompany you to Newgate and show you many such." With this proposition, they were highly pleased, and agreed to accompany the officer.

"The thieves in London," said Mentor, "are, after all that has been said of them, a most singular set of people.

"Perhaps, you will think that I am wandering, when I give you a panegyric upon thieving, for I undertake to prove, that filching is as old as the world; that it has been the practice of all nations and ages; that the best of men have endeavoured to keep it in countenance; and, in short, that, without it, we had, as the song says, neither philosophers, poets, nor kings. In a word, I can prove, that all men are thieves, though very few have the honesty to confess it.

"The first theft was committed in Paradise; and the first thief was our universal mother, to the honour of the fair sex be it spoken; who, influenced by so good an example, have to this day kept up their laudable appetite for pilfering, as appears by the numerous complaints you hear of doleful swains whose hearts have been purloined. In this, I think, they have got the start of us: we can prove our first sire no more than a receiver, at best; and the proverb will not allow the receiver to be as good as the thief.

"After this, n body will controvert the antiquity of this art: it remains, then, that something be said for the honour of our own sex, who, though they cannot boast of being the inventors of it, yet I hope to show, that they have made as many improvements on it, and carried it to as high a pitch, as it would bear.    The *Jews* stealing every thing they could *wrap and rend* from the Egyptians at their departure, is an exploit that we shall come in for at least half the glory of, though it should be allowed that the ladies, as it often happens in modern marches, carried the knapsacks, and the men only bore the arms.

"He must be very ignorant of history, who knows not that the Egyptians, a learned and wise nation, held this art in such high esteem, that they punished severely ignorant pretenders to it. Ancient writers assure us, that a theft, cleverly performed, entitled the artist to the booty purloined; but, if he was so awkward as to be detected before the completion of his purpose, he was turned over to the hands of old *Father Antique*, the Law; as Butler says,—

> ' *For daring to prophane a thing*
> *So sacred, with vile bungling.*'

The Lacedemonians were so well apprised of the great use and advantage of this art, that they early instructed their children in the commendable art of filching; and every one knows that the Lacedemonians were always reputed a wise and famous people, though it be certain that no other of the polite arts or sciences ever got footing among them.

"So remarkable an instance as that of Romulus must not be admitted: he very wisely raked together a party of thieves; and they became the progenitors of a set of people, who, while they kept up to the virtues of their ancestors, were the most powerful, the most learned, and the most polite nation in the world: but, when they grew rich, and their opulence set them above practising those virtues, they dwindled into nothing.

"That it has been the universal practice (and often the only knowledge) of all philosophers, will be evident upon a comparison of their several notions and systems.    I would avoid an ostentation of learning, or I could make you stare in discussing the tenets, and discovering the thefts, of the ancients, one from another; but familiar examples will perhaps be more suitable: therefore it is only necessary to mention the South Sea scheme, the bubbles of 1824-5, &c. &c.

"Authors and parsons are great pilferers; particularly the former, who possess themselves of some author's work, of ancient date, and steal out the good things it contains; or, if they fortunately hit upon a manuscript that has been hid for centuries in some library, it is indeed a harvest!—they transcribe its essence, and send it out to the world, as their own *original;* as poor Dibdin sings—

> ' My uncle, the author, stole other men's thoughts;
> My cousin, the bookseller, sold them.

"The parsons are sad dogs at purloining.—If you pay attention,
28.

you will find many of their sermons are made up out of Porteus, Hurd, Lowth, &c. &c. and better so, than preach nonsense of their own composition."

"You are talking of pilferers, sir," said the officer, "of whom I have no knowledge. As for my part, I think the impostors are more numerous than thieves in London, and many of their tricks far more reprehensible than the depredations of the robbers.

"I was told yesterday," said Wilmot, "of a vile trick played off on a young student, by an old soldier: his mode for provoking compassion was to get some sheep's blood and a handful of flour, which he put so artfully upon his knee, as to make the passengers who saw it believe it to be a mortification in his leg and thigh. —This fellow had taken his stand one morning in a part of the Borough, where this young surgeon, who was walking one of the hospitals, happened daily to pass. The lamentation of the *Gagger* at once seized his ear and attracted his eye. Being a young man, full of the milk of human kindness, he stopped and demanded of the impostor, whether he did not dread a mortification; the gagger replied that, " he was in great pain, and that was all he knew about the matter." The young student gave him sixpence, and promised to get him into the hospital, whither he scoured away, assembled the pupils, and informed them of the shocking case which had occurred to him that morning as he passed along the Borough: he had seen a poor man sitting upon some straw, whom he believed to have gotten a mortification in his leg and thigh; and he begged them for the sake of humanity to join him in soliciting the head of the hospital to admit the poor wretch as a patient. The head of the hospital was applied to; but a negative was given to the application.

"This disappointment excited a double spirit in the young gentle men, who immediately subscribed upwards of five guineas; and one of them was desired to hire a room with a bed in it. The next thing was to get two men with a hand-barrow and some straw, when off they set, in a body, to fetch the old soldier. My friend arrived first, and desired him to be of good cheer, for, though they were not going to take him to the hospital, he should be full as well treated where they would carry him; and he doubted not but that they should make a cure of him without cutting off his leg. When the *gagger* saw the two men, the hand-barrow, the straw, and the young surgeons, he jumped up, and scampered through the crowd, as if the devil was in him; to the admiration of the mob, who huzza'd the surgeons, by way of applauding their skill in surgery.

"I am sorry to interrupt you, gentlemen," said the officer, " but if you wish to go to Newgate to-day, you must go directly." The reckoning was immediately paid, and the four took a hackney-coach and drove to the prison; the inside of which filled the visitors with dismay, in witnessing such a mass of wretchedness, misery, and crime. The officer told them it would be desirable for them to leave their watches, handkerchiefs, and money they had about them, with his friend, before they entered the prison, for fear some one should take a fancy to them.

"That man," said the officer, "with a great scar across his forehead, you must take particular notice of: his companions in crime call him captain; he is a man of great reputation among birds of the same feather, who I have heard say thus much in his praise, that he is as resolute a fellow as ever cocked a pistol upon the road. And, indeed, I do believe he fears no man in the world but the hangman, and dreads no death but choking. He's as generous as a prince; treats any body that will keep him company; loves his friend as dearly as the ivy does the oak; and will never leave him till he has hugged him to his ruin. He has drawn in twenty of his associates to be hanged, but had always wit and money enough to save his own neck from the halter. He has good friends at Newgate, who give him now and then a squeeze, when he is full of juice; but promise him, as long as he's industrious in his profession, and will but now and then show them a few sparks of his generosity, they will always stand between him and danger.

"That tall curly-pated Irishman, sitting alongside the fellow with a wooden leg, is a notorious offender: he is under the sentence of transportation for life, for swindling the wife of a poor sailor out of £50, the hard savings out of a seven years' voyage. She accompanied her husband to receive his pay, and, on their return, they were accosted by a stranger, who said he could procure 'Roger' a ship; and, for the purpose of giving a direction, took them into a public-house in Fetter Lane. At this house they found a man sitting in the parlour, and shortly after the prisoner entered, in a swaggering manner, saying he was a Welsh farmer, and had just received £1100 at the Bank. He then began to 'flash' some notes and sovereigns, and a bet was made between him and the stranger about some chalks, and they requested witness's husband to put his hand on a pint-pot, under which they placed a halfpenny; he did so, and on the pot being lifted up, the stranger said he had won a sovereign, which the prisoner paid, but the former returned it. During the transaction, they pretended not to know each other. The prisoner soon after said they were all poor people, and wanted to rob him. Witness at this time was putting the direction in her pocket-book, when her husband said, 'Let him see the notes, and that we are not poor people, or want to rob him.' The stranger instantly snatched tne notes, threw them into the prisoner's hat, and ran off. The prisoner also endeavoured to escape, but was prevented, when he returned the notes, and begged witness to let him go. This, however, was refused, and he then began destroying what appeared to be Bank-notes, but, in reality, were nothing but sham-notes, one of them commencing with, 'One Bonassus.—Pay to the Governor and Company of the Bank of England one most extraordinary Bonassus,' &c. Do you perceive," said the officer,

' that lad, with a plaid cap on ?    He is here for trial.    He played
off cruel and malicious hoaxes on some people in Dundee, some
time since.    One gentleman was informed that his mother, residing at the Spittal of Glenshee, had died suddenly—he arrayed
himself in the necessary funeral garb, with a large knot of crape
flowing from a hatband of the same, and proceeded post haste to
the abode of his parents, where, to his utter astonishment, he beheld the aged dame amusing herself with a spinning-wheel, and
" crooning o'er an auld Scots sonnet."    Both parties stood dumb-
founded for a time—the one at seeing the other arrayed in
black, while the son stood petrified with joy at beholding his
mother in the body.    A merchant got a similar route, and,
having had a new suit of black prepared, set out at midnight on a journey of nearly thirty miles.    Another was informed that his father, a commissioner of supply, was at the
point of death ; and, having procured the attendance of an eminent
physician, both set out together to the family mansion, where
neither  death nor the doctor found a patient.    A clergyman was
informed at a late hour that it was necessary he should also be-
take himself to a death's dance ; but, not being prepared, he put it
off till another day, when, luckily, the hoax was detected.    Another person was told a similar errand awaited him ; and the in-
formant, as usual, having demanded a sum to procure lodgings for
himself and horse, was asked where the latter was stabled, but did
not give a satisfactory answer.    The person, however, procured
and paid for a bed for him ; but, having entertained doubts as to
the veracity of the mission, next morning went and secured the
juvenile, just as he was preparing to depart, and lodged him in
gaol.

"And who, pray, sir," said Mentor, "may that genteel youth be,
who seems in such bitter anguish, talking to the elderly lady ?"
"He, sir, was a confidential clerk at a merchant's house ; but,
having, unfortunately, become a frequenter of those horrid sinks of
iniquity, the saloons at the west end of the town, he fell a prey to
the artful snares of a woman of the town ; and, to support her in
her extravagance, he first robbed his employers, and then, in the
false and fatal hopes of making things better, fell to gambling ; and
when, poor fellow, he could no longer keep the woman—wretch, I
mean—in her luxury, she went and informed his employers, who
apprehended him ; and, on his trial, became the principal evidence
against him—producing the identical things he stole at her request.
Women, sir," continued the officer, "can either make themselves
angels or devils—they can render the marriage state a heaven or a
hell.—This poor fellow is much pitied : great intercession is being
made for him ; and, it is generally expected, his sentence will be
mitigated.    The lady he is talking to is his unfortunate mother.

"Here is a lesson," said Mentor to Peregrine and Wilmot, "for
all young men,—another martyr to that dreadful mania of gambling :
but the corruption of the times has made gaming a trade.    Be very

careful that playing is only followed as an amusement; for, if you suffer it to become a passion, it will presently terminate in a rage for play. A professional player, who exposes to the hazard of the dice, or a card, his paternal fortune, or the dowry of his wife, generally ends his days in a wretched workhouse, with the bitter remarks of the public on his conduct. You will never see a man of information, who is master of his passions, sacrifice the pleasures of a fine day or a tranquil night, in the foolish expectation of obtaining a fortune, which is but very seldom acquired, and never but at the expense of honour. Keep in your memory the saying of Madame Deshoulieres on a gamester, who is one that 'begins by being a dupe, and ends by becoming a rogue.' We are lost if, after judicious reflection, we still resolve to have recourse to gaming. Madame Deshoulieres played, but she did not gamble; she had felt all the bitterness of disgrace, and all the pains of severe illness; however, although death menaced her with his icy hand, and sickness preyed on her beauty, and misfortune haunted her like a spectre, yet she fortified her mind by solid reflections, and indulged in innocent pleasures; she played no more than two hours a day, and then on so low terms, that she never felt the hope of winning, nor the fear of losing.

"There are some games very proper to be learned, such as chess; this game, when well played, may reasonably give rise to feelings of exultation; however, they should not be indulged in.

" It has been said that the disposition of a man is better known when he has taken a quantity of wine, or when he is engaged in play, than in any thing else; this is not a certain way of arriving at a correct conclusion of his disposition: however, I am inclined to believe that he who is ready for dispute under the effects of wine, or who regrets the money he has lost in play, is not either very liberal or very pacifically inclined. Inquietude betrays a narrowness of mind, and anger or avarice shows a littleness of soul. If a person has sufficient strength of mind to hide his defects and his vices, even if he is naturally rude or avaricious, he will appear complaisant or generous; but if he does not support this hypocrisy when playing, if an accidental failure in an expected event arises, and the individual is soured by it, we may judge, without fear of inaccuracy, that the natural temper is exposed, and that the mind is unmasked; and we may reasonably conclude that the first movement which escapes, is a better criterion to judge of his character, than all the parade of those false and studied virtues: he thus loses in one moment all that had been acquired by long expedients.

" When you play at innocent games, do not play as though you cared nothing about them; on the other hand, do not exhibit either lively inquietude, or foolish joy, or ridiculous fear; take the middle course between anxiety and inattention; learn that, if play dishonours those who make a shameful commerce of it, if it brings to light all their avarice or folly, it is not without advantages to the polished man, since it gives him an opportunity of showing, without an ostentatious parade, the nobleness of his sentiments, the justness of his mind, the politeness of his manners, and the equanimity of his temper.

"That fellow near the pump," said the officer, "is one of the way-layers, a contemptible class of thieves, who attend the waggon and coach-yards, pretending to be porters; they watch the country people, and offer their services to carry their parcels or call a coach; and no sooner do they get any property in their hands, than they sneak off with it.

"He with his arm in a sling is an advertising swindler, and belongs to a gang, who live upon robbing people, by advertising to borrow or lend money, or procure situations. If they borrow, they have sham deeds, and make false conveyances of estates: if they lend, they artfully inveigle the borrower out of his security, which they take up money upon, and convert to their own use, without the poor deluded person's knowledge, and, by absconding, leave him to the mortification of descanting on their roguery. It is the greatest folly to pay any attention to advertisements in the papers, offering assistance of the above nature. Not long ago, a person was tried on an indictment charging him with a fraud, in obtaining the sum of £100, under pretence of procuring for him the situation of a clerk in the Treasury. The prosecutor said, he had inserted in a morning paper an advertisement, offering to pay a moderate premium to any one who would procure for him a *permanent mercantile situation*. Two or three days after, he received a note, inviting him to come to Purton Street. He proceded to the house, and saw the defendant, who, after some conversation, informed him that he could procure him the situation of one of the clerks in the revenue department of the Treasury, as a gentleman who then held the situation was about to retire from it, and that the sum to be paid for it must be £150. At the same time he said that he could not mention the name of the gentleman through whose interference it was to be procured. ℡e salary, he said, was £100 a year, with perquisites. It was then agreed that Mr. A. was to call again in a few days, when he was to make up his mind on the subject. Mr. A. called again and saw the prisoner, who, after some discussion, agreed to take £140 for the situation. While they were conversing on the subject at this second interview, and before the bargain was closed, a young man knocked at the door, and the defendant told Mr. A. that this young man had also been in treaty for the place, that he had come to settle the business finally, and pay a part of the money: therefore, he should close with him, unless Mr. A. would agree to the terms proposed, and lay down £20 at once on account.— Mr. A. did accordingly close with the defendant, and paid him down £20, for which he had his promissory note; and a sum of £80 more was to be paid as soon as Mr. A. received his warrant of ppointment. The remainder was to be paid by instalments.

From that time until the middle of October, the prosecutor and defendant had several interviews. On the 15th of October, Mr. A. received a note appointing a meeting in Villiers Street, York Buildings, and announcing that he should have his appointment with him on that day, and desiring the prosecutor to bring with him the £80. Mr. A. was punctual to the appointment, and met the prisoner at the time and place fixed on. The latter produced a note, purporting to be from Lord Lowther, one of the Lords of the Treasury, and addressed to the prisoner. In this note it was required that the money should be paid to the prisoner, before he let the appointment out of his possession. He also showed the prosecutor a written parchment, with these words on the back of it, '*Appointment of Mr. J. Anderson.*' The document purported to be signed by Mr. Vansittart, Lord Lowther, and the Earl of Liverpool; and countersigned by Mr. Lushington, one of the Secretaries of the Treasury. After seeing such a document as this, the prosecutor could no longer entertain any suspicion; he paid the £80, and gave up the promissory note for the £20 which he had previously advanced. The prisoner then said he must go over to the Treasury to have the warrant entered, and promised to return in half an hour. He did not return; and, in an hour after, Mr. A. received a letter from him, acknowledging that the whole business was a fraud; that he was obliged to commit the same on account of his poverty; but promising that he should shortly have it in his power to repay him the £100; and, at the same time, he sent a written acknowledgment of his owing him that sum.

" The jury immediately found the prisoner guilty; and he was sentenced to pay a fine of £100 to the king; to be imprisoned twelve months in the House of Correction; and to be further imprisoned until the fine be paid.

" I could tell you of many other cases of fraud. I remember being in Bow-Street Office, when a young man—one of the simple ones, presented himself before Sir Richard Birnie, requesting the intervention of the police between himself and a Mr. Reading, a gentleman, he said, who, having undertaken to procure him a place under government for a *douceur* of £400, pocketed the *douceur*, and forgot to get the place.

" The magistrate expressed his surprise that, after so many public expositions had been made of this stale trick, any person should be found green enough to be gulled by it.

" The young man proceeded to detail the particulars of this affair. He inserted an advertisement in a morning paper, describing his qualifications, and offering £400 to any person who would procure him a permanent mercantile situation. To this advertisement he received a multitude of answers—the zeal with which many persons ' of great influence' came forward to offer him their services, was really quite gratifying; but, had it not been for the advertisement, it's a hundred to one if he had ever known what lots of good people there are in the world. Amongst others, there came to him the above-mentioned J. J. Reading, *Esquire*, as he called himself. 'So, young man,' said he, 'you are in want of a situation?' The advertiser bowed. 'Very good,' continued the patron—'very good—you seem a likely young man; and, fortunately, I have just now an opportunity of procuring a situation—an excellent situation, worth £500 a-year, young man; what do you think of *that?*' The advertiser bowed again—'Should be very happy,' &c., and the patron proceeded. 'But then there must be a set-off, of three years' purchase, you see, for these things are not to be had every day; and three years' purchase is but a trifle for such a chance.' The advertiser admitted it, but observed that he could not raise so much money. 'Oh, I don't want your money, young man,' replied the patron—'I don't want your money; if I did, I must be mad, and should require a strait jacket. But you had better consider of what I have said, and consult with your good lady'—meaning advertiser's wife, who was in the next room. Having thus broken the ice, as it were, he took his leave, requesting the advertiser to call upon him, when he had duly considered the matter, at his house in Cirencester Place. The advertiser did call accordingly, and found him living in considerable style. He talked largely of his connexions and his influence, of his intimacy with Sir T. Maitland, Sir J. Throckmorton, the Lords of the Admiralty, and a nobleman lately deceased; and finally said the situation he had hinted at was that of an accredited agent for one of our colonies in the Mediterranean. The advertiser departed from this interview deeply impressed with the political importance of his patron; and the more so, as he said, because he had been told that this identical gentleman had once been had up at the bar of the House of Commons, about the sale of a borough, in consequence of his intimate connexion with the deceased nobleman above mentioned. Other interviews took place, sometimes at the advertiser's house, and sometimes at the Museum Tavern; and at last the advertiser gave him an assignment of a reversionary interest he had in his mother's will, to the amount of £389, &c.; and, in consideration thereof, he, Reading, *Esquire*, undertook to procure him to be appointed 'accredited agent at Liverpool for the Ionian Islands, with a salary of £500 per annum.' There was a farther agreement with respect to the three years' set-off from the salary in favour of Reading; and, as a sort of collateral security for the assignment, the said Jeremiah accepted the advertiser's bill for £200. All these things arranged, the munificent Reading told the advertiser he had sent out the necessary documents to Sir Thomas Maitland, by the Blucher packet; and his appointment would take place immediately on the return of that vessel to England. The Blucher returned, and the advertiser *naturally* expected to pop into his place *instanter*—but, no! week after week passed away, Jeremiah became more and more difficult of access, and, at last, he told the simple advertiser that *he* could not have the situation on any consideration whatever; and the young man lost his money.

" That Hibernian, with his toes out of his shoes, is here," con
tinued the officer, " for making too free with the heads of his
brethren by breaking some of them, at their wakes, as they call
them." " He looks like the man," said Mentor to Peregrine, " who
ut such a conspicuous figure in

The Doings at an Irish Wake.

In St. Giles's, at which we were visitors. Did you ever witness
one of these curious ceremonies, Wilmot ?" Never," he replied
" Indeed they are worth seeing ;" continued Mentor. " The one a
which we were, was in a cellar in Diot Street; and we were re
ceived with all that generous feeling for which the natives of Ire
and are so celebrated. The corpse was laid in a decent coffin,
on a low table, and by its side were placed several lighted candles
ornamented with cut paper ; the coffin was covered with flowers, the
snowdrop, the primrose, and the ever-green ; on the right and left
were several men and women bewailing the loss of the deceased, and
in apostrophising the inanimate clay, they ran over every endearing
quality that he possessed. In a short time a shrill voice, in a sort
of howl, exclaimed, ' Arrah, by Jasus, what did you die for ?' ' Bad
luck to you ! what did you die for ?' re-echoed an old woman ; and
taking up the hand of the deceased, ' There, sir,' said she, ' that
never *will*, nor would take a thump from any one, without returning it !' In one corner sat several *devil-may-care* fellows—every
inch of them Irishmen--generous, eccentric, good-natured, and

grateful—drinking, crying, howling, praying, and swearing; in another, were some descanting on the virtues of the deceased; and, in the centre of the cellar, were two friends most unmercifully be-abouring each other, with tremendous shilelahs.

"Yet the immorality of these beings is not so great as it has been represented: the seeds of virtue remain uncultivated in their hearts, while the vices and follies germinate in the foul atmosphere of obscenity. Their absurdities, though many, are generally ludicrous; and their actions form a tragi-comic series, indicative of feeling and humour.

"The bodies are generally carried to St. Pancras; and, by the time the corpse is interred, the liquor having begun to operate after several agreeable jests, some man of nicer feelings than the rest takes offence at them; then loud sounds of discord are vociferated, in the Irish language, by the opponents; blows succeed, and a battle, of perhaps a dozen combatants, presents an animated scene in the road opposite the cemetery. When they have vented their passion, and bestowed a number of contusions on each other, they shake hands, and march off the field of battle to the next ale-house, where they drown their animosity in generous liquor.

"In the report of the committee on the state of the police of the metropolis, we find the following examination of a beadle of St. Andrew's, Holborn, which gives a melancholy picture of the wakes in that parish; it says:—

"'Do the Irish hold wakes on the death of their relatives or friends?' Yes, they do. Last Tuesday a woman died; and, on the Saturday following, her daughter. The father asked me what the parish could do for him? I said to him there are at this very time from ten to fourteen gallons of porter before you, and more than that,—surely you can bury your wife and daughter and all.'

"'I remember a capital wake; it was for the wife of James Corcoan. I think I counted about sixty-four or sixty-five gallons of porter that they had before them to drink, in gallon pots, and two-gallon pots, and so on: I counted them for curiosity: the pots that were there held, I think, about sixty-four gallons. I have seen them, likewise, when they have got drunk, quarrel, and throw down the corpse, and fight over it.'

"'At what hour in the morning?' 'About three or four o'clock in the morning, when they get drunk.' 'Do they commonly fight at wakes?' 'Very commonly.'"

"In Ireland," continued Mentor, "they conduct the wakes with greater solemnity and form than they do here.

"'It was on a frosty October evening,' says the author of *Tales of Irish Life*, 'that the peasantry of the parish of Dunmore began to assemble around the corpse of a man, whose recent misfortunes and death gave additional notoriety to his *wake*; which was more numerously attended than is even usual on similar occasions; although the natural sympathy and good humor of the

Irish people conspire to cause, at such places, a congregation, for the double purpose of honouring the dead and amusing the living.

"'The body, which once bore the name of Ned Kilpatrick, was laid out in a spacious barn, which was converted, for the occasion, from the purpose of a granary, into a melancholy hall of mourning. Around the dead man's bed were hung, with artful contrivance, large sheets of white linen ; which, as they inclined towards the wall, displayed many fantastic images of flowers, angels, and seraphims. Over the corpse was spread a cloth to correspond with the canopy, which was strewed with roses, marigolds, and 'sweet-smelling flowers,' while an image of our Redeemer on the cross reposed, as it were, upon a dove—emblematic of the dead man's faith. There is something very terrible in death, when divested of those circumstances which add a solemn gloom to the awful presence of a lifeless body ; but, in Ireland, those scenes, which remind us of what ' stuff we are made,' receive a desponding influence from the circumstance of the nearest friends of the deceased being arranged around, according to their degrees of affinity ; and, as the poor have more cause than the affluent to lament the dreaded departure of their relatives, there is seldom a want of loud and copious sorrow ; for simple nature cannot learn to modulate her woe by the rules of fashionable grief. At the head of the venerable deceased sat his wife, overwhelmed with a sense of her own loss ; and, in regular succession, agreeably to their respective ages, were seated her four daughters, the mournful attendants of the scene. At the extremity of the bed, stood the only son of the defunct, who bore his father's name. Numerous aunts, uncles, and kindred, pressed around, to share the general grief; whilst neighbours, as they came in, after falling on their knees to repeat the Lord's prayer, fell back to a respectful distance, where pipes and tobacco were supplied in gratuitous profusion. On this night, decorum, for a while, was preserved, and the mourners received the most respectful attention ; but a dull scene of silent meditation was neither accordant with their wishes nor their habits. A song from one of the party was the signal for the commencement of sport, which soon began to engage the young and thoughtless ; nor were the old averse from the scenes which once had charms for themselves.'

"The ' Irish Hudibras' (1682), thus humorously describes an Irish wake :—

' To their own sports (the masses ended)
The mourners now are recommended.
Some sit and chat, some laugh, some weep,
Some sing *cronans*, and some do sleep ;
Some court, some scold, some blow, some puff,
Some take tobacco, some take snuff.
Some play the trump, some trot the hay,
Some at *machan*,* some noddy play :
Thus mixing up their grief and sorrow,--
Yesterday buried, kill'd to-morrow."

* A game at cards.

"Most certainly," said Mentor, "the laying-in-state, as it is called in England, is a part of the ceremony of waking. Browne, in his 'Vulgar Errors,' gives us a curious detail of the various customs formerly observed at deaths, and several of which are yet retained in different parts of England; he says—

"'The passing bell, so called from its denoting the passing or parting of any one from life to death, was originally intended to invite the prayers of the faithful for the person who was dying, but was not yet dead; and, though in some instances superstitiously used, has its meaning clearly pointed out in a clause in the 'Advertisements for Due Order, &c.' in the seventh year of Queen Elizabeth, which enjoins 'that when anye Christian bodie is *in passing*, that the *bell be toled*, and that the curate be speciallie called for to comfort the sicke person; and, *after the time of his passing*, to ringe no more but one short peale; and one before the buriall, and another short peale after the buriall. Grose, referring to the old Catholic belief on this subject, treats it rather ludicrously, though its intention, as just described, was evidently serious. 'The passing-bell,' says he, 'was anciently rung for two purposes: one to bespeak the prayers of all good Christians for a soul just departing; the other, to drive away the evil spirits who stood at the bed's foot, and about the house, ready to seize their prey, or, at least, to molest and terrify the soul in its passage; but, by the ringing of that bell (for Durandus, a writer of the twelfth century, informs us evil spirits are much afraid of bells), they were kept aloof; and the soul, like a hunted hare, gained the start, or had what is, by sportsmen, called law.'

"In the diary of Robert Birrel, preserved in 'Fragments of Scottish History,' &c. is the following curious entry :—

"'1566, the 25 of October, word came to the towne of Edinburghe, from the Queine, yat her majestie was deadly seike, and desirit ye bells to be runge, and all ye peopile to resort to ye Kirk to pray for her, for she was so seike that none lepsied her life', (expected her to live). Bourne supposes, that from the saying mentioned by Bede, 'Lord have mercy on my soul,' which St. Oswald uttered when he fell to the earth, has been derived the distich so often introduced in ballads on the melancholy occasion of a coming execution :—

'When the bell begins to toll,
Lord have mercy on my soul!

"In a very rare book, entitled 'Wits, Fits, and Fancies,' (1614) the author relates a droll anecdote concerning the ringing-out at the burial of 'a rich churle and a beggar, who were buried at one time, in the same churchyard, and the bells rang out amaine for the miser. Now, the wiseacre, his son, and executor,' says he, 'to the ende the worlde might not thinke that all that ringing was for the begger, but for his father, hyred a trumpetter to stand all the ringing while in the belfrie, and between every peale, to sound his trumpet, and proclame aloud and saye, sirres, this next peale is not for R, but for maister N,—his father.' There seems to be nothing more intended at present by tolling the Passing Bell, but to inform the neighbourhood of some person's death.'

" The Jews used trumpets instead of bells. The Turks do not permit the use of them at all. The Greek Church under their dominion still follow her old custom of using wooden boards, or iron plates full of holes, which they hold in their hands and knock with a hammer or mallet, to call the people to church. China has been remarkably famous for its bells. Father Le Compte tells us, that at Pekin, there are seven bells, each of which weighs 120,000lbs.

" WATCHING WITH THE DEAD.—This is called in the north of England the *Lake Wake*, a name plainly derived from the Anglo-Saxon *lic* or *lice*, a corpse, and *wæce* or *wake*, a vigil or watching. It is used in this sense by Chaucer, in his ' Knight's Tale :'

'Shall not be told by me
How that arcite is brent to ashen cold,
Ne how that there the Liche-wake was y-hold
All that night long.'

" Pennant, in describing Highland ceremonies, says, ' The Late Wake is a ceremony used at funerals. The evening after the death of any one, the relation or friends of the deceased meet at the house, attended by a bagpipe or fiddle : the nearest of kin, be it wife, son, or daughter, opens a melancholy ball, dancing and greeting—that is, crying violently at the same time; and this continues till daylight, but with such gambols and frolics among the younger part of the company, that the loss which occasions their meeting, is often more than supplied by the conse-quences of that night. If the corpse remain unburied for two nights, the same rites are renewed. Thus, Scythian-like, they re-joice at the deliverance of their friends out of this life of misery." The custom in North Wales, we are informed by the same writer, is, the night before a dead body is to be interred, the friends and neighbours of the deceased resort to the house the corpse is in, bringing with them some small present of bread, meat, and drink (if the family be something poor), but more especially candles, whatever the family may be, and this night is called *wyl noss*, whereby the country people seem to mean a watching night. Their going to such a house, they say, is *i wilior corph*, to watch the corpse; but *wylo* signifies to weep and lament, and so *wyl nos* may be a night of lamentation. While they stay together on that night, they are either singing psalms, or reading some part of the Holy Scriptures. Whenever any body comes into a room where a dead body lies, especially on the *wyl nos*, and the day of its interment, the first thing he does, he falls on his knees by the corpse and says the Lord's Prayer.'

" LAYING OUT, OR STREEKING THE BODY.—Durand, at the remote period at which he lived, gives a pretty exact account of some of the ceremonies used at laying out the body, as practised at present in the north of England, where the laying out is called *streeking*. He mentions the closing of the eyes, the decent washing, dressing, and wrapping up in a clean winding-sheet, or linen shroud, as well as other ancient observances. The interests of our woollen manufacture have interfered with this ancient rite in England. To the laying-out may be added the very old custom of *setting salt*, and placing a lighted candle upon the body, both of which are used to this day in some parts of Northumberland. The salt, a little of which is set upon a pewter plate upon the corpse, is, according to the learned Morex, an emblem of eternity and immortality. It is not liable to putrefaction itself, and preserves other things that are seasoned with it from decay. The lighted candle, the same author conjectures to have been the Egyptian hieroglyphic for life.

"Aubrey, in some miscellanies of his, among the Lansdown MMS., at the British Museum, mentions a very curious custom at deaths, observed in a degree until his time (reign of Charles II), which he describes under the name of Sin-Eaters. "In the County of Hereford,' says he, 'was an old custome at funeralls, to hire poor people, who were to take upon them the sinnes of the party deceased. One of theme (he was a long lean ugly lamentable raskal), I remember, lived in a cottage on Rosse highway. The manner was, that when the corpse was brought out of the house, and layed on the biere, a loafe of bread was brought out and delivered to the sinne-eater over the corpse, as also a mazar bowl, of maple, full of beere (which he was to drink up), and sixpence in money: in consideration he took upon him, *ipso facto*, all the sinnes of the defunct, and freed him or her from walking after they were dead.' This custom, he supposes, had some allusion to the scape-goat under the Mosaical law.

"FUNERAL SERMONS.—Speaking of the frequency of these formerly, and their present disuse :—' Even such a character as the infamous *Mother Creswell*, the procuress in the reign of Charles II.,' our author observes, ' must have her funeral sermon. She, according to Granger, desired by will to have a sermon preached at her funeral, for which the preacher was to have ten pounds, but upon the express condition that he only spoke well of her. A preacher was with some difficulty found, who undertook the task. He, after a sermon preached on the general subject of morality, and the good uses to be made of it, concluded by saying—" By the will of the deceased, it is expected I should mention her, and say nothing but what is *well* of her. All I shall say of her, therefore, is this—she was born well, she lived well, and she died well, for she was born with the name of Creswell, she lived in Clerkenwell, and she died in Bridewell." '

" For heaven's sake," said Mentor, " let us retire from this prison ; the very air seems infectious. What oaths ! what blaspheming ! what a clashing of chains !" " Not in such haste, 'riend," replied Wilmot ; although it is hell in miniature." " But look in yonder cell—a dreadful sight, indeed," said Mentor : " I see a poor wretch loaded with chains, stretched at his length upon the earth, beating his breast in the utmost agonies of despair, and a woman lying dead by his side. What's the meaning of this ?" " The man," answered the officer, " was an industrious young tradesman, who married the woman you see dead by him, and has had by her five children, now living. Never was a more affectionate couple : but an unavoidable misfortune in trade, and the severity of his inhuman creditors, soon reduced him to want bread. Unable to bear the piercing sight of wife and children who were perishing, in the utmost distraction of mind, he loaded his pistols, and robbed an old miser of about a dozen shillings. He was soon taken, tried, and condemned, and is to be executed to-morrow. His wife, who came to take her last leave of him, expired in his arms, and the parish are to take care of their children." " But is this justice ?" said Peregrine ; " if it is, how near is rigid justice akin to cruelty ! Can those who thus send an almost innocent man to death, have any bowels? O thou eternal Being ! wert thou to judge each action of those men with the same severity they have judged this poor wretch, unless thy boundless mercy interposed, how dreadful would be their portion ?"

" In the next cell is an intrepid hero : he is a rare tongue-pad ; he can out-flatter a poet, out-wrangle a lawyer, out-cant a Methodist, out-cringe a beau, out-face truth, and out lie the devil. He hath for many years raised contributions in this metropolis. Justice hath overtook him at last ; but, true as steel, he resolves to die with the same resolution he lived.

" Next to him you see a young woman who was condemned for murdering her bastard child ; but, having youth and beauty on her side, she has been reprieved.

" The next is a bailiff's follower, who murdered a person he had a warrant to arrest. It is true, he might have performed his duty without bloodshed, as his unhappy victim made no resistance ; but he chose effectually to secure his prisoner by knocking his brains out. However, as he has the honour of being a limb of the law, his sentence will not be put in execution.

" Observe the youth fervently praying upon his knees.—His case is hard, but not singular—he must suffer for a crime he never committed. An old Jew, being engaged in an amorous conflict with a Cyprian of Drury, lost his watch in the dispute ; but, not missing it till he came into the Strand, he seized this young fellow, whose misfortune it was to be walking close to him, charged him with the robbery, and, upon the trial, swore positively he caught his hand in his pocket." " Perjured, murdering villain !' cried Peregrine, " if the truth should ever come to light, must he not run distracted ?" " Only shrug up his shoulders," cried the officer ; " cry he is sorry, and return to his bulls and bears in 'Change Alley.

" Turn your eyes into yonder room, which seems too elegant

for a prison. The gentleman in a splendid dressing-gown, who is making merry with his friends, was committed for murdering a poor watchman in one of his drunken frolics ; but, being a man of family and fortune, he has this morning got his pardon."

" Let us go, for I will not stay here one moment longer," said Peregrine. " With all my heart," replied Mentor ; " we will once more breathe the pure air ; and pray our rulers to spare the innocent, and punish the wicked." They then rewarded the officer for his trouble, and retired.

" Since you forced me to leave Newgate so abruptly," said Mentor, " I will introduce you to a place you will like as little. We will go to Bedlam, where you may make observations, and see what miserable spectacles the lords of the universe are, when deprived of their senses. Yet remember, when you pity their condition, that vices and folly are often the occasion of their coming to this dismal place.

" The raving creature in the first cell is a merchant, who had once acquired a plum and a half in trade, but, losing fifteen hundred pounds on the insurance of a ship, it hath turned his brain ever since.

" The young woman next him, who is continually talking of love, flames, darts, sighs, and vows, is descended from an ancient family in the west of England, and was seduced by a young nobleman, famous for exploits of this sort, who made her a promise of marriage which he never intended should be performed ; and her senses have paid the price of her folly.

" The young man you see with his arms across is certainly a happy man He ran mad upon the loss of the mistress to whom he was betrothed, and who married another : he had a lucky escape, for there is not such another termagant in hell. Her unfortunate husband is continually imploring the gods that he may change his condition with the lover."

" Heyday," said Wilmot, " what have we here ; this is a madman with a vengeance : how swift he runs round the room. Now he stops suddenly and shakes his head, while the tears run down his cheeks." " That, sir," said the keeper, " is a poet, whom the managers of the theatres have driven hither, by refusing to perform a tragedy he had written. The title is ' The Death of Patroclus,' and he himself is now acting the part of Xanthus, one of Achilles' horses, which he intended to have introduced upon the stage.

" The hump-backed lad next him, was sent here by the same gentleman, who would not permit him to act the part of Bevil, in the Conscious Lovers.

" The grave gentleman that walks so sedately, is really to be pitied. He was possessed of a plentiful fortune, liberal to the poor, and generous to his friends. He was driven mad by the ill-behaviour of his wife, as many others are.

" Take notice in the next cell of that cobbler strutting along.

He exacts of every one that passes by him, the title of my lord. His good fortune was his ruin ; having scraped together twenty pounds with hard labour in the space of twenty years, he purchased a lottery ticket with the money, and soon after found himself possessed of ten thousand pounds, which was the cause of his removal from his stall to this place.

" That old woman you see mounted upon a joint-stool, and preaching to a crazy audience, was a follower of the field-preachers, who terrified her out of her senses, by threatening her with hell and damnation, for not contributing more than was in her power, towards the support of her godly pastors. It has long been matter of doubt to me," said Mentor, " whether these field-preachers are not more knaves than fools." " They have certainly most of the former in their composition," said the keeper. " However, they rant with an enthusiastic madness of heaven and hell, they generally take care to fill their own pockets.

" The next is an odd sort of a madman, who had both learning and genius; but a visionary turn of mind, and over studying, have almost reduced him to the state of the man recorded by Horace, who used to sit alone in the theatre, imagining he was hearing the most excellent plays. This gentleman believes he is among the dead, and conversing with Pluto, Socrates, Aristotle, and all the far-famed sages of antiquity. In my opinion, his lot's rather to be envied than pitied; nor do I believe, if he was to be restored to his senses, that he would thank the friendly hand that worked his cure.

"The next object you see, is a female, a citizen's wife, who ran distracted, because she was refused entrance into St. James's, on a ball night; and is now in imagination the greatest duchess in the land.

" In the next dwellling, are the remains of a city beauty, who, being seized with the small-pox, desired to view herself in a looking-glass, and immediately, upon the sight of her own face, despatched her senses in search of her fugitive charms.

" In the next cell is a lawyer, who made the last will and testament of an old nobleman, when he was at the point of death, and, by some strange fatality, forgot to insert his own name.

" Take notice of yonder venerable matron, with a dead animal in her arms. This heroine bore not only with patience, but resignation, the death of fourteen husbands, and at last ran distracted upon the decease of her favourite monkey.

" Near this pattern of conjugal affection is a weaver, who was brought hither in consequence of being interrupted in the midst of an oration at a debating club, by the baker's hammer.

" In the next dungeon lies the body (for the soul is almost departed), of an eminent physician, who, being sent for to his elder brother when he lay in the utmost extremity, declared all human aid was vain, and refused to prescribe for him. This saved his life, for nature, having no drugs to combat, recovered her patient ;

2 O.

yet, by saving one brother his life and estate, she occasioned the other to lose his senses.

"The next is a naturalist, who is still in debate with himself, whether a curiosity he unluckily found one day upon the top of a very high hill is common pumice-stone, or an antediluvian human excrement."

"But we have seen enough of these unhappy creatures; let us now, if you please," said Peregrine, "witness some joyous happy scene." "Agreed," replied Mentor and Wilmot; so let us go to that delightful fairy spot, Vauxhall. They returned home to dress, and, in the evening, drove to the gardens.

"This enchanting and elegant place of summer resort," said Mentor, "is named from the manor of Vaux Hall, or Fawkes Hall; but the tradition that this house, or any other adjacent, was the property of the Popish conspirator, Guy Fawkes, is entirely fictitious. The premises were, in 1615, the property of Jane Vaux, widow. It was formerly little more than a tea-garden, enlivened with instrumental music; but its rural beauty, and easy access, soon rendered it a place of universal attraction. Since it has become the property of the present spirited proprietors, these gardens have assumed an entirely different character. Instead of the simple singing and music, and the dark walk, and the brilliant promenade, you will here witness the representation of ballets, &c. after the manner of the minor theatres.

"There was nothing that more distinguished the environs of the metropolis a few years since (before the building-rage commenced), than the number of gardens open for public entertainment: I do not mean simplay tea-gardens, but places on the plan of Vauxhall Gardens; where concerts of vocal and instrumental music were to be heard, and where the eye was regaled with displays of fire-works, illuminated walks, and other embellishments.

"MARY-LE-BON, or MARYBONE GARDENS.—These stood a little northward, on the sight of the present Manchester Square. They were opened some time previously to 1737; and, till that year, were entered *gratis* by all ranks of the people; but, the company resorting to them becoming more respectable, Mr. Gough, the owner, demanded a shilling as entrance-money; for which the party paying was to receive an equivalent in viands. They afterwards met with such success as to induce the proprietor to form them into a regular place of musical and scenic entertainment; and the late Charles Bannister, Dibdin (who both made their first public appearance here when youths), and other eminent vocalists, now no more, contributed to enliven them with their talents. Different splendid fêtes, during the run of the season, were given here, as at Vauxhall, which are to be found advertised in the papers of the day. In one of these, given on the king's birth-day, June 4, 1772, after the usual concert and songs, was shown a representation of Mount Etna, with the Cyclops at work, and a grand fire-work, consisting of vertical wheels, suns, stars, globes &c.; which was afterwards copied at Ranelagh : and, on another occasion, great part of the gardens were laid out in imitation of the Boulevards of Paris, with numerous shops, and other attractions.

" The Royal Park, called Marybone Park, once occupied the site of these gardens, and a large tract of land around, and had a fine stock of game. In Queen Elizabeth's ' Progresses,' it is recorded, that ' on the 3d of February, 1600, the ambassadors from the Emperor of Russia, and other the Muscovites, rode through the city of London to Marybone Park, and there hunted at their pleasure , and shortly afterward returned homeward.' What a contrast to the present state of this spot and parish, now entirely covered by magnificent streets and squares, which form so elegant a part of the metropolis !

" BERMONDSEY SPA.—These gardens were situate in the Grange Road, Bermondsey, and received their name from some waters of a chalybeate nature, which were discovered there about 1770; a few years before which a Mr. Thomas Keyse opened the premises for tea-drinking, and exhibited, with great success, a collection of his own paintings, chiefly of still-life subjects ; and which, considered as the works of a self-taught artist, had great merit. Abundance of persons (for the gardens have not been closed many years) still recollect his natural representations of butchers' shops, greenstalls, fishmongers' stalls, &c. Keyse afterwards procured a licence for opening his gardens with musical entertainments, in the manner of Vauxhall ; and they were accordingly opened during the summer season, at one shilling admission. Songs, duets, &c. were sung, sometimes in character, as well as burlettas performed, on small stages, erected in the garden. Occasionally, also, fireworks were exhibited, not inferior to those at Vauxhall ; and, a a few times in the course of the season, on what are called ' gala nights,' a very excellent representation was given of the siege of Gibraltar, with fireworks, transparencies, &c. ; the whole of which were constructed and arranged by Mr. Keyse himself, and did great credit to his mechanical abilities. The height of the rock was above fifty feet, and its length two hundred. The whole of the apparatus covered above four acres of ground.

" Of RANELAGH, so recently in remembrance, I shall only say a few words. This celebrated and fashionable place of entertainment had been the seat of Lord Ranelagh, and was situated at Chelsea. At his decease, in 1733, the estate was sold to one Timbrell, a builder, for £3,200, who re-sold it the following year; when, some gentlemen and builders having become purchasers, a resolution was taken to form the spot into a place of public amusement; and which was completed and opened in the year 1740. The great attraction here, and which constituted the chief place for the assemblage of company, was a magnificent rotunda, which will be better known from the prints of it than from any description. The internal diameter of this splendid receptacle was one hundred and fifty feet, and it was fitted up with boxes, an orchestra

&c.  Concerts of vocal and instrumental music were given here, in a superior style, and occasionally other amusements; but the resort of company dropping off of late years, the site was sold, and has been since built on.  Ranelagh usually opened on Easter Monday, and closed on the Prince of Wales's birth-day.  It had a convenient landing-place and entrance from the Thames, and carriage-ways from Hyde Park Corner, and Buckingham Gate.  The price of admission was two shillings and sixpence.

"The APOLLO GARDENS, and DOG and DUCK (both, until ately, standing in St. George's Fields) were a direct contrast in oint of respectability to Ranelagh.  The former stood opposite the Asylum in the Westminster Road, and was very prettily fitted up, on the Vauxhall plan, by a Mr. Clagget.  The orchestra, in the centre of the gardens, was large, and particularly beautiful: a want of the rural accompaniment of fine trees, their smallness, the situation, and other causes, soon made them the resort only of the low and vicious; and, after an ineffectual struggle of two or three seasons, they finally closed, and the site has been since entirely built on.  The Dog and Duck was more obstinate, and far less worthy of patronage.  At this place there was a long room with tables and benches, and, at the upper end, an organ.  The company which assembled in the evening consisted chiefly of women of the town, their bullies, and such young men as could, without reflection, supply them with inflaming liquor.  Becoming a positive nuisance on these and other accounts, it was, after many complaints, put down by the magistrates, and that useful, though melancholy charity, Bethlem Hospital, now occupies the spot.

"TONBRIDGE WELLS, or ISLINGTON SPA, was formrely in full favour with the public, and opened for the summer on the 5th of May.  The proprietors admitted dancers for the whole of the day, on Mondays and Thursdays, provided they did not appear in masks, for whom music was provided.  The Princess Amelia, in 1733, rendered this place, for a time, fashionable, by drinking this water for the benefit of her health.  These gardens were beautiful, particularly at the entrance, where pedestals and vases were grouped with a good deal of taste, under some extremely picturesque trees.  The subscription was one guinea for the season, and concerts, with public breakfasts, were occasionally given.  They were latterly very little frequented, which occasioned the site to be built on.  They stood nearly opposite Sadler's Wells.

"The following are still open, but much degenerated.  They are quite of an inferior species, at best—

WHITE CONDUIT HOUSE, by Islington:—Much resorted to formerly, particularly on Sundays, as tea-gardens, and forming then a pleasant rural walk from town:—

> " Human beings here
> In couples multitudinous assembled,
> Forming the drollest group that ever trod

Fair Islingtonian plains—male after male,
Dog after dog, succeeding—husbands—wives—
Fathers and mothers—brothers—sisters—friends—
Around, across, along the shrubby maze
They walk, they sit, they stand.'

"BAGNIGGE WELLS.—These gardens are said, by Mr. Lysons, to have opened, for the first time, about 1716; in consequence of the discovery of two spings of mineral water, chalybeate and cathartic. The gardens were originally small, but made the most of in walks, fountains, trees, Dutch nymphs, and Cupids, &c. &c. The old-fashioned manner of gardening—clipped trees and formal lines, characterized this place. It was formerly much frequented on Sundays, for tea-dinking, but is now curtailed, and nearly deserted. The prologue to *Bon Ton* notices it among the places of low fashion :—

'Tis drinking tea, on Sunday afternoons,
At Bagnigge Wells, in china, and gilt spoons.' "

While Mentor and his friend were parading Vauxhall Gardens, and admiring the animated scene before them, Peregrine remarked on the increasing fashion with gentlemen, in wearing beards on the upper lip, and some with it on the chin, while others have such a quantity of hair on their heads. "These only serve to show," said Mentor, " that the ' Vagaries of Fashion' were at all times as prevalent as at present; for the Anglo-Saxons appear to have worn their hair and beards long, merely dividing that on the head from the crown to the forehead; and the men a sort of bonnet, when not engaged in war. At their first invasion of this country, their dress is supposed to have resembled that of the ancient Germans, their neighbours, which Tacitus describes as having been a close habit, fitted to their shape, with fantastic patches of different-coloured skins set on it, and a large mantle fastened over one shoulder. This costume was in many respects considerably altered afterwards. The Normans shaved away the enormous mass of hair, which the Saxons had suffered to disfigure their faces. William of Malmsbury says this began in the reign of Harold, at which time the hair on the upper lip only was retained; but when the conqueror came in, he had such an aversion to whiskers, that he expressly commanded his new subjects to part with them. The dresses of the upper ranks, at this period, were of the finest cloth, or most beautiful furs, and ornamented with jewels. The colours were various, but *yellow* they appropriated as a mark of infamy to the Jews. The lower classes wore a doublet tied about the waist, which, having sleeves to the wrist, was put on over the head : these reached only to the middle of the thigh.

" The variety, and we may say absurdity, in the article of shoes, which began near this reign, and continued until that of the Tudor family, far exceeds any thing we have witnessed in these days. In 1135, they were made without heels, like those of the blue-coat boys at present, came up to the ankles, and had a slip on the in-

PUBLISHER'S NOTE

PP.238-239 ARE MISSING.

of your parrots feathers  This snows that dyes for the hair were in use long before the present age."

Mentor and his friend now left Vauxhall Gardens, highly gratified with the treat of the evening, having agreed to meet Wilmot the next morning; he, having completed his studies, and passed his examination at college, intended to take his departure for the country; and Mentor and Peregrine accompanied him to the coach office. While waiting for the coach, they observed a poor woman in tears, with an infant at her breast, and a countryman bargaining with her for a *new hat*. Mentor, leading his friends to a convenient situation, desired them to take a side glance at the parties, and they would see what is called 'doing a yokel' with a plated hat. The countryman purchased the hat, and departed, well satisfied with his bargain. Mentor explained to his yet inexperienced friend, the roguery practised on the present occasion. "That woman," said he, "whom you supposed in tears, is one of the many impostors who frequent the streets of this great metropolis for the purpose of defrauding the unwary. She pretends she has just arrived in London from Portsmouth, or some other sea-port town, that her husband was killed at Navarino, or died in an hospital, that she is obliged to part with all his apparel to defray the expenses of his funeral, and that this is a hat he had purchased just previous to his death for twenty-five shillings, and for which she would be glad to obtain twelve or fourteen shillings. The countryman, who evidently listened with great attention, felt a spark of humanity for her distressed situation, and, although not wanting the hat, yet from its very low price asks, 'Is dat hat for sale?' The woman says 'Yes, but I have offered it to this gentleman for fourteen shillings.' 'Vell,' says the Jew, 'if he von't give you that price, I will.' Thus the poor countryman is thrown off his guard, presuming, that if it is worth fourteen shillings to a *Jew*, it must be to him; and he is *regularly* let in for the hat, which, on inquiry, he finds is not worth more than two or three shillings."

Peregrine was again astonished at (to him) this new species of villany. "And this," said he, "reminds me of a lady at Pontefract, a connoisseur in zoological specimens of the canine tribe, who purchased from an itinerant dog-dealer a most beautiful little French poodle. His sparkling eyes, half hid amidst a profusion of silken curls, his sleek and glossy sides, aided by a multiplicity of innocent gambols, attracted the hearts of all beholders, and made him the pet of his mistress and the family. In a few weeks, however, the poor little fellow was observed to grow unaccountably dull and stupid; his mirthfulness and vivacity were lost; he became snappish, refused his food, and ultimately crept into a corner, where, in spite of blain and brimstone balls, he gave up the ghost. Having been a very great favourite, and, although defunct, the beauty of his silvery coat not being wholly spoiled his mistress determined upon having him stuffed, and sent for an amateur dog-fancier, who immediately discovered it was a little cur, sewed in the skin of a French poodle.

The coach now drove up, and Mentor and Peregrine bade adieu to Wilmot, who left London a little wiser than he entered it.

At this moment their attention was drawn to the riotous behaviour of a woman; who, although in a state of sad inebriety, gave evident proofs she was not of the lowest class : she was under the charge of two officers, for demolishing the glasses and windows of a public-house, and they were conducting her to Bow Street; she was the celebrated *Lady Barrymore*; and, as Mentor and Peregrine were anxious to hear her examination, they followed her to the office, not being tired of witnessing the melancholy, laughable, depraved, and interesting

**Doings at the Public Office, Bow Street.**

In a few minutes after they entered the office, this " fallen angel," was placed at the bar, and exhibited a melancholy proof of the dreadful effects of drunkenness : there were yet many pleasing remains in her countenance of former beauty; but she was in a state of madness, produced by the drinking of the deadly gin ; and, when told by the magistrate that she must find bail, or go to prison, she vociferated with an oath, " Bail!—where the h—l do you think I can get bail ?" " Then," replied the magistrate, " you must go to prison." To h—l with you," she answered, " and take that with you;" and actually threw her shoe at the magistrate. With great difficulty she was taken from the bar, and secured in the

31. R

lock-up room. Nothing particular being before their worships, the hearers withdrew.

Mentor and Peregrine now agreed to visit Westminster Abbey; and, on their way thither, Mentor remarked to Peregrine that the story they were talking of that morning, of the cased dog, was not a solitary instance of fraud; "for I remember," said he, "a gentleman, who saw what he thought a beautiful small poodle dog in a cage at Charing Cross, which struck his fancy, and, after much chafering between the seller and himself, he became the purchaser for twelve shillings: in a few days he observed symptoms of uneasiness in the animal, when all on a sudden he saw a brown nose just under the white one, and, with a little assistance, out walked as dingy ill-looking a cur, as ever breathed : the poodle's skin had been curiously fastened on the animal's body, *and he was bit.*"

Mentor had now conveyed Peregrine to the interior of Westminster Abbey. "Observe," said Mentor, " yon stern figure bursting from his sepulchre; how formidably he frowns—in his very looks he seems to upbraid the degeneracy of the age. And see, he points to the *fleur-de-lis* on his shield, and seems to say, ' Britons, remember Cressi !'

" But turn your eyes from the kings and princes, who are no more secured from the stroke of death than the meanest hynde, and observe yonder bust of a person who left, by will, five hundred pounds to be expended in a monument, resolving to do himself that justice, it is more than probable an ungrateful country would have denied him. Such is human vanity, which ends not with life, but flutters even o'er the tomb.

" The next monument is that of an actress; who, having often personated queens and princesses upon the stage, was judged by her admirers worthy to mingle her dust with theirs." .

" What absurd vanity," said Peregrine ! " But to whom belongs that magnificent tomb on the right hand ?" " That, replied his companion, " is one monument (I wish there were many more) of British freedom, and British gratitude. It was erected to the memory of a hero, who lost his life in a sea-fight, to preserve his admiral's, and maintain the glory of his country.

" See where yonder lies the greatest philosopher the world ever produced. His name will be reverenced by the learned of every nation, and his works will remain as long as the orbs, whose course he traced, shall continue to move. Look into the tomb, and you will see the mighty remains of human greatness—Dust !

" To give the virtuous dead their due praise," continued Mentor, " is the duty of every generous mind ; to lament them is folly.

" Take notice of that figure of a lady weeping ; her breast, when living, was as cold as her statue, nor could it be warmed by the most ardent vows and sighs of her lovers, till, having passed her fortieth year with the purity of a vestal, she formed a resolution to be useful in her generation, and accordingly married her coachman ; but the ceremony was scarcely performed, when death laid his icy hand upon her, and sent her to sleep with her forefathers."

"What clumsy heap of stones is that next?" said Peregrine. "I is the resting-place of a rich old miser," answered Mentor, "who, drinking water to save the expense of better liquor, when he was warm, was seized with a violent fever: in his extremity, he made a thousand vows and protestations to amend his life, and restore what he had unjustly amassed, if ever he should recover. His vows were heard, and his health returned. But, instead of amending, he was more rapacious than ever; till, at last providence, resolving to rid the world of such a monster, cut him off as he was putting his hand to a mortgage, and saved a family from ruin.

"On the left hand, is interred a young nobleman, of whose growing virtues the world had the greatest expectations; and he would have fulfilled them, had his life been of longer date: but, going into a tavern one evening along with his most intimate acquaintance, and drinking pretty freely, a discourse arose concerning the orthography of a word, which terminated in the death of them both. Such are the blessed effects of drinking to excess!

"The next monument is to the memory of a beau, who spent all his time in dancing, singing, and dressing, till Death, who purposely put on the form of a beautiful young lady, danced away with him in the middle of a minuet."

"What do I see?" said Peregrine, "cannons, muskets, swords, and spears? that must be the monument of a warrior." "That," rejoined Mentor, "belongs to a general; who, in several campaigns, never lost one battle: and, indeed, to do him justice, I cannot tell how it was possible he should, for he could never prevail upon himself to run the hazard of one."

"Whose superb monument of pure white alabaster, is that?" asked Peregrine. "It is to the memory of one of the fairest of the daughters of Britain: she belonged to the Russels, and was 'as pure as ice, as chaste as snow;' and, I believe, she was so spotless as even to escape calumny. She was such another being as the accomplished and virtuous

*Margaret Roper,*

the beloved daughter of the learned and inflexible Sir Thomas

More, Lord Chancellor of England; who, for judgment, humility, devotion, sweetness of temper, contempt of the world, and true greatness of soul, was the ornament of his own, and an example to every other age. She was not only panegyrized by Erasmus, Ludovicus Vives, and all the learned men of her time, for the acuteness of her judgment, and the profundity of her learning, but was further held up to public view as a pattern of daughterly perfection and the most exalted piety. This extraordinary female, being seized with a sweating sickness, which put an end to her earthly career in the course of a very few hours, conducted herself on this trying occasion with such consummate fortitude, that shere sembled much more an expiring Seneca of the Roman school, than a  id daughter of Albion's isle. Margaret Roper was also the grand-daughter of

Sir John More,

who  as on of the judges of the King's Bench, and a man of r re abilities and integrity.

"But yonder is a sight, indeed,—a superb and elegant marble, erected by a most disconsolate husband, to the memory of his dear departed wife. View the inscription—how lavish he is in her praise—how tenderly he laments her loss. Such instances of conjugal affection are not very common: but our wonder at this will a little abate, if we reflect that she lived but three days after the priest had joined their hands. *Æternæ memoriæ sacrum.* Ay, of a scoundrel," continued Mentor. "This fellow had formed a design to extirpate the female sex from the earth. He poisoned six wives, and intended the same favour for the seventh, but she luckily escaped, and soon after gave him his passport to the other world, in a glass of Rhenish."

"Well, my good friend," interrupted Peregrine, we have seen enough here. Let us, if you please, shift the scene, and move to another quarter. But, before you go, tell me whose monument that is?" "It is for a man of very great merit," said Mentor, "and he was rewarded for it; his works were universally applauded, and he himself perished for want. This monument was placed here, not long since, by a man who was desirous of purchasing immortality at the cheap rate of two hundred pounds, which was laid out in carving the poet's bust, and his own name at the bottom."

"Now let us leave this depository of the dead," said Peregrine, and take a survey of the city." "Yes," replied Mentor; "and, after dinner, I will show you my collection of drawings—a living panorama of scenes from real life, of daily occurrences in the city—'most strange and most unnatural, and yet not more strange than true.'

"Behold this drawing," continued Mentor: "it is a temple dedicated to Venus; whose venerable priestess is continually employed in finding out means to satisfy the wants and necessities of youth. In plain English, it is a brothel; where, for the value of half-a-crown, you may purchase diseases that will attend you to your grave. Yet are the poor wretches who inhabit it, really to be pitied. That miserable object you see expiring on a flock bed, in the garret, is the only daughter of an old baronet, who is possessed of a large estate. Having unluckily a heart too susceptible of love, she married a young fellow of no fortune, who had privately paid his addresses to her. The father, who before seemed passiouately fond of his daughter, upon the news, acted as many fathers do when they are disobliged,—absolutely refused to see, forgive, or succour her, and the next morning married his cook-maid, and settled his whole estate upon her. The lovers struggled a long time with want and grief, till death, at length, in pity, sent the husband to rest. His widow again applied to her *humane* father, was refused admittance, and—but let humanity draw the veil of oblivion over her errors. Let it suffice, that poor shrinking virtue fled the field, when want, clothed in all its bitter terrors, stared her in the face.

"The girl you see yonder, crying in the corner, is just brought into this blessed *mansion*. Being very beautiful, and deprived of both father and mother, she was importuned a long time by a young gentleman to submit to his inordinate desires; a large settlement was offered, but she nobly refused it. He then offered marriage; the proposal was accepted, and a sham parson performed the ceremony; but a mouth's cohabitation sated the hero; who after undeceiving her, flung out of the room, and left her without a penny. The master of the house, who was entirely at the devotion of his landlord, arrested her for the rent. The lady with whom she now is, being purposely sent by the mock husband, compassionately paid the debt, and carried her to her own house. —It is easy to guess the rest.

"The person you observe in the arms of a rotten strumpet, is an eminent merchant, who has a virtuous loving wife and several fine children at home; but his dirty grovelling soul prefers the feigned embraces of a perfidious harlot to all the soft endearments of a virtuous love.

"In the next room, you see Bacchus and Venus are met together. See that company of young fellows, with each his girl upon his knee; how jovially they carouse! They are apprentices and journeymen to tradesmen, and take care to fleece their masters to maintain their doxies.

"Here is a view of a public-house, with a company of blackguard fellows drinking in a little room. That man you see giving another a watch, is a watchman; who, having conducted a gentleman safe home, who was a little in liquor, thought proper to pick his pocket of his watch. He is also giving information to the thieves of a house he found left open by negligence, that they may rob it, while the *honest* guardian is going his rounds.

"That quarrel you see, is between two who go by the name of man and wife; she has plunged a knife into his bosom: the tragic effects of gin and jealousy.

"Here is a humourous scene," continued Mentor,—"an old fellow and his servant quarrelling. The latter saved the life of the former not half-a-year since, by cutting him down (like a fool as he was) when he had hanged himself in the stable. His *generous* master, being about to part with him, has deducted a groat from the fellow's wages, for the halter he had cut in order to preserve him.

"In the parlour of this spacious house, on the left hand, is a young nobleman, paying his addresses to a merchant's daughter. His great soul condescends to mix his illustrious blood with a plebeian's, in order to recover his estate, which he has lost at play. The lady, fond of title and equipage, will now despise her father's clerk, and bear a coronet for life.

"Here is a man talking in his sleep; he is a lawyer, who dreams he is in the lower world, and making his defence at the bar of *Minos.* When he goes there in earnest, he will find the practice of that court different from any he ever saw in his life. Near this lawyer is a young fellow—what horror and grief appear in his looks!—he has dreamed that his father is come to life again, and demands his estate.

"This old citizen is drawing on his boots: he is going to dine at Hammersmith, which is the longest journey he ever went in his life, and has compelled his family to get up very early to accoutre him for the expedition.

"That old fellow, sneaking out of the corner house, is a clergyman, whose austere looks, and devout appearance, make him pass for a saint; he has just quitted a girl whom he privately keeps.

"This is a representation of an old man on his death-bed, and his chamber crowded with his nephews and nieces, who are beating their breasts, and tearing their hair, with all the expressions of frantic grief. But his last breath is parted from his lips. The voice of sorrow is hushed, and they have already begun to rummage his coffers." "Then amongst those floods of tears, not one honest one was shed." "Yes," replied Mentor; "the old groom in the stables is paying his last tribute to the memory of his deceased master.

"The next drawing represents an old woman sitting by the fire-side. She was first married to an eminent banker, who promised his eldest daughter to a young merchant, but, dying before the marriage could be consummated, he left his widow the management of his whole fortune. The lover, after a proper time, attended the dowager, in hopes to obtain the daughter. But how great was his surprise, when the good lady carried him into her closet, and accosted him in these terms: ' Look ye, sir,—I will deal honourably with you. You shall have my daughter, if you insist upon it, but not one farthing fortune. *Mr. Sgueezum* died worth fifty thousand pounds; if you think the money will compensate the loss of the girl, here is my hand; you shall be master of me and mine to-morrow.' The young fellow, who was a true pounds, shillings, and pence citizen, agreed to the match, and they were married the next day.

"Here is a representation of an old dog, who has just done the only good action in his life. He has hanged himself in the cellar. He lent a gentleman, who at the time was in want of cash, twenty pounds, but took care to deduct fifteen out of it for three months' interest. An action was soon commenced against him for usury and extortion, and he has done that justice to himself the hangman should have done for him.

"Observe this woman embracing her husband with the utmost tenderness. This poor man was married six years, and never knew a happy moment till this. Her tongue, which came the nearest of any mortal thing to the perpetual motion, has never been still all that time, till within a quarter of an hour of this embrace, when this reverse of *Socrates*, unable to bear his sufferings any longer, strapped her heartily, and you see the consequence. Now, here, on the contrary, is a merciless rascal, who is kicking his wife about the room, has been out all night with the strumpets, and is making his wife, whom he left without a morsel of bread, this recompense for sitting up for him. But this is the least of his torments, for she died under her bruises, and the villain was hung.

"What! is that a ghost," said Peregrine, "walking at the break of day?" "No," replied Mentor; "he is a roguish sexton, who, having dressed himself in a white sheet, frightens the people out of their senses, whilst his associates are robbing the church.

"These two fellows, with a farthing candle burning dimly before them, are of the race of *Cain*. They are stock-jobbers; they sit up all night to contrive a lie for the next day, in order to sink the stocks that they may purchase the cheaper. Gibraltar is to be swallowed up by an earthquake; and fifty thousand troops, with young Boney at their head, are to land in Ireland.

"Here is a representation of a company of jovial beggars in St. Giles's, singing and dancing: they are bred up in laziness, and are enabled, by the misplaced charity of easy good-inclined people, thus nightly to indulge themselves in riot and debauchery.

"I do not know how it is," said Mentor, "but I always read with avidity every history or anecdote that relates to beggars; and I find St. Giles's mentioned by Strype, in the time of Elizabeth, as one of the frequent places of resort 'for such misdemeaned sort of persons,' who used to haunt the fields about here and Islington in such numbers, and were so audacious in their importunities, as, on one occasion, to have beset the queen's coach (Elizabeth's) as she rode out for air, and cause her considerable trouble, 'of which Fleetwood the recorder,' says, he (the anecdote has before been quoted) 'being informed, sent out warrants into the same quarters, and into Westminster and the Dutchy, and in the morning he went abroad himself, and took that day seventy-four rogues, whereof some were blind, and yet great usurers and rich, who were sent to Bridewell and well punished.' In continuing his observations on the subject, as well as remarking on the various proclamations issued to prevent the influx of country people and paupers in London, he assigns as a cause of their particularly choosing this spot, that it lay nearest to the court (a few fields then only separating it from Westminster), to which numbers of strangers (and particularly Irish), flocked about that period, under pretence of presenting petitions, &c., and that this, with the general disposition which began to prevail among mechanics and others from the country, to settle in London as a better market for labonr, soon caused this, among other places, to become overstocked with poor, and especially to abound with beggars and vagrants. What were the then manners and habits of such, the first quoted author (Hollingshed) further informs us: 'Some,' says he, 'do practice the making of corrosives, and applying the same to the more fleshie parts of their bodies, and also the laieng of raisbane, sparewort, crowsfoot, and such like, into their whole members, thereby to raise pitifull and odious sores, and move the harts of the goers by such places as they do lye in, to yern at their miserie, and thereupon bestow large almesse upon them. How artificiallie they beg, what forcible speech, and how they select and force out words of vehemence, whereby they do in a manner conjure or adjure you to pitie their cases, I pass over to remember,—as judging the names of God and Christ to be more conversant in the mouths of some, nor the presence of the heavenly majestie further off than from this ungracious companie; which maketh me to think that punishment is faire meeter for them than libertie and almesse.'

"'Another sort,' he continues, 'more sturdie than the rest, and having sound and perfect limbs, do counterfeit the possession of all sorts of diseases. Others, in their apparell, are like *serving men and labourers*. Oftentimes they can plaie the marriner, and seake for ships they never lost. But, in fine, these thieves and caterpillars are of various stocks,' &c.

" Noticing their use of the ' cant or slang language,' he says, ' Moreover, in counterfeiting the Egyptian rogues, they have devised a language amongst themselves, which they name *canting*, a speech compact thirty years since of English, and a greate number of od words of their owne devising, without all order or reason, and yet such as none but themselves are able to understand. The first deviser thereof was hanged by the necke, a just reward, no doubt, for his deserts, and a common end of all that profession. A gentleman of late,' he adds, ' hath taken great paines to search out the secret practices of this ungracious rabble; and, amongst other things, he setteth down and describeth twenty-three sorts of them, whose names it shall not be amisse to remember, whereby one may take occasion to read and know, as also by his industrie, what wicked people they are, and what villanie remaineth in them.'

" Many entries occur in the reign of James I. and Charles I. in the parish-book of St. Giles's, on the subject of these newly-intro duced paupers and beggars, who are spoken of under the names of ' new-comers, undersitters, and cellar-mates, dwellers in straight places, lodgers in divided tenements,' &c., and had become then such an annoyance, that an assistant beadle (Giles Hanson) was appointed with a particular dress, and a salary of forty pounds a-year, to prevent their further settlement, but without effect. The items of relief in the churchwardens' accounts preserve the names of some of those early mendicants, apparently then well known, and are curious, such as—

|                                             | *s.* | *d.* |
|---------------------------------------------|------|------|
| To Tottenham Court Meg, being very sicke    | 1    | 0    |
| To Mad Bess                                 | 1    | 0    |
| To olde Guy, the blind poet                 | 1    | 6    |
| To the ballad-singing cobbler               | 1    | 0    |

" Those we may suppose were objects more particularly distressed, or better behaved. Those that were less deserving were generally confined in the cage, and not unfrequently died there, several entries occurring similar to the following :—

To Ann Wyatt, in the cage, to buy her a truss of straw, &c. *2s. 6d.* And a few days afterwards :

To Anne Wyatt, to buy her a shroud, *2s.*

" The places they more particularly congregated about at this period, are not mentioned, but appear to have been in the neighbourbood of Dyot Street, which they have since rendered so notorious. This spot was then called Maidenhead Close, and afterwards Maidenhead Row, from the Maidenhead Inn adjoining (the old public-house now pulling down), and abounded principally with cottages and a low kind of dwellings, the residence of the gentry being chiefly about Drury Lane. Richard Dyott, Esq., Messrs. Bainbridge and Buckridge, and other builders, erected on this site, in the reign of Charles II., the several streets bearing

32.

their names, and which, being generally let in lodgings, invited the settlement of fresh numbers of Irish, as the building of the Seven Dials, soon afterwards, did that of distressed French Protestants. Hogarth, in his 'Four Stages of Cruelty,' satyrizes, in the person of Tom Nero, a St. Giles's charity-boy, the then state of this neighbourhood, who is represented with other wicked boys tormenting poor animals to death, literally dressed in rags, a beginning which at length leads him to the gallows ; and, though there are no particular marks to identify it, the scene of 'Gin Lane' is supposed to be laid in the same quarter.  Fielding (the author of *Tom Jones*), also, in a pamphlet published by him near the same time, relative to the police of the metropolis, has some forcible observations on the depravity and wretchedness of the lower orders here, as have several other writers, but which, describing circumstances similar to what we have ourselves witnessed, it is needless to quote from.  They serve to convince us of one fact, however, amidst all the dissoluteness they notice, viz.—that these parts of the parish, as well as their inhabitants, are at least somewhat improved in modern times.  The widening of the high street, and several other causes, might be enumerated, as having contributed much to this.

"The beggars are always sure to find a mart for such articles as they steal or beg, in the receivers of stolen goods, of whom Mr. Colquhoun, in his Police of the Metropolis, says—'There are upwards of three thousand receivers of various kinds of stolen goods, and an equal proportion all over the country, who keep open shop for the purpose of purchasing, at an under price, often for a mere trifle, every kind of property brought to them, and this without asking a single question.  He further supposes that the property purloined and pilfered in a little way, from almost every family, and from every house, stable, shop, warehouse, &c., in and about the metropolis, may amount to about £700,000 in one year.  The vast increase and extensive circulation of counterfeit money, almost exceeds credibility ; and the ingenuity and dexterity of these counterfeits have enabled them to finish the different kinds of base money in so masterly a manner, that it has become extremely difficult to distinguish the spurious from the real manufacture.  In London, regular markets, in various public and private houses, are held by the principal dealers, where hawkers, pedlars, fraudulent horse-dealers, gamblers at fairs, itinerant Jews, Irish labourers, market-women, rabbit-sellers, fish-criers, barrow-women, and many others, get supplied with counterfeit money, with the advantage of nearly £100 per cent. in their favour.

"There exists in the metropolis a class of dealers extremely numerous, who keep open shops for the purchase of rags, old iron, and other metals.  These are divided into wholesale and retail dealers.  The retail dealers are the immediate purchasers, in the first instance, from the pilferers or their agents ; and, as soon as they collect a sufficient quantity of iron, brass, or other metals, worthy the notice of a large dealer, they dispose of it for ready money. Others are employed in the collection of rags, and other articles purloined in the country, which are conveyed to town in " single horse carts," kept by itinerant Jews, and other doubtful characters, who travel to Portsmouth, Chatham, Woolwich, and Deptford, for the purpose of purchasing metals, &c., from persons who are in the habit of embezzling the king's stores.

" The connexion between the thieves and the police is so un-equivocal, that it has become necessary for persons who have been robbed, and who suspect that their goods are at the houses of certain receivers, to apply for search-warrants at hours when some of the officers of the establishment are absent from the offices. The moment the information is given, the trap, or police-officer, if he happen to learn what is going forward, gives the word to the ' fence,' who acts accordingly; and the chance of regaining the property is gone, except a pecuniary compromise can be effected. In this compromise the officer is a large sharer. There are generally four partners in the produce: the thief has a fourth, the receiver a fourth, the officer a fourth, and the attorney, or Newgate agent, a fourth; but of late attorneys are very shy of dabbling in robberies: the exposure some time ago of their agency with respect to bankers' parcels has in a great measure diminised their profits in this particular department of the profession. The Jew agents, some of whom have been tried at the Old Bailey themselves, and who are in the habit of getting up *alibis* and other modes of defence by means of perjury, now monopolize the stewardship of the plunderer. At an investigation into the circumstances of the escape of Ikey Solomons from justice, it was ascertained beyond all doubt, that, ' the thing' was planned by a Jew agent; and almost the only meritorious determination, per-haps, ever arrived at by the magistrates as a body, that of exclud-ing the projectors of this base enterprise from the police-offices for ever, was instantly made. It would be well if they made a proper use of a far higher power, which they allow to lie in so shameful a state of inaction, as to exhibit the symptoms and effects of positive connivance. We are, however, glad to observe one proof of virtuous indignation upon the part of the magistrates. The agent in the nefarious business alluded to, admits that he used to put upwards of £1000 a year into his pocket by his trade. His exclusion from the police-offices and the prisons of the metropolis necessarily checks the tide of his prosperity, and operates as a redeeming spirit in the conduct of those who have expelled him. The main articles upon which the receiver depends are silk and broadie (broad cloth.) The broadie at once finds purchasers amongst the Jews, and the silk finds customers, not only amongst that class of dealers, but amongst some of the most affluent trades-men. A very great house in the neighbourhood of Finsbury has been known so far to transgress the rules of fair competition, as to act the part of receiver upon many occasions. The proprietor, however, who had all the sinister ingenuity of an accomplished thief, managed things so well as to escape such a detection as would compel him to hold up his hand at the Old Bailey. The price it was, at which his tricks had enabled him to sell the article, and the acknowledgment of his confederates, who never failed at one time or other to tremble in the grasp of retributive justice, that fixed his participation beyond all doubt. The name of this congenial soul has not of late appeared in the police vocabulary, and some ascribe the change to fear, and some to virtue.

" There is not, we will venture to say, a warehouseman in Wood Street, who does not know that there are houses which are daily selling Bandanas at twenty-five per cent. cheaper than the price at which the fair dealer can afford to dispose of articles of the same description—nay, even at twenty-five per cent. under first cost. The ladies at the west end of the town are not aware, that when they are making bargains with persons who hawk about silks, they are encouraging the system of robbery upon which we have animadverted. There is scarcely a shawl purchased as a ' bargain' in this way, that has not been in the possession of some desperate house-breaker, who has risked his neck to get hold of what afterwards adorns the shoulders of many a beautiful woman. In fact, many a lady of rank and fortune may say with truth, when she looks at her new purchase, ' This passed through the hands of a man who was or will certainly be hanged.' The removal of Ikey Solomons', who, from the moment Dudfield was ' lagged,' became the most extensive fence in the metropolis, caused the greatest possible excitement amongst the Jews. Indeed, to the spirit of rivalry and jealousy amongst them on the subject of an adequate substitute, is to be attributed the very accurate information which led to the development of so many facts as have reached the public since his escape. He is now beyond the reach for ever of the poor, spiritless, corrupt, contemptible police, whom he was always able to manage, having resolved to introduce into America the system which he carried on here for so many years with impunity. The energy of the worthy magistrates, and the corresponding zeal and vigilance of the police, are strikingly exemplified by the terrible fact that thieves have no less than five or six times visited, by means of false keys, or false servants, the premises which they afterwards robbed; that they have postponed their last visit to a period when the ' swag' was sufficiently bulky, not choosing to lay their hands upon property of inconsiderable amount, when they knew that a little patience would reward them for their forbearance; and that they have often filled a cart or hackney-coach with goods, within a few yards of a watchbox, the inmate of which shammed sleep. Sleep, however, is so well known a characteristic of the watchman, that he generally gets credit for the reality, when he is actually silent for a share of the plunder.

" Receivers of stolen goods are always in droves about the police-offices. Those gentlemen, also, have their privileges. An interchange of civilities frequently takes place between them and some of the officers, who are willing to smoke a pipe, crack a bottle and a joke with them, and the proprietors of houses of accommodation for both sexes of all ages, the owners of gaming-houses, and those respectable thieves who disdain to do a dirty action, but plunder where some character is to be got by the achievement, for which they may be, if not ' scragged' for death, at all events ' lagged' for life.

" There is a low public-house close to the noses of their worships, in which many of those ruffians are in the habit of sitting the greater part of the day. A stranger who should look in, and see them playing cribbage and smoking and drinking, would suppose that they snatched an hour for relaxation from the labours of their several occupations. But it is not so : there they sit every day from morning till night, waiting for the arrival of their *nose* (a man deputed to pick up news of robberies), and the moment any thief is ' pulled' at the office, off they scamper to watch the examination, and ascertain whether they cannot get hold of the ' swag,' before it can be brought forward in judgment. There never is an occasion when what they call a ' good' robbery is known at the office to have been committed, upon which they do not receive immediate intelligence. Some of them act as ' touters' to those who may have got the ' swag,' and the moment they find that the thief is ' grabbed' (apprehended), they run off to the fence, and give him the wink to ' lumber it in another crib.' A notorious receiver, named Reuben Josephs, who was some time ago transported for fourteen years, was in the habit of visiting this house, into which some of the officers often look, to say, ' Tom, or Bill, or Benjamin, how do you do?' and throw off a half-quartern of ' jackey' to the health and at the expense of the company. It has been the fashion with the police (for what reasons may be easily guessed), to say in defence of their practice of associating with thieves and receivers, that it is necessary for them to do so for the protection of the public,—that, in fact, stolen property could not be recovered if the connexion were not kept up. The true meaning of this is, that, if the natural hostility which exists between an honest officer and a rogue be acted upon, all chance of participation is at an end. The officer is shut out from his perquisite, but the thief and the receiver run a thousand hazards, which they know not in the ordinary compact, and the public are sure to be benefitted when the thief-taker acts independently of the reptiles whom he is employed to hunt.

" The receivers pay to the thieves for swag in the following proportion :—for silver, four shillings an ounce; but the reason they pay so high for this description of commodity is, that the crucible is always ready, and they can, immediately after the purchase, sell it at the full price, without the slightest hazard of detection. For a chest of slop (tea), £15; but for tip-top slop they will not hesitate to give £20. For broadie, they pay ten shillings a stretch (a yard); and for bull-dogs (lumps of sugar stolen from grocers), half price. The fences always have the ready money about them, and the dealing is strictly according to the maxim of 'honour amongst thieves.' Ikey Solomons was known to be in the habit of carrying £1,000 in his side-pocket, and to have purchased bandanas as they were carried along the street. There is one class of thieves who do an immensity of mischief, and who are seldom or never restrained in the slightest degree, although the officers well know that, if they frisked a bit (searched), a great deal of swag is sure to be forthcoming. Those are the fellows who seem to be employed as costermongers; but nothing is too hot or too heavy for them. They take their rounds in the suburbs of the town with their donkeys and panniers, and dispose of their greens and herrings, and other commodities; after which they substitute in the place of such articles as much smut (copper or lead) as they can stow away. If they fail in stripping a house of the smut, they pick up a stray fowl, or any thing which is convertible into cash, and they are always ready to lend a hand at a burglary, the simplicity of their ostensible trade acting as a security against detection. It is usual with them to operate largely in the glass line. If they can prig a 'shiner' (a looking-glass), they immediately transport it to the neighbourhood of Wentworth Street, where the Jews knock off the frames, and so transform it in other respects, as to destroy all identity. Some of the lower order of fences turn a penny by the purchase of the plate-glasses which the thieves remove from gentlemen's carriages. Those glasses are converted into 'shiners,' and are often sold to the trade, who are sometimes unconscious that they are instrumental in disposing of stolen property. The swarms of 'buzzes' who infest the neighbourhood of the theatres, exercise their ingenuity in a great variety of ways. During the last season they practised a trick, which succeeded every night to an extraordinary degree. One of them would go in front of the horses of a gentleman's carriage, and play such tricks as would induce the coachman to rise from his seat to whip the fellow away. The moment he rose, another of the gang, who waited under the coachman's seat for the movement, would pull down the great-coat, upon which the owner had sat for security's sake, and away he would run, the coachman in vain calling out that he was robbed. At the last Guildhall dinner many were plundered in this manner by some of the west-end 'out-and-outers' (thorough-bred thieves). But the plunder which has in its list the most able, desperate, and ingenious professors, is that which the housebreaker commits, and the city of London is the place in which that species of depredation is carried on to an extent greatly beyond credibility.

" It is to the receivers of stolen goods, giving such facility to the theives disposing of their ill-gotten booty, that we must ascribe, in a great measure, the numerous robberies that are committed daily by servants on their masters. Almost all parts of the town abound with prigs, cracksmen, and flash dragsmen; but, certainly, if in any one part more than another, it is in the vicinity of Covent Garden; and, to obtain an adequate idea of the nightly occurrences in the desperate vicinity of Bow Street, it would be necessary for a stranger to visit it, under the protection of an officer (for the officer is admitted into all the flash-houses at all hours), at different periods of the night. Immediately before the theatre-doors are opened, a gang of thieves assemble at a public-house close to Drury-Lane Theatre, and they simultaneously drop their pipes the instant notice is given, and issue forth to plunder the struggling crowd. As soon as the press is over, they return to their 'smoking crib,' dispose of their plunder to the landlord, and enjoy themselves until the performances are concluded. The signal for industry is then repeated; down go the pipes, and off the

ieves scamper, to levy fresh contributions upon the public. Their plans are arranged by such strict rules, and the beat of each is so accurately ascertained, that when a gentleman happens to miss his watch, and gives symptoms of liberality—for robberies are now-a-days difficult to be found out without the precursor of a reward—he has only to say in what part of the house he believes the transfer to have taken place, and the 'buzz' (pickpocket) can be in most cases easily found, and the property restored. The loser, at all events, will have the gratification of knowing from the officer whom he employs, that Jack such-body had 'the thimble,' whether it is ever recovered or not. Each of the thieves who thus, by constant practice, attain a wonderful degree of excellence in transfering watches, pocket-books, shawls, cloaks, handkerchiefs, &c. has what he calls his 'pal,' or blowing, to assist him. This 'pal' is a girl of the town, as great an adept as her 'pal' in the art of prigging. They sometimes come across a drunken man; and, if the female can prevail upon the unfortunate fellow to accompany her to White-Hart Yard, or Swan Yard, or any other infamous place, in which the most dangerous houses of accommodation are kept, a robbery is sure to take place, and fear of exposure is generally calculated upon as a security from punishment.

"About two or three o'clock in the morning, the flash-houses in this hopeful part of the town abound with buzzes, prigs, cracksmen (housebreakers), and flash dragsmen (coachmen who associate with thieves, and occasionally lend a hand.) There are also to be seen, sprinkled about the bars and parlours of the flash-houses, watchmen, whose silence is purchased with gin. Those 'terrors of the robber,' have a little game of their own, but the thieves are never played upon by them. Gentlemen are their aim. If a well-dressed man happens to pass along Bow Street, or any of the neighbouring streets, at a late hour, he must not be surprised at eceiving a push from a watchman, and then being accused of a

violent breach of the peace.    It is necessary, however, to tell him
that, if he behaves respectfully to the watchman, who will not
scruple to call him a thief, he may be allowed to depart upon a
compromise of five shillings, and that, if he resists, his watch and
purse and clothes are in the greatest peril.

"I supppose," continued Mentor, "you have read of the ex
ploits of the celebrated Jonathan Wild; or, as he was termed by
the French, Jonathan Wild the Great?"   "Most certainly," rejoined Peregrine.    "Well, then, here is his portrait—an unquestionably faithful, likeness of that prince of villains,

Jonathan Wild.

Who, to give the devil his due, was a man of most extraordinary
abilities, which had he, fortunately for himself and society, employed them in a proper manner, would have been an ornament to
society, instead of a curse: his whole life has more the appearance of romance, than the real incidents of an unlettered villain,
as Byron says—

"Truth is strange,
Stranger than fiction."

"I will show you," continued Mentor, "the remainder of my drawings, and then we will dress for our evening's party.

"Here is a representation of a middle-aged woman, who, regardless of drums, hurricanes, routes, and operas, is contemplating in her closet, like Solomon; she has tasted of all the pleasures of life, and found all is vanity, except her favourite amusement, that of getting drunk by herself.

"And pray," said Peregrine, "who are these two men, seemingly so deep in conversation? Ministers of state, I suppose." "No, indeed, they are not: they are planning which of their horses are to win at the ensuing races." "What, then," said Peregrine, "is it settled before the races which horses are to win?" "Most certainly, my friend," said Mentor, "nothing more common; but sometimes even the knowing ones are outdone by the riders, who, getting information how the bets are laid, make the horse win that was intended to lose."

'I am afraid, my friend," said Peregrine, "we shall be too late for our party, as I am more than anxious to witness

The Doings at Lady Spade's Rout.

Her ladyship's invitation-card says, 'At home at ten,' and now it is near that time." "We shall be in good time," said Mentor, "if we are there by twelve: but we will prepare to dress."

As the clock struck twelve, Mentor and Peregrine were set down at the door of the celebrated Lady Spade, and were both immediately introduced to the gay and vicious hostess.

33.                              s

" I am now going to present to your sight," continued Mentor, as they entered the rooms, " one of the politest assemblies—a collection of all the celebrated beauties, beaus, lords, and scoundrels, in town.—Here Vice appears in her gayest clothing, but Modesty, Virtue, and Honour, are never suffered to enter; or, if they enter unadvisedly or by mistake, are never permitted to retire untainted.

" Behold, at that table, the greatest monster the world ever produced; no object the sun ever shone on is half so deformed." " Heavens! what can that be?" replied Peregrine; I see you point to a very lovely young lady at cards; but what, in the name of wonder, can you mean?" " A FEMALE GAMESTER," returned Mentor; " her name is Leonora.—Her story is as follows :—She was married very young to a noble lord, the honour and ornament of his country, who hoped to preserve her from the contagion of the times by his own example, and, to say the truth, she had every good quality that could recommend her to the bosom of a man of discernment and worth. But, alas, how frail and short are the joys of mortals! how soon is virtue, when it begins to totter, degenerated into vice! As the blooming flowers of the spring are instantly destroyed by the cold blasts of winter, so, the moment the lust of gaming takes possession of the human heart, every virtuous consideration that can render man supportable to himself, is utterly lost and eradicated.—Of all vices, gaming, in my opinion, is the most pernicious to mankind. Ambition may be satisfied; lust most commonly loses ground as age and debility come on; hatred often sinks into contempt; and the snakes of envy have, ere now, been lulled to repose: but the monster, Gaming, is never satisfied; for the more it devours, the more it craves. Behold its votaries, as unhappy with thousands as when possessed of one single shilling; leading a life so fluctuating and so uncertain, that it is scarcely more eligible than that of a malefactor going to execution. But to proceed.—One unfortunate hour ruined his darling visionary scheme of happiness : she was introduced to the infamous woman under whose roof she now is—she was drawn into play— liked it—and, what is the unavoidable consequence, was ruined: having lost more, in one night, than would have maintained a hundred useful families for a twelvemonth, she was obliged to prostitute her body to the wretch that had won her money, to recover her loss. From this moment, she might justly have exclaimed, with the *Moor*—

‘ Farewell the tranquil mind! farewell content!’

The affectionate wife, the agreeable companion, the indulgent mistress, were now no more. In vain she flattered herself the injury she had done her husband would for ever remain one of those secrets which can only be disclosed at the last day. Mistaken woman! the cries of justice are too strong for any human power to stifle—though the paths before her seemed easy and pleasant, impending thunder filled the air, vengeance pursued her steps, and infamy spread her venomous wings around her—while she triumphed in her security, she was lost. The villain who enjoyed her, boasted of the favours he had received.—*Modern Humanity* conveyed the fatal news to the ears of her injured lord; he refused to believe what he thought impossible, but honour obliged him to call the boaster to the field.—The hero (for he had all the qualifications our modern romances require—namely, drinking, duelling, and gaming, to complete one) received the challenge with much more contentment than concern : as he had resolution enough to murder any man he had injured, so he was certain, if he had the fortune to conquer his antagonist, he should be looked upon as the head of all the modern bucks and bloods; esteemed by the men as a brave fellow, and admired by the ladies for a fine gentleman and an agreeable rake."

" You must pardon me," said Peregrine, " if I am obliged to question the truth of this part of your relation. Is it possible that woman, who was formed for the happiness of mankind, can take delight in, or suffer, the company of the wretch who has destroyed his brother ?" " There is nothing more common," replied Mentor. " What greater pleasure can a *fine* lady receive, except cheating at cards, than to see the dear, brave, heroic man, who will run an innocent person through the body, for accidentally treading upon his corns, dying at her feet, and existing only by her smiles ? In a word, the fine ladies look upon courage, in our sex, to be equal to chastity in theirs : at least, the appearance of both must be preserved." " You must certainly mean," said Peregrine, " that such women are to be found among the female gamblers, and not in general society ; for—

' I wonder why, by foul-mouthed men,
 Women so slander'd be,
Since it doth easily appear
 They're better far than we.

' Why are the *graces*, every one,
 Pictur'd as women be,
If not to show that they, in grace,
 Do more excel than we ?

' Why are the liberal *sciences*
 Pictur'd as women be,
If not to show that they, in them,
 Do more excel than we ?

' Why are the *virtues*, every one,
 Pictur'd as women be,
If not to show that they, in them,
 Do more excel than we ?

' Since women are so full of worth,
 Let them all praised be,—
For commendations they deserve,
 In ampler wise than we.'

So sings the old poet, Sir Aston Cockayne." " You are **very** right," said Mentor. " But, to resume the thread of my story, which you have interrupted, the hero and the husband met: the former, not content with declaring, exulted in his guilt. But his triumph was of short date—a bullet drove his indignant soul from its frail tenement, to the great mortification of all the men of frolic and pleasure of the age.

"Lucius (for that is the husband's name), after a long conflict in his bosom, between justice and mercy, tenderness and rage, resolved on what is very seldom practised by an English husband—to pardon his wife, conceal her crime, and preserve her, if possible, from utter destruction. But the gates of mercy were opened in vain—the offender refused forgiveness, because she had offended. The lust of gaming had absorbed all other desires. She still plays on, while her easy lord is hastening, by a quick decay, to that place where '*they are neither married, nor given in marriage.*'"

"Execrable murderess, for such she doubly is," exclaimed Peregrine. "How can she appear in public? how wear that smile upon her face? hath conscience entirely deserted her?" "Only nods a little," replied Mentor; "it will soon awake, and sting her into horror. When that carnation bloom (as shortly it will) hath left her cheeks, and those eyes, that now shine so brightly, are become weak and languid, what a despicable creature must she be, without innocence or peace of mind to comfort her! But no more of this.

"Observe that well-dressed gentleman: with what philosophy he loses his money to the lady that sits over against him?—But see, he rises—his stock is now exhausted, and he must raise contributions on the public for more." "Is it possible he can be a person of that description?" cried Peregrine. "Yes," said his companion; "there are many more gentlemen of his like in the room." "Does the lady he played with suspect his employment?" said Peregrine. "Her suspicion is lost in certainty," returned Mentor; "she is too well acquainted with the town, not to know a great many gentlemen, without fortunes, live upon their means. To be plain, she is as great a cheat as he is a thief."

"But you have not told me, my good friend, the name of that meagre person, on whose countenance want and despair seem to sit; methinks he is but meanly dressed, in comparison with his gaudy companion." "That," answered Mentor, "*was* the gay, the gallant, the agreeable *Florico*, first in the box, the ring, and the mall :—

'Pause—turn thine eye, and view, with pitying scan,
That wasting remnant of what was a man;
In youth a worldling, seeking transient joys,
He barter'd his best hopes for worthless toys.
Why that hung lip? that sad dejected air?
Is that the face which rev'rend age should wear?
The loss of vig'rous health hath sour'd his mind,
And misspent youth no solace left behind.
Did Beauty more than earthly lure him on,
Whilst gay he sported, Fortune's favour'd son?

In age he owns no magic in her sigh,—
He reads no language in her beaming eye.
Did wild ambition mock his reas'ning powers,
And partial conquests strew his path with flowers?
Age steals their odour and their hue away,
And low'rs a cloud o'er glory's brightest day.
Did Bacchus round his brows the chaplet fling,
And topers pledge him their anointed king?
In age the port is cork'd, the claret sour;
He sheds his honours, and resigns his pow'r.
Did thousand gawsy shadows woo his stay?
And Luxury's minions fan his years away?
In age no painted bauble charms his eye,
And pleasure's phantoms devious pass him by.
The gamester's chance,—ay, all the arts that live,
Now fail a respite to his thoughts to give:
Cool staid reflection lays his vices bare,—
Relentless Conscience goads him to despair.
Down to the grave (yet fearing still to die,
Though all life's blessings from his blessings fly),
He sinks without a hope his soul to cheer,—
His mem'ry lifeless—grave without a tear.

He *is now* many degrees worse than nothing, having squandered away an almost princely estate in one eternal round of vice and folly; he is obliged to live on the assistance he receives from the very men who caused him to ruin his fortune, and shared the plunder. He hath just now issued proposals for publishing a treatise he hath written, in which he endeavours to prove the mortality of the soul, and it is to be dedicated to the most beautiful women now living. It is thought this performance will, in some measure, retrieve his affairs, as people of quality are very desirous of being assured, that, when dead, they shall share the fate of dogs and monkeys—*wisely* giving up all pretensions to another world, so that they may be permitted to gratify their appetites and passions in this." "Good heavens! is it possible there is a wretch who disbelieves the existence of a God?" cried Peregrine. "There is not," answered Mentor: "the gentlemen who dignify themselves with the title of *Free-Thinkers* endeavour to disbelieve, but their efforts are vain. View a pretended Athiest on his death-bed, and your indignation will soon be turned into compassion, when you hear him, in the agonies of despair, cry out for mercy from that Supreme Power whose existence he hath denied. Where, then, is his fallacious reasoning? his boasted philosophy? his contempt of death? Can all the quaint superficial arguments of Tindal, Hobbes, Toland, and Colins, the abusive reasoning of Woolston, or the vain blusterings and absurd dogmas of the restless factious Bolingbroke, first a traitor to his king, and then to his God, afford him comfort? To such a man how terrible are his last hours: the wretch upon the rack is at ease, when compared with him."

"And is this the way the gentry in London pass their time?" asked Peregrine. "Most certainly not all of them," replied Mentor. "I obtained an invitation for this party, in order that, before you left the metropolis, you might be an eye-witness of the

depravities in high life, as well as in low. But these senseless
routs, card-parties, &c., are the very acme of fashion in the higher
circles. To invite more people than your house can hold, and to
make those who are fortunate enough to gain admittance and ' be
presented,' as wretchedly miserable as over-crowded rooms,
heated almost to suffocation, can make them, is the height of
ambition with the leaders of *Ton*." " But why so many women?"
asked Peregrine. " Why?" replied Mentor. " Mr. Croly, in
his *Pride shall have a Fall*, tells you :—

> ' What are your sleepless midnights for, your routs,
>    That turn your skin to parchment? Why, for man !
> What are your cobweb robes, that, spite of frost,
>    Show neck and knee to winter ? Why, for man !
> What are your harps, pianos, simpering songs,
>    Languish'd to lutes ? All for the monster, man !
> What are your rouge, your jewels, waltzes, wigs,
>    Your scoldings, scribblings, eatings, drinkings, for ?
>    Your morn, noon, night? For man ! ay,—
>    Man, man, man !'

" To be sure," continued Mentor, " these poor pitiable creatures, having no employment, are happy any how to murder their
time. Such inconsistencies are generated by idleness; which,
Barton says, is the badge of gentry, the bane of body and mind,
the muse of naughtiness, the chief author of all mischief, one of
the seven deadly sins, the devil's cushion (as Gaulter calls it), his
pillow and chief reposal: for the mind can never rest, but still
meditates on one thing or other; except it be occupied about some
honest business, of its own accord it rusheth into melancholy. It
fills the body full of phlegm, gross humours, and all manner of
obstructions, rheums, catarrhs, &c. They that are idle are far
more subject to melancholy than such as are conversant or employed about any office or business. Plutarch reckons up idleness for a sole cause of the sickness of the soul.—Idleness is
either of body or mind. That of body is nothing but a kind of
benumbing laziness, intermitting exercise, which causeth crudities,
obstructions, excremental humours, quencheth the natural heat,
dulls the spirits, and makes them unapt to do any thing whatever.
A horse in a stable that never travels, a hawk in a mew that seldom flies, are both subject to diseases: an idle dog will be mangy
—and how shall an idle person think to escape? Idleness of mind
is much worse than that of the body : wit without employment is a
disease—*erugo animi, rubigo ingenii*—the rest of the soul, a
plague, a hell itself. As in a standing pool worms and filthy
creepers increase, the water itself putrifies, and air likewise, if it
be not continually stirred by the wind,—so do evil and corrupt
thoughts in an idle person ; the soul is contaminated. Thus much
I dare boldly say : he or she that is idle, be they of what condition they will, never so rich, so well allied, fortunate, happy,—let
them have all things in abundance and felicity that heart can wish
and desire, all contentment,—so long as he or she or they are

idle, they shall never be pleased, never well in body and mind; but weary still, sickly still, vexed still, loathing still,—weeping, sighing, grieving, suspecting,—offended with the world, with every object, wishing themselves gone or dead, or else carried away with some foolish phantasie or other. And this is the true cause that so many great men, ladies and gentlewomen, labour of this disease in country and city, for idleness is an appendix to nobility; they count it a disgrace to work, and spend all their days in sports, recreations, and pastimes, and will therefore take no pains, be of no vocation. They feed liberally, fare well, want exercise, action, employment,—and thence their bodies become full of gross humours, wind, crudities; their minds disquieted, dull, heavy, &c. When you shall hear and see so many discontented persons in all places, so many unnecessary complaints, fears, suspicions, the best means to redress it is to set them a-work, so to busy their minds: for the truth is, they are idle. An idle person knows not when he is well, what he would have, or whither he would go; he is tired out with every thing, displeased with all, weary of his life; neither at home nor abroad; he wanders and lives beside himself.

"Do you see that tall gentleman," said Mentor, "in earnest conversation with two young ladies? His name is Malvolio; and he is perhaps the greatest dupe to villains in this country. The following extraordinary case is one of the numerous instances in which his vanity and credulity were worked upon with success:— About seven years ago he rented a furnished house in Park Street, where he was surrounded by the most dashing swindlers in England. One of the fraternity, a captain in the army, wormed himself into his confidence, whose house was immediately opposite to that of a noble lord, who had two or three beautiful daughters. Malvolio fancied himself beloved by one of those young ladies, and his friend encouraged the fancy for his own purposes, and told Malvolio that, if he had spirit, and managed the thing well, he might get the girl. The first thing to be done was to procure an interview, and Malvolio's friend recommended an immediate correspondence. A love-letter was written to the lady by the lover, and the captain's servant, who was to be well paid, was employed to deliver it. This trusty messenger delivered the letter to his master, who wrote an answer in the lady's name, stating her regret that she could not see her dear Malvolio, as she was obliged to go off to Ireland, in consequence of his majesty's determination to visit that country, where she hoped to see her beloved. Malvolio, delighted at this avowal, proposed an immediate journey, and requested the captain's company. The latter replied, that the thing required great caution and tact, and that, as he owed £300 or £400 in Ireland, he could not face that country without the sum. This difficulty was soon removed.

"The captain got the required amount from his dupe, and off to Dublin they went, where the correspondence was resumed, the answers of the young lady becoming so warm, that Malvolio wrote to her to 'run off with him at once.' 'Yes,' said she, in her reply, 'I will run away with you; but, unfortunately, my family have become acquainted with my passion for you, and are resolved to take me off to the seat of a nobleman, about sixty miles from town. I shall, however, write to you, and let you know how to proceed.' The letter concluded with strong approbation of the address and talent of the servant in managing the correspondence. This was a severe check to Malvolio's hopes, but the captain cheered him up, and told him that his servant's assistance would release a girl from the protection of the devil himself. Another letter was sent, and another received. The lady described her situation as wretched in the extreme, and vowed that she could only be happy with her lover, but she could not move without bribing the servants; for which purpose she required a couple of hundred pounds. The money was supplied, and the time of starting was appointed. Malvolio was to be ready with his carriage at the spot adjoining the estate on which she was on a visit. He was punctual. After having waited for some time, in great suspense, he perceived a lady, elegantly attired, running hastily towards him. 'Oh! dear Malvolio!' she exclaimed, 'I am pursued—the servants are after me—save me, save me!' 'With my life,' cried Malvolio, and he lifted her into the carriage. 'Halloo!' said two or three savage-looking fellows, who just sprang out of a ditch with cudgels in their hands, 'where are you galloping with our young mistress?' and, without more words, they laid their sticks so heavily upon the poor *inamorato's* shoulders, that he yielded up his prize without any farther effort, and drove off in a state of mind and body not easily to be described; but, although Malvolio's ardour sustained some abatement, that of the young lady was as ardent as ever. She wrote to him deploring the mishap, and told him that her father had resolved to send her to Paris, where she hoped to see the only man she ever loved, and marry him. The credulous fool still believed that all was real, and asked his friend, the captain, to accompany him; but the captain spoke of the expense, and said, that upon such an occasion they ought to have at their command at least £1000. Malvolio had already overdrawn at his bankers; but, at the suggestion of his friend, he accepted bills to that amount, and handed them to the captain, who promised to go at once to France, and said that the money should follow them, as his friend, who discounted them, had promised to forward the amount to Paris. The advice was adopted, but no girl was to be found, and no money was forthcoming. The captain then said he would return to ascertain the cause of the delay; but Malvolio was not long by himself, before he learned that his disinterested friend had got the bills cashed, and determined to keep the produce for the trouble he had been at in aiding the acceptor in his project of a noble connexion. At the same moment that he received this disheartening intelligence, a letter arrived from the lady, dated London, and recalling her lover from France. At length he suspected that he was humbugged; and, upon his return to England, he despatched a friend to the nobleman, with the whole of the correspondence; which was at once declared to be nothing but a hoax, by his lordship, who said his daughters had been in Hampshire all the time Malvolio was wandering about on his Quixotic expedition. So blind was the unfortunate Malvolio, and so completely imposed upon by the captain, that, although the latter scarcely took the trouble to disguise his hand-writing, Malvolio was indebted to the post-office inspector for the information, that the captain's letters and love-letters were all in the hand-writing of the same person. The next step the poor dupe took was after his acceptances; but his worthy friend had obtained their value, and Malvolio was compelled to take them up. The robbery thus effected upon the wretched man, within four months, by the captain and his servant, who was no other than the captain's half-brother, amounted to no less than £1,700.

"But enough of this company," said Peregrine; "pray let us hasten home." On their way thither, it was remarked by Mentor, that it was curious to notice the various styles of living and variations of the manners of the great. "Now the gentry turn the night into day, and their living consists of the most trifling, but most expensive foods. How different from those of our forefathers.

" The Northumberland Household-book (or account of the annual expense of housekeeping of the Earls of Northumberland in the reign of Henry VII.), furnishes us with much curious information as to the style of living among the great at that time, and, connected with other documents relating to the same subject, affords a competent idea of the manner in which our ancestors contrived to nourish their frail clay, though unfurnished with many of the luxuries of modern days.

" In this official record (for such it may be properly termed), the particulars of each day's fare, according to the several seasons, whether festival or farce, are minutely stated, and the ratio, as well as kind of provision for each table specified. During Lent the earl and countess had for breakfast, on the Sundays, Tuesdays, Thursdays, and Saturdays, as follows :—' A loaf of bread in trenchers, two manchetts,* a quart of beer, a quart of wine, two pieces of salt fish, six bacon'd herrings, and four white herrings, or a dish of sprats.' The officers of the household and menial servants were confined, at the same season and days, to bread of different qualities, according to their degrees, beer, and salt fish. On ' Flesh Days,' my lord and lady breakfasted on ' half a loaf of household bread, a manchett, a pottel of beer, and a chicken, or else three mutton bones broiled. The servants had, in addition to bread and beer, also boiled beef. On other days, the earl and countess's breakfast-table was set out, in addition to manchett bread, beer, wine, &c., with ' forty sprats, two pieces of salt fish, a quarter of

* A manchet was a loaf of the finest white bread, weighing six ounces.

3 1.

salt salmon, two slices of turbot, a side of Flanders' turbot baked, or a dish of fried smelts." The dinners were of a similar character.

" At Wolsey's mask and entertainment of Henry VIII. and the French ambassadors, noticed in Shakspeare's play, there were two hundred covers of eatables put upon the tables ; the cardinal drank of Ypocrass from a cup worth 500 marks, and every thing displayed more than regal splendour. Stowe mentions the eating establishment of this proud churchman. He had in his hall kitchen two clerks, a clerk controller, a surveyor of the dresser, a clerk of the spicery, two cooks, and three assistants, and children, amounting to twelve persons : four scullions, two yeomen of the pastry, and two paste-layers. His larder had a yeoman and groom ; the scullery and buttery an equal number of persons each ; the ewry, the same ; the cellar, three yeomen and three pages ; and the chaundry and waifry two yeomen each. His master-cook wore a superb dress of velvet or satin, decorated with a chain of gold. He had six assistants and two deputies.

" The Earl of Lancaster's account of housekeeping for a year, in the reign of Edward II., was, for his buttery, pantry, and kitchen, £3045 (a prodigious sum, considering the value of money in those days); for grocery ware, £180. 7s. ; for 184 tons and two pipes of claret and white wine, £104. 17s. 6d. ; for six barrels of sturgeon, £19 ; and for dried fish of all sorts, as ling, haberdines, (or barrelled cod), and others, £47. 6s. 7d.

" At the town-house of the great Richard Nevil, Earl of War-wick, in Warwick Lane, Newgate Street, in the time of Edward IV., there are said to have been oftentimes six oxen eaten at a breakfast. This is accounted for by Stowe's informing us that, at that nobleman's, every one that had an acquaintance of the household, might have as much roast and boiled meat as he could prick and carry away upon the point of a long dagger. Many more of these kind of examples might be produced in ancient times.

" In the houses of our nobility at these periods, they dined at long tables. The lord and his principal guests sat at the upper end of the first table, in the great chamber, which was therefore called the Lord's Boar-end ; the officers of his house and inferior guests, at long tables below in the hall. In the middle of each table stood a great salt-seller, and, as particular care was taken to place the guests according to their rank, it became a mark of dis-tinction, whether a person sate above or below the salt. Among the dishes in ancient cookery, are mentioned, swans, bustards, sea-gulls, cranes, peacocks, porpoises, boars' heads, oysters in gravy, stewed partridges, venison with furmenty, and several other kinds of food now but little or not at all known. Trenchers, ashen cups, and other utensils equally simple, furnished the common tables ; the superior ones sometimes had pewter, but this was too costly to be frequently used, and was thought so much of, that in Rymer's Foedera, there is a licence, granted in 1430, for a ship to convey from this country certain articles express for the use of the

King of Scotland, among which are particularly mentioned a supply of pewter dishes and wooden trenchers.

" It was then the custom in great families to have four meals a day—viz. breakfasts, dinners, suppers, and liveries, or deliveries. They had their breakfast at seven, dinner at ten, supper at four, and the livery between eight and nine, in their chambers. The household-book, just quoted, mentions the latter to have consisted of bread, beer, and wine spiced. The hours of the middle rank of life were more rational, as they breakfasted at eight, dined at noon, and supped at six. The hours had somewhat changed in the reign of Elizabeth; ' the nobilitie, gentrie, and students,' as an author of the time tells us, dining then ordinarily at ' eleven before noon, and at supper at five, or between five and six, at afternoone. The merchants,' he adds, ' dine and sup seldome before twelve at noone and six at night, especiallie in London. The husbandmen dine always at high noone, as they call it, and sup at seven or eight.' But out of the Term, at the Universities, the scholars still continue to dine at ten. The tables, at great feasts, were decorated with pastry in various figures, which were labelled with witty remarks suited to the occasion of the feast, and which on that account were called ' *subtleties*,' and, though these were not to be eaten, three courses are mentioned to have been served; and the time occupied in drinking was usually two hours, from eleven till one.

" The number of meals in 1627 is to be inferred from a sermon of that year, called ' The Walk of Faith,' which asks, ' Why should not the soul have her due drinks, breakfasts, meals, under-meals, bevers, and after-meals, as well as the body?' Well might Reeve, in his ' Plea for Nineveh,' written 1657, say the glutton must then have ' his olios and hogoes, creepers and peepers, Italian sippets, and French broth,' &c.

" As to some of the old customs respecting particular things eaten at certain seasons of the year, a writer of Charles the Second's days says, ' Before the late civil wars, in gentlemen's houses at Christmas, the first dish that was brought to table was a boar's head with a lemon in the mouth; and at Queen's College, Oxon, the custom was in his time retained, the bearers of it bringing it into the hall, singing to an old tune an old Latin rhyme, *capri caput de fero, &c.* The first dish formerly brought up to dinner on Easter Day was a red herring riding away on horseback—*i. e.* a herring ordered by the cook something after the likeness of a man on horseback, set in a corn sallad. The eating of a gammon of bacon at the same season (until of late kept up in some parts of England) was done to show an abhorrence of Judaism, at that solemn commemoration of our Lord's resurrection. We shall just further observe, that that most useful table utensil, a fork, was not known in England before the reign of James the First. Coryate, in his Crudities, ' mentions his introducing this from Italy, the only place where he had ever in all his travels met with it, and that himself, on his return home, had thought it good to imitate the Italian fashion, by this forked cutting of meate;' and that a familiar friend of his had from that cause named him *Furcefer.* His description of first seeing this use of the fork is ludicrously quaint 'The Italians,' says he, ' doe always at their meals use a little fork when they eat their meat; for while with their knife, which they hold in one hand, they cut the meat in the dish, they fasten their fork, which they hold in the other, upon the same dish.' The reason of this custom he states to be, that the Italian cannot endure to have his dish touched by fingers, seeing all men's fingers are not alike clean. The use of glass at table (though long used in churches) seems also to have been of comparatively late introduction."

While Mentor and his friend were at breakfast, the waiter brought in a parcel directed for Mr. Peregrine Wilson, who instantly desired the carriage to be paid, thinking it came from his home; but, lo! on unpacking it, he found that it contained a quantity o rubbish. At the discovery of the cheat, Mentor laughed heartily, to think how cleverly Peregrine had been defrauded, telling him, that such cases in London were very common. It is not long since a fellow was sentenced to three months' imprisonment for defrauding the Earl of Templeton of six shillings, by delivering at his house a basket of rubbish, under pretence that it contained game. Innumerable other cases I might give you.

Those fellows who get their livelihood by such means are most of them what are termed Way-layers, or Kidders; and country-men and errand-boys to shops are the best customers they have. The mode they adopt to cheat the countrymen, I have already told you. Where these Way-layers perhaps do the most mischief, is in robbing errand-boys, which they do by getting into conversation with them, and thus learning the articles they are carrying to Mr. Such-a-one's, their master's name, business, and residence; which obtained, away goes the Layer, to inform his mates of the prize they have in view, and to give them the necessary intelligence and instruction, in order to obtain the same. If the boy happens to inquire his way, he is directed by one of them, and, within a few yards of the house, is met by another, who asks him if he has not brought such and such things from his master, tells him his name, takes the parcel from him, and sends him back for other articles, which he is ordered to return with immediately, as a customer is waiting for them: the unsuspecting boy goes home, gets the fresh order, and brings it to the house where he should have left the first when, too late, he is made sensible of his error in trusting to strangers in the streets, however feasible or probable their story o. being the person he was directed to may appear.

"It is not a long time since," continued Mentor, "that an apprentice to a composition doll-maker in Long Lane was going through Bow-Church yard, Cheapside, with a large parcel of dolls, when ' a gentleman' tapp'd him on the shoulder, and said to him

My boy, that gentleman wants to speak to you'—at the same time pointing to an accomplice, who was standing in a passage of one of the warehouses there, without his hat. The boy walked towards him, and said he to him—' My lad, I want you to run into Cheapside and call a cabriolet for me; and I'll mind your parcel for you the while, and give you sixpence for your trouble.' Sixpence is a large sum to a doll-maker's apprentice, and the unsuspecting lad instantly put down his parcel at his feet, and ran off into Cheapside for the cab: with which he returned in about two minutes, and found that his parcel and the man were both missing from the passage in which he had left them. Luckily for him, however, his *parcel* had been stopped *in transitu*, by one of the city officers, who, in the meanwhile, chanced to be passing through Bow Church-yard, and, seeing a gentleman whom he knew to be a professor of *kidding*, trotting along with a parcel, he naturally suspected how he came by it; and by virtue of his office he seized him by the collar—or, rather, he made an attempt so to do; but the professor, suspecting his intention, threw the parcel at him and bolted.

" It is the bounden duty of all masters to particularly instil into the minds of their servants not to part with any parcel, but to the person to whom it is directed: if they were to do so, we should not read of similar tricks being played off daily.

" It is to carelessness that tradesmen ought to ascribe most of their losses, added to neglect and extravagance; and then they are for ever complaining of the want of money, and of business; let an impartial person take a retrospective view of the habits of tradesmen a century past, and compare them with those of the present day, and they will soon find one of the principal causes of the outcry.

" A tradesman of 1728, never aspired higher in his dress than a second-cloth coat and waistcoat, a pair of leather breeches— that were hardly ever without a guinea in their pockets—a felt hat, and worsted stockings; and, as for a greatcoat, it was quite out of the question.

" A tradesman of 1828, never condescends to wear any other than a superfine coat and trousers (or *small-clothes*, as they are now termed, agreeably to the modern *refined* nomenclature), whose pockets are seldom gladdened with the company of even a single shilling—silk waistcoat, silk stockings, superfine hat, with a superfine greatcoat or two, exclusive of chaise-coats, &c. &c. Indeed, so great is the pride of the generality of tradespeople now, that I am bold to declare they expend more money for clothes alone, than their forefathers did for house-rent and housekeeping.

" A tradesman of 1728, used to take a pride in showing his sons and daughters, when grown up, the coat in which he was married; so careful were they of their clothes.

" A tradesman of 1828, can scarcely show you a coat he has had twelve months.

" A tradesman of 1728, used to open and shut up his shop, scrape his shop-floor, and be behind his counter, never later than seven o'clock in the morning.

"What tradesman of the present day opens and shuts his shop? not one in a thousand; for it is considered ungenteel, and that, by so doing, he would injure his consequence. If the shopman is out getting drunk, or the errand-boy loitering his time about the streets, Mr. Tradesman gets the watchman to shut up his shop for him—it *only* costs sixpence; and what is sixpence for performing such a service? a mere *bagatelle*. Suppose the watchman is employed three times a week, why it is only 1s. 6d. not quite £4 a year; and what is that for a tradesman to pay, to save his *feelings* from being hurt? Besides, the watchman, in shutting up the shop, becomes well acquainted with the fastenings, and learns where the most valuable part of the stock lies, and then he can the better inform the thieves. And suppose the shop is robbed; why that misfortune is far better to bear, than to be so *mean* as to shut up his shop: any thing but that, in the present *refined* state of society.

"As for scraping their shop-floors, the major part of tradesmen now, poor devils! have no need of that labour. I remember, when I was a boy," continued Mentor, "in going along the streets of a morning early, what a confounded scraping was there at almost every shop-door. Now you may march from Hyde-Park Corner to Whitechapel, and hear no scraping, except at the *Pawnbrokers* and the *Gin-Shops*, they being the only people now who have any custom.

"A tradesman of 1728 was satisfied with a humble pot of porter; and, upon extraordinary occasions, with a bowl of punch which cost him two shillings and sixpence.

"A tradesman of 1828, must have his sherry with his dinner, and his port afterwards.

"A tradesman of 1728, never used to travel farther in summer than Hampstead, or Calk Farm, on a Sunday; and, perhaps, in the week, on an evening, take his pint and pipe at the Goat and Boots, in Marybone Fields, and have a game at skittles.

"A tradesman of 1828, must have his country house, and his chaise, or buggy, or sulky, or Tilbury, or whatever you please to call it. The more economical go to Margate or Ramsgate, by steam, for a *few weeks* in the summer, while their servants are robbing them at home; and then at Christmas they find they are minus.

"A tradesman of 1728, was satisfied with a small house, and a snug shop.

"A tradesman of 1828, must have a large house and a capacious shop, such as are in our new grand streets: the heart sickens at beholding those masses of egregious folly and splendid misery! No sooner are the major part of the tradesmen in them, than they are out, or their windows ornamented with printed bills, "This House to Let." "The Lease, Goodwill, and Stock of this House to be Sold," &c. &c. These melancholy mementos of distress are seen, unfortunately, in most of the leading streets of the me tropolis.

"A tradesman of 1728, used to have the assistance of his wife in his business, by either attending to his shop when her husband was out, or, when he was busy at home, going to the various customers with parcels, &c., in order to save the expense of shopmen and errand-boys.

"A tradesman of 1828 would fairly swoon, if his wife was so *ungenteel* as to carry out a parcel, or to see to her husband's business, by doing the work of a shopman or errand-boy.

"A tradesman's daughter of 1728, was to be seen scouring her father's house, and cleaning his windows.

"A tradesman's daughter of 1828, is to be seen hum-strumming on the piano, or learning to dance.

"A tradesman of 1728, was always ready in his shop before breakfast.

"If you want your mushroom tradesman of 1828, at ten or eleven o'clock in the morning, you are told he is *a-dressing*; and he will be down in half an hour. This is not an exaggerated picture; it is unfortunately too true : and thus this beggarly pride descends from the master to the servant.

"Now I ask," continued Mentor, "if it is to be supposed trade can support such accumulated pride and extravagance, and if it is any wonder so many tradespeople should be so short of money?"

"But pray," said Peregrine, "is not the present want of money owing to the paucity of trade and the heavy taxation?"

"No, IT IS NOT! It is occasioned by the dreadful extravagance of tradespeople, by taxation, and by redundant population.

"But the remedy is working itself with a vengeance. The time *will come*, and that shortly, when these gentlemen tradesmen will find they must retrace their steps, and follow those of their forefathers. They must *stick* to their counters, those who are fortunate enough to have them—open and shut their shops—lay by their wines and superfine clothes. Their daughters must learn to handle a scrubbing-brush and a pail, instead of playing with the keys of the piano, or the chords of the harp—their wives must lay by their silks, and put on their check aprons, as their grandmothers used to do. This alteration will take place,—ay, assuredly as day is day, and night is night. Necessity, stern necessity, *will* cause it, and *is* causing it daily. Yes, my jolly masters, ' To this complexion you must come at last.'

"Yet there are men who grumble at the present times. Why should they? They expected to have all the fun of the late war for nothing: then—

‘ They were all of them monstrous jolly,
    And they covered their houses with holly !'

" Well, then came the peace—the glorious peace. Then fol-

lowed the payment of the bill for the expenses of the war.  Then
came long faces; for—

> ' Most folks laugh until the feast is o'er,
> Then comes the reckoning, and they laugh no more !'

Curses are heaped upon the poor ministers' heads, because
they impose taxes to pay the interest on the money borrowed for
carryiug on the war.   Well, all this time tradespeople forget
to lower their expenses, or abridge their luxuries : and what is the
consequence—they become beggars !"

"But how," said Peregrine, "can one of the causes of the
present distress be ascribed to the population?   I always thought
the wealth of a nation consisted in the number of the people."
"So it does," replied Mentor, "if the people are legitimately
employed, that is, working for profit; not in digging holes, and
filling them up again, and all that nonsense.   Now, for instance:—
Supposing I have twelve children, and each child costs me 10s. a
week for board and other expenses, and they earn me 12s. a week
each, the consequence is, I am 24s. a week richer by having so
many children.   But, if I can find no employment for my
children, I am, at the week's end, £6 minus.   Therefore, in such
a case, no man must tell me my wealth consists in the number of
my children.   Such is exactly the case with a nation : if profitable
employment is found for the people, they are enabled to purchase
more largely of all articles ; and the consequence is, government
receive more taxes from the extra quantity of articles consumed,
and the tradesman, because he vends more goods.   But, if the
population be not employed, the consequence is, taxes are not so
productive—the tradesman's business falls off, and, added to which,
he has, out of his straightened income, to pay a part of it to support
those who have no employment ; and he becomes poorer daily.
In such case, the wealth cannot consist in the number of the people.   It is of no use for Malthus and others to preach about the
matter.   Find employment—profitable employment, and that will
remedy one of the evils ; unless you can kill off the people by a
war, as fast as ' new comers' make their appearance in the world.
The plain matter of fact is this, that in England, since the peace,
trade has *not* fallen off, but, on the contrary, has increased ; but
it cannot increase in the same ratio as the population increases—
hence the want of employment.

"Such is exactly the case with the shipping interest, as it is
called : they complain of the want of employment for their ships,
foolishly expecting that trade will increase as fast as they build
new ships : that is impossible.   Let them refrain, for a few years,
from launching any more vessels, and they will soon find employment for those already manned.   But the shipping interest are for
ever crying out, as if they were worse off than the rest of the trading
community ; when, in fact, in many cases, they are infinitely better.
The truth is, they want a war, so that their ships may be taken on

for the transport service, at a good round sum per month for
tonnage. In short, let the tradesmen become more moderate in
their out-goings and dress, and stick closer to their counters; let
the ministers curtail all extravagant expenditure, and let the detested
corn laws be repealed—the principal source, perhaps, of English
misery—and manufactures, trade, and commerce will increase.

"So much for political economy!" exclaimed Peregrine; "but,
sir, you will remember, it was agreed we should visit Smithfield."
"Certainly," replied Mentor: "so take up thy hat, and, in a few
minutes we shall be in that celebrated mart, just in time to witness

The Doings in the Horse-Market, Smithfield.

"It will be best," said Mentor, "for us to go through the middle
of the market, and there we shall see the doings of the gentlemen
of the whip, in all their ramifications, trickeries, and impositions.
We can sit upon the side of the pens unnoticed, and quietly view
the busy scene before us." They had scarcely seated themselves,
before a true Smithfield racer was being shown out to the best advantage, to a sort of Jemmy Green cockney, who said he was in
vant of a *norse*—a good 'un and a cheap 'un. "Do you, master?"
said a well-known gammoning cove, ever on the look-out for flats.
"Here is vone, sir, that vill suit you to a hair—I'll varrant him
to be free from vice, sound vind and limb, regular in his paces;
von't shy at any thing; he never slips; is sure-footed; goes well in
harness, is a master of twelve stone, and is a good roadster; in
fact, he is such a horse as you von't see in a day's ride." "He

18. T

seems," said the cockney, "much out of order, and half starved."
" Lord bless you, master," replied the jockey, " he did belong to
an old miser, who not only starved himself, but all about him.
All this here horse vants is good corn, and if I did not think,
master, you vould give him plenty, I vould not sell him you: I
can soon see who's who. I have not attended this here market
these twenty years for nothing. I can tell a gentleman in a twink-
ling; and I knows vat suits a gemman—I knows vats o'clock,
master; you may trust to me." " That may be," said the cockney, " but somehow I don't much like the horse. He don't look
*quite* the thing." " Vell, sir, there's no harm done, if you don't
buy." Just at this moment up comes a confederate, dressed like
a coachman, with a whip in his hand, and, addressing the jockey,
said, " Ah, Tom, what have you Mr. B.'s roan mare here? Is the
old rogue dead?" ".Yes, he is," replies the jockey, " and I have
the job of selling his favourite horse; and, as you sold it to old
B., and knows her well, perhaps you will give your opinion to this
here gemman." " Vy, as for that 'ere," said he, addressing the
cockney, " I knows the mare vell. I sold it to old B. for sixty
sovereigns eleven months ago, and all that is the matter with her
is, that she is starved; and, if my stables vas not so full, I do not
know any horse I would sooner buy; what do you ask for her?"
" Twenty pounds," replied the jockey. " As cheap as dirt,"
continued the coachman, "and look here, sir," taking the cockney
by the arm,

" There," said he, pointing to the poor jaded mare, " is the countenance, intrepidity, and fire of a lion.

" There's the eye, joint, and nostril of an ox.

" There's the nose, gentleness, and patience of a lamb.

" There's the strength, constancy, and foot of a mule.

" There's the hair, head, and leg of a deer.

" There's the throat, neck, and hearing of a wolf.

" There's the ear, brush, and trot of a fox.

" There's the memory, sight, and turning of a serpent.

" There's the running, suppleness, and innocence of a hare."

" I should like," said the cockney, " to see him run." " Why,
as for that 'ere," replied the jockey, " you see this poor mare has
been without shoes for six months,—the old miser would not give
her any; and I had her shod yesterday with the best patent
shoes, and that you see makes her valk lamish." " Ah! that, to
be sure, makes all the difference," said the cockney, who, after
standing all this *gammon* and *patter*, agreed to give fifteen pounds,
which, with a deal of cavilling, was agreed to; and all the
parties, with the poor mare, hobbled off, seemingly well pleased.

" And is this the way," said Peregrine, " that you *do* the natives?" " Seemingly so," replied Mentor. " I do not suppose there
can possibly be more roguery practised in any trade, than is daily
among some of the dealers in horses." At this instant, Peregrine
caught the eye of a farmer and dealer in the crowd, a neighbour of

his in the country. After the usual salutations, Peregrine informed him what he had witnessed. "There is no excuse," said the farmer, "if people will be so foolish as to buy as bargains things they do not know the value of : the best way is, if a person is in want of a horse, for instance, to give some competent judge a guinea for his advice, and then it is a thousand to one if he is cheated. There is a combination of circumstances, tending so much to perplex and confuse, that urges the necessity of care, caution, and circumspection, in purchasing horses. The eyes of *Argus* would hardly prove too numerous· upon the occasion, a bridle being as necessary upon the tongue, as a padlock upon the pocket ; for, amidst the great variety of professional manœuvres in the art of horse-dealing, a purchaser must be in possession of a great share of good fortune and sound judgment, to elude the ill-effects of deception and imposition. The greatest cheats are to be found among the ostlers ; and I would advise you to adopt the good old maxim of ' never trusting them *further* than you can see them.' I remember the *false manger* having been discovered at a principal inn in the town where I was born. Always look sharp after them, for, if your eyes are not sharper than their hands, they will certainly deceive you. Always make it a constant rule *personally* to attend to see your horses fed, and put the corn in the manger *yourself;* thus guarding yourself against *invisible* losses, experienced by the destructive roguery of ostlers, the bad ness of hay, the hardness of pump-water, and the scarcity of corn.

"When an ostler speaks about feeding a horse, never say ' Go' and do this, that, and the other to him, but ' let *us* go.' Never let an ostler do for you what you can do for yourself. A little attention in these matters will save you hundreds.

"It is the custom, now, for landlords of inns to let their stables to their ostlers, while they themselves carry on the business of the inn. A landlord on the Sussex road, who had lost by horses, and by hay and corn, in the course of six years, near seven hundred pounds, determined to let his stables, and accordingly advertised for a man capable of taking care of them. A Yorkshireman applied, who agreed on a hundred a-year rent, to buy his own hay and corn, to act as head ostler, to keep an under ostler, and to pay the rent quarterly. In a few years, the landlord accumulated a fortune by the inn, and the ostler by the stables, by stinting the horses of their food ; making them ill, and then receiving a handsome bonus for curing them ; making horses belonging to riders and other travellers lame, and selling them others, and such like impositions."

"But, come, gentlemen," said the farmer, "evening is drawing on ; and, as we all seem fatigued, I shal feel happy if you would accompany me, and take a glass of wine and some refreshment at the inn where I put up, Freeman's, the King's Head Inn, Old Change, Cheapside, where are always to be found the best of liquors and eatables, and reasonable charges, polite treatment, and the greatest attention."

In a short time the trio found themselves comfortably seated in the parlour of the King's Head Inn. "Come," said Mentor, "this a snug room; I like every thing that is *snug;* there is an enchanting sound in the very word, for it is purely English, and I believe you will not find the word in any other language; the reason is, because no people on earth but the English know its meaning: the very sound makes one warm and comfortable; it brings with it a picture of a nice carpeted room, good fire, good company, good conversation, a good hostess, together with old wine, old ale, and old friends. I wish Wilkie would paint us a picture of ' a Snug Party:' the king, God bless him, would buy it immediately; for he, being every inch of him an Englishman, would feel a pleasure in possessing such a picture, having passed so many happy *snug* hours. And I pray," continued Mentor, " he may pass many, many more.—

> ' May he live
> Longer than I have time to tell his years !
> And, when old Time shall lead him to his end,
> Goodness and he fill up one monument!'

"Bravo!" cried Peregrine. "Bravo!" echoed the farmer.

"Did you see that gentleman leave the room?" said Mentor to Peregrine; "he is a particular friend of mine: his name is Hale, as good a creature as ever broke the bread of life. I don't suppose he noticed me; but here he returns, and I'll ask him to give us a song." "Stephy, my boy," said Mentor, " I hope you are well?" "Never better," he replied. "Then," said Mentor, "give us ' Here's to the King, God bless him.' " With all my heart, Georgy;" and, to the pleasure of the company, he sang it with all that ardour and taste for which he is so eminent.

After a few more songs and toasts, and as the generous wine was going round, Peregrine intimated to his neighbour, the farmer, that he should like to know a little more about the horse-jockeys.

"Certainly, my young friend," said the farmer; " whatever knowledge I have of the various cheats and frauds of the horse trade, I will gladly impart to you, for your guidance. In the first place, you should never attempt to obtain a high-priced horse from the hammer of a modern repository, without the advantage of an assistant perfectly adequate to the arduous task of discrimination. Let it be remembered, at such *mart of integrity,* a horse is seldom, if ever, displayed in a state of nature; he is thrown into a variety of alluring attitudes, and a profusion of *false fire,* by the powerful intermediation of *art*—that predominant incentive the *whip* before and the aggravating stimulus of the *ginger* behind (better understood by the appellation of *figging*), giving to the horse all the appearance of *spirit* (in fact, fear), which the injudicious spectator is too often imprudently induced to believe to be the spontaneous efforts of nature.

"During the superficial survey, in the few minutes allowed for inspection and purchase, much satisfactory investigation cannot be obtained; for, in the general hurry and confusion of 'showing out,' the short turns and irregular action of the horse, the political and occasional smack of the whip, the effect of emulation in the bidders, the loquacity of the orator, and the fascinating flourish of the hammer, the qualifications of the object are frequently forgotten, and every idea of perfection buried in the spirit of personal opposition.

"When a horse is lame of one foot, the knowing ones put a common horsebean under the shoe of the other foot, on the night previous to being sold, the pain of which will cause both feet to appear alike. As, also, when a horse is subject to the *glanders,* they trim the nostrils with a pair of scissors, blow a little pepper and salt up his nostrils, which will cause him to sneeze, and clear his head; they then sponge the nostrils, and grease them with a tallow candle; this will cause the filth to run off the nostril, and the defect will not be perceiveable for an hour or two.

"To prevent the detection of a *broken-winded horse,* they give him a pound of hog's lard, and a quarter of a pound of shot, on the night previous to being offered for sale : this will prevent its being discovered for a day, perhaps two, according to the work the horse does.

"The best way to discover a *Roarer,* is, to hold the head of the horse close to your ear, hitting him at the same time over the back with a stick, which will cause a roaring noise in the head.

"Those who traffic in stolen horses have also the faculty of altering and disguising them, in a manner which is scarcely to be conceived of. An instance occurred not long since of a gentleman losing a valuable mare, which he afterwards purchased, and kept some time without recognising, until, an accident befalling her, she was killed, when the farrier ascertained, from the remaining mark of an operation which had been performed, that she was the identical animal which had been stolen. Horses which have been stolen, it is well known, have run for a length of time in night coaches, not far from the very neighbourhood from which they were stolen. It is not an uncommon thing for dealers in stolen horses to rub the hair off the knees, or otherwise blemish a valuable and thorough-bred horse, for the purpose of having a reason for selling it into harness; and thus many a horse, worth an hundred guineas, has been sold for £35 or £40; which sum would, however, afford a handsome profit to the receiver.

"During the last two or three years, the crime of horse-stealing has prevailed to an extent scarcely to be credited : in the course of this time, probably thousands of horses have been stolen throughout England. So great has been the apprehension of losing these animals, that in many places persons have not ventured to turn them out into the fields, but have been constrained to keep them in the stable, on dry food, much to the injury of their health. The actual stealers of horses are generally low fellows, of desperate character, who fetch them from different parts of the country, and supply the receivers in London, and other large towns. The price which the latter give is very small—probably, in many instances, not one-tenth of the real value. Some time back two horses were stolen from the stable of a clergyman and magistrate, about thirty miles from London; for one of these, which was a thorough-bred hunter, the owner had been bid 150 guineas a short time before; yet for both the horses, it has been ascertained, the parties who stole them really received only £10, which, however, was pretty well for one night's work. An opinion has generally prevailed, that many stolen horses are exported; and this opinion has been encouraged for the purpose of inducing parties to give up further inquiry as hopeless. The truth is, very few horses are sent abroad; the receivers have connections in various parts of this country, to whom their consignments are made: the counties of Hants, Kent, and Sussex, and the west of England, have been supplied very liberally.

" 'There is reason to believe that the iniquitous traffic has lately received a considerable check. A pretty large proportion of notorious dealers have become entangled in the net of the law, and several of them have experienced that it is possible that that hempen ligature, called a halter, which is used for restraining the generous and useful quadruped, can, by order of a court of justice, be applied to another purpose. It is said that the operations of the stealers and receivers of horses are likely to experience a further check, in consequence of information which has been given by a convict, who was found guilty, not long since, upon three several indictments, for each of which he was sentenced to fourteen years' transportation. There is, perhaps, no measure more likely to prove embarrassing to criminal offenders, than to make it appear to them that they are constantly in danger of being betrayed by their associates. In general, thieves are stanch to those of their own character, to a degree which would be honourable in a good cause; whatever, therefore, may have a tendency to shake the confidence which these persons repose in each other, cannot fail to prove advantageous to the public security."

" Can you tell me," asked Peregrine, " as we are speaking of horses, the origin of horse-racing ?" " I remember reading," replied Mentor, " in an interesting work, called 'The History of Epsom,' that the first information we have of horse-racing in this country is in the reign of Henry II.; there can be no doubt that Epsom Downs early became the spot upon which the lovers of racing indulged their fancy; and perhaps the known partiality of James I. for this diversion will justify us in ascribing their commencement to the period when he resided at the Palace of Nonsuch, near Ewell; and his reign may be fairly stated as the period when horse-racing became a general and national amusement. They were then called bell-courses, the prize being a silver bell, and the winner was said to bear or carry the bell. The first Arabian which had ever been known in England as such, was purchased by the royal jockey of a Mr. Markham, a merchant, at the price of £500. During the civil wars, the amusements of the turf were partially suspended, but not forgotten; for we find that Mr. Place, stud-master to Cromwell, was proprietor of the famous horse, White Turk, and several capital brood mares, one of which, a great favourite, he concealed in a vault during the search after Cromwell's effects at the time of the Restoration, from which circumstance she took the name of the coffin mare, and is designated as such in various pedigrees. King Charles II., soon after his restoration, re-established the races at Newmarket, which had been instituted by James I. He divided them into regular meetings, and substituted, both there and at other places, silver cups, or bowls, of the value of £100, for the royal gift of the ancient bells. William III., though not fond of the turf, paid much attention to the breed of horses for martial purposes, and in his reign some of the most celebrated stallions were imported. George, Prince of Denmark, obtained from his royal consort, Queen Anne, grants of royal plates for several places. In the latter end of the reign of George I., the change of the royal plates into purses of 100 guineas took place. In the time of George II. there were many capital thorough-bred horses in England, the most celebrated of which were the famed Arabians, Darley and Godolphin—from the former descended Flying Childers. To continue a list of celebrated horses would exceed the limits; we shall therefore close with a brief account of the famous Eclipse This horse was first the property of the Duke of Cumberland, and was foaled during the great eclipse in 1764; he was withheld from the course till he was five years old, and was first tried at Epsom. He once ran four miles in eight minutes, carrying twelve stone, and with this weight he won eleven king's plates. He was never beaten, never had a whip flourished over him, or felt the tickling of a spur, nor was he ever for a moment distressed by the speed or rate of a competitor, out-footing, out-striding, and out-lasting every horse which started against him. When the races on Epsom Downs were first held periodically, we have not been able to trace with accuracy, but we find that from the year 1730 they have been annually held; for a long period, they were held twice in every year; it was then customary to commence at 11 o'clock, return into the town to dinner, and finish in the evening; but this arrangement has been long discontinued."

"You told me, Mentor," said Peregrine, "some few weeks gone, that there were sad cheats practised at horse-racing. Do you think there are, sir (addressing himself to the farmer); and do you imagine horse-racing is on the decline in the country?'

"I do know," replied the farmer, "that the most disreputable

tricks are resorted to by the black-legs, but not by the generality
of the nobles and gentry who patronize horse-racing. And, with
regard to horse-racing being on the decline, I will tell you what
Mr. Taplin, the great author on the diseases of horses, and on the
tricks of horse-jockeys, says :—' The falling off of racing,' says he,
' may be justly attributed to a combination of obstacles : the constantly increasing expense of training, the professional duplicity
(or rather family* deception) of riders, the heavy expenditure
unaviodably attendant upon travelling from one seat of sport to
another; the very great probability of *accidents*, or *breaking down*
in running; with a long train of uncertainties, added to the infamous
practices of " The Black-Legged" fraternity, in perpetual intercourse and association with both trainers and riders, leaving the
casual sportsman a very slender chance of winning *one* bet in *ten*,
where any of this *worthy society* are concerned, which they generally
are by some means, through the medium of occasional emissaries,
mercenary agents, or stable dependants, in constant pay for the
prostitution of every trust that has been implicitly reposed in
them by their too-credulous employers.

" ' Such incontrovertible facts may perhaps appear matters of
mere conjecture and speculation to the young and inexperienced,
who will undoubtedly believe, with reluctance, what is so
evidently calculated to discourage the predominance of inclination;
and, not having explored the regions of discovery, they may be
induced to flatter themselves with an opinion, that such representation is a delusion, intended much more to entertain, than com-
municate instruction. However, that the business may be elu-
cidated in such way as will prove most applicable to the nature of
the case, and the patience of the reader, it will be necessary to
afford their practices such explanation as may render the facility
of execution more familiar to the imagination of those whose
situations in life, or contracted opportunities, may have prevented
their being at all informed upon the subject in agitation.

" ' That these acts of villainy may be the better understood, it
becomes applicable to observe, that it is the persevering practice
of *the family* to have four, five, or six good runners in their possession; though, for the convenience and greater certainty of
public depredations, they pass as the distinct property of different
members : but this is by no means the case, for they are as much
the joint stock of *the party*, as is the stock in trade of the first firm
in the city. The speed and bottom of these horses are so accurately known to each individual of the brotherhood, and they
are in general (without an unexpected accident, which sometimes
happens) as well convinced, *before starting*, whether they can
beat their competitors, as if the race was absolutely determined.
This, however, is only the necessary groundwork of deception,
upon which every part of the superstructure is to be raised : as
they experimentally know how little money is to be got by *winning*,

* Gamblers are known by the appellation of " The Black-Legged Family."

they seldom permit that to become an object of momentary consideration; and, being no slaves to the specious delusions of *honour*, generally make their market by the *reverse*, but more particularly when they are the least expected *to lose;* that is, they succeed best in their general depredations, by losing when their horses are the favourites at high odds, after a heat or two, when expected to *win to a certainty*, which they as *prudently* take care to prevent.

" ' This business, to insure success and emolument, is carried on by such a combination of villany, such a systematic chain of horrid machinations, as it is much to be lamented could ever enter the minds of degenerate men for the purposes of destruction. The various modes of practice and imposition are too numerous and extensive to admit of general explanation; the purport of the present *epitome* or contracted description being intended to operate merely as a guard to those who are totally unacquainted with the *infamy* of the party whose *merits* we mean to describe.

" 'The principal (that is, the ostensible proprietor of the horse for the day) is to be found in the centre of the "betting ring" previous to the starting of the horse, surrounded by the sporting multitude; amongst whom his emissaries place themselves to perform their destined parts in the acts of villany regularly carried on upon these occasions, but more particularly at all the meetings within thirty or forty miles of the metropolis. In this conspicuous situation he forms a variety of pretended bets with his confederates, in favour of his own horse; such bait the unthinking bystanders eagerly swallow, and, proceeding upon this show of confidence, *back him themselves:* these offers are immediately accepted to any amount by the emissaries before mentioned, and is, in fact, no more than a palpable robbery, as the horse, it is already determined by the family, is *not to win*, and the money so betted is as certainly their own, as if already decided.

" ' This part of the business being transacted, a new scene of tergiversation becomes necessary; the horse being mounted, the rider is whispered by the *nominal owner* to win the first heat if he can; this it is frequently in his power to *do easy*, when he is consequently backed at still *increased odds*, as the expected winner, all which proposed bets are instantly taken by the emissaries, or rather principals, *in the firm;* when, to show us the versatility of fortune, and the vicissitudes of the turf, he very unexpectedly becomes a loser, or perhaps *runs out of the course*, to the feigned disappointment and affected sorrow of the owner, who publicly declares he has lost so many " score pounds upon the race," whilst his confederates are individually engaged in collecting *their certainties*, previous to the *casting up stock*, at the general rendezvous in the evening.

" 'To this plan there is a direct alternative, if there should be no chance (from his being sufficiently a favourite) of laying on money in this way; they then take the longest odds they can obtain, that

17.

he wins, and regulate or vary their betting by the event of each heat; winning if they ean, or losing to a certainty, as best suits the bets they have laid, which is accurately known by a pecuniary consultation between the heats. From another degree of undiscoverable duplicity, their great emoluments arise.—For instance: letting a horse of capital qualifications *win* or *lose* almost alternately at different places, as may be most applicable to the betting for the day; dependent entirely on the state of public opinion, but to be ultimately decided by the latent villany of the parties more immediately concerned.

" These, like other matters of magnitude, are not to be rendered infallible, without the necessary agents; that, like the smaller wheels of a curious piece of mechanism, contribute their portion of power to give action to the whole. So true is the ancient adage, " birds of a feather flock together," that *riders* may be selected who will prove inviolably faithful to the dictates of this party, that *could not* or *would not* reconcile an honourable attachment to the first nobleman in the kingdom. These are the infernal deceptions and acts of villany upon the turf, that have driven noblemen, gentlemen, and sportsmen of honour, from what are called country courses, to their asylum of Newmarket, where, by the exclusion of the family from their clubs, and their horses from their subscription sweepstakes and matches, they render themselves invulnerable to the *often envenomed* shafts of the most premeditated (and in general well-executed) villany.'

" I have often thought," continued the Farmer, " that in giving the pedigree of horses, and expatiating on their perfections, great nonsense is displayed, to say the least of it; and I have here a description of a horse, sent me this morning, which an Irish gentleman offers for sale, which I will read you; it is a fair burlesque:

' SPANKER,

The property of O'—— D——, Esq.

Will be sold, or put up for sale,

at Sligo,

On Saturday, September the Sixteenth,

A strong, stanch, steady, sound, stout, safe, sinewey, serviceable, strapping, supple, swift, smart, sightly, sprightly, spirited, sturdy, spunky, shining, surefooted, sleek, showy, smooth, wellskinned, sized and shaped

SORREL STEED,

of superior symmetry, called SPANKER,

with small star and snip, square-sided, slender-shouldered, sharp-sighted, and steps supereminetly stately:—free from strain, sprain, spavin, spasms, sinus, strangles, stringhalt, stranguary, sufflation, seed-shedding, sciatica, staggers, sceling, scouring, sellander, sarcocele, star-gazing, surfeit, strumous-swelling, seams, sorrances, scratches, shingles, splint, squint, squirt, scurf, scabs, scars, sores, scattering, shuffling, shambling, scampering, straddling, slouching, or skue stunted gait, or symptons of secretion, or sickness of any sort. He is neither stiff-mouthed, shabby-coated, sinew-shrunked, spur-galled, slight-carcassed, star-footed, saddle-backed, shell-toothed, splay-footed, slim-gutted, short-winded, sag-eared, surbated, skin-scabbed, star-coated, slack-sleazy, or shoulder-shotten, or slipped, and is sound in the shanks, sword-point, spine, and stifle-joint;—has neither sleeping evil, snaggle-teeth, sanious-ulcers, sick-spleen, sand-cracks, setfast, schirrous, scissures, scrofulous, or subcutaneous sores, swelled sheath, sarcoma, stegnosis in staling, or shattered hoofs. Nor is he sour, sulky, surly, stubborn, or sullen in temper;—neither shy or skittish, slow, sluggish, squabby, or stupid;—he never slips, strips, strays, stalks, starts, stops, shakes, strides, snivels, snuffles, slavers, shudders, scambles, snorts, spatters, scranches, swallows his wind, stumbles or stocks in his stall or stable, and scarcely or seldom sweats. Has a showy stylish switch tail or stern, and a safe set of shoes on; can subsist on soil, stubble, sainfoin, sheaf-oats, spoon-wort, straw, sedge, sorrage, or scutch-grass; carries sixteen stone with surprising speed in his stroke, over a six-foot sod or stone wall. His sire was the sly Sobersides, on a sister of Spiddle-shanks (from the select stud of Squire Splashaway), by Sampson, a sporting son of Sparklers (by that seminific superlative stallion, Stingo), who won the sweepstakes and sub-scription plates last season at Strangford. His selling price, 76l. 16s. 6d. sterling.

" ' At same time will be Sold or Swapped, a snug, safe, substantial, serviceable, second-hand Saddle, with secure stuffing, seat, skirts, straps, stirrups, studs, and a strong Surcingle; also a solid silver Snaffle and sharp steel Spurs.'

" And pray," said Peregrine," are there not any tricks played with cows, as well as horses?" "Unfortunately, there are too many," replied the farmer. "Cows, you are well aware, tell their age by the number of wrinkles on their horns. When the dishonest vendor wants to keep their age a secret, he files off the ridges or marks on the horns, in order to deceive the buyer; in the same manner as the horse-jockeys do with the horses' teeth. Among the innumerable schemes of fraud, they have one, of what they call *stocking the cows,* that is, not to milk the cow for two days before she is offered to be sold, in order to cheat the buyer as to the quantity of milk: they then wash the udder with red ochre.

" I remember," continued the farmer, " reading an account of a person being imposed on, by having an old cow foisted upon him as a young one. The man applied to the Lord Mayor, when he made the following statement:—' About a fortnight ago, a farmer residing at Epping Forest, having rather an elderly cow

which began to be very slack of milk, he determined to get rid of
her, and to purchase another.  He accordingly took her to Romford fair, and sold her to a cow-dealer for about 4*l*. 10*s*., but he
did not see any cow in the market promising enough in appearance, and returned home without a cow, but satisfied at the price
he had got for the ' old 'un.'  The cow-dealer calculated upon
Smithfield market as a better *emporium* for disposing of his bargain, and accordingly drove her there, in order to sell her to the
*polony*-pudding merchants ; but there was a glut in that description of dainty, in consequence of the late floods, which have
proved fatal to many poor beasts.  The cow would not sell even
for the money which had been just given for her, and the owner
was about to dispose of her for less, when a doctor, who had
been regarding the beast for some time, offered, for a fee of 5*s*.,
to make her as young as she had been ten years before.  The fee
was immediately paid, the doctor took his patient to a stable,
carded her all over—prescribed some strange diet for her—sawed
down her horns from the rough and irregular condition to which
years had swelled them, into the tapering and smoothness of
youth, and delivered her to the owner, more like a calf, than the
venerable ancestor of calves.  The cow-dealer was struck with
the extrordinary transformation, and it immediately occurred to
him (a proof that a cow-dealer can be dishonest as well as a
horse-dealer) to sell her for the highest price he could get
for her, without saying a word about her defects and infirmities.
Having learnt that the Epping farmer was in want of a cow, he
thought he could not send his bargain to better quarters than those
she was accustomed to, and he forthwith despatched her to Romford market, where her old master was on the look-out for a beast.
She immediately caught his eye.  He asked her age.  The driver
did not know, but she was a ' fine young 'un.'  ' I've seen a cow
very like her somewhere,' said the farmer.  'Ay,' said the driver,
' then you must have seen her a long way off, for I believe she is
an Alderney.'  ' An Alderney ! what do you ask for her ?'  The
price was soon fixed.  The driver got the sum of £15. 7*s*. for the
cow, and the farmer sent her home.  The ingenuity exercised
might be guessed at from the fact, that the person who drove the
beast home had been at her tail for the last seven years, at least
twice a-day, and yet he did not make the discovery, although
she played some of her old tricks in the journey, and turned into
the old bed, with all the familiarity of an old acquaintance.  At
length the discovery was to be made.  The cow was milked, and
milked, but the most that could be got from her for breakfast was
a pint, and that was little better than sky-blue.  The farmer, in
grief and astonishment, sent her to a cow-doctor, who had been
in the habit of advising in her case, and complained that she
gave no milk.  ' Milk !' said he, ' how the devil should she,
poor old creature?  Sure it isn't by cutting her horns, and giving
her linseed oil-cakes, and scrubbing her old limbs that you can

expect to make her give milk.' The farmer was soon convinced of the imposture, and would indeed forgive it, if the laugh against him could be endured.

" Mr. Hobler regretted that the Lord Mayor could not interfere. He believed that the farmer must be content with the benefit derived from his experience, which, it was to be hoped, would make him take a judge with him the next time he went to purchase a cow. Some facts had reached him about the transformation of old jaded horses into spirited steeds, but he had not heard before of the effect filing down a cow's horns had in restoring old age to youth. He supposed this was what was meant by 'grinding young.' "

" Smithfield," says Mentor, " seemingly, by toe papers, will soon cease to be a place of notoriety, endeavours being used to prevent it remaining any longer a market for cattle. Its history, however, is full of interest.

" In former times, there was in it a great pond called Horse Pool, for men watered their horses there, which pond was supplied by the river Wells, or Turnmill Brook, near which was a place called *The Elms*, for that there grew many elm trees; and this was the place for punishing offenders in the year 1219, and, as it seems, long before. Here, in 1530, John Roofe, a cook, who, for poisoning seventeen persons, was boiled to death: and, in 1541, Margaret Davie, a young woman, suffered also here in the same manner. At this period Smithfield must have been very large, says Stow, for now remaineth but a small portion for the old uses; to wit, for markets of horses and cattle: military exercises, as justings, tournaments, and great triumphs, have been there formerly performed before the princes and nobility, both of this realm and foreign countries.

" In 1357, the 31st of Edward III., great and royal jousts were then holden in Smithfield; there being present the kings of England, France, and Scotland.

In 1362, the 48th of Edward III., Dame Alice Perrers, or Pierce, the king's concubine, who assumed the appellation of the ' Lady of the Sun,' rode from the Tower of London through Cheapside, accompanied with many lords and ladies; every lady leading a lord by his horse's bridle, till they came into West Smithfield, and then began a great joust, which lasted seven days.

" In the 9th of Richard II. was the like great riding from the Tower to Westminster, and every lord led a lady's horse's bridle; and on the morrow began the joust in Smithfield, which lasted three days.

" In the 14th of Richard II. royal jousts and tournaments were proclaimed to be done in Smithfield, for many days. At the day appointed, sixty coursers came from the Tower, and upon every one of them an esquire of honour; then came forth sixty ladies of honour, mounted upon palfries, riding on the one side, richly appareled; and every lady led a knight with a chain of gold.

Those knights which were of the king's party, had their armour and apparel garnished with white harts, and crowns of gold about the harts' necks; and so they came riding through the streets of London to Smithfield, with a great number of trumpets. The king and queen were placed in chambers, to see the jousts.

"In the year 1393, the 17th of Richard II., the Earl of Mar challenged the Earl of Nottingham to joust with him; and the Earl of Mar was cast, and two of his ribs broken with the fall; so that he was conveyed out of Smithfield, and so towards Scotland, but died on the way, at York.

"In 1409, a royal joust took place in Smithfield, between the Earl of Somerset, and other knights, against the Seneschal of Hanault and some Frenchmen.

"In the year 1430, a battle was fought here, before the king, between two men of Faversham. In 1442, Sir Philip la Beautfe and 'Squire Astley fought here, with sword, spear, axe and dagger, but neither were killed; also with Thomas Fitz Thomas, and Butler, Earl of Ormond. In 1467, the bastard of Burgoigne challenged Lord Seales, with spear, axe, and pole, which lasted three days. This was the last tournament in Smithfield.

"Stowe relates that, in the year 1446, John David appeached his master, William Cator, of treason; and, a day being appointed them to fight in Smithfield, the master being well beloved, was so cherished by his friends, and plied with wine, that being therewith overcome, was unluckily slain by his servant. But that servant lived not long unpunished, being afterwards hanged at Tyburn for felony.

"Grafton says the master was an armourer, and the incident has been introduced by Shakspeare into his play of Henry VI. The dramatist has, however, altered the names to Horner and Peter. The original document in the Exchequer, acquaints us, that the real names of the combatants were John Daveys and William Catour; and the following is the last article of the record of expenses:—

"Also paid to officers to watchying of ye ded man in Smythfelde ye same day and ye nyghte after yt ye batail was doon, and for hors hyre for the officeres at ye execution doying, and for ye hangman's labour xjs. vjd.

"Also paid for ye cloth yat lay upon ye ded man in Smythfelde, viijd.

"Also paid for 1 pole and nayllis, and for setting up of ye said mannys hed on London brigge, vd.

Sum, xijs. vijd.

"In Smithfield, Wat Tyler, in 1381, met his death by the hands of the mayor, William Walworth—or some one else.

"This place was also held for *Autos de Fé*. Here our martyr, Latimer, preached patience to Friar Forest, agonized under the torture of a slow fire, for denying the king's supremacy. Here

Cranmer forced the reluctant hand of Edward to the warrant to send Joan Bocher, a silly woman, to the stake. The last poor creature who suffered at the stake, in England, and burnt here, was Barth Leggatt, in 1611.

" Smithfield thus became, from being a place of honourable exercises and entertainments, the scene of the most appalling spectacles; and afterwards it was resorted to for settling private quarrels for all loose sorts of men, at a place then called Ruffian's Hall.

" In 1614 it was paved, and became a market-place for cattle, hay, straw, and provisions; for which purposes it is used till this day; but how much longer it will continue, a few months will show : some of the citizens, having too much *gentility* about them, petitioned to have the market removed; and, in consequence, a committee of the members of the House of Commons was appointed to inquire into the subject, on the motion of Mr. Gordon.

" It is said that there never was such a mass of conflicting and opposite evidence offered to any committee of the House of Commons, as that received by the committee on the Smithfield Market question. Clergymen have been called to prove that the Sabbath day is violated; medical men in proof of cruelty; butchers, salesmen, drovers, and a long list of others, on general points. One party distinctly states that every thing would be gained by changing the market-day; another as confidently asserts that that would make no alteration for the better, and cannot be done before changing the provincial market-days throughout England, and arranging with all the retail butchers and families in London. One witness states, that for about thirty years he has attended Smithfield Market, and has only heard of a few isolated cases of cruelty during all that time; whilst another says that cruelty the most revolting may be witnessed there on the eve of every market-day. One talks of the conveniency of having the market in the suburbs; another says that such a change would merely affect the families in the vicinity of Smithfield, and those who may reside in the neighbourhood of the new one. Whilst there are doubts, however, as to the expediency of wholly removing the market, there are none as regards the size of the market-place : all agree in saying that it is too small."

" The market-days are Mondays and Fridays; on these two days, are weekly brought upwards of three thousand oxen, or beasts; thirty thousand sheep and lambs; with a proportionate number of pigs and calves, all alive.

" This market has actually been disgraced by fellows taking their wives there with halters about ther necks, and selling them : but, thanks to the civil authorities, such practices are discontinued.

" Whoever has not seen Smithfield on a market morning, can scarcely form any idea of the scene; but, to be viewed to advantage, it should be visited at the witching hours. Methinks, if the neighbouring graves did give up their dead, the frightened sprites would fain retreat to their former habitations. Here are half a thousand beasts bellowing in concert to the bleating of ten thousand sheep, mingling with the shouts and oaths of hundreds of drovers, enlivened by the barking of dogs, the blaze of innumerable torches, the sound of blows, the trampling of hoofs : although forming a scene unparalleled, yet amidst all this din, the worthy inhabitants repose undisturbed.

" Here, also, is a fair once a year, commencing on Saint Bartholomew's day, and continuing three successive days ; but it is dwindling away to insignificance, and in a few years, doubtless, it will be extinct."

" Ward, in his London Spy, thus makes mention of it in his time : ' At the entrance,' he says, ' our ears were saluted with the rumbling of drums, mixed with the intolerable squeaking of cat-calls, and the discordant noise of penny rattles. The impatient desires of the innumerable throng to witness Merry Andrew's grimaces, led us ancle deep into filth and nastiness, and crowded us as close as a barrel of figs, or candles in a tallow-chandler's basket, sweating and melting with the heat of our own bodies. We next went,' continues Ward, ' into a cook-shop, where a swinging fat fellow, who was overseer of the roasted meat, was standing by the spit in his shirt, rubbing of his ears, breast, neck, and arm-pits, with the same wet cloth which he applied to his roasting pigs, which brought such a qualm over our stomachs, that we scouted out of the parlour, and deferred eating till a more cleanly opportunity.'

" The facetious George Alexander Steevens thus gives us the following just description of it, about 1762 :—

" Here was, first of all, crowds against other crowds driving,
  Like wind and tide meeting, each contrary striving ;
  Shrill fiddling, sharp fighting, and shouting and shrieking,
  Fifes, trumpets, drums, bagpipes, and barrow girls squeaking,
  Come, my rare round and sound, here's choice of fine ware,
  Though *all* was not sold at *Bartelmew* Fair.
  There was dolls, hornpipe-dancing, and showing of postures,
  With frying black-puddings, and opening of oysters :
  With salt-boxes, solos, and gallery-folks squalling,
  The tap-house guests roaring, and mouth-pieces bawling,
  Pimps, pawnbrokers, strollers, fat landladies, sailors,
  Bawds, bullies, jilts, jockeys, tumblers, and tailors :
  Here's Punch's whole play of the Gunpowder-Plot,
  Wild beasts all alive, and pease-pudding all hot,
  Fine sausages fried, and the Black on the wire,
  The whole court of France, and nice pig at the fire ;
  Here's the up-and-downs, who'll take a seat in the chairs ?
  Though there's more up-and-downs than at *Bartelmew* Fair,
  Here's Wittington's cat, and the tall dromedary,
  The chaise without horses, and Queen of Hungary ;
  Here's the merry-go-rounds, ' Come, who rides ? Come, who rides,' sir ,
  Wine, ale, beer, and cakes, fire-eating, besides, sir
  The fam'd learned dog, that can tell his letters ;
  And some men as scholars, are not much his betters."

" Such," continued Mentor, " is a description of Bartholomew
Fair, in 1762. How different from the present time! the shows
and booths now not occupying a quarter of the space they used
to do, even ten years ago !"

" Come, gentlemen," said the farmer, " as I do not like to
encourage late hours, I think it would be well for us all ' to go to
our night-caps,' as Mons. Tonson says." To this proposition
Mentor and Peregrine immediately assented ; and, wishing the
worthy farmer a good night's rest, took their departure, highly delighted with the evening's entertainment at the King's Head Inn.*

On the morrow, Peregrine accompanied Mentor to the college
of *Banco Regis,* or *Abbot's Priory,* as it is *classically* termed, on a
visit to an unfortunate gentleman, who was ruined by being concerned in the late Joint-Stock Companies. They were not long
within its melancholy walls, before they beheld, with sorrow, surprise, and pity,

The Doings in the King's-Bench Prison.

Peregrine gazed with wonder on the motley scene before him :—
Black-legs, Gamblers, Dandies, Fortune-hunters, fraudulent Bank-
rupts, Lawyers, Pigeons, Greeks, Quacks, Chimney-sweeps,
Pimps, Bawds, Prostitutes, Bullies and Panders, Clergymen,
Soldiers, Sailors, Thieves, Sprigs of Nobility, upstart Gentry ; and
last—*and least*—the Honest Unfortunate ;—the whole forming such
an heterogeneous group, such a sad, merry, careless, dissolute,
confused mass of society, and yet such an animated and true picture

* In page 276 it is, by mistake, called the George Inn.

of *real life*, that it bewildered Peregrine while he beheld it. In the midst of his reverie, he was led by his friend Mentor to a room where he witnessed a different scene of distress and dissipation. Mentor's poor friend was stretched out on a pallet with little or no covering over him, sleeping, or trying to sleep, to starve out hunger, or to shut out the scene before him. "There," said Mentor to Peregrine, pointing to his friend, "there lies the once lord of thousands!" Mentor went up to him, to awake him. "Pray do not, sir," said a kind-spoken woman; "he seems fast asleep: pray don't disturb him. You little know what a luxury sleep is to the wretched. Perhaps he is dreaming of his former home, of his happy state—when the sun of prosperity shone on him. Hark! he is talking—he mutters, 'Mary, Mary! heaven's blessings be on thee!'" "Ah!" replied Mentor, "Mary was his wife: she broke her heart on witnessing him so suddenly hurled to destruction, by taking the accursed persuasive advice of a villanous stock-jobber." "Indeed, sir," said the woman, "he often sighs out Mary! But he *must* starve, sir," continued the woman: "he has no money; and without that, sir, this is a wretched place indeed!" "But he shall *not* starve!" exclaimed Mentor, as the tears trickled down his cheeks. "Never!" sobbed out young Peregrine. "Yes, gentlemen," continued the woman; "he will though, for he has not tasted a mouthful of meat for these three days; and has had nothing but a little tea!" "Good heavens," ejaculated Mentor; "but hush—he wakes!" "Ah! Mentor, is it you?" he said, looking wildly on him. "I did not wish to see *you*, my friend, or any one else I formerly knew. I have been dreaming," continued he, taking hold of Mentor's hand—"I have been dreaming of Mary and the two little ones; and—" but grief denied him utterance—he looked on Mentor—then on himself—then around his room—when a flood of tears came to his relief. At length, after much persuasion, he walked out on the *Parade* with Mentor and Peregrine, and consented to take some refreshment, and afterwards a dinner; when it was arranged, and consented to by him, that some of his old friends should be made acquainted with his present distress, and that the necessary steps should be taken for him to be liberated. In the course of conversation, he gave a description of his *chums*, or fellow-lodgers. "That old cobbler," said he, "you saw at work, ruined himself by meddling with politics: he was once in a good way of business; he neglected it by running after every brawler for public liberty; and he became bankrupt: but he bears his misfortunes with fortitude. That good kind-hearted woman to whom you spoke, is the wife of a fellow-prisoner. I hardly know how to mention her in sufficient terms of admiration and gratitude. She has attended me with all the care of a wife. Ah! it is indeed true, as Lord Byron says,

'Woman!
When care and anguish wring the brow,
A ministering angel thou!'

That person who sat at the table, with a cap on, drinking, is a most singular creature : his history seems more like romance, than incidents of real life.   He is a foreigner : his *real* name is S——, and, while abroad, he acquired, by the depredations which he committed in the night, the respectable and even pompous appearance which he made during the day.   He was handsome in person, and accomplished in mind ; and, having received an excellent education, and gone through a regular course of studies, the pleasure which this afforded, combined with his respectable appearance, caused him to be received in the best houses of T——.   Amongst others, he was introduced to M. B——, mayor of T——, who, pleased with his prepossessing appearance and gentlemanly address, invited him to his house, where he soon became a favourite with the whole family.   Among its members was Adeline, the eldest daughter of the mayor, nineteen years of age, and whose personal charms and high accomplishments soon attracted the attention of S——.   It may easily be supposed that a man like S——, possessing a handsome person, a well-informed mind, elegant and prepossessing manners, and, in addition to all these, the appearance of great wealth, which he spent in a manner which gave an equally high opinion of his liberality and generosity—it may easily be supposed that such a man easily won the affections of a young and artless girl.   The attachment soon became known to the family, and S——, who thought that by marrying the wealthy and beautiful Adeline, to whom he was really attached, he would secure at once his happiness and a respectable rank in life, actually carried his audacity so far as to make a formal proposition of marriage to the mayor of T——.

"It is a fact well known to the inhabitants of T——, that the mayor, deluded by the appearance of S——, by his pretended rank, his supposed wealth, by the amiability of his disposition, the elegance of his manners, and, above all, by the resistless powers which men of talent ever did and ever will have over inferior minds, not only listened to the proposals of S——, but readily gave his assent to the proposed union between him and his daughter. The intelligence was, of course, made known to the mother of Adeline, who sanctioned the consent given by her husband ; and preparations were at once begun for the approaching ceremony. The delighted Adeline soon imparted the joyful news to her young friends, and the report having spread throughout the town, this intended marriage soon became the subject of general conversation. In the meantime, the epoch of the annual *fête*, celebrated at P—, was approaching, and the Prefect invited the Mayor of T—— and all his family to spend a few days with him during the approaching festival.   The invitation, of course, included S——.   The Mayor of T—— thought it advisable, on account of the state of his health, and the approaching marriage of his daughter, to decline the invitation for himself and his family, but he requested S—— to go and thank the Prefect, in their name and his own, for the honour

thus conferred upon him.  S—— eagerly availed himself of this
proposition.     Arrived at P—, S—— was received in the kindest
and handsomest manner possible by the Prefect, into whose good
favour he soon ingratiated himself so much, that he begged and insisted that he should remain with him a week or two.   To this
S——, at length, consented ; and, during his stay at P—, he was
introduced to the principal inhabitants of the town, who vied in
giving marks of attention and politeness to the amiable, and, as
they thought, distinguished foreigner.   One day that the Prefect
had invited a party to dinner, purposely to introduce his new friend
to them, he was, about the middle of the repast, requested to attend in his study a person who had just arrived with a message on
business of importance, which required immediate attention.
Having apologized to his friends, the Prefect left the dining-room,
and, on entering his study, found an officer; who informed him
that an order had been received at T——, the preceding evening,
from the head of the police, immediately to arrest S——, to put
him in prison, and, with all possible speed, to proceed to his trial
for the numerous depredations he had committed, and which, it
seemed, had not escaped the all-searching eye of the police.   The
Prefect, as may be supposed, was struck with astonishment, but,
as the officer showed him a written order, he saw no means of
avoiding this most unpleasant *eclat*, and, stepping into the dining-
room, he called out his new guest, who was immediately made
prisoner by the officer, who informed him of the nature of the order he had to put in execution.   S—— was at first confused, but
soon recovered his *sang-froid*, which has so frequently carried him
through the most unpleasant circumstances : he assured the officer
and the Prefect that this must be the result of some mistake, and requested the latter to apologize to his guests for his absence. Having
said this, he took leave of the Prefect with perfect composure, and
with apparrent *nonchalance* followed the officer and his men to T——;
on reaching which he was immediately put into strict confinement,
and informed that preparations were being made for his trial, which
would take place in a few days.   You may easily suppose what
were the consternation of the mayor, and the distress of his unhappy
daughter, on being made acquainted with these unexpected events;
but such was, however, the degree of confidence with which S ——
nad inspired them, and their infatuation with regard to this man,
that they looked forward rather with hope than with fear to his
approaching trial.   The anxiously expected day at length arrived,
and S—— appeared in the court, before the assembled multitude,
unmoved and unabashed.   As soon as he made his appearance,
every eye was fixed upon him.   His handsome appearance, his
elegant and gentlemanly deportment, and the honourable reputation
which he had hitherto borne, inspired the audience with the liveliest
interest and commiseration in his favour.   When the proceedings
commenced, the attention seemed to be rivetted to the words of
the principal witness, and consternation, as well as astonishment,

was visible in every countenance, when it was evident from the report read to the court by this officer, and from the evidence of numerous and respectable witnesses, that S—— was only enabled to keep up the splendid appearance he carried on during the day, by the depredations he committed during the night; and that this much esteemed and beloved man, the friend of the Prefect of P— and the intended son-in-law of the mayor of T——, was no more than a desperate gambler, and a common and audacious swindler. When the proceedings were terminated, and nothing remained but the defence of the accused, he rose, and in a dignified manner, and with a composed accent, he addressed the court. ' Even if it were possible,' he said, ' I would not now atttempt to deny the accusations brought against me. Weak minds may dissapprove my conduct, but those who think and reflect, instead of blaming, will approve of it; and, so far from being ashamed, I am proud of what I have done. Born of a good family, and having received an excellent education, these advantages would have become use-less, if, when misfortune fell upon me, I had sunk under the weight of adversity. I saw but one way of remedying the evil, and I took it; who will blame me for doing so? The means, I may be told, are wrong—I deny it. I never injured the poor, the oppressed, the needy, the unfortunate. I appeal to the inhabitants of this city now here assembled to say whether I have not always been willing—nay, anxious, to lend a helping hand to those who wanted help, and whether my purse was not always open to the necessitous. What has, then, been my crime? I have taken from the rich to give to the poor! The proud, the avaricious, have been deprived of their useless wealth; and that wealth has become, in my hands, the instrument of relief to the humble and the unfortunate. Such, gentlemen, has been my crime. I once obtained the approbation of this town, because a young man, in an humble rank of life, compelled by necessity, having made an at-tempt to rob me, and being discovered, was not prosecuted, but relieved by me—an action which, however humble in itself, has been a source of great pleasure to me, since the young man, thus saved from ruin, is now comfortably settled in life, and has since become, by his prudent and upright conduct, an ornament to so-ciety—that society, whose vindictive laws I might have called upon his head, as they are now called upon mine. I could say and advance more in defence of my conduct, but I read in the countenances of my judges, that to say more were useless; and feel certain, also, that a favourable decision will be given in my be-half, and will meet with the approbation of the assembled multitude, whose looks now assure me of the interest they feel, and the wishes they form for my liberation.' Having thus spoken, he sat down; and, when the judge rose to deliver his charge to the jury, he was evidently affected by the strange and unexpected address which he had just heard. The jury soon after withdrew, but, having had time to recover from the effect which S——'s address had also produced upon them, they soon returned a verdict of *guilty* against the prisoner, who was condemned by the court to be confined for fifteen years, to be exposed for one hour in the pillory on the public place of T——, and to be branded on the shoulder, by the public executioner, as an impostor. This sentence, which, although it appeared harsh at first, was afterwards considered as perfectly just, was put in execution a few days after, and, at the first opportunity, S—— was conveyed to —— with the condemned criminals. His deportment during all these trying events was such as it had always been, easy and dignified; and he had rather the appearance of a man patiently suffering the injustice of others, than of one undergoing the punishment of his crimes. He was put on board one of the galleys, where he soon distinguished himself by the propriety of his conduct. Assiduous in performing the tasks assigned him, kind to his companions, respectful to his superiors, he soon gained the esteem and affection of every one. Among others, the governor, appointed to superintend the galleys, took particular notice of S——. His good conduct and regular deportment led him to suppose that his punishment might be the result of some act committed in the rashness of youth; and, having conversed several times with him, and found him a man of excellent education, and possessing very extensive information, he conceived the project of asking him to give his younger children the first principles of instruction, especially as it was extremely difficult to find a preceptor in such a place as R——. S—— readily accepted the offer, as it was likely to render his confinement much less irksome and disagreeable than it otherwise would have been. He was therefore admitted at certain hours, during the day, to the governor's house, and soon rendered himself as great a favourite there as he had formerly been at T——. Such a circumstance offered a chance of escape from confinement, but S—— was too wise to make an attempt, which, if frustrated, would not only deprive him of the hope of liberty, but render his situation more horrible than it had ever been. He met, in the house, and at the table of the governor, the priest who was appointed to act as chaplain to the prisoners, and who, therefore, had a lodging within the citadel; which, however, he was at liberty to leave when business or pleasure called him to the town. This man, possessing great information and superior literary talents, had been for a considerable time engaged in a work of some magnitude. Finding in S—— a person who he thought could assist him, he obtained of the governor permission to take him to his rooms, where he sometimes remained late in the evening, copying some of the chaplain's manuscripts, or otherwise assisting him in his literary undertaking. One afternoon, while they were thus engaged, a message was sent to the chaplain that one of the prisoners, having met with an accident, and being at the point of death, requested his immediate attendance. He gave S—— several books to examine, which would take him some hours, and left him, to attend to the dying man. After he had been gone some time, and as evening approached, a thought flashed across S——'s mind, that this was a favourable opportunity to regain his liberty. He examined the room in which he was, and found in one of the drawers a clerical dress belonging to the chaplain, and which he had not put on, as it was not his intention to go to town that evening. S—— put on this dress, placed his own in the drawer, of which he took the key, and, putting on the gown and clerical hat of the chaplain, walked demurely, with a book in his hand, toward the gate leading to the city. He knocked; the porter asked, as usual, who was there, when, fortunately for S——, a soldier who had reached the gate at the same time, and was deceived by the dress, answered—'Don't you see it is the chaplain?' The man opened the gate, bowed to the reverend personage, who returned the salutation, and hastened to pass through the town. The chaplain on his return home, having been detained some hours, found the room in perfect order; and, as the books were carefully put away, he concluded that S——, having finished his task, and tired of waiting for him, had gone to the governor's house; while the governor, on going his rounds, and not seeing S—— at his post, recollected that the chaplain told him in the evening that he was in his room, where he would be employed in writing till late in the evening. This combination of circumstances left the fugitive the whole night at his command, and he used it so well, that in the morning, when his flight was discovered, every search was made in vain.

"He arrived in England some few months since, got in debt, and that brought him here. He has a feeling heart, and, I assure you, I lay under many obligations to him for his kind assistance.

"Begging your pardon, sir," said Peregrine, "how are the prisoners used?" "I will tell you, my young friend," replied the gentleman. "The morning after committal to the King's Bench Prison, the prisoner is roused early from whatever couch he may have got for the night, by the sonorous voice of the turnkeys, calling, 'Pull up, pull up,' and is obliged to enter the lobby through two lines of curious, and often impudent and unfeeling faces, to have, what is technically denominated, 'his likeness taken,' i. e. to be again personally and particularly scanned by the whole of the turnkeys, and then is 'quizzed' by the fellows who are in waiting to observe his return. Female prisoners (and there are several) are compelled, however delicate or respectable, to go through the same disgusting ordeal, and be the subjects of the same coarse buffoonery.

"There are, or rather were, a number in the King's Bench, who take an especial pleasure in tormenting those whose simplicity or undisguised melancholy point them out as fit objects for the cruel sport. These poor beings are made to believe all sorts of horrible stories connected with the prison. The 'strong room,' which is dreadful enough in itself, is exaggerated beyond description; and sometimes simple countrymen are persuaded that the officers are about to carry them to those places of punishment. A poor man, a few months ago, was goaded to distraction in this way; and, on his tormentors assuring him that the turnkeys were coming for him, he threw himself from a top window to the pavement below, and was nearly dashed to pieces; yet those who had so worked upon his feelings, were seen immediately afterwards playing at rackets, laughing and rioting, as though nothing had happened.

"About the second day of a prisoner's committal to the Bench, he receives a chum ticket, and may enter the apartment on which he is chummed, or receive five shillings per week from the occupant. If he resolves upon going into the room, he hires a bed and other furniture, which will cost him four or five shillings per week. The accommodation he will have may be imagined from the following statement:—There are about 240 rooms in the Bench; of these about eighty are occupied by the prisoners who 'pay out' all chums, and keep their room to themselves. There have been as many as 900 prisoners at once in the prison, but the average in term time may be taken at about 650. From the 240 rooms, deducting eighty, and from the 650 prisoners, deducting eighty, there will remain 570 of the latter to occupy 160 of the former— *i. e.* about three and a half persons to one room of twelve feet long and ten broad. In the hot summer months, the consequences of this crowding may be better conceived than described.

" In addition to the eighty prisoners who keep their own rooms, and can afford to 'pay out' two or three chums, other encroachments are made upon the little accommodation left for the mass of the prisoners. The turnkeys, instead of being paid by the marsha., or otherwise, have rooms given them in the prison, which they are not called upon to inhabit, and which they do not in fact inhabit, but are allowed to let out, and receive thereby a handsome sum weekly.

" The emoluments of the officers constitute an exaction upon the prisoners—upon persons who cannot pay their own debts—who cannot engage in any employment—who, if honest, must be destitute of sufficient to procure their own subsistence; yet they, and they alone, are made to defray the charges of this vast establishment.

" Thus, the income of the King's Bench arises from :—

" 1st. The fees on committal and discharge, amounting together to upwards of one pound, which, unless paid, the prisoner is detained, though all his debts are settled.

" 2d. The rent of the rooms, which is one shilling per week each on 240 rooms. If not paid, the wretched inmate is threatened to be ejected, to find a lodging where he can.

" 3d. Fees on granting the rules, which are, I believe, according to the amount of the debts; £8 for the first hundred, and £4 for every succeeding hundred; and the fees on term bonds.

" 4th. A guinea and half, I believe, upon every butt of porter, stout, and ale, admitted into the prison, which amounts to a very large sum.

" In addition to these is the rent, or gratuity paid by the persons who keep the coffee-room, who are not prisoners, but who are nevertheless allowed a room opposite, which they sublet; the rent of the *public* kitchen—I believe £50 per annum.

" By a mistaken law, spirituous liquors are not allowed to enter *civil* as well as criminal prisons; though why a person who is merely unfortunate, and not guilty of any offence, should be subjected to this privation I know not:—the *malaria* occasioned by the high walls; the damps and the underground cells and stone floors of the Fleet; and the habits and necessities of hundreds who are annually taken to the Bench, may render an occasional glass absolutely requisite, yet such indulgence is by law prohibited, though not in practice. In both prisons there is not a single prisoner who does not know where to apply for spirits when he wants any.

" In the King's Bench prison, where the law is more rigidly enforced than in the Fleet, the risk is much greater, and the punishment more certain. The consequences of the prohibition are to make the spirits twice as dear, and a hundred times more deleterious, than they can be got outside. Both in the *Bench* and the *Fleet, spirits of wine, vitriol,* &c. have been frequently found in rooms in which a search has been made; while the purposes to which these maddening incentives were intended to be applied could not be mistaken. No wonder, therefore, that so many instances of desperation, recklessness, and premature death occur, the results of the foolish attempt to prevent people getting that which they are determined to have, and which they might have good, wholesome, and cheap, but for this enactment.

" Whilst some persons *do* get in their spirits most unaccountably, and in large quantities too, others are most severely punished if they attempt to introduce the smallest portion, and for the most necessary purposes. Some months ago, a poor prisoner, being afflicted with a strangury, desired a little girl to procure for him on the outside a quartern of gin; the girl did so; she and the gin were seized at the gate—the purpose for which it was procured was mentioned—no matter—the gin was not suffered to reach its destination: the child was sent for a month to the House of Correction, and the miserable prisoner died. Whether a jury of prisoners, as is customary, sate upon the cause of his death, I know not, but, even were that the case, I can easily believe that few prisoners, unless very bold men, not having the fear of the strong room before their eyes, would venture to return a verdict that

38.

might lead to unpleasant consequences,  The consequences of allowing the turnkeys to search whoever they please on entering the prison, to discover concealed spirits, are sometimes both gross and disgusting.  Women are sometimes subjected to this revolting ordeal.  Elegantly dressed females may, perhaps, escape ; but it is a fine treat to a set in the lobbies to thrust their hands about a poor and pretty girl's person, and gloat over her blushes and feelings of shame.  There are one or two turnkeys who are incapable of such conduct.

" I would hint to Mr. Hume, Mr. Buxton, and other benevolent legislators, that there would be no harm in moving for a return of the number of persons who have died, during the last five years, in the King's Bench and the Fleet, or shortly after they have been removed from either of them, and the average number of persons confined during that time in these prisons.

" The self-degradation engendered by long imprisonment, is horribly exemplified in many persons who have been lately, or are now, in the King's Bench and Fleet prisons.  As to the former, the case of poor Meredith has been mentioned in the Herald ; but there is another individual in the Bench, who is son or nephew to a most distinguished literary person of the last century, and who has been himself a gentleman, a scholar, and a polished citizen. What is he now?  Besotted by habitual intoxication, he is a moving mass of filth—a locomotive nuisance—the scoff of the lowest and the vilest—not to be approached, even when sober, but by carefully keeping to the windward ; yet, in this horrible condition, does a scholar and a gentleman of former times verge towards the grave, a filthy, besotted old man.

" I could multiply instances of this nature, but one is sufficient to show the influence of imprisonment for debt, in producing self-degradation.  Let us next see its consequences upon the morals of many who are its victims.

" What I may consider as the climax of imprisonment for debt, as exemplified in the prison, is the utter depravation of morals to which it leads.  Imprisonment, as I have before said, produces idleness and want ; idleness, again, engenders gaming ; and want, theft.  There is a set of abandoned wretches in this prison (of whom poor Meredith was one of the victims) whose principal object is to discover what new comer possesses money—to induce him to play —to cheat him ; and, if that cannot be speedily or sufficiently done, to pick a quarrel, throw down the lights, and rob him of every farthing he has, before he leaves the room.  If he afterwards complain, they laugh at him, and tell him there is no redress to be had in the prison.

" A new comer is surprised, especially in term time, by the frequency with which the common crier is called upon to advertise different articles as lost, and offer a reward to the finder.  It would appear at first sight, that people within a prison, who had little to lose, were infinitely more careless than people without ; but a little reflection, and the invariable addition to the reward, soon puts another light upon the matter. The notice the crier vociferates is as follows :—' Lost, from No.      in          , last night, (a great coat): whoever has found it, and will bring it to the crier, shall receive ten shillings' reward, and *not* ONE QUESTION *asked.'*

" The strong room is liberally enough awarded to individuals, however respectable, who attempt to recreate their idle and unhappy hours by a little harmless mimicry of a popular election—but to the midnight gamester, cheat, and robber, it has no terrors.

" While we have such specimens of roguery within the walls, to one another, it can scarcely be expected that there are more honest feelings to their creditors outside. In fact, while imprisonment lessens the ability of the debtor to pay, it is sure, in a still greater degree, to lessen his inclination. There are two clubs, called, I think, ' Harmonic Societies,' held during different nights in the week, at the ' Coffeehouse' and ' Brace,' the places for the sale of beer in the Bench, at which many prisoners, having nothing to do, will assemble to while away their time, in listening to the songs and drinking the toasts. What sort of lessons in honesty and morality they may learn at these places, may be gathered from a song that is frequently, if not constantly sung, detailing the mode of taking the benefit of the Insolvent Act, by prisoners pawning their goods, committing perjury, and cheating their creditors ; and by drinking a standing toast, to the following effect :—

" ' May our opposing creditors be taken ill on Monday, get worse on Tuesday, send for a doctor on Wednesday, take to their beds on Thursday, be given up on Friday, die on Saturday, and go to h—, &c., on Sunday !'

" Neither a prisoner's wife nor his children are allowed to sleep in the Bench, however long he may be confined there—they may be scattered by the winds of heaven, widowed and fatherless, without food or shelter ; but *a gentleman*, who can afford it, may easily get ladies inside. Many of the females who *were* resident in the prison, belonged to the class of those who humble themselves beneath the honour of their sex. Nothing is more easy than to get *them* in—the paramour causes his mistress to be arrested and removed by a Habeas to the Bench, which being done, the cohabitation is easily effected.

" Call a prison a ' College,' indeed !—If it be a college, it certainly is one in which the Prince of Darkness is principal professor—and the various vices the sciences that are taught. A student here may take a degree in artifices, if not in arts—and learn, if not to extract the cube root, to extract the ' root of all evil.' In point of dissipation and debauchery, indeed, among the majority of those who, by hook or crook, can ' raise the wind,' the College of Banco Regis is nearly as bad as its brethren on the banks of the Cam and the Isis. To use the metaphor of an Irish orator, many a simple countryman who goes into it, ' pure as the mountain snow, may come out hardened, in dishonesty and debauchery, as the mountain adamant.'*

" It was well observed by Dr. Johnson, in the Idler," continued the gentleman, "that ' the misery of goals is not half their evil; they are filled with every corruption which poverty and wickedness can generate between them; with all the shameless and profligate enormities that can be produced by the impudence of ignominy, the rage of want, and the malignity of despair. In a prison, the awe of the public eye is lost, and the power of the law is spent: there are few fears; there are no blushes. The lewd inflame the lewd; the audacious harden the audacious. Every one fortifies himself as he can against his own sensibility; and endeavours to practise on others the arts which are practised on himself; and gains the kindness of his associates by similitude of manners.

" ' Thus, some sink amidst their misery, and others survive only to propagate villany. It may be hoped that our law-givers will at length take away from us this power of starving and depraving one another: but, if there be any reason why this inveterate evil should not be removed in one age, which true policy has enlightened beyond former time, let those whose writings form the opinions and the practices of their contemporaries, endeavour to transfer the reproach of such imprisonment from the debtor to the creditor, till universal infamy shall pursue the wretch whose wantonness of power, or revenge of disappointment, condemns another to torture and to ruin, till he shall be hunted through the world as an enemy to man, and find in riches no shelter from contempt.

" ' Surely, he whose debtor has perished in prison, though he may acquit himself of deliberate murder, must at least have his mind clouded with discontent, when he considers how much another has suffered by him; when he thinks on the wife bewailing her husband, or the children begging the bread which their father would have earned. If there are any made so obdurate by avarice or cruelty, as to revolve their consequences without dread or pity, I must leave them to be awakened by some other power, for I write only to human beings.' Such are the just opinions of the learned, moral, and philanthropic Dr. Johnson; who urged, on all occasions, a revisal of the Law of Arrest. He, from the number of his acquaintances, made himself master of all the vices committed in our prisons, and of the folly, to say the least of it, of confining persons for debt. I have been told," continued the gentleman, that he wrote another essay, besides the one which appeared in the Idler, as also a descriptive poem on this subject; but I never saw either. *Apropos*, a gentleman lent me yesterday, *an Elegy, written in the King's Bench Prison*, giving a true picture of this place. It was written by one of our most favourite dramatists, and appeared in a little work, called ' Prison Thoughts, by

* See Morning Herald, June, 1828.

a Collegian.' It is a parody on Gray's celebrated Elegy in a
Country Church-Yard :—

> The turnkey rings the bell for shutting out,
>     The visitor walks slowly to the gate ;
> The debtor chum-ward hastes in idle rout,
>     And leaves the Bench to darkness, me, and fate.
>
> Now fade the high-spiked wall upon the sight,
>     And all the space a silent air assumes !
> Save where some drunkard from the Brace* takes flight,
>     And drowsy converse lulls the distant rooms.
>
> Save that from yonder Strong Room,† close confined
>     Some noisy wight does to the night complain
> Of Mister Jones, the marshal, who, unkind,
>     Has, by a week's confinement, check'd his reign.
>
> Within those strong-built walls, down that Parade,
>     Where lie the stones all paved in order fair,
> Each in his narrow room by bailiffs laid,
>     The new-made pris'ners o'er their caption swear.

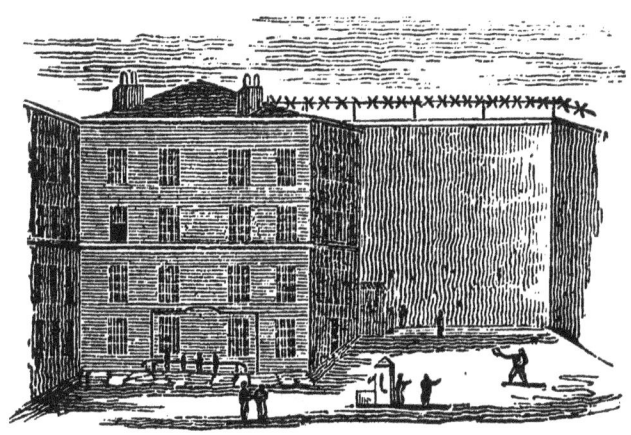

\* The Brace :—

A sort of under-tap, in the interior of the Bench, in which porter is sold by
authority of the marshal, to the debtors.

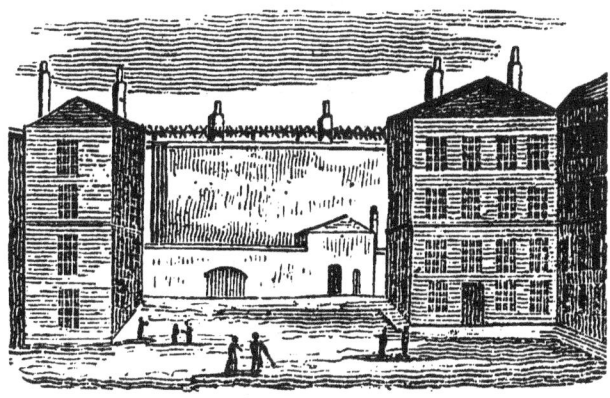

† The Strong Room :—

A solitary place of confinement for such as break the rules of the prison.

The gentle morning bustle of their trade,
  The 'prentice, from the garret overhead,
The dapper shopman, or the busy maid,
  Will never here arouse them from their bed.

For them no polish'd Rumfords here shall burn,
  Nor wife uxorious ply her evening care;
No children run to lisp their dad's return,
  Or climb his knees, the sugar-plums to share.

Oft did the creditor to their promise yield,
  As often they that solemn promise broke;
How jocund did they drive the duns a-field!
  Till nick'd at last within the bailiff's yoke!

Let not ambition mock their heedless fate,
  And idly cry, their state might have been better;
Nor grandeur hear with scorn while I relate
  The short insolvent annals of the debtor.

The boast of heraldry, the pomp of pow'r,
  All wealth procures, its being to entrench,
Await alike the writ's appointed hour:
  The paths of spendthrifts lead but to the Bench.

Nor you, ye proud, impute to these the fault,
  That they are here, and not at large like you,
That they have bills at tailor's, and wine vault—
  Bills that, alas! have long been over due.

Can story gay, or animated tale,
  Back from this mansion bid us freely run?
Can honour's voice o'er creditors prevail,
  Or flatt'ry soothe the dull cold ear of Dun?

Perhaps in this confined retreat is shut
  Some heart, to make a splash once all on fire:
Skill, that might Hobhouse to the rout have put,
  Or loyally play'd Doctor Southey's lyre.

But prudence to their eyes her careful page,
  Rich in pounds, shillings, pence, did ne'er unroll;
Stern creditors repress'd their noble rage,
  And froze the genial current of their soul.

Full many a blood, in fashion an adept,
  The dark, lone rooms of spunging-houses bear
Full many a fair is born to bloom unkept,
  And waste her sweetness, none know how or where.

Some Cockney Petersham, that with whisker'd cheek
  Once moved in Bond Street, Rotten Row, Pall Mall,
Some humble Mrs. Clark for rest may seek,
  Some Burdett, guiltless quite of speaking well.

The applauses of admiring mobs to gain,
  To be to threats of ruin, prison, lost;
To see they have not spent their cash in vain,
  And read their triumph in the Morning Post.

That lot forbade; nor circumscribed alone
  Their growing follies, but themselves confined;
The bailiff grimly seized them for his own,
  And turnkeys closed the gates on them behind.

The struggling pangs of conscious truth to hide,
  To quench the blushes of ingenuous shame,
The King's Bench terribly pulls down our pride —
  For high or lowly born, 'tis all the same.

Far from the city's mad ignoble strife,
  They still retain an eager wish to stray;
They hate this cool sequester'd mode of life,
  And wish at liberty to work their way.

And on those walls that still from duns protect—
  Those fire-proof walls, so strongly built, and high,
With uncouth rhymes and mis-spelt verses deck'd,
  They ask the passing tribute of a sigh.

Their names, their years, writ by th' unletter'd muse
  The place of fame and brass-plate fill up well;
And many a lawyer's, too, the stranger views,
  With pious wishes he may go to hell.

For who, to dumb forgetfulness a prey,
  His pleasing anxious liberty resign'd,
To Banco Regis bent his dreary way,
  Nor cast one longing lingering look behind.

On some one out, the prisoner still relies,
  Some one to yield him comfort, he requires;
E'en from the Bench the voice of nature cries,
  E'en though imprison'd, glow our wonted fires.

For thee, who, mindful of the debtor's doom,
  Dost in these lines their hapless state relate;
If chance by writ or capias hither come,
  Some kindred spirit may inquire thy fate.

Haply, some hoary bailiff here may say,
  " Oft have we watch'd him at the peep of dawn,
But, damn him, still he slipp'd from us away,
  And, when we thought we had him, he was gone.

" Where Drury Lane erects its well-known head,
  And Covent Garden lifts its domes on high,
Morning and noon and night we found him fled,
  Most snugly pouring on us passing by.

" On Sundays, ever smiling as in scorn,
  Passing our houses, he would boldly rove;
We gave his case up as of one forlorn,
  And for his person pined in hopeless love.

" One morn we track'd him near th' accustom'd spot
  Along the Strand, and by his favourite she,—
Another came; yet still we caught him not,
  But, on the third, we nabb'd a youth,—'twas he.

" The next, with warrant due, we brought our man,
  Snug to the Bench, here all the way from town:
Approach and read the warrant (if you can),
  You may a copy get for half a-crown."

## THE WARRANT.

Here rests his head, in " seventeen and one,
    A youth to fortune aud to fame well known.
But tradesmen trusted and began to dun,
    And Mister Sheriff mark'd him for his own.

Great were his spendings, he naught put on shelf,—
    To send a recompense law did not fail :
He gave his cred'tors, all he had—himself,.
    He gain'd from them (all he abhorred) a gaol !

No further seek his doings to disclose,
    Or draw his follies from this dull abode,
(Here he'll at all events three months repose),—
    Th' Insolvent Act may open then a road.

" Perhaps, sir," said Mentor, " one of the most remarkable events in the history of the King's Bench Prison, and which seemed fully to develop the real manners of its inmates, was the humours of the *Mock Election,* which took place in July, 1827, and from which ceremony Mr. Haydon painted his celebrated picture that was exhibited in Picadilly, and is now in the King's Gallery, his Majesty having purchased it for £500.

" Mr. H., in his explanation of this picture, says ' Nothing, during the last year, excited more curiosity than the mock election, which took place in the King's Bench Prison ; as much from the circumstances attending its conclusion, as from the astonishment expressed that men, unfortunate and confined, could invent any amusement at which they had a right to be happy. At the first thoughts, it certainly gave one a shock to fancy a roar of boisterous merriment in a place where it was hardly possible to imagine any other feelings to exist than those of sorrow and anxiety ; but, on a little more reflection, there was nothing very unprincipled in men, one half of whom had been the victims of villany, one quarter the victims of malignity, and, perhaps, not the whole of the remaining fourth justly imprisoned by angry creditors, in hope to obtain their debts ; it was not absolutely criminal to prefer forgetting their afflictions in the temporary gaiety of innocent frolic, to the dull, leaden, sottish oblivion produced by porter and cigars.

" ' I was sitting in my own apartment, buried in my own reflections, but not despairing at the darkness of my own prospects, and the unprotected condition of my wife and children, when a sudden tumultuous and hearty laugh below brought me to the window. In spite of my own sorrows, I laughed out heartily, when I saw the occasion. I returned to my room, and laughed and wept by turns. Here was a set of creatures who must have known afflictions, who must have been in want and in sorrow, struggling (with a spiked wall before their eyes) to bury remembrance in the humour of a farce ! flying from themselves and their thoughts to smother reflection ; though, in the interval between one roar of laughter and another, the busy fiend would flash upon ' their inward eye,' their past follies and their present pains! Yet, what is the world but a prison of larger dimensions? We gaze after the eagle in his flight, and are bound by gravitation to the earth we tread on; we sail forth in pursuit of new worlds, and after a year or two return to the spot we started from; we weary our imagination with hopes of something new, and find, after a long life, we can only embellish what we see; so that, while our hopes are endless, and our imagination unbounded, our faculties and being are limited, and, whether it be six thousand feet or six thousand miles, a limit still marks the prison."

"You must now leave, my friends," suddenly exclaimed the gentleman; "for hark—

'The turnkey rings the bell for shutting out.' "

Peregrine and Mentor accordingly immediately arose, the latter having previously furnished his friend with means for procuring his future comforts; and, with the promise of returning again in a few days, he wished him good night.

As Mentor and Peregrine were walking slowly to the gate, they agreed, on the morrow, to change the scene, and witness the ioyous

Doings on Board a Steam-Vessel.

On leaving the prison, "Once more," said Mentor, "thank heaven, we taste the sweet air of liberty! After the sight that we have seen, Peregrine, we may exclaim, with the inimitable Sterne,

39.                                    X

It is thou, O Liberty ! thrice sweet and gracious goddess, whom all in public and private worship ; whose taste is grateful, and ever will be so, till nature herself shall change ; no tint of words can spot thy snowy mantle, or chymic power turn thy sceptre into iron : with thee to smile upon him, as he eats his crust, the swain is happier than his monarch. Gracious Heaven ! grant me but health, thou great bestower of it, and give me but this fair goddess, Liberty, as my companion, and shower down thy mines, if it seem good unto thy divine Providence, upon those heads that are aching for them !

> ' Oh Liberty ! how fair thy angel face,
> Which gives to every thing a double grace.
> How wretched he who lives and is not free,—
> For show'rs of gold I would not part with thee ;
> For, nothing Fortune gives or takes away,
> Could for thy loss, sweet Liberty, repay !' ”

On their way homewards, Peregrine asked his friend the name of the place they were in ? " St. George's Fields," replied Mentor. " And do you call these streets *fields* ?" said Peregrine. " Yes the land all about here is still so denominated. The building of Westminster and Blackfriars' bridges first contributed to effect the amazing change which, within the comparatively short period since their erection, has taken place.

" The name of ' Fields,' before that, was strictly appropriate, as a designation for all the lands hereabout, for  , considerable extent, and had been so for ages. To omit, for a moment, a description of its very ancient state, we may observe that, in the long view of London and Westminster, from Lambeth, by Hollar, takes in the reign of Charles II. the whole space of land from Lambeth town to Bankside (including St. George's Fields) appears nearly unbuilt on. Lambeth Marsh, through which the Westminster Road now runs, is shown completely walled in, and most of the grounds eastward of it divided into fields and inclosures. The whole extent, for a considerable way north and east, is thickly wooded, and a few scattered dwellings only occasionally peep out from among the trees. Some particulars in this curious view are worthy of remark. Before St. George's Fields, on the Lambeth side, lies the tract of land on which the Asylum and its neighbourhood, as well as Tower Street, Melina Place, &c., now stand ; opposite is the way formerly called " the Back Lane," now Hercules Buildings, a retired country lane ; and further west, Lambeth Palace-Gardens (as formerly laid out), the entrance to Lambeth town, with Norfolk House, Carlisle and Bonnor Houses, and a number of other interesting objects ; and in the distance, eastward, appears part of the Borough, the wall of Winchester Park, Bankside, &c.

" Before the settlement of the Romans, St. George's Fields, and all the ground next to the Surrey side of the river, as far as to the hills of Camberwell and Dulwich, is thought by antiquaries to have been a swamp, inundated by the tides, and, at low water, a

sandy plain; and that it was not inhabited until that people had
fixed themselves in England, when it is supposed that they improved it by banking against the Thames, and by draining. It is
also generally admitted that the Romans had a station in some
part of St. George's Fields, though on what particular spot is not
ascertained; and the abundance of Roman antiquities discovered
here, as mentioned by Dr. Gale, Dugdale, and other old writers,
as well as the great quantities recently found on cutting the new
sewer by Bethlem, leave no doubt of this. It is not stated when
all this ground was first drained, but various ancient commissions
are remaining, for persons to survey the banks of the river, here
and in the adjoining parishes; and to take measures for repairing
them, and to impress such workmen as they should find necessary
for that employment; notwithstanding which, these periodical
overflows continued to do much mischief; and Strype (edit. of
Stowe's Survey) informs us that, so late as 1555, owing to this
cause, and some great rains which had then fallen, all *St. George's
Fields* were covered with water.

"Several of the names of particular plots of land, during the unbuilt state of St. George's Fields, are transmitted to us in old
writings, as well as some amusing notices of certain places here,
or in the neighbourhood, in scarce books. Among others, the
parish records of St. Saviour's mention Checquer Mead, Lamb Acre,
and an estate denominated the Chimney Sweepers, as situated in
these fields and belonging to that parish; as also a large laystall,
or common dunghill, used by the parishioners, called St. George's
Dunghill. The open part, at the beginning of the last, and end of
the preceding century, like Moorfields, and some other void places
near the metropolis, was appropriated to the practice of archery,
as we learn from a scarce tract published near the time, called
' An Aim for those that shoot in St. George's Fields.' The Dog
and Duck, within memory, of infamous notoriety, in the plan of
London, as fortified by Parliament, is marked as a ' Fort with four
half bulwarks,' the remains of which are described by De Foe, in
his Tour through Great Britain (1724), who says, the moat of the
Fort then existed, and was called the *Ducking Pond.* Hercules
Buildings, near the Asylum, took its name from an inn called the
Hercules, which was opened just after the completion of Westminster Bridge, and the forming of the roads to it. It had large
stables, and a spacious garden, but, not answering, was sold in 1758
and the Asylum built on its site. The figure of Hercules, which
belonged to it, lately stood over the door of the public-house
opposite. This ground was granted by Edward VI., in 1551, to
the citizens of London, by the description of ' one close of ground,
late in the possession of John Billington, lying in Lambeth Marsh,
late part of the possession of Charles, Duke of Suffolk."

"Before the building of Westminster Bridge, the only communication between this large district (including Lambeth), and
Westminster, was by the ferry-boat near to Lambeth-Palace gate,

which belonged to the archbishops, and was granted by Parliament, under a rent of twenty-pence. On opening the bridge in
1750, this ceased, and £2,205 was given to the See of Canterbury
as an equivalent. Previously to that time there were two considerable inns in Lambeth town, for the reception of travellers, who,
arriving in the evening, might not choose to cross the water at such
an hour, or who, in case of bad weather, might prefer waiting for
better.

" It has been disputed among antiquaries, whether Canute's
Trench was cut through this neighbourhood, or rather, whether the
trench here (for it seems agreed that there was something of the
kind) was the work of that monarch or not. Dr. Gale supposes
it to have been of Roman origin, and afterwards to have been
altered by Canute, and says that the remains of it, when London
was fortified by the Parliament, in 1642, were used for a like
purpose to that intended when it was first constructed. This was
one of the ancient curiosities of St. George's Fields, and Dr.
Stukeley supports the opinion, that the Roman roads, leading to
different parts of the kingdom, met here, as the centre of so many
*radii ;* but that, when London became considerable, Stangate
Ferry became partly disused, and hence so little of the road that
ran through these fields, towards the Lock Hospital, Deptford,
&c. then appeared; and he thinks it probable that its materials were
long since dug away to mend the highways. Upon this road many
antiquities have also been discovered, particularly a *Janus,* in
stone, which was in the possession of Dr. Woodward.

" From being, in former times, so frequently overflown by the
tides, as we have stated, the whole, nearly, of the ground here-
abouts remained for ages of little value, and, in fact, it has only
become valuable since the building of the bridges. It was long
before a proper mode of draining was adopted, and in this state it
only afforded, at times, a scanty pasture for the cattle of those
who occupied lands that were out of the reach of the floods.
Right of common diminished from time to time, by the erection of
new buildings, but the value seems to have been considered so
small, that scarcely any interruption was given to these encroachments. But in the case of public buildings, the authority of Parliament was generally procured for extinguishing such claims. At
length (viz. in 1810), in consequence of the great improvements
which were taking place, the city obtained an act of Parliament
for the total extinguishment of such rights. Since this, the New
Bethlehem Hospital, the Blind School, and other public buildings
have been erected; streets of handsome houses are forming on the
sites of poor ones which have been destroyed, and the whole, by
the building of Waterloo and Southwark bridges, is concentrating
into an immense and populous neighbourhood.

" Thus you see, my friend," said Mentor, " how this overgrown
metropolis has increased, is increasing, and will continue to increase, until it becomes in splendour and magnitude a second Rome;

when, like that once mighty city, it will decay, and the inquisitive traveller will be told, while walking o'er its ruins—

' Here once imperial London stood !' "

Peregrine and Mentor having now arrived at the end of Briage Street, they wished each other good night, and repaired to their homes, agreeing to meet the following morning, to join in an " Excursion to the Nore," one of the present fashionable modes of blending pleasure with charity, although it does not reflect much credit on the cockneys, to think they cannot " *do* a little bit of charity," without having, what they *call*, some pleasure for it.

Accordingly, the next morning, our heroes were punctual to their time of meeting at Billingsgate, where they found many non-descript dandies in waiting for their several parties, crawling about backwards and forwards, like so many straggling caterpillars in a grove of sycamores.

Mentor and his friend bent their course to the Tower Stairs, where their ears were astounded with the bawling of hundreds of watermen plying for fares ; at length, after having " run the gauntlet" of these noisy fellows, they descended the stairs, when a jolly grizzled-pated charon hands them into his boat, whips off his jacket, whereon was a badge, to tell whose fool he was, bids them surlily to trim the boat, and, after much rioting and confusion, being in danger of having their sides stove in, with the sculls of the innumerable contending watermen, and of being capsized, at length puts them safe on board the steamer, when, in a few minutes after, a fellow bawled out, in the voice of a stentor, close to the ear of Peregrine, " let go the wharp !" which so astounded him, that he almost lept over-board. " *About*" the steamer goes, and Peregrine, for the first time, found himself in the bosom of the " King of Floods"—the river Thames, which is, as Denham has well described it—

" Though deep, yet clear ; though gentle, yet not dull ;
Strong without rage ; without o'erflowing, full."

The first group that presented itself to the eyes of Mentor and his friend, was a party of fat landladies, every one of them as slender in the waist as a Dutch skipper's stern, and looked like a litter of squab elephants. On the steamer gently gliding down with the tide, one of these ladies took a " long last lingering look behind," and sighed out, " It will be a some hours before we see that dear monument again." " Ah!" said a surly old cynic— The monument, indeed ! '*tis a monument* to the city's shame, the orphan's grief, the Protestant's pride, and the Papist's scandal, and only serves as a high-crowned hat, to cover the head of the old fellow who shows it." " I beg," retorted one of the landladies, whose face resembled the sun on a frosty morning, " nothing may be said against the poor orphans, as this excursion is for their benefit." " Avaunt, woman," replied the cynic ; " I want no converse with you," and instantly arose from his seat, and went to the fore part of the vessel.

" At this instant, Mentor espied an acquaintance, who was an eccentric fellow, a bachelor, and a disciple of Malthus; to whom he introduced Peregrine as a young gentleman from the country, anxious to witness all that was worthy of observation in the metropolis.    After the usual salutations, this curious fellow, Mr. Francello, began immediately, without ceremony, to give Peregrine some gratuitous advice ; especially to beware of the women, and never to think of matrimony; "for," said he, " if men and women were not so foolish as to get married, there would be no orphans, and then we should not be obliged to have taken this trouble to-day." " I am satisfied in my own mind," replied Peregrine, " that, with respect to matrimony, it is either a heaven or a hell, which ever the parties choose to make it." " Did you hear this gentleman, madam ?" said Peregrine to a lady sitting by the side of him.   " He's not a man, sir, but a beast that totters on two legs." " And pray, madam," replied Francello, bitterly feeling the reproach, "what is woman ?"   " Ah! what is she !" retorted the lady, "how should *you* know ?"   " But I *do* know," replied Francello :—

' What's death ? what's life ?  Oh, painted vanity !
What *is* she ?  She's a freak—a froth—a bubble—
A humour bred of drink and salt provision.
What is she ?  She's a painted bit of clay,
That falls to pieces, like a lump of sugar
(Save that she's not so sweet).  Her white and red
Are kept in health by murdering crowds of sheep,
Into whose skins she creeps, and cries ' Adore me !'"

" You're as cold as adamant," said the lady, looking at poor Francello most contemptuously, " and not worthy of notice," and immediately left him and joined her party.

A jolly-looking tradesman, who had listened to the conversation, and heard Francello's remarks with seeming disgust, addressed himself thus to Peregrine : "I tell you what, young gentleman," said he—

" ' Woman is
In infancy, a tender flow'r,—
   Cultivate her ;
A floating bark, in girlhood's hour,—
   Softly freight her.

When woman grown, a fruitful vine,—
   Tend and press her ;
A sacred charge in life's decline,—
   Shield and bless her !"

" Ah, woman, indeed," said a seafaring gentleman ; " she's—

' Form'd in benevolence of nature,—
   Obliging, modest, gay, and mild ;
Woman's the same endearing creature,
   In courtly town and savage wild.

When parch'd with thirst, with hunger wasted,
   Her friendly hand refreshment gave ;
How sweet the coarsest food has tasted,
   What cordial in the simple wave !

Her courteous looks—her words caressing,
Shed comfort on the fainting soul:
Woman's the stranger's general blessing,
From sultry India to the pole.'"

When Mentor and Peregrine looked round to hear what Fran-cello had to say to these true quotations, they found he had sneaked off.

"Good heavens! cried Peregrine, with great earnestness and surprise, "there is the very girl that poor Julia Desmond relieved, and whom, I recollect, she told me she first knew by working with her at a fashionable dress-makers; but, on the account of the scanty pay, and falling-off of employment, she became, like poor Julia, 'a fallen creature.' But she looks well, and seems happy. Thank heavens! some of my money has been the means of producing happiness. I should like dearly to speak to her—but I will not: she does not recollect me, and I cannot make myself known to her, without harrowing up her feelings."

"I remember well what you told me respecting the girls that work at the dress-makers," said Mentor, "and of the true picture you gave me of that white slavery.* But I am glad to learn that, since that time, the subject has been taken up by several correspondents in that mighty engine, the Times newspaper. I have preserved all their communications, in my pocket-book, intending, some days ago, to give them you, but it escaped my memory; and, as we have a few minutes to spare, before the company begin their dancing, I will read them you. The correspondent Argus, says :—

"It is, I think, too notorious to need further confirmation from me, that milliners and dress-makers experience more hardships and privations, from the confinement and over-fatigue of eighteen or twenty hours' exertion every day for several months together, than is experienced by any other class of individuals in the metropolis, and, at the same time, receive proportionately less emolument, sympathy, and respect; though surely, from the natural delicacy peculiar to their sex (for I do not allude to man-milliners), none are more justly entitled to these advantages.

"'Those who do not think the subject beneath their notice would find, on inquiry, that many of the individuals of which this class is composed, are the scattered wrecks of fortune,—daughters of genius and affluence, nursed in the lap of plenty, but, by 'some alarming shock of fate,' for ever divided from a home no longer happy, if remaining;—many whose minds have been rendered more sensitive, and 'feelingly alive to each fine impulse,' by the practice of early virtue, and the effects of a liberal education, and whose manners and address bespeak the domestic calamity that doomed them to a life of celibacy and fatigue, for which slavery is only another name. But I will not enumerate or particularize the numerous ills which are the consequent, though not the necessary, concomitants

* See page 83.

of such a situation : these, with kind treatment from those for whom they sacrifice their health, may be, and often are, endured with cheerfulness and contentment, till exhausted nature sinks beneath the pressure, and early death (which every season annihilates its thousands) becomes not less desirable than it is inevitable.

" ' But how shall a sensitive female, at such a frightful crisis, bear to be insulted by those to whose opulence she is longer unable to add, and at an hour's warning turned out of doors, without a friendly asylum near ?   And what punishment were enough for such inhumanity ?   It may be doubted whether such brutality exists in a civilized nation.   Fortunately, such instances are rare ; but, disgraceful as it is, such an occurrence actually did take place a few days ago, attended with the most fatal effects, and the actors in the affair were deservedly censured by most of the daily and weekly journals, the leading features of which were,—The unfortunate individual (who, I think, was an apprentice), becoming, from excessive fatigue, so seriously ill as to be unable longer to pursue her almost ceaseless avocations, was removed to an adjacent hospital, where she ultimately died, and was buried, before her friends were made acquainted with the circumstances of her indisposition.'

" Another correspondent, under the signature of ' An Old Physician,' remarks, with great truth, ' I am quite convinced, if publicity were given to the privations and hardships which are endured by this class of individuals, something would be done to render their lives less wretched than that which thousands are compelled to lead at present.   Sincerely do I wish they had many such able advocates as your correspondent, and then surely, in England, happy England, some kind-hearted persons in the higher ranks of society—and many such, thank God, are to be found—would interest themselves in behalf of their suffering fellow-creatures ; and I can from experience safely affirm, few are more deserving of compassion than those in whose cause I am induced to take up my pen, which I have long wished to do, but have abstained from doing, as I always wrote with difficulty ; and I had great hopes that, in this age of liberality and improvement, when many of our greatest orators in both houses of Parliament are endeavouring to abolish slavery in far distant lands, where such a proceeding may be attended with great disadvantages, they would not have left entirely unnoticed those who spend a life of perfect slavery in their own native country, under their very noses, and for the purpose of attiring their rich countrywomen, most probably their own wives and relatives.   That something may soon be done to alleviate the sufferings of the poor, hard-worked, ill-paid, and unpitied milliners' apprentices, is my sincere prayer.'

" But," continued Mentor, " I am indeed delighted with the following remarks of Cosmopolite ; they speak volumes of truth. The English nation are too systematic in their charities—too cold, and too proud—and they seem really to imagine that no other people on earth are charitable but themselves : however, they are as inconsistent on this as on every other subject. But to proceed ; Cosmopolite says,—' I am sick to my soul of the constant twaddle about the charitableness of the people of this country, and the epithets of " happy England."

" ' There is no country in the world, and I appeal to the traveller, where the health, amusement, or happiness of the lower orders are so little thought of, cared for, or promoted, as in this same egotistical opinionated England. Nor is there any civilized place where the gratifications and amusements of the rich are more ably catered for, or more luxuriously promoted.

" ' I make these unqualified remarks, because it seems to me that the English sleep over their prosperity, wrapping themselves up in their proud system of exclusiveness, and blinded by self-satisfaction and the increasing sneers of their less refined, but acute neighbours, to which deep-rooted prejudice alone could subject them.

" ' The feelings clearly evident by these remarks, are called from me by some letters relating to the unhappy state of those hard-worked girls, the milliners' apprentices. The ladies,—the fashionable, the well-dressed, the charming, kind, and charitable, —are the real cause (do not wrong me, I dearly love the sex); but, owing to their constitutional thoughtlessness, they are the cause.

" ' A dress is wanted—say, for example, for the hortricultural *dejeuné,* a *fête* that it is well known will happen months before it really occurs. A lady must of necessity have a new dress, hat, or cap, for that particular occasion. Her numerous occupations, —viz. the paramount ones of calls, &c. and pursuits of equal importance,—drive the circumstance from her mind. Two days previous to the time her dress should have been finished, away she drives to her milliner, her orders are given, the dress must be ready for Saturday, the —, without fail, or it will be of no use whatever ; if it be not sent by the day, she will order her servants not to take it in. The consequence is, the mistress is obliged to comply : then the poor girls are desired to work day and night, to complete my lady's dress. Fifteen or sixteen hours in such cases are the utmost limits of their time. Pallid looks, sickly appetites, a physical action on their morals—for such is the case, and I appeal to the Old Physician if the derangement of the system from sedentary employment, without proper exercise, does not act physically, so as to endanger the morals,—are the painful results of the system. How often does it happen—I speak to the consciences of the fair sex—that an unnecessary delay or procrastination in the giving their orders occasions a necessity for an expedition that can only be accomplished by the working extra hours—not only extra, but unreasonable hours—not simply unreasonable, but unhealthy ones ? How often is a dress ordered to be ready for a particular Sunday by church-time, and the bedecked form offers her prayers

40.

to that Power for blessings which she, from the absence of thought,
has been an instrument in withholding, viz. health and content,
from the humble agent of her finery.

"'The English, no doubt, are a charitable people, and wish to
be thought so.   Charities are well supported, and wealth is not
wanting to further its ends; but the English are not a discriminating
race—they are prejudiced.   You must receive relief according to
their own way of applying it, and not from the broader principles
of humanity.   The exclusiveness of the age will be the national
bane.   Sympathy for our fellows will be blunted, if enjoyment is
made attainable by the poor.   The rich are envied, because they
alone possess the key to pleasure.   Open the door for harmless
and rational enjoyment, the rich will then not be envied, but admired, because they participate in common with the pleasure of a
people, but have, from their means, the power of benefitting their
fellows.   Envy would then fade into admiration, and ostentation
dissolve into real charity.'

"As a proof," continued Mentor, "of the truth of these assertions, a young girl, named Catharine Aram, aged only nineteen
years, died suddenly in July, 1828, who had been employed by
one of the fashionable dress-makers at the west-end of the town,
where it appeared, by the evidence before the coroner and jury,
that she had been obliged to sit up the whole of the night to finish
the dresses she was engaged upon; and where she frequently
worked eighteen hours out of twenty-four.   One of the jurors said
it was a notorious fact, that at almost all the principal dress-makers
at the west-end of the town, the apprentices actually worked day
and night, and even the Sabbath was devoted to labour, to satisfy
the tastes of ladies of fashion.   He considered some measures
ought to be immediately adopted to prevent young females from
such confinement.   He was of opinion that, had this poor girl been
allowed more exercise, she would have been still in existence;
and it was frightful to think human life should be sacrificed to the
whim of fashion."

"It would be well, sir," said a gentleman, "if, while so many
persons are strenuously striving to abolish the black slave-trade,
they would first put an end to the Bristish white slavery."

At this instant, poor Francello made his appearance upon
deck, and took his seat comfortably in the aft-part of the vessel,
expressing his surprise at the number of ships in the Pool.   "They
are nearly all colliers, my friend," said Mentor to Peregrine;
"and the amazing extent of the coal-trade in the port of London
may be imagined, when it is ascertained that, in one year, 6810
ships entered the pool, laden with coal, and that their cargoes contained the enormous quantity of 1,600,229 chaldrons and a half.
A history of coal and the coal-trade would form a very interesting
volume, and what is much wanted.   Upon a calculation, it is
supposed that, when all the deputy sea-coal meters are on duty,
no less than 2084 persons are daily employed in delivering coal in

the pool, from the ships to the barges, exclusive of the crews of the different vessels, which cannot be reckoned at less than between fifteen or sixteen hundred. This trade also gives employment to numerous watermen, and is the ' soul and substance' of the *coast* of Wapping; and very partially so, of the south side of the Thames. When the number of land coal-meters, and the coal-heavers, at the different wharfs, are taken into the calculation, together with the bargemen in the country barges, the barge-builders, clerks at the various counting-houses, the coal-market, &c., it is evident that the coal-trade alone finds employment for *ten thousand persons.*

" It is curious to watch the progress of the consumption of coal in London.

" In 1615, 30,000 chaldrons were imported into London.

" In 1708, 613,823 chaldrons.

" In 1798, 786,200 chaldrons.

" In 1826, 1,600,229 chaldrons.

" Anderson says that coal was first introduced into London in 1305; but I find from the city papers, that it was introduced in the reign of Henry III. (1216—72), when a portion of coal from every ship was sent in a small basket to the Lord Mayor, as a sample. Coal, in the time of Edward I. (1272—1307) was only used by dyers, brewers, &c.; and Richard II. published a proclamation, in 1398, forbidding the use of coal as a public nuisance.

" In 1563, the House of Commons passed a bill to restrain the carriage of Newcastle coal over sea.

" In 1642, Parliament published an ordinance, prohibiting wood-mongers, wharfingers, &c., from selling coal in London above 23*s.* per chaldron.

" In the household book of the fifth Earl of Northumberland, 1512, a record of a singular curiosity, equally throwing light on our ancient manners, and reflecting lustre on the great family whose extensive love of domestic economy it so minutely displays, mention is made of coal, which, it seems, they had not yet learnt to use by itself, for this reason—' because,' observes this authority, ' colys will not byrne withowte wodd.'

" In Harrison's description of England, prefixed to Holling-shed's Chronicle, edited in 1577, it says—' There are old men yet dwelling in the village where I remain, which have noted the multitude of chimneys lately erected; whereas, in their young dayes, there were not above two or three, if so many. When our houses,' continues he, ' were builded of willowe, then we had oaken men, but, nowe that our houses are come to be made of oake, our men are not only become willows, but a great many altogether of straw, which is a sore alteration.'

" When coal became somewhat in general use, great inconvenience was felt for the want of a proper person to *weigh* it; and accordingly the Lord Mayor of London was applied to, and he actually weighed the coal in *propriâ personâ*, and turned it over into the barges, he being the first sea-coal meter; and he continues the principal sea-coal meter to this day.

"In 1599 (41 Eliz.) the coal-trade increasing, an act was passed to regulate the office of coal-meter.

"In 1602, the sea-coal ship meters did not exceed ten.

"In 1662, they were increased to fifteen.

"In 1824, they were increased to one hundred and fifty-eight; at which number they now remain. I know many of these sea-coal meters well," continued Mentor; "and I am bold to say, without fear of contradiction, that, take them as a body, there are not more respectable officers in the city of London, or any where else; there are among them many who, by their talents and demeanours, would not disgrace any rank in society. Many on whom—

'Misfortune smil'd deceitful at their birth.'

Many who have been masters of thousands, but, by the vicissitude of trades, are not now so wealthy as they were; yet, amidst all the clashings and jarrings of their employment, they preserve an unsullied probity of character, that many in higher walks of life would fain enjoy. I don't know whether the city of London are proud of them as officers, but this I know, they ought to be. The reason I am so explicit to you on this subject, Peregrine, is, that doubtless you have read some of the slanderous paragraphs in the daily papers, inserted by interested rogues, in the hopes of lessening them in the estimation of government, of the corporation of London, and of the public in general. But to such dastardly calumniators, I can only say—

'Cease, vipers,—you bite against a file.'"

At this instant, the decks were ordered to be cleared, the band struck up, and the old and young, the handsome and the ugly, the straight and the crooked, all simultaneously, like a party of light-hearted Frenchmen, began to trip it on the light fantastic toe.

This pleasing and healthy amusement agreeably beguiled the time, while the vessel arrived at the Nore, when the company left off, and each party sat down in groups to their dinner; to which most of them did ample justice. The steamer then commenced its return to "Smoky London," amidst the bewailing of a dandy, at having his new coat spoiled by one of his party (accidentally, or on purpose, no matter which), pouring the remains of a giblet pie on it. "I hate," said Mentor, "a new coat: it is like a troublesome stranger that sticks to you most impertinently wherever you go, embarrasses all your motions, and thoroughly confounds yourself-possession. A man with a new coat on is not at home, even in his own house; abroad he is uneasy—he can neither sit, stand, nor go, like a reasonable mortal. All men o sense hate new coats, but a fool rejoiceth in a new coat. Without looking at his person, you can tell if he has one. *New Coat* written on his face; it hangs like a label out of his gaping mouth, there is an odious harmony between his glossy garment and his smooth and senseless phiz—a disgusting keeping in the portrait. Of all vile exhibitions, defend me from a fool in a new blue coat with brass buttons."

As the vessel had nearly reached the metropolis, Mr. Green ascended in the air, mounted on his pony, suspended in the place of a car. "This foolish exhibition reminds me," said Peregrine, of an exploit of some Frenchmen, in two balloons. I remember reading, in the New Annual Register (1808), of M. de Grandpree and M. Le Pique having quarrelled about Mademoiselle Tirevit, a celebrated opera-dancer, who was kept by the former, but had been discovered in an intrigue with the latter : a challenge ensued. Being both men of elevated mind, they agreed to fight in balloons, and, in order to give time for their preparation, it was determined that the duel should take place that day month. Accordingly, on the 3d of May, 1808, the parties met at a field adjoining the Tuilleries, where their respective balloons were ready to receive them. Each, attended by a second, ascended his car, loaded with blunderbuses, as pistols could not be expected to be efficient in their probable situations. A great multitude attended, hearing of the balloons, but little dreaming of their purpose : the Parisians merely looking for the novelty of a balloon race. At nine o'clock the cords were cut, and the balloons ascended majestically, amidst the shouts of the spectators. The wind was moderate, from the N. N. W., and they kept, as far as could be judged, within about 80 yards of each other. When they had mounted to the height of about 900 yards, M. Le Pique fired his piece ineffectually : almost immediately after, the fire was returned by M. Grandpree, and penetrated his adversary's balloon ; the consequence of which was its rapid descent, and M. Le Pique and his second were both dashed to pieces on a house-top, over which the balloon fell. The victorious Grandpree then mounted aloft in the grandest style, and descended safe with his second, about seven leagues from the spot of ascension."

"I remember, when I was a boy," said the sea-faring gentleman, "what a number of depredations were committed on this river Thames. There were then *river pirates*, who plundered ships and small craft in the night. *Night plunderers* consisted of watchmen, who formed into gangs of five or six each, and used to lighten small craft. The *light horsemen* used to confine their depredations to West India ships. The *heavy horsemen* used to go on board, either by connivance or under the pretext of selling some articles, having peculiar dresses, which had pockets all round, and bag-bladders and pouches affixed in various parts, which they filled with sugar, coffee, cocoa, or any portable article ; and in the night they would plunder more largely, and were rowed by what were called *game watermen*, who were always ready to receive what was thrown to them. The *mud-larks, scuffle-hunters, cope-men, &c.* are now, like the others, nearly extinct.

" Mr. Colquhoun, whose meritorious exertions contributed to the establishment of a regular Thames Police, estimated that about ' *eleven thousand* persons, inured to habits of depravity, and long exercised in all the arts of villany,' were engaged in this species of plunder; and that the amount of their depredations upon floating property was upwards of five hundred thousand pounds sterling, annually.

" The extent and constancy of the depredations were so notorious as to call loudly for some special interference, and hence the ' Marine Police Establishment,' which was opened at Wapping New Stairs. Its importance will be admitted, when it is recollected that in this single river are engaged 13,444 ships and vessels, which discharge and receive in the course of a year *three millions of packages,* many of which contain very valuable articles, greatly exposed to depredations, not only from the criminal habits of many of the porters, labourers, &c., but from the temptations to plunder arising from the confusion unavoidable in a crowded port, and the facilities afforded in the disposal of stolen property.

" The West India trade suffered annually to the amount of £232,000, the East India, £25,000, the United States, £30,000, and the coal trade alone £20,000.

" So successful was the system pursued at the Thames Police Office, that, in the first year, the savings to the West India merchants alone was upwards of £100,000, and to the revenue more than half that sum."

Mentor thanking the gentleman for his company, and wishing those around him good evening, he and Peregrine took boats and landed at Wapping; where a boat's crew had just come on shore with their hammocks,* in search of those land debaucheries which the sea denies them, looking such wild, staring, uncouth animals, so rude in their demeanour, and so mercurial in their actions, that a woman could not pass by them but they fell to sucking their lips like so many horse-leeches.

A sailor is, indeed, as Sir Thomas Overbury says, " a pitched piece of reason, caulked and tackled, and only studied to dispute with tempests. He is part of his own provision, for he lives ever pickled; a fair wind is the substance of his creed, and fresh water the burden of his prayers. He is naturally ambitious, for he is ever climbing out of sight; as naturally he fears, for he is ever flying; time and he are every where, ever contending who shall arrive first; he is well winded, for he tires the day, and outruns darkness; his life is like a hawk's, the best part mewed, and, if he lives till three coats, is a master; he sees God's wonders in the deep, but so that they rather appear his bedfellows than stirrers of his zeal; nothing but hunger and hard rocks can convert him,

---

* The natives of Brazil used to sleep in nets, composed of the rind of the hamack-tree, suspended between poles fixed in the ground; and from that the sailor's hammock is derived.

and then but his upper deck neither, for his hold neither fears nor
hopes; his sleeps are but reprievals of his dangers, and, when he
awakes, 'tis but next stage to dying; his wisdom is the coldest
part about him, for it ever points to the north, and it lies lowest,
which makes his valour every tide o'erflow it; in a storm, it is
disputabte whether the noise be more his or the element's, and which
will first leave scolding; his keel is the emblem of his conscience:
till it be split he never repents, and then no farther than the land
allows him.   His language is a new confusion, and all his thoughts
new notions; his body and his ship are both one burden, nor is
it known who stows most wine, or rolls most,—only the ship is
guided; he has no stern, and barnacle and he are bred together,
both of one nature, and, it is feared, one reason; upon any but a
wooden horse he cannot ride, and, if the wind blows against him,
he dare not; he swarms up to his seat as to a sail-yard, and cannot sit, unless he bear a flag-staff; if ever he be broken to the
saddle, 'tis but a voyage still, for he mistakes the bridle for a
bowling, and is ever turning his horse's tail; he can pray, but it
is but by rote, not faith, and, when he would, he dares not, for his
brackish belief has made that ominous.   A rock or a quicksand
pluck him before he is ripe; else he is gathered to his friends at
Wapping.   Such," said Mentor, " is the character of a sailor of
the seventeenth century.   They are now dwindling into a maukish,
puritanical, sighing, grunting set of drivelling psalm-singing sons
of—— (you remember what Lord Cochrane called his commander.)
The bold, open, generous, eccentric Bristish sailor is now nearly
extinct: one of the blessed effects of modern improvement."

"I cannot but reflect," said Peregrine, " on the unhappy lives
of these sea-water eccentrics, who are never at home but when
they are at sea, and always are wandering when they are at
home, but never contented but when they are on shore: they are
never at ease till they have received their pay, and never easy till
they have spent it.   And, when their pockets are emptied by
their landladies (who cheat them of one half, if they spend the
other), as a father is by a son-in-law, who has beggared himself to
give him a good portion with his daughter.

"These sons of Neptune were not long on shore, before they were
surrounded by plenty of tawdry trulls, dancing to a Scotch bag-
piper, in a public-house where were a party of coal-heavers, who
were drinking the fine of a gallon of beer, from a brother labourer,
who had had the misfortune of falling off a barge into the water.   "It is
too bad," said Peregrine, " for a poor fellow to pay a fine for being unfortunate."   " It is a custom observed among them," replied Mentor, " some time ago, a man, while working out a barge laden with
coals at Queenhithe, had the misfortune to slip off the plank into
the river.   His companions, on hearing the splash in the water,
ran to his assistance, and instantly succeeded in getting hold of
his jacket, but, instead of immediately dragging him out, they barely
kept his head above water, and began vociferating ' beer, beer.'

The man in the water in a short time endeavoured to speak, but had no sooner opened his mouth, when a wave, owing to his head being kept so low, gently glided down his throat, and prevented him; he was then allowed to stand up, the water being at the spot about four feet deep, but not to get out, and, as well as the water in his throat would allow, bawled out 'beer.' His black companions, on hearing him mention the word 'beer,' immediately assisted him in getting into the barge, and the whole gang of them shortly after repaired to the Farnham Castle, in Trinity Lane, and ordered the landlady to send in a gallon of beer. On inquiring into these curious proceedings, it turned out that the coal-heavers had a standing rule, that, if any man falls overboard, he is to be fined a gallon of beer; but, as many of them, after being safely got out, have refused to comply with the rule, they now keep the unfortunate fellow in the water till he gives his consent, by calling out 'beer,' when they take him out, proceed to a public-house, and drink a gallon at his expense."

On the return of Mentor and Peregrine homeward, near Billingsgate, they heard the praying, singing, and brawling of a sailor-looking mendicant preacher, holloaing to a rabble of crack-brained followers, who were fools enough to listen to his specious oratory. And near the same spot, was a drunken fiddler, scraping away to a party of vulgar swearing trulls and their flashmen, who afforded mirth to plenty of by-standers, some of whom were laughing at the fiddler's audience, and some at the preacher's eloquence. What a place for the worship of God!

Among the crowd was a fellow, with some watch-stands for sale, which appeared as if made of marble, and they particularly attracted the attention of Peregrine, who, believing the vender, thought they were manufactured of alabaster: he was about giving the sum demanded, when Mentor informed him there was much deception in them, for they were made of nothing else but *rice.* "Well, then," said Peregrine, "as I am rather thirsty, I suppose I may safely purchase some of these Orlean plums—there can be no deception in them: see what a beautiful bloom is on them!" "Very beautiful, indeed," replied Mentor, "and very natural, is it not? Why, this *beautiful* bloom is manufactured—it is artificial: they take the plums, breathe on them, and then dip them in powdered blue (such as laundresses use), and that gives them the appearance of fresh bloom!" "Ah!" said Peregrine, "London is the school for a man to finish his education in."

They had scarcely reached the top of Thames Street, when they saw a crowd assembled round a decent-looking man, who was telling them how he had been *done:* he took a seat on the *dickey* of one of the stages, a few miles out of town, and in a few minutes afterwards, a queer-looking fellow got up, and seated himself close beside him: when, after riding about a couple of miles, he alighted. On the coach arriving at the foot of London Bridge, he felt in his waistcoat pocket, and found all his money was gone. "That," said a by-stander, "is not so bad as I was served; for the other day, when I alighted from the stage, I found one of my coat-pockets cut off, in which was a pocket-book, containing, fortunately, only some private memorandums. People ought to be careful, when they ride in the dickies, not to let the flaps of their coats hang over the railing; for the thieves get behind, at dusk, and cut off the pockets."

"But come," said Peregrine, "let us make haste home, for I am tired; and to-morrow we will visit poor Farmer Metcalfe, in the Fleet Prison."

Accordingly, the next morning, they made good their engagement with the farmer; and, while talking with him, they were surprised by the hurraing and music which proceeded from the parade. "Come with me," said the farmer "and you shall witness the Doings at the

Chairing the Cook of the College,

an officer of some consequence and emolument in the Fleet Prison, as he is elected annually. The following is a copy of the bill of one of the candidates:—

"'CANDIDATE FOR THE KITCHEN.

"' J. M'C—— respectfully announces to the ladies and gentlemen of the College, that it is his intention to offer himself a Candidate to fill the situation of Cook; and he trusts, if successful, from his long experience in the Baking business, he shall be found to give ample satisfaction.

41.                                    Y

" ' *J. M'C*—— *begs to add, that he has a wife and a family of children depending on him for support; that he has been an inmate of the College some time; and, from peculiar circumstances, he is likely to continue so a considerable time longer.*'

" ' *Fleet, Dec.* 1826.' "

" It is consoling, really," said Mentor, " to think the prisoners can be allowed to indulge themselves in such a manner as we have witnessed : it must tend much to rub off the rust of care, and beguile a few hours in innocent mirth.

" This prison," continued Mentor, " is, I believe, the most ancient in London; formerly called *Prisona de la Fleet*, or the Queen's Gaol of the Fleet.  I find that Richard I. confirmed to Osbert, brother to William Longshampe, chancellor of England, and elect of Ely, the keeping of his Gaol of the Fleet at London, so called from the fleet, or water, running by it.

" King John gave to the Archdeacon of Wells the custody of his gaol of the Fleet.

" About 1586, the prison was let and set to farm to the victualling and lodging of all the house and prison to John Harvey, and the other profits to Thomas Newport; and these men used to extort so much from the poor prisoners, whereupon they petitioned the lords of the council, and a commission was granted for the relief of the Fleet.

" The Fleet Prison was afterwards used for the reception of the prisoners committed by the council-table, then called the Court of the Star-Chamber : this assumed authority being found an intolerable burden to the subject, it was dissolved in the sixteenth year of the reign of Charles the First.

" After the passing of this act, the Fleet Prison became a prison for debtors, and for contempt of the Courts of Chancery, Exchequer, and Common Pleas only.

" The Fleet was consumed in the fire of London; and, during its rebuilding, the prisoners that were therein at that time were removed to Cerron House, in South Lambeth, which was made into a prison; and, upon the finishing of this place, the prisoners were brought back, and it has ever since continued as a prison.

" Jacob Mendez Solas, a Portuguese, was the first prisoner for debt that ever was loaded with irons in the Fleet : he was turned into the dungeon (a place like those the dead are buried in), without chimney or fire-place—neither paved nor boarded. Capt. John Mackphedris, a merchant, was another victim of the warden Bambridge.  These atrocities came to the ears of Charles, who declared that they might raise their walls higher, but that there should be no prison within a prison.

" In 1728, a Mr. Edward Arne, father of the celebrated Dr. Arne (then 81 years old), while in the Fleet Prison, was suddenly seized, and forced into a damp, nauseous, and unwholesome dungeon, without fire or covering; where, through excessive cruelty for the space of six weeks, he lost his senses and died. John Huggins, the warden of the Fleet, was tried for murder, and acquitted; but James Barnes, his agent, was commited, but he fled. Various other cruelties, committed by these wretches, gave rise to the committee, which the humane Thompson has thus celebrated in his Winter :—

' And here can I forget the generous band,
    Who, touch'd with human woe, redressive search'd
  Into the horrors of the gloomy gaol ?
  Unpitied and unheard, where misery moans;
  Where sickness pines; where thirst and hunger burn,
  And poor misfortune feels the lash of vice.
  While in the land of liberty, the land
  Whose every street and public meeting glow
  With open freedom, little tyrants raged;
  Snatch'd the lean morsel from the starving mouth;
  Tore from cold wintry limbs the tatter'd weed;
  E'en robbed them of the last of comforts—sleep,
  The free-born Briton to the dungeon chain'd,
  Or, as the lust of cruelty prevail'd,
  At pleasure mark'd him with inglorious stripes;
  And crush'd out lives, by secret barbarous ways,
  That for their country would have toil'd or bled.
  O great design ! if executed well,
  With patient care, and wisdom-temper'd zeal.
  Ye sons of mercy ! yet resume the search ;
  Drag forth the legal monster into light,
  Wrench from their hands oppression's iron rod,
  And bid the cruel feel the pains they give.
  Much still untouch'd remains : in this rank age
  The toils of law (what dark insidious men
  Have cumbrous added to perplex the truth,
  And leng then simple justice into trade)
  How glorious were the day ! that saw these broke,
  And every man within the reach of right.'

"Of the old prison," continued Mentor, " we know but little of its architecture; but the body of the present prison is a handsome, lofty, brick building, of a considerable length, with galleries in every story, which reach from one end of the house to the other: on the sides of which galleries are rooms for the prisoners. All manner of provisions are brought into this prison every day, and cried as in the public streets. Here, also, is kept an ordinary : with a large open area for exercise, enclosed with a high wall.

"The following lines you will find in a poem called the 'Humours of the Fleet :'—

' Near Fleet's commodious market's miry verge,
  This celebrated prison stands, compact and large,
  Where, by the jigger's * more than magic charm,
  Kept from the power of doing good or harm,
  Relenting captives inly ruminate
  Misconduct past, and curse their present state :
  Though sorely griev'd, few are so void of grace,
  As not to wear a seeming cheerful face ;

* The door-keeper.

Y 2

In drinks or sports, ungrateful thoughts must die,
For who can bear heart-wounding calumny?
Therefore, cabals engage of various sorts,
To walk, to drink, or play at different sports:
Here on the oblong table's verdant plain,
The ivory bull bounds and rebounds again;
There at backgammon two sit *tête a tête*,
And curse alternately their adverse fate;
These are at cribbage, those at whist engag'd,
And as they lose, by turns become enrag'd:
Some of a more sedentary temper, read
Chance-medley books, which duller darkness breeds;
Or politics in coffee-room, some pore
The papers and advertisements thrice o'er.

Here, knotty points at different tables rise,
And either party's wondrous, wond'rous wise:
Some, of low taste, ring hand-bells, direful noise!
And interrupt their fellow's harmless joys;
Disputes more noisy now a quarrel breeds,
And fools on both sides fall to loggerheads:
'Till, wearied with persuasive thumps and blows,
They drink as friends, as though they ne'er were foes.

Without distinction, intermix'd is seen,
A 'squire quite dirty, a mechanic clean:
The spendthrift heir, who in his chariot roll'd,
All his possessions gone, reversions sold;
Now, mean as once profuse, the stupid sot
Sits by a runner's side, and damns his lot.

Beneath a tent some drink, and some above
Are slily in their chambers making love:
Venus and Bacchus each keep here a shrine,
And many votaries have to love and wine.'

" I have read," said Peregriue, " with great attention and plea-sure, several papers in the Morning Herald, *on the present state of the two great debtors' prisons of the kingdom—the King's Bench and the Fleet,* by a Prisoner for Debt, in which the author says—

" 'There is an individual at this moment in the Fleet, who is a fit representative of the victims of " contempts of Chancery." Poor wretch! He is like Edgar in King Lear. His madness, however, is not feigned, and the tattered coat, or rather spencer, that hangs loosely from his shoulders, is not put on for deception; yet, like " mad Tom," it may almost be said of him,

> Rats and mice, and such small deer,
> Have been his food for many a year.'

" ' In the callous and joyless mirth of the prison he is bantered about his property, and his prosecutor, who is, I believe, a female; and the name by which he is known, and to which he answers, is, " the Lord Chancellor!" When broken victuals are placed be-fore him, not knowing, like Captain Dalgetty, when and where he is to get more provender, he swallows them with inconceivable rapidity, and is ready, in return, to fetch and carry water, &c., for his benefactors. With a shipwrecked mind—in tatters—in desti-

tution, he lingers out his youth and manhood (for he is in the prime
of life), and with his look of vacuity, his arms folded across his
breast, and the holes in his wretched garments, he seems to be
inwardly muttering—

'Poor Tom's a-cold.'

" 'The scenes in this prison sometimes beggar description.
Every prisoner, before he can get a chum ticket, entitling him to
4s. 6d. per week, or the half of a room, must pay his entrance-fee,
amounting to about 30s. Many are utterly destitute when they
enter, and cannot raise 30s. in the world—these persons must
either go to the 'poor-side,' or take a room in the 'fair,' and in
either place give at least 2s. 6d. per week for the loan of a bed,
out of 3s. 6d. per week, which they are allowed as 'county money,'
on swearing they are not worth £10 in the world; thus they have
just 1s. per week to provide food, fire, and clothes ! But sometimes, too, this 'county money' is not paid, on the ground that the
funds are exhausted, in which case they are left for weeks to beg,
steal, or perish !

" ' I forget—there is " the grate," they can " declare on the grate."
But what does the reader think the grate is ? Why that little place,
in which through thick iron bars, during the middle of each day,
you may see a human form, and hear a voice saying " pity the poor
prisoners," from a room looking into Fleet Market; which, I have
been told by those who have been in it, is, during the winter and
rainy seasons, so unhealthy, that even few young men can be in
it for an hour or two a day, without imminent hazard to their lungs
and limbs.

" ' Nor are the rooms in the " fair" much better, if at all. They
are underground. Many feet beneath the surface of the damp
earth. They have a light somewhat like that of cellars. The
entrance to them, however, is much worse, being, in midday,
" darkness visible." You must grope to find each door, and the
air, of which there is no current, is from one end, within a few feet
of the high wall. Many are the prisoners who have died here, or
who have been taken from here to die.

" ' The last death I heard of in the " fair" was a most melancholy
one. A poor old man, upwards of eighty, who had been a respectable tradesman at the west end of the town, sacrificed himself
for a near relative. It was necessary, to prevent worse consequences to that relative, that he should acknowledge a signature to
be his, which was not; but which acknowledgement cast him,
in his old age, into the Fleet Prison. At first he came to the
" poor-side," but, as his venerable and loving wife, or, as he used
to call her, " his ain kind dearie, oh !" offered to make him more
comfortable by sharing his imprisonment, he took a room in the
" faire." Few were the weeks the faithful couple dwelt together !
The damp, the bad air, or, it may be, want, in addition (for he
" could not steal, and to beg he was ashamed"), laid the affectionate woman low, and she went from a cell in the heart of the city

of London to "a house not made with hands, eternal in the heavens."

" ' The " poor-side," to which a prisoner must go who has not money to pay his entrance-fees, is composed of four rooms, I think, each containing about seven spaces for bedsteads, divided by a slight partition of wood, extending to near the ceiling; these rooms have two windows each, for air and light; and, in each room, seven prisoners may be mingling their healthy or unhealthy breath nightly—some coming in at one hour, others at another—some sober and quiet, others drunk and noisy, and these four rooms, by the way, being just opposite the high wall of the prison, at a distance of a few feet, and immediately above the common sewer, and the common temples for a nameless purpose.

" ' Yes, in London the city of charities; in London, the capital of " the envy and admiration of surrounding nations;" in London, where a thousand voices are daily talking about " Freedom," " Independence," " the British Constitution," &c., in the very heart of the " heart of England," there are human beings, for no crime, incarcerated, and not being able to pay thirty shillings, are obliged to reside in the " fair," or in the " poor-side" of the Fleet Prison, with an uncertain three-and-sixpence per week, two-and-sixpence of which must be paid for a bed, and the remaining shilling is all they have to spin out the thread of life as well as they can! Talk of the " march of intellect," indeed! when will the march of intellect, or of benevolence and enlightened legislation, march into the King's Bench and Fleet prisons?

" ' It certainly is a great advantage that the Fleet possesses beyond the bench, in allowing the wives and infant children of prisoners to abide with them. Nothing is so horrible as the separation exacted by the regulations of the Bench, nor is any thing so consolatory as this privilege allowed in the Fleet.

" ' Yet the poor prisoner can have no wife or child to abide with him, save in the cells of the fair, unless he pay his entrance-fees. Without thirty shillings :

" Nor wife, nor children, more shall he embrace,
Nor friends, nor sacred home—

" ' One poor fellow, who had been a postmaster and stamp-distributor in a country town, was brought into the prison utterly destitute. After he had been there three weeks, a bone, such as a dog would scarcely thank you for, was offered to him by a fellow-prisoner; he took it with tears of gratitude, saying he had not tasted animal food since he had been within those walls. His wife was confined to her bed, and his children were starving. At last his prospects brightened with the shoes he got to brush.

' " Another, a sensible man, who had moved in good society, took a large dose of laudanum a few months ago, to release him from the poor-side and his woes at once. He was saved from an immediate death, to linger out what I should call a daily one. How can it be otherwise? How can a respectable man live on three shillings and sixpence per week, and endure the society—

the compulsory society, by night of the habitual drunkard, the blas-
phemer, the debauchee, the heartless and impudent blackguard, to
which he may be subjected by being on the " poor side ?"

" ' When you enter the lower rooms of the Fleet, you respire with
a thickness that is palpable. Nor is this surprising : the Fleet is
in the centre of London, and occupies altogether a space, the inside circumference of which is, I think, only about the ninth part
of a mile. The upper rooms, in point of light and air, are not
bad ; but, during the summer months, the heat to which they are
exposed, and the vermin which that heat calls into life, are intolerable. The vaulted roof, when you enter the " hall," or first
gallery, and the dim light while the sun is blazing in meridian
glory on the outside, give an appearance of a place in which you
would think owls and bats alone would love to live. To a sensitive imagination, these scenes would recall the forcible language
of Dante's " *Inferno*"—

*"All hope abandon, ye who enter here !"*

" ' I do not wish to instance the numerous cases which, both
in the Fleet and the Bench, show the horrible demoralization
caused by imprisonment. Were I to do so, I should be compelled
to lift up a veil that, for the sake of the beings behind it, had better never be withdrawn. Those, after long imprisonment, who once
moved in the foremost ranks of society—were brilliant among the
gay, dignified among the high, erudite among the learned, what
are they now ? Who is that youth in the Fleet, whose hollow
cheeks and sunken eyes—whose tattered coat and haggard look,
speak of utter and reckless dissipation ? Is he the once glittering
and fashionable ——— ? Who is that old gentleman, with whom
the name of the deity is sport, and his greatest condemnation a
by-word ; who carries his God about him, and drinks it to the
destruction of his appetite, his peace, and his morals ;—is he the
son of the celebrated, the almost immortalized ——— ? Who is
that wild and desperate ruffian, whose language is that of an
Indian savage—a cannibal ; who could tomahawk, " kill, and eat,"
his victim ? Is he the once classical, erudite, and highly-respected
——— ? Alas ! it is so ; but the dark and merciful waves of
oblivion will pass over them ; and their creditors may feast their
voracious revenge like Zanga—*they have damned both body and soul.*

" ' But there is another, and a different class, with whom the
good may sympathize without shrinking. There are, in the Fleet,
victims of the chancery system, whom even oppression and privation have not weaned from the charities of our better nature.
There is one, at least, who cannot forbear sharing his last shilling
with the destitute—who has given bread to the hungry, and
*wholesome liquor* (not ardent spirits) to the weak and pennyless.
" Verily I say unto ye, he shall not go without his reward."

" ' And the Warden, with very limited means, is ready to listen
and relieve. Even those who have wronged him—deeply and ir-
revocably wronged him, he has, on application, though smarting
beneath the wrong, pitied and succoured.' "

"'I have known the Warden some years," said Mentor; "and have had many opportunities of witnessing his kind and charitable disposition. I followed him one day along St. Paul's Church-Yard, over Blackfriars Bridge, and I did not see one beggar but what he relieved, and that in the kindest manner; and I could give you numerous other instances of his charity, were it necessary."

"I thank, you, my friend," said Peregrine, "for your interruption; it has given me a little breathing-time. But, to proceed: our author continues thus:—

"'I shall merely add to this catalogue of evils, the common modes of irritation resorted to by vindictive creditors of sending their victims backwards and forwards, from term to term, from the Bench to the Fleet, and from the Fleet to the Bench. Many a miserable debtor has been harrassed to death, and put to vast expense, in this way. It is an annoyance of easy accomplishment, and of most frequent occurrence. They have nothing to do but get up two actions—one in the Pleas or Exchequer, and one in the King's Bench, and at every process in each they can send their victims like a shuttlecock, from one to the other, destroying his domestic prison arrangements, or putting him to the heavy expense of a 'speedy habeas.' Why is this? why do the courts permit it? why cannot declarations, &c. be served upon prisoners where they are, without this annoyance and expense?'

"The following remarks," continued Peregrine, "are worthy of every consideration:—

"'It now only remains to be shown, or rather discussed, whether it would not be better to abolish the practice of imprisonment for debt altogether than to attempt to remedy its abuses?

"'I propose to view its consequences under three heads: 1. *Upon the Debtor;* 2. *Upon the Creditor;* 3. *Upon the Community.*

"'1. The effects upon the debtor are, first to disable him, and next to disincline him, to pay his debts. Whatever means he possessed while at liberty, these means must, in most cases, be greatly abridged during confinement. He cannot see after his own affairs, but must trust to the agency of others. If he be embarrassed, but in a train to relieve himself from his embarrassment, his object is effectually frustrated; as, from the circumstance of his imprisonment becoming public, all are ready to sink and none to save him. If he be poor, he cannot labour, but is driven to the alternative of feeding upon what property of his creditors he has left, or starving—he must be dishonest or die. The creditor who elects to seize his person cannot seize his goods; hence those goods may be, and are, generally, sold at a ruinous loss, or pledged, to provide for the debtor in prison.

"'As the debtor is thus *driven* to dishonesty, he begins to habituate his mind to that which he cannot help. Instead of viewing his creditors, the merciful as well as the unmerciful, as persons to whom he is bound by a *moral obligation,* he considers that they have ceased to have any claims upon him, save those which they can satisfy by *legal force.* In this feeling he is en couraged by what he sees around him. He sees numbers relieved monthly under the Insolvent Act, who have defrauded their creditors of every farthing, by committing what to him, and to most of the others who hear them, is *notorious perjury*. He hears the songs and toasts before alluded to, and must have a mind strongly fortified by a disinterested sense of moral duty, not to be debauched by the almost universal example.

" ' Nor is *dishonesty* the only vice which imprisonment engenders. Dissipation and gaming next follow. Man cannot be idle. Imprisonment says *he shall*—Nature says *he shall not*. The mind must be employed—otherwise, as Byron poetically observes, like a sword undrawn, " it eats into itself, and rusts ingloriously." Defoe has well described Robinson Crusoe's longings for even a savage associate; and Baron Trenck risked his life in the prison of Magdeburg for a mouse. So, in the King's Bench and Fleet, men must do something—and what do they?—what do most of them, but—

" *Game* by night and *tipple* all the day ?"

" ' I speak not again of the sufferings of those who are poor and honest—I speak not again of those who, after having given up " their all," are thrust into a gaol to pine upon 3*s*. 6*d*. per week, afforded but not assured by the county, or extracted by a legal process from the inhuman creditor after execution. I speak not again of sleeping upon inverted tables in the Bench with a score of associates, or being turned to the " poor side" or the " Fair" of the Fleet—I speak only of the moral consequences to the debtor ; and I am satisfied with having shown that the tendency of imprisonment for debt is, and must be, to the debtor, *dishonesty, dissipation, gaming*, and *desperation*.

" ' 2. Its consequences upon the creditor are nearly as bad—he loses his money and feeds his revenge. Is revenge a Christian virtue? Yet Christianity is " part and parcel of the law of the land"—that same law which allows its subjects to feast their revenge even to satiety !—to visit upon their miserable debtors, and upon the wives and children of their miserable debtors, the loss—it may be, of health, of morals, of society, and of happiness, to make up for the nonpayment of their goods ! Is it beneficial in a state to encourage such a spirit as this? Is it beneficial to the individual who indulges it? Is it calculated to fit him for better discharging his duties to his own family—his own country—his God? It cannot be.

" ' And then, in reference to his pecuniary interests, we have seen that imprisonment lessens the ability and lessens the inclination of the debtor to pay : the consequence, then, is, that, in the average of cases, the creditor *loses* by incarcerating his debtor—he loses, at all events, the money necessary for subsistence during his imprisonment—he loses the costs of law—he loses the value of those goods which are sold or pledged by his debtor—and he loses all that the disinclination of the debtor to pay, even when he has it in his power, can compel him to lose.

42.

" ' I know a striking instance of this latter evil. A gentleman of family was arrested for about £400, and removed to the Bench. Being able to command £200, he offered 10s. in the pound to his creditors, with his own security for the payment of the remainder in twelve months. This was refused; and, as he could not mend his offer, he remained in prison, living upon his £200. After being about eighteen months confined, a large property was bequeathed to him, unknown to his creditors: this property he declared he would enjoy in prison, rather than pay his creditors a farthing—he considered their claims cancelled by his long imprisonment. His friends remonstrated, but in vain. At last, one of them made an offer to his creditors, on his behalf, of *five* shillings in the pound: this was eagerly accepted by them, but utterly refused by him, until that friend informed him that he had made himself *personally responsible* for the amount. It was then paid as a debt of honour to the friend, but as a debt of constraint to the creditor. Such are the feelings of those upon whose minds a long imprisonment is allowed to operate.

" ' The only good which creditors expect from possessing the means of imprisoning their debtors, is the *terror* which such imprisonment is likely to excite; but, unfortunately, that terror is only for those who cannot pay—not for those who can. Men who have money, and who wish to keep it, can live very comfortably and very economically in a prison. They can command a room well furnished, for about a guinea per week, at the top of the building—they can have what wines and delicacies they choose—they can keep their mistresses, though they cannot their wives and their families; there is always *some* genteel society to be had; and, having the money of their creditors in their pockets, they can spend it in whatever manner they choose. Imprisonment has no terrors for them. But imprisonment is terrible to the good, the poor, and the honest—to those who love their wives and their families, and who would wish never to be deprived of their company—to the virtuous, whose daily prayer is " lead us not into temptation"—to the industrious, who cannot endure idleness—to the sober, who detest drunkenness—to the prudent, who like not gaming.

" ' 3. To the community at large the evils of imprisonment for debt are most seriously felt. Of course, as the community is made up of units, so, whatever affects those units severally, affects the whole community jointly. But, to the particular consequences to debtors and creditors of imprisonment for debt, must be added the force of those consequences, as examples upon society at large. A creditor who is in the habit of exercising a revengeful spirit, in locking up the unfortunate who cannot pay, cannot be expected to be untainted with the same spirit in his conduct to those who are not his debtors, but who are yet under his control; while a debtor, who has learned such lessons of roguery while in prison, and become idle from necessity, and dissipated from choice, cannot be expected to shake himself free from his vices and his fetters at once. What, then, is the inevitable result to the community, but an increase of evil and a decrease of good, in both cases?

" ' Holland is without imprisonment for debt, and yet the Dutch understand their interests as well as any nation on the earth. Scotland is comparatively without imprisonment for debt—yet who will doubt the sagacity of Sawney? Two of the most thinking and commercial people carry on their business largely and thrivingly without imprisonment for debt—why, therefore, cannot England? *Which loses the most money by their several systems? Let avarice himself be the judge upon this occasion, and determine whether or not imprisonment for debt ought to be continued.*' "

" There is certainly," said Mentor, " a vast deal of truth, sense, and feeling in these remarks; and they do the author great credit; but there must be some severe check on dishonest extravagant people. I was looking, the other day, among some papers, and I found an account of a foreigner, a prisoner in the Fleet, against whom a commission of bankruptcy had issued. He had been several times under examination before the commissioners, and had been desired to furnish the particulars of certain items which appeared in the statement of his accounts delivered to his assignees, one of which was as follows:—" Family expenses in the Fleet and at my dwelling-house for 219 days, for thirteen persons in and out, and different visitors, £1,888;" of which he gave the following remarkable explanation:

" ' EXPENSES IN THE FLEET.

| | £. | s. | d. |
|---|---|---|---|
| Sugar, tea, coffee, spices, chocolate, rice, cocoa, sago, &c., at the average of £1. 10s. per day . | 328 | 10 | 0 |
| Bread, flour, biscuits, &c., at the average of 10s. per day . . . . . . . . | 109 | 10 | 0 |
| Cheese, butter, eggs, &c., at the average of 12s. per day . . . . . . . | 131 | 8 | 0 |
| Meat, at £1. 1s. per day . . . . . | 229 | 19 | 0 |
| Poultry, at 5s. per day . . . . . | 54 | 15 | 0 |
| Beer and ale, at 10s. per day . . . . | 109 | 10 | 0 |
| Brandy, &c., at 10s. per day . . . . | 109 | 10 | 0 |
| Wine, 10s. per day . . . . . . | 109 | 10 | 0 |
| Confectionary, 6s. per day . . . . | 65 | 14 | 0 |
| Fish and oysters, 6s. per day . . . . | 65 | 14 | 0 |
| Vegetables, 5s. per day . . . . . | 54 | 15 | 0 |
| Coals and wood, 4s. 6d. per day . . . | 49 | 5 | 6 |
| Cooking in the kitchen, 1s. 6d. per day . . | 16 | 8 | 6 |
| Oils, soap, salt, &c., 11s. per day . . . | 120 | 9 | 0 |
| Fruit, 3s. per day . . . . . . | 32 | 17 | 0 |
| Tallow-candles, 1s. 6d. per day . . . | 16 | 8 | 6 |
| Family washing, 4s. per day . . . . | 43 | 16 | 0 |
| Sundries, 15s. per day . . . . . | 154 | 5 | 0 |
| | 1,802 | 4 | 6 |
| Deficiency not fully explained, but which must have been expended during my confinement | 84 | 15 | 6 |
| | £1,888 | 0 | 0 |

" These *moderate, reasonable,* and *probable* charges not appearing altogether to satisfy the minds of the commissioners, and the bankrupt pertinaciously declaring himself incapable of affording further elucidation, he was committed to Newgate.

" I have often thought," continued Mentor, " that a History of the Fleet would make a very interesting work; especially if it were possible to give the lives of the most eminent and remarkable characters which have been there incarcerated.   We have portraits of several persons who have been inmates of this celebrated prison, one of the last of whom was the celebrated Mrs. Cornely, who died here in 1797; not forgetting the notorious Johnson, the Smuggler, who made his escape out of the Strong Room, and, by means of a patent sash-line, descended safely into the street; and also the Frenchman who took *French leave,* and ascended by a rope ladder, and got over into the Belle-Sauvage Inn Yard; but the walls were not so high then as they are now."—" It would indeed," said Peregrine," be a truly interesting work, especially, as you say, *if* every inmate would give a *true* detail of his adventures."

Peregrine having now arranged his affairs with the farmer, took leave of him, and in a few minutes found himself, with his friend Mentor, once more in Fleet Market.   " But stop awhile," said Mentor to Peregrine, as in all probability, by the next time you come to London, this market-place will be annihilated; for, as it appears it is soon to be removed from its present site, in order to make way for a variety of projected improvements on the spot, it may be as well to give you a little of its history.   It arose about the year 1736, in consequence of the wish of the city to erect a mansion-house or residence for the Lord Mayor; and who, conceiving Stock's Market, near the entrance to Lombard Street, the most centrical situation for that purpose, obtained permission to arch over a part of the Fleet ditch, and transfer it thither.

" In a preparatory petition of the city, presented Feb. 26, 1733, to the House of Commons, by the sheriffs, several particulars are stated relative to the then nature of the site, which, connected with others known of it in remote times, are highly interesting.   It sets forth, that, by act of Parliament, 22d Car. II., entitled an Additional Act for Rebuilding the City of London, &c. the channel of Bridewell Dock, from the Thames to Holborn Bridge, was directed to be sunk to a sufficient level to make it navigable, under certain limitations therein prescribed, which was done; but that the profits arising from such navigation had not answered the charge of making; that part of the said channel, from Fleet Bridge to Holborn Bridge, instead of being useful to trade, as was intended, was filled up with mud, and become a common nuisance, and that several persons had lost their lives by falling into it; that the expense of cleansing and repairing the same would be very great, and a larger annual charge would be required to keep it in r pair, without answering the intent of the act; it therefore prayed that a bill might be brought in to repeal so much of that act as related to the said channel, and to empower the petitioners to fill up that part of it from Fleet-Bridge to Holborn-Bridge, and to convert the ground to such uses as they should think fit and convenient.

" 'The creek or channel alluded to had its entrance from the Thames, immediately below Bridewell, and reached as far as Holborn Bridge, at the foot of Holborn Hill, where it received into it the little river Fleet, Turnmill Brook, and another stream called Oldbourne, which gave name to that vast street. The tide flowed up as far as Holborn Bridge, and brought up barges of considerable burden. The Fleet river flowed in a valley, which may still be traced from this spot to Battle Bridge, near the Small-Pox Hospital, and though .t might once have been celebrated for its transparent waters (and " possibly some of our very, very early ladies," as a certain writer observes, " might have honoured it by smoothing and adorning their shining tresses from its surface)," it had several centuries back become occasionally so filthy as to be almost intolerable. So long since as 1290, we learn from the Parliament Rolls, that the White Friars, whose convent lay on its west side, complained of the putrid exhalations arising from Fleet River, which were so powerful as to overcome all the frankincense burnt at their altar during divine service, and even occasioned the death of many of the brethren. They begged that the stench might be immediately removed, lest they should all perish. The Black Friars on the opposite side, and the Bishop of Salisbury, who then lived in Salisbury Court, united in the same complaint.

" ' But little redress, however, appears at this time to have been obtained, for the great Henry Earl of Lincoln, who had his mansion somewhere near Shoe Lane, strongly reprobated the existence of this nuisance, in a Parliament held at Carlisle in 1307, in which he was joined by the city of London, who represented, by petition, that the course of the water which ran at London under the bridge of Holborn, and the bridge of the Fleet into the Thames, was wont to be so large and broad, and deep, that ten or twelve ships used to come up to the said Fleet Bridge with merchandize, &c., some of which ships went under the said Bridge unto Holborn Bridge; but that the course was then obstructed by the filth of tanners, and other stoppages made in the said water; but chiefly by the raising of a quay, and by diverting of the water, which they of the New Temple had made for their mills without Baynard's Castle, and praying for an inquest as to the same. And this was further explained by the commission itself for such inquiry; which states it to have been asserted, that the course of the water of Fleet, running down to the Thames, as well by dung and filth, as by the exhalation of a certain quay by the master, &c. of the New Temple, for their mills upon the Thames, near Castle Baynard, newly made, was so stopped up, that boats with corn, wine, faggots, and other necessaries, could not pass up as thentofore.

These representations occasioned the removal of the nuisances complained of, and we hear little of the Fleet River until the year 1606, when nearly £28,000 was expended in cleansing it. On this occasion, numerous Roman vessels, coins, and other antiques, were discovered, besides remains of the Saxons, in spurs, weapons, keys, seals, &c.; also, medals, crosses, and crucifixes, most of them supposed to have been flung in at different times of alarm.

" ' It changed, after this period, its nobler name of Fleet River for Bridewell Ditch, and Fleet Ditch, which designations were applied respectively to those parts of the stream which ran next Bridewell and the Fleet Prison, near each of which was a wooden bridge for foot passengers. And in this condition it continued until the small tenements, sheds, and laystalls, on the banks of it, were burnt down in the fire of London. A commission and inquiry to make it navigable to Holborn or Clerkenwell were moved for two years after this calamity by the celebrated William Prynne, in consequence of which, in the act for rebuilding London, just mentioned, it was enacted, " that the channel of the River Fleet to Holborn Bridge should be sunk to a sufficient level to make it navigable;" and it was accordingly finished and re-opened in 1673.

" ' By the directions of this act, a passage was to be left on each side the channel of not less than 100, no more than 120 feet wide. The stream itself was 2,100 feet long, and 40 feet in breadth; so that two lighters might meet, and pass each other without difficulty in any part of it; and the style of finishing it, with its roads, wharfs, bridges, &c. must have rendered, at first, the appearance of the whole extremely handsome. It was wharfed on both sides with stone and brick, laid with terras; had a strong campshot all along on both sides, above the brick wharfing, with land-ties in several places; and was guarded with rails of oak breast-high, above the campshot, to prevent danger in the night. The depth of water, at the head at Holborn Bridge, was five feet, at a five-o'clock tide, which is the slackest of all tides; but, at spring and other neap tides, there was much more water. It had wharfs on both sides its whole length, constructed in a uniform manner, with appropriate buildings, and four stone bridges; viz. Fleet Bridge, Holborn Bridge, a bridge facing Bridewell, and another, anciently called " Smalee Brigge," opposite the end of Fleet Lane. The Fleet and Holborn Bridges were of stone, before the fire, but were afterwards enlarged and beautified with iron gratings, and carved work in stone; those opposite Bridewell and Fleet Lane are described as " two fair bridges standing upon two stone arches, over the river; having two steps to ascend and descend on either side, and half a pace over the arches, all of Purbeck and Portland stone."

" ' That it became subsequently much neglected, we learn from the city petition in 1733; and though great sums of money are said to have been, from time to time, expended on this Stygian Lake, the task of keeping it clean appears to have been as fruitless as that of Sysiphus, for we find Pope, near the period mentioned, inviting his heroes in the *Dunciad* to its filthy stream:

> "Here strip, my children—here at once leap in;
> And prove who best can dash through thick and thin."

"By the act for converting the site into a market (6 Geo. II. c. 22.), the fee simple of the ground and ditch is vested in the Lord Mayor, commonalty, and citizens of London, for ever; with a proviso that sufficient drains shall be made in or through the said channel or ditch, and that no houses or shed shall be erected therein exceeding fifteen feet in height. The ditch was arched over with a double arch, with a common sewer, from Holborn to Fleet Bridge, and the market finished, and proclaimed a free market, on the 37th of September, 1737, of which the following notice is given in the *Gentleman's Magazine* for that month: "Friday, 30. The stalls, &c. in Stocks Market being pulled down, the Lord Mayor, &c. proclaimed Fleet Market a free market."

"'From a contemporary publication, describing it as then erected, it seems to have since undergone but very little alteration. "In the middle a long building is covered in, containing two rows of shops, with a proper passage between, into which light is conveyed by windows along the roof. Over the centre is placed a neat turret, with a clock in it. From the south end of this market-house, piazzas extend on each side of the middle walk to Fleet Bridge, for the convenience of fruiterers. At the north end are two rows of butchers' shops; and from thence to Holborn Bridge, a spacious opening is left for gardeners and herb-stalls. The whole market is well paved."

"'The north end has been of late years improved by a good pavement, and the erection of many convenient stalls, and the south by two handsome shops; but the centre part, with its pretty little spire, remains in its original state. This market is busy at all times, but particularly so in the fruit and vegetable seasons. Considerable quantities of earthenware are also sold within it, besides every kind of flesh and fish. The never-ceasing hammers of the undertakers, for which this spot was formerly noted, appeared at one time to have almost driven away the more quiet inhabitants, but there are now a variety of good shops carrying on other trades, at its sides.

"'The market ceases at Fleet Street; from whence Fleet ditch continued open till 1764, when the building of the new bridge at Blackfriars suggested the expediency of converting the remainder into an open street, and the archwork was continued (but with a single arch only) from Fleet-Bridge downward to the river, and Bridge Street and Chatham Place were built. This improvement, exclusively of other reasons, seems to have been in a great measure a matter of necessity, from the accidents passengers were liable to; for on Thursday, Jan, 11, 1763, we find from the papers, that " a man was found in Fleet Ditch, standing upright, and frozen. He appears to have been a barber, from Bromley in Kent; had come to town to see his children, and had unfortunately mistaken his way in the night, had slipped into the ditch, and, being in liquor, could not disentangle himself."

" ' Of the nature of the Fleet marriages, we may form a guess, from the complaint of a female correpondent to the *Gentleman's Magazine* for 1735, who deplores the many ruinous marriages that are every year performed in the Fleet, "by a set of drunken, swearing parsons, with their myrmidons, that wear black coats, and pretend to be clerks and registers to the Fleet, plying about Ludgate Hill, pulling and forcing people to some peddling ale-house or brandy-shop, to be married; and even on Sundays stopping them as they go into the church."—2,954 marriages (it appeared in evidence) were celebrated in this way, from Oct. 1704 to Feb. 1705, without either licence or certificate of banns. Twenty or thirty couple were sometimes joined in one day; and their names, if they chose to pay for it, were concealed by private marks. Pennant says, in walking by the prison in his youth, he had been often tempted with the question, *Sir, will you please to walk in and be married?* and that signs, containing a male and female hand conjoined, with the inscription, " *Marriages performed within*," were common along the whole of this lawless space. A dirty fellow invited you in. The parson was seen walking before the shop—a squalid profligate figure, clad in a tattered plaid night-gown, with a fiery face, and ready to couple you for a dram of gin or a roll of tobacco. The warden of the Fleet, and his register of marriages, made large gains from this trafic, and were convicted before a committee of the House of Commons, of forging and keeping false books. This abuse was the foundation of the present Marriage Act."

" ' The negotiation for the loan of £150,000 for the removal of Fleet Market from its present site, was closed on Wednesday, July 14, 1824. Alderman Sir Charles Flower took it. Bonds of £100 were issued, and the whole sum was taken by the baronet at $3\frac{1}{2}$ per cent. interest.

" ' The new market is to occupy nearly the whole of Shoe Lane, on one side; it is then intended to build a new prison in St. George's Fields, between the King's Bench and Bethlehem Hospital, and take down the present Fleet Prison; to remove most of the houses; to open, on the north side of the foot of Holborn Bridge, a grand street to Islington, to be on a line with the Obelisk in Bridge Street, Blackfriars. This, when completed, will certainly be one of the greatest and most useful improvements in the city since the rebuilding of the houses after the great fire.

"I cannot do better," said Mentor, "then now re ate to you the prelude scene to becoming an inhabitant of this immense fabric which is here most faithfully portrayed in

The Doings at a Meeting of Creditors.

"Being a loser of some amount by the thoughtlessness of a man in whom I placed the greatest reliance. We met at one of the City coffee-houses, and I was surprised at the very scanty number of creditors present, there being only, besides myself, an enraged Scotch baker, a fat boisterous butcher, and a contented tailor. The accounts he presented were by no means satisfactory, especially his bill for wines, which certainly excited the wrath of those present: he would not for some time give any reason why he was so indebted; at length, after much questioning, he acknowledged, very reluctantly, that he had the wines to treat his friends with, who were his wretched companions at the gambling-tables; and that his ruin was occasioned by frequenting the various 'Hells' at the west end of the town; in which horrid receptacles he had not only lost an independent fortune, but also some thousands of pounds of other persons' property: for he had not one single pound to share among his creditors. To imprison him was of no use; his friends refusing to assist him, knowing the uselessness of it; for his love for gaming was such, that he would even play for the coat on his back. We, therefore," continued Mentor, "agreed to give him a discharge, after much grumbling on the part of the baker and

43.

butcher. The poor, lost, wretched man, seemed truly thankful; telling us, that his miserable existence, he felt assured, would not be of long endurance; for all he had to depend on now, was to get a situation of a *workman* at one of the banks in the gambling-houses. These workmen," says Mentor, " are ruined men, who attend these places to do any disgraceful work, such as bilking or cheating, they are ordered to do.

" Yes, Peregrine, this infatuated man, by his love of gaming, reduced himself and the best of wives to a state of the most deplorable misery and want. I asked him, privately, how he could possibly lose so much property in so short a period? He replied; " A few months since I was introduced to one of the first ' Hells,' by a Colonel M., who took me in his coach; on alighting I was led into a most splendid room, where many persons were at supper; the magnificence of the room, the brilliant looking-glasses, in massive gilt frames; the lamps, wax candles; the many tables laid out with costly plate, and the happiness which *seemed* to reign throughout the whole of the place, quite enchanted me. I was soon invited to partake of some of the high-seasoned dishes, and their rich and savoury flavour gave the greatest zest to the champagne and claret, which passed round with rapidity. Well, Sir, by the time these worse than devils thought I was nearly intoxicated, and ripe for *bleeding*, cards were introduced. They took care not to give me enough to make me drunk, only to stupify me; for, as the proverb has it, ' When the wine is in, the wit is out,' and a man under its influence does many things which, if sober, he would shudder at. At first I refused, in which my friend, the colonel, as I *then* thought him, highly commended me, but I was so completely *set* by the gang, that I agreed to play a game at ' Blind Hookey;' and before I left my seat, I was a loser of fifteen hundred pounds! I little thought they were playing with concave and convex cards.' ' How do you mean, Sir,' said I. ' Why you see,' he replied, ' the *low* cards are *convex* at the sides, and *concave* at the top; the *high* cards *concave* at the sides, and *convex* at the top and bottom. When cards are wanted to be cut low, for ' blind hookey,' or you are cuttting simply for high or low, you take the cards across for low, and lengthways for high. Indeed it is almost impossible to manage a game at ' blind hookey' with fair cards. I now found, Sir, that peculiar spell on me which all are cursed with who once enter these dens of iniquity. The next morning, the transactions of the preceding night seemed to me as a dream. I thought of my loss; then heaped curses on the heads of the robbers; then swore I would never again visit such places; then I thought, by *one* more trial, I might regain what I had lost. In this state of indiscribable agitation I remained the whole of the day; at length, night came. I dressed; walked I knew not wither; at length found myself at the entrance of the ' Hell.' I shuddered back with horror, and hastened away, but in a few minutes all my virtue and philosophy forsook me, and I involuntarily once more traced my steps to the horrid den; into which I entered, and became in a few minutes reckless of myself, my wife, or my family. Well, Sir, to be brief : in six months I lost every farthing of my own, all my wife's property, all my furniture, and five thousand pounds of my creditors' ! And here I am, a lost, disgraced, wretched, and miserable man. Shunned and spurned by every one, *except my wife*—she forgives me, and tries, to the most of her power, to comfort me. O God! had I but had half the love and regard for her then, as she shows me now, I should be a happy man. For myself, I care not what becomes of me; but to see her want—and the little ones, too—' Here the poor fellow, overpowered by his feelings, left the room.

"Such, my friend Peregrine, are the cursed effects of gambling; and before you return to the country, I would strongly recommend you to take with you that invaluable work, *Life in the West.* Peruse it with attention; it will pay you for your trouble; and read it also to all your young friends who are about visiting London. It will be to them, indeed, an incomparable monitor.

"I have," continued Mentor, "some communications that appeared in the Times newspaper; and, as they cannot possibly be too much promulgated, or too widely disseminated, I will read them to you; they depicture, with such great truth, the enormities committed at the ' Hells' at the west end of the town. One of the communications commences thus :

### " ' TO THE EDITOR OF THE TIMES.

" ' SIR,—' Fishmongers' Hall,' or the *Crock*-odile Mart for gudgeons, flat-fish, and pigeons (which additional title that ' Hell' has acquired from the nature of its ' dealings,') has recently closed for the season. The opening and closing of this wholesale place of plunder and robbery, are events which have assumed a degree of importance, not on account of the two or three unprincipled knaves to whom it belongs, and who are collecting by it vast fortunes incalculably fast, but for the rank, character, and fortunes of the many who are weak enough to be inveigled and fleeced there. The profit for the last season, over and above expenses, which cannot be less than £100 per day, are stated to be full £150,000. It is wholly impossible, however, to come at the exact sum, unless we could get a peep at the black ledger of accounts of each day's gain at this Pandemonium, which, though, of course omits to name of whom, as that might prove awkward, if at any time the book fell into other hands. A few statements from the sufferers themselves would be worth a thousand speculative opinions on the subject; however, they might be near the fact, and they would be rendering themselves, and others, a vital benefit were they to make them. Yet some idea can be formed of what has been *sacked,* by the simple fact, that *one thousand pounds* were given at the close of the season to be divided among the waiters alone, besides the Guy Fawkes of the place, a head servant, having half that sum presented to him last January for a New Year's Gift. A visitor informed me, that one night there was such immense play, he was convinced a million of money was, to use a tradesman's phrase, turned on that occasion. This sum, thrown over six hours' play of 60 events per hour, 360 events for the night, will give an average stake of £2777 odd to each event. This will not appear very large when it is considered that £10,000, or more, were occasionally down upon a single event, belonging to many persons of great fortunes. Allowing only one such stake to fall upon the points of the game in favour of the bank per hour, full £16,662 were thus sacrificed; half of which, at least, was hard cash from the pockets of the players, exclusively of what they lost besides.

" ' Now that there is a little cessation to the Satanic work, the frequenters of this den of robbers would do well to make a few common reflections : that it is their money alone which pays the rent and superb embellishments of the house—the good feeding, and the fashionable clothing in which are disguised the knaves about it—the refreshments and wine with which they are regaled, and which are served with no sparing hands, in order to bewilder the senses to prevent from being seen what may be going forward, but which will not be at their service, they may rest well assured, longer than they have money to be plucked of; and, above all, it is for the most part their money, of which are composed the enormous fortunes the two or three keepers have amassed, and which will increase them prodigiously while they are blind enough to go. To endeavour to gain back any part of the lost money, fortunes will be farther wasted in the futile attempt, as the same nefarious and diabolical practices by which the first sums were raised, are still pursued to multiply them. One of these ' Hellites' commenced his career by pandering to the fatal and uncontrollable appetites for gaming of far humbler game than he is now hunting down, whose losses and ruin have enabled him to bedeck this place with every intoxicating fascination and incitement, and to throw out a bait of a large sum of money well hooked, to catch the largest fortunes, which are as sure to be netted as the smaller ones were. Sum up the amount of your losses, my lords and gentlemen, when, if you are still sceptical, you must be convinced of these things. Those noblemen and gentlemen just springing into life and large property should be ever watchful of themselves, as there are two or three persons of some rank who have themselves been ruined by similar means, and now condescend to become ' Procureurs' to this foul establishment, kept by a 'ci-devant' fishmonger's man, and who are rewarded for their services in the ratio of the losses sustained by the victims whom they allure it.

" ' They wish to give the place the character of a subscription club, pretending that none are admitted but those whose names are first submitted for approval to a committee, and then are ballotted for. All this is false. In the first place the members of different clubs are at once considered eligible; and, in the next, all persons are readily admitted who are well introduced, have money to lose, and whose forbearance under losses can be safely relied on.   Let the visitors pay a subscription—let them call themselves a club, or whatever they choose—still the house having a bank put down from day to day by the same persons to be played against, which have points of the game in its favour, is nothing but a common gaming-house, and indictable as such by the statutes, and, in the eye of the law, the visitors are rogues and vagabonds. Were it otherwise, why do not the members of this club be seen at the large plate-glass windows of the bow front, as well as at the windows of reputable club-houses ?   No one is ever there but the creatures of the hell, dressed out and bedizened with gold ornaments (most probably formerly belonging to unhappy and ruined players), to show off at them, and who look like so many jackdaws in borrowed plumes ; the players, ashamed of being seen by the passers-by, sneak in and out like cats who have burnt their tails.   Some of the members of the different clubs will soon begin to display the real character of this infernal place—those who will ultimately be found to forsake their respectable club-houses, and merge into impoverished and undone frequenters to this hell.

" ' The hellites at all the hells, not content with the gains by the points of the games in favour of the banks, and from the equal chances, do not fail to resort to every species of cheating.   The ' croupiers' and ' dealers' are always selected for their adeptness in all the mysteries of the black art.   Sleight-of-hand tricks at *rouge et noir*, by which they make any colour they wish win— false-dice and cramped-boxes at French hazard, which land any main or chance required ;—all are put in practice with perfect impunity, when every one, save the bankers and croupiers, are in a state of delirium or intoxication.   About two years ago, false dice were detected at a French hazard bank in Piccadilly, of which the proprietors of Fishmongers' Hall had a share.   A few noblemen and gentlemen had been losing largely (it is said £50,000 among them), when the dice became suspected.   One gentleman seized them, conveyed them away, and next morning found that they were false.   Were not things of this kind constantly done, it would be wholly impossible for these gentry, with all their great advantages, to make their fortunes quite so rapidly.   What with cheating, the points of the games, and the bewilderment of the senses of the players, it would be a miracle indeed, if any others could win but the hellites themselves.

" ' I am, Sir, your obedient Servant,

" ' *London*, Oct. 9, 1824.                    EXPOSITOR.'

___

" I will," continued Mentor, " read to you the whole of the communications of ' Expositor,' for I have carefully preserved them ; in the following letter he exposes, in its true light, the tricks and frauds resorted to.

" ' TO THE EDITOR OF THE TIMES.

" ' SIR,—The system of plunder and robbery in what is called the sporting (rogueing) world, never was so extensive or ramified as at the present time. The machinery of fraud and ruin is to be seen, with a little scrutiny, in all boxing matches; in trotting matches; in most races; in pigeon matches; in the gaming-houses, the keepers of which are sure to be active co-operators in all the various plans of robbery. They are laid with infinite cunning, and often are many months in maturing. The vast sums of money they amass enable them to command so many auxiliaries to aid their nefarious schemes, that they reduce them to a certainty of gain. The sacrifice of a few thousands to farther their views, is never a consideration, when, for every one, they make sure of sacking twenty or more. The recent transaction of ' the general,' for the Derby, in which the proprietors of the hell called ' Fishmongers' Hall' were deeply implicated, is a glaring instance of this fact. There is a ' secret' in almost every match that is made. This ' secret' means the knowledge how to lay bets with the dead certainty of winning them. The technical phraseology used among the tribe of black-legs is, ' Are you in the secret?'—' How is it to be?'—' Which is to lose?'—' Is it a cross?' &c. All persons, therefore, must lose, who do not possess this talisman, this ' secret,' excepting a few betters ' out of the ring,' who may happen to bet the right way among themselves. The legs always bet on the sure side, or they never bet at all, excepting to make fictitious bets one with another, in order to gull and deceive the better.' "

" And is there no possibility," said Peregrine, " of putting a total stop to such horrid places." " I am afraid not," said Mentor : " they are continually being indicted; but in general, before trial, the indictments are withdrawn. The compromise of one indictment was thus announced in a letter of ' Expositor,' in the Times of Friday, July 23, 1824, prefaced by some excellent leading remarks of the editor.—' We trust our readers will give due attention to a letter in this day's journal, on the subject of gaming-houses. This is every man's affair—every honest man's grievance : that of the young who have fortunes to be robbed of, and reputations to be disgraced; as of the old who have the inheritance of character and money to leave to their yet uncorrupted and unpolluted offspring. The evil is, that, in exact proportion to the depth of their guilt, the criminals enjoy the means of disappointing justice, and of paying for impunity. It appears from our correspondent's letter, that those prosecutions on which so many sanguine hopes had been raised, of crushing, if not destroying, one overgrown nest of villany, have been, unhappily, compromised, and that the work of robbery and desperation has begun again with undiminished vigour. Will the legislature leave the law as it stands? for the fault, we believe, is not at present with its ministers.'

" ' TO THE EDITOR OF THE TIMES.

" ' SIR,—The action against the keepers of a certain notorious ' hell,' which was noticed in the different journals as 'coming on,' is withdrawn; or, more properly speaking, is 'compromised.' Thus it will always be; and the different 'hells' still flourish with impunity, to the enrichment of a few knaves, and the ruin of many more thousands, till more effectual laws are framed to meet the evil. As they net thousands a night, a few hundreds or even thousands can be well spared to smother a few actions and prosecutions, which are very rarely instituted against them, and never but by ruined men, who are easily quieted by a small consideration, which, from recent judgments, will not be withheld; therefore we shall see recorded but very few convictions, if any at all. At the head of these infamous establishments is the one yclept ' Fishmongers' Hall,' which sacks more plunder than all the others put together, though they consist of about a dozen. This place has been fitted up at an expense of near £40,000, and is the most splendid house, interiorly and exteriorly, in all the neighbourhood. It is established as a bait for the fortunes of the great, many of whom have already been severe sufferers. Invitations to dinner are sent to noblemen and gentlemen, at which they are treated with every delicacy, and the most intoxicating wines. After such ' liberal' entertainment, a visit to the French hazard table, in the adjoining room, is a matter of course, when the consequences are easily divined. A man thus allured to the den may determine not to lose more than the few pounds he has about him; but in the intoxication of the moment, and the delirium of play, it frequently happens, that, notwithstanding the best resolves, he borrows money on his checks, which are known to be good, and are readily cashed to very considerable amounts. In this manner £10,000, £20,000, £30,000, or more, have often been swept away.

" ' They left King Street, about three years ago, when, in conjunction with T——, (a man who a few years ago took the benefit of the act, and subsequently kept one or two ' hells' in Pall Mall, but has amassed full £150,000 of plunder) and A——, who has £70,000 of plunder, they opened a club-house in Piccadilly, with a French hazard bank of £10,000, when in a short time they divided between the four, after all their heavy expenses were covered, upwards of £200,000. In proportion to the extent of the bank and the stakes, so do they collect the plunder. It is to be hoped that some notice will be taken of the subject next session of Parliament, and that a committee will be appointed to collect evidence, in order that a stop may be put to the evil.

" ' I am, Sir, your humble Servant,

" 'London, July 22, 1824. EXPOISTOR.'

———

The announcement of a fresh indictment, and also an action for large penalties, was made in another of the same writer's letters in the Times, December 10, 1824.

## "' TO THE EDITOR OF THE TIMES.

"' SIR,—The invulnerability of 'Fishmonger's Hall,' or **the** *Crock*-odile Mart for gudgeons, flat-fish, and pigeons, is likely soon to be put to the proof. The principal mover and actor in this ' Hell' is now under indictment, charged with having had a share in the lowly one of King Street, St. James's; and unless, like the rest, it is compromised (which, for the sake of humanity, let us hope will not be the case), the trial will come on in a few days. An action is also pending against the same party, wherein the penalties sought to be recovered for moneys gained by illegal gaming at the ' Hell,' are stated to be £160,000.

"' This ' Hell' has recently commenced the infernal trade again, after a short vacation of about two months, during which time the procureurs to it, who are broken men of fashionable notoriety, have been very active. Melton Mowbray, Brighton, Cheltenham, and other places of high and wealthy resort, have been visited in their turns, and it is pompously announced that no less a number than two hundred names of young nobility and gentry are down upon the black list as admissible to this ' Hell'—I beg pardon— to this ' Club ! ! !' as it is called.

"' Tremble, ye parents, lest your fond hopes in those who will be the representatives of your honours and estates be blasted for ever in this gigantic house of ruin, and that all devolve upon deluded, infatuated visitors to it. It will—it must, prove the grave of many a fortune, mind, and honour, like other ' Hells' have been, over which the very same parties who keep this have heretofore presided. It would be shocking to see your ancient patrimonies, handed down to you by your forefathers, melt away like snow before the sun, to enrich a *ci-devant* fishmonger, and an exwaiter of a faro ' Hell.' Their fortunes are already immense, created by the same means, but composed of those lost by many, some of whom have met with violent deaths, and others are now struggling with wretchedness and despair.

"' I am, Sir, your humble Servant,

"' *London, Dec. 8.*                                    EXPOSITOR.'

--------

" These remarks must, I think," continued Mentor, " convince every person of the dreadful consequences of gambling, which has, arrived in England, to a most frightful pitch : it is even getting strong hold of the boys in our streets; for, in the evidence given before the Committee of the House of Commons, appointed to inquire into the state of the Police of the Metropolis, (1828) it is said, speaking of the neglect of children, and gambling among them :

"' With more propriety may reliance be placed on the neglect of children as a primary source of mischief. Notwithstanding that we hear of schools having been established, continuing to be munificently supported, and receiving in each for instruction from 200 to 300, and even larger numbers of children; and notwithstanding that we find such seminaries existing in every quarter of the town, and in most of the adjoining districts, we yet find that in the parks and outskirts of the metropolis, on each returning Sabbath, and not unfrequently on other days, young persons assemble in numerous gangs or parties for the express purpose of indulging in the vice of gaming, and continue in the uninterrupted pursuit of that most seductive and immoral propensity from hour to hour on each succeeding day; and, what is still more surprising, and perhaps is more appalling, we find that instances are not unfrequent of parents so totally regardless of their children's welfare, as to view with careless indifference their expulsion, for misconduct, from those seminaries to which alone such parents could look with any hope of saving from ruin their unhappy offspring.

" ' To remedy an evil so glaring, becomes an object of primary importance, but so difficult as to have hitherto baffled the efforts of all the practical and intelligent persons who have applied their minds to this interesting subject.

" ' Education may have done something, but it clearly has not done enough; for never was juvenile depravity so unlimited in degree, or so desperate in character; but still, upon that effort of the humane great reliance must be placed, and on their unabated zeal in the prosecution of their charitable object the hopes and expectations of future amendment must in great measure depend; but police regulations may be superadded as a corrective, not unlikely to prove beneficial. It has been represented to your committee, that were the day patrol sufficiently numerous to admit of their disturbing and driving from their haunts the gambling boys, without at the same time leaving the streets in an unprotected state, the disgraceful and mischievous practice might be rooted out, as is shown in the following evidence of a police-officer:

" ' What are the instructions that you give to your men with respect to the gambling in the streets ?—We always drive them away, but we do not see it once a month.

" ' Is the Green Park in your district ?—No.

" ' Would there be any difficulty in preventing the constant gambling that is going on in the open daylight in the Green Park ?— If there were some spirited young men that could go into it, men that could jump and run about, they could soon put a stop to it.

" ' Do not you see it in other parts of the town ?—I have seen it; I have seen it near St. Martin's Church; but they get into the avenues, and the moment we go away they run back again.'

" In the same Report (which will be read with the highest degree of interest) the causes given for the increase of crime, are the extended population, want of employment, and the low price of gin. It says :—

" ' Your Committee, considering that the order of the House under which their investigation has been prosecuted, was divisible

44.

into two distinct heads of inquiry, applied themselves in the first instance to ascertain (if possible) whether the increase of commitments was to be attributed to a proportionate increase of crime, or whether much of it might not reasonably be supposed to emanate from circumstances and changes in the state of society; which, whilst they serve to exhibit conspicuously offences that have been committed, and to swell the catalogue of criminals that have been apprehended, by no means warrant the inference that there has been a proportionate perpetration of crime.

" ' Your committee having had laid before them, by the Secretary of State for the Home Department, " summary statements of the number of persons charged with criminal offences, who were committed to the several gaols in the cities of London and Westminster, and county of Middlesex, since the year 1810," have selected two series of years, for the purpose of ascertaining what has been the progressive increase of committals, and for the purpose of showing what proportion that increase bears to the increase in the population, have commenced each series with the period at which the previous population return had been completed. But as, in an investigation into that which immediately affects the security, as well of the person, as of the property of each individual member of the community, it may be convenient further to show, by a classification of the offences, how the one or the other are endangered, your committee have subjoined tables, in which the cases contained in the same two series are divided into classes, distinguishing those of ordinary occurrence which are aimed at the person, from those also of ordinary occurrence by which property most immediately under the protection of the person is invaded, and both of these form offences of rare occurrence; and those perpetrated on property necessarily left in a less protected state.

" ' Thus, the 1st class will contain—murder, manslaughter, shooting, stabbing, and poisoning.

" ' The 2d class will contain—burglary, embezzlement by servants, frauds, housebreaking, larceny of all descriptions, stealing from letters, highway robbery, receiving stolen goods.

" ' The 3d class will contain—cattle-stealing, horse-stealing, sheep-stealing.

" ' The 4th class will contain—rape, assault with intent to commit rape, ———, assault with intent to commit ———.

" ' The 5th class will contain—arson, bigamy, cattle-maiming, child-stealing, game laws (offences against), perjury, piracies and murder, sacrilege, sending threatening letters, treason, traffic in slaves, transports at large, felonies and misdemeanors not otherwise described.

" ' The 6th class will contain—coining, coin putting off and uttering, forgery and uttering forged instruments, forged bank notes having in possession.

" ' To complete the tables, from which to deduce a result, it is

**necessary** to add such as will show the amount of the population of London and Middlesex at the periods of the three last returns.

In 1801, the population of London and Middlesex was 845,400

In 1811, it was . . . . . . . . 985,100

Being an increase of . . . . 139,700

(which is about 17 per cent).

In 1821, the population of London and Middlesex was 1,167,500

From which, if that of 1811 be deducted . . . 985,100

There will remain an increase of . . 182,400

(which is about 19 per cent).

" ' And, as nothing has occurred to check the progressive addition to the population, but, on the contrary, much to stimulate and advance it (as, for instance, the invitation held out by the new buildings to occupants to come from distant quarters ; and the introduction of multitudes of workmen and labourers from various parts of the empire, to assist in the erection of such numerous and widely extended structures), there is satisfactory ground to suppose that between 1821 and 1828 the advance on the then population has not been less than it was between 1811 and 1821.

" ' If so, the fair deduction is, that the population has again increased 19 per cent.

" ' And, as the population-returns show an increase of 19 per cent. within the same periods of time, 19 per cent. of the increase of commitments and convictions may be accounted for by a proportionate surplusage of population, and that there remains attributable to other causes, only    per cent.

" ' If the foregoing be a reasonable mode of accounting for of the average increase of convictions being nineteen per cent., there will remain to be accounted for    , for the existence of which it would be most gratifying to your committee could they suggest such a cause as would enable the house to apply a direct and effectual remedy.

" ' Several prevalent evils are indeed relied upon by the police justices, and by various of the intelligent witnesses called before your committee, as being sufficient to solve the difficulty. Without doubt they must injuriously influence the state of society, and deteriorate public morals ; your committee therefore recapitulate them, more perhaps in the hope that, by the attention of the house being attracted to them, every opportunity will be taken for the application of correctives, than in the expectation that thereby, or, indeed, by any means, can vicious habits, in such a thickly inhabited district, be so far eradicated as to restore to the returns of criminal commitments that appearance which they presented when the population was at least thirty-six per cent. less dense.

" ' In addition to extended population (the leading assignable cause) are to added—

" ' The *extremely low price* at which spirituous liquors are *(since*

*the repeal of duties)* sold, a general want of employment, and neglect of children.

" ' The *lamentable effects of the first* are *too apparent* to require
much detail of evidence or lengthened argument to support; the
truth of the hypothesis will be upheld by a reference to the evidence of a remarkably intelligent officer, whose duty requires a
constant and accurate observation of what passes in the streets;
by which, also, may be impressed upon the house the magnitude of the evil occasioned by that erroneous though well-in-
tentioned financial measure.

" ' What effect has the reduced price of gin had in your district?—I think there is a great deal more drunkenness; I THINK
IT WAS ONE OF THE WORST THINGS EVER DONE IN THE
WORLD; if they had RAISED it a penny instead of FALLING it,
it would have been a very good thing.

" ' What is the price it is retailed at?—You may have very good
gin at $2\frac{1}{2}d$. a quartern—10*d*. a pint; but what they call famous, is
3*d*.,—that is, 1*s*. a pint; that is what is called " blue ruin."

" ' Do you find there is a great deal of drunkenness among
people who are not thieves?—Most certain; the first days in the
week you will always find somebody drunk, because there are
very few tailors and shoemakers that will work on the first days
in the week.

" ' Although it has been assumed that want of employment
has occasioned much criminal conduct, yet your committee do not
find that such is the case in the metropolis; that there may be
very many persons, who, having been attracted by the variety of
works which are now carrying on, and tempted by the rumours of
high wages to quit their ordinary residences, have been disappointed in their expectation of finding immediate occupation, and
are, with others (the dupes of folly or the victims of extravagance),
reduced to extreme distress, is more than probable : but when,
upon referring to the following evidence, viz—

" ' Do you mean that the wages received by those people for one
or two days in the week, are sufficient to support them for the remainder of the week?—There are many trades who do not go to
work till Friday morning; in some of those trades, two or three
days is all they work, beause they have piece-work.

" ' What trades are those?—Shoemakers and tailors in par-
cular.

" ' From your experience, do you think there is more decency
than there used to be among the lower classes?—I do; I think
since the day-police has been formed there is a wonderful alteration."

" ' Your committee find that it is not uncommon for those engaged in some trades altogether to abstain from work till the
Friday morning; and that in others, two or three days in the
week are all that they devote to industrious labour, the high
rate of wages enabling them to earn in one, two, or three days,

sufficient to maintain them the whole of the week; they conceive that there cannot be such a superabundance of labourers as to warrant the apprehension that want of employment can, in London and the vicinity, be ranked as one of the causes to which an increase of crime can justly be attributed.'

"Thus," says Mentor, "we are, thank heaven! certain that the rulers of the country are now acquainted with the fact of the melancholy doings of spirituous liquors. Drinking leads to loss of virtue and character, laziness ensues, and thieving follows.

"The subject of compounding felonies, and of the receiving of stolen goods, in the said Report, is well worth attention: it says—

"'This statute of Geo. I. was repealed, and its provisions re-enacted last ression, by statutes 7 and 8 Geo. IV. c. 29, s. 58; but which makes the offence no longer capital, and limits the highest punishment to transportation for life. The statute 6 Geo. I. c. 23, s. 9. (which is still unrepealed) enacts a reward of £40 to the person prosecuting any such offenders to conviction. It is to be observed, that while these severe penalties against such compromises have been provided, the offence of compromising felony, or theftbote (as termed by older law-writers), to perfect which there must be an actual agreement not to prosecute, and connivance at the impunity of the felon, has continued, and still remains a misdemeanor at common law, punishable only by fine and imprisonment. Lord Coke, indeed, lays down, that if the owner of stolen goods, in addition to the offence of theftbote, " receive the thief himself, and aid and maintain him in his felony, then is he accessary to the felony," viz. of robbing himself. It seems that for many years the statute 4 Geo. I. c. 11, has been very ineffectual, perhaps arising merely from the difficulty of detecting such offences, to which Sir R. Birnie seems to impute it; as he says, " I believe there is law enough against compounding a felony, but the great thing is to get a discovery." The severity of the punishment, under stat. 4 Geo. I. c. 11, may have discouraged prosecutions; or the decisions, that money or bank-notes were not within the meaning of such acts, may have afforded the officers a pretence for considering themselves as committing no crime in most of the late compromises. This latter omission has been rectified by the act of last session, the provisions of which have, it is hoped, had a beneficial effect on various offenders. One officer has stated, that his brethren had agreed " to give up all transactions of the sort, as they thought some mischief would come of it under Mr. Peel's Act." But it does not appear that this agreement took place till after the inquiry before alluded to had been instituted by order of the Home Office. Another witness says, with respect to the " fences," " I know that these persons, since the passing of Mr. Peel's bill, are more timid of receiving property than they were before." It is extraordinary that the police-officers, with the severe act of Geo. I. in existence, should, as it were, have considered themselves as committing no crime; and your committee infers some deficiency in the law, which the statute of last session may not have completely remedied. Your committee therefore submit, as well worthy of consideration, whether it would not be advisable to make it at least a misdemeanor in the party paying a reward for the restitution of stolen goods, as well as punishing the party receiving it. This has been recommended by an intelligent witness, well acquainted with such parties, and the nature of such transactions. The advertising a reward for stolen goods, "no questions asked," was by statute 25 Geo. II. c. 36, subjected to a penalty of £50; which provision was re-enacted by Mr. Peel's bill of last session, before cited. Your committee, therefore, see no injustice in making the payment of that reward a substantive offence, the published offer of which has so long been subject to a penalty. Your committee, moreover, submit, that the due gradation of crime would be better regarded, by affixing to the offence of compounding felony a higher punishment than that of merely paying or taking a reward for the return of stolen goods. Whether, in order to effect this, it may be advisable to mitigate the punishment now enacted by 7 and 8 Geo. IV. c. 29, for the latter offence, or to make the compounding a higher felony, belongs to future deliberation on the details of the measure.

" 'Your committee are well aware that it may seem severe to proceed with rigour against an act which at first sight contains nothing repugnant to honesty—namely, helping an owner to regain, or he himself regaining, the property of which he had been robbed. But their inquiries have too satisfactoriy convinced them that the frequency of these seemingly blameless transactions has led to the organization of a system which undermines the security of all valuable property, which gives police-officers a direct interest that robberies to a large amount should not be prevented; and which has established a set of " putters-up," and " fences," with means of evading, if not defying, the arm of the law; who are wealthy enough, if large rewards are offered for their detection, to double them for their impunity; and who would in one case have given £1,000 to get rid of a single witness. Some of these persons ostensibly carry on a trade; one, who had been tried formerly for robbing a coach, afterwards carried on business as a Smithfield drover, and died worth, it is believed, £15,000. Your committee could not ascertain how many of these persons there are at present, but four of the principal have been pointed out. One is the farmer of one of the greatest turnpike trusts in the metropolis. He was formerly tried for receiving the contents of a stolen letter: and, as a receiver of tolls now employed by him was also tried for stealing that very letter, being then a postman, it is not too much to infer, that the possession of these turnpikes is not unserviceable for the purposes of depredation. Another has, it is said, been a surgeon in the army. The two others of the four have no trade, but live like men of property; and one of these, who appears to be the chief of the whole set, is well known on the turf, and is stated, on good grounds, to be worth £30,000. It is alarming to have observed how long these persons have successfully carried on their plans of plunder; themselves living in affluence and apparent respectability, bribing confidential servants to betray the transactions of their employers, possessing accurate information as to the means and precautions by which valuable parcels are transmitted; then corrupting others to perpetrate the robberies planned in consequence; and finally receiving, by means of these compromises, a large emolument, with secure impunity to themselves and their accomplices. It is scarcely necessary to point out the difficulties which must obstruct these persons, even after they may have amassed a fortune, 'in betaking to any honest pursuit. This, your committee have evidence, is deeply felt by themselves; and the fear of being betrayed by their confederates, should they desert them, and of becoming objects for sacrifice by the police, to whom they at present consider themselves of use, leaves little hope of any stop to their career but by detection and justice. The owners of stolen property have thus purchased indemnity for present losses, by strengthening and continuing a system, which re-acts upon themselves and the community, by reiterated depredations committed with almost certain success and safety. Your committee believe they have not drawn a stronger picture than the evidence before them warrants; and whatever measures may be necessary to abolish such a system, such measures, however severe, should be provided.'

"That some magistrates think the compounding of felonies not only no crime, but a positive merit, is certain," said Mentor, "as the following circumstance, of the truth of which there is no doubt, will serve to show:—Some time ago, a gentleman had his pocket picked at Doncaster races of a very valuable gold watch. He immediately came to town, and proceeded to one of the police-offices, where he stated his case, and applied for the assistance of an officer to help him to recover the watch. The magistrate to whom the gentleman applied, referred him to one of the principal officers, who, on hearing the case, and receiving a description of the suspected party, promised his assistance. 'But,' said the officer, 'you must advertise the watch, and offer a reward for it before I can do your business.' The gentleman accordingly caused advertisements to be published, describing the watch, and offering forty guineas for its recovery. When this was done, the officer called upon him, saying, 'Your business is in a good train, sir; I have discovered where your watch is, but you must pay something more than the reward for it. The fellow who has it is a d—d Jew.' The gentleman consented to give twenty guineas more. 'If you will step to the office at twelve o'clock to-morrow, sir, you shall have your watch,' said the officer. The gentleman attended at the appointed hour, and the officer was called in. 'Well, B.' said the magistrate, 'what have you done about this gentleman's watch?' 'I have recovered it for him, your worship,' said the officer, 'and here it is,' drawing the precious bauble from his fob, and presenting it to the magistrate with one of his best bows. 'Upon my word,' said the magistrate emphatically, 'you have done it well; you deserve great credit.' Then, turning to the gentleman, and handing him the watch, he said, 'You see, sir, what we can do when we like to go about it.'

" 'Considerable sums have been paid to regain their property by the parties robbed, generally stipulated to be paid in cash, for fear of the clue to discovery of those concerned that notes might give. These sums have been apportioned, mostly by a per centage, to the value of the property lost; but modified by a reference to the nature of the securities or goods, as to the facility of circulating or disposing of them to profit and with safety.

" 'A great majority of these cases have taken place where large depredations have been committed upon bankers. Two banks that had recently been robbed of notes to the amount of £4,000, recovered them on payment of £1,000 each. In another case, £2,200 was restored out of £3,200 stolen, for £230 or £240.

" 'This bank having called in their old circulation, and issued fresh, immediately upon the robbery, the difficulty thus occasioned was the cause of not much above £10 per cent. being demanded. In another case, Spanish bonds, nominally worth £2,000, were given back on payment of £100. A sum, not quite amounting to £20,000, was in one case restored for £1,000. In another, where bills had been stolen of £16,000 or £17,000 value, but which were not easily negotiable by the thieves, restitution of £6,000 was offered for £300. The bank in this case applied to the Home Office for a free pardon for an informer, but declined advertising a reward of £1,000, and giving a bond not to compound, as the conditions of such grant. In another case, £3000 seems to have been restored for £19 per cent. In another case, where the robbery was to the amount of £7,000, and the supposed robbers (most notorious " putters-up" and "fences") had been apprehended, and remanded by the magistrate for examination, the prosecution was suddenly desisted from in consequence of the restitution of the property for a sum not ascertained by your committee. In the case of another bank, the sum stolen, being not less than £20,000, is stated to have been bought of the thieves by a receiver for £200, and £2,800 taken of the legal owners as the price of restitution. The committee does not think it necessary to detail all the cases which have been disclosed to them; but, though it is evident they have not been informed of any thing like all the transactions that must have occurred under so general a system, they have proof of more than sixteen banks having sought, by these means, to indemnify themselves for their losses; and that property

"It is, perhaps, not extraordinary that bankers, who have lately been so repeatedly subject to heavy losses, should take measures to procure indemnity. A highly respectable banker has said before your committee, "I have no hesitation in mentioning that, at a meeting in our trade, I have heard it said, over and over again, by different individuals, that, if they experienced a loss to a considerable amount, they should compound." This your committee consider by no means to be universal. I shall reserve," said Mentor, "for a future occasion, some other remarks from the same report; which, as they so truly develop the manners and depravities of London, are highly worthy your most serious attention.

"We agreed," continued Mentor, "to-morrow to visit the inns of court; therefore, if you will meet me at the Rainbow Coffee-house, I will accompany you to Lincoln's Inn, and witness

The Doings in the Court of Chancery.

"You will easily find the Rainbow: it is by the Inner-Temple Gate, opposite to Chancery Lane."

The next morning Peregrine and Mentor met. "This coffee-house," said Mentor, "is one of the most ancient in London. Aubrey, in his Lives, speaking of Sir Henry Blount, a fashionable of Charles the Second's day, tells us, 'when coffee first came in, he was a great upholder of it, and had ever since been a constant frequenter of coffee-houses, especially Mr. Farre's, at the Rainbow, by Inner-Temple Gate. Here Johnson used to sit. How

changed the scene ! as the author of Wine and Walnuts says,—
" How changed, indeed ! for, in this old-fashioned room, now
newly beautified, where, half a century ago, congregated worthies
—chiefly men of known repute, and of long standing—as, physi-
cians, authors, certain learned printers, topping publishers, and
others, opulent traders, friends, and social neighbours,—in this
old room, instead of those, you behold the boxes filled with young
pale-faced lawyers. The change is grievous to behold.

" Mackay, in his Journey through England, gives an entertaining
account of the chocolate and coffee-houses of the metropolis in
1724, and the different sorts of company by which they were then
frequented.

" The character of Tom King's coffee-house, in Covent-Garden,
immortalized by Hogarth, in his print of ' Morning,' in his ' Four
Times of the Day,' and the sort of company who frequented it,
about 1735, is thus given in some lines in ' A Covent-Garden
Eclogue ' of the time :

> " The watch had cried *past one* with hollow strain
> And to their stands returned to sleep again.
> Jephson's and Mitchell's hurry now was done,
> And now *Tom King's* (so rakes ordained) begun.
> Bright shone the moon, and calm around the sky ;
> No cinder-wench, nor straggling link-boy, nigh ;
> When in that *garden*, where, with mimic power,
> Strut the mock-purple heroes of an hour,—
> Where, by grave matrons, cabbages are sold,
> Who all the live-long day *drink gin* and *scold*."

" The coffee-houses of London, which have become extremely
numerous since this period, are no longer distinguished, as in
former times, for the meeting of particular sets of company ; such
as Spiller's Head Club, in Clare Market, where Colly Cibber, Orator
Henely, Count Heidegger, and others used to congregate : then there
was the Old Slaughter's, in St. Martin's Lane, the resort of Jonathan
Richardson, Harry Fielding, Lambert, the landscape-painter,
Woollett, and the whole herd of painters and engravers, for the
' Academy ' was then held in St. Martin's Lane. Now we
have none, if we except Garraway's Coffee-House, and a
few others in the city, such as Tom's Coffee-House, in Cornhill.
Plenty, the parent of cheerfulness, seems to have fixed her residence on this spot; while Joy, which is the offspring of Folly,
seems to be utterly unknown. Industry, the first principle of a
citizen, is an infallible specific to keep the spirits awake, and
prevent that stagnation and corruption of humours, which make
our fine gentlemen such horrible torments to one another and to
themselves. Decency in dress is finery enough in a place where
they are taught from their childhood to expect no honours from
what they seem to be, but from what they really are. The
conversation here turns chiefly on the interests of Europe, in
which they themselves are principally concerned ; and the busi-

ness here is to enlarge the commerce of their country, by which the public is to gain much more than the merchant himself. Of their generous principles, I need only give an instance : it is that, in this place, was first projected the subscription for the relief of Mrs. Clarke, the aged and only surviving daughter of the glorious Milton, in 1727.

"Of the ancient taverns in the metropolis, a few noticed by Stowe are yet in existence.

"The sites of others are still preserved, as tne Boar's Head, in Eastcheap. A boar's head, cut in stone, and painted blue, is the only memorial that now marks the site of this very ancient scene of conviviality, which has for many years ceased to be a tavern, and was lately occupied by a wholesale perfumer. Maitland, speaking of the Boar's Head, says ' In this street (Eastcheap), is the Boar's Head, under the sign of which is written " *This is the Chief Tavern in London.*"

"Goldsmith, in his delightful essay, called ' A Reverie at the Boar's Head Tavern, in Eastcheap,' appears to have been unmindful of the original mansion being destroyed by the fire of London. The introductory mention of it must only, therefore, be taken as a specimen of his beautiful description :

"' Such were the reflections that naturally arose while I sat at the Boar's Head Tavern, still kept in Eastcheap. Here, by a pleasant fire, in the very room where old Sir John Falstaff cracked his jokes, in the very chair which was sometimes honoured by Prince Henry, and sometimes polluted by his immoral merry companions, I sat and ruminated on the follies of youth; wished to be young again : but was resolved to make the best of life while it lasted, and now and then compared past and present times together. The room also conspired to throw my reflections back into antiquity : the oak floor, the gothic windows, and the ponderous chimney-piece, had long withstood the tooth of time,' &c.

"Shakspeare furnishes us with a specimen of the charges at the taverns of his time, in the bill which Peto takes out of Falstaff's pocket, of the expenses of his supper and night's drinking at the Boar's Head.

"' Item, a capon, 2s. 2d. ; sauce, 4d. ; sack, two gallons, 5s. 8d. ; anchovies and sack after supper, 2s. 6d. ; bread, a halfpenny.'

"So much for the Boar's Head.

"The *Bush* is, perhaps, one of the most ancient of alehouse signs ; and hence has arisen the well-known proverb, ' Good wine needs no bush ;' that is, nothing to point out where it is sold.

"The subsequent passage seems to prove that ancient tavernkeepers kept both a *bush* and a *sign;* a host, in speaking, says :—

' I rather will take down my *bush* and *sign,*
Than live by means of riotous expense.'

"In the British Apollo, fol. Lond. 1710, vol. 14, we have the following verses on some of the signs in London :—

' I'm amaz'd at the signs
  As I pass through the town ;
To see the odd mixture—
  A *Magpie* and *Crown*,
The *Whale* and the *Crow*,
  The *Razor* and *Hen*,
The *Leg* and *Seven Stars*,
  The *Bible* and *Swan*,
The *Ax* and the *Bottle*,
  The *Tun* and the *Lute*,
The *Eagle* and *Child*,
  'The *Shovel* and *Boot*.'

"Indeed, many of the alehouse and tavern signs are so incongruous or ridiculous, that it is difficult to conceive how they originated.

"But come," said Mentor, "time is stealing on us; so let us begone, else you will lose a sight of the Lord Chancellor." Accordingly, our heroes walked up Chancery Lane into Lincoln's Inn, and soon found themselves in the Court of Chancery.

"This court of equity," said Mentor, "is worthy your attention. Many eminent lawyers have presided here: of these may be mentioned Sir John Fortescue, one of the fathers of the English law, who held the great seal under Henry the Sixth; that virtuous chancellor, Sir Thomas More, who was beheaded by order of the sanguinary Henry VIII. It was his general custom to sit every afternoon in the open hall, and, if any person had a suit to prefer, he might state the case to him without the aid of bills, solicitors, or petitions. And such was his impartiality, that he gave a decree against one of his sons-in-law, Mr. Heron, whom he in vain urged to refer the matter to arbitration, and who presumed upon his relationship. He was also so indefatigable, that, though he found the office filled with causes, some of which had been pending for twenty years, he despatched the whole within two years, and, calling for the rest, was told that there was not one left; a circumstance which he ordered to be entered on record ; and which has thus been wittily versified—

' When *More* some years had chancellor been,
  No *more* suits did remain ;
The same shall never *more* be seen
  Till *More* be there again.'

"The learned antiquary, Sir Henry Spelman, was chancellor; as also that pious judge, Sir Matthew Hale, Lord Chancellor Egerton, &c., and not least, that upright and conscientious judge, Earl Eldon, who, I believe, held the seals longer than any chancellor. The present chancellor you see there, is Lord Lyndhurst, well known as Sir John Copley: he is the son of Mr. Copley the celebrated painter, and rose to his present exalted station by his talents and integrity. That gentleman on the right, is

Mr. Heald; and he sitting by his side, is Mr. Sugden, one of the members for Weymouth, who, in his address to the electors, told them that he was once as poor as any of them, and that it was to his perseverance in his profession he had to ascribe his present station in society : and he ought to have added, his honour, ability, and integrity : for certainly a more conscientious upright man does not exist. I do not believe," continued Mentor, "there is any profession wherein a man of talent and integrity can rise to greater honours than in the law; but he must not be a *common star*. He must possess rare transcendent talents, and consummate industry and application, never to feel tired or alloyed;—such a man was Lord Eldon, who, from a very humble state, rose to be Lord Chancellor of England!—an honour that probably awaits his prototype, Mr. Sugden.

" At this instant the Lord Chancellor rose, and the court broke up; and Mentor and Peregrine, having viewed the armorial bearings in the windows, &c., strayed into Lincoln's Inn. " The term is now over," said Mentor, " and in a few days what a forlorn state this square will be in, which is well told in the following poem, called ' Long Vacation, by Jemmy Copywell, of Lincoln's Inn :'—

> ' My lord now quits his venerable seat,
> The six clerk on his padlock turns the key,
> From bus'ness hurries to his snug retreat,
> And leaves vacation and the town to me.
>
> Now all is hush'd,—asleep the eye of care,
> And Lincoln's Inn a solemn stillness holds,
> Save, where the porter whistles o'er the square,
> Or Pompey barks, or basket-woman scolds.
>
> Save that, from yonder pump, and dusty stair,
> The moping shoe-black and the laundry maid,
> Complain of such as from the town repair,
> And leave their usual quarterage unpaid.
>
> In those dull chambers, where old parchments lie,
> And useless draughts, in many a mouldering heap,
> Each for parade to catch the client's eye,
> Salkeld and Ventris in oblivion sleep.
>
> In these dead hours, what now remains for me,
> Still to the stool and to the desk confin'd :
> Debarr'd from autumn shades and liberty,
> Whose lips are soft as my Cleora's kind.'

" Now," continued Mentor, " the dispensers of the law retire to take a little recreation from the toils of the terms, and drink ' to the glorious uncertainty of the law :' of this uncertainty, Mr. Baring, in his speech on the Court of Chancery, thus gives a proof :—' A question had been before the Court of Chancery for thirty years, as to the disposal of £150,000. Owing to the long delays, most of the suitors had been reduced to the greatest poverty and distress. From 1791 to 1825, this sum had been locked up in the Accountant-General's hands, owing to reports, exceptions to reports, masters' reports, and other delays ; and the consequence was, that some of the suitors, who had formerly been in good circumstances, were absolutely living on charity. One of the solicitors of the parties happened to be his own solicitor, and he one day asked him when he thought the suit would be at an end. He replied, that he thought it was impossible it would soon come to a conclusion, as some of the parties were dead. He said that, even if the Chancellor did give judgment in the case, it might be on some quibble of the law. Hearing this, he (Mr. Baring) applied to the solicitor on the other side, and asked him if it would not be better for the interests of all parties to settle the matter out of court. He replied, that he believed it would, and it was a proposition which was much wished for, and he was sure would meet the approbation of the parties. They met him the next day, and the parties asked him to sit in judgment on the matter; but, as he did not wish to take on himself alone to give a decision on a matter involving so large a sum of money as £150,000, he deemed it advisable to call to his aid the talents and experience of another individual, and he suggested to the parties that Mr. John Smith should sit with him in judgment on the case. The parties approved of his choice ; they sat for an hour and a half on two days on the matter, and, in the course of those two days, they settled this suit, which had been pending nearly thirty years in the Court of Chancery !' ”

“ And are there as many inns of court in France, as here in London ?” inquired Peregrine. “ No,” replied Mentor; “ the fact is, people in England are too fond of law—from the peer, who prosecutes a poor wretch for stealing a rabbit to give to his starving family, down to the drunken fish-fag, who *takes the law* on some of her companions for *defamation of character*—all is now law— from the Lord Chancellor to the parish beadle. If Spain and Portugal be priest-ridden, certain it is England is law-ridden. Which is worst, Peregrine ?” “ In faith,” replied Peregrine, “ I know but little of either the one or the other.” “ Ay, then,” rejoined Mentor, “ your ignorance is bliss ; and proves the words of Pope—

> “ ⟶ı ignorance is bliss,
> It's folly to be wise.' ”

Peregrine accompanied Mentor to his apartments, to meet a gentleman who had undertaken to arrange the affairs of Mentor's friend in the King's-Bench Prison ; where, on their arrival, they found the gentleman waiting, who informed Mentor that every thing was arranged, and that his friend would almost instantly get his discharge. On dinner being served up, Mentor inquired of the servant-girl for more spoons. when the poor creature, after many excuses, with tears in her eyes, was obliged to inform her master that she had given, or lent, them to a fortune-teller, to make up a certain sum which she wanted, to tell her the history of her future destiny. Mentor, though much vexed, mildly rebuked the girl (knowing her to be an invaluable servant, and that she had been the dupe of some crafty wretch), and told her of the crime she had been guilty of, in giving away his property, who had been so good a friend to her. The poor girl acknowledged his kindness, and, falling on her knees, craved forgiveness; on which Mentor Instantly raised her. " Bend thy knee, Martha," said Mentor, " to none but to thy God! I forgive you; and may you prove, by the faithfulness of your future service, that you are worthy of my forgiveness!"

After the girl had left the room, " I think," said Peregrine, " you have acted with your servant as every *Christian* ought to do." " I hope so!" said Mentor. " Now, supposing I had discharged her, I could not have given her a character—and what would have been the consequence? Why, in all probability, she would have gone on the town. If I had prosecuted her, she would have been sent to prison, and ruined for ever; and then, in either case, I should not have got back my spoons, but have been the same loser as I am now, and could only have to reflect on her unfortunate fallen state : but now I hope to see her yet comfortable and happy, and a valuable member of society. Which reflection do you think, Peregrine, will tend to make my dying moments the more happy?" " The latter, most certainly," replied Peregrine, " and I hope you will receive as much mercy at the last day, as you have now shown your servant." " Amen!" responded Mentor. Not a word more was spoken during dinner—both of them seemed thinking of that indescribable something beyond the grave. At length, Peregrine broke the silence—" Curses on those fortune-tellers," said he; " in this day's paper, there is the following, among the thousand proofs of the folly of girls listening to those confounded cheats, the fortune-tellers : it says—

" ' Bow Street.—Ruth Smith, a gipsy woman, was charged with having been concerned in stealing twenty sovereigns from Miss L. P., a young lady who resides at Knightsbridge.

" ' It appeared from the evidence of a young woman, Miss P.'s servant, that a gipsy woman, who very much resembled the prisoner, called upon her at the house of her mistress, and, after a short conversation, offered to show her the secrets of futurity for the trifling consideration of a sovereign, to be paid in advance. The poor girl not being provided with the sum, the gipsy consented to take the amount in clothes; and the girl was so anxious to know her future fortune, that she actually parted with the best part of her wardrobe to receive the wished-for information. Accordingly, the old sibyl assured her that a great fortune, a handsome husband, and a large family, were the blessings which the Fates had in store for her. Overjoyed with this glowing prospect, the girl communicated her good fortune to her young mistress, who felt an equal anxiety to read the book of fate, and accordingly a meeting was appointed between the lady and the fortune-teller, who remained closeted together in private for a considerable time. The result of the conference did not transpire, but it from what followed, that the old gipsy was as successful in raising the expectations of the mistress as those of the maid. The sibyl told the young lady that, in order to complete a charm which she had in preparation for her especial benefit, it would be necessary for her to *deposit* 20 *sovereigns between the sheets of her bed.* The young lady did as directed, and on the following day the gipsy called at the house in a great hurry, telling the young lady that the charm was proceeding as happily as her heart could wish, but that, in order to bring it to a speedy close, it would be necessary for her (the gipsy) to have the 20 sovereigns in her own possession. The lady foolishly consented, and it is unnecessary to add that the gipsy, having taken her departure, forgot to call at the expiration of the three days, which she had fixed for the working of the charm. Miss P., perceiving her folly when too late, gave information of the circumstance to an active officer of this establishment, who soon apprehended the prisoner, upon whose person he found several cards, and other matters used by itinerant fortune-tellers; and said, that, from information he had received, he had good reason to believe that the prisoner was concerned with the other woman, and that she was near the house at the time when the young lady was robbed of the 20 sovereigns.'

" It is but the other day," said Mentor, " that Catherine Dillon, a county of Cork girl, of very comely appearance, was brought before Alderman Farebrother, at the Mansion House (who sat for the Lord Mayor), charged with being a most dangerous conjuror, and having stolen a silver thimble, a pocket handkerchief, and an apron, the property of a tradesman's wife, in Moorfields.

" 'The conjuror, it appeared from the statement of the complainant, walked into the shop where the latter was sitting at work with her two children, and said, ' Ma'am, I'll tell you what is to become of you, if you please to give me a trifle of money.' ' No,' said the lady, ' I don't wish to have my fortune told.' The conjuror, however, seized her hand, and, looking into the palm with a very wise countenance, ' Hear it, my jewel,' cried she; ' as sure as you live, you will have another husband.' ' Another husband!' said the complainant; ' why my husband is alive, thank God! and well.' ' Arragh! then,' added the Irishwoman, ' that's no matter. How can it be helped if the stars will have it so? As sure as you're born, dear, you'll have another husband, and very shortly too, and by him you'll have seven children.' (A laugh.)

" ' Alderman Farebrother.—And you have a husband and children already?

" ' Complainant.—My husband is here, your worsh p (pointing to a well-looking man, who eyed the sorceress in no very favourable manner): but she was not content with telling me so abominable a story,—she said that there was a great deal more about me, and asked me whether I had any gold or silver to let her look at, and that it was necessary to her charm to look at any sovereigns or shillings I might have in my possession.

" ' Conjuror.—Indeed, your worship, I only tould her that she might have another husband and seven children; and that's plain enough, for I'm sure she's young enough.

" ' Mr. Hobler (to the conjuror.)—Why, you are an Irishwoman, are you not?

" ' The Conjuror.—God knows, I am; and I'm so poor, I'm obliged to tell people that they'll have all sorts of good luck. If I was to tell them the other thing, the d—l a halfpenny I'd ever get from them at all at all. (A laugh.)

" ' Mr. Hobler.—It is but seldom people of your country take to this sort of deception. I thought you had left fortune-telling to the Bohemians and other foreigners.

" ' The Conjuror.—The Bo—who? I don't know who you mean. I know that we are just as well able to tell people's fortunes in Ireland as they can tell them in Jericho or Dingledy Cooch.

" ' Mr. Hobler.—Were you ever on the tread-mill?

" ' Conjuror.—No, nor don't intend it, your honour

" ' Alderman Farebrother.—But we'll lock you up as a rogue and vagabond. We'll give you something to do for a few months, to keep you out of harm's way.

" ' Conjuror.—Thank your worship. It's often you give us nothing.

" ' The complainant then stated, that the prisoner took up the thimble and rolled it up in a handkerchief which lay upon the counter, and that she also took up an apron with which she pretended to be performing a charm. Suddenly, however, watching an opportunity, she slipped out, after she had said to the complainant ' Take your eyes off me, or the charm won't work.' (A laugh.) She had not, however, gone far when she was apprehended.

" ' Conjuror.—Why, you were mad to have your fortune tould, and you gave them bits of things to me to tell you the good news. (Laughter.) You even took off your rings and put them into my hands, and I would not keep 'em.

" ' The complainant said that she certainly had handed a ring to the conjuror, but the observation made by the woman was, ' I know by the stars that the ring is copper, and copper has no power over my charm.' (Loud laughter.)

" ' Alderman Farebrother.—Well, well; we'll see whether she can charm the inmates of Bridewell. Although she can dive into futurity, I dare say she could not tell what sort of amusement she'll be at a few hours hence.

" ' Mr. Hobler.—These people are very dangerous.

" ' Alderman Farebrother.—I know that. They often prevail on servants to rob their masters and mistresses, but the best I can do here is, to convict the prisoner as a rogue and vagabond, and order her to be set to hard labour;' to which she was accordingly sentenced.

" At any rate," observed Peregrine, " these cases do not give much proof of the ' march of intellect.' " " No, indeed, they do

46

not; but, talking of the 'march of intellect,'" said Mentor, "here
is a real instance of the present *enlightened* state of society :—
' In May, 1828, a numerous body of fanatics had a camp meeting
on Combe Down, Bristol. Early in the morning two waggons were
placed for the preachers, including three females; the preachers
stood in the waggons, when singing commenced. One of the
female preachers chose for her text, Gen. xxiv. 58, ' Wilt thou go
with this man?' After a few preliminary remarks, she said, ' All
those that are willing to go, hold up their hands,' when a great
show of hands was exhibited. She then said, ' To you Christ is
precious;' when a stout countryman, half drunk, a collier, bawled
out, ' Ah! he is precious to I.' After the sermon was finished,
the director of these people commanded all to separate into different lots :—' You Camerton friends, go to the left;—you, Frome
friends, go to the right;—you, Coleford friends, go out in the
front;—the Bath and the Combe-down friends will stay near the
waggons; and may the Lord pour out his spirit upon you all; don't
be long in prayer, but be earnest, that you may pull down the
blessing of God on your heads, and drive the devil out of your
heels.' Each company then began singing different tunes, and
went to their stations stamping with their feet as they proceeded
with their hats off, and pocket handkerchiefs tied round their heads.
After the singing was finished, they kneeled down, and began
praying with their heads close to each other, their eyes shut,
swaying their bodies backwards and forwards, bawling as loud as
they possibly could, until quite black in the face, and suffused with
perspiration. During this time the director of these people went
from company to company, telling them ' to pray in the faith.'
One man said, ' Thou hast promised to come down to thy people;'
when the director patted the man on the back, and bawled out,
' Thou sha't come down,—ah! thou sha't come down,' striking his
hands together. Cries of ' Amen,' resounded from these people,
and groans were uttered incessantly. This continued until the
evening, when they separated.'

" What do you think of this delectable history?" continued
Mentor: " this period is called the age of reason. Fie on it!
Why, the uneducated Hindoo, or Indian, or Esquimaux, are more
enlightened beings than the above wretched creatures, who are
inhabitants, too, of England!—the most *polished* nation on the
face of the earth, as it is sometimes called."

Mentor's servant now entered the room, and informed her master
that James, her late fellow-servant, wished to speak to him. Accordingly, he was ordered to walk up, when the poor fellow told him,
that he had paid two half-sovereigns (all the money he was in
possession of, owing to the long time he had been out of employ)
to an advertising office for servants, and that, after keeping him
attending at the office for three weeks, they informed him it was out
of their power to obtain him a situation; " And so, Sir," said
James, " I made bold to ask you whether I cannot get my **money**

back?" Mentor told him it would be of no use to try, and that he must put up with the loss; but at the same time intimated, that in all probability in a few days a friend of his would engage him; which intelligence poor James received with thankfulness, and retired.

"I am glad," said Mentor, "that the Times newspaper has taken up the subject of these office-keepers, by exposing their frauds, as appears by the following communications to the editor:

"'SIR,—Your excellent paper has already done immense good in exposing some of the numberless frauds carried on in this great Babel; permit me to draw your attention to another, of no less enormity, among the humbler classes of society,—I mean the unprincipled frauds committed on the public by a set of fellows called office-keepers, or situation-procurers. Their titles, indeed, are numerous, as land-surveyors, school and house agents, &c. Now, Sir, the plan of those fellows is, to hunt out all the newspapers they can find containing advertisements, which they extract and post up at their doors. It is evident, therefore, that *The Times* is their principal resource. The numerous flats (many of them respectable persons), seeing such a profusion of situations stuck up, imagine they cannot fail of obtaining one among so many, and think the conductors of those precious places men of immense business and respectability; while I may safely affirm that they are not employed to transact one case out of 500 of those they exhibit to the gulled public. But, Sir, this is not all: an entrance-fee (generally half-a-guinea) is always required by these fellows, who, when they pocket the money, think nothing farther of their deluded applicant, who is never repaid, whether the situation is procured or not; and, to prevent all disclosure or redress, a condition-paper is signed by the gulled flats, who, in their high hopes, never read the honest office-keeper's conditions. Ludgate Hill, Newgate Street, the Old Bailey, &c. have exhibited curious specimens of this sort. In the first of these I have been taken in myself, among many hundreds of others; but the place has, at length, exploded, and the losers of half-guineas and guineas will now, no doubt, enjoy a laugh at the explosion. If persons in want of situations had advertised in the regular channels, they would have the benefit of the most extended publicity, and ninety-nine chances to one of obtaining their ends by such a mode rather than by a system of unprincipled audacity. It is high time the public should be put on their guard against such fellows, and there is no mode of doing so more effectually than by describing them. By giving this a corner in your valuable columns, you will prevent many simple people from throwing away their money in similar places, and will have exposed a most unprincipled system of pick-pocketing.

"'I remain, Sir, your obedient servant,
"'J. B.'

" ' TO THE EDITOR OF THE TIMES.

" ' SIR,—While your columns are always kindly open to communications designed to caution against fraud, there is one trap laid to catch the unwary which I have not observed pointed out by any one, but against which you would be conferring a kindness on many, if you would guard them, especially young men recently arrived in the metropolis, and who are desirous of meeting with employ. I refer to what are designated as " Agency Offices," established professedly for the purpose of procuring and supplying appointments and situations. Now, sir, when application is made at such places, a handsome deposit is demanded; you are told that every effort will be made to accomplish your object, and that such effort will continue for a given time, generally a month. After this, it rarely happens that you hear any thing further of the business, but when a call is made within the limited time, the applicant is almost sure to meet with the reply, " Mr. —— is unexpectedly called out of town," or " Mr. —— is so engaged that he will not be able to see you to-day." Thus you are put off from one day to another, till the month is expired, when you are very coolly told that nothing farther can be done without a second deposit. Few, I should apprehend, suffer themselves to be so duped a second time, but, if this should be a means of preventing it in the first instance, it will answer the design of

" ' Your's, &c.          A CONSTANT READER,
              AND AN ENEMY TO IMPOSITION.'

" When you mention advertising," said Peregrine, " I think of the extraordinary and objectionable mode of advertising for wives and husbands; and of the ill effects of which, the case of the late ruffian, Corder, is a convincing and melancholy proof: here was an ignorant profligate, who, by twice puffing his personal qualities in a lying advertisement, turned the heads of ninety-eight indiscreet spinsters, silly boarding-school girls, or wanton widows; but, had no channel existed for such objectionable communications, his unfortunate wife would not have had to prepare her weeds as the widow of a murderer! Female credulity is proverbial; but that sex to whom we owe all that is excellent in life—from whom our children receive the first and best lessons of morality—whose presence cheers adversity and brightens prosperity, and whose unwearied attentions shed a gleam of comfort even in the hour of death—that sex should remember that, while a man of sense will not descend to such an expedient, and a man of rectitude has no reason to obtain a wife by means of public advertisement, it is seldom or never resorted to, except by fools or designing villains."

" This disgraceful mode of gaining a wife," said Mentor, " deprives a man of the most agreeable part of his life, which is generally that which he passes in courtship, provided his passion be sincere, and the party beloved kind with discretion: love, desire, hope, and all the pleasing emotions of the soul rise in the pursuit.

" ' It is easier,' says the Spectator, ' for an artful man, who is not in love, to persuade his mistress he has a passion for her, and to succeed in his pursuits, than for one who loves with the greatest violence. True love has ten thousand griefs, impatiencies, and resentments, that render a man unamiable in the eyes of the person whose affection he solicits; besides that it sinks his figure, gives him fears, apprehensions, and poorness of spirit, and often makes him appear ridiculous, where he has a mind to recommend himself.

" ' I should prefer a woman that is agreeable in my own eye, and not deformed in that of the world, to a celebrated beauty. If you marry one remarkably beautiful, you must have a violent passion for her, or you have not the proper taste of her charms; or, if you have such a passion for her, it is odds but it will be embittered with fears and jealousies.

" ' Good nature and evenness of temper will give you an easy companion for life; virtue and good sense, an agreeable friend; love and constancy, a good wife or husband. When we meet one person with all these accomplishments, we find an hundred without any of them. Marriage enlarges the scene of our happiness and miseries. A marriage of *love* is *heaven;* a marriage of *interest* is *hell :*

" ' Naught but love
Can answer love, and render bliss secure.'

" Perhaps," continued Mentor, " you will not think it amiss were I to read you, out of the last improved edition of ' *Bourne's Vulgar Antiquities,*' a slight account of the different rites, cere-monies, and customs, adopted formerly, both in the manner of making and of celebrating this solemn contract, particularly as regards this country.

" ' The first grand preliminary to marriage, called " BETROTH-ING," is a custom of immemorial antiquity, and was differently practised by different countries. Among the Danes, it was called *Hand-fasting,* and is explained to mean a contract between par-ties to marry, ratified by the taking of hands, &c. Sir John Sin-clair illustrates this custom, by mentioning a similar one, which obtained, until lately, in a part of Scotland, where, at an annual for the unmarried persons of both sexes chose a companion ac cording to their liking, with whom they were to live until that time twelvemonth. This was called *hand-fasting,* or hand in fist. If they were pleased with each for that time, they continued toge-ther during life; if not, they separated, and were free to make another choice as at first. The fruit of the connexion, if any, was always attached to the disaffected person. An old author (1543), in his " Christen State of Matrimony," does not speak over favourably of this custom, which, as might be expected, was far from producing desirable effects. " Yet in thys thynge," says he, " also must I warn everye reasonable and honest person to beware that in contractyng of maryage they dyssemble not, nor set forthe any lye. Every man lykewyse must esteem the person to whom he is *hand-fasted,* none otherwyse than for his owne spouse, though as yet it be not done in the church nor the streate. After the hand-fastyng and making of the contracte, the church-going and weddyng should not be differed to long, lest the wick-edde sowe hys ungracious sede in the mean season." A thing which probably happened so often in the interval between this sort of contract and marriage, that it was one of the interrogatories to be put to the clergy in the early part of Elizabeth's reign, "whe-ther they had exhorted yonge folk to absteyne from privy con-tracts, and not to marry without the consent of such their parents and freyndes, as have auctority over them."

" ' Singular as it may seem in the present day, the MARRIAGE CEREMONY, or part of it, was performed anciently in the *church-porch,* and not in the church. Chaucer alludes to this custom in his ' Wife of Bath :'—

> ' She was a worthy woman all her live,—
> Husbands at the *church-door* had she five.'

" ' By the Parliamentary reformation of marriage and other rites under Edward VI., the man and woman were first permitted to come into the body or middle of the church, standing no longer, as formerly, at the church-door. Part of the old mar-riage form of words, from a missal in the time of Richard II., follows :—

" ' Ich M. take the N. to my weddid wyf, to haven and to holden, for fayrere for fouler, for bettur for wors, for richer for porer, in seknesse and in healthe, from thys tyme forward, 'til dethe do departe, zif holi chirche will it ordeyn, and zerto Ich plizh the my treuthe.' And, on giving the ring, ' with this ring I the wedde, and zis gold and silver Ich the zee, and with my bodi I the worschepe, and with all my worldly castelle I the honoure.' The woman says, ' Iche N. take the M. to my weddid husbond, to haven and to holden, for fayrer for fouler, for bettur for wors, for richer for porer, in seknesse and in helthe, to be bonch and buxum in bed and at borde, tyl dethe us departe, fro thys tyme forward, and if Holi Churche it wol orden, and zerto Iche plizh the my truthe.' This form a little differs in some of the other missals, but the variations are not material.

" The Hereford missal enjoined, as part of the marriage cere-mony, *the drinking of wine in church,* and by the Sarum missal, *sops* were directed to be immersed in it, and that the cup that contained it, and the liquor itself, should be blessed by the priest. An illus-tration of which occurs in Shakspeare's Taming of the Shrew, where Grumio describes Petruchio in church, at his wedding, as calling for wine, giving a health, and, having quaffed off the muscadel, throwing the sop in the sexton's face.

" Of the other attendant ceremonies on marriage, both before and after its solemnization, an enumeration merely would occupy some space. The principal were the giving of the RING, the BRIDE-CAKE, BRIDE-FAVOURS ; as TOPKNOTS, GLOVES,

SCARFS, GARTERS; the having of BRIDEMEN, and MAIDS; use of ROSEMARY and BAYS, wearing of GARLANDS, drinking of SACK-POSSET, throwing of the STOCKING, *Reveilles* in the MORNING AFTER MARRIAGE, &c. &c.

"The RING.—This seems to have been in use from the remotest antiquity, being to be traced to the Gentile nations, in their making of agreements, grants, &c.; from which practice it no doubt became emblematic of one of the most solemn engagements, and was adopted as such by the Christian world. Hudibras laughably insinuates that the supposed *Heathen* origin of this emblem nearly occasioned its use to be prohibited in the time of the Puritans, or Interregnum :—

> ' Others were for abolishing
> That tool of matrimony—a *ring*.
> With which th' unsanctify'd bridegroom
> Is marry'd only to a thumb;
> (As wise as ringing of a pig
> That's us'd to break up ground and dig),
> The bride to nothing but her will,
> That nulls thee after marriage still.'

"The wedding-ring is worn on the fourth finger of the left hand, because it was anciently believed, though the opinion is exploded by modern anatomists, that a small artery ran from this finger to the heart.

"The practice of marrying with the ring, for the female, was adopted by the Romans : the bride was modestly veiled, and, after receiving the nuptial benediction, was crowned with flowers. The ring, symbolic of eternity, was given and received as a token of everlasting love.

"RUSH RINGS were sometimes substituted for those of gold, by designing men, but were never used in lawful marriages. Mr. Douce refers Shakspeare's expression—" Tib's *rush* for Tom's forefinger," which had so long puzzled the commentators, to this ancient but pernicious custom.

"BRIDE-CAKE may be mentioned with the gift called Bride-favours, which consisted, besides that refreshment, as we have observed, of top-knots, gloves, scarfs, garters, &c. agreeably to a remark in an old writer, who, speaking of a certain wedding, says, ' No ceremony was omitted of bride-cake, points, garters, and gloves.'

"Of TOP-KNOTS, or favours of ribands, &c., to be worn by the married couple, which, though now *white*, formerly consisted of various colours, our author gives an amusing account. The book he quotes is called ' The Fifteen Comforts of Marriage,' and the conversation related is as to the choosing of these bridal colours. Many difficulties suggest themselves as to which colour is most conspicuous, until the milliner fixes the colours as follow :—For the favours, blue, red, peach-colour, and orange-tawney : for my young lady's top-knots, flame-colour, straw-colour (signifying plenty), peach-colour, grass-green, and milk-white; and for the garters, a perfect yellow, signifying honour and joy.

"The custom of BRIDE-MEN and BRIDE-MAIDS, being in part retained in the present day, need not be described. It is to be traced to the Saxon times.

"ROSEMARY, which was also used at funerals, was an accompaniment of ancient marriages, according to the poet—

> "The rosemary branch,
> Grows for two ends, it matters not at all,
> Be't for a bridall, or a buriall."

"Eating of SACK POSSET, throwing the STOCKING, and other customs, on the wedding eve, are sufficiently honoured by a bare mention. The REVEILLEZ, or morning salute after marriage, is ludicrously described by an old author, in a work called 'Comforts of Wooing,' &c. He says, ' Next morning come the fiddlers, and scrape him a wicked *Reveillez*, the drums rattle, the shaumes tole, the trumpets sound tan-ta-ra-ra-ra-ra, and the whole street rings with the benedictions and good wishes of fiddlers, drummers, pipers, and trumpeters; you may safely say now the wedding's proclaimed.'

"I suppose," continued Mentor, " the *Reveillez* gave rise to the marrow-bones and cleavers welcoming new-married people with a serenade: a custom practised to this day in London, by those rude minstrels. The following is a copy of a card presented by the men with marrow-bones and cleavers, to a young couple lately married.

## HIS MAJESTY'S ROYAL PEAL

OF

# MARROWBONES AND CLEAVERS,

OF THE

*County of Middlesex.*

### Instituted 1719.

" ' Honoured Sir,—With permission, we, the *Marrow Bones and Cleavers*, pay our usual and customary respects, in wishing, Sir, you and your amiable lady joy of your happy marriage; hoping, Sir, to receive a token of your goodness—it being customary on these happy occasions.

" ' Sir,—We being in waiting your goodness, and are all ready to perform if required.—Book and medal in presence to how.

"This book, it seems, they carefully preserve. By the proceedings against the St. George's Marrow-bone and Cleaver Club, at Marlborough-Street Office, by the Dowager Lady Harland, in their attempting to extort from her newly-married daughter, to whom they presented their silver plate, ornamented with blue ribbon and a chaplet of flowers, it appears the constable presented before the magistrate the book belonging to them, containing the names of a great many persons of the first consequence, who had been married at St. George's, Hanover Square; all of whom had put down their names for a sovereign. In the course of a year, the sums gathered by these greasy fellows, as marriage-offerings, amounted to £416.

"So you see, Peregrine," said Mentor, "what ways there are in London for men to raise the wind. It is certain that no person, if he has a mind to exert his wits in the metropolis, need be without money."

Peregrine, wishing his friend good night, retired to his inn; having previously made an appointment to visit the Eagle Tavern City Road, the next day, to see

The Doings of the Wrestlers.

They arrived at the Eagle Tavern just in time to witness a grand match between the wrestlers of Devonshire and Cornwall; when the skill displayed by Abraham Cann, the Devonshire champion, elicited universal applause.

"I am glad," said Mentor, "to see wrestling, one of the most

47                    2 B

ancient games of Englishmen, coming again into fashion. For the advantages of it are felt through the whole body : it exercises both legs and arms; excites every muscle; strengthens the chest, and circulates the blood. If we wish youth to possess courage, patience, and perseverance, no exercise is more fitting for the purpose than wrestling; nor is there one which calls forth, in such rapid and varied succession, all the muscular powers.

"In ancient times it was customary to celebrate the anniversary of the day of martyrdom of St. Bartholomew, by a wrestling-match, at the place appointed for that sport in Moorfields. The Lord Mayor and sheriffs were present at the recreation, and it was their duty to bestow the prize on the successful struggler. In the sixth year of the reign of Henry the Third, the citizens of London held their anniversary meeting on St. James's Day, near the Hospital of St. Matilda, St. Giles in the Fields, where they were met by the inhabitants of the city and suburbs of Westminster; and a ram was appointed for the prize, which was customary in those days, as we learn from Chaucer. The Londoners were victorious, having greatly excelled their antagonists; which produced a challenge from the conquered party, to renew the contest upon the Lammas Day following, at Westminster. The citizens of London readily accepted the challenge, and met them at the time appointed; but, in the midst of the diversion, the bailiff of Westminster, and his associates, took occasion to quarrel with the Londoners; a battle ensued, and many of the latter were severely wounded in making their retreat to the city.

"Thus, my friend Peregrine," continued Mentor, "by comparing the manners of the present race of the citizens of London and Westminster, with those of the fourteenth century, we can judge which is the most conducive to health and strength, and the most rational. Now, the major part of the citizens' thoughts are entirely engrossed on the accumulation of wealth; and, when I show you the Stock Exchange and the Royal Exchange, you will there see many proofs of their rapacity."

The wrestling-matches were now over, and as our heroes were steering their course towards Cornhill, they saw a mob assembled round a blind beggar, singing and praying,—a kind of itinerant ranter—a real blind guide; at last he came to the terrible words, "hell and damnation," which he sang out with such an emphasis, that he put all the people a trembling, so they all sneaked off one by one, wondering how a blind man should remember to sing by heart, without the help of his eyesight.

Peregrine, feeling rather hungry, expressed a desire to take a little refreshment at a pastry-cook's. "I do not wish," said Mentor, "to debar you, but perhaps you are not aware that some of these pastry-cooks use an enormous quantity of Derbyshire white, burnt bones, and other calcareous matter, and with complete impunity, too, as they are a sort of *ad-libitum* dealers, and can venture, by catching the eye with beautiful colours, and the palate with sweet tastes, to adulterate infinitely more than the baker can: they also use the following poisons, in great quantities, to give colour to their confectionary: *chromate of lead, copper, verdigris, iron, rose pink, vermillion, and powder blue!!*"

Mentor and Peregrine had now reached Cornhill, where the latter, perceiving a large building, asked his friend what place it was. "This," said Mentor, "is the Royal Exchange: here you may see the most honourable characters in the world—the English merchants! who meet here every day at 'change hours; and, for the more regular and readier despatch of business, they dispose of themselves in separate walks, each of which has its appropriate name.

"The figures you see in those niches are the statues of some of the kings and queens of England; and that on a pedestal, in the centre of the area, is Charles II. in a Roman habit. That figure under the pediment, is Sir Thomas Gresham, who founded this Exchange, in 1566; the other whole-length statue, is of Sir John Barnard, which was placed here in his life-time by his fellow citizens."

"And pray," asked Peregrine, "who is that very lusty gentleman, who is talking so anxiously to that Jew?" "Why, he is one of the most eminent stock-jobbers," replied Mentor. "Pardon my ignorance," said Peregrine; "what is a stock jobber?" "A stock-jobber, my friend, is a speculator; a compound of knave, fool, shop-keeper, merchant, and gentleman. His whole business is tricking: when he cheats another, he's a knave; when he suffers himself to be outwitted, he's a fool. He's as great a lover of uncertainty as some fools were of the lottery; and would not give a farthing for an estate got without a great deal of hazard. He's a kind of speculum, wherein you may behold the passions of mankind, and the vanity of human life. To-day he laughs, and to-morrow he grins; is the third day mad; and always labours under those two passions, hope and fear; rising one day and falling the next, like mercury in a weather-glass. He is never under the prospect of growing rich, but at the same time under the danger of being poor. He spins out his life between faith and hope, but has nothing to do with charity, because there's little got by it. He is a man whose great ambition is to ride over others, and, in order to do which, he resolves to win the horse, or lose the saddle.

"'The practice to which the term *stock-jobbing* is applied is that which is carried on amongst persons who possess but little or no property in any of the funds,' says the author of the Picture of London; 'yet who contract for the sale or transfer of stock at some future period, the latter part of the day or the next *settling-day*, at a price agreed on at the time. Such bargains are called *time-bargains*, and are contrary to law; and such practice is *gambling* in every sense of the word. Those who resort to it ought not to be trusted without caution. But the business of *jobbing* is carried on to an amazing extent; it is of this character:—A agrees to sell B £10,000 of bank stock, to be transferred in twenty days, for £12,000. A, in fact, does not possess any such property; yet, if the price of bank-stock on the day appointed for the transfer should be only £118 per cent., he may then purchase as much as will enable him to fulfil his bargain for £11,800; and thus he would gain £200 by the transaction. Should the price of bank-stock advance to 125 per cent., he will then lose £500 by completing his agreement. As neither A nor B, however, may have the means to purchase stock to the extent agreed on, the business is commonly arranged by the payment of the difference—the profit or the loss—between the current price of the stock on the day appointed and the price bargained for.

" ' In the language of the *Alley*, as it is called, (all dealings in the stocks having been formerly transacted in 'Change Alley) the buyer, in these contracts, is denominated a *bull*, and the seller a *bear*. As neither party can be compelled to complete these bargains (they being illegal), their own sense of ' honour,' and the disgrace, and the loss of future credit that attends a breach of contract, are the sole principles on which this singular business is regulated. When a person refuses, or has not the ability, to pay his loss, he is termed a *lame-duck*; but this opprobrious epithet is not bestowed on those whose failure is owing to insufficient means, provided they make the same surrender of their property voluntarily, as the law would have compelled had the transaction fallen within its cognizance. This illegal practice, which we have already termed *gambling*, is nothing more than a wager as to what will be the price of stocks at a fixed period; but the facility which it affords to extravagant and unprincipled speculation—speculation that is not checked by the ordinary risk of property, and the mischief and ruin which have frequently followed it, is incalculable.

" It was among these worthies, with Mr. Law at their head, that the speculation of the South-Sea Scheme, in 1719, was concerted : this oddest and most calamitous *bite* upon the town was followed immediately by the following schemes for companies, to raise *twenty-eight* millions of money—twice as much as the current coin of the realm; and, as the knowledge of these projects will doubtless be of service to you, I will read you an abstract of them, together with the places where the *flats* were to pay their *deposits!*

" ' For a general insurance on houses and merchandize,—at the Three Tuns, Swithin's Alley, £,2000,000.

" ' For building and buying ships to let or freight,—at Garraway's, Exchange Alley, £1,200,000.

" ' To be let by way of loan on stock,—at Garraway's, £1,200,000.

" ' For granting annuities by way of service-ship, and providing for widows, orphans, &c.,—at the Rainbow, Cornhill, £1,200,000.

" ' For the raising the growth of raw silk,—£1,000,000.

" ' For lending upon the deposit of stock, goods, annuities. ' tallies, &c.—at Robins's, Exchange Alley, £1,200,000

" ' For settling and carrying on a trade to Germany,—£1,200,000, at the Rainbow.

" ' For insuring of houses and goods from fire,—at Sadler' Wells, £2,000,000.

" ' For carrying on a trade to Germany,—at the Virginia Coffee-House, £1,200,000.

" ' For securing goods and houses from fire,—at the Swan and Rummer, £2,000,000.

" ' For buying and selling of estates, public stocks, government securities, and to lend money, £3,000,000.

" ' For insuring ships and merchandize, £2,000,000,—at the Marine Coffee-house, Birchin Lane.

" ' For purchasing government securities, and lending money to merchants to pay their duties with, £1,500,000.

" For carrying on the *undertaking* business, for furnishing funerals, £1,2000,000,—at the Fleece Tavern, Cornhill.

" For carrying on trade between Great Britain and Ireland, and the kingdoms of Portugal and Spain, £1,000,000.

" ' For carrying on the coal-trade from Newcastle to London, £2,000,000,—Cooper's Coffee-house.

" For preventing and suppressing of thieves and robbers, and for insuring all persons' goods from the same, £2,000,000,—at Cooper's.

" ' A grand dispensary, 3,000,000,—at the Buffaloe's Head.

" Subscription for a sail-cloth manufactory in Ireland,—at the Swan and Hoop, Cornhhill.

" ' £4,000,000 for a trade to Norway and Sweden, to procure pitch, tar, deals, and oak,—at Waghorn's.

" ' For buying lead-mines and working them,—Ship Tavern.

" ' A subscription for manufacturing dittis or Manchester stuffs of thread and cotton,—Mulford's.

" ' £4,000,000 for purchasing and improving commons and waste lands,—Hanover Coffee-House.

" ' A royal fishery, Skinner's Hall.

" ' A subscription for effectually settling the islands of Blanco and Saltorturgus.

" ' For supplying the London markets with cattle,—Garraway's.

" For melting lead-ore in Derbyshire,—Swan and Rummer.

" ' For manufacturing of muslins and calico,--Portugal Coffee-house.

" ' £2,000,000 for the purchase of pitch, tar, and turpentine,—Castle Tavern.

" ' £2,000,000 for importing walnut-trees from Virginia,--Garraway's.

" ' £2,000,000 for making crystal mirrors, coach-glasses, and for sash windows,—Cole's.

" For purchasing tin and lead mines in Cornwall and Derbyshire,—Half-Moon Tavern.

" ' For preventing the running of wool, and encouraging the wool manufactory,—King's Arms.

" ' For a manufactory of rape-seed oil,—Fleece Tavern.

" ' £2,000,000 for an engine to supply Deal with fresh water,—Black Swan.

" ' £2,000,000 at the Sun Tavern for importing beaver-fur.

" ' For making of Joppa and Castile soap,—Castle Tavern.

" ' £4,000,000 for exporting woollen stuffs, and importing copper, brass, and iron, and carrying on a general foundry,—Virginia Coffee-House.

" ' For making pasteboard, packing-paper, &c.,—Montague Coffee-House.

" ' A *hair* co-partnership, permits 5s. 6d. each, at the Ship Tavern, Paternoster Row; *by reason all places near the Exchange are so much crowded at this juncture.*

" ' For importing masts, spars, oak, &c., for the navy,—Ship Tavern.

" ' This day, the 8th inst., at Sam's Coffee-House, behind the Royal Exchange, at three in the afternoon, a book will be opened for entering into a joint co-partnership for carrying *on a thing* that will turn to the advantage of those concerned.

" For importing oils, and materials for the woollen manufactory, permits 10s. each—Rainbow.

" ' For a settlement in the Island of St. Croix,—Cross Keys.

" ' Improving the manufacture of silk,—Sun Tavern.

" ' For purchasing a manor and royalty in Essex,—Garraway's.

" ' £5,000,000 for buying and selling lands, and lending money on landed security—Garraway's.

" ' For raising manufacturing madder in Great Britain,—Pensylvania Coffee-House.

" ' £2000 shares for discounting pensions, &c.—Globe Tavern.

" ' £4,000,000 for improving all kinds of malt liquors,—Ship Tavern.

" ' £2,500,000, for importing linens from Holland, and Flanders' lace.

" " A society for landing and entering goods at the Custom House, on commission,—Robins.

" ' For making glass and bottles,—Salutation Tavern.

" ' The grand American fishery,—Ship and Castle.

" ' £2,000,000 for a friendly society, for purchasing merchandize and lending money.—King's Arms.

" ' £2,000,000 for purchasing and improving fens in Lincolnshire, —Sam's.

" ' Improving soap-making,—Milford's Coffee-House.

" ' For making English pitch and tar,—Castle Tavern.

" ' £4,000,000 for improving lands in Great Britain,—Pope's Head.

" ' A woollen manufactory in the north of England,—Swan and Rummer.

" ' A paper manufactory,—Hambie's Coffee-House.

" ' For improving gardens, and raising fruit-trees,—Garraway's.

" ' For insuring seamen's wages,—Sam's Coffee-House.

" ' The North-American Society,—Swan and Rummer.

" ' The gold and silver society.

" ' £2,000,000 for manufacturing baize and flannel,—Virginia Coffee-House.

" ' For extracting silver from lead,—Vine Tavern.

" ' £1,000,0000 for manufacturing China and Delt wares,—Rainbow.

" ' £4,000,000 for importing tobacco from Virginia,—Salutation Tavern.

" ' For trading to Barbary and Africa,—Lloyd's.

" ' For the clothing and pantile trade,—Swan and Hoop.

" ' Making iron with pit-coal.

" ' A co-partnership for buying and selling *live hair*,—Castle Tavern.

" ' Insurance-office for horses dying natural deaths, stolen, or disabled,—Crown Tavern, Smithfield.

" ' A rival to the above, £2,000,000,—at Robins's.

" ' Insurance-office from servants' thefts, &c., 3000 shares of £1000 each,—Devil Tavern.

" ' For tillage, and breeding cattle,—Cross Keys.

" ' For furnishing London with hay and straw,—Great James Tavern.

" ' For bleaching coarse sugars to a fine colour, without fire or loss of substance,—Fleece.

" ' £1,000,000 for perpetual motion, by means of a wheel moving by force of its own weight,—Ship Tavern.

" ' A co-partnership for insuring and increasing children's fortunes,—Fountain Tavern.

£4,000,000, for manufacturing iron and steel,—Black Swan Tavern.

" ' £2,000,000 for dealing in lace, &c. &c.—Sam's.

" ' £10,000,000 for a royal fishery of Great Britain,—Black Swan.

" ' £2,000,000 to be lent upon pledges,—Blue-coat Coffee-House.

" ' Turnpikes and wharfs,—Sword-blade Coffee-House.

" ' For the British alum works,—Salutation.

" ' £2,000,000 for erecting salt-pans in Holy Island,—John's Coffee-House.

" ' £2,000,000 for a snuff-manufactory,—Garraway's.

" ' £3,000,000, for building and rebuilding houses,—Globe Tavern.'

" It has been well observed of the Englisn people," said Mentor, " that they are like a flight of birds at a barn-door: shoot amongst them, and kill ever so many, the rest will return to the same place, in a very litttle time, without any remembrance of the evil that had befallen their fellows. Never was a more faithful remark; for who could have believed, after the knowledge of the fatal effects of so many hundreds of people being ruined by the above projects, that the public would again so easily fall in, as they did, with those schemes of speculators, or swindlers, which produced the memorable *panic* of 1825—the era when every species of fraud was at its summit. In that year of folly and villany, the following companies were in existence, and on which payments to the amount of nearly eighteen millions of money were paid. This list, which was compiled with great care, I have preserved" said Mentor, " as a curious and valuable record of the gullibility of the citizens of this overgrown metropolis :

## LOANS.

|  | Deposits paid. £ |
|---|---|
| Brazilian Loan of 1824 | 350,000 |
| Do. 1825 | 1,500,000 |
| Danish do. | 2,625,000 |
| Greek do. | 1,130,000 |
| Guatimala do. | 357,143 |
| Guadalajara do. | 246,000 |
| Mexican do. | 2,872,000 |
| Neapolitan do. | 1,750,000 |
| Peruvian do. | 480,480 |

## MINES.

|  |  |
|---|---|
| Anglo-Mexican Mining Shares | 250,000 |
| Anglo-Chilian | 75,000 |
| Arigne Iron and Coal | 42,000 |
| Bolanos | 12,500 |
| Boliva | 30,000 |
| Castello | 50,000 |
| Chilian | 50,000 |
| Cobalt and Copper | 5,000 |
| Chili and Peru | 50,000 |
| Cornwall and Devonshire | 150,000 |
| Consolidated Copper | 5,000 |
| English Mining | 25,000 |
| Equitable | 8,000 |
| Famatina | 12,500 |
| General Mining | 100,000 |
| Gwennappe | 5,400 |
| Haytian | 50,000 |
| Hibernian | 20,000 |
| Hoomeavy | 15,000 |
| London United | 75,000 |
| Manganese | 4,000 |
| Pasco-Peruvian | 50,000 |
| Potosi | 100,000 |
| Polbreen Tin and Copper | 3,000 |
| Royal Irish | 56,000 |
| Real del Monte | 165,000 |
| Royal Stannary | 40,000 |

|  | Deposits paid. £ |
|---|---:|
| Waldeck | 5,000 |
| South Wales | 10,000 |
| Scottish National Mining | 30,000 |
| Tywarnhale | 30,000 |
| Halpuxahua | 20,000 |
| Tarma | 5,000 |
| United Mexican Mines | 60,000 |
| Do. (New) | 180,000 |

## COMPANIES.

| | |
|---|---:|
| Welsh Iron and Coal | 150,000 |
| Do. Slate, Copper, and Lead | 100,000 |
| Protector Fire Assurance | 500,000 |
| British Gas | 80,000 |
| International Gas | 50,000 |
| London Portable | 15,000 |
| New Imperial | 100,000 |
| Provincial Portable | 30,000 |
| Independent Gas | 30,000 |
| Phœnix Gas | 45,000 |
| United General | 160,000 |
| Birmingham and Liverpool Railway | 20,000 |
| Manchester and Liverpool | 12,000 |
| Anglo-Mexican Mint | 50,000 |
| American and Col Steam | 60,000 |
| Australian | 20,000 |
| Atlantic and Specific | 100,000 |
| Egyptian Trading | 10,000 |
| British Iron | 500,000 |
| British Rock and Patent Salt | 300,000 |
| British and Foreign Paper | 300,000 |
| British, Irish, and Col. Silk | 40,000 |
| British Ship Canal | 10,000 |
| Steam and Packet Navigation | 25,000 |
| British and Foreign Timber | 100,000 |
| British, Chuan, and Roman Cement | 5,000 |
| Canada | 50,000 |
| Canal Gas Engine | 5,000 |
| Colombian Agricultural | 65,000 |
| Canada and Nova Scotia | 10,000 |
| Devon Hayton Granite | 8,000 |
| Droitwich Patent Salt | 50,000 |
| Elbe and Weser Steam | 2,000 |
| East London Drug | 10,000 |
| French Brandy | 4,000 |
| General Steam | 50,000 |
| Gold Coast | 50,000 |
| Great Westminster Dairy | 48,000 |
| Guernsey and Jersey Steam | 40,000 |
| Ground Rent | 10,500 |
| Hibernian Joint Stock | 250,000 |
| Honduras | 50,000 |
| Irish Manufactory | 20,000 |

|  | Deposits paid. £ |
|---|---|
| Imperial Plate Glass | 4,000 |
| Imperial Distillery | 120,000 |
| Imperial Estate | 10,000 |
| Investment Bank | 2,000 |
| London Brick | 30,000 |
| London and Gibraltar Steam | 1,000 |
| Do. Window-Glass | 2,000 |
| Lower Rhine Steam | 1,000 |
| London Drug | 5,000 |
| London Smelting | 4,000 |
| London and Portsmouth Steam | 2,000 |
| Do. and Gravesend | 4,000 |
| Mexican Company | 100,000 |
| Metropolitan Dairy | 24,000 |
| Medway Lime and Coke | 20,000 |
| Netherland Patent Salt | 18,750 |
| New Brighton | 10,000 |
| New Corn Exchange | 15,000 |
| National Drug and Chymical | 10,000 |
| Patent Bricks | 30,000 |
| Pacific Pearl Fishery | 20,000 |
| Pearl and Coral Fishery | 60,000 |
| Provincial Banks | 200,000 |
| Patent Distillery | 90,000 |
| Rio de la Plata | 50,000 |
| Roman Bricks and Tile | 7,000 |
| Scarlet Dye | 7,500 |
| Swedish Iron | 4,000 |
| Steam Engine Machinery | 9,000 |
| Tobacco and Snuff | 4,000 |
| Thames and Medway Brick and Lime | 12,000 |
| Do. and Rhine Steam | 3,000 |
| Do. and Loire do. | 1,000 |
| West India Company | 100,000 |
| United Pacific | 200,000 |
| United Chilian | 50 000 |
| Do. London and Hibernian Corn and Flour | 10,000 |
| Foreign Stock and Share Investment | 5,000 |
| Thames Tunnel | 40,000 |
| Hammersmith Bridge | 40,000 |

£ 17,582,773

" A vast many other companies I could mention," continued Mentor, " of which it is uncertain what deposits were paid; for the people were so maddened with the greedy idea of realizing fortunes, that they took no time to inquire into the plausibility of the schemes: their cry was, ' For G—d's sake, let me subscribe to something—I don't care what it is!' So that many adventured in some of the grossest cheats and improbable undertakings that ever the world heard of. At length the bubbles burst; and hundreds were hurled from a state of affluence to the most abject ruin—the fatal effects of their rapacity and folly!

"The words of Mr. Philips, 1720, may be well applied : ' Oh, my fellow-citizens! you have joined with the spoilers, yet you have not added to your stores. Let me print the remembrance of your past inadvertency upon your hearts, that it may abide as a memorial to us and to our children. The wealth, the inheritance of the island, are transferred to the meanest of the people; those chiefly have gained who had nothing to lose. All the calamities have we felt of a civil war, bloodshed only excepted. They who abounded suffer want; the industry—the trade of the nation has been suspended, and even arts and sciences have languished in the general confusion : the very women have been exposed to plunder, whose condition is the more deplorable, because they are not acquainted with the methods of gain to repair their broken fortunes. Some are driven from their country, others forced into confinement; some are weary of life, and others there are who can neither be comforted, nor recovered to the use of reason.'

"The following *memorandum* of the career of Mr. W., one of the most active projectors of the various schemes, is interesting, as giving a true picture of the *mania* of the times :—

"Before 1823, he had so little professional business, that he endeavoured to obtain money and popularity as an author. He wrote a patriotic life of the late queen ; also, a biographical dictionary of pious people. He paid great attention to the Dissenters, and figured in the ' Evangelical Magazine;' in which he inserted an advertisement, expressing his willingness, upon a payment of a suitable premium, to admit into his family, as an articled clerk, a youth of pious ways, provided it could be shown satisfactorily that he had received a sound religious education from his parents. Mr. W., also, as the public are already aware, endeavoured to get up a Joint Stock Company to obtain the due observance of the Sabbath, by enforcing the laws passed for that purpose in the reigns of Elizabeth and Charles I. His merits were not, however, appreciated by the sects in whose paths he walked. His activity was, perhaps, too great for them ; and, being straightened in circumstances, and indisposed to wait for the success which otherwise he would, no doubt, have obtained in that line, towards 1824 he started another project for a Joint Stock Company of a different character. This was contrived, and it succeeded. Scheme after scheme followed until the end of 1825, when he found himself surrounded by lords, ministers of state, members of Parliament, a large portion of the aristocracy, who, with merchants and bankers, courted his favour and patronage in the bestowal of directorships, &c., &c., in Joint Stock Companies ; the proceedings of which, as they never had been, there was no reason to apprehend would ever be, exposed to the public gaze by the interference of the press. In the year mentioned he had a sumptuously-furnished house in New Broad Street; he was possessed, also, of a splendid mansion at Mill Hill, where he kept three carriages and fourteen carriage-horses, four servants for his equestrian establishment alone, and a corresponding number for the interior of what may be called his palace. The Lord Chief Justice of all England, who resided in comparative obscurity in the same neighbourhood, and drove to town in a carriage and pair, was often compelled to make way, in order to avoid being overset by the vehicle which contained Mr. W., who was driven to town in a carriage and four, frequently preceded by outriders. He gave princely entertainments, to which men in office were not strangers; and the neighbourhood of his residence was crowded with the splendid equipages of his guests. He had an establishment at Ramsgate during the summer, and, during the winter, apartments at Long's Hotel, where he gave audience to men of distinction at the west end of the town; and thrice accredited and supremely happy was the member who could win his smile of recognition, when he joined the ride in the park. At this period, it was proudly declared in Parliament, that the stable prosperity of the companies of his formation was equal to that of the Bank of England. He then declared to his friends, that that was but a step to greater things; that within twelve months from that time, they would see him possessed of power and patronage to reward their zeal and services. His parliamentary phalanx was broken. He was now "deserted in his utmost need:" defeat after defeat, expulsion after expulsion followed, until he had not a single company left. He was now beset on all sides, but he still disputed every inch of ground with his enemies. He rallied vigorously in the House of Commons on the subject of the Cornwall and Devon Mining Company. He made his last desperate effort in the Court of Chancery to compel the payment of forty thousand pounds from the directors of the latter company. Being defeated there, and having failed in his efforts to establish a weekly paper, he was reduced to a state of the greatest financial embarrassments, and was only preserved by the exercise of his parliamentary privileges from imprisonment for debt. Having lost all the money he had made, he stood little chance of regaining confidence or professional employment in the city, where success is considered the best evidence of merit. He was now deprived of all resources, and he wandered through Wales, with what design is unknown. A respectable member of his family, it is generally stated, consented to give him a small annuity, on condition that he quitted this country and remained abroad."

"I thank you much," said Peregrine, "for the trouble you have taken to make me acquainted with the memorable bubbles of 1701 and 1825; and, believe me, it will be a long time ere they are obliterated from my memory.

"As I have never yet been over St. Paul's Cathedral, pray accompany me hither on our way home." "Certainly," replied Mentor; and accordingly, in a short time, Peregrine had the pleasure of beholding one of the most gratifying sights in the metropolis—that of beholding the " forest of London" from the dome of St. Paul's. " The most interesting time to have a view," said Mentor, " is early in the morning, to mark the gradual symptoms of returning life, until the rising sun vivifies the whole into activity, bustle, and business." " Certainly, it must be," replied Peregrine ; " but even now the view before us fills the mind with wonder and admiration ; and it is lost in contemplating this second Rome, and in reflecting on the various vicissitudes it has undergone, and how it has increased." " Indeed, my friend Peregrine, few cities have undergone more vicissitudes than London : scarcely may it be said to have been founded, or rather laid out (for it at first was little more than a fortified inclosure), when it was burnt, and the inhabitants massacred by the vindictive Boadicea, in the reign of Nero. Overcoming this calamity, it was again threatened, and would, no doubt, have been destroyed by a body of Franks, who had quitted the army of Constantius, in the year 296, who intended to pillage it, and then retreat to their own country with the plunder, by seizing the vessels in the Thames. But a part of the Roman fleet, which had been carried into the river, drove them off with great slaughter. On this occasion, our chronicles say, *L. Gallus* was slain, in the brook which ran through the middle of the city, and from him took the name of ' Na█gall," in British, and *Walbrook* in English ; which name still remains in the street, under which, it is stated, is still a large sewer to carry off the filth.

" In the year 314, London, York, and Colchester, appear to have been accounted the three principal cities of Roman Britain, three bishops taking their titles from them, at the synod held at Arelate, in Gaul. At this time, York had the first rank, London the second. That of London, on this occasion, occurs in the lists of ecclesiastics—' *Restitutus episcopus de civitate Londinensis provincia suprascripta.*' And, in 360, its consequence was further evinced, by Lupicinius being ordered by Julian to march here previous to his attacking the Scots and Picts, who were then harassing Britain, as it must have been a place of considerable importance, when the Roman general came here to concert the operations of the campaign with the provincial governor. In 367, Theodosius, having defeated these barbarous invaders, made a triumphal entry into *Londinium* (then called *Augusta*, and a colony, as all towns of that name were), which was saved from ruin or pillage by his seasonable arrival. Bishop Stillingfleet supposes that Augusta was at this time the capital of all Roman Britain ; and he quotes the opinion of Velserus, that all towns dignified with that name were *Capita Gentium*, the chief metropolis of the provinces. Perhaps a better argument for its supremacy may be derived from the treasures of the province being deposited in it, as we learn from the *Notitia Imperii*.

" Not long after, on the decline of the Roman power in Britain, this city, according to the fate of the whole island, fell under the dominion of the Saxons, but in what manner histo  do not relate. But it is thought Vortigern gave it up to Hengist to procure his own liberty; it being in the territory of the East Saxons, which historians agree was surrendered by the former to the latter on that condition. At this time both the city and church suffered dreadful calamities; the pastor being put to death or banished, the flocks dispersed, and all the wealth, whether sacred or profane, carried off.

" In 730, and probably long before (for the notice is connected by Bede with events of the year 604), London, though the capital of one of the smallest kingdoms in England, was a mart for many nations, who resorted thither by sea or land; and now, the gentle gale of peace beginning to breathe on this harassed island, by the Saxons generally embracing Christianity, it flourished with renewed splendour. Ethelbert, King of Kent (under whose favour Sebert reigned here) built a church in honour of St. Paul, where it is said had been before a temple of Diana, which afterwards became a great and magnificent structure; from which time it became the seat of the bishops of London. This calm of peace, however, had not continued long, when the West overcame the East Saxons, and London fell into the hands of the Mercians; and scarcely had the intestine commotions, caused by this transfer, ceased, when a new, and one of the worst storms it had ever yet experienced, broke in from the north. The Danes, who had already ravaged England in a miserable manner, and given a terrible blow to London (in which, however, they met with some repulses), first surprised and took that city in the reign of Ethelwulph (639), and massacred the citizens in the most inhuman manner. To recount, in a circumstantial manner, the many calamities that succeeded, would take up too much room. In 851, these ferocious invaders again sacked it, after totally routing the army of Beornulph, King of Mercia, who came to its relief. In the reign of Ethelred, 872, they again took it, and wintered in it. In 994, after a long resistance to Anlaff, and Sueno, King of Denmark, who besieged it, the citizens forced them to raise the siege. In 1016, it was hard pressed by Canute, and was forced to permit him to winter, and purchase peace with a considerable sum of money.

" It suffered greatly in the insurrections of Wat Tyler and Jack Straw, in the reign of Richard II. (1381); of Jack Cade, in the reign of Henry VI., and of Falconbridge in 1481, in the reign of Edward IV. These were the chief hostile attacks.

" In 983 it was greatly damaged by fire. In 1077, in the Conqueror's reign, it was laid in ruin in one night by such a fire as had not happened, says the *Saxon Chronicle*, since it was founded.— The greater part of the city, with the cathedral, was again destroyed by fire in 1086; again, in 1135 (1st Stephen) with the bridge, which was afterwards rebuilt of stone; but, within four years of its being finished (1212), all the houses on the bridge were burned.   This fire happened in Southwark, and the flames communicating from the south end of the bridge to the north, that also took fire : a multitude of persons on it were, by this second accident, put between two fires, and, crowding into boats on the river, overset them in the confusion, whereby 3000 persons perished. The last and most terrible calamity of this sort was the great fire of 1666, of which there being numerous accounts, it will be enough merely to mention it to you.

" From this period the importance and present splendour of London may be dated, in the manner we now see it.   Hence, in a few years, it rose again with extraordinary strength and magnificence, far surpassing its former state both in buildings and inhabitants ; insomuch that Sir William Petty, in his *Political Arithmetic*, compiled from the number of burials and houses, says, that London, in or about 1682, was as big as Paris and Rouen, the two best cities of France together ; and, since his time (about seven parts of the fifteen having been new built since the fire, and the number of inhabitants increased one-half, the total amounting to nearly 700,000), it is become equal to Rome and Paris put together.   Maitland, reckoning *seven* to a house, calculated, in 1738, the number of inhabitants of the city and suburbs at 725,903.   Dr. Brakenridge, who persuaded himself the numbers had decreased (viz. 120,000 from 1742 to 1754), sets them down at 680,700 ; which Governor Barrington, in his answer to him, denies.   A MS. paper in the Harleian Library estimates the total of houses in London, Westminster, Southwark, and Middlesex, within the bills of mortality, at 993,104.   The enumeration in 1801, made by order of Parliament, makes the total number of houses 120,414, and of persons, 854,845.   The additional buildings, which have since that time run out a great way into the fields, on every side, form many noble squares and handsome streets, and must have amazingly augmented the number.   This prodigious increase of inhabitants in the suburbs has rendered the out-parishes immoderately large, many of which have been divided, and many new churches erected, exclusive of the churches erected in the reigns of Anne and George I., and their successors ; and, as this building rage still continues, where may we expect the metropolis to stop ?   The rents in Maryle-bone parish, which in 1706 amounted only to £4000 per annum, were found, in 1782, to have advanced to £26,000, and have since more than doubled.

" I will read you," continued Mentor, " an interesting description of the streets of London, said to be from the travels of Theodore Elbert, as it appeared in that popular periodical, *The Athenæum*:—

" 'The streets of London,' says the author, ' have a twofold nature, a double existence ; there are the dead streets and the living streets, the stucco chaos of Mr. Nash, and the great collective majesty of John Bull.   I have a respect for both, but more, I confess, for the masonry than the men.   Go through London when its highways are deserted, and see those long vistas of silent habitations,—they have as much of human interest about them as a million of Englishmen. They are the works and homes of men; but they carry with them comparatively little of that jar and bustle of the present moment, the element of an Englishman's existence; they have a past and future. Here is a line of tall irregular houses, beneath which Milton has walked; yonder are the towers that point to the stars from above the tomb of Isaac Newton and of Edmund Spenser. Along this magnificent street our children's children will linger and wonder, but will not, like us, be able to discover a dim and distant patch of hill, and believe that it is green with God's verdure. Below stretches, with its wide and broken outline, the prospect which is made boundless by such big recollections. There Charles was executed; there Cromwell has ridden on a charger which may have seen Naseby or Worcester; there Vane has mused and sauntered. And beyond rolls the river, reflecting bridges and towers, with their myriad cressets, and the cyclopian shadows of domes, and palaces, and lifting its mist around those chambers from which have proceeded more lastingly powerful decrees than from the Roman Curia, and which (once, perhaps, or twice) have been filled with the grand presence of better statesmen than ever declaimed in Paris, or muttered in the Escurial. Away, again; and, heeding neither that cathedral front, which spreads like the wings of an archangel, nor that star which gleams so high above it, nor the hundreds of buttressed pinnacles which glimmer upwards like holy thoughts, stand for a few moments beneath those square, black, massy, and unwindowed walls; they are a prison. The rain is driving fast and slant along the gusty street; the distant rumble of some lagging vehicle is all the sound that I can hear, except the pattering of the rain-drops, and the voice of the lonely wind; and now rings out, with slow and lingering strokes, the chime which in a few hours will knell to his execution some wretched criminal within a few yards of where I am now placed. There is a slit over my head, one edge of which gleams in the lamp-light. It opens, perhaps, into the very death-cell; and there is, amid the gloom which it doth not illumine, a choking agony which stifles the prayer that desperation would force into utterance. Far away again, a shadowy intertexture of masts and cordage stretches between me and the skies, and some round antique towers rise against it. Within them Raleigh thought for years, and Jane Grey knelt to beseech forgiveness from Heaven for her innocent and beautiful life. These things—so much less dreams or fancies than our own wretched selfish interests—throng round us in the streets of London; but they only come to be repelled.'

"Do you perceive that crowd beneath us?" said Peregrine; "they look, from hence, a swarm of Lilliputians." "Yes, certainly," replied Mentor; "and let us haste into the street, and you will there witness one of the oldest and most favourite amusements of John Bull, in the adventures and changeable

Doings of Punch and Judy.

Accordingly, Mentor and his friends made the best of their way down the almost numberless stairs, and soon mingled with butchers, sweeps, pick-pockets, milk-girls, old fools and young fools, forming a motley but a merry audience, who had assembled to see the exploits of that great actor and hero of tragedy, *Mister Punch*;—some looking wise and dignified with all their might; others, without shame, "holding both their sides;" several Irish labourers, fresh from Munster, roaring with glee; and a troop of children, who, at every blow of that magic wand on the head of Mrs. Punch, re-echoed it with shouts and chimes of laughter. "Some Scotchman," says Theo. Elbert, in his account of Punch, " at my elbow, has been complaining that Punch has not partaken of the improvements of the age—that he is behind the nineteenth century. The malison of every quiet good-humoured traveller on the eternal upstart insolence of this nineteenth century! The world is improving—who doubts it? but the human mind and men's affections are the power that pushes it on; they were, before the nineteenth century, as they were before the first; and they will be, after it, as they will be after the nineteenth. I love the people for loving what their fathers loved, and what they themselves have loved from the earliest, most bawling, most turbulent years of infancy. There was, perhaps, but little of creation in the original devising of these puppet-shows; there is assuredly none in the minds of those who exhibit them; but how much is there in the hearts of the labourer and the child, whose open mouths and dancing eyes are so instinct with imaginative joyousness."

At the end of the performance, Peregrine accompanied his friend Mentor home; and, after dinner, the conversation turned on the puppet-show they had that afternoon seen. "It is remarked by the Editor of the Literary Gazette (No. 577, p. 83), "that Punch, though a fellow of wood, is, after all, a fair repretative of human nature: he has his foibles and his good qualities, his vices and his virtues, his crimes and his contritions; he is, indeed, a thorough man of the world,—selfish, as all men are, and reckless of the results to others, when he desires to remove any obstacle which stands in the way of his own gratification. Punch does not like to be thwarted: who does? Punch hates to be dog-bitten, hen-pecked, opposed, physicked, imprisoned, hanged, bedevilled; is there aught unnnatural in this? It may be that his mood is hasty, that he is too violent and pugnacious, and that he has a Turkish disregard of mortality; but then—his buoyancy of spirit, his boldness, and his wit, are not these redeeming points, which shed a lustre over even his worst faults? Punch is certainly not a very moral personage; but then was there ever one more free from hypocrisy? and profligacy is, beyond compare, the lesser sin of the two.

"The original family name of this renowned personage, was probably, Pulcinella, or Punchinello: he came into existence at Acerra, an ancient city, at a short distance from Naples, about th end of the fifteenth century.

"In a letter to the editor of the Every Day Book, it is said 'In some of the old mysteries, the devil was the *buffoon* of the piece, and used to indulge himself most freely in the gross indecencies tolerated in the early ages. When those mysteries began to be refined into moralities, the *vice* gradually superseded the former clown, if he may be so designated; and, at the commencement of such change, frequently shared the comic part of the performance with him. The *vice* was armed with a dagger of lath, with which he was to belabour the devil; who, sometimes, however, at the conclusion of the piece, carried off the *vice* with him. Here we have something of the club wielded by Punch, and the wand of Harlequin, at the present time, and a similar finish of the devil and Punch may be seen daily in our streets.

"The famous comedian, Edwin (the Liston of his day), acted the part of Punch, in a piece called 'The Mirror,' at Covent-Garden Theatre; in which he introduced a burlesque song, by C. Dibdin which obtained some celebrity; evidently through the merit of the actor, rather than the song.

" In the *New Monthly Magazine,* appears the following :—

## " STANZAS TO PUNCHINELLO.

Thou *lignum-vitæ* Roscius, who
Dost the whole vagrant stage renew,—
    Peerless, inimitable Punchinello!
The queen of smiles is quite undone
By thee, all-glorious king of fun,—
    Thou grinning, giggling, laugh-extorting fellow.

At other times mine ear is wrung,
Whene'er I hear the trumpet's tongue,
    Waking associations melancholic.—
But that which heralds thee recalls
All childhood's joys and festivals,
    And makes the heart rebound with freak and frolic.

Ere of thy face I get a snatch,
Oh ! with what boyish glee I catch
    Thy twittering, cackling, babbling, squeaking gibber ;
Sweeter than siren voices—fraught
With richer merriment than aught
    That drops from witling mouths, though utter'd glibber

What wag was ever known before
To keep the circle in a roar,
    Nor wound the feelings of a single hearer ?
Engrossing all the jibes and jokes,
Unenvied by the duller folks—
    A harmless wit, an unmalignant jeerer.

The upturn'd eyes I love to trace,
Of wondering mortals, when their face
    Is all alight with an expectant gladness ;
To mark the flickering giggle first,
The growing grin—the sudden burst,
    And universal shout of merry madness.

I love those sounds to analyse,
From childhood's shrill, ecstatic cries,
    To age's chuckle, with its coughing after ;
To see the grave and the genteel
Rein in awhile the mirth they feel,
    Then loose their muscles and let out the laughter

Sometimes I note a henpeck'd wight,
Enjoying thy martial might,—
    To him a beatific *beau ideal ;*
He counts each crack on Judy's pate,
Then homeward creeps to cogitate
    The difference 'twixt dramatic wives and real.

But, Punch, thou'rt ungallant and rude,
In plying thy persuasive wood ;
    Remember that thy cudgel's girth is fuller
Than that compasionate thum-thick,
Establish'd wife-compelling stick,
    Made legal by the *dictum* of Judge Buller.

When the officious doctor hies
To cure thy spouse, there's no surprise
    Thou should'st receive him with nose-tweaking grappling;
Nor can we wonder that the mob
Encores each crack upon his nob,
    When thou art feeling him with oaken sapling.

As for our common enemy,
Old Nick, we all rejoice to see
    The *coup-de-grace* that silences his wrangle;
But, lo, Jack Ketch!—Ah! well-a day!
Dramatic justice claims its prey,
    And thou in hempen handkerchief must dangle.

Now helpless hang those arms which once
Rattled such music on the sconce;—
    Hush'd is that tongue which late out-jested Yorick—
That hunch behind is shrugg'd no more—
No longer heaves that paunch before,
    Which swagg'd with such a pleasantry plethoric.

But Thespian deaths are transient woes,
And still less durable are those
    Suffer'd by *lignum-vitæ* malefactors.—
Thou wilt return, alert, alive,
And long, oh, long, mayst thou survive,
    First of head-breaking and side-splitting actors!'

"The editor of that clever work, *Punch and Judy, with Illustrations drawn and engraved by George Cruikshank,* says, 'In Germany, Punch is known by the name of *Hans Wurst,* among the lower orders; the literal translation of which is our Jack Pudding—*Hans* being John or Jack, and *Wurst,* a sausage or pudding.

"'In Holland, about ten years ago, we were present at one of the performances of Punch (there called *Toonelgek,* "stage fool," or "buffoon"), in which a number of other characters, peculiar to the country, and among them a burgomaster and a Friesland peasant, were introduced.

"'The current joke (at which date it originated seems uncertain) of Punch popping his head from behind the side curtain, and addressing the patriarch in his ark, while the floods were pouring down, with "Hazy weather, Master Noah," proves that, at one period, the adventures of the hero of comparatively modern exhibitions of the kind were combined with stories selected from the Bible.'

"We find frequent mention of him in the Tatler; and even the classical Addison does not scruple, in the Spectator, to introduce a regular criticism upon one of the performances of Punch.

"That the dress and appearance of Punch, in 1731, were, as nearly as possible, like what they now are, will be seen by the following popular song, extracted from vol. VI. of the Musical Miscellany, printed in that year. In other respects, it is a curious production, and, perhaps, was sung by Punch himself, in one of his entertainments. It is inserted under the title of—

" ' PUNCHINELLO.

' Trade's awry—so am I—
    As well as some folks that are greater;
But, by the peace we at present enjoy,
    We hope to be richer and straighter.
Bribery must be laid aside,
    To somebody's mortification;
He that is guilty, oh, let him be tried,
    And exposed for a rogue to the nation.
            I'm that little fellow
            Called Punchinello—
    Much beauty I carry about me;
            I am witty and pretty,
            And come to delight ye—
    You cannot be merry without me.

My cap is like a sugar-loaf,
And round my collar I wear a ruff;
I'd strip and show you my shape in buff,
    But fear the ladies would flout me.
My rising back, and distorted breast,
Whene'er I show 'em, become a jest;
And, all in all, I am one of the best,—
    So nobody need doubt me.
Æsop was a monstrous slave,
    And waited at Zanthus's table;
Yet he was always a comical knave,
    And an excellent dab at a fable.
So, when I presume to show
    My shape, I am just such another—
By my sweet looks and good humour, I know,
    You must take me for him or his brother.
            The fair and the comely
            May think me but homely,
    Because I am tawny and crooked;
            But he that by nature
            Is taller and straighter,
    May happen to prove a blockhead.

But I, fair ladies, am full as wise
As he that tickles your ears with lies,
And thinks he pleases your charming eyes
    With a rat-tail wig and a cockade:
I mean the bully that never fought,
Yet dresses himself in a scarlet coat,
Without a commission—not worth a groat—
    But struts with an empty pocket.'

" It is both curious and entertaining," continued Mentor, " to notice the variety and nature of the sports and amusements of the citizens of London; for, says the learned and elaborate John Peter Malcolm, in his *Anecdotes of the Manners and Customs of London,* Amusement necessarily attends congregated population: the activity of the human mind must have new sources of attraction; the man who labours through the day should not fall into his bed wearied by exertion; time ought to be allowed for recruiting his spirits; and amusements, which are relaxations of the mind from oppressive thought, prepare it for that happy state of quiet—the cause of refreshing sleep and renovated vigour.

" ' The rich man, at perfect ease with respect to the animal wants of life, has no employment for his time, unless he devotes great part of it to amusement: the necessity thus urged, it will be far more difficult to define the term. What one individual would call amusement, a second would call a crime, a third labour, and a fourth folly. The depraved mind asserts that bull-baiting and cock-fighting are manly amusements; but, happily, the majority think otherwise: and it gives me real pleasure to reflect, that those, in common with all our ancient royal sports, are becoming unfrequent, and gradually giving place to that frivolity which renders the human mind gay and cheerful, and consequently innocent.

" ' The reader must agree with me, that a laughing is better than a sullen or ferocious age.'

" " Such," continued Mentor, " are the opinions of Mr. Malcolm; but certainly, if any one amusement is more censurable than another, it is the private theatricals; and the following remarks on the subject, in a morning paper, fully bear me out:—

" ' There is no practice more ridiculous, or more pernicious to the morals and interests of young people, than private stage-playing. If the persons who engage in it intend themselves for the profession, they adopt bad habits, the eradication of which is more difficult than the acquirement of good ones. If they do not intend themselves for the profession, they squander on extraneous pursuits that time which would have been better devoted to their respective employments. They become neither good actors nor good men. The misery of many starving on provincial boards may be traced to this source. How many useful members of respectable trades and professions have been lost by this destructive habit. It steals into the retreats of science—it goes from the college to the counting-house—from the counting-house to the shop. The academic gown has been resigned for the tragic cloak—the truncheon has taken place of the yard—SHAKSPEARE of COCKER—

> " Not young attorneys have this rage withstood,
> But chang'd their pens for pistols—ink for blood—
> And, strange reverse! died for their country's good."

Even the softer sex has not been free from this pestilence which goeth by night. Not a few belonging to those respectable classes named milliners and haberdashers, have, from making dresses, aspired to make speeches—from flouncing gowns, to flounce on carpets. To judge of the time and money thrown away on these pursuits, we should consider the process usually gone through, in order to what is called getting up a play. A number of young men subscribe to gratify an audience with the exposure of their follies and incapacities. Five or six weeks generally elapse before the play is fit to be murdered. During that time they nightly assemble in taverns, not to drink of that poetical fountain which flows near the abode of the Muses—not even to gather the mists of Helicon, but to inspire themselves with plain mortal beverage—gin, rum, and beer. Night after night, the cleft walls of some unfortunate dwelling resound with the ravings of Othello, or the bellowings of Richard. These wooers of the coy sisters now want nothing but women. A Desdemona, an Ophelia, or a Bel videra, is at length procured. The long-wished-for time arrives, and the work of havoc commences. I was once amused at one of those private plays. It was, of course, a tragedy, and no less than Richard the Third. Some delay was occasioned by the absence of the Queen. The performers, through a respectable consideration, did not wish to commence without her Majesty's presence. After the audience had waited with the greatest patience an hour and a half beyond the stated time, the Lord Mayor stepped forward, and announced her Majesty's arrival. Richard growled, and mouthed through his opening soliloquy as well as might have been expected. As soon as he had killed King Henry according to the rules of art, a wag threw an orange at the anointed head of the slain monarch. The body instantly became galvanized, betrayed convulsive symptoms of returning life—started up—took his bonnet in his hand—grinned horribly at the audience, and made his exit. In the apparition scene, *King Henry*, offended at the indignity offered his sacred person, did not come on, and consequently gave up the ghost. Most of the other ghosts were damned. Instances as ludicrous as this frequently occur in such performances. If young people were to use a little reflection, they would not engage in practices which vitiate their morals, make away with their time, and may eventually lead them to a disgraceful end.'"

"I beg pardon," says Peregrine, "for interrupting you; probably you forgot we agreed this evening to visit the House of Commons." "Indeed I did," answered Mentor, "but it is not too late; so, therefore, let us take coach and make the best of our way to Old St. Stephen's Chapel." In a short time Peregrine had the pleasure of being within side of the British House of Commons. "That person," said Mentor, "who is sitting, dressed in robes, with the mace before him, is the Speaker of the House; that part of the House on his right is called the ministerial side, and that on his left, the opposition. The bench on the floor, extending from his chair to the division in the centre, is known by the appellation of 'The Treasury Bench;' on which his Majesty's ministers usually take their seats. The bench on the opposition side is occupied by the leaders of the opposition. That on which the mace is placed, is the table, on which are also a certain number of the journals: it is here the various petitions, &c. are put when not taken immediately into consideration; and hence you hear so much in the parliamentary proceedings, 'Ordered to be laid on the table.' Those galleries on the right and left are the members' galleries."

Peregrine having been fortunate enough to gain admittance

on an evening when Canning, Mackintosh, Brougham, Burdett, and other illustrious men, delivered their opinions, left the house highly delighted with the eloquence of those eminent orators, and retired to his friend's residence to take some refreshment.

"Pennant," said Mentor, "in his *London*, informs us, that 'the House of Commons was built by King Stephen, and dedicated to his name-sake, the proto-martyr. It was beautifully rebuilt by Edward the Third, in the year 1347. By him it was made a collegiate church, and a dean and twelve secular priests appointed. Soon after its surrender to Edward IV., it was applied to its present use. The revenues at that period were not less than £1,085 a year. The west front, with its beautiful Gothic window, is still to be seen as we ascend the stairs to the Court of Requests; it consists of the sharp-pointed species of Gothic. Between it and the lobby of the house is a small vestibule of the same sort of work, and of great elegance. At each end is a Gothic door, and one in the middle, which is the passage into the lobby. On the south side of the outmost wall of the chapel, appear the marks of some great Gothic windows, with abutments between; and beneath some lesser windows, once of use to light an under chapel. The inside of St. Stephen's is adapted to its present use, and is plainly fitted up. The under chapel was a most beautiful building; the far greater part is preserved, but fitted into various divisions, occupied principally by the passage from Westminster Hall to Palace Yard. In the passage stood the famous bust of Charles I. by *Bernini,* made by him from a painting by *Vandyke,* done for the purpose. Bernini is said, by his skill in physiognomy, to have pronounced from the likeness, that there was something unfortunate in the countenance. The far greater part of the under chapel of St. Stephen is *(was)* possessed by his Grace the Duke of Newcastle, as auditor of the Exchequer. One side of the cloister is entirely preserved, by being found convenient as a passage; the roof is Gothic, *so elegant as not to be paralleled even by the beautiful work-manship* in the chapel of Henry VII. Several parts are walled up for the meanest uses; a portion serving as a coal-hole. That which has the good fortune to be allotted for the Steward's room, is very well kept. * * * In what is called the grotto-room, are fine remains of the roof and columns of the sub-chapel. The roof is spread over with ribs of stone, which rest on the numerous round pillars that compose the support. The pillars are short; the capitals round and small, with a neat foliage intervening. In a circle on the roof is a martyrdom of St. Stephen, cut in stone. In another circle is a representation of St. John the Evangelist cast into a cauldron of boiling oil, by command of the Emperor Domitian.

" ' I cannot but remark,' observes Pennant, in concluding this portion of his work, 'the wondrous change in the hours of the House of Commons, since the days in which the great Earl of Clarendon was a member: for he complains—of the house keeping *those disorderly hours,* and seldom rising till after *four* in the *after-noon !'*

" The *History of Parliaments*, from its earliest periods, would form an invaluable work; detailing the days of meeting, times of sitting, fines, purity, steadiness, privileges, such as being free from arrest, franking of letters, &c.

" In the reign of Edward III. the town of Chepyng Toriton, in Devon, prayed, on account of its poverty, to be excused the burden of sending a member to the King's Parliament; which was complied with. How different from the present time, when cities and towns are praying to have the privilege of sending members. In the tenth of the same Edward, the citizens of London were commanded to elect four discreet merchants, and send them to Oxford.

" ' In 1468, Essex and Hertford were so bare of substantial inhabitants, that the sheriff could only find Colchester and Maldon in Essex, and not one town in Hertfordshire, which could send burgesses. It appears, therefore, that it lay much in the choice of the sheriff whether or no a town should send any representative; and that the so sending was considered a severe hardship.

" In ancient times, Sunday appears to have been an usual day on which to convene Parliaments. From the rolls of Edward II. and VI. there are various tested writs, in which the king commands the attendance of Parliament on the Sabbath-day, principally at York and Lincoln.

" The Parliament of 1426 was called the Parliament of Bats; since the senators, being ordered to wear no swords, attended with clubs or bats. This meeting was held in Leicester, to avoid the tumult of a London mob.

" What we have seen this evening," continued Mentor, " suggests to me the following excellent remarks, which I will read to you out of the Morning Herald; and which proves, as 1 before remarked, that the British Constitution holds out to every subject, without reference to birth or fortune, the prospect of rising to the highest office in the executive.

" ' This facility of acquiring power and influence in a state might be supposed to lead to dangerous results, because men's ambition is known to increase with their advancement, until, intoxicated with success, they are unwilling to set any bounds to their career, or any limits to their authority. History supplies numerous instances of men of talent who, encouraged by the applause of the people, sought and obtained office with the purest intentions, but afterwards perverted them to the worst ends. The long possession of place and authority produces their wonted effects: power corrupts and changes the virtuous purpose; the successful aspirant, hitherto unconscious of its extent, and giddy with the elevation to which he has been raised, pierces through the cloud which before concealed the summit from his view, and, kicking away the ladder by which he mounted, seats himself upon it, or falls in the attempt. This is human nature—

50.

" I shall do well,—
The people love me, and the sea is mine.
My power's a crescent, and my auguring hope
Says, it will come to the full."

" ' History shows that Pompey, to whom Shakspeare gives those
sentiments, was not the only man of antiquity who, from being
the favourite, desired to become the master—who, from being
the protector, aimed at becoming the tyrant of the people. Rome
and Athens furnish abundance of examples to illustrate this. In
the age of Solon, Pisistratus was at the head of the popular
party in Athens. Uniting in himself all those qualities that captivate
the minds of the people—illustrious birth, great wealth, acknowledged courage, a commanding figure, and persuasive eloquence—
Pisastratus professed to maintain equality among the citizens. He
accordingly declared himself their protector, and an irreconcileable
enemy to every innovation which might tend to the destruction of that
equality. His virtues seemed to increase with his popularity, but his
conduct soon discovered that he concealed the most inordinate ambition under the mask of an affected moderation. With the guard which
the people gave him for the defence and for the honour of his
person, he took possession of the citadel, disarmed the multitude,
and seized without opposition on the supreme authority. In the
Athenian republic afterwards, when a citizen became popular or
powerful, he became at the same time culpable and obnoxious. The
constitution giving no other security, recourse was had to the
ostracism, by which the formidable citizen was banished for a certain number of years. Rome was, even in her greatness, perpetually
agitated by those citizens who rose through the favour of the
people to an eminence that threatened danger to the state, and
finally paved the way to despotism—such as Spurius, Cassius,
Manlius Capitolinus, Marius, Sylla, Cinna, and Cæsar. The
constitution of Rome afforded no remedy against a dangerous
ascendancy but the dagger or the Tarpeian rock.

" ' But it is a singular characteristic of the constitution of England, that it affords security against the contingency of any subject ever rising to a pre-eminence dangerous to the safety of the
state. No person, even though he possessed the most shining
talents, the highest rank, the largest fortune, and most extensive
connexious, joined to indefatigable industry, could entertain a rational hope of settling himself above the constitution. To the inordinate ambition of an individual, the royal authority in England
is a sufficient counterpoise, because the king is the depository of
the whole executive power. If any subject would hope to dazzle
the multitude, and elevate himself over his fellows, by the splendour of his rank and fortune, he is sure to be eclipsed by the
glare of royalty, because the king, at the head of the state, is in-
vested with all the pomp, all the personal privileges, and all the
majesty of which human dignities are capable, and he is the very
source and fountain from whom the other derives his honours. In-

deed, the king himself, who is confessedly supreme in station as well as in authority, cannot render his power dangerous, because that power is very wisely limited by the constitution, and made entirely dependent on the people, who can arm or disarm it, by refusing or granting supplies. Should any man aspire to dangerous greatness by the weight of his own abilities, by his eloquence, by his public services, or by his popularity, he would find himself ultimately disappointed. Our constitution, making the people share in the legislature by their representatives, has prevented the momentary ebullitions and irresistible violence which in ancient states arose frequently from those numerous and general assemblies of the people, who, when raised to fervour by flattery and eloquence, nominated their orator chief, or dictator, or emperor. The people of England, besides, are too prudent to listen to, and too phlegmatic to be excited by, such oratory. Should such a man traverse the country in search of proselytes to his ambitious designs, and should the people attend to him, yet all he can expect is barren applause. The heat which his address inspired in one county would cool before he assembled a meeting in the next. He cannot proceed far, if his designs be wicked, before he excites the suspicions and the vigilance of the government, and then all his projects are foiled. Should a member of the House of Commons attempt to climb the dangerous height, by influencing the other representatives of the people by his eloquence, by enumerating his own services or their grievances, the only door the constitution opens to his ambition is a place in the executive government, or a seat in the House of Peers. But the very moment he takes office, and becomes one of the administration, his career of popularity is closed. The people, who are always in opposition to men in power, cannot be persuaded but their favourite has deserted their cause. This position requires not any illustration. It would be difficult to produce an instance of any person in this country, who, however good his intentions might be, did not lose the confidence of the people the very moment he took office, or even defended the measures of ministers. The acceptance of a peerage produces the same effects. It operates on the individual like banishment. Mr. Pulteney was, in the reign of George the Second, one of the most popular men in the kingdom, yet the very moment he was created Earl of Bath, he lost the love of the people, and, without enjoying any share of the royal confidence, he remained the victim of his own treachery, as Mr. Belsham says—"A solitary monument of blasted ambition." Mr. Pitt, another friend of the people, in the same reign, distinguished by the flattering appellation of the Great Commoner, lost in popularity and in power what he gained by the dignity of the peerage. The title of Chatham operated on him like the ostracism of the Athenians. It is therefore always in the power of the king to obviate the dangers arising from popularity, by calling the favourite to his councils, or by raising him to the honour of peerage. But, should the individual's ambition when in office prompt him to pervert to selfish and unconstitutional purposes the power with which he has been trusted, a word from his sovereign dismisses him, and a dismissal consigns him to merited infamy. The only instance in English history in which even a suspicion of this nature was entertained, was the case of the Duke of Marlborough. He was at the head of a powerful and victorious army, among whom he was greatly beloved. He had a numerous and strong party at home, and he was favoured by the allies of England abroad; yet the very moment he was called on by his sovereign to lay down his commission, he submitted without hesitation. " He knew," as a philosophical observer of our constitution says, " that all his soldiers were inseparably prepossessed in favour of that power against which he must have revolted. He knew that the same prepossessions were deeply rooted in the minds of the whole nation, and that every thing among them concurred to support the same power. He knew that the very nature of the claims he must have set up would instantly have made all his captains and officers turn themselves against him. And, in short, that, in an enterprise of that nature, the arm of the sea he had to repass was the smallest of the obstacles he would have to encounter."

" ' Hannibal, the Carthaginian general, placed in circumstances somewhat similar to those of the Duke of Marlborough, carried on the war in Italy against the will of the senate and government of Carthage, to gratify his private vengeance. Cæsar, also, continued the war in Gaul, to satisfy his thirst for glory—that infirmity of noble minds—notwithstanding the frequent remonstrances of the senate and Roman people. Settting himself at length above all authority, he discovered his real designs, crossed the Rubicon, and marched to Rome, not to surrender his commission, but to establish a military despotism. But the laws and the constitution of England " open no door (says M. De Lolme) to those accumulations of power, which have been the ruin of so many republics. They offer to the ambitious no possible means of taking advantage of the inadvertence, or even the gratitude, of the people, to make themselves their tyrants; and the public power, of which the king has been made the exclusive depository, must remain unshaken in his hands, as long as *things continue to keep in their legal order.*" The nomination of Cromwell cannot be considered as an exception to this position. His rise was subsequent to the destruction of the monarchy and to the dissolution of the legal and established order. The state of society in England then bore some resemblance to that of Athens, when Pisistratus seized the supreme authority; or of Rome, on the usurpation of Augustus. The essential advantage, therefore, of the English government above all those that have been called free, and which, in many respects, were apparently so, is, that no person in England can entertain so much as a thought of his ever rising to the level of the power, charged with the execution of the laws. All men in the state, whatever may be their rank, wealth, or influence, are thoroughly convinced that they must, in reality, as well as in name, continue to be subjects, and are thus compelled really to love, to defend, and to promote those laws which secure the liberty of the subject.' "

Mentor and Peregrine were now amused in hearing the wonderful tales of a gentleman, who had paid Mentor a visit, and who was a sort of a Munchausen, having seen so many astonishing sights, and escaped such dreadful dangers : at length, what with talking and the effects of the wine, he fell asleep. " This friend of mine reminds me," said Mentor, " of an anecdote I was reading a few days ago : it was this. In an assualt case at York Assizes, a witness named John Labron was thus cross-examined by Mr. Brougham :—What are you—I am a farmer, and melt a little. Do you know *Dick Strother* ?—No. Upon your oath, Sir, are *you* not generally known by the name of *Dick Strother* ?—(much confused.)—That has nothing to do with this business ! I insist upon having an answer : have you not, from the notoriety of your character as a *liar*, obtained that name ?—(Very reluctantly.) I am sometimes called so.—(*Laughter*.)—Now, *Dick*, as you admit you are called so, do you know the story of the hare and the ball of wax ?—I have heard of it. Then pray have the goodness to relate it to his lordship and the jury.—I do not exactly remember it. Then I will refresh your memory by relating it myself. *Dick Strother* was a cobbler, and, being in want of a hare for a friend, he put into his pocket a ball of wax, and took a walk into the fields, where he soon espied one. Dick then very dexterously threw the ball of wax at her head, where it stuck, which so alarmed poor puss, that, in the violence of her haste to escape, she ran in contact with the head of another; both stuck fast together, and Dick ! lucky Dick ! caught both.—Dick obtained great celebrity by telling of this wonderful feat, which he always affirmed as a truth, and from that time every notorious liar in Thorner bears the title of *Dick Strother*. Now, *Dick*—I mean John—is not that the reason why you are called *Dick Strother* ?—It may be so ! Then you may go."

Mentor's friend, having now awoke, yet full of the generous grape, insisted upon the company toasting his favourite lady, or be fined, which desire, to pacify him, was immediately complied with.

It was remarked by Peregrine, that in the merry thoughtless days of Charles the Second, it was the custom, when a gentleman drank a lady's health, by way of doing her greater honour, to throw some part of his dress into the fire, an example which his companions were bound to follow. One of his friends, perceiving that Sir Charles Sedley had on a very rich lace cravat, when he named his toast, committed his cravat to the flames, and Sir Charles and the rest of the party were obliged to do the same.

The poet observed it was a good joke, but that he would have as good a one some other time. When the party was assembled on a subsequent occasion, he drank off a bumper to some beauty of the day, and ordered a tooth-drawer into the room, whom he had previously brought for the purpose, and made him draw a decayed tooth, which had long plagued him. The rules of good fellowship required that every one of the company should have a tooth drawn, also, but they naturally expressed a hope that Sedley would not enforce the law. Deaf, however, to all their remonstances, he saw them one after another put themselves into the hands of the operator, and, whilst writhing with pain, added to their torment by exclaiming " Patience, gentlemen, patience, you promised that I should have my frolic too."

" You are correct, indeed," said Mentor, "in calling them the ' merry thoughtless days' of the second Charles; and whosoever doubts it, let him read the memoirs of Mr. Pepys, who held the important office of secretary to the Admiralty, and who gives the following description of Life in London, in the ays of the merry monarch.

" ' 14th.—After dinner, I went with my wife and Mercer, to the Bear Garden, where I have not been, I think, of many years, and saw some good sport of the bulls tossing the dogs—one into the very boxes; but it is a very rude and nasty pleasure. We had a great many Hectors in the same box with us (and one very fine went into the pit and played his dog for a wager, which was a strange sport for a gentleman), where they drank wine, and drank Mercer's health first, which I pledged with my hat off. We supped at home, and very merry, and then about nine o'clock to Mrs. Mercer's gate, where the fire and boys expected us, and her son had provided abundance of serpents and rockets, and there mighty merry (my Lady Pen and Peggy going thither with us, and Nan Wright), till about twelve at night, flinging our fireworks, and burning one another, and the people over the way; and, at last, our business being almost spent, we went into Mrs. Mercer's, and there mighty merry, smutting one another with candle-grease and soot, till most of us were like devils; and there I made them drunk, and up stairs we went, and then fell into dancing, W. Ratelier dancing well, and dressing him, and I, and one Bannister, who, with my wife, came over with us, like women; and Mercer put on a suit of Tom's, like a boy, and mighty mirth we had; and Mercer danced a jig, and Nan Wright and my wife and Peggy Pen put on perriwigs; and thus we spent till four in the morning, mighty merry, and then parted and to bed.'

" What, in the name of patience," said Mentor to Peregrine, have you got there?" " *True* Dutch salt of lemons," he replied, " which I bought of a man in the street, who assured me they were genuine; and I thought they would be useful when I was in he country." " N ever, my friend," replied Mentor, " purchase articles of those wandering hawkers ; always go to respectable shops. This true salt of lemons, is composed of five parts of cream of tartar, and one of oxalic acid. A honest tradesman of Islington was cheated, some few months ago, in purchasing a quantity of it, on being promised to be appointed *sole agent* for the place. There are also a parcel of Jews who go about with pencils ; and, when they see a new shop opened, or fresh occupants, they agree to appoint them *agents*, tell them a fine flattering tale, and generally contrive to get rid of their pencils, which are good for nothing. I was at a police-office where a Jew was taken before the magistrate for vending *true* Dutch drops without a licence : just as the magistrate was going to convict him in the penalty, he acknowledged that he made them himself, and, therefore had no need of a licence. ' Make them !' said the magistrate, ' of what ?' ' Why, your worship,' replied the brazen-faced Jew, ' of *coal tar!* there's nothing else in them, as I hope to be saved.' The Jew, by this *honest* confession, was spared the fine.

" These facts ought to put the public against buying any thing of such vagabonds, who live by their wits and scheming, and cheat all who are foolish enough to listen to them.

" Of the innumerable modes adopted in London, to gain a livelihood, I know of a curious one, pursued by a respectable-looking man, and that is, of going, in the season, to all the auctioneers, and procuring catalogues from them ; perhaps obtaining of some of them, in the hurry of their business, two or three in a day, and, in the evening, he sells them for waste paper. There are also sprung up some gentlemen who levy pretty heavy contributions on booksellers and publishers, by representing themselves as hawkers or canvassers, and procuring from them their catalogues and prospectuses, on purpose that they may sell them for waste paper. This, I am told, has been to them, hitherto, a good speculation but I hope their swindling career is nearly at an end, as the trade in general is acquainted with the trick."

" Such trickeries are almost incredible," said Peregrine ; " and the mind is lost in amazement, while contemplating the vile uses man too often puts the talents which God has endowed him with, to such bad purposes. Thinking of the wickedness of mankind, reminds me of the trial of the man to-morrow for murder ; pray, my friend," continued Peregrine, " will you indulge my curiosity, and accompany me to hear his trial at the Sessions House, Old Bailey ?" " You are mistaken, Peregrine,"replied Mentor ; " the trial took place yesterday ; and I am surprised you have not read the report of it in the morning papers. This murder, like most that are committed, was occasioned through drunkenness. The brief melancholy history of the affair is this :—the perpetrator had been a faithful, honest, sober servant, for many years, to a soap-maker ; until, one Saturday night, he unfortunately met a countryman of his, whom he had not seen for many years, and they retired gossip over days ' auld lang sine ;' and, before they parted, were both in a state of inebriation, having been all the evening drinking that deadly damnable poisonous liquor—*gin!* This poor creature, while labouring under the maddening effects of that execrable drink, in a state of fury, went home and beat his wife's brains out! He was found guilty; and is to be executed next Monday, together with another murderer. I wish the learned judge had expatiated on this melancholy proof of the horrid effects of drunkenness: it might probably have done great good, coming from such a personage, and on such an occasion.

"Now hear another deplorable statement of the cursed consequences of gin-drinking. I will read it you as it appeared in the Times newspaper—

"'MANSION HOUSE—Gin—Allen, the officer, who is principally employed in clearing the streets of paupers, apprehended a woman who had been begging with a wretched emaciated child, about two years and a half old, in her arms, a few days ago. She had levied contributions upon the public to the amount of three shillings, and was sent to the usual place of confinement after examination. The feeling excited by the appearance of the unfortunate woman and her child was one of commiseration, so that she was sent to prison to be protected rather than to be punished. As the officer was escorting her, she complained of weakness, and begged that he would be so good as to pay out of her money for a drop of something that would comfort her at the next public-house. He immediately consented, and they entered a public-house together, but he stood at the door while she went to the bar for the drop of comfort. He was rather surprised at her delay, and upon turning round he saw the child swallow a glass of gin, without hesitation or making "faces" at it. Upon inquiring how much was to pay, he found that the mother and child had taken between them no less than nine-pennyworth.

"'Allen mentioned that *the child had breathed its last, and the last cry from its throat was " gin, gin." The poor little wretch could not be prevailed upon to take a drop of medicine, or gruel, or any thing else up to its dying moments, but " gin, gin."*

"Numerous other cases I could relate to you, of daily occurrence," continued Mentor, " of the deplorable doings of drunkards; but I hope I have stated enough to satisfy your mind on that point." Indeed you have," replied Peregrine, " and I thank you kindly; but I am going to ask you another favour; and that is, whether you will try to get me an admittaace into Newgate on the morning of the execution of those miserable men who are to suffer on Monday next." " I will try," said Mentor, "and as I have the pleasure of knowing one of the sheriffs, in all probability I can procure you and myself admittance. But I would advise you to decline the sight: you, nor no one else, can form any idea of the horror of the scene." " I do not wish," answered Peregrine, " to go there merely to gratify my idle curiosity; nor shall I witness the scene without a proper feeling; yet I should like to behold the sad ceremony." Accordingly, Mentor wrote to the sheriff, and obtained an order to admit them. They were punctual to their time, and were soon conducted to the Press-yard, where they saw

The Dreadful Doings in Newgate.

The officer was knocking out the bolts from the irons of one of the culprits who was intended for execution, and in whom there was a firmness that surprised every one: the sheriffs, chaplain, and the other officers were in attendance, presenting, on the whole, a sight the most melancholy to be imagined; and at which Peregrine turned away with horror. "Let us, for heaven's sake," said he to Mentor, "leave this scene: I had no conception it was half so impressive, or so terrible: see, the gaoler, who, they say—

'Is seldom the friend of man!'

is absorbed in tears. I cannot remain;" and, taking hold of Mentor's arm, he rushed from the dreadful scene, expressing his sorrow that he had ever witnessed it. "It is proved beyond doubt,' said Mentor, "that these executions fail in their intended purposes—that of awing the wicked. Hard labour, as Mr. Harmer observed, has a thousand times more terror to the thief than death; and, if executions were resorted to only in cases of murder, depend on it, we should not find an increase in any of those crimes, the committing of which is now punishable with death. But the reformation of the criminal code is now engaging the best attention of our rulers, and when we reflect the great good that enlightened man, Mr. Secretary Peel, has already done, we are sure it cannot be left in better hands.

" ' It cannot be denied,' observes Mr. Martens, ' that in these latter times some individuals, actuated by cordial zeal in the cause of their suffering fellow-creatures, have attempted, and in part effected, improvement to their advantage; but how barren their exertions have on the whole been, is but too clearly shown. The greatest criminal, of whatever description he may be, still retains, even amidst the most licentious and wicked course of life, a spark of that noble feeling, which seems to cease only with the natural end of man. If this spark be but truly appreciated, and sedulously and constantly cherished, it may be almost taken for granted, that he is still capable of being in some measure, if not wholly, reformed."

" How grateful," said Peregrine, " we ought to be that we have escaped the snares that have brought those two wretched men we just now saw, to such an ignominious end. I have now more cause than ever to be grateful. It is indeed true, as Addison says in the Spectator, ' There is not a more pleasant exercise of the mind than gratitude. It is accompanied with such an inward satisfaction, that the duty is sufficiently rewarded by the performance. It is not like the practice of many other virtues, difficult and painful, but attended with so much pleasure, that were no possible command which enjoined it, nor any recompense laid up for it hereafter, a generous mind would indulge in it, for the natural gratification that accompanies it.' "

The crowd having now dispersed before Newgate, Mentor and his friend rose and took their leave of the worthy and enlightened keeper, thanking him for his kind attention.

On reaching the street, Peregrine was struck with the splendour of the liveries of the sheriffs' servants. " This fashion of wearing liveries," observed Mentor, " is of very ancient date. The best account handed down to us is from Mr. Douce, who, in his *Illustrations of Shakspeare*, says, that ' the practice of furnishing servants with *liveries*, may be traced in some of the statutes ordained in the reign of Edward IV. Badge and livery were synonymous, the latter word being derived from the French term, signifying the delivery of such a thing. The badge was then, as at present, the armorial bearings, crest, or device of the master, executed in cloth or metal, and sewed to the left sleeve of the habit. Greene, in his *Quip for an Upstart Courtier*, speaking of some serving-men, says 'Their cognizance, as I remember, was a peacock without a tayle.' Hentzer mentions it as a great fashion in the reign of Queen Elizabeth for the nobility to be followed by whole troops of servants, bearing their masters' arms in silver, fastened to their left arms, and reprehends it as a piece of ridiculous English vanity. And we find, from Fynes Morison, that it had been the custom for gentlemens' servants to wear ' *blue coats,* with silver badges of their masters' devices on their left sleeve,' but which, in his time, had become less fashionable ; ' and they commonly had cloaks edged with lace, all the servants of one family wearing the same livery, for colour and ornament.' This fact leads to the supposition, that the badge on the sleeve was disused in the reign of James the First (when he wrote), though it had before been so constant an accompaniment to a blue coat, as to have occasioned the proverbial expression of ' like a blue coat without a badge.' Liveries and badges, however, were not wholly confined to menial servants formerly. The retainers of the great—a class of men of considerable importance in the feudal times, kept up for ostentation long afterwards, may also be numbered among them ; for, though they did not reside with their employers, attending them chiefly on days of ceremony, they regularly received an annual allowance of a suit of clothes, a hat or hood, and a badge. A quotation from ' A Health to the Gentlemanly Profession of Serving-Men,' or ' The Serving-Man's Comfort' (1598), explains the description of persons accepting the office of retainer. ' Amongst what sort of people,' it asks, ' should this serving-man be sought for ? Even the duke's son preferred page to the prince, the earl's second son attendant upon the duke ; the knight's second son the earl's servant ; the esquire's son to wear the knight's livery ; and the gentleman's son the esquire's serving-man : yea, I know at this day,' says the author, ' gentlemen, younger brothers, that wear their elder brother's blue coat and badge, attending him with as reverend regard and dutiful obedience as if he were their prince or sovereign.'

" Stowe (Survey of London) gives numerous instances of the excess to which this fashion of wearing liveries had been carried a little before, and within his memory. Richard Neville, Earl of Warwick, in the reign of Edward IV., came to town, he tells us, with 600 men, all in red jackets, embroidered with ragged staves (his cognizance), before and behind. West, Bishop of Ely (1532), kept 100 servants, to every one of whom he gave, for a winter gown or livery, four yards of broad cloth ; and, for his summer coat, three yards and a half. The Earl of Derby had 220 men in check-roll, who wore his livery. Lord Chancellor Audley, in the reign of Henry VIII., gave to his gentlemen, who rode before him, coats guarded with velvet, and chains of gold; and, to his yeomen after him, the same livery, not guarded : every silvery coat had three yards of broad cloth. Old John Paulet, Marquis of Winchester, near the same time, gave his gentlemen and yeomen a livery of ' Reading tawny.' The livery of Cromwell, Earl of Essex, was ' a grey marble cloth,' the gentlemen guarded with velvet, the yeomen with the same cloth, ' yet their skirts large enough for their friends to sit upon.' The Earl of Oxford, at the same period, has been seen, the same author informs us, to ride into the city, to his house by London stone, with four score gen-

tlemen in a livery of Reading tawny, and chains of gold about
their necks, before him, and one hundred tall yeomen behind him,
in the like livery, without chains, but all having his cognizance of
the blue boar, embroidered on their left shoulder.

" Henry the Seventh gave the first check to the custom of
keeping and clothing numerous retainers ; that polite monarch had
no sooner obtained the crown than, aware of the formidable consequence this class of men had given to the nobles in the preceding
civil wars, he determined to restrain them. He issued the strictest
orders for this purpose to all his nobility, and it is well known that
he severely fined his own father-in-law, the Earl of Derby, for daring to break them. Henry the Eighth, not having his father's
fears, was less scrupulous, and most of the examples of great
numbers of livery servants just mentioned, took place in his reign.
At length the custom, from producing quarrels between different
families, as well as licentious excesses, was found so pernicious
as to suggest the propriety of licensing them. Strype, mentioning
the latter fact, declares that Queen Mary granted thirty-nine licences of retainer during her reign, but Queen Elizabeth only
fifteen. Gardiner, the prelate, had two hundred retainers ; the
Duke of Norfolk, in the latter reign, was allowed one hundred,
which the Queen never exceeded. Archbishop Parker had no
more than forty.

" ' Before we dismiss the present subject,' says Mr. Douce, ' it
may be necessary to observe that the badge occurs in all the old
representations of posts, or messengers. Of the latter of these
characters it may be seen, in the 52d plate of Strutt's first volume
of ancient dresses, &c., where, as in most of the early instances,
the badge is affixed to the girdle ; but it is often seen on the
shoulder, and even on the hat or cap. These figures extend as
far back as the thirteenth century, and many of the old German
engravings exhibit both the characters with a badge that has sometimes the device or arms of the town to which the post belongs.
He has, generally, a spear in his hand, not only for personal security, but for repelling any nuisances which might interrupt his
progress. Among ourselves, the remains of the ancient badge are
still preserved in the dresses of porters, firemen, and watermen,
and, perhaps, in the shoulder-knots of footmen. The blue coat
and badge still remain with the parish and hospital boys.'

" As you are determined, to-morrow, to take your departure
for the country," said Mentor to Peregrine, " we will, this afternoon, pay one more visit to the west end of the town." They arrived in the park, about the time when the ladies arise from their
downy couches, and walk to refresh their charming bodies with
the cooling and salubrious breezes of the gilded afternoon. They
could not have chosen a luckier moment to have seen the delightful park in its greatest glory and perfection ; for the brightest stars
of the creation were moving here, with such an awful state and
majesty, that their graceful deportment bespoke them goddesses.

Such merciful looks were thrown from their engaging eyes upon every admiring mortal, so free from pride, envy, or contempt, that they seemed to be sent into the world to complete its happiness. The wonderful works of heaven were here to be read in beauteous characters. Such elegant compositions might be observed among the female quality, that it was impossible to conceive otherwise than that such heavenly forms were perfected after the unerring image of divine excellence. " I could," exclaimed Peregrine, " gaze for ever with inexpressible delight, finding, in every lovely face, something new to raise my admiration, with gratitude to heaven, for imparting to us such forms of celestial harmony, in that most beautiful, yet curious creature—woman !"

After some hours' enjoyment, they began to think of some new objects to feast or refresh their senses; and strayed along the Green Park into that of St. James's. " This once fashionable promenade," said Mentor, " how altered it is since the time when Hogarth painted his celebrated view of it, with Rosamond's pond, then an enclosed piece of water; but many suicides having been committed here, occasioned it, several years since, to be filled up.

" Le Serre, a French writer, in his account of the visit of the Queen Mother, Mary de Medicis, to her daughter, Henrietta Maria, and Charles the First, in the year 1633, mentions several particulars of St. James's Palace, as well as of the Park, and the then state of the neighbourhood. The Palace he calls the ' Castle of St. James's;' and describes it as embattled, or surmounted by crenelles on the outside, and containing several courts within, surrounded by buildings, the apartments of which (at least, such as he saw) were hung with superb tapestry, and royally furnished. ' Near its avenue,' says he, ' is a large meadow, continually green, in which the ladies always walk in summer. Its great gate has a long street in front, reaching almost out of sight, seemingly joining to the fields, although on one side it is bounded by houses, and on the other by the Royal Tennis Court;' and, after noticing the gardens, and the numerous fine statues in them, he adds, ' these are bounded by a great Park, with many walks, all covered by the shade of an infinite number of oaks, whose antiquity is extremely agreeable, as they are thereby rendered the more impervious to the rays of the sun. This Park is filled with wild animals; but, as it is the ordinary walk of the ladies of the court, their gentleness has so tamed them, that they all yield to the force of their attractions, rather than the pursuit of the hounds.'

" In the time of Henry VIII., the founder of the palace, the park is described as a marsh, which had formed part of the grounds of St. James's Hospital. That monarch first laid it out and planted it (perhaps with the venerable oaks Le Serre mentions), and caused the whole to be enclosed with a wall. Charles II. added several fields to it, planted it with rows of lime trees, and laid out the mall, which an old writer describes as a ' vista half a mile in length, formed into a hollow smooth walk, skirted

round with a wooden border, and with an iron hoop at the further
end, for the purpose of playing a game with a ball, called mall.'
This prince, also, the same author informs us, ' formed the canal,
which is 100 feet broad, and 2,800 feet long, with a decoy and
other ponds for water-fowl.'    Jorevain, another French traveller,
speaking of it at this time, says, ' it is filled with all sorts of deer ;
the mall is above 1,000 paces long, bordered on one side by a
great canal, on which are to be seen water-fowl of all sorts ; and
an aviary near it, where are birds of divers countries and different
plumage, which serve to divert the king, who frequently visits
them.    There is, at the beginning of the canal, upon a pedestal,
a brazen figure of a gladiator, holding his buckler with one hand,
and his sword with the other.    The attitude of this statue is much
esteemed.'

"  The decoy and ponds mentioned by the first writer, stood on
a piece of ground, or little island, situated at that corner of the
park enclosure which faces Storey's Gate, and a plan of which may
be seen in ' Smith's Antiquities of Westminster.'    It was called
' Duck Island,' from the circumstance of Charles II. being accustomed to feed and amuse himself with his ducks here, which,
Colley Cibber informs us, drew numbers of people to see him.
Of this place he is said, by Pennant, to have constituted Monsieur
St. Evermond governor, with a pension of 300l. a year.    William
III. afterwards built a tea-drinking room in it.    Birdcage Walk,
adjoining, the same author asserts, was so named, from the cages
which were hung in the trees with the king's birds.

"  ' A Tour through Great Britain,' (1753) says, ' King Charles
II., after his restoration, gathered some acorns from the royal oak
at Boscobel, and set them in St. James's Park, or garden, and
used to water them himself.'

"  Mr. Nathaniel Rench planted the elm-trees in the Bird-cage
Walk : it was he who introduced the moss-rose tree into this
country ; he died in the same room in which he was born, 1783,
aged 101.

"  Here," continued Mentor, " formerly stood Buckingham
House, built by John Sheffield, Duke of Buckingham, of whose executors it was bought, as a residence for the late Queen Charlotte,
and where the major part of the present royal family were born.
It was pulled down, or altered to the present building, which is
called, by some persons, a palace.    It is a disgrace to the English
people, that their king does not possess even a respectable town
dwelling—but such is the fact !"

From the Park, Mentor and his young friend proceeded to take
water at Westminster Bridge, and enjoy the genial evening
breezes of the Thames ; and, on their way, Peregrine's attention
was arrested, by viewing the exterior of Westminster Hall.

"  This structure, it is well known," said Mentor, " only forms
a single apartment of a once extensive and magnificent royal palace, many minor parts of which still exist, though much altered,

or hidden by later erections. To attempt a history of such a place, and of the many important events of which it has been the scene, would be to write a history of England. But it may be amusing to those who have not been accustomed to make researches of this kind, to have some idea afforded them of its ancient appearance, and how grand a pile of building it must have been, when the whole was standing and perfect.

" The foundation of the palace of Westminster was the work of King Edward the Confessor, and might have taken place near the time he rebuilt Westminster Abbey. It is probable that it was not large at first, as William Rufus found it consistent with his royal dignity to make many additions to it, and, among the rest, to build the fine hall in question. In 1262, great part of the palace was destroyed by fire, and in 1298 a similar calamity again happened.—These accidents, it is likely, occasioned Edward III. and his successor, Richard II. to build so largely here, that they may be justly styled re-founders. The two chief works of these monarchs were the erection of St. Stephen's chapel, and the re-building of the hall, in its present form. A third fire, in the reign of Henry VIII., did some damage, but not considerable. The old range of building, in what is called the Tudor style, adjoining the hall, probably arose in consequence of this event, though that prince himself appears to have only occasionally resided here. Elizabeth built the Star Chamber, and remainder of that side of New Palace-yard, standing next the Thames, a doorway of which had lately on it the date 1602; but, like her father, she only lived here occasionally, Whitehall and St. James's Palace being her chief places of residence. After a time, it was, in a great measure, deserted, except for state purposes.

" There are no representations of this palace in its very ancient state; but Hollar, and other artists near his time, have left us views of it, when much of its original appearance remained, and which are extremely interesting. From these, and other authorities, we learn, that it was formerly divided into two great areas or squares, bearing, as now, the names of Old Palace-yard, and New Palace-yard, which were separated and inclosed by walls and gates. Of these, the Old Palace-yard was by far the superior in point of architectural elegance, exhibiting in one group, on the north and east, the Abbey, with Henry the Seventh's Chapel, Westminster Hall, St. Stephen's Chapel, the Painted Chamber, and other ancient buildings, scarcely to be matched for grandeur and effect, when in their perfect state. Old plans show this yard with three gates: one, parting it from New Palace-yard; another (with a wall running parallel with the south end of the hall), and a third, which stood somewhere near the top of Abingdon Street, by College Street, and which seems to have formed its boundary that way. The two outer, or first and third gates, are represented of considerable size, and embattled. The most curious building in the New Palace-yard, exclusively of the hall, &c.,

were the clock-tower and conduit. These, as well as the yard, generally are very satisfactorily delineated in Hollar's Views, taken near the Restoration, and show us the nature of the alterations which have since taken place. The clock-tower was a high building, resembling the steeple or tower of a church, and was erected by Edward III. It stood where is now the terrace opposite the hall, and contained the famous bell, called Great Tom of Westminster. The conduit stood near the middle of the yard, and on grand occasions was, as were all the other conduits of London, made to run with wine. It appears to have been a large and ornamental erection. From the clock-tower to the end of King Street ran a wall, which inclosed the Palace-yard that way, and which turned up from the end of King Street, towards St. Margaret's Church, where was a magnificent gateway, built by Richard III. (whose foundations were discovered in making the late alterations there), and which formed the principal entrance on the land side to the palace, King Street being the only avenue to it (anciently through the Whitehall gate), and which was so named from being the usual way the sovereign came here from St. James's and Whitehall.

" With the exception of the Hall, we can form but little conception, either of the nature or number of the different buildings which composed this palace when entire, nor are we rightly able to ascertain the sites of several places mentioned in old accounts, but now gone. The notice of the fire in 1298, by Leland, specifies, among the buildings burnt, the Little Hall, Queen's Chamber, and the King's House, within the Palace (*domus regis in pal' apud Westmonaster'*), which must have been some part more exclusively devoted to the residence of the sovereign, and might have been the same as is elsewhere called the ' King's Privy Palace,' as an entry in an official book, among the Harleian MSS., at the British Museum, mentions ' John Apulby to have the keeping of the King's Privie Palois, in Westminster.' Important as these places might have been, however, they were all eclipsed by St. Stephen's Chapel, which must have been, when perfect, the glory of this palace. This, before the Reformation, had its dean and canons, similar to St. George's Chapel, at Windsor, and, from the residence of such canons there, the present Cannon Row has its name. The mutilations of the interior of this fine fabric took place on its being converted into the House of Commons. The outside was ruined by the clumsy repairs it afterwards underwent; but we are enabled, from existing remains, and different graphical illustrations of it, to judge sufficiently of its original elegance. The cloister attached to it, which is still nearly perfect, is exquisitely beautiful. The Painted Chamber, one of the very ancient apartments of this palace, may be termed a treat for the lovers of ancient art. This room, which acquired its name from its walls being entirely painted over with historical or allegorical subjects, after being wainscotted up for ages, has, in some late alterations, been laid open, and affords one of the most interesting specimens of the state of painting in this country, about the reign of Edward III., that we know of. There are various others of the old apartments here, well worth notice, but not necessary to enumerate : amongst its architectural remains, are to be found examples of almost every style, from its foundation to the present time.

" In the New Palace-yard, in the time of Cromwell, was a celebrated tavern for political discussion, called the Turk's Head, at which Sir James Harrington, Sir John Penruddock, Birkenhead, and other eminent republicans, met nightly, just before the Restoration, to debate on government affairs. They had a large oval table, purposely made, with a passage in the middle for the landlord to deliver his coffee, around which sat Harrington's disciples, and other select auditors. A writer of the time says, the room was every evening as full as it could be crammed, and that the arguments in the Parliament House were flat, to the discourses here. Several of the Parliamentary soldiers (officers), were accustomed to attend these debates, and they went so far as to have (very formally) a *balloting-box*, and to ballot how things should be carried ; but General Monk coming in, made all their airy models of government vanish. The Rhenish Wine-House was another celebrated tavern here, about the same time. These, and various other houses and erections, opposite and adjoining to the Hall, may be reckoned among the early defacements of the Palace, and similar encroachments continued until very lately—a recurrence of which, it is probable, the present improvements will do away for ever.

" I believe, I have now," continued Mentor, " shown and given you the best description I was able of the principal Doings of this vast metropolis, with the exception of one of the grandest and most magnificent in the world,—that of the annual meeting of the charity children of the metropolis, at St. Paul's Cathedral ; and, as to-morrow is the day appointed for the celebration, I would advise you, by all means, to embrace the opportunity." " Certainly I will," replied Peregrine ; " and therefore, if you will breakfast with me, we can make the necessary arrangements for my leaving London, and then I will accompany you to St. Paul's."

Accordingly, the next morning, Mentor and his friend, having gained tickets of admission, entered the Cathedral, when the sublimity of the scene struck Peregrine with amazement :—to behold so many thousands of poor children snatched from ruin, and trained up in the paths of virtue and industry, created in his mind sensations of indescrible pleasure and admiration. " Well, indeed," said Peregrine, " might the Emperor Alexander of Russia, say, that the meeting of the charity children in St. Paul's was the grandest sight he ever beheld." These schools are the greatest instances of public spirit the age has produced. They are most laudable in-

52.

stitutions, if they were of no other service than that of producing a race of good and useful servants, who will have more than a liberal—a religious education. The wise Providence has amply compensated the disadvantages of the poor and indigent, in wanting many of the conveniences of this life, by a more abundant provision for their happiness in the next. Had they been higher born, or more richly endued, they would have wanted this manner of education, of which those only enjoy the benefit who are low enough to submit to it; where they have such advantages without money, and without price, as the rich cannot purchase with it. The learning which is given is generally more edifying to them than that which is sold to others; thus do they become more exalted in goodness, by being depressed in fortune, and their poverty is, in reality, their preferment.

The service being ended, Peregrine and Mentor waited for some time in the church-yard, to notice the dresses of the children of the various schools. "There is only one fault," said Mentor, " I find with some of the dresses of the girls : they are rather too showy—not simple or plain enough ; for I am afraid, in their tender age, it gives them too early a *love of dress*, which has been, and is, the ruin of hundreds of girls." " I don't know any thing about that," replied Peregrine, " but really I think it is impossible to make any objection to the neatness or cleanliness of their clothing ; and they look so innocent, so modest, and so unassuming, that most of them seem more like celestial beings than mortals. This is a sight, indeed, that London has reason to be proud of." " It is so," said Mentor. " I mentioned, the day I first had the pleasure of seeing you, that there is not a calamity to which ' flesh is heir to,' but what can here find an asylum to assuage its anguish. To convey to you some idea of the immensity of the various charities in the metropolis, it may be well, at first, to tell you that there are, at least,—

" 1239 National Schools, containing 180,000 scholars.

" 45 Free Schools, for educating 5000 children.

" 239 Parochial Charity-Schools, in which from 12 to 14,000 children are annually clothed and educated.

" 17 other Schools for deserted and poor children.

" Three Colleges.

" 23 Hospitals for the sick and lame, and for pregnant women.

" 18 Institutions for the support of the indigent of various other descriptions.

" 20 Dispensaries for the gratuitous supply of medicine and medical aid to the poor, besides innumerable other private institutions and Pension Societies, among them being the Printers' Pension Society, one of the most laudable among the many.

" Exclusive of these, the companies of the city of London distribute above £80,000 annually in charities ; and the sums expended yearly in London for charitable purposes, independent of private relief, have been estimated at £900,000. In fact, the number of charitable institutions is immense; and yet the inhabitants think little about the matter, they being as eccentric in their charitable feelings as in every thing else : for instance, Kean's benefit always netted him £800; but when he gave the produce of his benefit-night to the starving Irish,* the produce of it was little more than £200. Performances at our theatres for charitable purposes generally fail of the intended design. John Bull will only be charitable in his own way; he will not be dictated to or told how he is to appropriate his money.

" It is astonishing," continued Mentor, " that though we have splendid accounts, printed in gold, of coronations—though our libraries groan with histories of our battles, we have not one book which gives an account of the charities of England, with the exception of Mr. Highmore's. This is the more extraordinary, as it is a subject on which every Englishman has reason to be proud, his country standing proudly pre-eminent above all other nations in the exercise of benevolence. Yes," continued Mentor, " *if* England *is* superior to other nations, it cannot be in valour, for that is to be found in every quarter of the globe—it cannot be in the superiority of her fine or mechanical arts, for many of those are inferior to other nations—it cannot be from the number of her historians and poets, for abroad there are her equals. No, Peregrine, *if* England is superior to other nations, it is in the *extent* of her *charities;* and pray Heaven may she ever continue so !" " Amen !" responded Peregrine.

The clock struck six, when Mentor and his young friend had finished their dinner. " In a couple of hours," said Peregrine, " I shall bid adieu to London; but I cannot leave it, without expressing to you the delight I have experienced during my residence in it, and I trust you will grant me one favour, Mentor, in return for the many I have received at your hands; and that is, to honour me with a visit at Marlborough, and I will show you ' The Doings in the Country.'—" I will with pleasure," replied Mentor; " and I hope then to find you in health, and happy."

" Perfect happiness is certainly incompatible with the nature of man; but there are several qualities, which, if possessed at once, may, in my humble opinion, make him approach very near to it, which are as follows : a sound constitution, joined with a distinguishing judgment, and a general good taste of books, men, and things; and possessed of virtue and art to direct them, so that they may afford him such pleasures as he need not be ashamed of enjoying, or ever have cause to repent.

" Remember, Peregrine, there are three things necessary for a

---

* By-the-bye, had their rich countrymen had the justice to have raised half as much money, then, for their perishing poor, as they do now for the Catholic rent, they would have had no occasion to have drawn so largely as they did on the charitable feelings of John Bull—it is past; and John is a kind-hearted forgiving creature; but it was not right; for occurrences prove they had the means, but not the inclination.

man to possess, whatever may be his profession, if he intends to be eminent—viz: nature, study, and exercise.

"In prosperity always prepare yourself for adversity. In summer we have time to lay up provision for the winter. In prosperity, we have friends in abundance, and our path is smooth and pleasant. It is wise, then, to be provided for evil times, for there is need of all in adversity. Thou wilt do well not to neglect thy friends, for a day may come when thou wilt be fortunate in having some, even those whom thou art heedless of now. Obscure men never have any friends, for in prosperity they know none, and in adversity no one knows them."

At this instant, the waiter came into the room, to inform them the mail was waiting. Peregrine arose, and, accompanied by his friend, entered the coach-yard, and, taking hold of Mentor's hand, —"Farewell, my friend," said he,—

## "VALE, LONDINIUM!"

# INDEX

## A.

## B.

# D.

# E.

# F.

# G.

# M.

# N.

# O.

# P.

# Q.

## T.

## V.

## W.

# INDEX TO THE ENGRAVINGS.

THE END.

www.ingramcontent.com/pod-product-compliance
Lightning Source LLC
Chambersburg PA
CBHW080817020726
47501CB00009B/2326